HOT MOON

HOT MOON

ALAN SMALE

CAEZIK
SF & FANTASY

ARC MANOR
ROCKVILLE, MARYLAND

✳

SHAHID MAHMUD
PUBLISHER

www.caeziksf.com

This is a work of fiction.

Cover art by Christina P. Myrvold; artstation.com/christinapm

Interior illustrations by Udimamedova Leylya; facebook.com/lkiudlkiud

ISBN: 978-1-64710-050-6

First Edition. First Printing July 2022.
1 2 3 4 5 6 7 8 9 10

An imprint of Arc Manor LLC

www.CaezikSF.com

CONTENTS

SOYUZ SPACECRAFT

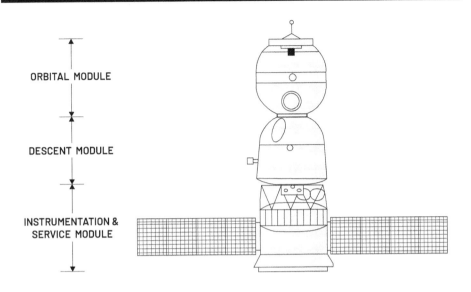

ORBITAL MODULE

DESCENT MODULE

INSTRUMENTATION &
SERVICE MODULE

LK LANDER

LEK LANDER

1

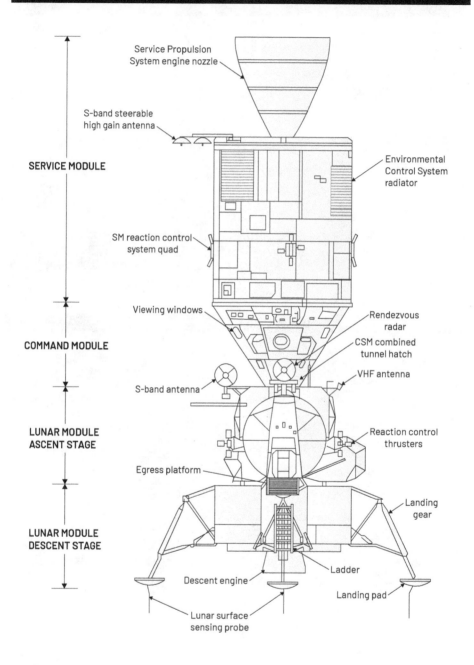

SERVICE MODULE

Service Propulsion System engine nozzle

S-band steerable high gain antenna

Environmental Control System radiator

SM reaction control system quad

COMMAND MODULE

Viewing windows

Rendezvous radar

CSM combined tunnel hatch

VHF antenna

S-band antenna

LUNAR MODULE ASCENT STAGE

Reaction control thrusters

Egress platform

LUNAR MODULE DESCENT STAGE

Landing gear

Descent engine

Ladder

Landing pad

Lunar surface sensing probe

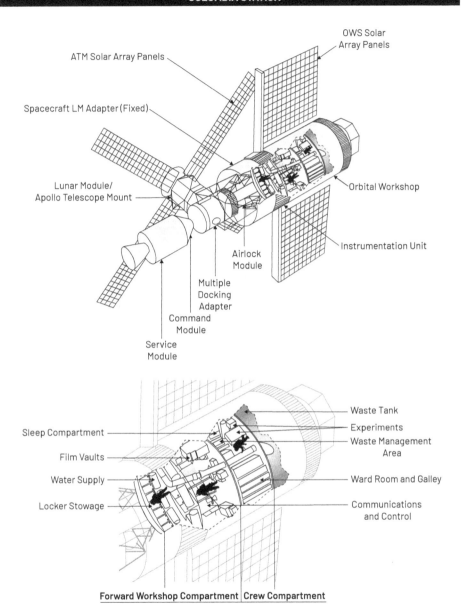

ATM Solar Array Panels

OWS Solar Array Panels

Spacecraft LM Adapter (Fixed)

Lunar Module/ Apollo Telescope Mount

Orbital Workshop

Airlock Module

Instrumentation Unit

Multiple Docking Adapter

Command Module

Service Module

Sleep Compartment

Film Vaults

Water Supply

Locker Stowage

Waste Tank

Experiments

Waste Management Area

Ward Room and Galley

Communications and Control

Forward Workshop Compartment | Crew Compartment

3

NORTH POLE

MARE FRIGORIS

MARE
IMBRIUM

Archimedes
Crater

Hadley Base

MARE
SERENITATIS

Marius Hills

APENNINE MTS

MARE
CRISIUM

Copernicus
Crater

MARE
INSULARUM

MARE
VAPORUM

OCEANUS
PROCELLARUM

MARE
TRANQUILLITATIS

Zvezda Base

MARE
FECUNDITATIS

MARE
COGITUM

MARE
NECTARIS

MARE
HUMORUM

MARE
NUBIUM

SOUTH POLE

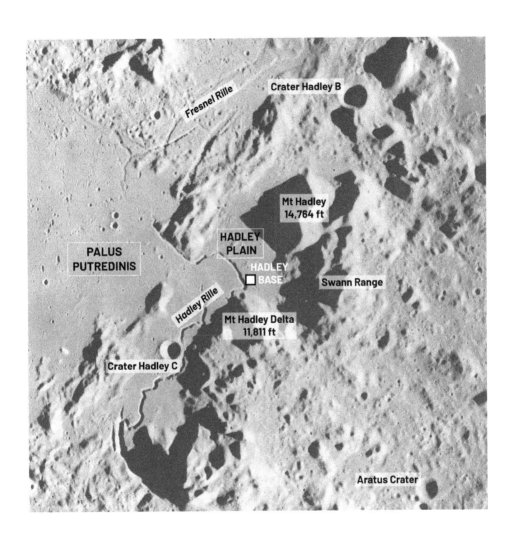

Fresnel Rille

Crater Hadley B

Mt Hadley
14,764 ft

HADLEY
PLAIN

PALUS
PUTREDINIS

HADLEY
BASE

Swann Range

Hadley Rille

Mt Hadley Delta
11,811 ft

Crater Hadley C

Aratus Crater

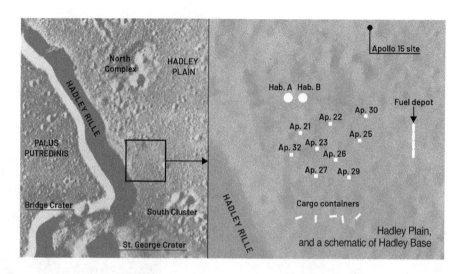

North Complex

HADLEY PLAIN

HADLEY RILLE

PALUS PUTREDINIS

Bridge Crater

South Cluster

St. George Crater

HADLEY RILLE

Apollo 15 site

Hab. A Hab. B

Ap. 30

Ap. 22

Ap. 21

Fuel depot

Ap. 25

Ap. 32 Ap. 23

Ap. 26

Ap. 27 Ap. 29

Cargo containers

Hadley Plain,
and a schematic of Hadley Base

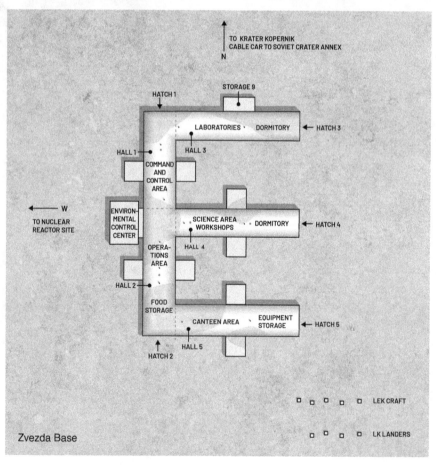

TO KRATER KOPERNIK
CABLE CAR TO SOVIET CRATER ANNEX

N

STORAGE 9

HATCH 1

LABORATORIES · DORMITORY ← HATCH 3

HALL 1

HALL 3

COMMAND AND CONTROL AREA

ENVIRON-MENTAL CONTROL CENTER

SCIENCE AREA WORKSHOPS · DORMITORY ← HATCH 4

← W
TO NUCLEAR REACTOR SITE

OPERA-TIONS AREA

HALL 4

HALL 2

FOOD STORAGE

CANTEEN AREA · EQUIPMENT STORAGE ← HATCH 5

HALL 5

↑
HATCH 2

LEK CRAFT

LK LANDERS

Zvezda Base

6

PART ONE: MOONFALL

December 1–2, 1979

CHAPTER 1

Apollo 32: Vivian Carter
Mission Elapsed Time (Hours): 105:40:16

IN orbit around the Moon, ferocious bees assaulted a tin can.

Spacesuited, untethered, and in free fall, Vivian Carter struggled to focus her thoughts and make sense of the scene before her. Woozy from pain and shock, she heard no voices in her headset, nothing but the seething white-noise hiss of jammed S-band communications.

That can't be right.

It was that empty hiss that freaked her out the most. She was alone in the void, between spacecraft, and as isolated as she had ever been. Comms were critical, and Vivian had none.

She'd been out of it for long, precious moments. Ever since the Soviet cosmonaut's bullets smashed into her shoulder and raked her helmet and sent her tumbling slowly in space, sixty miles above the mares and uplands, the basins and craters of the Moon. Since the impact trauma, she'd been suspended in a stunned reverie.

C'mon, Viv. Snap out of it. Work to do.

She dragged in a long, shaky breath. It was stale with pressure-suit odors, an odd blend of metal and rubber, Vivian-smell, and the acidic tang of pure oxygen.

An assault rifle in space? No reason why it couldn't fire in a vacuum—ammunition had its own oxidizer—but dissipating the heat was another matter. Hopefully the weapon would jam before the cosmonaut could fire again.

Vivian blinked hard to shake away the drops of sweat that wouldn't fall from her eyelashes in zero G. Glanced down at the compressed-air gun she was still clutching in her gloved hand and not using. Squinted at the pressure gauge on her wrist. Low, but steady. Her suit was probably compromised at the shoulder and maybe the calf as well, even with its twenty-one layers of thermal and micrometeoroid protection. But the holes must be small, and her PLSS—the portable life support system that she carried on her back—could replace the leaking oxygen at that rate.

If she could get back to her ship soon, she should be all right.

Okay, fine. I've got this.

Maybe.

There was no time for self-doubt. A hundred yards ahead of her was the Apollo stack Vivian had seen in her dreams for a decade. A Command and Service Module mated with a Lunar Module, in glorious orbit around the Moon. NASA's iconic image, the fundamental visual of the US space program since Apollo 11. Under its shiny hood, Apollo 32 was better equipped than the crate that brought Armstrong and Aldrin to the Moon ten years ago, but from the outside it looked pretty much the same.

A similar distance behind her, Columbia Station was a patchwork beetle, a blocky cylinder with an X of solar panels resting on its shoulders. It was a converted Saturn V third stage, flown from the Earth to the Moon and decked out as a Skylab. Inside it was a relatively luxurious living space with three separate levels, each a circular deck twenty feet in diameter. Vivian had just come from there, having escaped through the airlock of the third port in some weird slow-motion version of the nick of time.

And then there were the three Soyuz interceptors and the uncrewed Progress cargo tanker, stalking over and around Columbia Station in a careful ballet. Sinister predators from the USSR, come to assault the US orbiting platform. With oddly curved lines compared to the blocky angularity of Columbia and Apollo 32, each Soviet craft resembled a bell with a ball affixed to its top. Two of the vessels were black and the other two mostly dark green, and each had "CCCP" emblazoned in red on its side.

They'd appeared from nowhere. And they were jamming NASA's communications so hard that Vivian couldn't talk to her crew, Columbia Station, or Mission Control.

Even with the collapsing détente between the Cold War adversaries, and with Soviet tanks rolling into Afghanistan, this was an astonishing development. Who'd have guessed the Soviets would be so bold?

Four days ago, Vivian had been at Kennedy Space Center preparing for launch and dreaming of the Marius Hills: a pristine lunar landscape with volcanic domes and rilles, regolith yet to be trodden by human boots, a thousand scientific discoveries yet to be made. A landing site she had studied in so much detail that it was inscribed on her soul. And, ironically, that was the area she was passing over right now: the wide basaltic plain of Oceanus Procellarum.

Her Moon. Her mission. Her life, for so many years. And now it was all going to hell.

Three of the Soviet vessels were clustered around Columbia, with the Progress tanker apparently attached to the US station like a limpet, close to the airlock module. The final Soyuz interceptor still stood apart from the others, above Columbia from Vivian's perspective, and rolling gently.

Vivian was about to concentrate her thoughts back onto her trajectory and use the gas gun to correct her course to the Apollo stack, when she caught a motion from the rotating Soyuz. The cosmonaut who'd just minutes ago shot bullets at her—with, what? An AK-47?—had reappeared in the hatchway. He was easy to spot in his orange-tinged Orlan spacesuit, and even easier because he was lugging a tube that must be six feet long.

A tube he was now settling into a suit attachment on his shoulder, and aiming in her direction.

A rocket launcher?

Jesus H. Christ. You have got *to be kidding me.*

The Ocean of Storms, unrolling beneath her, might be the last thing Vivian ever saw.

CHAPTER 2

Apollo 32: Vivian Carter
Mission Elapsed Time (Hours): 103:11:05

TWO and a half hours earlier, strapped into the right-hand seat of her Command Module, Vivian Carter had watched the pocked, ashen lunar surface roll by sixty miles below; they'd just passed the terminator out of eerie darkness into full Sun, throwing the broken walls of Mendeleev Crater and the impact basin of Mare Moscoviense into sharp relief. At this phasing, the Moon's "dark side" was truly dark for most of their passage over it, with only the last thirty degrees of rocky, broken uplands illuminated by sunlight.

She fidgeted, glanced at the clock. "Three minutes till acquisition of signal, guys."

"Roger that," said Ellis Mayer, snapping a film magazine into his Hasselblad camera. Dave Horn just grunted, his attention on the radar and the guidance computer.

Vivian leaned back and breathed deep. For the time being she had no checklists to run, no switches to set, no decisions to make. Orbital rendezvous was Horn's gig. A rare opportunity for her to kick back and enjoy the ride. This should have been relaxing, but it just gave her the itch. She was so used to having every instant of her time precisely scheduled that these empty minutes were almost physically painful.

They also allowed for a trace of apprehension to creep in at the edges. A shadow of unusual foreboding that she pushed aside impatiently.

"Man, that'll never get old," said Mayer, and took a picture.

Dead ahead and right on schedule, the Earth rose over the Moon's limb, a startling blue crescent against the deep black void. The radio crackled. "Apollo 32, this is Houston. Do you copy?"

Vivian reached for the comms board and pushed-to-talk. "Five by five, Houston."

"Burn status, 32?"

She scanned the gunmetal-gray control panels, dense with switches and indicators. "Trim burn occurred on time, duration two minutes fifteen, zero residuals. Boards are green, and everything's peachy."

"Aaand we have Columbia Station in our sights," said Horn, from the commander's seat on the left side of the tiny cabin where Vivian normally sat, but was for Dave's use while he controlled their maneuvers. "Be advised that we are closing in for the kill." From the center seat, shoulder to shoulder with them both, Ellis grinned.

In their headsets came an amused Texas twang. "32, Columbia Station. We see you clear and bright in the early Sun, and we're for-sure quakin' in our boots at your approach."

That was Josh Rawlings, current commander of Columbia Station. Vivian knew him well from astronaut training, particularly the desert survival exercises in Nevada, where he'd thrived, and the jungle exercise in Panama, where none of them had. He was a good guy.

"Apollo 32, Houston," CAPCOM chimed in from a quarter million miles away. "We confirm you as Go for docking."

His tone was mildly reproving. Mission Control wasn't big on astronaut levity during critical maneuvers.

Vivian grinned, and tightened her lapstrap. She preferred it when Michael Collins or Charlie Duke sat Capsule Communicator duties, as they sometimes still did. Liked it when those legends of spaceflight were on the loop, working *Vivian's* mission, talking to *her*. Back when Apollo 11 had flown to the Moon in July 1969, Vivian had been a scrappy Navy ensign trying to persuade her captains that she deserved a slot as one of the first women to enter the Aviator Training Program at Pensacola. In 1972, when Charlie Duke walked on the Moon as Lunar Module Pilot for Apollo 16, Vivian had been logging as many flight hours as she could on Douglas A-4 Skyhawks while trying her damnedest not to get tossed out of Naval Air Station Corpus Christi for "insubordination," which mostly meant shoving back hard when her male colleagues dismissed her efforts, passed her over for promotion, or otherwise disrespected her.

Back then, she'd just wanted to fly. She'd certainly adored watching the Moon landings on the mess-room TV, but going herself would have seemed impossible.

Now, in 1979, Vivian's Moon looked almost close enough to touch.

"We copy, Houston," Horn said, now laconic. "32 is a Go for docking with Columbia."

"Looking forward to it," Vivian said, and releasing the button on the comms panel, added: "Looking forward to getting this over with, is what I mean."

"You got that right." Ellis pressed buttons on the guidance computer keyboard and eyed the green numbers on its display. "I have us at three thousand, braking down to twenty. On the money." Columbia Station was three thousand feet away, and they were approaching it from slightly beneath at a rate of twenty feet per second.

"Doing the twist." Dave juiced the thrusters to rotate the craft, then burped the jets again to cancel the rotation. They peered forward along the line of the Cargo Carrier that had blocked their view until then. That Carrier was half again as big as their spacecraft and attached firmly to its nose. "There's Columbia. Damn, I'm good."

The only other Skylab Vivian had seen had been in Earth orbit on her first flight, two years ago, and she hadn't gone inside it. This one looked newer and shinier. "Yay Columbia Station. Home of the Brave."

"Range twenty-eight hundred, velocity eighteen, and nominal."

Columbia Station was all angles on the outside. Inside, it was kitted out with all modern conveniences. Sleeping berths. A shower, even. Basically, a cushy posting. Whereas the Command Module that Vivian and her crew had been living in for the past three days had a couple hundred cubic feet of space in total, three couches and a bunch of instrument panels and storage, and had smelled like a locker room since shortly after the translunar injection burn.

The distinctive cylinder-and-cone Command and Service Module combinations jutted from two out of three of the radial ports around Columbia Station. Four more CSMs were arranged in a neat row along an extensible boom that spread left and right from the docking adapter. Parked there for months at a time, with augmented batteries and heaters to keep their electronics humming through the long exposure to cold, heat, and vacuum.

Dave Horn, her Command Module Pilot, was matching orbits with Columbia, and doing it like it was nothing. Horn had followed in Buzz Aldrin's footsteps in getting his PhD in orbital mechanics and rendezvous techniques, pushing the high boundaries with even higher math, and this kind of maneuvering was in his blood. Which was good, since their current rendezvous was complicated by the bulk of the Carrier.

"Twenty-five hundred, fifteen," said Ellis.

Vivian leaned in. "Columbia, 32. Good-looking station you've got yourself. Damn fine." She cut the comms long enough to say. "Massage a guy's pride, he'll love you forever."

"Take your word for it," said Horn.

"Oooh," said Rawlings over the loudspeaker. "I've come over all aflutter. Do I have the honor of addressing *the* Miss Captain Vivian Carter?"

"Delivery girl, TV star, lunar explorer?" came another voice. "Woman of many talents?"

Horn nodded solemnly. "Triple threat."

"The commander's a danger, all right," Ellis added. "To people who *put her down*."

"Guys, guys," Vivian said. "Cool your jets."

They heard two laughs from Columbia, and then Rawlings said, "No offense, Vivian."

"Sure, you say that now."

"32, Houston. Range and rate?"

"Twenty-one hundred, fifteen." Ellis was still frowning. He looked at Vivian, and said, off-comms: "'Delivery girl'? Really?"

Vivian raised her hand. "Drop it. Doesn't matter. And we *are* delivering." She had other worries.

Until now, Apollo flights had been classified as missions of either exploration or development. Those of exploration traveled to new sites on the lunar surface, while the development missions focused on growing NASA's space infrastructure by placing Skylabs in orbit around the Earth and Moon, and establishing the US Hadley Base on the surface.

Now, the boundaries had blurred. Shortly before launch, Apollo 32 had become a hybrid. The ten-day trip to Marius was still its prime mission, but on the way they'd stop off in lunar orbit to dock with

Columbia Station to deliver this Cargo Carrier containing a far-ultra-violet spectrograph and a new large-format optical camera, plus additional air, water, and food.

That was already one complication too many as far as Vivian was concerned. But then, since this delivery would complete Columbia's science complement and bring it to full operational status, the NASA Public Affairs geniuses had decided to make a song and dance of it and scheduled a prime-time TV broadcast, which Vivian would have to go aboard Columbia for. To be followed by a largely pro forma spacewalk back to her own vessel, while zooming over the Moon at about a mile a second.

Vivian resented the cluttering of her mission timeline, but she didn't have a whole lot of choice. Before she could go skid her Lunar Rover around in her pristine volcanic corner of the Moon with a camera mounted on her chest and a geologist's hammer in her gloved hand, this was the price she'd have to pay.

Vivian looked down again. As the lunar surface unrolled beneath them, she could see the flat volcanic expanse of the Sea of Serenity to the north, with what must be the Hadley-Apennine range rising jagged on the Moon's limb beyond. Hadley Base was located on the other side of that range. It would be another ten minutes before the Soviets' Zvezda lunar base at Copernicus Crater came over the horizon, five hundred ground miles distant from Hadley.

Low Earth orbit had felt safe, even comfortable. The blues, greens, and golds of the living planet were warm and familiar, its fuzzy atmosphere like a blanket, there to cushion them. Zipping across the harsh moonscape was another kettle of grit entirely. Vivian could pick out individual craters and mountains and valleys as solid three-dimensional chunks of terrain, and *close*, so close that it felt like her Apollo spacecraft might tumble down into them at any moment. The magnificent desolation of the Moon was stark, gray, under some Sun angles a little brown. Angular. Soulless. Unforgiving.

Vivian couldn't wait to get down there.

"Fifteen hundred feet out, braking to ten feet per second."

"Seriously, can't you guys get here any faster?"

Josh again, joshing from Columbia Station. No one dignified that with a response. Despite the boldness of its missions, NASA was a careful and conservative agency, and their flight plan required them to make haste painfully slowly.

That care and dedication to detail was why NASA's astronauts came home alive. The Soviets' relative recklessness was why a bunch of their cosmonauts didn't come home at all.

And it was also how the Soviets had rushed a man to the Moon just a few short months ahead of the Americans. Damn their asses.

Hey, who cares who was first, right?

Everyone, apparently. Everyone except Vivian.

In truth, Vivian had several reasons to be grateful to the Soviets. If the third cosmonaut to tread the Moon's surface hadn't been a woman, and if Brezhnev hadn't made it such a screaming propaganda centerpiece that men and women were treated equally in the Soviet Union, a sign of Communist superiority, NASA might not have opened its doors to women as astronaut candidates as early as it had. And even before that, without the blare of Soviet propaganda it was also unlikely that women would have been accepted as US naval aviators early enough for Vivian either.

Vivian hadn't been the first American woman in orbit, and she wouldn't be the first to walk on the Moon either. Even now, there were two American women among the eighteen astronauts at Hadley. But Vivian Carter was the first woman to command an Apollo, and that had to count for something. Right?

Vivian had worked *really* hard. But she'd had some good luck too.

Please God, don't let that luck change yet.

"A thousand feet, ten feet per second."

Horn juiced the RCS jets again, and the Cargo Carrier swung to block their view of Columbia Station once more. "Houston, 32. Switching to TV camera."

"Hmm." Ellis studied the blurry black-and-white image on the small TV screen from the camera on the far side of the Cargo Carrier. "*That's* our picture? Holy cow."

Horn cracked his knuckles, and twisted his head left and right to work the tension out of his neck. "All I wanna do is go the distance," he said, and grinned at Vivian.

Vivian groaned. At the end of their last sleep period Houston had woken them with the "Gonna Fly Now" theme from the Rocky movie, blaring horns and all, and since then her crew had been dropping Rocky Balboa quotes into the conversation to yank her chain.

Ellis nodded sagely. "Hey. 'It ain't over till it's over.'"

Horn pointed at the displays Ellis was supposed to be reading from. "Okay, let's get serious."

As they closed, Ellis and Horn fell into their rhythmic call-and-repeat of numbers, now not just range and speed but angles: pitch, yaw, roll. Ellis read with smoothness and precision, just as he'd call numbers for Vivian tomorrow as she flew the LM down to the lunar surface.

And, damn it, Vivian wanted her Lunar Module back.

The early Apollos had jettisoned their spent Saturn V third stages after the translunar injection burn. Once they'd used the mighty booster to propel them out of Earth orbit, they didn't need that big empty tank anymore. So, on the long coast moonward they'd separate the CSM from the third stage, turn it through a 180, then move back to dock with the LM and pull it free. On they'd go, leaving the third stage to smash down onto the Moon, or careen off into orbit around the Sun.

A decade later, NASA wasn't so profligate with useful hardware. Apollo 32 had kept its third stage all the way, and used the last of its fuel to insert them into lunar orbit. They'd separated from it just minutes earlier, leaving it in orbit a mile behind them. After delivering the Cargo Carrier, Horn would steer the CSM back to pull the LM free of the third stage. Then back to pick up Vivian and off they'd go, down to the Moon, tra-la-la. Having done their chores, they could go play.

Meanwhile, the six-man crew of Columbia Station would have themselves a fine home improvement project. They'd go retrieve that third stage and dock it to their axial port, doubling their living space and adding volume for larger experiments.

The Columbia astronauts wouldn't go down to the surface. They'd circle the Moon a couple thousand times and then hurry on home at the end of their tours of duty when their replacements showed up. Vivian felt a bit sorry for them. She hadn't joined the Astronaut Corps to float around the Moon for months and never land. Even if the view was outstanding.

Which was why she'd obsessed about geology, starting the very day she'd received the letter welcoming her into the Astronaut Corps. Vivian was no egghead, but the better you knew your lunar science, the better your chances of being assigned to a landing crew.

NASA was still leery of taking academics out of universities and tossing them into orbit. With Soviet rhetoric ratcheting up into ever-higher gear, and the risks of spaceflight increasing as the hardware complexity redoubled, it was best to keep the effort as military as possible.

That's what they'd signed up for when they'd joined the military, right? Lives on the line for their country? Yeah. That was it.

Hopefully it wouldn't come to that.

But it might. Even with no human enemy in sight, there was no shortage of ways to die up here.

Apollo 32 docked with Columbia Station with all the delicacy of a bull ramming a gate. The crew lurched into their straps. An unsecured pencil flew past them to ricochet off the instrument panel. Vivian snagged it on the rebound, and bit her tongue.

"Three capture latches engaged," Ellis said calmly, scanning the board.

Horn placed his left hand against the wall of the Command Module, feeling for vibrations. "Yeah. Okay, stable. Retracting probe."

Vivian counted to eight as the docking mechanism pulled the two craft closer, and right on time, heard the twelve docking latches snap into place around the flange.

"Hard dock," said Horn. "Columbia, 32: honey, we're home."

"Ouch," came the aggrieved response from next door. "32, Columbia: We felt that down to our toes. The target is bruised."

Vivian grinned. "Houston, be advised that 32 has acquired the target. Emphatically."

Delayed by signal travel time, Mission Control came in late and dry. "Roger, 32, we confirm."

Horn broke comms to say privately: "You always need a bit of extra shove at the end to get the latches to engage. Guess I overdid it, given how heavy the damned Carrier is."

"Okay, Navy," Ellis said. "Time for you to go and out-propaganda the Russkies."

"Ha." Vivian snapped free from her harness. "Sure, I'll go smile for the cameras while you guys have *all the fun* getting 32 put together and ready to hit the road."

"A woman's work is never done."

"Shut the hell up, soldier," she said companionably, and started unstowing her suit.

Caution in all things. If the act of opening the hatch at the far end of the Carrier somehow exposed a weakness in the seal and it blew out, she'd be dead in seconds. Everyone on the Apollo program took hard vacuum very seriously. And Vivian was quite okay with that.

Horn and Mayer pushed back into their couches to give her room as she wriggled in through the back zipper of the suit. Its construction required her to squirm into it simultaneously at shoulder and hip to get her arms and legs situated properly. As her head popped out the top, Ellis said, "Help you with your zipper, ma'am?"

"Let me give it a go," Vivian said casually. In theory she could pull a long cord that would zip her up from her crotch to the back of her neck, but it often snagged on the way up. Normally astronauts helped one another into their suits, but however relaxed Vivian felt around Ellis and Dave, it still felt odd to have one of them helping with that particular zip.

This time it went smoothly. "Whaddaya know, I can dress myself without help."

"What a champ." Horn was already setting switches, beginning the checklist for undocking.

Ellis leaned forward to ease Vivian's gloves over her hands. "For what it's worth, I'm still not a fan of all this razzmatazz."

"Me neither, man," Vivian said. "But them's the breaks. Ready for helmet."

"Helmet, aye." Ellis carefully lowered it over her head, tucked her hair in, locked it firm, checked the seals. "Comms check, Viv."

She was hearing him now through the headphones under the Snoopy cap that covered her scalp. She spoke into the microphone at her chin. "Comms live, how me?"

"Loud and clear. Houston, Vivian is a Go for egress."

"Columbia, 32," Vivian said over the wire. "Us villains are all set. You?"

"Yes sirree, ma'am, 32."

"Then roll out that welcome mat," she said, " 'coz here comes Viv."

Ellis pulled open the top hatch of the Command Module to reveal the long, darkish tunnel that led through the center of the Cargo Carrier. Vivian kicked up, and Ellis grabbed her boots to steer them into the tunnel. "Thanks, soldier."

As she drifted farther into the tube, the couches of the Command Module receded away from her. After three full days crammed into that tight space, it was an odd view.

"Hey." Dave nudged Ellis. "Wanna play some rock'n'roll while Mom's out?"

"Hell no," Ellis said immediately, and Vivian laughed. Musically, Horn was old school, locked into Elvis Presley and the Rolling Stones. For him, it was like the seventies had never happened. By mutual consent, they never played cassette tapes in the Command Module.

The sides of the tunnel came up around her shoulders. "No fighting, guys. See you on the flip side."

Ellis mock saluted. "Take care."

He floated forward to close the hatch, shutting Vivian out. It locked with an odd finality, right in front of her visor.

Nope. That's not weird. Not at all.

The tunnel was twenty feet long and barely wider than her suit, lit only by a trail of small red lights. It wasn't difficult to propel herself along it feetfirst. As with everything in zero G, the trick was not to overdo it. She gave the closed hatch a gentle push, and off she went.

Yeah. Definitely feels longer than it is.

Her boots met the hatch at the far end. Vivian stuck out her elbows to anchor herself. "Columbia Station, Vivian. I'm standing on you. Let me in?"

Beneath her feet, a vibration. Then a bright light spilled up and past her. She felt her ankles grasped and tugged gently downward.

She slid through, twisted, and found herself in a broad airlock with two guys in spacesuits. One of them reached up to dog the hatch she'd just come through. The other grinned, his face magnified by the curve of his visor.

"Josh, you slack bastard," she said.

"Vivian, you son of a gun."

"Equalizing pressures. Hold," said the guy she didn't recognize. Vivian drifted in place, watching the gauge. There was a half-pound difference in pressures between the CM plus Cargo Carrier and the Skylab, because Apollo 32 was on a pure oxygen system, and Columbia Station was on a 70/30 oxygen/nitrogen mix. It wasn't healthy to breathe pure oxygen for the extended time the Columbia crew would be aboard.

"Okey dokey," the non-Josh astronaut said. "Clear for ingress."

Josh opened the airlock hatch, and the three of them drifted into Columbia Station.

After the Command Module, and especially the tight tunnel through the Cargo Carrier, the domed area in the forward part of Columbia Station seemed cavernous. Also, bright and unsettling. Vivian swallowed, said casually: "So that's what being born feels like." She could faintly hear her own words coming through the speakers mounted on Columbia's inner walls, slightly delayed.

"Breech birth?" said someone in her headset.

Feetfirst. Right.

A different voice: "Need someone to slap you on the butt, Carter?"

Vivian knew who *that* was. "Not just now, *Jackson*. I seem to be breathing just fine."

Skylabs had been designed from the get-go with a definite up and down in mind, in the belief that their occupants would feel comforted by a clear sense of direction. In reality, astronauts had adapted quickly to the lack of a favored orientation.

Vivian had entered through the Multiple Docking Adapter area at the top—fore—end of the module, and now was floating in a high dome area, twenty-two feet across. Ringing the walls at the level where the dome straightened into a cylinder were bands of lockers, cupboards, freezers, and water tanks, and beneath those was the forward workshop compartment, a working space lined with scientific equipment and storage. The floor was an open aluminum grid, with a hexagonal cutout in its center. On this grid she recognized materials science experiment cases and other paraphernalia, including an infrared spectrometer, a radiometer, and some avionics boxes with their covers removed. She also saw several cameras and three empty spacesuits. Mounted against one wall was a radar unit and comms system, all lit up, with an astronaut in the usual blue jumpsuit strapped into the seat in front of it, staring up at her.

Vivian's brain might tell her that all the equipment apparently scattered on the floor was fastened there with clamps and ties, but the visual impression was that she was mysteriously hovering just beneath the ceiling of a tall, round-walled room.

Josh glanced at her. "Okay?"

"Sorry. Bright in here, after the tunnel."

"That it is," he said readily, and it was true: the paintwork across the dome was a light green that almost shimmered, and the cupboards and containers below were green and white. Artfully done, but to Vivian the paint job seemed a little precious.

The guy at comms left his perch and propelled himself up toward her. "They really made you suit up for a whole half-pound pressure differential?"

"Hey, safety's our number one priority," Vivian said.

"Let's get you out of all that," Josh said, and she obligingly held out her arms to him as they turned slowly in the air. He unfastened the clamps that held her gloves on and twisted them through a quarter turn to release them. Meanwhile the other guy reached for her helmet.

"Vivian Carter," she said.

"Danny Zabrinski."

"He's one of the good Russians," Josh said.

Zabrinski eye-rolled. Vivian figured he got that joke a lot. "Third-generation American," he said.

"And second-generation US military," she said. Although she hadn't met him previously, Vivian knew Zabrinski's grandparents had fled the Russian Revolution over fifty years ago. The family had been true-blue American ever since.

He grinned. "Done your research."

"Always." The helmet came off, and Vivian took a gulp of air. "Ooh, nitrogen. Yummy."

"You can't smell that."

Vivian had now drifted upside down relative to the forward compartment, boots pointing to the hatch she'd come in through, and was determined not to comment on it. "Can so." She ducked her head down into her suit as they peeled it off her. She knew that it used to take well over an hour to get into or out of the original Apollo moon suits. Was glad NASA had fixed a few things in the decade since, because she didn't have that kind of time.

Once Josh and Danny Zabrinski freed her up from the suit, they let it go and it billowed beside them like a headless corpse. Her gloves had already traveled twenty feet away and were bouncing off the water tanks. "Powerful fans you have in here."

"Yeah. Air conditioning's a bit fresh."

Another blue-suited jock came flying up through the hexagonal gap from the compartment below. "Woo-hoo, Rocket Girl!"

"Give it a rest, Jackson," Vivian said. "I mean, c'mon, damn."

"Well, sorry there, uh, Captain Carter." Jackson gave her a broad grin that he probably thought smoldered, and reached out to shake her hand. Vivian took it warily, but there were no tricks, no spinning-the-rocket-girl-in-zero-G, so that was okay. Though now Jackson leaned forward and sniffed, and pretended to recoil. "Jesus. I gotta be honest with you, Rocket Girl: you do not smell good."

"Neither would you if you'd been flying with those lunks for half a week," Vivian retorted.

"Columbia, 32: you do know we can still hear you?" came Ellis's voice over the loudspeaker and in her headphones.

"That's a roger, 32. I was aware."

Vivian had feared that Columbia Station might greet her with a bouquet of plastic flowers, or some other crap. That would've pissed her off. If she was just to be ribbed about personal hygiene, she could live with that.

"Okay, Jackson," Rawlings said. "Now you're embarrassing your stupid self. Float away from Commander Carter and give her some space."

The intercom crackled, and Horn's voice boomed out. "Vivian, 32. Let me know if you need me to rattle that tin can again and shake some sense into those knuckleheads."

"32, Viv. I'm surrounded by feral jackasses, but I think I can hold 'em at bay. All's tight as a drum here. You're free to disengage."

You are free to leave me here and go off on your own. Damn it. "Go fetch my Lunar Module, Dave. And don't slam it like you slammed Columbia. Vivian out."

Introductions continued. Rawlings and Jackson she already knew, and Zabrinski she'd just met. The other guy in the airlock with them was Ed Mason, broad shouldered and sandy haired, another guy she'd met in Houston and at the Cape but didn't know that well. The latest crewmember to arrive, he was still a little tentative in weightlessness. Up from below now came the last two, Marco Dardenas and Gary Wagner. Dardenas was short and smiley with dark hair and moved with quick, confident motions; Wagner was more reserved, a New Englander by his vowels, and appraised her shrewdly as he shook her hand.

God, there were a lot of people in here. Even six was a crowd after the past few days.

After the glad-handing, Dardenas and Zabrinski went back to their posts, but Jackson hadn't given up baiting her yet. "So, you show up, and suddenly we're booked onto the *CBS Evening News?* Guess you're rock-star important."

"Yeah, well. I wouldn't ride into *this* one-horse town for anyone less than Cronkite." Vivian looked past Jackson to Rawlings. "Seriously, let's get this done. Time's a-wasting, and as Jackson so kindly informs me, I need to freshen up."

Rawlings pushed off toward the opening that led to the lower compartments. "Copy that. Walk this way."

Vivian dived through headfirst, like anyone would, but now flipped over so that she'd meet the floor feet-foremost, like Josh had done. She reached out to brake herself using a wall mount with, she thought, a certain amount of professionalism. Her movements weren't as smooth as Josh's—he'd had several months to accustom himself to wide open spaces—but she hadn't embarrassed herself. Yet.

The crew compartment was divided into four main areas. In front of her was the wardroom, with a galley. In its center against the wall was a table, with four chairs bolted to the floor around it. The crew must eat in shifts. To her right she could see past an accordion-pleated privacy curtain into the waste management area—shower, toilet facilities, and the crew's personal lockers. Behind her was the doorway to the sleep area, where each crewman would have his own private niche with a bunk, sleep restraints, blankets, and additional locker space. To her left was an operations zone with a bicycle ergometer and rowing machine, yet more boxes and equipment chests, a teleprinter, and a low, flat computer unit. "This place is huge."

Rawlings mock shuddered. "Please. I'm practically claustrophobic. After almost a year in this dump, my skin is crawlin'."

"Weenie," she said.

In the Command Module and Lunar Module, every available surface on the floor, walls and ceiling was filled with instrument panels, storage lockers, and other equipment. Here on Columbia, all that stuff was only on the walls. On this level at least, the ceiling and most of the floor were clear. "Weird."

Rawlings cocked an eye. "The mess?"

"The uppy-downness. The verticality."

He nodded, shrugged.

25

In fact, it *was* all kind of a mess, but Vivian wasn't about to remark on it. That might open her up for comments about the place needing a woman's touch. But it still made her teeth itch to see so much junk so loosely tethered, and some items even carelessly floating free, when there was a perfectly fine ceiling they could have clamped it to.

Not her circus, not her monkeys. She looked at the waste management compartment. "I'll need to primp for this. How long does it take?"

"Full-up shower? Maybe twenty minutes, including cleaning the area up after. Which one of us could do in a pinch."

"So, thirty then," she said, then took in his quizzical expression. "What? You guys all have buzz cuts. I have actual hair."

Vivian hadn't washed her hair since launch four days ago, and since then she'd been limited to infrequent wipe downs with damp cloths laced with germicide. Despite the distraction of the Columbia stopover, Vivian secretly welcomed the opportunity to get clean.

She checked her watch. An hour and a half until CBS go-live time. Right now, Columbia was directly between Moon and Earth. The broadcast would begin promptly once they reacquired signal with Houston after swinging around Farside again.

Her shower could wait a little longer. "Let's review, first. I haven't really given any thought to this since the last briefing a couple weeks back. That way I can run the script in my head while I'm, uh, in the head."

"Hungry?" Josh said. "Could eat while we talk."

It was well known that the Skylab crews had better food than the Apollos. "Okay, sure. Buy me dinner."

Before she knew it, she was seated at the wardroom table, a tray clipped to the surface in front of her with three small heated containers and three more of cold food; her legs held gently with thigh restraints; and her feet slid under a toe bar. And the food smelled great. "This is one sweet billet you've got yourself here, brother."

"Yeah, it's a blast. Just between us, this boat is fallin' apart. Tech headaches twenty-four twenty-nine." Geek astronaut humor: twenty-four hours per Earth day, 29.53 Earth days per lunar day. Like twenty-four seven, but more so. "Getting second-guessed by Houston every step of the way. I'd like to enjoy the view but I'm too busy fixing the plumbing. So, y'know. Just like being at home. Hey, look, your people are leaving you."

The only window in Columbia Station was the circular one over the wardroom table. Vivian leaned forward. Sure enough, thirty-five feet above her, Apollo 32 was firing jets, reversing gently away, leaving the Cargo Carrier in place. The gap was opening up: five feet, ten feet.

She sighed. "Damn it," was all she could find to say.

"Hey, you get to walk back," he said. "Spacewalks are cool."

"Sure." It would be the first zero-G spacewalk by a US woman astronaut, but Vivian would have willingly given up that footnote in history to stay with Mayer and Horn for the mating of Athena, her Lunar Module, with Minerva, her Command and Service Module.

Vivian had known it would hurt to not be aboard for the docking. She hadn't realized it would hurt *this* bad. "The things we do for Cronkite. Jeez."

"Copy that. So, let's get this done and get you back to your crew."

Vivian sampled one of the hot containers. Chicken cacciatore. Damn, that was good. She waved her hand. "Talk."

"Okay." Josh unhitched a clipboard from the wall by his chair and studied it. "So, three takeaways that Public Affairs wants us to drive home. First and foremost, your mission. Science goals. Evidence of awesome volcanic activity in the Moon's past, possible lava tubes, we're now inches away from a complete understanding of how the lunar surface came to look the way it does, evolution of the Earth-Moon system, blah blah blah."

"That part I've got down cold."

"General audience, drinkin' a brew after dinner. Nothing too technical."

"Got it."

"But remember, the Soviets are claiming our lunar bases are military rather than scientific. Which is obviously just so much noise. But make sure you say enough to sound smart and science-y. Tough path to walk."

"Yeah, yeah. Next?"

"Two. First female commander of such a mission. I'll handle that part so you don't have to brag on yourself. We'll lead in with establishing shots of Columbia, then the mission stuff is all you. Cronkite will probably only jump in if you get tongue-tied. Then after a few minutes you throw it to me and I'll talk you up, lob softball questions."

Vivian gulped down food, opened another hot container. Beef something. "Do you have to ask me how it feels to be a woman in a man's job?"

"Nope. We're gettin' away from that. Now it's role-model stuff. Blazing the trail, space is for everyone. Positive. Mostly just human interest on you personally."

"Positive it is."

"By then, 32 will be mated and almost all the way back, so we'll show cool shots of the stack approaching. This'll mostly be Cronkite waxing lyrical. Meanwhile, you're suiting up again with Dardenas and Mason assisting. Cronkite will bounce some questions to me for the third takeaway: completion of Columbia, new light on the heavens through the UV spectrograph. Closer study of the surface using the fancy-pants large-frame camera you also brought us.

"Then it's back to you as you start the spacewalk. Cronkite talks, we follow along on camera as you float around Apollo 32, inspecting it. We're done whenever Cronkite pulls away or if your ingress to the CM runs into snags. Because we want you back inside 32 by the time you cross the terminator into dark."

Vivian gave him a look. "Uh, yes we do, so no snags."

"Hopefully."

"I've crawled through a hatch before, you know."

"Sure. Anyway. That's—"

Alarms blared all around them.

CHAPTER 3

Columbia Station: Vivian Carter
Mission Elapsed Time (Hours): 103:52:35

THE loudspeaker above their heads brayed, almost deafening her. Then: "Incoming," came a terse voice. "Bogies. Emergency."

"Bogies?" Vivian looked at Josh.

He was already leaping for the Comms button. "What, Jackson? Say again?"

"Incoming craft. Unidentified."

"Like who? From where?"

"Unidentified, I said. Get up here, Josh."

Vivian shot a look out of the window. "I see nothing but 32."

Rawlings shoved off and soared past her. "Talk to me, Jackson! If this is a joke—"

"No joke." Dardenas was speaking now. "I confirm three objects on radar, coming up fast. Fast and *together*. From underneath us."

Vivian abandoned her food and pushed on out of the wardroom, following Josh up into the forward compartment. Rawlings had already arrived at the comms console and was floating there, staring intently at it. "No transponder pings?"

"None," Dardenas said. "They're not ours. Just the radar blips."

"Could they be ghost images? Artifacts? Meteors?"

"Too bright, no, and not unless meteors can change direction and decelerate *in effing formation*."

29

Vivian peered at the small radar screen. Three faint blobs at its edge. *That's it?* "It's not 32 and my third stage, somehow?"

Jackson gave her an *idiot-girl* look. "Not unless they're suddenly three hundred miles away."

Dardenas pointed to another blip almost at the center of the circular screen. "That's your third stage."

"Has to be Soviets," Jackson said.

"Let's see." Dardenas pressed buttons. "Houston, Columbia. We have a problem, possible hostiles. Three unidentified incoming craft. Assuming Soviet unless advised otherwise. Houston, do you copy?"

A crackle from CAPCOM. "We copy, Columbia. We're—"

"Four!" said Jackson. "Look. Parallel trajectory but well behind." The rendezvous radar only worked to about 350 miles out. Apparently now there were four ... bogies.

"Houston, *four* incoming. Confirm not friendlies?"

"We have nothing anywhere near you, Columbia. You say three or four?"

"Four now. In formation. Sort of. Together, a few miles apart."

A pause. "You're sure?"

"Yes, of course we're bloody sure. Stand by." Josh reached past Dardenas to mute the microphone. "Fat lot of good they are."

Mason was frowning. "Think they came up from the Moon? From Zvezda Base?"

"Doubt it," Vivian said, just as Jackson said "Not necessarily." Just because the Soviets were approaching from beneath hardly meant that they'd come from the surface. Like the Americans, the Soviets went to rendezvous by bringing the active vehicle up from a faster, lower orbit to match the slower, higher orbit of the target. And launching from Zvezda they'd have needed to match planes with Columbia's orbit, which would be nontrivial. So in all likelihood they'd come straight from Earth and whipped around the Moon, injecting themselves into an eccentric orbit with its highest point at Columbia's altitude.

Even so, converging with Columbia's location was a considerable feat of orbital mechanics. To achieve their various docking maneuvers the Apollos used radar transponders and a whole rack of computing power to derive ranges, angles, and velocities. To even attempt it, the Soviets must have tracked NASA communications accurately enough to derive their ephemeris and state vector with high accuracy, and they'd still need to figure out the final approach in real time.

Vivian wasn't the only one thinking this. From behind her, Ed Mason said, "Whichever cosmonaut is driving this bus is a stone-cold pro."

"Doesn't matter *how* they're doing it," Rawlings said with some impatience. "They're *doing* it."

Suddenly, Wagner said, "Guys, are these *missiles?*"

"Prrrobably not," said Dardenas.

Vivian's blood ran cold. "Could you try to sound more definite about that?"

Jackson gave her the look again. Once more and she was going to slap him, crisis or no crisis. "They're small. Much smaller than your third stage. Closer to CSM-scale. And they're braking, aren't they?"

"Are they?"

"Well, at least a bit. Yes. This is a rendezvous."

Rawlings reached forward to punch the Comms button. "Houston, Columbia. Tell us something we can use."

"We're sending a request for information up through channels."

"So you'll get back to us in two or three days?" Rawlings demanded. *Gee,* Vivian thought; *even I've never snarked Mission Control that badly.*

She looked at the wall clock. "Dardenas, Jackson, whoever. What's their likely ETA?"

Jackson snorted. Dardenas said, "Well, that depends."

"Obviously. Guess?"

"Hour, hour and a half?"

"That's the best we can do?"

"Well, if they brake like normal people, it would be like … an hour, minimum? I mean, I've got nothing on them except what I see on the radar."

"They're not gonna do this like normal people," Jackson said. "Guaranteed."

"Depends how much risk they're willing to take," said Dardenas. "They'll have to be a bit careful on the approach. We'll be going into orbit night soon. I'm thinking they won't come in for final approach till we pass back into sunlight."

So: fifteen minutes until they crossed the terminator into darkness. Another ten after that until loss of signal with Houston. And, since they spent an hour of every two-hour lunar orbit in orbit night, they'd cross back into sunlight in an hour and a quarter. *Perfect.*

Rawlings had been doing the same math. "Yeah, that's exactly how they'll play it."

Vivian leaned in "Apollo 32, Columbia, you read?"

"Here and paying attention," came Ellis's prompt response.

"Good. So, we have possible Soviet incursion. What's your status?"

"Uh, nominal? Still outbound. Three quarters of a mile to the LM."

Vivian ran the numbers in her head. The original schedule gave the boys almost two hours to get there and back; it took forty-five minutes or more just for all the activities that needed to take place between docking with the LM and pulling it free of the third stage. "Earliest ETA back here if you speed it up?"

"Still assessing," Ellis said. "There's a limit to how much we can safely compress the checklist."

Vivian could picture Horn beside him, punching buttons and trying not to swear on open loop. He'd hate changing the mission timeline. Even for Soviets.

Ellis again: "What do we anticipate the Reds will do on arrival?"

"Nothing good, we're guessing," Rawlings said grimly.

"Okay, okay, we copy," Horn said in exasperation. "We'll crank it up, especially on the return. But right now we've *really* got to concentrate on the docking, Viv, okay?"

"Sure, yeah, push on."

Rawlings shook his head. "Houston, this is Columbia Station. What do you have for us?"

"Situation unclear," said CAPCOM. "Use your best judgment."

Josh looked like he was having trouble not pounding the console with his fist. "Roger. Great. Thanks."

"Hung out to dry," Jackson said, to no one in particular.

"Can we hail 'em?" Wagner asked, floating behind them.

"*Hail* them? The Soviets?" Jackson shook his head. "Why don't we beam aboard while we're at it? Attack them with photon torpedoes?"

"Jesus, they must have *radios.*"

Vivian leaned in again. "Houston, Columbia. We don't even know what frequencies the Soviets use?"

"Well, yeah, but …. Stand by," CAPCOM said. "We're working this. Calls placed. Phones are ringing all over Moscow and in the Soviet embassies."

"Our radios are hard-tuned," Zabrinski said. "Exact frequencies, for precision and transponder tracking. We'd have to—"

And then all communications dropped out completely, replaced by a loud roaring hiss.

"Mother of God!" Dardenas reached for the board and threw switches, and the hiss disappeared.

"Sons of bitches!" Jackson shouted at the same time, and a babble burst out from the rest of the crew.

"Hey, hey! Pipe down!" Rawlings barked. "Everyone! Quiet!"

Vivian turned and shoved off. She banged her hand on the edge of the hatch, but swung herself down and through, into the wardroom, back to the window.

She saw one bright dot in the distance that had to be a glint off Apollo 32, or the Saturn third stage. It was a hell of a long way out. *Hurry it up, guys.*

She looked beyond, squinting into the black of the sky. Turned to shut off the lights in the wardroom, put her hand up to block the Sun, and peered again.

There they were, teeny tiny specks reflecting sunlight. *They're real. Goddamn it.*

So much for Cronkite. Got ourselves a breaking story here and we can't even tell him.

"So we've got nothing?" Josh was demanding as she swung herself back up into the forward compartment. "Was I not clear? No radio, no communications at all, no better ETA on the Soviets?"

"We're jammed, man," Jackson said. "S-band jammed, VHF jammed, we're *jammed*."

"This is not a coincidence," Vivian said. "Soviets arriving while 32 is here and vulnerable? Can't be just chance."

"I know that," Rawlings said.

Dardenas checked the wall clock. "Terminator. We're now in darkness."

Radar, of course, didn't care whether the ship was in sunlight. But there was no reason why they had to make it easy for the Soviets. Vivian was just opening her mouth when Josh beat her to it. "Mason! Turn off the docking lights. Block off the wardroom window. Let's make ourselves tough to see."

"I already turned off the wardroom lights," Vivian said.

33

"That window has a cover, too."

"They'll still see us if they have IR detectors," Jackson pointed out.

"Yup. But we do what we can."

They floated in silence, watching the radar blips getting steadily closer. *Predators stalking us in the darkness*, Vivian thought. *Nice*.

Wagner cleared his throat. "Uh, should we maybe prepare—"

"Hey, heads up, we have VHF back," said Dardenas, his hand up to his headset. "Part of it. But S-band is still hosed."

Rawlings twisted himself back to the board. "Yeah? What the hell is *part of it?*"

"Well, the Russkies are transmitting to us. On *our* frequency."

He flipped a switch to send the signal to loudspeaker, and they all heard a heavily accented voice saying: "… lumbia Station, you are operating illegally in Soviet space. We have been commanded to take control of your facility. Do you read? Columbia Station, Soyuz. We—"

Rawlings pushed-to-talk. "Soyuz, this is Columbia Station. Take control? On whose authority? This here's US sovereign territory. You will stand off. I repeat, do not approach."

The Russian voice sounded almost apologetic. "Nyet, Columbia. You trespass in Soviet airspace. You will surrender and allow us to board."

"Soviet airspace?" Rawlings laughed shortly, the tension clear in his voice. "Are you kidding? Am I on *Candid Camera?*"

A different Russian voice, now. Louder. Harsher. "Be advised that we are not joke, Columbia Station. Surrender, and we will allow you to return to Earth. If not surrender, if evasive action or resist, we have power to take you by force. Or to destroy you."

Destroy?

The first voice came back. "Columbia Station, Soyuz. Do not compel us to take such uncomfortable action. Allow us entry, and no one will be harmed. You have my word. Over."

Rawlings's tone was icy. "Soviet craft, listen up. You will pass us and continue on your way, or face the consequences. Be advised that we will consider an incursion within a twenty-mile radius of our station to be a contravention of international law, and an act of war."

Vivian blinked, and looked around into the sudden silence. Men were looking at one another.

An act of war.

The first voice again. "Columbia Station, Soyuz. We regret we cannot comply."

Presumably Horn and Mayer would be listening into this, would know what was up by now. That, at least, was helpful.

Of course, she had no idea how the LM docking was going. It might be smooth and nominal. It might not. Contingencies happened.

"Keep talking," Vivian said urgently. "We have to stall. This line has to stay open."

"Yeah?" Jackson's face was set. "Not sure how much good *talking* is going to do us with these jokers."

Vivian shook her head, frustrated. Rawlings stepped in smoothly. "Transponders. Apollo 32 needs the transponder signal from the LM to dock effectively, and from us to get back here. If that frequency is jammed, Horn has to do it all purely on radar and visual."

"Which Horn can handle," Vivian added. "Given enough time. Which we don't have. We need him to do this *fast*."

Jackson nodded, chastened. "Oh, yeah, crap. Wasn't thinking. Sorry."

"No problem, man," Vivian said graciously. "Lots going on."

"Yeah."

She spoke crisply into the microphone. "Soyuz aggressor, good afternoon. Please identify yourself: name, rank, serial number."

A pause. Then: "I am Major-General Nikolai Makarov. Soviet Air Force. 'Serial' is what?"

Vivian's jaw dropped. "Okay, *now* you're kidding us."

She looked around at the crew of Columbia. Eyebrows raised, all around.

Nikolai Makarov. The second cosmonaut to walk on the Moon, just over ten years ago. Now, apparently, attempting to invade.

At any other time, Vivian might have liked to make Makarov's acquaintance. In a bar in Switzerland, say, with plenty of napkins to draw on.

She lifted her finger off the Comms button. "Well, that explains their flying chops, at least."

Rawlings looked baffled. "What the hell does *Makarov* want with us?"

"Let's find out." Vivian pressed the button again. "This is Captain Vivian Carter, of the US Navy and NASA. Commander of Apollo 32, shortly to descend to the surface on a peaceful scientific mission." *That's public knowledge. Nothing they don't already know.*

"*Dobryy den'*, Kapitan," Makarov said. "I am sorry indeed that we meet under such circumstances."

"Yeah, Ivan, so are we," Jackson muttered. Vivian cut the mic and gave him an arch look. "Hey, man. Diplomacy."

"Huh."

"They're decelerating for real at last," Dardenas said, studying the radar.

"What's their ETA now? And 32's?"

"Give me a minute."

"Well, let's ask them." Vivian pushed-to-talk. "Soviet vessels, Columbia Station. What is your anticipated time of arrival here?"

The Russians gave no reply. Rawlings grinned, shook his head. "What?" she demanded. "Worth a try, right?"

"Maybe … thirty minutes to Russkies?" said Dardenas. "I still can't resolve 32 from the third stage."

"Damn it." Vivian pressed the Comms button again. "Major-General Makarov, we respectfully request a few minutes to discuss among ourselves. We'll get right back to you."

She turned off the microphone. Rawlings looked around at them all. "Okay, guys. What can we do to defend ourselves in here?"

"Defend?" Jackson shook his head.

"We need to seal up the station hard. We're not going to make it easy for 'em."

Vivian took a deep breath. "Sure. But before you do that? Josh … I've got to get across to 32. Soon as they get back."

Jackson snorted. "Don't be daft."

Even Rawlings looked at her askance. "I think your spacewalk may be off, Viv. Under the circumstances."

Dardenas was still studying the radar traces as if trying to scry the future from tea leaves. "Soviets will probably be here by then."

"Or, they might not."

"There's no way, Vivian," said Rawlings. "Seriously."

"Come on," she said. "Don't do this to me, man. Let me try it."

Rawlings wrinkled his forehead. "We still have no idea whether 32 will make it back in time. Even if they do, we can suit you up but … ." He looked at her, his eyes troubled. "It'd be no tether or umbilical. Ad hoc. Free-form."

Vivian had already figured that out. "I can do it."

"I can't let you."

"Josh, come on, damn it. My place is with my crew. I *need* to be with my crew."

"If she can do it, she should," Dardenas said. "No point having her stuck here in the line of fire too, and losing her mission."

"No point in letting her kill herself on an off-plan spacewalk either," Jackson said. "She dies, it's on us."

Vivian glared. "If I die, it's on *me*. But I won't. I've trained."

"Not for this." Rawlings looked at the board. Looked at the clock. Then he saw the expression on Vivian's face. "I dunno. But okay, fine, let's at least start prepping so we're ready for anything."

He turned to face the rest of the crew, his voice carrying clear through the habitable space. "Listen up! Emergency EVA for Vivian, to get Apollo 32 clear on return, soonest. Mason! Prep Port Three for evac. Don't skimp the checklist, but do it *fast*. Wagner, grab her suit and help me wrap her." Both Wagner and Mason kicked off upward, streaking through the high open space of the forward compartment.

"We can't signal 32 to let 'em know," Jackson said. "Not by radio, or the Russkies will hear. Not by lamp, or they'll see."

"My boys will know I'm coming," Vivian said.

"Will they?"

"We'll figure something out," Rawlings said impatiently. "If there's even time. Dardenas, where do we stand with the Soviets?"

"Well, they're still incoming," said Dardenas. "And ... wait. Okay, yeah, I'm now seeing separation on 32. Horn and Mayer are on their return."

"About fricking time," she said.

"Vivian, catch." Wagner had thrown her suit, and it was twisting and turning in the air as it drifted down to her. Rawlings helped her grab it and held it steady while she wriggled into it. Wagner was still scooting around up in the dome, grabbing Vivian's gloves and helmet.

Vivian got her head up and out through the collar in record time. She hardly registered it when Rawlings zipped her suit up the back. *Priorities.* "Open the loop for me."

Dardenas flipped the switch.

"Major-General Makarov, it's an honor and a privilege to speak with you. I regret that we will not be able to meet in person, as I have other duties to perform." That would clue Ellis and Dave in that she was still coming. "Meanwhile, please cease jamming our S-band as soon as we have direct line of sight with Earth, so that we may reestablish communications with Mission Control. Understand that Commander Rawlings can neither allow your approach, nor relinquish the station, without orders from his superiors."

Vivian looked at Rawlings and grimaced. For a moment, the commander of Columbia seemed almost amused.

Now they heard a third voice, a woman's. Heavy Ukrainian accent. "Captain Carter and Columbia, please be assured that we are not bluffing. We have capability of taking your station with or without your permission. We have full authorization to use that capability. But we would prefer no loss of life."

"Well, hi there, fellow spacewoman," Vivian said. "Who are you, now? In your case I'll settle for just a name."

To that there was no response.

Rawlings broke comms. "Must be Svetlana Belyakova. She and Makarov come as a matched pair."

The second Russian voice came back again, the harsher-toned man. "Columbia Station, this is simple. You will allow us to board, or we will do this the hard way. Apollo 32, your surface mission is canceled. You will jettison your Lunar Module and return to Earth."

Vivian's blood ran cold. *Jettison. Jesus Christ.*

She'd been clinging to the hope they'd just *let her go.* A peaceful mission to the surface? The Russians might mistake Columbia for a military facility, but a classic Apollo with a science mission plan? They'd just let them go on, right?

Wrong. She wondered how she'd ever let herself think otherwise.

"Break, comms off," Dardenas said. "Apollo 32 has pedal to the metal. Coming in hot. Horn had better start a retro fire soon or he'll overshoot."

Vivian shook her head. "That's exactly what he'll do, overshoot. Right now, he's behind us in orbit. And the Soviets are coming from behind and under. If Horn goes beyond, Columbia ends up between the Soviets and 32."

Even Jackson looked impressed. Rawlings nodded. "Yeah, okay. Cool."

"But we need more time." Vivian glanced up. Wagner was bringing her a PLSS—a portable life support system. Zabrinski was holding her gloves and helmet ready. *Shit's getting real.*

She hated it that this level had no windows. How did these guys stand it? She looked at the clock, but her mind had gone blank. "How long till daylight?"

"Ten minutes till night-day terminator," Rawlings said promptly. "Ten minutes longer till AOS with Houston, except that the Russkies will for sure not let us talk to them."

"Yeah." Vivian winced as Wagner tightened the PLSS harness across her shoulders. Josh was snapping in hoses and connectors.

Vivian should really be paying more attention to this. She'd be in vacuum real soon now. She glanced at the displays on the control unit on her chest. *Um.*

"Vivian, are you ready?"

I dunno. Am I?

Despite her bravado, the answer was a clear No.

Dardenas flinched. "Apollo 32 is passing … ouch, holy smokes, range indistinguishable from zero. Okay, they're past. Still braking. Looks like they'll take up station a couple hundred yards beyond us. Maybe farther."

A couple hundred yards? A short walk. A hell of a long spacewalk.

Vivian wondered what that had looked like from Apollo 32's perspective. Completely different from their first sedate approach. *Ellis can't even have had time to call numbers. Must have been total seat-of-the-pants from Dave Horn. Scary as hell.*

"Soviets almost on us," Jackson said. "Coming in … a bit more moderately than your guys." He looked back at Vivian, and this time there was no disdain or humor in his expression. "It's now or never. Good luck, Rocket Girl."

"Well, so much for stalling the bastards," Rawlings said. "Vivian, go."

He took Vivian's right glove. Wagner her left. Vivian raised her arms, watched as the men made the connections, snapped the gloves tight, double-checked and cross-checked them. Josh was now holding her helmet and a zip gun, and Vivian began to focus in on what she'd signed up for.

Alexei Leonov's first spacewalk had been performed with an oxygen backpack and a tether; Ed White's, with a twenty-five-foot umbilical to bring him oxygen, a tether, and a zip gun like the one Josh had in his hand.

In fact, almost all spacewalks to date had been tether-and-umbilical. Vivian's spacewalk for TV would have been, too. Now, it could not be.

The original plan had called for Dave Horn and Ellis Mayer to bring the Apollo stack back to within fifty feet of Columbia Station.

39

Vivian would egress, tethered to Columbia and with an umbilical for oxygen, and conduct her photo-op spacewalk. She'd perform a largely redundant visual inspection, then clamber through the open hatch into her Command Module. Disconnect the pipes and wires, seal up the capsule, and off they'd go.

It wasn't supposed to be hard. Just another US first to check off: spacewalk by female astronaut, done and done.

Now, with four Soviet craft in the mix and no time margin, it would be a completely different animal. Hence the PLSS for life support. Vivian would be going way too far for an umbilical, too far for even a tether. She'd be doing this free-form, steering with a gas gun.

"You can still abort. Order 32 to disengage into a higher orbit, wait to see what happens here with the Soviets. There might be a safer solution."

Couple hundred yards was a hell of a distance. And this wasn't on the plan. Everything was moving a bit too fast for Vivian to keep up with.

No. She wasn't throwing in the towel. She'd got it right: her place was with her crew. Her ship. Her mission.

Rawlings was studying her face. "Vivian? You good to go?"

"Roger that," she said. "Vivian is Go for return to Apollo 32."

"Okay. Good luck." Rawlings lowered the spacesuit helmet over her head, pushed down to lock it into the neck ring.

"Pressurizing," she said to the microphone by her chin, and heard her own voice dimly through the station loudspeakers.

Josh raised his forefinger to his lips in the age-old gesture of silence.

Oh yeah. Anything I say now, the Soviets can also hear. Way to go, Viv.

She shoved off against the floor. Rawlings and Wagner came with her, one on each side, helping to steer her now-bulky form toward the airlock hatch where Mason was waiting.

Oxygen hissed through her suit. Vivian took long, deep breaths. No turning back now.

CHAPTER 4

Cislunar Space: Vivian Carter
Mission Elapsed Time (Hours): 105:22:09

THE zip gun was simple in design. It had two nozzles on stalks pointing backward, and one pointing forward. You aimed it where you wanted to go and pulled the trigger. Pressurized nitrogen vented out from the backward-facing nozzles, and away you went. On arrival you flipped a switch, pointed and fired again, and this time nitrogen squirted out the front, to slow you down. A bit of care about your center of gravity and you'd be fine.

Sure. Except the only way you could train for this on Earth was underwater, in a buoyancy tank. And water tended to hold you in place.

Vivian Carter jetted across the void toward Apollo 32, rolling gently around her center of mass at a rate of maybe a cycle every ten seconds. It had been worse just a few moments ago, and she'd worried that she might throw up into her helmet before she made it across the abyss that separated her from 32. So she'd used the zip gun to slow her roll, and not done it well. She'd messed up her trajectory toward her spacecraft, and then she'd had to fix *that*.

Photo-op spacewalk, my ass.

But at least she was heading toward Apollo 32, her safe haven.

Her ship, at least, looked nominal. The Apollo Command and Service Module, two triangles separated by a cylinder, a sleek bullet, joined to the most ungainly space vehicle ever devised. The Lunar Module was

41

a bug with a gray aluminum head, windows for eyes and a hatch for a nose, gold foil wrapping its thorax, and skinny tubular legs.

Vivian had obviously never seen her combined spacecraft before with her own eyes. Now she was floating toward it. And sixty miles below, the Moon scrolled past—that same Moon she'd stared at from the Earth's surface all her life.

Behind her, Columbia Station was now swarmed by the four Soviet craft, their hatches open and cosmonauts on umbilicals floating around them. One of the four ships, she could now see, was a Progress cargo tanker. The Progress craft were almost the same shape as the Soyuz, but uncrewed and remotely piloted.

Vivian was not being pursued. None of the Soyuz were chasing her. But what the hell was about to happen to Josh and his Columbia crew?

One thing at a time. Concentrate on where you're going. Nothing you can do to help Rawlings and the others now.

The closer Vivian got to Apollo 32, the more off target she realized she was. She did the briefest of nitrogen jet squirts at an offset angle of around twenty degrees. That helped a bit. But 32 itself was moving again, she was sure of it; easing slowly back toward her, powered by its reaction thrusters. And even as Vivian was rolling, 32 was in a slow roll of its own.

Was Horn trying to match trajectories with her? *Might be better if he didn't.*

Vivian couldn't communicate with her crew. The Soviets had stopped talking to Columbia and their jamming was once again live in her ears. Mason had signaled 32 with a flashlight once they'd arrived on the far side of Columbia. Her crew knew she was hurrying back to them.

Hurrying? Well. She still had several hundred feet to go. Her spacecraft was growing in front of her, but how fast was she going? It was really hard to figure out her relative speed. It would be bad if she smacked into her Lunar Module so hard that she damaged it. Or bounced off and away.

Everything was in motion around her. The Moon rotated beneath her, craters and plains and mountain ranges in stark monochrome. The Sun shone obliquely across the lunar landscape, bringing it into brutal sharp relief. Vivian felt intensely vulnerable, as if she could tumble down onto the Moon's surface, to be smashed in an instant.

Right now she was orbiting head-down, and she experienced a disorienting mental shift. The Moon loomed *over* her, burned and lifeless and hostile, ready to crush her at any moment.

Her breathing sounded very loud in her ears. She wondered if her heart was laboring—if stress was getting to her. *Can't imagine why that might be.*

She couldn't hurry this. Needed to get closer to 32 before she did anything else. Couldn't go too fast, couldn't get impatient.

She started taking longer breaths and glanced back again.

Three cosmonauts were working on the number-three airlock that Vivian had exited through, since the other two were blocked by CSMs. The Progress was now clamped to the outer skin of the station. Another Soyuz floated over the station's solar panels, its threat to Columbia's primary power system obvious. The hatch of the third Soyuz was open, the top half of a cosmonaut jutting out. Pointing something in her direction.

She saw the muzzle flashes at the same moment as she heard her own voice shouting, a din in her helmet: "No! What? No!"

The cosmonaut was firing an assault rifle at her? In space? *Holy crap* ....

Vivian squeezed her own trigger, the one on her gas gun, and everything lurched. She stopped quickly. She wasn't flying a jet, couldn't just take evasive maneuvers. If she missed Apollo 32 altogether, she'd be totally screwed.

More muzzle flashes, and then a mule kicked her in the shoulder and there was a hideous screech that certainly hadn't come from Vivian's throat.

Vivian swung back, tumbling, the sudden motion sickening. Columbia Station and its attackers slid away, and the Moon scythed across her field of view. Dizziness and nausea swept her, and she felt an intense and growing pain in her shoulder.

The cosmonaut had shot her. A deep scratch marred the upper part of her helmet visor that hadn't been there a moment ago. And she was in a dangerous roll.

Vivian felt drenched in a hot wave of dazed unreality. *If I ignore all this, it'll go away. No?*

Maybe ... ?

With a jolt, full consciousness came back, and Vivian realized that she'd mentally drifted off, dissociated from what was going on around her. *Snap out of it. Come on.*

She looked down at her gauge. Her air pressure was low, but holding steady. If she was holed, it wasn't by much. But that mule had just slammed its hooves into her shoulder, and she felt a new hot dampness down by her ankle that could only be blood. Had she taken a bullet there too? No time to bend and look.

As for the bullet scratch across her visor, she really didn't want to think about what would have happened if that bullet had slammed into her helmet face-on.

Instead, she looked ahead to Apollo 32. Raised her gas gun and gave a short squirt back over her shoulder, against her direction of spin. Not enough. She gave it another pulse, and another, and managed to cancel her rotation, mostly.

Glanced back at the Soyuz craft clustered around Columbia. Saw the cosmonaut hefting his rocket launcher into position on his shoulder.

Oh, oh, oh. Hell's teeth.

If that rocket had a heat seeker, it would get either her or Apollo 32. Out here in sunlight they'd both be glowing like crazy in the infrared.

She would die. Or Horn and Mayer would die first, and then she'd die soon after.

The bastard hasn't fired yet. Why not?

The cosmonaut was holding still, holding position. He must have the rocket launcher aimed right at her, because it now looked like a tiny disk rather than a tube.

Vivian gritted her teeth and looked away. She was currently facing Columbia, flying backward. Apollo 32 now appeared to be behind her and off to the left. She lined the zip gun up roughly with her center of mass, and gave that trigger a good long squeeze. *Caution be damned. Kind of beyond that now.*

The Command Module side hatch was open. Well, thank God, but Vivian's current trajectory was taking her squarely toward the LM. *Damn it.*

The LM had a pretty thin skin. Vivian didn't want to come barreling in and smack into it. She could leave a major dent, even damage something critical. She sent a pulse of gas off to one side, again corrected too much.

She had to twist in her suit to fix it. Another wave of intense pain flooded her. "Aaah, for the love of …" All this swinging her arm around was killing her shoulder, but she wasn't about to switch hands. The gas gun was tethered to her, so she couldn't lose it, but even with a banged-up right shoulder she didn't want to steer left-handed. She wasn't that ambidextrous.

She steeled herself, leaned into the pain, and corrected yet again.

Glanced back at the Soyuz. No change. No movement. No missile. Still, the cosmonaut was waiting.

Oh. I bet I know why.

She swung to look back at her Apollo. The closer she got, the faster she realized she was going. Once seemingly immobile in the black, Apollo 32 now seemed to be bearing down on her like a freight train. Twenty feet per second, minimum. Probably more. Way too fast …

Vivian flipped the switch on the gas gun, pointed directly at 32 and applied full braking thrust. It slowed her, but not enough. In the seconds she had left she kicked her legs up, tried to fold herself so that it wouldn't be her injured shoulder that impacted first, but the stiff suit resisted her—

She hit Apollo 32 butt-first, taking the brunt of the impact on her left hip, slamming into the Service Module just above the big conic rocket nozzle at its base. Her PLSS hit next, with a thud and a muffled clang that reverberated through the inside of her suit … and then she bounced off.

"God *damn* it to *hell!*"

Vivian fired the gas gun again, largely on instinct. Slewed around dizzyingly, but got her gloved left hand onto the handrail that Command Module Pilots used during EVA on the long coast back from the Moon to fetch film canisters out of the Service Module. Released the zip gun, got her right glove onto the rail, started pulling herself along it hand over hand.

The Service Module was only thirty-some feet long. It seemed much longer. But there was Dave Horn, suited up and leaning out of the CM's side hatch, waiting for her.

If the cosmonaut had been waiting to kill two birds with one stone, the missile would be arriving any second now.

Or maybe they'd save it in case they needed to use it on Columbia. They probably weren't carrying many missiles that size. *Shit.*

Or … there was another, even more ominous possibility. One that Vivian chose to put out of her mind for now. *Nothing I can do about it. First things first.*

Still only that goddamn hissing in her ears. The Soviets were doing a swell number on them today. Good job Vivian actually had nothing to say to anyone right now. And a good job no one could hear her whimper and curse.

Ten feet separated her from Dave, then five. He was beckoning with both hands, urgently, *hurry up Viv, hurry up*. He was right. No time for subtlety, they had to get out of here.

Vivian heaved, let go, practically launched herself at him. Dave gripped her left arm with both hands. She swung, pivoting around him.

Oops. Too keen. Damn it, I can do better than this.

Her momentum had flipped her so that her feet were now pointing at the LM—"down," said her brain, since she was looking at it from what would be above, if the Module was resting on a surface. Vivian twisted to get her legs under her and felt a stab of protest from her wounded left ankle. "Okay, I got it," she said, but Horn couldn't hear her, of course, so she did a thumbs-up, in that half-assed way that was all her suit glove would allow.

Horn retreated backward into the CM. There wasn't room in the hatchway for both of them. Suited up, it was barely wide enough for one. He ducked in and to the side, still gripping her, and she grabbed at the edge of the hatchway with her free glove.

Ideally, she'd have maneuvered to come in feetfirst. No time for that. Vivian let go of Horn and dove through the hatchway, grasping it on either side and hauling herself in, heedless of the pain in her shoulder.

As she slid into the CM, Vivian experienced an instant of claustrophobia followed by a flare of panic. It was just her and Horn. *Where the hell was Ellis?*

She cried out, a strange moan of desperation. And then realized that, of course, Ellis Mayer would be in the Lunar Module. There had been no time for both Ellis and Dave to suit up. Ellis must have helped Dave into his suit and then retreated to shut himself into the LM while Dave depressurized the Command Module. Vivian had even seen the lights on in the Lunar Module, but hadn't thought it through. *Must still be cold as hell in there.*

Good thing, though, because space was at a premium in the CM with Dave and Vivian both bulky in suits. Dave had folded up the center couch to make more room, and Vivian pulled herself in between the two that remained, hunching and bending her legs to bring

46

her boots in, clear of the hatch. Horn threaded himself around her to close it up.

Taking off the PLSS would cost them minutes they didn't have. Vivian wriggled and twisted, trying to position herself over the right couch as Dave got the hatch closed. She still couldn't talk to him, didn't know whether they'd take the time to repressurize the cabin before—

Nope. Dave pushed himself into the left couch, glanced at the eight ball that showed the CM's orientation relative to the Moon's horizon, and jabbed the keyboard on his guidance computer with a gloved finger.

Vivian fumbled for her seat restraints but had no time to even find them, let alone adjust the straps. The seat lurched and thrust hard into her, jamming the PLSS into her spine. Her CMP had initiated a pre-programmed burn with zero warning and no double-checking. Dave swung his head back and forth inside his helmet, studying switches and gauges, the eight ball, the stars outside the window. She could see his lips moving as he talked to himself.

Vivian held on. No danger right away, not with the G-forces pushing her into her seat. The problem would come when the burn ended. That ceasing of acceleration would eject Vivian out of her seat and might send her slamming into the instrument panel. That was not at all what they needed, right now.

Vivian wasn't counting seconds, but Dave was. His finger tapped as he watched the clock.

As the burn continued, Vivian could see a small part of Columbia Station through the windows, and Soviet craft still clinging to it like limpets. But mostly what she saw was the Lunar Module above them, and the Moon beyond. Then Columbia slid away and out of sight. Half a minute later, the burn ended, gently. Dave had attenuated it gradually. Neither of them slammed into anything.

Horn checked numbers. From his posture and stillness Vivian could tell he was thinking intently, could almost see that fierce brain working.

She waited. The burn had been retro, opposing Apollo 32's direction of motion. Due to the perversity of orbital mechanics this would actually speed them up, dropping them into a lower elliptical orbit to quickly put distance between themselves and the Soviets. To match their course, a Soyuz would have to estimate their track by eye and attempt to duplicate it. Had Apollo 32 been broadcasting a radio signal that the Russians could latch onto for range and velocity, it might have been possible, but of course they weren't.

Darkness fell as they crossed the terminator. They were free from pursuit, but not from a shoulder-mounted heat-seeking missile.

Hopefully, if a missile hadn't found them yet, it wasn't going to.

Dave waved generally around them, and gave her the high sign. Vivian nodded. Time to repressurize this baby and get their helmets and gloves off.

And figure out what the hell to do next.

"Where are we?" Ellis demanded, as soon as they opened up the tunnel to the LM.

Vivian had asked the same question once she'd gotten her helmet off, and so by now she knew the answer. Besides, Dave ignored Ellis. He was busy now with the CM's sextant and telescope, his lips moving silently as he measured star offsets and punched numbers into the guidance computer, fine-tuning their ephemeris.

"Elliptical orbit," Vivian said. "High point still sixty miles, lowest point now twelve miles. Equatorial plus the necessary boost to take us north. Perilune not ideally timed, but not too bad either. With an extra-long burn, we can initiate Marius PDI two orbits from now." Two lunar orbits: four hours. They wouldn't be able to finish preparing the LM for the powered descent initiation burn sooner than that anyway. Vivian grinned tautly. "As it turns out, Dave doesn't suck at this."

"Thanks." Horn grunted, frowned, did more math.

Ellis drifted in and pulled himself to the window, looking back at Columbia. "What the living hell is going on here?"

"The Soviets? Damned if I know. Apparently they're willing to go to war over the Moon?"

Ellis just shook his head, momentarily speechless.

Vivian took a long breath, looked at them both. "You guys okay?"

"I guess."

"The LM still nominal?"

"Sure." Ellis turned away from the window. "Wait, you still think we're a Go for Marius after *that*?"

Vivian shrugged, and tried not to wince at the pain this induced in her shoulder. Was *she* okay? For now. She'd piloted through worse. "No one has yet told me we're not."

"Well, no." Ellis grimaced. Obviously, no one had yet told them anything at all. The hiss in the headsets was attenuating, and sometimes they heard a ghostly voice trying to fight through the murk, but they were still jammed and would remain so until they achieved sufficient distance from Columbia, or put the Moon in between themselves and the Soviet transmitter. The jamming equipment was presumably aboard the Progress cargo tanker, Vivian now realized. Jammers weren't small.

"What about *them?*" Ellis gestured, meaning the Columbia crew.

"I have no freaking clue," Vivian said. "Nothing we can do for them now, though. Wish there was."

"We might have to abort to Earth," Ellis said. "Drop the LM and scoot."

Vivian gave him a look.

"Just saying, those might be our orders."

"Or they might not. NASA—the US—might decline to get chased off the Moon by the Reds. And why should we be? You think Makarov will follow us all the way to Marius just to shoot at us again? He doesn't even have a lander."

"Someone has shot you already," Horn pointed out.

He didn't need to remind her. "Let's not get sidetracked."

"What?" Ellis said. "Wait, shot you, what?"

She told Ellis the same minimum she'd told Dave—probable AK-47 bullets to the shoulder helmet, ankle. "Pretty sure nothing is broken."

Ellis didn't buy it. He scanned her in alarm. "Show me where. *Now*, Vivian."

"Jeez, fine." She touched her shoulder. "Here, mainly."

Together, they studied her suit. It was scuffed and abraded in three places at the shoulder, the marks several inches apart. At the calf it was tough to find the impact site at all. "Bullets bounced off," she said.

"Yeah, great," Ellis said. "What about *you?*"

"I'll take a look in a while," she said impatiently. "But I'm guessing general bruising to chest and shoulder, maybe abrasions at the calf. I'll patch the suit before the next EVA to be safe. Okay?"

"Well." Ellis frowned.

"*Moving on.* Moonwise: possession is nine-tenths of the law, right? It's all about occupancy. We're here to explore. For the US, and all mankind."

"Right," Dave said sardonically.

"If we were to go on ... the Soviets only have to wait ten days and we'll leave anyway. It's not like we can stick around any longer. After ten days we're out of supplies, lunar night is closing in, and Apollo 32 is heading home. There's no percentage in chasing us down. Ellis?"

Ellis had pulled out her helmet to peer at the bullet scratch across the visor. He cocked an eye at her. "Trying to persuade us, or yourself?"

"She's right." Horn nodded. "Columbia and Hadley have to be the Commies' priorities. The permanent stations in orbit and on-surface."

"Even *that* is nuts," Vivian said. "Take over Columbia? Why?"

"So's we can't see what *they're* doing," Horn said.

They swiveled to look at him. "Doing? What are they doing?"

"What are *we* doing?" Horn demanded. "Surveillance, that's what. Columbia flies over Zvezda Base twelve times a day. You think Columbia isn't watching Zvezda just as hard as our MOLs around the Earth are watching Baikonur and Tashkent and everywhere else the Soviets have facilities? What other use is it?"

"It's part of our long-term plan for Apollo Applications," Vivian objected. "Improved mapping of the lunar surface. Permanent stations on and around the Moon. Then Venus and Mars flybys. Then—"

"Oh, please," said Horn. "Spare me."

"What? Come on. What could the Soviets be doing at Zvezda that's so important that they wouldn't want Columbia to look down and see?"

"Well, that's the sixty-four-million-ruble question, isn't it, Comrade?"

"No," Vivian said. "I don't buy it. That *can't* be what all this is about."

"You have a better theory?"

Ellis was shaking his head. "I'm with Viv."

Horn glared. "Like Rawlings said, the Soviets just committed a damned *act of war*. You think they did that for shits and grins? This isn't some wild plan they cooked up last Wednesday. It was a really well-thought-out military strike, with a concrete strategy behind it. What do *you* suppose that is?"

"Break," Vivian said. "We stop arguing. It doesn't matter for now." She gestured at the radio. "Listen up. By the time we swing back around to Nearside we should have enough distance from the Soviets to talk to Houston again. Where do we want to be by then?"

"Close to the end of the LM activation list," Ellis said promptly. "Ready to initiate descent to landing on the next go-around. Just in case we do still get to go down."

"And where are we now?"

"Okay, Commander Obvious, enough already." Ellis grinned and kicked off to propel himself up into the narrow tunnel that led to the LM. "Let's get to it."

"Fine." Horn frowned and busied himself with the CM guidance computer again. "I'll, y'know, do math and stuff."

She paused. "Dave. Hey. You still okay with this?"

"Sure. I don't want to get chased off the Moon by Soviets any more than you do. This is the mission. It's just, after all that we're not quite in the right orbit any more, and it bothers me."

This is the mission. Vivian nodded, glanced once out the window at the fast-receding Columbia Station, and then pulled herself up through the narrow docking tunnel into the Lunar Module.

CHAPTER 5

Apollo 32: Vivian Carter
Mission Elapsed Time (Hours): 107:06:49

ON the early Apollos, much of the LM checkout had happened between the Earth and the Moon, and it still took three lunar orbits—six hours—to prepare for landing. That process had been streamlined in the years since, but it would still be an unholy rush.

Vivian and Ellis had rehearsed this in the simulator on Earth a dozen times, slowly and carefully. They'd never experimented to see how *fast* they could do it.

Pretty fast, as it turned out.

Even though they had to do it all out of order. Ellis obviously hadn't had time to do a proper initialization when he'd first rushed into the LM, so they had to backtrack, reset all the circuit breakers, and laboriously check all the switches and initial settings on the consoles. Next should have come the stocking and reprovisioning, moving food and equipment back and forth between the LM and CM, but they needed Horn for that, and he was busy. The VHF and S-band comms checks would obviously need to wait, too. So they jumped straight to fully activating the electrical power system, environmental controls, and guidance systems for landing.

Despite their hurry and their on-the-fly rework of the checklists, the activity calmed her. This was known territory, a steady workflow that Vivian understood in every detail. It kept her hands full and her mind mostly occupied, and Ellis's scrupulous care was reassuring.

Vivian couldn't imagine doing this without a partner, but the first man on the Moon, Alexei Leonov, had done the bulk of his prelanding preparation—and, of course, the landing itself—entirely alone. That landing, in May 1969, had beaten Apollo 11 to the punch by a humiliating two months, winning the Space Race for the Soviets with a brief ninety-minute solo excursion onto the Moon's surface.

Well, perhaps that wasn't fair. If anyone had won the Space Race it was the shadowy figure of the Chief Designer. The Soviets had kept the Designer's identity hidden, for fear that the CIA would try to assassinate him. After the landing he was revealed to be Sergei Korolev, a leading Soviet rocket engineer. A giant in his field, a true brother in technology to pioneers like Konstantin Tsiolkovsky, Hermann Oberth, Robert H. Goddard, Werner von Braun.

And so now Korolev was immortalized, rather than von Braun. The Soviets had spun themselves a fine propaganda yarn about how Korolev had been brought low by a heart problem in January 1966—had been at death's door—but that due to the superiority of Soviet medicine and his stout heart and love of country, had survived his illness and returned to the Soyuz factory floor just ten days later to continue his leadership of the Soviet space effort.

In stark contrast to his previous anonymity, Korolev had stood side by side with Leonov in the post-Moon-landing victory parades, twenty-seven years older than Leonov but still a vigorous man and now a People's Hero.

Though, Vivian thought, Leonov's task had likely been less complex than theirs. Korolev might well be a genius, but to US eyes Leonov had been largely cargo with little control over his fate. Yuri Gagarin, the first man in space, hadn't even been able to take the controls of his own craft. Even by 1969 the Soviets allegedly still relied heavily on computer control and kept operations as simple as possible. By contrast, the Apollo astronauts like her and Ellis were a highly skilled team who understood their craft inside and out. Armstrong and Aldrin may have landed later than Leonov, but they'd done it in a hell of a lot better style.

Stunt or not, the glory was Moscow's. The lunar landing was just the latest in their chain of linked successes: Sputnik, Laika, Gagarin;

Valentina Tereshkova the first woman in orbit; Luna 10 the first satellite of the Moon, and Leonov the first man to set foot on its surface. Cosmonauts Makarov and Belyakova, repeating Leonov's feat four months later, landing with far more control and pinpoint accuracy, and Belyakova the first woman on the Moon. Domino after crushing domino, achievement piled on top of achievement, demonstrating the Soviets' mastery of the high frontier.

Khrushchev trumpeted these successes far and wide, a demonstration of the compelling advantages provided by the Communist system. And American confidence, already taking a beating due to race riots at home and a failing war in Indochina, had crashed.

Something had to be done, and quickly. With the Vietnam war projected to be a long-drawn-out failure, President Nixon had cashed in his chips. Cut America's losses, pulled out unilaterally, and thrown those billions at the "Moon issue" instead.

There were Soviet footsteps on the Moon, but that hardly meant the Space Race was over. The US still led on the technical front. A few cheeky stolen bases could not negate the impact of the solid and repeatable home runs scored by the Americans.

The American eagle had surpassed the Russian bear in a vicious and convincing two-clawed attack. NASA had established a permanent scientific presence on the Moon, while—with less fanfare—the USAF's ongoing Manned Orbiting Laboratory program created a similarly rock-solid surveillance presence in Earth orbit, utilizing an updated variant of NASA's Gemini spacecraft. One of Vivian's closest friends in astronaut training, USAF astronaut Peter Sandoval, now worked that program. The Soviets had a similar program: their Salyut orbiting stations were a thinly veiled cover for their Almaz spy stations, and Vivian and the all the other NASA and USAF astronauts knew it.

Nixon had stayed the course through his two terms, and the President that followed him in 1976, Ronald Reagan, had taken up the torch, dedicated to establishing US dominance in space. And Vivian had the feeling that Reagan wasn't about back down now.

"Five minutes to acquisition of signal," said Horn.

Apollo 32 was a few minutes from swinging out from behind the Moon and having line of sight to Houston. At which point, assuming the Soviet jamming transmitter on Columbia was not of epically superhero proportions, they'd be back in contact with Mission Control.

All the Lunar Module systems had come online and checked out fine, with no unexpected anomalies, but Vivian couldn't shake the thought of those assault weapon bullets spraying past her toward her spacecraft. What if one or more of those slugs had hit her LM? Ellis and Dave claimed they'd heard nothing out of the ordinary. Then again, they'd been busy, and Dave had already been suited up by then.

Don't worry about what you can't change.

Bad enough to be in a tiny spacecraft, alone around the far side of the Moon. Even now, only a few dozen human beings alive had experienced this degree of isolation. And yet, with the Soviets attacking US installations in lunar orbit, this separation from the rest of humanity seemed almost incidental.

But at least Vivian had her ship. She still had her command. Still might make it to the lunar surface.

"Houston, 32, do you copy?"

Noise.

"Houston, 32—"

"32, Houston. We have you. Welcome back."

"Well, now, Houston, that's warm and comforting."

"All healthy? Report."

"Everyone's alive and healthy. All spacecraft systems nominal." *As far as we know.* "Houston? Status of Columbia Station?"

"Switching to secure radio, 32."

"Uh." Vivian and Ellis looked blankly at each other. Apollo expeditionary missions broadcast publicly for everyone on Earth to hear who had a radio set powerful enough to pick them up.

"Hang on." Horn pulled out a binder from a side pocket and flipped through it. "Hang on, hang on ... okay, got it. Houston, switching to secure radio in ... well, a minute or two." He toggled some switches on the comms panel, compared them against the checklist, then held the binder out to Vivian. "Your side too. And then the comms station in the LM. They all need to be set identically or nothing works."

"Okay." Vivian found the relevant switches and set them, then Ellis took the binder up into the LM. "Done," he called down shortly.

"Houston?"

"32, Houston. Roger on secure comms. Be advised that Columbia Station is now in Soviet hands."

Vivian and Ellis looked at each other grimly. Horn frowned. "How?"

"Rawlings surrendered it to them, to prevent destruction and loss of life."

"What? Why would he do that?"

Vivian leaned forward. "Hush, Dave. Houston, go ahead."

"The Soviets gave the crew of Columbia an ultimatum. They could open up and yield the station peacefully, or they could sit tight. If they sat tight, the Soviets would cut their way in. Forcing an explosive decompression if need be."

Vivian shuddered. *Explosive decompression. Jesus Christ.* Even if Rawlings and the other astros aboard Columbia had had time to suit up, they might not have survived the shock. She had a sudden, vivid mental picture of the chaos inside the Skylab if that had happened.

Would the Soviets truly have gone so far? Or were they bluffing?

I guess now we'll never know.

Horn shook his head, obviously angry. "How about the choice where they let our astronauts return to Earth *peacefully* in their Command Modules?"

"Apparently that one wasn't on the table," said CAPCOM.

"Josh wouldn't have done that, anyway," Vivian said. "Abandon his post, his command? He wouldn't have done it."

"Plus, once the astros had abandoned, the Soviets would just have cut their way in anyway," Houston added.

"So what?" Horn demanded. "An explosive breach would have destroyed most of the equipment on board, stopping it falling into Soviet hands."

Vivian shook her head. "Jeez, Dave."

"Anyway," came the voice of CAPCOM, at the same moment. "Rawlings had to make a decision on his own initiative. And we think he made the best call. If the crew of Columbia had bailed, the Soviets would likely have spun it that they'd abandoned ship, and claimed the station as salvage. And cut their way in at their leisure, as you say. The way it is now, the Soviets have committed acts of piracy and kidnap. They're illegally detaining US citizens. This solution means higher stakes all around."

"No kidding," Vivian muttered.

"And we're doing what, about it?" Horn demanded.

"Politicos are screaming and shouting in the UN."

Horn threw up his hands. "That's it?"

"Of course that's not *all* we're doing," CAPCOM said.

"Well?" Vivian said. "What else?"

"I don't know. Above my pay grade. But we've been assured that other forces are in play, behind the scenes."

Ellis looked around the small cabin at his crewmates. "Houston, none of us have any idea what that means."

"And neither do we, Apollo 32." CAPCOM said, with exaggerated patience.

"This way, a diplomatic solution is possible," Vivian said slowly. "This is now a hostage situation, like the US citizens currently being held in our embassy in Iran. Given enough pressure, the Soviets might withdraw and we'd still have the station. Abandoning, or forcing the Soviets to trash the station to gain ingress—"

"Would still have been better choices," Horn insisted. "Either of them."

"That's not the feeling down here," CAPCOM said. "Although, the USSR is claiming that our people are prisoners of war. Uniformed combatants."

"Combatants?" Ellis said. "For crying out loud …"

Vivian held up her hands. "Houston, 32. We're going to take a minute of private time here. Okay?" She didn't wait for an answer, but flicked off the comms, cutting out Mission Control. "Hey, guys? Chill out, okay? In that scenario, I'd have done the same as Josh."

Horn stared at her, baffled. "Surrender? Let the Reds in?"

"Yeah. And hoped to get the better of them later on."

They all thought about that. "Interesting," Ellis said.

"Josh's guys know the station inside and out. The Soviets don't. And these aren't just *Soviets*. It's Makarov, and presumably Belyakova. Cosmonauts. Moonwalkers. Heroes of the Soviet Union. They're trained astros first, soldiers second. Surely."

"Maybe not so much difference in the USSR," Horn said darkly.

"Once they're all together in the Skylab, talking like reasonable human beings …"

"I admire your confidence," said Horn.

"Okay, the hell with it." Ellis spread his hands. "Don't we have other stuff to do, here?"

Horn bit his lip. "Yeah. Okay."

Vivian hesitated. "But there's something else, first. You ready for this?"

They looked at her. "What?"

"The Soviets had a rocket launcher trained on us. Maybe on me, maybe on 32. But definitely aimed right the hell *at us*."

"Oh." Ellis leaned back in his couch. "I get it."

"God *damn*," said Horn. "*We* were the hostages."

"Yeah," Vivian said. "At least in that moment. I'm betting that the Soviets told Rawlings that we were toast if he didn't open up. And so he opened up. That's my best guess."

"Clever," Ellis said.

Horn's expression was dark. "I wanna kill someone."

"Me too," Vivian said. "But now? We are where we are. Moving on. Right?"

"I guess," said Ellis.

"Dave? Moving on?"

He blew out a long breath. "We're not telling Houston that part?"

"Later. Let's not complicate things for now. They seem fine with it the way they think it went down, and I don't want the burden of it being *us* that were the patsies here. But I don't keep secrets from you guys, and maybe this'll be important later on, who knows. Are we cool?"

Horn nodded. "Roger that. For now."

Vivian hit the button to reestablish contact. "Hey, Houston, Apollo 32. The Lunar Module checks out fine so far. So, we aim to head on down to the Moon on schedule. Are we Go?"

Was that pause longer than usual? Maybe she'd been a bit flippant for open loop. Then CAPCOM came back: "32, Houston, roger. We would like to read you up a PAD for your lunar descent."

Vivian broke comms, and to Mayer, said: "Be still my heart."

Mayer exhaled. "Thank God."

Immense, saturating relief. A PAD was pre-advisory data, a voice upload of the parameters the crew would need to enter into their guidance computers. For lunar descent.

So that was the call: they were going down to the surface after all.

"However, we, uh, regret to advise," said CAPCOM.

Vivian froze. "Yes?"

"PAD will contain new landing coordinates."

"Say again, Houston?"

"Apollo 32, sorry to tell you this, but you're diverted to Hadley Base."

It was a punch to her gut, even worse than being shot. With a similar effect: for a moment, Vivian was stunned. "What?"

"No way to spin this nicely, 32. Your Marius mission is off."

She glanced at Dave, then at Ellis. Both were similarly frozen in place. Ellis was blinking rapidly. "To *Hadley*? Why? Who the hell decided this?"

"It comes from the top, 32."

She looked out the window at the Moon endlessly rolling by beneath them. They were over the eastern Nearside; soon they'd come up on Mare Tranquillitatis again, where Neil and Buzz had landed. "Uh, *which* top, Houston?"

"Direct from the White House. 32 is a No-Go for Marius. You are diverted to Hadley Base. There can be no argument on this issue. Tell me that you copy."

The crystal sharpness of the lunar landscape blurred. Vivian said nothing. Ellis glanced at her, glanced away. They all waited.

CAPCOM broke protocol. "Vivian, the Marius Hills are five hundred miles *west* of the Soviet base at Copernicus Crater. Under current circumstances, the White House has deemed it too risky for you to be on the wrong side of Zvezda, for a Soviet moonbase to be in between you and Hadley. We couldn't guarantee your safety from further Soviet military action. So, you're still going down, but to Hadley. To conduct further scientific exploration there. To continue your mission, *a* mission anyway, and prove to the Russians that the US is not running scared, that we are still actively proceeding with our lunar operations. I'm sure you understand."

Vivian's heart was breaking. *Houston, I do not copy, say again.*

Except that she'd heard just fine.

Her mission, *her* explorations, everything she and her crew had worked so hard on for two years, was evaporating before her eyes.

"But … Houston, *five hundred miles*. Why would the Soviets go all that way to remove a crew that will leave soon enough anyway—"

CAPCOM, remorseless: "32, we cannot take that chance. You are No-Go for Marius. You are Go for Hadley. Do you copy?"

She looked at Ellis helplessly.

Ellis cleared his throat. "Houston, 32. Our flight plan is for Marius. Our current orbit is tuned for Marius. How could we even make landfall at Hadley from this orbit? We are honestly unclear on this point."

"32, Houston. We have a plane change PAD ready for upload."

"Plane change? Change our orbit that much?" Horn was muttering, looking at the guidance computer numbers, at tables in his binder, at a lunar map he'd pulled out and set floating in front of him. "Naw. From here, Hadley's not even *half*-possible."

"That would be one mother of a plane change, Houston," Vivian said forcefully.

'Well, good job FIDO's been working it for the past couple hours," CAPCOM said dryly. FIDO was the Flight Dynamics Officer at Mission Control. "We're going to spend out the SPS, mark the CSM zero-return until refuel."

Horn rocked back. "Uh, we're doing *what*, now?"

"You're using up Minerva's main engine?" Vivian said.

The Service Propulsion System rocket engine that powered the CSM had plenty of fuel left for trans-Earth injection, once it was time to leave lunar orbit and head home. But apparently Mission Control now intended them to burn all that fuel to put them into a new orbit, so their LM could land at Hadley Base.

"That leaves Dave stuck in orbit with no margin," Vivian said bluntly. "Come on. That's ... that's not acceptable, Houston. I can't risk my crew like that."

"32, Houston. Here's the complete plan. We put eighty percent of the CSM fuel into trajectory shaping for your landing at Hadley. Later, we figure out a fuel resupply run for Dave."

Vivian shook her head. "Later? Later when?"

"We're working that," CAPCOM said. "Don't have the details for you yet."

"Haven't pulled it out of their asses yet," said Horn, sotto voce.

"Soooo, this is no longer a ten-day mission, is what you're saying?"

"Still evaluating that too. Your mission duration is open ended at this time."

Horn and Mayer looked perplexed. Vivian blinked. "Open ended? Then, that's a hard negative, Houston. I can't just hang my CMP out to dry like that, with no recovery plan in place, while we go down to the surface." She took a deep breath. *Damn it. Damn it all.* "Come up with a better plan. We'll wait."

Horn raised his hand, shook his head, gestured.

Vivian reached toward the communications panel. "Uh, stand by Houston, we need a few moments to discuss, here."

The CAPCOM voice changed. "Vivian, this is Michael Collins. I understand your position completely. And I am very sorry. But you are aborting to Hadley, ASAP."

Michael freaking Collins? Command Module Pilot for Apollo 11, commander of Apollo 20, the seventeenth American in space, and also the seventeenth to walk on the surface of the Moon. National hero. Legend.

Oh, for God's sake. That's not fair.

But it doesn't change anything.

Actually, it did. Mission Control was trying to manipulate her, and she didn't like it one bit. "Okay, fine, Commander Collins. *You* tell me what sense this makes. How long would you have liked to orbit the Moon alone?"

"Whoa," said Ellis. "Vivian?"

Silence on the loop for eight seconds. Then: "32, we didn't copy that," Collins said. "Reconfirm, stand ready for new PAD. How do you read?"

As Vivian took in a deep breath, Ellis shook his head. Pointed at her mouth, mimed a zipping.

Vivian stared at him for a moment, nonplussed. Then looked up through the window at black eternity. "God *damn* it."

Ellis had muted the microphone. Houston hadn't heard it. "Vivian. If we had any choice? Even the smallest say in this? But we don't."

"I … know that."

"I hear you Viv. I do. But … Going to VOX." Voice-activated communications. Now, every word spoken would be heard in Mission Control.

She closed her eyes. "Houston, 32, we read you five by five. We are No-Go on Marius landing. We are ready to receive new PAD for the plane change."

Horn picked up a pencil. "Houston, proceed."

Numbers filled the air, verbs and nouns in numerical form. Horn faithfully transcribed the litany of coordinates, repeated them back, then began to punch them into the Command Module's guidance computer. Houston followed along.

After a pause, Michael Collins' voice came back. "Maps of Hadley in backup packet, 32. Confirm?"

Vivian dug them out, stared at photographs of a completely new terrain. A landscape she had not studied in the simulator, not even once.

"Houston, 32, maps for Hadley in hand." They were a blur of craters and mountains. She could barely comprehend what she was looking at, but her voice was steady, almost robotic. A good NASA soldier. "Uh, Houston, I apologize for my earlier communications glitch. That was rude. My error."

"No apology necessary, 32. Your disappointment is understandable. And rest assured, we'll take good care of your crewman."

"Thank you for that. Please confirm time to plane change burn? I was ... occupied."

"Viv, Houston, copy. We'll be doing the burns consecutively at one hour fifteen from now: plane change, and then descent orbit injection to put you on trajectory for landing."

Michael Collins had just called her "Viv," on open loop. On any other day, that would have been really freaking cool.

"Tons of time." Maybe the Hadley maps she was holding would come into focus by then. "Roger that, Houston. Apollo 32 will be ready for Hadley."

"I know you will, Viv."

"Thanks, uh, Mike."

Well. Okay, then. She turned to Dave Horn. Lowering the pitch of her voice to mimic the earlier CAPCOM's, she repeated: "So, 'Your mission duration is open ended at this time.'"

"Sure looks like it."

"Consumables?"

Horn looked around his Command Module. "Should be fine, at least for a while. We're stocked for the return to Earth plus lots of contingency. We'll transfer all your food and water for the Moon back into here as well. That's another twenty man-days worth. You can eat Hadley's food once you're down. I'll eat all this, and you can reprovision us from Hadley for Earth return. And oxygen is no issue."

"We estimate that current air, power, water, food in 32 should be sufficient for forty-five days," their original CAPCOM confirmed.

Horn glanced at the loudspeaker. "Yeah, I just said that."

"Forty-five days." Vivian looked around the confined space of the Command Module. Dave Horn might spend a *month and a half* all alone in this tin can? *Shit*, she mouthed at Dave when he next looked at her.

Horn didn't even blink. "Larder will be pretty bare by then. But I won't be exerting. Maybe I could even go sixty."

"You're crazy," she said. "Two *months*?"

"Hey, go Army," he said. "Don't worry. I'll live."

"Make sure you do, man."

Vivian shook her head. *We're really doing this? Really?*

Ellis gave Dave a long stare, then looked away. "Houston, 32. I'll be ready to receive the updated Lunar Module PAD in a couple minutes. Heading into Athena now."

Vivian's mind was still a whirl. Even once the fierce plane change adjustment was taken care of, this was still a complete game changer.

To land at the Marius Hills, Vivian would have flown her LM in from the east across the Oceanus Procellarum, Ocean of Storms. The only lunar ocean, largest of the mares, Procellarum was the dark basaltic plain on the left of the Moon as seen from Earth's surface. They'd have begun their descent burn 250 miles east from a position just north of Kepler Crater. The approach would have been over largely level terrain until the volcanic domes of Marius came into view. The approach to Hadley, on the other hand, would take them over a giant mountain range—

"Wait," she said, interrupting the steady quiet stream of numbers coming over the loop and Ellis's careful repetition and entry of them into the LM's computer. Both came to an abrupt halt, and Ellis called down to her with as much irritation as he ever showed. "Vivian, what now?"

"Houston, we have a problem."

Collins came back onto the loop. "And what would that be, 32?"

Marius would have been the farthest west on the Moon that humans had ever landed, with Earth permanently down near the horizon as viewed from the surface. Hadley was pretty much central on the lunar disk, as seen from Earth.

Marius and Hadley were only fifteen degrees apart in latitude, but over fifty in longitude. The Apollo 32 launch date and mission profile had been chosen for optimum side-lit illumination for a Marius landing. Now, instead, they'd be landing fifty degrees farther east, putting the Sun at a sixty-degree angle. "We're way out of bed on solar elevation at the Hadley landing site, Houston."

"We're relaxing that requirement, 32."

Yeah, of course they were. She'd be the first commander ever to land a Lunar Module in Sun-soak, with high-angle glare washing out the surface features. *Not one of the records I was looking for.*

"Relaxing the requirement?"

"Roger that."

All right, fine. Fine.

The steady roll of numbers began again over the loop. With a hopeless shrug, Vivian picked up the contingency packet and pushed off upward to pull herself into the LM. Somehow, she wanted to be in the same space as Ellis while she did this. He barely spared her a glance, his attention on his notepad and the sixteen-character keyboard that was his link to the guidance computer, but his solid competence lent her strength.

Now she could focus. She scanned the plan.

It was even worse than she'd thought.

The ground track for the Hadley approach also—naturally—began 250 miles to the east of the landing site. They'd make the burn passing over Mare Serenitatis, the Sea of Serenity, the Moon's northern central mare, with the Sea of Tranquility to its southwest. They'd yaw to vertical over the western mare. Update their landing radar as they passed over the ten-degrees-east latitude line. Still all rolling terrain, ancient lava flows, with hummocks and a few craters.

But shortly after that they'd be flying into mountains. Serious mountains.

They'd come in over the Swann Range to Hadley Plain, to land just sixteen miles from Mount Hadley itself. The range was higher than the Rockies, and Mount Hadley was about the same height as Mount Whitney in the Sierra Nevada, the tallest peak in the contiguous US.

She'd acquire Hadley Delta, a different mountain eleven thousand feet tall, out of her left window when she hit the nine-thousand-foot mark. So its peak would be *above* them. *Mountains to the left, the right, above, and beneath. Gack.*

Ellis paused, took a drink of water. "Hey, newsflash," Vivian said. "Because of the mountains, the angle of our final descent after high gate is gonna be twenty-five degrees." They'd trained for a fourteen-degree descent.

Ellis barely looked up. "Fine. Fourteen is boring anyway."

"Yeah, kiddie slope."

Then, for the actual landing, Vivian would have to thread the needle and avoid the US assets already strewn over Hadley Plain. She had a map of them right here in her hand, accurate as of a week ago. Hopefully they hadn't moved too many things around in the meantime.

The Hadley folks would surely put down radar beacons, marking out a "safe" area for landing. Maybe safe as far as not hitting the Habs and fuel dumps, but sure as hell not safe where natural obstacles were concerned. They could hardly shift every boulder and iron out every crater from an area several hundred feet on a side. And the Sun would prevent Vivian from seeing those boulders and craters clearly.

This was going to be hairy as hell.

She looked out the window at the real lunar surface beneath them. Right now they were in daylight, but loss of signal was coming up in ten minutes, as Apollo 32 slid around the back of the Moon and out of contact with the Earth for the final time before they did the descent burn.

So, here was what was about to happen, provided Ellis finished his reprogramming before loss of signal—which looked likely, judging by the relaxation that was beginning to appear in the creases around his eyes.

On the far side of the Moon, Horn would fire the CSM main engine to initiate the plane change burn, and then the descent orbital insertion burn. The DOI burn would slow them into an elliptical orbit, sixty miles by nine.

Having done them that service, the CSM would separate from the LM. *Bye, Dave. Enjoy your weeks alone in space.*

Vivian and Ellis would swing around the Moon in Athena, losing height all the while as they dropped to the low point of their orbit. Then, at that lowest point, a little over fifty thousand feet above the surface, they'd fire the Lunar Module engine for the PDI burn. Powered descent initiation. And down they'd go.

Twelve minutes after PDI burn, they'd be on the Moon. One way or another.

With Ellis's critical help calling the numbers, Vivian would bring the Lunar Module down onto the surface. Woman, man, and machine in perfect harmony.

What could go wrong?

CHAPTER 6

Apollo 32: Vivian Carter
Mission Elapsed Time (Hours): 108:31:21

"I really wanted Marius, Ellis. I wanted it ... a lot."

"Well, we don't always get what we want."

His words were blunt, harsh. His eyes weren't. He was totally with her on this. But he was a tough guy, and he had to say tough-guy things, even when his soul was tearing. When his entire demeanor was radiating other emotions entirely.

"All right, fine," she said. "Fine. Screw Marius. Hadley's where it's at. I want Hadley. I want it bad."

Ellis nodded. "There you go. And it could be a hell of a lot worse. At least Hadley has mountains, A rille. Real geology. Scott and Irwin had themselves a blast there. Thought it was the best thing ever."

Her heart hurt. "Yeah, but they were the first ones in. They owned it. It was *theirs*."

Dave Scott and Jim Irwin. Apollo 15. The first and arguably most productive of the four Apollo J-mission lunar landings, devoted to science in an awesome location.

Their big discovery at Spur Crater: the Genesis Rock, formed at least four billion years ago in the early days of the solar system. That had been a huge deal nearly a decade ago, but was old news now. What had the two geology-trained astros currently on-surface at Hadley discovered since?

Vivian knew the answer to that because she'd been trained by the best of the Apollo geology instructors. And the answer was: not a whole lot. Science-wise, Hadley was probably tapped out.

She just shook her head at Ellis, and he grinned wryly, waved a hand. *What else can we do?* She blew out a breath, frowning.

They huddled in to study an approach they'd never simulated, or even visualized.

The burns were nominal. Almost anticlimactic, since they happened on the far side of the Moon, where Houston couldn't talk to them, and in the dark. Very long and steady, though, pushing them into their seats. The plane change burn used a hell of a lot of fuel. After that another thirty seconds of gentle thrust for the descent orbit insertion burn, and then Dave Horn nodding with satisfaction.

"Well, have fun." Ellis unbuckled, clapped Dave on the shoulder, and drifted up toward the tunnel into the LM.

"Sure thing," Horn said.

"We'll be back for you, Dave," Vivian said. "One way or another."

"I know you will."

Vivian hesitated. "Uh, look, man. We …"

Horn held up a hand. "Don't sweat it. You guys focus on the landing. Everything's gonna happen pretty fast from here on out."

That much was certain.

Vivian shut up. It was Horn's ass on the line. If this mysterious Houston recovery plan never happened, or got derailed by the Soviets, Horn might orbit forever in his own tomb. He no longer had the fuel to even adjust his orbit back to the plane of Columbia Station, to throw himself on the Soviets' mercy.

No point in dwelling on it. Vivian shook his hand, nodded once, and headed up through the docking tunnel after Ellis.

No reason to wait, and every reason to get ahead of the schedule while they could.

By the time they'd secured the hatches and unlatched, and Dave had done his separation burn to give them a delta-V of 2.5 feet per second, Vivian had already filed his predicament as a problem for another day and was thinking ahead to the next phase.

All the Apollo commanders trained for landing in the simulators on Earth for three hundred hours or more, memorizing the terrain and rehearsing for every possible anomaly, till they could do it in their sleep. But just because no one had crashed a descent yet hardly meant it was routine. And none of the others had landed at a site they hadn't trained for. In Sun-soak.

Literally a thousand things could go wrong, even in a Lunar Module with no AK-47 bullets lodged in it. They'd have to execute every aspect of a familiar but extremely complicated procedure, under very unfamiliar circumstances, and with mountains a few thousand or a few hundred or a few dozen feet below them.

Vivian still had a lot to do before landing. A hell of a lot.

The Apollo Lunar Module was outfitted for utility rather than comfort. From outside it looked like a wide-eyed bug, a squat head perched directly over an oddly short body with four splayed legs. Inside, the crew compartment was shaped like a short section of a tube, propped up on its edge: seven feet in diameter and less than four feet front to back. The LM had about the same internal volume as the Command Module, but oddly configured. Even stripped down to jumpsuits and in zero G it had seemed cramped. Now, wearing their spacesuits, there was just enough room for Vivian and Mayer to stand side by side.

In front of them were two triangular windows. Between the windows, and around them to the sides, stretched a complex array of instrument panels: avionics, guidance systems, communications boxes, circuit breakers, environmental controls. High and central above the front panels was an alignment optical telescope that Ellis would use to take star sightings to confirm their alignment and state vector. Bumping up against the backs of their legs was the ascent engine housing, and right behind that was the rear equipment bay with their comms gear and life support systems, and a mess of white and silver stowage locations for their suits, PLSS backpacks, tools, and food.

Above Vivian's head was the docking tunnel and hatch they'd entered through. Down in front of their feet was the hatch she'd eventually crawl out of, to get onto the porch and then down the ladder to the lunar surface. If they lived that long.

Vivian stood on the left with Ellis to her right, held in place with waist harnesses, footholds, and armrests. Umbilicals brought oxygen and cooling water into their suits. On Vivian's primary instrument panel was the eight ball that served as an attitude indicator, various other engine and guidance controls, and a ton of warning lights and other displays.

Her left hand held the thrust/translation controller assembly, her right the attitude control. To the right of that was her guidance computer display and keyboard, identical to the one on the Command Module but with different programs in its guts. Ellis had his own set of controls, in case of need.

The aluminum skin of the Lunar Module was only twelve-thousandths of an inch thick, and the walls visibly bowed outward when it was pressurized. But it was tough. Vivian had long since stopped worrying that it might pop like a balloon.

Despite the complexity and confinement of the LM cabin, Vivian felt completely at home. Standing here in the Lunar Module was as familiar to her as sitting in the cockpit of her T-38 jet, and a lot more comfortable than standing in the LM trainer at Kennedy Space Center in Earth gravity.

"Five minutes to AOS," Ellis cleared his throat. "So, Vivian: who takes the landing?"

"Uh, hi?" Vivian waved at him.

He studied her. "Let me see you move that shoulder."

Vivian raised and lowered her arms, rotated her wrists, made a chopping motion with each hand, then did a flamenco finger snap, left hand raised over her head and the other forearm sideways across her body. "Full range of motion. As far as the suit allows. I'm good to go."

It still hurt like hell, but she wasn't about to tell Ellis that. Her shoulder hadn't stiffened up yet, and she'd worked through worse pain. It wouldn't make any difference to her piloting.

Ellis reached forward, switched off the mics.

"Uh-oh," she said.

In LOS their voice band wasn't being monitored anyway. But by switching off the mic, Ellis was ensuring that their words wouldn't even be recorded for later playback in Houston. "Vivian, you took hits, big ones. And we're landing off-plan. New terrain. I need to know you're sure."

They'd been crew for two years, colleagues for longer. Vivian knew exactly what Ellis was driving at. If their positions had been reversed, she'd have pressed him on the same question.

But still. "The commander lands her. Always."

"Everything is always till it's not."

They'd both trained extensively in the simulator for landings. Anything could happen, so the crews cross-trained rigorously. If need be, Mayer certainly *could* land the LM. And Vivian would trust him to do it—if it came to that. She had no doubt that Mayer could bring them down to regolith. If Vivian had really been too injured to fly, she'd have handed the landing to Mayer without a qualm.

But she wasn't.

"It's mine," she said.

Ellis patted the air, and she realized that had come out of her mouth a little harsh. "And I *want* you to do it. You kick my ass most times in the simulator. That's not in question. But ... I just wanna be sure that ..." He looked at her intently. "Vivian. Pride?"

"First female Apollo commander? Sure, I'm proud. But that's not it."

"Okay. But I wanted you to know that, hypothetically, if you happened to be in any doubt, it would be a brave decision to punt on this and call the approach for me. I want us to be smart, here." He glanced at the mission clock. "Acquisition of signal in three minutes."

"In three, roger that," she said. "Honestly, Ellis. I'm fine. I can do this. It's okay. But thanks for checking."

He studied her again. His hand hovered over the mic switch. "Last chance. Anything I need to know?"

She should probably tell him her left foot was still sticky with blood. "Nope."

"No visual issues? Your eyes okay?"

"Jesus H. Christ, Ellis. *That* I would have told you right away."

"But, getting shot .... Your concentration still okay? It hasn't made you jumpy?"

"No more agitated than you, crewman."

"Fair." He grinned. "Okay, boss. Let's go smack this."

Ellis flicked the switch, and they were live again. "AOS in sixty seconds."

The Earth rose before them once again, over a lunar surface brightly lit. "Houston, 32," Vivian said calmly. "We're back around the block, you copy?"

Her headset crackled. "Apollo 32, Houston."

Acquisition of signal, right on schedule. Additional confirmation that Horn's DOI burn had been exactly on the money. *Thanks, man.*

"Houston, Athena. We're go-go-go."

"Houston, Minerva," came Dave Horn's voice from the CSM.

"32, Houston, we're ready to receive your burn report."

"Plane change burn fully successful," Dave said simply. "DOI burn likewise. Separation achieved with no issues."

"Athena is in center lane for final descent," Vivian said.

"Roger. Batteries, Athena?"

Ellis double-checked. "Ascent stage and explosive devices batteries solid at 37 volts."

Explosive devices. If they suffered a failure in the descent engine and were forced to abort, they'd have to fire the pyros, explosive bolts to drop the descent stage. And then hope the ascent stage engine fired and hightailed them back up into orbit, saving them from a long plummet down into the surface.

Vivian had flown that contingency a dozen times in the simulator. Hoped like hell she'd never have to do it in real life.

Ellis and CAPCOM were updating and verifying state vectors, coordinates. Vivian's eyes roved across her displays, double-checking every setting. Eventually he turned to her. "Okay. Time to go."

"Roger that," Vivian said, and they slid into the procedure with the ease of long practice.

"Throttle, soft stop," Ellis said.

"Soft stop, roger."

Houston: "Check DPS, APS, RCS, ECS, EPS?"

Vivian had already done all that. But she checked them again. "All nominal, Houston."

More chatter, this time with Horn about positions and settings for the high-gain antenna. Dave Horn, alone in the CSM some 350 miles behind them. Who would just stay up here and hang in orbit by himself, till Houston figured out what the hell to do with him.

The CSM would pass over Hadley as Vivian and Ellis landed. Horn might even snatch a glimpse of them through the 28× magnification lens of his onboard sextant.

The lunar surface was already getting pretty close beneath them. Even before the descent burn, their ellipse was swinging them down to fifty thousand feet. *Yep. That's the Moon all right. Sure enough.*

"Switching to VOX." No privacy from now on. No chatter, no BS. Everything on strict protocols. Vivian flexed her fingers.

71

"Roger, VOX loud and clear."

"P63 initiated." Ten minutes to powered descent burn, ten minutes to the principal braking phase. Twenty-two minutes till landing.

Ellis Mayer worked quickly and calmly beside her. "DECA gimbal AC closed, Command Override logic closed, Attitude control circuit breakers closed."

"Closed, confirm." Separate electrical busses. If her power failed, Ellis could take over.

Vivian felt herself relax as she went into the zone. *I got this. Even in Sun-drench.*

Ellis: "Attitude translation, four jets."

"Four jets," she agreed. Always nice to know the steering rockets worked.

On went the litany. Eventually: "Pings, Aggs to auto," Ellis said.

Pings: PGNS, the Primary Guidance and Navigation System, would control the initial braking and maneuvers. Aggs: AGS, the emergency Abort Guidance System, sitting calm and quiet as a backup in case of need. *Yay redundancy.*

"Pings auto, Aggs auto," she said.

"Throttle to minimum."

"Minimum, roger."

"Stand by for five minutes to PDI."

Five minutes, wow, time flies. "Go for final trim," she said.

"Athena, you are Go for powered descent," said CAPCOM.

"Go for PDI," Vivian said. "Nuthin's gonna stop us now."

"Roger that, Athena."

More checks, more careful adjustment of switches, more numbers. Vivian's breathing and heart rates eased. She was getting calmer, even as the critical moment approached.

"Mark: one minute," said Ellis.

Vivian flipped switches. "Master Arm on. Descent engine armed. Guidance A-OK."

"Here comes the ullage burn."

Even as Ellis said it, they felt the kick: a quick burst of the LM's jets to settle the propellant at the bottom of the tanks. They swayed in their harnesses.

"Ullage burn, no kidding," she said.

On her computer display two green figures blinked: 63. At the same time, Ellis said: "P63, confirm?"

P63 was the program for the braking burn. Vivian had five seconds to confirm and commit. The alternative was to abort, let their elliptical orbit swing them back up and away from the Moon.

Vivian calmly pressed the PROCEED button. "Proceeding."

"We have ignition."

The descent stage engine was firing steadily now, at 10 percent of maximum thrust. A form of gravity returned, nudging Vivian against her boots and the floor of the LM. She felt a twinge from her leg. Stupid thing. *Jeez, Vivian.*

She looked out of the window at the lava fields of Mare Serenitatis fifty thousand feet beneath them. Counted seconds as the guidance system gimballed the engine to align the LM's center of gravity over the major thrust that was coming.

"Throttle up," she said, with something like joy, and the descent engine kicked in hard. Nine thousand, nine hundred pounds of thrust, braking them for real, shoving her into the floor.

"Boom," Ellis said, flipping through tables, comparing numbers on paper to those on his display. "Descent rate good. Fuel, oxidizer good."

Houston fed them targeting updates. Vivian watched her twin guidance systems, PGNS and AGS, and compared their numbers. Under ideal conditions both systems should read the same, and they did. Close enough for rock and roll, anyway.

Ellis was watching too. "Aggs and Pings in good agreement."

"On my mark: three minutes into PDI burn," she said. "Aaaaand around we go. Goodbye, Moon. For now."

Ellis's lips twitched. The LM rolled smoothly. The illuminated lunar surface slid out of their windows. Vivian was now looking up into the blackness of space. Beside her, Ellis continued to call numbers. Vivian checked them, checked her systems. They were at forty-three thousand feet.

Behind their backs in the LM, the landing radar locked onto the surface and began to give them ground-truth numbers. Altitude and velocity. The numbers were good.

"Accept," Vivian said. From now on they'd rely on ground radar rather than predictive numbers. *Ground truth.* She liked that, especially as the "ground" would be giant-ass mountains anytime now.

"Thirty thousand feet," said Ellis. "We're a little long, a little south."

Vivian poked at her keyboard, scrutinized the numbers. "What's a *little*?"

"A few hundred feet. We'll fix it on pitch-over. Hold on a minute."

The square she was supposed to land in was only a couple hundred feet on a side. NASA assets dotted all around it. So that didn't sound like *a little* to Vivian.

And at any other time, Ellis would be giving her exact numbers. She glanced away from the computer. He was frowning. "Ellis, what?"

"Uh, we may have an issue."

At the same time, Houston piped up. "We read your oxidizer ten percent low. Athena, you copy?"

"Copy that, Houston, ten percent low." Ellis sounded relaxed, almost sleepy, which meant he was tense and completely focused.

"Altitude now five hundred low. H-dot, fifty high. Fuel good to two percent. Oxidizer now reading fifteen percent low."

Vivian scanned her instruments, said nothing. She didn't need to. No point in interrupting. Her pilot and CAPCOM were engaged in a quick-fire back-and-forth, staccato numbers, and Vivian completely understood what she was hearing.

What, but not *why*.

The Lunar Module rocket engines were powered by hypergolic propellants. The fuel, Aerozine 50, spontaneously ignited when mixed with the oxidizer, nitrogen tetroxide. They had separate tanks of each, and the mix happened in the engine.

They obviously needed both to get to the lunar surface. And now the oxidizer level had dipped dramatically right after they'd initiated full braking thrust. That could only mean a leak. And they were also suddenly five hundred feet lower than they should be, and dropping hard—their downward speed, H-dot, was fifty feet per second higher than it should have been.

A leak, and also a blockage? Had to be small—a large blockage would have stopped the engine cold. But this wasn't good.

Vivian felt the descent engine of the LM adjust to the new flow rate. That's what computers were for. "Now?" she demanded.

"Altitude two hundred low, H-dot twenty, fuel good, oxidizer stable at fifteen percent low."

Vivian realized she was breathing short, and took a big inhale. All right: bad, but not getting catastrophically worse. They were low on propellant, but it wasn't continuing to drop. They weren't falling out of the sky. Too much. "Hey, at least we're not landing long anymore, am I right?"

"Huh." Ellis didn't appreciate the levity.

And then the LM juddered, hard. Ellis swore.

"Houston, we have shimmy," Vivian said. Even to herself, she sounded oddly calm. "Medium intense. Copy?"

"Shimmy, roger, Athena. Continuing?"

"Abating."

Ellis shook his head convulsively, as if he couldn't believe it, or was trying to shake waterdrops out of his ears.

"We see it," CAPCOM reported a few moments later. "Can't explain it, though."

Ellis cut in, started barking numbers to Houston. They numbered right back at him. Vivian scanned her instruments and looked out at black sky. Beneath her the surface would be coming into relief as they dropped. Craters, the lava plain of Mare Serenitatis no longer seemingly a flat plain but a fully featured landscape of creases, dips, and small hillcrests. She itched to see it. Even with radar, not being able to see with her own eyes where they were going was … disconcerting.

Ellis fell silent. Vivian waited. She had no idea what the shimmy had been. From the interchange she'd just monitored, Ellis and Houston didn't either.

She held her breath, waiting for the abort call.

Then, through her headset: "Athena, Houston, you are Go at six. Twenty-eight thousand feet."

"Confirm Go, Houston. Proceeding."

Six minutes through the burn. And they were Go. Not aborted. Moving right along.

But they'd be desperately low on propellant for the landing. Vivian thought it through, doing barnyard math for the final descent. Fingers literally itching inside her gloves.

They still had their backs to the Moon. They had to be over the Swann Range now. Vivian couldn't wait for pitchover. She didn't like mountains she couldn't see.

"Seven minutes. Five hundred low. H-dot nominal. Fuel, oxidizer okay." Ellis looked at her. "Relatively speaking."

Meaning, not getting any worse. Staying on a lower trajectory, because why not, but not falling too fast. But at this point, Vivian was quite ready to strangle the Soviet soldier who'd taken potshots at her and her ship.

An AK-47, in space. Good grief. Her shoulder still ached like hell.

She found her mouth repeating numbers that her ears had heard. "Throttle down, seven plus twenty-two, copy." She checked attitude: no red flags. "Tell me where I stand with landing."

"Hold that thought. Eight thousand feet altitude … P64 is Go."

"Roger on P64." Vivian felt a surge of relief. "Bring it."

P64 was the code for final approach. Already they were pitching upright. And all of a sudden there was a mountain in her left window, looming above them. That was Mount Hadley Delta, rising eleven thousand feet above the valley floor, and the LM was at an altitude below eight thousand.

A huge crater on its northwestern slopes. St. George Crater. Vivian wondered what size crater the LM would make, if they kept on falling from right now, if the engines quit.

C'mon, now. That's not how we think.

"Houston, I have Hadley Delta, visual, left window." Still just drifting on by beside them. *Dang.*

"Ahead, I have Hadley Plain. The rille." Ellis glanced left at her to make sure she was ready. "Vivian has LPD."

"Roger on LPD." Vivian grasped her hand controller. The computer was still in overall charge, but now she had access to the Landing Point Designator. She could manually alter their projected landing target with a flick of the wrist, and the computer would recalculate the thrusters and trajectory for that new spot.

As they continued to pitch up, that target was coming into view.

Their desired landing site wasn't hard to see. A big old green beacon shone, center right on Hadley Plain, set out by the crew of Hadley Base. Unfortunately, Vivian already knew there was no way in hell she could reach that target, and when Ellis started giving her angles, heights, fuel readings, that clinched it.

It added up to this: by the flight plan, Vivian had three minutes from the P64 call through to the landing. But now she didn't, nothing like. In two minutes they'd be on reserve fuel. And at two minutes thirty or less, they'd be making a crater directly at the end of whatever trajectory they were flying at that point.

Alive or dead, Vivian and Ellis would be on the lunar surface a little over two minutes from *right now.*

Vivian felt completely calm, and if anything, CAPCOM and Ellis calmed further too. Every last trace of emotion cleared out of their voices. They all knew the score. Only clear heads would get them through this.

That, and some very quick and precise action.

Of course, it would help if Vivian could *see* any surface features aside from the mountain now passing behind them, the sinuous Hadley Rille far ahead, and the bright green dot of the beacon.

"Very few craters resolving, Houston. Sun-angle issue."

The glancing Sun angle of ten degrees that they'd trained with threw crater rims into sharp relief. The craters around Hadley were relatively shallow, and everything was washed out in the high glare.

She glanced at the map of the NASA assets she'd strapped to her arm. Naturally, landing short would put them down right by Hadley's fuel depot. Massive tanks of inflammable propellant. *Wouldn't that be the perfect way to make an entrance?*

Vivian flicked the controller to select a new landing spot, short and south of the light but long of where she thought the dump must be. Get the computer working on that while she kept trying to get her bearings.

Aside from St. George, she still hadn't identified a single crater. Hardly mattered now—because they were dropping like a stone. Final approach was supposed to take just over ninety seconds and take them all the way down to five hundred feet, and that was a pretty good lick. But Vivian was low on gas. They had to do it quicker.

At twelve hundred feet, it all suddenly began to make sense. At the same time, Ellis saw where they were too. "I have Index Crater on my four. Eleven hundred feet. Minus twenty."

"Index Crater. Roger." Vivian glanced at the map one last time. She wouldn't have the leisure of looking down again. For that matter, Ellis should be calling numbers off the displays, not looking out the window. "Eyes inside. I'm taking P66 early. Let's do this."

She flipped a switch near the attitude controller, moving the computer to the program for final descent.

By now the LM was almost vertical, balanced on a plume of rocket exhaust.

"Assuming full manual control."

Vivian wasn't even thinking any more, just acting, summoning up all of her skill and training. Her right hand gripped a controller that powered the sixteen attitude control thrusters. Her left controlled the thrust on the descent engine.

"P66 aye," Ellis said. "You have the com. Zone of Unforgiveness. The beacon is out."

"In the Zone, roger." At this altitude they couldn't abort to orbit. It was land or crash.

She could still see the glow of the beacon, well long of their current track. By "out," Ellis was stating the obvious, for Houston's benefit: that they couldn't make it that far on the fuel they had left.

"P66, thousand feet altitude. I'd call your angles, but ..." Ellis left that hanging. He could only call angles relative to a landing site, and he didn't know where Vivian was planning to land. Neither did she. "Houston, we have Low Gate. Nine hundred. Delta is minus twenty-five now. Minus thirty. Viv?"

"Keep calling, man," she said. "No asks. We're booking, here."

"No kidding," Ellis muttered. "Eight hundred, minus twenty-five feet per second, fuel at eleven percent, whoa, Jesus, Vivian ..."

At eight hundred feet, dropping toward the surface—way too fast—Vivian had goosed the thrusters to shove them forward. "Heading longer," she said, to confirm she'd meant to do that.

They flew over the fuel depot. At least, Vivian hoped that was what it was. The long, low tanks flashed by in an instant, and she'd only glimpsed them out of the very bottom of her window.

"Athena, Houston, you are Go for landing."

"Quiet, please," she said. Like she could abort now anyway.

She was shutting up Houston, not Ellis. He knew that. "Six hundred, minus thirty. Five hundred, minus twenty-five. Four hundred. Ten percent of fuel remaining. Damn ..."

"Damn is right," she said.

Time to hit the brakes. Left hand quivering, she fired thrust to slow their plunging descent. Hopefully, by enough.

"Three fifty, minus twenty, three hundred, minus fourteen, seven percent on fuel. Six percent."

Braking soaked up fuel like a bitch, obviously. *That's physics for ya.*

"Two hundred fifty feet, two hundred, one hundred, five percent on fuel, quantity light, we have quantity light."

Vivian knew that; her own light had just lit up to the right of her window.

"We're bingo in sixty seconds," Ellis said, an oh-shit tone to his voice.

They weren't supposed to call it that any more, but all the pilots did.

The Propellant Quantity light came on at 5.6 percent of their original propellant load remaining. This started a ninety-four-second countdown. When that count reached zero, they'd be riding fumes, with a maximum of twenty seconds in hand to get to the surface before running dry and crashing.

Again, twenty seconds was the *maximum*. Zero seconds was the minimum. At bingo, they might well be out of fuel. They wouldn't know the actual number of seconds until they expired.

The map of Hadley Base was a mess. By now Vivian couldn't remember where all the assets were in detail, and had no time to look again. The big Habitats were by the rille, of course, but everything else was scattered.

Well. Anything Vivian could see, she'd try not to hit, but whatever. Even if the LM pitched over on contact, they might survive. *Any landing you walk away from is a good landing, right?*

As long as nothing actually explodes.

"Mark me on thirty seconds to bingo," she said.

"Three hundred, minus fifteen. Two hundred, minus eleven. One fifty … one hundred. Thirty seconds to bingo on my mark …. Mark."

They were still too high. Damn it all to hell, Vivian had been shedding height like crazy and they were *still too high*. Still a killing fall from here, even in one-sixth G.

An asset resolved out of the glare. As Vivian glimpsed it, she goosed the Lunar Module to push forward, go long past it, using fuel she couldn't spare. Was that a crater ahead of them now? And boulders? "God-the-hell-*damn-it*!"

"Vivian, bring it *down*."

"Keep your hair on," she muttered.

The assets shouldn't be clustered, so if they were just past one, here should be as good as anywhere to set down. Yeah?

No. More boulders. Giant ones, bigger than the LM. "Oh, give me a break."

Vivian recalibrated mentally. When her eyes told her she was forty feet up, that would mean her landing pads were actually twenty-four feet above the surface. And from three of those four pads dangled a contact probe six feet long. So she'd be effectively "down" when her eyes told her she was still twenty-two feet up.

Of course, they were still way higher than that ... and then it didn't matter anyway. "Dust," she said.

Dust was kicking up all around them. Bright dust too. Whiter than white in the solar glare. Under a hundred feet from the ground, and all she could see was the shadow of Athena's ungainly silhouette against the dust background, torn and flexing.

Sun above them, dust below. And a very hard surface below that.

"IFR," she said. Not a NASA acronym for once: Instrument Flight Rules were FAA regs for civil aviation, under poor visibility conditions.

Ellis got it, of course. "Roger IFR, but you're still coming in very hot, holy crap ..."

"Stay with me, man."

"And bingo!" Ellis called. "Zero margin. Twenty seconds, nineteen, eighteen—"

"Give me feet!" she snapped.

"Sixty feet at three. Fifty at three. Forty. Thirty at minus three. Twenty-five at minus two. Ten seconds. Vivian, we—"

"Numbers!"

"Fifteen at two .... Ten at minus one. Eight at minus one. Contact light! Contact, contact, contact!"

Vivian jerked her left hand—one final pulse of the descent engine, one last shove to diminish their descent rate, if there was even any fuel left for that. Six feet between probes and pads. And the LM's undercarriage was hardly robust.

The engine died.

CHAPTER 7

Apollo 32: Vivian Carter
Mission Elapsed Time (Hours): 109:47:29

THE Lunar Module slammed down onto the surface with a loud, startling crunch. Ellis stumbled, and Vivian reached out to grab him before he could fall into the instrument panel. A stab of pain lanced up Vivian's left leg and she raised her boot from the floor, rocking in her straps. Ellis flailed, while scanning the indicator lights for any anomaly.

They swayed in their harnesses. Standing upright. On the goddamned *Moon*.

Vivian held her breath. Around them, everything rattled. But they remained level. The four landing legs held. Nothing broke. No warning lights came on.

Over her headset, distractingly, she could hear applause, and CAPCOM breathing heavily but saying nothing.

"Houston, be advised that Athena has landed at Hadley Base." Vivian exhaled big-time, wondering how long she'd been holding that breath in. "Christ on a pony."

"We copy you down, Athena, and congratulations."

Her armpits were wet, her forehead slick. Heart still racing. She looked out the window. and there was the great mountain of Hadley Delta, disarmingly smooth. It didn't look as tall as Vivian knew it was. That preternatural lunar clarity, and of course the high Sun angle washed the hell out of the topography.

81

She peered downward out the window as best she could. No cloud of dust around their landing pads now, of course. That would have required an atmosphere for it to be suspended in. The disturbed dust grains had just settled right back down onto the surface. Commander after commander had been startled by that. Even Neil Armstrong. Especially Neil, because he'd been the first to see it. Knowing intellectually that something peculiar's about to happen doesn't make it any less strange when you see it with your own eyes.

"ECS looks good," said Ellis. The Environmental Control System was still working? Well, that was fortunate. It hadn't occurred to Vivian to wonder. She'd been more concerned about the LM's legs buckling beneath them.

"Holding steady," she said, eyes flicking back and forth across the instrument panel again, and added: "Hallelujah and thank you God, Newton, and Robert Goddard."

"We had six seconds left on bingo fuel!" Ellis was saying at the same time. "Ridiculous!"

"Eh, trivial."

"Six seconds!"

Hey, if even supernaturally calm Ellis was jazzed, that must mean something, she supposed. "Don't look at me, the damned Russkies somehow stole a thousand pounds of my tetroxide."

Vivian had no idea what the real number was. She'd done all the barnyard math she was capable of, today.

Ellis was still shaking his head. "God *damn*, Viv. I *so* did not sign up for that."

"Yeah, who did?"

He blew out a long breath. "Okay. Houston: I am standing by for T-minus-one."

T-1 was their opportunity to abort back to orbit using the ascent engine, in case of a disaster on the landing. A leg about to collapse. Sinking in regolith. A critical malfunction. Anything.

Vivian snorted. "If you think I'm taking off again after *that* carnival ride, you're out of your freaking gourd."

"Procedure, Viv."

"Procedure, my ass."

CAPCOM, dry as ever: "Athena, Houston. You are Stay for T-minus-one."

"Houston, Athena," Ellis said. "We certainly roger that on Stay."

Vivian stared upward, breathing. First woman to ever pilot a Lunar Module down to the surface. Could someone please mention that? She wasn't about to bring it up herself.

No one did. Everyone seemed stuck for something to say. Perhaps they were concentrating on breathing again too.

She grunted. They were alive: that would have to do. She looked again at her markers, and across at Ellis.

Finally, he tore his gaze from the control board, looked at her, nodded once, and smiled.

Belatedly, Vivian said: "Houston, please advise Minerva that we're safely on-surface."

"I copy you down, Athena," came Dave Horn's voice from far above. "I was following along in real time. Cuss words and all. Epic."

Vivian stretched as best she could, realizing that the whole sides of her body were wet with sweat. Good job her suit covered up the evidence. "That little thing? Stroll in the park, Minerva."

"Huh. I mean, roger that, Commander."

Ellis sobered. "Houston: status on Columbia Station, please?"

"Uh, still in Soviet hands," said CAPCOM. "No new information at this time."

"But still our Moon," said Vivian, looking out the window at the arid grandeur of it all. Avoiding looking at the assets, for now. Just looking at the Moon.

"Copy that, Athena: the Moon, for the United States of America and all mankind. Whatever the USSR may claim."

Vivian hoped that Josh and the other guys on Columbia would get through this unharmed. "Be sure to advise us of any … sudden changes."

"Will do, Athena."

A crackle, then a new voice. "Athena, Hadley. Welcome to the neighborhood."

Jeez. This had to be Rick Norton, commander of Hadley Base, a man Vivian had met a few times and didn't get along with all that well.

More to the point, she'd gotten so used to the reassuring triangle of Ellis, Dave, and CAPCOM that Norton's transmission seemed a crass intrusion. Couldn't they have had a few moments to revel in their escape, their allegedly epic descent and landing, before Norton muscled in?

She clicked the radio off, worried that one of them might break out swearing, but Ellis just grinned and stretched. "Guess we're in the right place."

Right place? "Guess so." Vivian opened the loop again. "Greetings, Hadley Base, and thank you. Between you and me, we frankly had other plans for today, But, hey, what can you do? Here's Apollo 32, making lemonade."

"Looking forward to making everyone's acquaintance," Ellis said, and on seeing Vivian shake her head emphatically, added, "... in the fullness of time."

CAPCOM intervened to save them. "Athena, Houston: be aware that you have been awake for twenty hours on my mark." He paused, dramatically. "Mark."

"Houston, we copy. Hadley Base, we'll be doing our own thing over here a while," Vivian said. "Tidy, rest up. Follow procedures and all. At least somewhat."

"I'd expect nothing different. We'll be here when you're ready. Holler if y'all need anything."

"Will do, Hadley Base. Houston, Athena is taking five."

"Roger, Athena."

Vivian turned off the radio, freed herself from her straps, and slumped back onto the ascent motor cover to cradle her head in her hands. "Awake only twenty hours? Not a week? Seems like a week. Must be a week." All she felt right now was a post-adrenaline flatness.

Ellis didn't respond, and after a few moments she opened an eye to peer up at him. He was grinning like a kid. "What?" she demanded.

"Hey, we're well off the plan anyway," Ellis said. "It's all free-form, starting now. Right?"

"Sure, I guess. Meaning?"

He looked out at the lunar surface. "Well. I see two choices. Hammocks and shut-eye? Or, y'know, we could ... ?"

"Could what? Spill it, man."

"Get our bearings." He gestured upward. "Have a look-see. Pop the top hatch and take a real look around."

Ellis's excitement was infectious. Suddenly, Vivian didn't feel tired any more. They weren't at Marius, but this was still *the freaking Moon*. "Hey, since we still have our suits on anyway ..."

"It *was* part of our original flight plan."

She shoved another twinge of sorrow away. "Yes. Yes, it was."

Vivian pushed-to-talk. "Houston, this is Athena at Hadley. Be advised we will be initiating SEVA in ten."

She unkeyed. "We do this whether or not they say it's okay, right? We worked hard today. We get a treat before bed."

"Sure. Where's the hurt?"

"Yeah, where?"

Houston came back, and to their eternal credit, didn't even sound surprised. "Initiating SEVA. Roger Athena, we confirm."

Vivian grinned and winked at her pilot. "Copy, Houston. Athena proceeding to SEVA."

SEVA was a stand-up extravehicular activity, as opposed to the straight EVA of a spacewalk or a lunar excursion. Technically, when Dave Horn had plucked Vivian out of vacuum and hauled her into the Command Module, he'd been conducting a SEVA.

As had the cosmonaut who'd had his torso outside his Soyuz, shooting at her.

Lunar SEVAs dated back to Dave Scott, who'd opened the upper hatch of his LM for an initial 360° reconnaissance right after landing Apollo 15 here at Hadley Rille eight years ago. In Scott's case, it was to give his roomful of mission planners and geologists back on Earth enough ground-truth data to finalize the details of the moonwalk that would follow their sleep period. The maps of Hadley they'd been working with had only twenty-meter resolution, and Scott's recce had located them accurately on Hadley Plain and enabled them to fine-tune their activities. Until then, they hadn't even known for sure whether they'd be able to drive the Lunar Rover. The boulder field on the Plain might have been too dense to allow it.

A post-landing SEVA would have served the same purpose for Vivian and Ellis at Marius. At Hadley it was an indulgence. But, hey— all work and no play.

"Houston, we are Go for depress."

"Roger, understood, Athena. Go for depress."

"Going open." Suited up and cross-checked, Ellis released the dump valve in the hatch above them that would bleed the precious air out of their LM, depressurizing it.

"Cabin pressure four-point-zero, three-point-five psi," Vivian said. "Heading to three point zero."

Ellis paused the venting, studied his chest gauge. "I confirm my suit pressure is holding. Yours?"

"Oh, sure."

"Well hey, Miss Casual," he said.

Vivian had barely checked her gauge. Prior to leaving orbit she'd slapped patches over the gashes in her suit, just in case. Now, after a day spent obsessing about her suit integrity, she knew she'd be aware right away if she was losing pressure at any significant rate.

"Athena, Houston, confirm pressures?"

Ellis pointedly looked at Vivian's gauge. "Confirm both suit circuits at four-point-five psi and stable. Going to full open on dump valves."

For the first moments, they could hear the hiss as the air escaped. After that, the cabin pressure was too attenuated to carry the sound.

Ellis opened the hatch, swung it down, and locked it in position. Light flooded the cabin, and they both hurriedly closed their visors. "Houston, overhead hatch is full open and latched."

"Athena, Houston, confirm full open."

They hardly needed those guys on the ground any more, Vivian thought. And it wasn't likely they'd get a whole lot of attention from Houston in the days to come. Hadley activities, all dozen-and-a-half astronauts, were monitored by a single and separate Mission Control. Wasn't practical to handle it any other way. She shook her head.

"No?" Ellis was looking at her oddly. "Not going up after all?"

"Sorry. Wool gathering. Yes." She shuffled toward the center point of the cabin. "Uh, foot me."

He grabbed her boot—fortunately, her right boot—and steered it up onto the flat top of the ascent engine. She hopped up, trying not to wince, reached up for the hatch edges, and pulled.

Up she went. Just like that, her head popped out of the top of the LM. She felt Ellis leaning on her torso to keep her straight. She kept pulling, twisting a little as she went, so her shoulders wouldn't bind, but it took very little effort.

"Okay?" Ellis said anxiously.

"Easy peasy."

She settled in, resting on her forearms. "Pullups are really trivial here. Even in a suit."

Already, and even through her helmet, Vivian could feel the heat on the top of her head. "Damned Sun is way too bright, though. Uh, shade around me to keep the instrument panels from heating up too much? Perhaps drape a thermal blanket?"

"On it, boss," he said, sardonically. Yeah, being Ellis, he'd probably been doing that already. Fine. Time to stop fussing.

Vivian looked up and around her.

Eight other Lunar Modules dotted the Moon's surface within a half-mile radius. The nearest was only a couple hundred feet away, presumably the one Vivian had bobbled over on her final approach. Although seemingly scattered at random, the LMs all faced west, since they'd all flown in from the east over the mountains as Athena had. They resembled a small squad of insects, silently staring over Hadley Rille into the distance.

Each LM had its own US flag set out in front of it. That bit of formal claim staking had remained traditional ever since the first US Moon landing. The flags stood as immobile as the Modules, as if frozen in the act of flapping. The nylon flags were deployed on telescoping shafts and hung from aluminum rods. Most were already bleached almost white by the harsh UV light of lunar day. A couple still looked fresh, obviously the newer arrivals.

Naturally, Vivian and Ellis had brought their own. One of their initial actions once they left the LM would be to set it up in pride of place outside their new front porch, and damn it, Vivian was absolutely going to do that, first thing tomorrow. No one, NASA or Hadley commander or Soviet thug, was about to take that moment away from her.

Even if the flag would be planted exactly 998 miles away from where it should have been.

Vivian blinked, squinted. *Too much Sun. Seriously.* With all the reflected light off the metal around her, her eyes were watering despite the visor.

Several LMs had Lunar Rovers parked outside them. In front of many were ALSEP stations or other experiments. Vivian saw messes of cables, boxes and containers strewn everywhere. Trash, plastic and metal, tossed under the Modules for later retrieval.

Ahead and to the north, within a hundred yards of Hadley Rille, sat two squat cylindrical modules, Habitats A and B. More rovers were parked outside them. Next to the westmost module was a small backhoe with skeletal frame, a seat but no cabin, and a ten-inch bucket.

Vivian swiveled to look the other way, turning herself with her forearms. Behind them a quarter-mile distant, and well separated from each other, were four large tanks of the hypergolic propellants that fueled the LMs. The new M- and N-class Lunar Modules could be refueled to make extra launches and landings using their descent stages, before their final launches back into orbit to take their crew home.

She twisted again. Even farther away, far to the south, were the remains of six Cargo Containers, cylinders hard-landed with shipments of oxygen, water, food, and all the other supplies that kept Hadley Base going. These modules were broken and discarded, hauled aside and piled up together once their contents had been unloaded.

Everywhere around Vivian, near and far, the lunar regolith was scuffed up with boot prints and tire tracks. This was a working base, established for nearly a year. And it sure looked like one.

Marius would have been pristine. Hadley was a grungy tragedy.

Aware her mic was live, Vivian swallowed the angry sob that threatened to erupt out of her throat. *It's still the Moon. No?*

Sure, babe. It's the Moon.

Okay, so much for the works of Man. Vivian looked past them.

Rising high to their north was Mount Hadley, dominant peak of the Hadley-Apennine chain. It stood nearly fifteen thousand feet above the plain and must be sixteen miles away, but in the absolute clarity of vacuum it looked like a hill they could stroll to in twenty minutes. Around them the terrain was rocky and hummocky, and behind to the east rose the Swann Range they'd flown over to get here. Craters pocked the near and middle distance. Vivian had to keep reminding herself, as if on a mental repeat loop, that everything was much farther away than it seemed. Mount Hadley looked like a bleak gray sand dune right next to her, not the immense mountain that it really was. It wasn't craggy like a young mountain on Earth; the Hadley-Apennines were *old*, older than any mountain chain she'd ever seen on Earth, their rough edges eroded away by millennia of micrometeorite impacts.

And then, in the distance to the west, was the great lava-flooded plain of Palus Putredinis, flat and level, looking nothing at all like the Marsh of Decay it had been named for. Beyond Palus, Vivian knew, stretched the Mare Imbrium, the Sea of Rains, a thousand kilometers across and four billion years old.

Four billion years. And still pretty much the same as when it had been formed, give or take a few meteor strikes. *Woo. Boggles the mind.*

Light behaved oddly on the Moon. With the Sun high over Vivian's left shoulder, much of the lunar surface gleamed silver-bright. But with no air to refract or scatter light, it was direct sunlight or nothing. Those few areas in shadow were night-dark, a dark beyond velvet, as if the terrain in those unlit areas had simply ceased to exist.

The Moon was bold. It was stark. It was beautiful.

Apollo 32 had brought a new type of Lunar Rover, a cut above the workhorse models in use here. *Okay, yeah. So we can go farther, right? We can get away from the base, Ellis and I, well beyond where anyone else here has been. There must still be some Moon here for me.*

I just need to fight to get to it.

Tooth and nail if she had to.

"Well?" said Ellis's voice in her headset.

"Kind of a dump, if you ask me," she said. "But hey. Mountains are always cool, right?"

She ducked in and sat back heavily on the ascent engine cover as Ellis took his turn to jump up and peer around.

Sure, fine. The Moon was pretty. But she and Ellis were no longer pioneers blazing a trail. For now, they were just extra warm bodies, unplanned new mouths to feed at an established base, with no real purpose.

Here at Hadley, she would answer to Norton. And orbiting above them, the Soviet Union had commandeered Columbia Base and imprisoned her friends, and God knew how *that* would play out.

Everything Vivian had trained for, and the mission she'd obsessed about for years, had gone to shit. Real fast.

The hell with it. If anyone heard her, let them think less of her. And screw them if they did.

Vivian Carter cried.

Hatch closed, cabin repressurized, they helped each other clamber out of their suits, pulled the window shades to try to keep out the blazing Sun. Those shades didn't fit well. It wouldn't be truly dark in there until sunset, in well over a week.

They'd shut out Mission Control as well, as soon as they'd got the cabin habitable again and stowed the suits, and spoke little to each other beyond the functional. Preparing for sleep was always a quiet time for the crew of Apollo 32. Today, without Dave Horn, it was even quieter, almost melancholy.

So: just the two of them, and with added awkwardness. Her wet cheeks had been obvious as soon as she took her helmet off. And it was obvious that Ellis didn't know quite what to do about it, or whether he should do anything at all. "Okay?" he said experimentally.

"Sure." And because he didn't make a big deal about it, she added: "Thanks."

Then she finally took off her boots and socks and sponged the dried blood off her left calf and ankle. The entire area was abraded, black and bruised, but she could still flex her foot. Nothing seemed broken. Ellis watched for a while without comment as she padded and taped up the untidy area where the skin was torn, then shook his head and went back to stowing gear.

They finished tidying the cabin and strung up the hammocks. Vivian remembered rehearsing all this in one G, the unsuiting and housekeeping for the sleep period, and the ribald comments of the sim supervisors.

The appropriate terminology is "sleeping simultaneously," not "sleeping together," you jerks.

Ellis, at least, had been professional about it. Always.

Vivian took the top bunk, strung front to back across the ascent engine, and managed to hop up into it without flailing or banging into the ceiling. The light pressure of the hammock against her back was oddly comforting after being in zero G for days. She lay there and breathed, didn't look down as Ellis stripped to skivvies, took his last leak, and set himself up for bed lying crossways beneath her.

Now unobserved, she peeled back the beta-cloth coverall from her shoulder and took a cautious look.

Christ. Three purple-black bruises stared back at her, reddened at the edges and merging into one another. She'd been very lucky that those bullets hadn't impacted closer together and lower down, or the combined blunt force trauma might have splintered a hole right through her ribs into her lungs.

Well, that was a cheerful thought just before bedtime.

Vivian wrapped up and lay back, still wide awake and ridiculously alert. Hyper, even. She didn't put her fingertips to her wrist to measure her pulse, didn't care to know what biometrics Houston would be seeing from her right now. What did that matter now?

She had expected to lie awake for hours, but she was dead to her new world as soon as Ellis quenched the module lights and her hammock stopped swaying gently in the one-sixth lunar gravity.

8

Manned Orbiting Laboratory 7: Peter Sandoval

IN low Earth orbit, USAF astronaut Peter Sandoval stared at the broad expanse of Asia as it rolled by beneath him, and thought of Vivian Carter.

She'd made it to the Moon. Living the dream. Except, not quite.

Sandoval had been a tiny bit jealous of Vivian ever since her crew assignment went public. Commanding a trip to Marius for ten days of fun in the Sun? Lucky swine. Along with Ellis Mayer, who was perhaps the luckier swine because he got to explore the Moon *with* Vivian Carter.

He certainly wasn't jealous of her being attacked in space by the Soviets. He was mad as hell about that, and about the capture of Columbia Station. He itched to kick some ass.

But at least Vivian was *down*, now. On the lunar surface and safe, even if she wasn't where she'd hoped to be. Alive and kicking, and no one's prisoner. That was something.

Back then, the NASA and USAF ascans—astronaut candidates— had shared most of the basic training. The fundamentals of spaceflight were the same whether you were an Apollo astronaut headed for the Moon or a Blue Gemini operative being trained to surveil the Earth from a Manned Orbiting Laboratory.

Sandoval glanced around him. His MOL was a cylinder ten feet in diameter and eighty feet long, with the huge DORIAN optical telescope taking up over half the internal volume, and limited functional space for only four guys besides. Even with four, when they weren't pulling shifts, they'd crash into one another constantly and get on each other's nerves over the course of a forty-five-day tour of duty. But on a staggered sleep schedule, one or two were immobile in the sleeping area at any given time.

There were only three other people Sandoval would really care to share a tin can this small with, and on this tour of duty they were all with him: Gerry Lin, Kevin Pope, and Jose Rodriguez, quiet guys who kept to themselves but got the job done with clockwork efficiency. Lin was currently Sandoval's shift mate, but he'd hit the sack early after a heavy workout on the exercise machinery in the middeck during orbital night, at a time when the vibrations from his activities wouldn't degrade the picture quality from the DORIAN. Pope and Rodriguez, on the opposite shift, they'd hardly spoken with in days.

The first five MOLs, now all defunct, had been two-person craft. Must have been exhausting doing alternate shifts with just one other guy, even when some whole orbits were passing over nations with only limited surveillance potential. Still had to monitor the independent panoramic camera that was always on the go, though. Still had to be on standby for any random tactical shots that the NRO, the highly classified National Reconnaissance Office, might require, even while flying over their allies' territory.

They'd become friends during the crazy jungle survival training episode in Panama. It had been Sandoval and Lin from the USAF, and Rawlings and Vivian from NASA, making fire by rubbing sticks together so they could cook their bugs rather than eating them raw. Another NASA astronaut, Terri Brock, had originally been assigned to that tour instead of Rawlings, he remembered, but both Vivian and Brock had scotched that idea right quick. *No chaperones, no gender-based buddy system, no BS. Women don't train and bunk only with other women, and men with men. We need to get used to functioning in mixed teams.*

And some guys had agreed, and they'd all been right, even though it gave the NASA PR folks a headache with dumbass media questions about Women Cohabiting with Men. Jeez. After the initial oddness wore off, it just wasn't that big a deal.

They'd had some good conversations, the four of them. A week eating snakes, bugs, and questionable rodents in almost constant rain had cemented their friendship. Lin and Rawlings were in happy marriages. Vivian was, as she had described it, "aggressively unmarried." She'd been engaged once, to another hotshot Navy pilot, but had refused to put his career prospects above her own. Once she made it into the Astronaut Corps and the other guy didn't, it had all fallen apart. And since then she hadn't had a whole lot of time for dating.

By contrast, Sandoval's marriage to Alice had already been on the rocks, pushed to the brink by his continuing acceptance of dangerous assignments he couldn't tell her about, coupled with his eternal absences. Problems that would only get worse once he'd gotten through astronaut training and started getting launched into space.

To begin with, he'd tiptoed around the topic with the gang. Didn't want Vivian thinking he was trying to play her by complaining about his home life to get her sympathy. *Poor misunderstood Peter, Alice doesn't get me, but you, Vivian, you understand.* That wasn't Sandoval's angle, he wasn't *that* guy. He genuinely just wanted to talk. But once they'd gotten past that hurdle it was good to be able to get into the details, get a woman's perspective, back in the days when he'd thought he might be able to keep his marriage together. That hadn't worked worth a damn, of course. The stresses ran too deep. But Sandoval was happy to say that the final ending fiasco hadn't been Vivian's fault.

He *did* wish he'd been able to be honest with Vivian about other stuff, though. The professional, hardcore stuff.

I'm more than you know, he'd wanted to say to Vivian, six times a day. And sure, to Josh Rawlings too, who seemed like a solid enough guy. *You think I'm just a USAF jock training to be an orbiting cameraman. A space voyeur. Lowest spy of the bunch. But as it happens, Lin and I are more like special agents. Covert ops. I'm a space-age James Bond. Yes, I am.*

None of which they could reveal to the NASA astronauts they trained with, of course. And so Vivian hadn't known what Sandoval was training to become, or what his job would be when he wasn't aloft on the Manned Orbiting Laboratory. And she probably never would.

Vivian took no bull. Flirted with no one. Didn't try to *use* the fact that she was a woman, unlike some of the other ascans. Didn't pitch and petition for slots. Just aced all the classes, learned every procedure till she had it cold—even the stupid ones—stepped up to every challenge with balls and willingness, and waited to be noticed.

Well, Peter Sandoval had noticed her, and he wasn't the only one. But office romances were off the table in the Astronaut Corps, whether

NASA or USAF, even if Sandoval hadn't still been married. Sure, people bent rules all the time just to get things done, but flouting the "no relationships" rule would have been career suicide.

Though he might wish Vivian's eyes lit up for him the way they lit up for … lunar volcanoes.

Vivian was as much an expert on the Moon as Sandoval was on the surface of the Earth. Her knowledge of lunar geography and geology had blown her instructors away, and grudgingly impressed just about everyone else. Vivian was a Navy pilot, not a scientist, so there was no reason to expect she'd excel at every Moon-related class she took. But she'd been real smart to focus on that. Competition enough to be an astronaut at all; even greater competition for flight slots. But flight assignments for lunar-surface missions? Brutal. And Vivian had left nothing to chance, just leaped up to ring all the bells and ring 'em loud.

Once, Sandoval had wanted the Moon himself. It wasn't a given that USAF high flyers had to move into Blue Gemini; there were plenty of Air Force officers in NASA's ranks as well. Sandoval had a solid background either way. He had hundreds of combat flying hours in Vietnam, piloting F-100 Sabers in Operation Rolling Thunder. He'd survived his share of strictly unofficial and unpublicized dogfights with Soviet MiG-17s. And, like many other astros, he'd followed that up with test pilot school at Edwards AFB and some precision work at the sticks of some pretty hairy flight prototypes. He could have switched over to NASA. He just decided not to.

And the MOLs—and the other, even more covert stuff—had turned out to be really good for him. Better than good: it was challenging, technically demanding, politically important work. Sandoval had spent more time in space and done more critical work up here than anyone else in the USAF space program. He'd gotten to spend countless hours looking down on Earth, pole to pole, in a way almost no one else ever got to do: for weeks and months, in all seasons and weathers, both out the window and through the biggest damn telescope humanity had ever flown.

Sandoval hadn't seen Vivian for two years, and whether Vivian's sojourn at Hadley succeeded or failed, he'd probably never see her again. The USAF astronauts had little enough to do with the NASA guys once they were all trained up: different missions, different orbital stations, even separate Mission Controls—NASA's was run out of Houston, Texas, and the USAF's from Cheyenne Mountain, Colorado. But Sandoval wished her well on the Moon. He'd be following along with interest.

Sandoval had been watching out the window with half an eye as the MOL had cruised over the yellow-tan expanse of the Arabian Peninsula and across Iran. He'd taken shots of some of the Iranian facilities. Good daylight, very little cloud cover. Didn't see much obscuration ahead of him over Kazakhstan, either. So this surveillance pass over Baikonur was going to be aces.

Sandoval pulled himself into his seat and strapped in. Not that he was expecting any bumps in the road: it just held him in place and made his work much more comfortable. He spun the verniers, peered quickly through the smaller spotting telescope to get his bearings, then moved to the main binocular eyepiece, which he preferred to the TV screen.

He saw plains, dunes, and some occasional splashes of color that marked oases. He was looking down on the Transoxiana region: a ton of central Asian history, with almost none of it left to see. He checked that all the telescope and camera systems were nominal, glanced at the flickering green numerals that indicated latitude and longitude, and fired off three quick shots of a nomadic caravan as it fortuitously passed beneath him, for kicks. Just to exercise his clicking finger, and who knows what they might see. After all, film was something he would *never* run out of. He had miles of it in the can.

Even with his naked eye he could see individual camels and their drivers through the scope, the colors of the blankets draped over the camels, their shadows against the sand. Could tell adults from children, heavily laden beasts from those that walked more easily. It was even pretty clear when individuals turned their heads, despite the shimmer of heat off the sand.

The rumor was that back in the 1950s the US had managed to identify Khrushchev and other ranking Soviets in photographs obtained from seventy thousand feet by the Lockheed U-2 aircraft. Sandoval had never seen those pictures, but he'd done the math: it might well be true. Then, in the sixties, the US CORONA and GAMBIT spy satellites had advanced to a resolution of two feet from much higher up, in low Earth orbit. And now, in the late seventies, the technology had leaped forward so far—the MOL was so much more stable as a platform, and trained officers like Sandoval and his teammates were so much faster and more efficient at identifying locations and setting up pictures—that the results had improved by a factor of ten.

Major Peter Sandoval was looking down at the Earth through the massive Eastman Kodak DORIAN telescope, with a six-foot-wide, one thousand-pound primary mirror. Set up properly, looking straight down and under good conditions with the Ross corrector to compensate for aberration and image motion compensation applied, the pictures he took on seventy millimeter film provided an image resolution of just a few inches—close to the theoretical limit—even stereo pairs, if that was his brief, that the ground folks could turn into 3D. In addition to the main telescope the MOL had the panoramic camera for terrain and attitude determination, and two small stellar cameras pointing in opposite directions to get orientation information from star fields. Sandoval was guessing that the computing power to deal with all this had to spread across multiple buildings at the National Reconnaissance Office.

Sandoval was rarely privy to the fine details the NRO and CIA coaxed out of his photographs. He certainly couldn't identify individuals by eye himself. But even so, the view through DORIAN was stunning to the point of being unsettling. Sandoval could look down onto a crowded city street or a country neighborhood, or—God help his soul—even a beach, and know for a fact that not a single one of the people he was scanning from his godlike perch could have any idea they were being scrutinized *from space*.

Okay, here came the Soviet launch facility. His MOL was zipping over the Syr Darya river—water level looked pretty low for the time of year—and here was the nearby city of Leninsk, there the railway line to Tyuratam … and yes, there was Baikonur. Sandoval was still viewing it obliquely through a ton of atmosphere—it would be a couple minutes before he was as close to overhead as he'd get on this pass—but he started snapping pictures anyway, hearing the *chunk* sound of the large-frame film advancing with every push of the button. The trick about Baikonur was to see what was sitting on the launchpads, what vehicles were moving around, whether there was any new construction or odd freight cars on the trains. Basically, work out what was where. Who knows what Sandoval might accidentally record on film that might be of some use to the CIA spooks. Besides, he didn't have to wade through all these images himself. They had a whole army of photointerpreters on the ground for that. Poor schmucks.

Sandoval zoomed out for context, swung in again for detail. He knew the layout of Baikonur by heart; knew every launchpad and building and fuel dump and parking lot and road. And so now he knew exactly what he was looking at. Rockets on pads. More than one. Three! *Cool beans.*

He had to move fast. The MOL was moving pretty quick, and it was surprising how rapidly Earth's surface unrolled. The very first time Sandoval had looked down on the streets of his own hometown in Racine, Wisconsin, he hadn't been able to figure out which street was which before he was well past. Next time around he'd done his homework and been ready, but of course everything had been at a different angle and he still hadn't cracked it. It had taken him until the fifth pass to confidently identify the house he grew up in.

He was much better at this nowadays, though.

And right now, he knew exactly what he was looking at. For a guy who'd never been closer to Asia than a couple hundred vertical miles— and probably never would—Sandoval knew this part of it like the back of his hand.

Amazingly, the first of the Soviet rockets began to lift off. He could see the cloud of smoke boiling up around its lower third. Whoa. Snap, *chunk*, snap, *chunk*, that was real pretty.

And then the second rocket began to launch too.

No. Come on. That never *happens. What are the odds?*

A chill hit the back of his neck, and hit it hard. These weren't N-1 launches, the rockets that took a Soyuz or a Progress up into space. And they weren't the massive Proton rockets either, that hauled the much bigger Soviet Salyut/Almaz spy stations.

N-1s and Protons were slow and ponderous. These rockets were smaller, sleeker, and *way* too fast.

And then, the third one launched.

Oh, holy living crap.

They were ICBMs. *Inter-fricking-continental ballistic missiles.*

Major Peter Sandoval might, this very moment, be witnessing the very first nuclear shots to be fired in World War III. *But from Baikonur? When I'm right here to see? Why would they do that?*

Unless the Soviets *wanted* the US to see this.

Sandoval pressed the button that would fire the shutter a dozen times in quick succession. Even before the sequence was complete, he was reaching for his comms panel.

It lit up before he got there. And at the same time a siren blasted throughout the MOL: five rising tones activated remotely by NORAD and routed through USAF Mission Control. Sandoval had never heard that alarm go off outside drills, tests, and bad nightmares. He could feel the damned sound in his teeth: it was fit to wake the dead, and would certainly waken the rest of his crew. That was kind of the point.

His ears rang, and into the void that remained after the siren cut out came a human voice. "MOL-7, Cheyenne. Maximum emergency. Respond immediately. MOL-7, Cheyenne. Maximum—"

Sandoval punched at his lapstrap to free himself, and pressed the Comms button. "Cheyenne, MOL-7, come in."

He sounded remarkably matter-of-fact for a man who might be about to watch his country vaporize in a nuclear holocaust on his next pass over it. Watch it, in fact, with excruciatingly fine spatial resolution.

"MOL-7, prepare for immediate evacuation. This is not a drill."

"Cheyenne: ICBMs launched from Baikonur. At least three—"

"Break, break. We're aware. Prepare to evacuate MOL immediately. DRVs, immediate launch. Crew to prepare for immediate return. Acknowledge."

Gerry Lin, wearing only shorts, rocketed onto the observation deck, bounced off a bulkhead and grabbed at a water pipe to arrest his motion. "Status?"

Sandoval raised a hand. "Evac, stat. Cheyenne, we're on the move."

But: evacuate the Manned Orbiting Laboratory? Why? They were probably safer here than anywhere else right now, and especially if the Cold War was about to turn hot. And one of the more ominous motivations for having the MOLs in the first place was to assess the devastation to the United States after a thermonuclear exchange. "Cheyenne, state rationale for evac. Over."

Beneath him, a commotion: metal cupboards banging, swearing. Pope and Rodriguez were out of their sleeping quarters, getting their kit on.

The cryptographic teleprinter right behind Sandoval started clacking. A message from Aerospace Defense Command. Sandoval didn't turn to look at it yet. "Rod, Pope, boot up power and heaters to the Geminis, prep for immediate depart. Short protocol. Move it!"

"Yeah, man, you got it," came from below decks. Lin hung there in place, half-naked. Sandoval glared. "Go get dressed, are you deaf?"

"I am, after *that*. Uh, evacuate why?"

"Hell if I know. Get on the stick, man."

"Roger." Lin flipped over, thrust himself back through the opening into the crew quarters. Next came the sound of a collision, and someone banged off metal again. "Chrissakes, Rod ..."

"Is this a fricking Three Stooges show?" Sandoval shouted. *Soviet missiles in the air and my guys are a goddamn slapstick act.*

"We're doing better than it sounds," Pope said, sounding muffled.

"Yeah, you'd better be."

DRVs immediate launch. That was next. Sandoval flew to the console, pressed buttons, heard the squeal of mechanisms deep within DORIAN as the remaining film spooled into drums at top speed. Next came the distant *ka-thunk* of pyros from way at the other end of the Manned Orbiting Laboratory as the automated Data Return Vehicles separated. Each was five feet in diameter and eighty inches high, and weighed two thousand pounds, over a quarter of which was film. Mission Control would direct the DRVs' return to Earth remotely. They'd be snatched out of the sky fifteen thousand feet over the Pacific by a C-130 Hercules transport aircraft. Or they wouldn't be. Either way, they were no longer Sandoval's concern.

The radio spoke to him again. "MOL-7, Cheyenne. Is this Sandoval?"

"Yessir, Sandoval here."

"Stand by for new information."

Bloody hell. "Cheyenne, clarify: do we continue evac or don't we?"

"Keep moving, but be ready in case situation changes, MOL-7."

"Christ's sake, Cheyenne." Sandoval released the mic switch and hit the intercom. "Pope, Lin: get the Geminis ready to fly. Rod, grab up all logbooks and paper. Leave your personal stuff. Jump the checklists, cut corners, we may need to be out of here in minutes."

"Roger that," Pope said from the lower level. "Suits or neg?"

"That's a negatory for now. No time." Their pressure suits were much less cumbersome than full EVA suits, but donning them would take time they didn't have. "Lowest priority, anyway. We may need to shirtsleeve the splashdowns."

Now he reached behind him, tore the paper out of the teleprinter and scanned it quickly. *Oh. Damn.*

Lin called up from below. "You setting the fuse, boss?"

"Yeah," Sandoval said bitterly. "God help me, I am absolutely setting the goddamned fuse."

He yanked the ops binder out of the wall pocket by the DORIAN controls, flipped to the back. The MOL's fierce air-handling system blew on his legs, rotating him gently in the middle of the observation deck, but from long familiarity Sandoval didn't even notice the motion.

He stared at the header of the back page. DESTRUCT SEQUENCE.

And there it was. A set of numerical codes that Sandoval needed to enter into the guidance computer. Right now, and without any error.

The last-but-one number was the length of the fuse in seconds, the countdown time until the pyros would ignite the explosives at the MOL's forward end. And the last was an activation code that was marked with six X's in the book, a PIN that had just arrived on the teleprinter behind him.

Once Sandoval entered that number the system would be fully armed, and after a thirty-second grace period the computer would ask Sandoval to confirm that he really, really meant it.

Sandoval would hit the DESTRUCT button. And after that there was nothing he or anyone else could do to stop the MOL from exploding silently into the void once that fuse number counted back to zero. It would be a gigantic fireball quickly quenched by vacuum, molten slag flying off in all directions, and God help them if they were still anywhere nearby when it happened.

The destruct sequence was longer than he remembered, so it was a good job he was getting started early. He'd pause before the end and pray that Cheyenne told him not to complete it.

Sandoval looked around at the instrument panels, the duct work, the blue-painted metal walls, the utilitarian furniture. This was his fourth MOL tour. All told, he'd spent seven months in this dump. But if he really had to blow it to smithereens, it would about break his goddamned heart.

But not blowing it up would be far worse. Rules were clear. The Manned Orbiting Laboratory was stuffed with above-Top-Secret tech, from the DORIAN optics and associated electronics down through the peripherals and computer equipment, to the software, the controls …

"Cheyenne, talk to me. I'm still awaiting clear—"

"Break. MOL-7, we have confirmation. Abandon ship soonest. Evac and torch, evac and torch. Destroy assets and return to Earth."

Destroy assets. Shit. Sandoval's mouth was suddenly very dry. "USAF Mission Control, repeat for the record: abandon and destroy Manned Orbiting Laboratory Seven. No drill?"

Was that exasperation? "MOL-7. We have been informed by the Soviets that you are targeted by three ICBMs. No drill. Get yourselves the hell out."

Sandoval thought about that. "Missiles definitely for us? Not a ruse?"

That would be just great, if the Soviets convinced the US they were terminating an orbiting asset, and those missiles instead flew by to form a first strike on Washington, DC, New York, or San Francisco. While, in the meantime Sandoval had fried his own MOL …

"We're sure, MOL-7. This is not World War Three. It's a single tactical strike. On you."

On *him.* Him and his crew. Sandoval's stomach lurched.

Well, it was better than the end of civilization. "ETA of missiles?"

"Ten minutes, less? Unclear. We cannot track."

"Ten, holy shit …"

"Set the fuse, *get out now.*"

"Roger, will comply." Finger off the comms, onto the intercom. "Hurry it up, you guys!"

"Got it, man," Pope said calmly. "No sweat."

Sandoval ran the math in his head even as he punched numbers into the computer. ICBMs were three-stage rockets. The Titan and Atlas rockets that launched Blue Gemini were variants of those in the US nuclear arsenal. Same for the Reds, presumably. ICBMs flew suborbital trajectories. They punched out of the atmosphere, and punched right back in again.

So, sure, these missiles could gain sufficient altitude to impact the MOL. Did they have the accuracy? Maybe so, and maybe not. And maybe that's why there were three of them, for redundancy. Sandoval wouldn't stick around to find out.

Ten minutes? Well, it took eight for a Blue Gemini to get into orbit from a standing start. MOL-7 had been right over Baikonur when the Reds had launched the missiles, which was obviously perfect if they were attempting a kill.

"Guys! Time till disengage?"

Intercom crackle from the Gemini. Lin's voice. "We're up. We can leave two minutes after you get your ass in here and close the hatch."

"Rod too?"

A Gemini could only hold two people. They needed both craft to work.

"Nearly there," Rodriguez said. "Fifteen seconds."

"Rod and Pope, you guys go as soon as you're ready. Disengage, get the hell away."

"Roger. Abandoning ship."

"Copy. Lin, make that one minute. And *wait for me.*"

"Okay. And, sure thing, man."

He felt the whole station vibrate beneath him. *Now what?* "MOL-7, Gemini," came Pope's voice. "We are clear of the station and applying maximum separation burn."

Oh yeah. "Godspeed, Gemini," Sandoval said. "Lin?"

"One minute, boss. Let's go."

Thank God Sandoval had had these guys with him. Some of his other crews wouldn't be this cool and efficient in a crisis. They'd still be struggling to get their acts together when the goddamn missiles slammed into the MOL and blew them into burning dust.

He typed "1000" into the fuse and hit the Enter key. A thousand seconds would be fine. If they'd read this wrong, if those missiles somehow held Soviet capture crews despite all evidence to the contrary, there was no way those crews could break into an armored MOL in less than twenty minutes. *We're no Columbia Station.* US secrets would be safe either way.

Then he typed the six-figure activation code in. *There's six numbers I'll see in my nightmares till my dying day.*

He pressed ACTIVATE.

"Self-destruct activated," he said into the microphone.

Sandoval pulled out his log sheet, code books, and other random crap and stuffed them all into a pouch. No time to think straight about what mattered and what didn't.

The thirty-second delay seemed endless. "Come on, come on …"

"Cheyenne, MOL, your status?"

"DRVs away. First Gemini launched and clear. Evac of second expected imminently. Self-destruct armed and awaiting confirmation." Finally, an orange bulb lit up. "Proceed with destruct, Cheyenne? Last chance."

"Proceed, MOL."

Aw, shit.

Don't think about it.

Sandoval hit the DESTRUCT button, which of course set the god-damn klaxon off again in the SOS pattern, three long, three short, three long. "Yeah, I know, I know ..."

He pushed off with both feet, hard. Flew through the hexagonal gap into the forward compartment faster than was sane. Slammed into the bulkhead on the far side, bounced off. He'd known that would happen. Didn't have time for finesse. Shoved himself up toward the Gemini hatch.

On NASA's version of the Gemini the hatch was in a sensible place, on the side of the capsule. On Blue Gemini, the hatch was in the heat shield. You came up inside the craft from the butt end and hoped to God the seal would hold through reentry. Hey, they hadn't lost one yet.

He thrust his sack of goodies through the hatch. Lin grabbed it from him. He pulled himself through more gently; the instrument panels were dead ahead of him and he didn't want to slam into them. Twisting himself to reorient within the cramped confines of the Gemini, Lin latched and dogged the hatch behind him. Connectors snapped into place.

"Would have been swell if that hatch had jammed, no?"

Lin shuddered. "Don't even joke, man."

Sandoval pushed his couch down. It locked, and he swung into it, fastened his harness, then pulled the right-hand couch down for his crewmate.

Lin scooched past him to take his seat. "Time check?"

Damned if Sandoval knew. He hadn't pushed the stopwatch on his wrist chronometer, hadn't ordered up an audible countdown, and none of that mattered worth a damn because they didn't know where the Soviet missiles were by now anyway.

"Dunno. Max avoidance."

"Max avoid, that's a roger."

It was honestly amazing that they could do this. This kind of quick egress was hardly typical for spaceflight. Normally it would take a two-hour checklist with every switch position and adjustment careful-ly marked, double-checked, and verified before moving on to the next. In space, pretty much everything took two hours. Except an emer-gency evac, which they'd drilled for, and—obviously—had down to minutes. An automatic, generic sequence to *get them the hell away from the MOL-7.*

"Go?" Lin's hand hovered over the PROCEED.

Sandoval braced. "Absolutely. Go!"

Lin hit PROCEED, and the world's biggest sledgehammer pounded them in the back as pyros guillotined their connection with the MOL and thrust them forward.

"God *day-amn*," Lin said.

"What, what?" Sandoval scanned the boards for red lights.

"Just painful, is all." Lin shoved at switches, tweaked dials. "You want to drive?"

"Nah, man, you already got it."

"Okay." Lin grabbed the hand controller mounted in between their seats, and twisted. Reaction control jets fired, yanking them left and swinging them dizzyingly in their seats.

The bulk of the MOL slid past Sandoval's window, still startlingly close. "Cheyenne, Gemini. Are you tracking those missiles yet?"

No response.

"Never mind." Lin pointed.

"Shee-it." There they were, three sparklies coming their way, all on the same trajectory; the first brighter than the second, which was brighter than the third. Glinting in the Sun and blazing with fire. Coming up from beneath them, already free of the atmosphere.

Yeah, they weren't coasting to gradually gain on the MOL. Those rockets were moving *fast.* That wasn't a rendezvous trajectory. It was an intercept, destroy, slam-the-MOL-to-hell-and-beyond trajectory.

"Grab on. Separation burn in three, two …"

Boom. The Orbit Attitude and Maneuvering System, OAMS, kicked in, harder than Sandoval had ever experienced before. *Cranking. Damn.* G-forces pounded them; he didn't want to know how many. They were hauling ass, gaining delta-V, *getting gone.*

He should really be figuring out the math while Lin handled the flying. Calculating probable relative speed, time to impact: in other words, how far away the Gemini would be when the missiles hit the MOL. But it hardly mattered. *We'll either be far enough away, or we won't.* They'd escape, or they'd die.

Sandoval grunted, tried to breathe in a series of short gasps against the lead weight that seemed to be resting on his chest, like he'd been trained. Watched the MOL receding. Watched the specks getting brighter. It was kind of hypnotic.

Time to start thinking about what they *could* control.

They were facing backward, flying blunt-end-first. The G-forces were eyeballs-in. So, yeah, Lin's emergency burn was a retrofire, fast-dropping them into a lower orbit, effectively accelerating them away from the MOL. But the MOLs flew close in to the Earth. They didn't have a whole lot of lower-orbit space beneath them until they hit atmosphere and started taking drag.

Lin's alternative would have been to push them into a higher orbit. Obviously with missiles coming up from beneath them, that wouldn't be supersmart. Most of the debris would fly *forward*. So, fine. They were doing the right thing. But—

"Time … till reentry?" Sandoval demanded, hissing out the words. They weren't in their pressure suits. Those suits were shoved under the seats, he'd seen the leg of one of them flapping by his feet. Suiting up would take quite a while and a bunch of contortions, the cabin being as tight as it was, and it would take them not being in however the hell many G's they were in.

He could see Lin swallow painfully. This was particularly hard on a couple of guys who'd been in free fall for weeks. Somehow, his pilot lifted a hand to punch buttons on his guidance computer. Green numbers lit up in succession. Lin pushed more buttons.

"I presume … you know *where* we're coming down."

"Uh, sure," Lin said unconvincingly.

The little lights in the sky had become streaks, like meteors, hot damn … "Brace!" Sandoval shouted, for all the good *that* would do them—

The sky right in front of them lit up. A bright nova, a globe of fire that spread outward. "Shit." Both men raised their hands in front of their faces instinctively.

Stupid, stupid. If that had been a nuclear blast, it would have blinded us both. Fried our eyeballs. Then what?

Well, then it wouldn't have mattered, because at exactly the same moment they'd have been strafed with ionizing radiation: neutrons, gamma rays, alpha particles, high-energy electrons, whatever else, much of it moving at the speed of light. And quite likely that radiation would have knocked all the Gemini's systems offline too. In principle, the spacecraft electronics were radiation hardened, but the

EMP from a nuke just a couple dozen miles away would likely have nailed them anyway.

That wasn't just kinetic-kill, though. Conventional explosives?

Debris strafed them. *Clatter clatter bang whump*, and now the Gemini was spinning. "Hot *damn*." Lin grabbed the controller again, fired thrusters to cancel the yaw and roll, bring them back.

Sandoval looked out the windows again, saw nothing. Not blindness-nothing; merely the Earth beneath them and the stars above. No MOL, no flaming wreckage, no chunks of metal drifting, *nothing*. Everything had blown by them already. As if his space station had just vanished. Which it *had*.

Lin was scanning gauges. "Integrity holding. Pressure maintaining." Sandoval looked too. They weren't holed, or not that he could see.

Screws, washers, pressure-suit pants legs started drifting in the breeze again and Sandoval belatedly realized they were back in zero G. "Burn okay?"

"All done. Nominal."

"Heat shield?"

Lin scanned the board. "No telltales." No red lights, is what he meant. Nothing to warn them that, say, the heat shield was fatally compromised and might crack and leak ionized plasma heated to thousands of degrees into their cabin during reentry.

Obviously, that damage might not become obvious until they were already in atmosphere.

Sandoval looked out at the Earth. Beneath them he saw only cloud. Before long they'd be coming up on the terminator into darkness. They'd been on ascending node when the alarm had sounded, heading northeast over Baikonur, and now it was ... how much later? "Hey man, no big deal, but ... reentry point?"

Then the cloud cover began to break up under them. Taiga forest, covered in snow. "Jesus Christ. That's still Mother Russia."

"*Da, Tovarishch*," Lin said.

"Uh, please tell me we're not aiming to come down in fricking *Siberia*."

"We'll skip across atmosphere," said Lin. "Gain some distance before we reenter for reals."

"Skip us across .... You've done that before, right?" If they got the angle too shallow, they'd bounce back out into space in a way that might be ... unfortunate.

"Uh, nope. Not as such."

Sandoval looked at him sideways. "As what, then?"

"Well, you know. Simulator." Lin flipped switches. "Should be okay."

"Great."

"Always has to be a first time, right?"

"Dang." Sandoval thought about it for a moment. "Okay, so once we've pulled that off, we're going to land in the North Pacific?"

"Yeah."

"In the dark?"

"Yes. Yes, we are."

Sandoval blew out a long breath.

"If we land at all," Lin added.

"You're not helping, airman," Sandoval said.

"Just keeping it real."

"Thanks. I sure hope there's a US naval vessel *somewhere* nearby." Sandoval flipped the comms switch. "Cheyenne, this is Blue Gemini. Copy?"

"Guam's probably out of range," Lin said. They listened to white noise for a moment. "Guess Pope and Rod are, too."

"When do we pick up Gilmore Creek?" The next NASA tracking station, near Fairbanks, Alaska.

"Not sure."

"Why do I keep you around?"

Lin grinned. "Because you suck at math even worse than I do. Wanna help me take star readings so's we can get some real answers?"

Sandoval shook his head in disbelief, but said, "Yes. I definitely want to help. And check your numbers, too."

"Be my guest, man," Lin said. "Be my frigging guest."

Their Blue Gemini hurtled on into darkness.

CHAPTER 9

Columbia Station: Nikolai Makarov

MAKAROV couldn't believe they'd pulled it off. Couldn't believe the Americans had thrown in the towel so quickly, opened up their airlocks, and meekly relinquished Columbia Station to his invading force.

To Makarov, that meant one of two things.

The first possibility was that there was nothing of military significance aboard Columbia Station after all, in which case Makarov would truly be the "pirate chief" that its commander, Joshua Rawlings, accused him of being. If so, instead of being feted for posterity as the second man to walk the surface of the Moon, Makarov might well go down in history as the commander of the first space military assault on unarmed civilians.

To Makarov, this frankly seemed the more likely scenario. He and Belyakova had been talking quite reasonably to Rawlings and Dardenas for several hours now. Getting to know them, charming them, and perhaps winning them over just a little, while ignoring the jibes that the Americans hurled back in their faces. These Americans, at least, were beginning to relax.

This is just a symbolic occupation. We will probably be ordered home by Friday.

Moscow is just making a political statement.

This is a very impressive facility. Large, very smooth. Pretty. Hats off to you Americans.

109

Let's sit tight and let the politicians sort it out.

Of course, it didn't help to have Lev Chertok sitting across from them in the forward compartment with his AK-47 over his shoulder and a revolver on his belt. No one was actually pointing a gun at any of the US astronauts right now, but none of them were mistaking this for a social call either.

Maybe soon we'll be able to let you go about your work as usual. We do not want to stand in the way of scientific progress.

There is no need for anyone to get hurt.

We hate this as much as you do.

You catch more flies with honey than with vinegar, and for now, honey was the plan.

Phase One was to collect as much data as possible by direct observation. This they had done at the outset, with Erdeli, Isayeva, and Salkov going over the station from end to end taking photos of every piece of equipment and every control board from every conceivable angle with their Zenit cameras. Salkov had taken that film out to the Progress to begin the laborious work of developing, scanning, and transmitting back to Baikonur. It would probably take several days just to complete that.

Phase Two was to extract as much information from the Americans as possible. Now that the iron fist had broken into Columbia Station, it was time to don the velvet glove.

Phase Three might be to rip that velvet glove back off, and drag intelligence from the astronauts by whatever means Yashin deemed expedient. And Makarov shuddered to think what that might mean.

Right now, Erdeli and Isayeva were down in the crew compartments area with the Americans Mason and Wagner, the astronauts briefing the cosmonauts on how the food preparation and toilet facilities worked. Even Rawlings had to admit that there was little point in withholding information about the station's larder and plumbing. Having fifteen people crammed into an orbiting facility designed for six was hard enough logistically without that.

Meanwhile, Yashin, Vasiliev, and Galkin were up in the Multiple Docking Adapter airlock area, taking stock of what was in the Cargo Carrier that Apollo 32 had brought, while riding herd on the final two Americans, Jackson and Zabrinski.

Going through that Cargo Carrier with a fine-tooth comb. Looking for ordnance.

Because of that nagging second possibility: that the astronauts' acquiescence was itself a trap, and it was the Soviets themselves who were being played. Yashin clearly believed this. He had been adamant from the very start that the KGB had iron-solid evidence that Columbia Station had hidden military capabilities.

It was hardly far-fetched. After all, the USAF MOL-6 spy station in Earth orbit had self-destructed prior to the impact of the Soviet missiles that had been launched to destroy it. The ICBMs had destroyed the other currently operational Manned Orbiting Laboratory, MOL-7, that had been flying right over Baikonur at the time, but in all likelihood its Blue Gemini astronauts had lit the fuse to blow that one as well before making their escape, rather than risk it falling into Soviet hands.

Which might mean that Columbia Station, too, was primed and ready to explode all around them. That would sacrifice the American crew as well, but politically the Soviets would certainly shoulder the blame for it.

Not that it would make any difference to Makarov, Belyakova, or the rest of them, because by that time they'd be blown to atoms. Well, not quite atoms. Bloody frozen meat, orbiting the Moon forever. It was a sobering mental image.

Even if Columbia Station had no warheads or major ordnance, it was surely too much of a stretch for its crew to be completely unarmed. Somewhere on this station there had to be rifles, pistols, grenades, *something* for self-defense. The Soviet Almaz spy stations had external machine guns mounted on them, and every one of the USSR's lunar missions had brought along … less obvious defensive capabilities. Surely the Americans must, too, and it would be a really great idea for Makarov, Yashin, et al. to find them before falling victim to them.

Fine. Look for weapons. But truth be told, Makarov was almost more apprehensive about Yashin—and Lev Chertok and Oleg Vasiliev, Yashin's crewmates—than he was about the Americans. It was Yashin who had pulled out an assault rifle and shot it at the Apollo 32 astronaut, Carter, without orders. It was Yashin who would have gone ahead and blown the Apollo stack to smithereens with a shoulder-mounted rocket launcher, even after they'd exploited that threat to attain entry to Columbia Station—if Svetlana Belyakova hadn't thrown herself almost physically into his face and demanded he stand down.

111

Makarov was nominally the commander of this operation, with Belyakova his deputy, but their authority was based entirely on their piloting skills. Without them, the flotilla of Soviet craft could never have rendezvoused with the American space station. From now on, Yashin would be looking over Makarov's shoulder from dawn to dusk—for whatever that phrase meant in cislunar space—and would certainly seize command of this mission by force if he, or his handlers back in the Lubyanka in Moscow, decided that was the superior approach.

Yashin was a stone-cold thug. Makarov had seen his fair share of them over the years. A hard line Communist as well, though that wasn't his major motivating force. Belyakova was an ardent Communist and a card-carrying Party member too, but Makarov was fine with that. Yashin, though … when it came right down to it, Yashin was a psychopath in Communist's clothing, and his crew were little better.

As if echoing his thoughts, they suddenly heard gunfire from above.

Shouting, banging … and another gunshot. The station itself quivered in resonance.

Rawlings and Dardenas flinched and glanced up, then both turned to glare at him. Makarov braced, certain that one or other of them was about to leap into action and attack him.

In a single smooth move, Lev Chertok swung the AK-47 off his shoulder and swept the safety lever down to firing mode. Before any of them could react, the chrome barrel of the semiautomatic rifle was pointing straight at Rawlings.

"Whoa, easy, man," said Rawlings, raising his hands slowly above his head.

Makarov shouted up. "Yashin? Yashin, what's happening? Galkin?"

From above they could hear Yashin swearing in Russian, and then the wet crack of punches being thrown.

"What the hell?" Makarov shouted. "What are you doing? Somebody talk to us!"

Svetlana pointed at the Americans. "You, stay exactly where you are. Don't even think of moving. Comrade Chertok is not afraid to shoot."

She shoved off, arrowing toward the hatch. Even as she arrived there, she collided with Jackson floating in the opposite direction. She grabbed at him and raised her fist, but Jackson had no fight left in him. His nose was bloody, his limbs limp. "Yashin?"

"Their little mutiny is over," came Vasiliev's voice. "We're coming down."

"Is he shot?" Rawlings shouted. "Is anyone hurt?"

Belyakova peered at Jackson, shrugged, pushed him down toward Makarov and Rawlings. "I see little serious injury. Do something with him. Keep him quiet."

Jackson, obviously stunned, raised both hands to his face as he tumbled through the air. Globs of blood scattered off him in all directions.

"Let me look after him," Rawlings called across to Chertok, whose gun was still pointed steadily at his head. "Yes? For the love of God, man, come on. Makarov?"

"Stand down," Makarov said in Russian, with all the authority he could muster, and Chertok reluctantly raised the barrel of his AK-47.

Rawlings seized Jackson and guided him into the seat by the radar console, fastening the harness around his waist. "Hold still, you're spraying blood everywhere. What the hell happened?"

"Thought we could take him," Jackson said, his voice blurring. "Sorry, chief. Sorry."

The other three were coming through the hatch, now: the stocky form of Vasiliev, followed by Zabrinski, who didn't look a whole lot better than Jackson, his face also bruised and bloody. Yashin brought up the rear, a coiled spring of muscle. He held a Soviet Tula PSM semi-automatic pistol in his hand, and his face was grim.

Well, so much for that. Given Zabrinski's Russian surname, Makarov had hoped he might prove more congenial than the other Americans. Perhaps be more reasonable, even quietly cooperate. But that clearly wouldn't be the case.

"Are you injured?" Belyakova demanded of Yashin. "Where's Galkin?"

Yashin shook his head curtly. "They thought me inattentive, and quickly learned their error. They are lucky I did not kill them then and there."

"It is a good job you did not. Galkin?"

"Checking for damage to the Carrier."

"Christ," said Rawlings. "Shooting a gun in there? Are you mad?"

Yashin stared at him, his expression dark.

Zabrinski made his way down to Jackson and anchored himself against the chair. He looked shaken. Dardenas raised a hand. "Uh, Nikolai? The flying blood drops, can we mop them up? If blood gets into the electronics, it could be very bad. For all of us."

"Yes," said Makarov, without waiting for Yashin's answer. "Proceed."

"Move slowly and carefully," Svetlana added. "Do not make Comrade Yashin nervous."

"Yeah, I get that." Dardenas grabbed a handful of wipes and headed off to round up the largest of the bloody globules, staying well clear of Chertok and Yashin. After a few moments, Vasiliev moved to assist him.

Erdeli peeked up through the hatchway from the crew quarters. "Everything all right?"

"Mason is our flight surgeon," Rawlings said. "Our medic? Let him come up, Nikolai. Let him look at Jackson and Zabrinski."

Makarov gestured helplessly, and Rawlings evidently took that for assent. "Ed!"

"Coming. 'Scuse me, Major Erdeli."

"Tell them they are lucky to be alive," Yashin said remorselessly to Makarov in Russian. "Tell them that this was their one warning. Next time it will be a bullet to the head, with no hesitation. Make them realize I am not joking about this. Then, we tie them up. All of them."

Belyakova looked at Makarov. Makarov looked at the Americans, who met his gaze blankly. Obviously, none of them understood Russian. Capitalist educational systems were badly wanting. "All? Is that really necessary? We will make much better progress if—"

Yashin cut him off effortlessly, without raising his voice. "We tried this your way. From now on, we free only two or three Americans at a time, to assist us, or to make use of the waste facilities. The rest: restrained, and always with two or more of us on watch. The next time we encounter any foolishness or failure to cooperate, an American dies."

"No killing," Makarov said bluntly. "Not unless we absolutely have to. Those were our mission orders, Sergei Ivanovich."

"You are the commander, of course," said Yashin. "Operational and piloting matters, matters of logistics, in all of these, you lead. But the *internal security* of our mission is my concern, and mine alone. We understand each other, I think?"

Well, Makarov thought, *that was fast*.

He straightened his posture. "Yes, Comrade. We understand each other very well."

"Good." Yashin shrugged. "And, of course, since the Americans will all cooperate from now on, nobody else needs to get hurt. So, everyone happy."

"Everyone happy," Svetlana agreed, and shot Makarov a warning look.

The Americans were all glancing around, but keeping their eye on Rawlings, alert for any hint of what to do next. Their faces were calm, but their body language belied this: all were taut, ready to jump into action. Makarov was convinced that if Rawlings gave the order, the Americans might attack them again even now. Svetlana knew it too; she moved out of Mason's reach as he brought his medical kit up to Jackson's side.

If they did attack, of course, it would be a massacre. Makarov switched back to English. "Josh. I beg you, be calm. For now, don't even move. Or someone may get killed."

Yashin held his pistol at the waist, his finger still looped around the trigger guard. Chertok had shouldered his rifle, but they had seen how quickly he could bring it to bear. If either man fired, bullets might ricochet everywhere.

"I suggest you heed my recommendation, Commander," Yashin said to Makarov. "We must restrain these men. Now, while they are cowed."

Yashin thought they looked cowed? Makarov didn't.

He licked his dry lips. Right now, the American space station that had looked so huge and sturdy when he and his crew had approached in their Soyuz capsules now seemed horribly fragile, tissue-paper thin. *One bullet in the wrong place . . . .*

Makarov nodded. "Of course, Comrade Yashin."

CHAPTER 10

Hadley Base: Vivian Carter

VIVIAN thought she'd awoken early, then looked at the green digits of the mission clock in the panel beside her. It was an hour later than she'd expected. Houston had let them sleep in.

Well, why not? Apollo 32 didn't exactly have a mission profile any longer—because they … didn't have a mission.

Goddamn it.

Even in repose, the LM cabin was noisy. The low grind of the air-handling system, the purr of a dozen electronics boxes. The whine of the multiple fans that moved the air and cooled the avionics. The creak and crack of the LM's thin skin and struts as the Sun angle changed, very slowly, above them.

No previous Apollo expedition crew on-surface had been allowed to sleep longer than nominal. A scheduled sleep period being canceled, or abbreviated? Sure, that happened all the time. Generally, the astronauts' time was so precious that Mission Control begrudged them the minutes it took to clean up the cabin after breakfast.

But not Apollo 32's time, apparently.

Well, Vivian called bullshit on that. "Rise and shine, crewman."

Ellis Mayer's eyes opened immediately. "Uh." He blinked and began to stretch, then remembered where he was and looked around carefully before reaching out. "Houston didn't wake us? Assholes."

Vivian grunted. "So let's get going anyway. Okay for me to climb down?"

116

"Uh, wait, I gotta pee," Ellis said apologetically.

"Yeah, me too, soldier, so hurry it up."

"Copy that."

Reaching forward, Vivian raised the shade over the left window.

Yup. She hadn't dreamed it. The Moon was still out there. *The goddamn Moon.*

Time to go make some tracks.

Her whole upper body felt stiff, and if anything, her shoulder bruising was worse. Her calf was still a painful weal, but at least the wound hadn't reopened overnight. Vivian figured she'd live, but while Ellis was taking care of business, she popped a pain med and when he asked how she was doing, just said Fine. It would all fix itself eventually, and wouldn't slow her down too much.

Now she pushed-to-talk. "Houston, this is Athena at Hadley. You forget about us?"

At least CAPCOM replied promptly. "Athena, Houston. Negative; just letting you stack some Z's after your heavy day yesterday."

That's an understatement. "How are our friends on Columbia Station?"

"Situation unchanged."

"Meaning, everyone's still alive?" Vivian demanded bluntly.

"Far as we know. We'll brief you further when we can."

Ellis cleared his throat. "Status of Minerva?"

"Nominal at last contact. But Minerva is running dark at this time."

Running dark? "Uh, Houston, Dave Horn is not a frigging submarine."

"Copy. But Minerva is in a holding pattern, set to receive but not transmit."

"Transponders off? Medical monitoring off?" Ellis demanded.

"Yes and yes. Obviously." CAPCOM sounded testy. "Apparently our Soviet friends have made it clear via diplomatic channels that they have no intention of hindering Command Modules that could return astronauts to Earth, as this would be counterproductive to their goal of removing the US presence from the Moon. But given what happened yesterday we're taking all precautions."

"All precautions?" Vivian said. "Sure. Roger that."

Okay, fine, up to a point. The tricky docking maneuvers that the Soyuz vehicles had executed to acquire Columbia in real time would have been impossible if they hadn't been able to track the US integrated S-band signal to establish range and velocity. Minerva was too small to track with regular radar outside a couple hundred miles. As long as Horn held radio silence, he was essentially invisible.

But he was also utterly alone. If he had a system failure or a medical emergency it might be hours, days, or never, before Houston found out about it. In the meantime, around and around the Moon he'd go until otherwise instructed. In a closed metal can eleven feet high and thirteen feet across the base.

His conical coffin.

Christ's sake, Vivian, you idiot. Cut that out.

"Well," Ellis said. "That's not good."

"Nor is it up for negotiation at this time," CAPCOM said. And then, perhaps regretting his tone: "Sorry, Athena. When we reestablish contact, you'll be the first to know."

Vivian and Ellis looked at each other. Vivian made a rude gesture at the comms panel. Ellis shrugged.

"Roger that, Houston," she said. "In that case … uh, we may as well prep for our first EVA, no? Get the lay of the land, get our Moon legs under us. Fly the flag." Silence from Earth. "Houston, are we go to commence EVA preparation?"

"Sure, Athena. Proceed."

Sure, Athena, do whatever; your mission's a bust anyway. "We thank you. Proceeding."

Despite the three sets of upgrades NASA and the Grumman Aircraft Engineering Corporation had made to the Lunar Module in the decade since Apollo 11, it was still as hard to get out of the damned thing as it ever was.

There wasn't much spare space in the LM, especially once they'd zipped themselves back into their spacesuits, so they had to be organized. The trickiest part was donning the PLSS backpack that would keep them supplied with oxygen and coolant water out on the Moon's surface. For the SEVA the previous night, they'd remained plugged into the LM's supplies through umbilicals. Today's venture would be very different.

Vivian's PLSS was mounted on the sidewall. She reversed into it, and Ellis helped her strap it to her back and then unhook it from the wall. Vivian's shoulder was still stiff as hell, and the PLSS weight increased the pain level to wincing point. She tried not to show it.

Turning awkwardly, careful not to bang into anything, she helped Ellis in return.

Once that was done, she positioned her microphone and made sure it was locked in place. There'd be no way to adjust it once she put her helmet on. "You hear me, soldier?"

"Yeah, of course."

"I meant through your headset, dummy."

He grinned. "There too."

"Okay. Now donning helmets and gloves."

Vivian lowered Ellis's helmet over his head, set it on the neck ring, shoved it down hard to lock it. Catches snapped and clicked into place. "Ow?" he said.

"Wuss. Do me."

Ellis helmeted and gloved her, and she fumbled his gloves over his hands. She hadn't been looking forward to putting her gloves on again. Her fingers felt like sausages, and her palms were sore and forearms aching from the effort she'd put in during yesterday's spacewalk. Already the gloves felt stiff, and she had to fight against them. "Integrity check."

They ran pressure integrity checks on each suit. "Airtight. Or good as."

"Good to go," she confirmed.

"Uh, we should probably at least let Houston know we're pulling the plug?"

Vivian shrugged, a motion almost invisible in the suit. "Or we could just do it and see if they notice."

In principle, Mission Control should be monitoring their systems, alert to any drop in cabin pressure. In practice, Vivian had a sneaking feeling they'd lost interest. Which was reasonable enough, since they'd also lost the mission *they'd* been training for, and were living in the middle of a tense international situation as well.

"Come on, let's play nice." Ellis pressed the button. "Houston, Athena, we're back and on PLSS comm. How do you read? Be advised we are ready for depress."

"Roger that, Athena, we read you fine. Go for depress. Please stay on VOX during egress, copy?"

"See?" Ellis said. "They still love us after all."

119

"Yeah, touching." Vivian flipped the VOX switch, then reached up to crack open the overhead dump valve.

She watched her pressure readings as the air drained out of the cabin again. *Yep, last night I was too casual about this. Shell-shocked, I guess. Need to pay attention at all times. We get sloppy here, we die.*

"Suit pressure holding. Integrity verified."

"Roger verify."

"Going open. Huh. Condensation."

"Ice crystals?"

"They are now. More like snow." Vivian hadn't even seen them until they formed a light spray out of the opening hatch, with the last of the air.

"Okay." Ellis scrunched, reached down to the front hatch latches. They were below his knee level, and in his newly stiff suit, it was a chore. "Okay. Here we go." The hatch swung inward. "Scootch left a bit, Vivian. Jeez, this is tight."

"Yeah. Next trip, we're springing for a larger cabin."

"Roger that. Now move back."

Vivian shifted again. Ellis got the hatch all the way open and shuffled right.

Clumsy in his moon suit, and with his movement at elbows and waist constrained, Ellis made his best effort at a pudgy but sweeping bow. "Ladies first."

"Age before beauty," Vivian agreed gravely. She was, after all, two years his senior.

As commander, it was Vivian's prerogative to exit the LM first. All prior Apollo commanders had been first onto the lunar surface, and Vivian had no intention of breaking with that tradition.

Yet it still hacked Vivian to the bone that she wouldn't be stepping out onto pristine ground. It weighted her soul, a wound more deep and raw than the bruising on her shoulder or the gashes on her calf. This was the sour end of a dream, not the culmination of one.

Yet, still: it was the Moon.

"Out you go, Commander."

"Roger that, Pilot. Can't wait to get my ass out of here." Vivian turned around, careful not to bump into any of the switches and circuit breakers. "Wow. Tight squeeze, wearing all this crap. Good job I'm a mere slip of a girl."

"Yeah."

"Uh, try to sound more convinced, Pilot."

"Yes, ma'am, you are absolutely a mere slip of a girl."

Maybe I should have thought that through. She grinned, flicked his shoulder with her finger. "Okay. Heading for the floor."

Vivian maneuvered herself down to an uncomfortable kneel. "Backing up. Am I centered? I need a goddamned mirror."

"Left a bit. That's it."

With Ellis guiding her, Vivian crawled backward through the hatch onto the platform between the hatchway and the top of the ladder. And distinctly felt the moment when her boot went past the porch edge and into the empty space beyond it. *Ooh.*

"Visor down, Navy. It's bright out, remember? Don't wanna get a sunburn."

"Uh, yeah." Their outer visors were electroplated with gold to protect them from solar UV radiation. She slid it down over her faceplate, shuffled back farther.

"That's it. Shoulders are clear of the hatch."

"Yep, thanks."

Nine rungs on the ladder, followed by a big gap down to the surface. Vivian pushed herself up onto her arms. *Yeah, it's bright.* Reached back with her left boot, found the rung. Then with her right, because of course, she couldn't see anything. There was a reason they simmed the hell out of all this.

"Okay, that's the nine steps." She paused on the bottom rung as she came vertical, looking around, eyes still adjusting. "Wow."

"Okay?"

She could feel the Sun beating down on her shoulders and legs even through the bajillion layers of her suit. *High noon on the Moon.* "Yeah, just …. Going to intermediate cooling. Minimum isn't cutting it anymore." She made the adjustment, then checked the pressure on the needle gauge on her wrist cuff. It read a little high, probably because she was hot and the air in her suit had expanded. "Okay, I'm feeling the swish swish swish of cool water through my LCGs now." Fine tubes of cold water threaded her liquid-cooled garments. "Even so. Might have to go to maximum to keep my cool."

"Roger," Ellis said, readily enough. This wasn't going to be an eight-hour EVA. They hardly needed to conserve resources.

Vivian looked down. The regolith glistened beneath her. "Now or never, I guess."

She stepped back into space, let go of the ladder. Came down onto the surface with the gentlest of bumps, right boot first. Hopped backward to keep her balance, then leaned forward to peer down through the lowest portion of her visor.

Her eyes watered with the glare, but sure enough, there they were. Her boot prints. Vivian's boot prints, on the *Moon*.

"That's one small jump, and I'm down. Vivian Carter, Apollo 32, reporting from the lunar surface. Very pleased and grateful to be here. My thanks to the hardworking and dedicated crews at Kennedy, Johnson, Goddard, and the other NASA Centers, and to our contractor family at Boeing, Rockwell, Douglas, Grumman, and all the rest. Sincere gratitude."

CAPCOM's crackle. "Roger, Vivian, and congratulations to you. First woman commander of an Apollo mission, and solid all the way from first assignment through to your historic landing yesterday. You should be proud."

A sudden lump came to her throat. "Uh, thank you very much, Houston. I appreciate that. Really do."

She felt like she should say more, but her mind was blank. It hardly mattered. They'd be lucky if this got a thirty-second mention on the evening news. Plenty of other stuff going on in the world, and in orbit. *Get to work, Vivian.* "All right. I'm off to check out the magic machine now, make sure all the bits are where they should be."

She walked a slow circuit around the Lunar Module, bouncing a little but keeping it under control, getting accustomed to locomoting as she scanned her LM from the VHF antennae that jutted out of its "head," increasing its resemblance to a giant squatting insect, down to its dish-like footpads.

It looked pretty damned good. In the past twenty-four hours her ship had been shot at with an assault rifle and then slammed down onto the surface of the Moon, but Vivian could see no signs of undue damage from either insult.

Whatever had caused that precipitous drop in propellant volume during their descent was invisible to her cursory inspection. They'd need to do a more detailed troubleshoot, and soon. Vivian didn't like mysteries. She was sure Ellis would be even more keen to give his beloved spacecraft a full physical.

She'd been doing a steady monologue as she walked, briefing Ellis on what she was seeing. "Okay, I'm back around. Now giving Quadrant One bay a closer look." Their rover was stowed to the right of the ladder, folded up against the side of the LM. "Thermal blanket looks in good shape. Hope the LRV is likewise." She could see parts of the wheels sticking out. They looked fine. Not even dusty.

"Itching to go for a drive, Commander?" That was Ellis.

"A road trip would be just the thing, wouldn't it?"

"Sounds swell."

Ten minutes, fifteen tops: that was all it would take to deploy the Lunar Roving Vehicle. Winch it out, lower it down, unfold it, lock the pins. Connect the battery. Mount the seats. Press some buttons. The rover had been painstakingly designed to be as easy to deploy as possible. She and Ellis could be heading for the hills within the hour.

And on the original mission profile, that would have been the plan. But not today.

"Clear for me to come out?"

"Uh, yeah, man, sorry. Come and join me. Moving to the base of the ladder to spot you."

Boots first, Ellis crawled backward out of the LM.

"Looking good," she said. "Even from this unusual angle."

"Closing the hatch."

For thermal control, and to keep the dust out. "Yeah, hey, don't lock it, okay?" A joke as old as the Moon landings.

"Roger that." Ellis shinned down the ladder pretty good, got himself positioned, then jumped, sliding his hands down the rail to steady himself as he plonked down beside her.

"Smooth."

"Thanks." He looked around, then down. "Your boots are already black. I need to play catch-up out here."

They were. Regolith dust coated them. "Guess it's not wrong, what they say about moondust getting everywhere."

"Yeah."

"Okay, man, let's do the Stars and Stripes."

Many of the components of the Apollo missions were ridiculously expensive. Not the flags, which by established tradition, cost a mere five dollars and fifty cents from a government supply catalog.

Ellis retrieved the flag from its steel case behind the ladder, and with solemnity and little chatter, they extended the telescoping aluminum tubes and planted the pole into the lunar soil. The double-latch locking mechanism on the horizontal bar gave Vivian a few moments pause, but eventually she snapped it into place.

They stepped back from the US flag, five feet by three, and gravely saluted it.

If they'd been at Marius, Ellis would have set up a camera to record the moment. Here at Hadley, neither of them had even broached the topic.

"Oh beautiful, for spacious skies," Ellis said, and tilted his body back at the waist as best he could, to look upward.

The sky over the horizon was pure black. With the Sun almost directly overhead, the terrain around them was lit way too brightly for them to see the stars. Although the fans in Vivian's helmet were purring smoothly, she could still feel the solar intensity on her shoulders, back, and feet through the suit. Her PLSS was getting a workout.

Vivian nodded. "From sea to shining sea. Mare to shining mare, anyway."

She took a long look around, turning in a complete circle. Ignoring the signs of human occupation, her eyes instead swept the tan-gray desolation, the uncannily rounded mountains at their almost unbelievable height and distance, the deep black of the sky behind them.

"Okay," Ellis said. "Let me do my own inspection, then we should drag out the solar arrays and soak up some of this sunlight for our batteries."

"Hey. Before you go running off?" She stretched out an arm.

Ellis paused, then solemnly shook her hand. It was tough to curl her thumb across the back of his glove where the knuckles would be, but she made a credible job of it.

She couldn't see his face for the gold visor, and he wouldn't be able to see hers either. That was good. He wouldn't see the small tears that were globbing in the corners of her eyes.

"Congratulations, Ellis Mayer, forty-third American to walk the surface of the Moon."

"Well, thank you. Congratulations, Vivian Carter, forty-second US moonwalker, fourth US woman, and" his helmet nodded ponderously, "as mentioned, the first commander. Woman commander, I mean."

"Yay Equal Rights Amendment," Vivian said ironically.

Ellis nodded again. "Maybe one day."

"In the meantime," came a third voice over their headsets. "Welcome to the Moon, Apollo 32."

It was Norton's voice, and a moment later Vivian saw a spacesuited figure bounding out from Habitat A with that two-footed lope characteristic of experienced moonwalkers. As yet, Vivian hadn't gotten herself cranked up beyond a gentle bouncing kangaroo-hop.

Damn it. That's all the time we get?

Yup. Their moment was over.

Norton slowed as he approached, raised his right arm to shoulder level. "Hey, man. Up high."

Ellis lifted his hand dutifully and the two men high-fived, a gesture only a few months old that Vivian had never seen anyone do outside a sports game. But when Norton turned to her she raised her gloved hand so he could swat at it. Easier than a handshake in a suit, that was for sure, and over quickly.

"Welcome to my neck of the woods. Thanks for dropping by."

"Least we could do, Rick," Ellis said.

"Good job me and my people were here to be your Plan B."

Yeah. "Ain't it just," Vivian said. "You really ran all the way over here just to say howdy?"

"More or less. Other stuff on my list to get done, now I'm out." Norton saluted their flag, then loped closer to Athena. "Looking good. You managed to not break it."

Would he have said that to a man? At least he hadn't made a "woman driver" crack. "Go figure."

"Came in a bit short, though."

"Well. Soviets and all. You know how it is."

"Sure." Norton turned, full-body. "We'll get a power line strung across, so's you can conserve your batteries, keep your cockpit cool. Some spare O_2 bottles. And we'll see if we can help you pin down that oxidizer leak."

"No rush." Vivian wanted as little from Hadley as possible, wanted Ellis to have the chance to check out his own ship. "Though, who knows, we might not be here long."

"Oh, you'll be with us a while," Norton said casually. "Ain't no one leaving this rock soon, 'specially now the Commies *want* us to. Which reminds me: council of war at fourteen hundred hours."

Ellis and Vivian both paused before saying at the same time, "Council of war?"

Norton looked back and forth between them with some amusement. "Cute. Yeah. We'll all get together in the Hab, so no one can overhear." Eavesdrop on any radio transmissions, was what he meant. "Habitat A, on the left. And that way we can get through all the introductions at once, get you two oriented here. Actually, you know what? Come at thirteen hundred, so we can get you out of suits and familiarize you with the Hab layout before the rest of the troops show up and it's so crowded that no one can swing a cat. Cool?"

"Go back to that 'council of war' part," Vivian said.

"Hey, you saw the first shots for yourself. Up there, yesterday, that was Lexington. Fort Sumter. The Gulf of Tonkin. Pearl Harbor."

Vivian raised her eyebrows. "History buff, eh?"

"You know it." Norton loped on, doing his own tour of their LM, just as Vivian had. It felt presumptuous, and she followed reluctantly. "All looks sound enough for now. I'll get your supplies sent over. You guys take it easy a while, you hear?"

"Uh, we got this, man," Ellis said. "Let's call it tomorrow for the cabling and air and such, okay?"

"Whatever you like," Norton said amiably. "Anyway, I need to do my rounds. Walk the perimeter, check the pressures at the fuel dump, a dozen other things. Busy, busy. See y'all at thirteen."

As he bounded away, Vivian beckoned to Ellis. They touched helmets, killed the radio. "Jeez. Does he think we broke his fuel tanks by flying over them?"

"Come on, Viv. You'd check too if you were in charge around here." Ellis's voice was quiet and buzzy, transmitted through the polycarbonate of the helmets rather than her headset. "It's probably on his checklist after every launch and landing. Be cool."

"Always," she said. "Okay, fine. Go stare at the LM. I'll wander around. Get the layout of this dump. Maybe go peer down into the rille."

"Uh, don't jump in."

"Seriously," Vivian said. "Don't tempt me."

Council of war? Holy crap.

11

Columbia Station: Josh Rawlings

THEY sat around the table in the wardroom, eating a long-delayed dinner: Rawlings, Zabrinski, Dardenas. Each man ate using only his left hand; his right was handcuffed to the table rail. Through the window, the Moon rotated lazily beneath them.

Outside the wardroom it was Oleg Vasiliev's turn to stand guard over them, his rifle held easily across his lap. Propped in place against one of the exercise machines, he was reading a book, his eyes glancing frequently over its top. Despite his apparent inattention, Rawlings was in no doubt about Vasiliev's ability to react quickly to any threat.

Jackson was asleep, bandaged up and shackled to his sleeping couch. Mason and Wagner were completing the unloading of the Cargo Carrier under the supervision of Yashin, Belyakova, and Galkin. Erdeli and Salkov were studying the control boards and experiments in the Forward Workshop. Makarov, Isayeva, and Chertok were grabbing some sleep. In the long days ahead, it would be important to stay well rested and maintain an organized shift schedule.

Zabrinski glanced out the door at Vasiliev and lowered his voice. "So, guys; you know how I've always claimed I don't speak Russian?"

Rawlings and Dardenas both swiveled to look at him.

"Hey, don't look *too* interested."

Rawlings turned his attention back to his egg salad. "Well, go on."

"Wasn't a lie, not exactly. I don't *speak* Russian worth a damn. But I understand it, maybe seven words out of ten, and I can usually figure out the rest. My grandmother spoke it at home and—"

Dardenas shook his head. "Doesn't matter *why*, man, hurry it up."

"I overheard our comrades, uh, 'Y' and 'V' talking, back while Jackson and I were in the Cargo Carrier. They thought we were out of earshot, but the curve of the Carrier walls—"

"Come *on*," Rawlings said, his voice low but urgent, but keeping his expression casual.

"Anyway. They need to make progress here as quickly as possible because more Soviets are on the way. More Soyuz and Progress, along with a regular flotilla of lunar landers. Didn't mention how many, but it's clear these wise guys are just the advance party, to secure Columbia as a beachhead."

"Landers," Rawlings said. "So, they *are* going after Hadley."

"Big time. And they're confident it'll be a surprise. Sounds like the Reds have destroyed our MOLs—"

"*Destroyed?* Both of them? Holy crap."

"—and also shot down a U-2 plane over Afghanistan—"

Dardenas put his hand up to his temple. He was Air Force, Rawlings remembered, and a veteran of the short-lived Vietnam conflict. Probably quite sensitive to the words *shot down*. "Gary Powers all over again."

"Afraid not. This time the pilot died. But the bottom line is that the US now has no means of monitoring Soviet launches, and it seems there have recently been a whole lot."

Rawlings' brow furrowed. "Damn."

"And it's worse than that."

"*Worse?* How much worse?"

"The next force is bringing major weaponry. Including *nuclear* weaponry."

A chill crawled up Rawlings's spine to his head, pausing en route to ice his heart. "You're sure? I'm doubting you heard those words around Granny's dinner table."

Zabrinski gave him a look, and lowered his voice even further. "*Atomnaya bomba?* It's literally the fricking same in Russian, man."

Despite the chill, sweat now beaded Rawlings's temples. "Well, shit."

"They're in no doubt they'll take Hadley, or destroy it in the attempt. They're *very* confident."

"Hadley has *no* weapons."

"Uh, yeah, I know that. And clearing Hadley out is just the next step. That's their next target, but it's clear there are more steps after this. A bigger plan."

A bigger plan? What kind of bigger plan could there be than this?

Doesn't matter. Yet.

"So, all this guff that Hunky Nik and Blond Svet are feeding us about symbolic occupation and home-by-Friday—"

"—is to lull us into cooperating. Oh, and the last thing Soviet ground control said to Yashin? They were kidding around. 'Try not to kill them all,' they said. About *us*."

"Jesus." Rawlings reached out, emptied more egg salad into his mouth and chewed without tasting it. He might need all his strength soon. "Okay, opinions: do Makarov and Belyakova know about this? You say Yashin was keeping his voice down?"

"They're *Soviets*. One team. The bastards are all in it together."

"Maybe so, maybe not. Can't hurt to try their own tactics against them. Befriend them. Play it cooperative. All buddy astronauts together, brothers and sisters in spaceflight, yeah? Make them think we're playing ball, get them to lower their guard. And look for opportunities to turn the tables."

"Okay. I guess."

Rawlings's mind was whirling. What to do next? What to do *first*?

Then his uncertainty moved aside, replaced with a grim, calculating calm. Rawlings looked at Zabrinski, then Dardenas. These were good men. He couldn't ask for anyone better at his side. And the other three were no slouches either.

"Okay. So. We don't have guns, but there's all kinds of stuff in this station that we can turn into weapons. We just have to be smart, prepare, bide our time. Right?"

"Right," Zabrinski said. "Except we can't wait too long, because one thing's for damned sure: if we can't figure out a way to warn the Hadley folks, they won't know what hit 'em. The Soviets will pound them into the regolith. They'll be sitting ducks."

PART TWO: HADLEY BASE

December 2, 1979 – January 6, 1980

CHAPTER 12

Hadley Base: Vivian Carter
December 3, 1979

AT fourteen hundred sharp, Norton stepped up and clapped his hands to bring the room to order. "All right, boys and girls, listen up. A lot has happened over the last couple days, so let's review. You've all met our new arrivals? Commander Vivian Carter and Pilot Ellis Mayer, Apollo 32. Let's make them welcome and bring them up to speed as quickly as possible."

A general murmur, a couple of waves. So far Vivian had only spoken to a few of the Hadley astros. Most had shown up moments beforehand. But she knew just about everyone here, at least by sight, from training or from meetings in Houston. Everyone's jumpsuit was labeled with their name and mission patch, anyway.

Assembling twenty astronauts in Habitat A wasn't trivial. Its upper level, the largest open space, was designed for a maximum of twelve. With all eighteen of the Hadley crew, plus Vivian and Ellis, it was uncomfortably crowded. Astros leaned against walls, squashed in side by side on the two bunks, or sat cross-legged on the floor.

It was Dan Klein, Apollo 27, who'd given them the tour of Habitat A, and it hadn't taken long. The Hab was a compressed, wider-but-shorter version of the Skylabs and Columbia Station. Squat and technically three stories tall, the Hab's lowest level was devoted to the airlock and environmental controls, and storage for spacesuits, tools, trash, and other supplies. The midlevel was divided into spaces similar to those on Columbia's middeck, with crew sleep areas, a wardroom for meals, a small area packed with science gear, and two personal-hygiene cubicles. The upper level was for command and control: their communications console and teleprinter, shelves of manuals and binders, and a couple of desks. Earlier, the room had also held exercise equipment that the crew used to maintain their bone and heart mass in the Moon's reduced gravity, but the Hadley astros had packed those away to make space. This level had two windows, on the north and south walls, currently shuttered and screened against the bright heat of lunar day. *Pity.*

Rick Norton and Casey Buchanan of Apollo 21 had been here since January. Two days after they'd touched down, Habitat A had been medium-hard-landed on automatic pilot, directly onto a beacon a couple hundred yards away from where they were sheltering in their LM. Even Vivian had to admit that it took solid steel balls to hang out on Hadley Plain in a flimsy aluminum can waiting for a hundred-ton cylinder to scream in and crash-land in front of you.

A week later had come Jim Dunlap and Ryan Jones in Apollo 22. Dunlap was old-school, square jawed, and clear eyed, but looked tired. Jones, who everyone called "Starman" after the Robert A. Heinlein novel, had short red hair and freckles and an aw-shucks bearing that belied his extensive experience. The other fourteen had arrived in twos and threes at regular intervals after that, and a few weeks ago Ben Epps and Jack Flynn of Apollo 31 had landed to complete the pack.

Now Norton turned to Jones. "Starman, take 'em under your wing once we're done here. Put together a schedule for supplying them with power and victuals, shielding, the usual deal. Everyone else: pitch in as required. Okay, Item One—"

Vivian raised a hand. "Shielding? So we're sticking around?"

Norton looked irritated at the interruption. "Word from Houston is that we wait and see. If the Soviet threat dissolves tomorrow, maybe you get to fly on to Marius after all. But nobody expects that to happen. My guess is that you're in a holding pattern for now, and if the standoff persists, you'll be commanded to ship home."

Home. That was a blow to the gut. "How? Our CSM is dry."

"Refueling options are being considered. Now, if you don't mind … ?"

Vivian had another dozen questions, but this obviously wasn't the time. "Sorry."

Norton nodded. "Item One: Columbia Station. The Soviets assure us that our astros are alive and well, and cooperating fully, helping to maintain the integrity of Columbia. We're assured that relationships are cordial." Norton's tone was sarcastic, and a ripple of dark amusement swept the room. *Cooperating fully. Sure, right; that or breathe vacuum. And good luck keeping up with the complexities of a Skylab, Ivan, if you harm them.*

"Oh, and also: in light of its liberation from capitalist oppression, Columbia Station has been redesignated. In future we're instructed to refer to it as Salyut-Lunik-A. Which certainly trips off the tongue, right?"

"What's Reagan's response?" Collier, the Apollo 25 commander, called out.

"The President has other things on his mind. Firstly, the Soviet occupation of Afghanistan, and the potential knock-on threats to Pakistan, Iran, and the Saudi oil fields. Second: the hostage crisis in the American embassy in Tehran. And, third? Hold onto your hats, kids: Brezhnev is accusing the US of developing a secret nuclear weapons stash here on the Moon."

Collier laughed, and it quickly spread. "Say what? You've got to be kidding."

"Is he senile?" That was Terri Brock, Collier's Lunar Module Pilot, sitting next to him. Vivian knew Brock well; she was Army, tall, lean, and no-nonsense, and on Earth the two of them had stood shoulder to shoulder a couple times to beat down some of the bureaucratic crap that the women astros had faced in training.

Norton shrugged. "Must be, to tangle with Reagan. Ol' Ronnie will eat him for lunch."

"But, nukes on the Moon?" Terri persisted. "What would be the point?"

Buchanan stirred. He was the oldest guy there, in his fifties and balding. Like Starman Jones, Buchanan was a Blue Gemini veteran who'd brought his experience over to Apollo, before they'd curtailed such transfers. "Second-strike capability? Third? Who knows."

"Third?" Vivian couldn't help herself. "That's crazy."

Ron Lawrence was also shaking his head. "Our aim would be lousy, and the damn things would take too long to get to Earth to be of any use."

"It's all just posturing," Norton said. "Brezhnev tossing out red herrings to justify his annexation of the Moon."

"So, uh, again: Reagan's response?" Collier persisted.

"He's meeting Brezhnev toe to toe and not blinking. What else can he do? Anyway, that's not our problem."

"Sure it is, if missiles start flying on Earth," Vivian said, and Ellis discreetly nudged her.

"Won't happen," Norton said. "Soviets will back down."

"Like they backed down in Indochina?"

The Hab got very quiet. Lots of frowns.

Yeah. I shouldn't have said that.

It was, of course, the US who had reversed out of the Vietnam conflict, back in 1968. Nixon had chosen to pour the money into the space program instead, to match the continuing Soviet achievements on the high ground, and today Vietnam, Laos, and Cambodia were all under Communist rule. US containment of Communism had failed then, and it looked like the Soviets had been emboldened by that message and were branching out again. Farther into Asia, and threatening the Middle East. And the Moon.

Carol Massey, Apollo 30, got on Vivian's case right away. "We didn't *back down*. We got the hell out of a stupid situation we shouldn't have been in in the first place. This," she gestured around them, "is way more important than wasting lives in a country no one cares about."

Vivian raised her eyebrows. "Our allies? Who we walked away from?"

"Whoa, hey." Norton raised his hands, palms out. "Y'all can bicker about politics later. For now, we have work to do."

Most everyone swiveled their attention back to Norton, though Collier, Massey, and a few others were still giving Vivian the stink eye.

Way to make an entrance.

"Here's the Soviets' generous offer. They'll allow any Apollo crew that evacuates from Hadley Base to rendezvous with their Command and Service Module at, uh, Salyut-Lunik-A. The Soviets will then release their CM pilot and allow them to continue on back to Earth. Those are the only circumstances in which the Soviets will permit any US approach to Columbia."

That was how the crew of Columbia Station had been built up in the first place. Rawlings had been Command Module Pilot for Norton and Buchanan, Wagner the CMP for Apollo 22, accompanying Dunlap and Jones, and so on.

"So that's the deal?" Dunlap said. "Pledge to go home, and you get to take your guy from Columbia with you?"

"Hells yeah," said Christian Vazquez. "Let's get Danny out of there." Danny Zabrinski, who'd come to the Moon as Apollo 26's CMP.

Joe Seaton and Carol Massey glanced at each other. Jackson was their CMP, if Vivian remembered right. They didn't seem quite so enthusiastic.

Lawrence looked thoughtful. "The more of our guys we liberate, the less able the Soviets will be to handle Columbia."

The offer did make sense. The Command Module Pilots were the experts for the final mission phase, from deorbit burn to splashdown. Vivian sure wouldn't want to hit atmosphere without a dedicated CMP at the helm.

Norton grimaced. "Well, that's the *offer*. For every pair of us who leaves the Moon, they'll free a prisoner. But it's not an offer we can accept."

"Why the hell not?" Dunlap demanded. "Starman and I are due to rotate back to Earth in a month anyway. So sure: let's go pick up Gary and get the hell home."

Gisemba, Apollo 29, shook his head. "You'd take the Soviets at their word?"

"On this, sure," said Luis Ibarra. "The Soviets *want* us out. That's the whole point. They shoot themselves in the foot if they renege."

Norton held up his hands again. "Guys, save your breath. Not gonna happen. This is a hostage situation, and the United States government does not make deals with hostage takers. No negotiating with kidnappers."

"Jeez." Dunlap sat back, frustrated.

"Absolutely," Vivian heard herself say, and over half the room shifted their unhappy gaze from Norton to her. "No other response possible."

"Yep," said Leverton.

"Easy for *you* to say," Dunlap retorted, turning on him. Two of the crews—Collier's Apollo 25, and Leverton's Apollo 29—didn't have anyone trapped aboard Columbia. Their Command Module Pilots, Ron Lawrence and Feye Gisemba, had come down to the Moon with them in their newer N-class Lunar Modules, capable of carrying three.

"Okay, fine," said Dan Klein. "So, what do we do next?"

"The real question is what *they're* going to do next. The Soviets," Norton said. "They can't evict us from Hadley from orbit. There's only nine of them aboard Columbia, and they didn't bring any landers anyhow."

"So, we just *sit* here?" Collier demanded.

"Those are our orders. Continue as if none of this is happening. Show that the US is not intimidated by this act of space piracy. Carry on with our materials science projects, our site clearing, all our other R&D, and do so just as publicly as before. You new guys?" He indicated Vivian and Ellis. "For now, settle in and get operational. Set out your science payloads, even though they're redundant. Send back TV footage of whatever geological work you can come up with, along with our other rock hounds. Job One is to reinforce the message that Hadley Base is a peaceful installation. A science camp. You know the schtick."

Vivian nodded. "Except it's not schtick for me."

"Then you'll be extra convincing. Anyway: we stay put. Call the Soviets' bluff. Stall, while the US rallies support in the UN."

Buchanan stepped up. "And in the meantime, quietly prepare to defend Hadley from ground attack."

Vivian's jaw dropped. "*Ground* attack?" She only beat Starman and Gisemba to the punch by a fraction of a second.

"From Zvezda Base." Leverton said, as if it was obvious.

The Soviet Zvezda moonbase was over five hundred miles west of Hadley. Way too far for US astros to traverse overland with their current equipment.

"Can they do that? Do they have the capability?"

Buchanan eyed Collier steadily. "We certainly can't rule out the possibility."

"Holy moly." Starman Jones sank his head into his hands.

"So, we dig in?" Dunlap demanded. "Come what may?"

Norton looked at him sideways. "You see it differently, Jim?"

"You bet I do. You're discussing a shooting match on the *Moon*?"

"Man, we set this base up together," Norton said quietly. "And you're ready to turn tail as soon as some Russkies growl at us?"

"This is more than a growl." Dunlap stood up. "I mean, guys, come on. I was in 'Nam. Two tours. And the day the Soviets storm Duluth, Minnesota, I'll be on the front line to push 'em back. I'll fight till there's no blood left in my body. But, Hadley? It's not worth any of us dying over Hadley."

"The US has made quite the investment here," Buchanan pointed out. "*We've* made quite the investment, each of us."

"This is a rock. It's a project. It's not home. I'm not about to dig trenches in the lunar soil and settle in for a goddamned *war*."

Several people started talking at once. Norton called for order. "One at a time. Joe next."

"Maybe there's some middle ground here," said Seaton. "We're not gonna cave. But maybe if a few people start leaving," he waved at Dunlap, "a couple volunteers, maybe that shows willing."

"You're saying we start a drawdown? In a foot-dragging sort of way?" That was Leverton. Vivian was already noticing that the commanders spoke more than the LM pilots.

"It buys us time, to see how far the Soviets are really willing to push this."

"The more of us that split, the weaker that leaves the rest of us," Buchanan objected. "And the less able we'll be to defend ourselves. No. We stay here. We stick together. And we wait." He sat back as if everything was settled, and perhaps it was.

Norton looked at his watch. "Joe, Jim? I hear what you're saying. So, here's what I'll do: right after this, I'll get on the horn to Houston and broach the idea of a gradual drawdown. I'm guessing they've already considered and rejected it. But it doesn't hurt to get a clear answer. Okay?

"But in the meantime, yes: we brainstorm ideas about defending Hadley Base in the event of an on-surface attack."

Astronauts looked at one another.

"Here's what we have, off the top of my head." Norton was remorseless. "Explosive charges, for site clearance, breaking up rocks and such. And the bridgewire detonators and blasting caps that go with them. And then, every LM has the four pyro bolts that separate the ascent and descent stages."

Explosive bolts: shaped charges, detonated using either gas cartridges or squib batteries. "Uh, hold on," said Starman. "We'll need those pyros if we do end up evacuating in a hurry."

"Betcha we don't." Buchanan reached up to grab a binder off a shelf and page through it. "If it comes to launching the ascent stages, I bet we can engineer the disconnect without the pyros. What I don't know is whether we can pry the pyros out of that midspace without breaking anything else in the process."

"Seems high risk," said Brock. "Would not recommend."

Ellis spoke up. "You don't keep spares, in case the ones in the LMs test dry?"

"Nope. We run lean on spares here, and pyros are generally pretty reliable." Buchanan held up a loose-leaf page he'd liberated from the binder. "But, y'know, we have all kinds of other pyros in the Hab systems to close bulkheads for atmosphere retainment in an emergency. And those are easy to get out. Designed to be replaced."

"Yes, but they're smaller charges," Brock said. "At least, I think they are."

Other people piped up again, but Norton cut them off with a hand gesture. "Okay, hold up. It's getting pretty toasty in here, and the CO_2 level is rising with all this hot air we're blowing out, so let's close this off for now. I don't want to waste time fielding wild ideas that nobody has thought through. This is homework, people. Talk among yourselves. Experiment. Even play around and rig up prototypes. Think about what we can use to harden Hadley against the Commie threat, and how to regain the initiative if we're attacked. Clear?" He clapped his hands. "That's it. Class dismissed."

"Back to bed, then." Epps and Flynn of Apollo 31, the crew that had been the newcomers until Carter and Mayer showed up, hustled for the stairs down to the next level. They were off shift, and obviously needed more shut-eye. Norton made to follow.

"So, Rick, wait," Massey said. "Apollo 32 gets to stay here and grandstand on TV while the rest of us work?"

Vivian eyed her. "What's your problem?"

Norton half turned. "You heard me. Nobody leaves the Moon for now. So, Carter and Mayer run around and play rock hound for a while."

"Per our mission as an exploratory Apollo," Vivian couldn't resist adding.

Massey frowned.

"We have a Lunar Module with probable damage to its rocket motor, and a Command and Service Module with insufficient fuel to break lunar orbit," Vivian said. "We're not going anywhere until both those issues are resolved."

"And what's the plan to resolve them?"

Jeez, lady, we've barely been here long enough to sleep. Vivian looked at Norton, who said, "That's down the queue. The Apollo 32 crew are safe and stable, and we have shorter fuse items to deal with. Now, if you'll excuse me ..."

Massey nodded curtly and moved off to join a knot of astronauts that were bouncing on the balls of their feet discussing pyros and detonators. Norton again headed for the stairs.

"Uh, Rick?" Vivian said. "Could we have a few more words?"

"Sure, but not right now." Norton took the steps four at a time, dropping quickly to the level below.

"Well, so much for that," she said.

"Norton's a busy man," Ellis said, levelly.

Well, fine. Norton didn't have to like her. "Mission Control never told *us* we were staying. They told him, but not us?"

"He's the base commander."

And Vivian was the commander of Apollo 32. Apparently, that had now been trumped. "Yeah. Guess so."

"Hey." Buchanan appeared by her side. "Hi there, Vivian. Good to meet you."

"Uh, good to meet you too, sir." As one of the older astros, Buchanan had been spaceside for most of Vivian's NASA career. She'd seen him maybe twice in Houston briefings.

"I'm not 'Sir,' I'm Casey." Buchanan eyed her thoughtfully. "You're not about to cause us any difficulties, Vivian, right? Because you seem a little confrontational, and here at Hadley we're all one team. Being one team is the only way this works. The odds against us are stacked high enough already, without internal dissent."

Vivian was hardly the only astronaut to have disagreed with Norton. But she knew how this worked: she was new in the room, a surprise arrival, not one of the established crew. They weren't used to her yet. *Not worth pushing back. Don't need to be on the wrong side of* both *the senior guys here.* "Copy that, Casey. Sorry, I've had a rough couple of days."

Buchanan nodded readily. "That, you have."

He was still looking at her, so Vivian added, "We'll give some thought to defense. And get our science up and running, as requested." *Ordered.* It hadn't been a request.

"And we'll obviously be happy to chip in on general maintenance tasks where necessary," Ellis said. "We'll pay our way."

"Outstanding. Welcome to Hadley, Vivian, Ellis."

"Thank you, uh, Casey."

"Hi, Vivian," said Terri Brock from her other side. "Sorry about your mission. Truly. That sucks."

First person to mention it. Vivian thought of hugging her for that, but played it safe and shook the other woman's hand instead. "It really does. Thanks for saying so."

"Give me a shout if you need anything, okay?" Terri smiled and moved on.

Starman Jones bounced up to them next. It was hard to walk in a dignified way on the Moon, and Starman obviously wasn't even trying. "I'm to lay a power cable out to Athena, stock you with food and air, provide whatever other help you may need. And bring some shielding out too. Just tell me when."

"Thanks," she said. "Excellent."

"But, you know?" He grinned at her. *Jeez, this guy is Mom and apple pie all the way down. My Gran would be pinching his rosy-red cheeks around now.*

Ellis looked at him sideways and grinned back, and Vivian remembered that he and Jones had been in the same astronaut class. "Okay, spit it out. What're you angling for, Starman?"

"Glad you asked. Truth be told, I'm kind of interested in your spiffy new rover. If you happen to need a hand with the deploy?"

Vivian and Ellis had brought the first of the new generation of dual-mode Lunar Roving Vehicles, with its radioisotope power option in addition to the usual pair of rechargeable batteries. The Apollo 32 Lunar Rover also had a telerobotic option, to allow it to be driven remotely from Hadley, or even from Earth. Slowly, because of signal travel time and the natural obstacles that the remote operator would have to deal with, but it was still a pretty cool capability. One that would have been more useful in an extended robotic exploration of Marius following the departure of the human crew of Apollo 32, but maybe they'd find a use for it here too.

Vivian bit back her first reaction. They certainly didn't *need* any help. But they could use a friend.

So, she gave in. "Sure. Why not?" She looked at the clock. "Probably still time to do that today. We're pretty anxious to check it out ourselves."

Starman grinned again. "I'll go prep. See you in vacuum."

Vivian noticed Bill Dobbs and Christian Vasquez, Apollo 26, listening in. These were Hadley's two on-site geologists. "Hi there, guys. Anything left to do around here? Or did you leave no stone unturned?"

"Oh, sure." They all shook hands, and Dobbs continued. "We've covered the local area pretty extensively. Focused heavily on the rille. We've made some traverses into the depths, taken a buttload of samples of bedrock, talus, debris. And done several trips to the foothills.

But if there's one thing the Moon has in abundance, it's rocks. We've literally only scratched the surface."

Ellis thought about it. "Mostly, the samples are packaged for Earth return?"

"Yes. We have a small X-ray fluorescence spectrometer in Hab B. A binocular microscope for petrographic analysis. That's about it for in situ work."

"We should put our heads together," Vasquez said. "Get some joint trips going. Maybe push the envelope a bit, while we have you."

"That would be great," Vivian said, agreeably enough.

"Sure." Ellis didn't even need to glance at her. "Let's me and Vivian do a few EVAs to come up to speed and put our rover through its paces. Take a look at some rocks, get ourselves calibrated. After that, let's talk."

Vivian considered. "So, that's how it works here, we all just make our own plans? Houston doesn't dictate our schedules?"

Vasquez laughed. "No. Sometimes the Earth geology team gives us suggestions, but we mostly populate our own timeline."

"We are empowered," Dobbs said. "We're the ones on the spot, and we're not limited by a ten-day window like you expeditionary flights. Norton, Jones, and Gisemba set the base development and maintenance schedules, and we take our turns like everyone else. But once we square away the mandatory stuff, we all get to work our specialties, and ours is rocks. We're working down an agreed list of target sites and objectives, but for timing and implementation, Mission Control leaves us to it."

Meaning they don't care a whole lot. Vivian couldn't imagine the geologists and other academics she'd worked with on Earth being indifferent to Apollo 32's schedule. She and Ellis had lifted off with a six-day itinerary laid out in minute detail, and the Houston geology backroom would have had the biggest say in planning their final four days as well, based on what they'd learned up till then, and which potential targets were voted highest priority after a rack-and-stack.

The schedules of the exploratory Apollos were not renowned for their flexibility. Evidently, the rules were different at Hadley.

Which was actually pretty cool. "Well, okay, then."

And with that, Vivian wanted to get the hell out of this all-too-comfortable Habitat. Back out onto the surface. She hadn't come all this way to sit in meetings.

She rubbed her aching shoulder, nodded professionally to Dobbs, and turned to Ellis. "Okay then, Army. Wanna blow this joint?"

"Yep, I do. But ..." He subtly gestured toward the knots of astronauts. "We should probably mingle for a few more minutes? Diplomacy?"

"Damn." Vivian sighed. "Yeah, okay. Probably should. But when I tug on my earlobe, we're leaving this party and heading out, right?"

CHAPTER 13

Columbia Station: Josh Rawlings/Nikolai Makarov
December 3, 1979

Rawlings

Six Americans. Nine Soviets. The odds were not in their favor. But Josh and his crew had the home-team advantage. They were intimately familiar with Columbia Station. They knew every useful piece of equipment, and all the handy places where they might stash such equipment till the moment came to use it. They were also fit, energized, and had several months more experience in zero G than the Russians.

Sergei Yashin, Lev Chertok, and Oleg Vasiliev were obviously the most dangerous of their captors. Tough and ruthless, they would kill first and ask questions later, if ever.

On the other end of the spectrum, Pavel Erdeli, Viktoriya Isayeva, and whoever-Salkov stood out as the techies and equipment specialists. Erdeli was big, bluff, and friendly, almost a caricature of the jovial Russian. Isayeva was small and polite; she seemed fit, with good muscle tone, but, even so, Josh was betting he could fend her off with one hand if he needed to.

The other Soviets called them "Pasha" and "Vika" in a comradely way. As for Salkov, he had no nickname, and apparently no first name and patronymic either: no one called him anything other than "Salkov." He got the scut work: developing film, scanning the resulting photos, and transmitting the data back to Mother Russia. Since much of that work needed to be done aboard the Soviet vessels, they rarely saw him inside Columbia Station, though he also handled some of the menial tasks the Soviets didn't trust their American captives to do: recharging oxygen bottles, maintaining spacesuits.

In between the soldiers and the nerds were the career cosmonauts: Nikolai Makarov, Svetlana Belyakova, and Yuri Galkin. Josh hoped they'd cave quickly if it came to a brawl, but that was by no means assured. Hunky Nik and Blond Svet were affable enough, but strong willed. Their clear eyes, chiseled features, and healthy bodies made them literal poster children for the Communist system. Galkin faded into the background by comparison, partly because his English wasn't so good. Josh wasn't about to count any of them out in a pinch.

Josh didn't give a toss what happened to the KGB goons, but he sincerely hoped he wouldn't have to damage big bear Pavel or pretty svelte Vika, or the veteran cosmonauts. He was guessing none of them were thrilled to be entangled in this mission of cislunar piracy.

But, damn it, Columbia was Josh's command. He wasn't about to let a bunch of Russkies rob him of it, even if he grudgingly liked some of them.

And with Yashin, Chertok, and Vasiliev in the mix, violence could break out at any moment. None was gentle. A few hours ago Chertok had, with no provocation, cracked Marco Dardenas over the head with his rifle butt while attaching him to the wardroom table at breakfast. All three drew out the process of releasing the Americans from their shackles, especially for bathroom breaks. Josh had begun asking half an hour before he really needed to go, because it might take that long for one of these assholes to find time in his busy schedule to undo the handcuffs and escort him down there.

Especially Yashin. He had dead fish eyes, and no inkling of humor, no signs of compassion. He looked like a stone-cold killer.

Thus, the Columbia crew timed their counterattack to take place during Yashin's sleep period.

Mason was briefing Galkin on the station radar, while Jackson was leading Vika and Pavel though the nitty-gritty of operating the large-frame optical camera that they'd uncrated from the Cargo Carrier. Chertok was their armed guard, but it was getting toward his shift end and he was yawning, spittle flying from his lips that he then had to wipe out of the air with his sleeve. Makarov was also on sleep shift; Josh was happy to keep him out of it.

Allegedly Wagner and Zabrinski were resting as well, loosely lashed to their bunks with lengths of metal cable. In fact, both were wide awake and ready for the fray.

Josh was handcuffed to the rail of the wardroom table. Across from him, Svetlana paged through one of the station's black-bound folders of checklists. Sometimes her brow furrowed and her lips moved as she read—the NASA checklists were terse instruction sets crammed with obscure acronyms, and Josh found it hard to believe that she understood much of it, but she had only asked occasional questions. Both were absently picking at food from trays next to them.

Svetlana was quite attractive, in that severe Soviet way. In another, very different world, Josh might have liked to take her to a nice restaurant and get to know her better.

Instead, he was about to hit her really hard.

No way of avoiding it. But while steeling himself for action, Josh recalled how she'd raised her fist to strike Jackson after the fracas in the Cargo Carrier. She'd have beaten on him without compunction if she'd seen the need. And now Josh would have to do the same to her.

Josh saw the flash through the ceiling from the wide open spaces of the level above at exactly the same time as he heard the crackle of electricity and Galkin's howl of pain.

According to the plan, prior to demonstrating the radar to Galkin, Mason—casually and without being noticed—had performed a simple rewiring under the panel. When Galkin had touched it, he'd taken 125 V directly from the station's electrical power system.

Even as Belyakova raised her head, there came a loud crunch and second yelp.

"Sorry about this," Josh said, and lunged across the table. His forehead caught the bridge of her nose, and her head snapped back. Blood gushed from her nostrils in a startling cloud.

Josh twisted. The US astronauts had been covertly loosening the bars along the underside of the wardroom table, and now he snapped the bracket out of position and slid his handcuff off the rail. *Free. Woo-hoo*—

But, holy hell: Belyakova was *fast*. Ignoring the pain and her sudden nosebleed she launched herself at him, swinging. The heavy binder slammed into Josh's arm and set him spinning, his head nearly smashing into the floor beneath him.

Josh windmilled his hands and legs. He got a foot to the floor and shoved off, sending himself flying up toward the window. He bounced off it and cannoned into the ceiling. Belyakova was coming for him again, but couldn't course-correct quickly enough to grab him. So Josh arrowed out of the wardroom door, seized its upper lintel, and swung himself up.

The last thing he glimpsed from the crew level was Zabrinski emerging from the sleeping quarters, having freed himself from his restraining cable using the bolt cutters they'd secreted at the foot of his bed eighteen hours before.

Wagner would still be in there. His job was to take Yashin out. Josh didn't begrudge him *that* task, but Gary had volunteered; he was a Marine, after all, and something of a hard-ass. Hopefully he'd still be alive to brag about it a few minutes from now.

Even as Josh thrust himself through the hexagonal cut that led to the fore level, gunfire erupted above him. He kept moving, still translating at quite the clip, with Zabrinski following, and took in the situation at a glance.

Shit.

According to the plan, Jackson would have looped a strand of thick wire around Vika's neck and used her as a hostage, a human shield to hold Pasha off. It clearly hadn't happened that way. Pavel Erdeli was floating back all right, wearing a stupefied look, but Viktoriya Isayeva had somehow flexed like an eel to twist herself out of Jackson's grasp. She was pummeling him, one-two, one-two, her fists accurately drilling into his face wounds from forty-eight hours earlier. Jackson was howling while still trying to kick her; it wasn't over yet, but they'd all badly misjudged "little Vika."

But that wasn't Josh's concern right now. *Where was the fricking KGB guy?*

There. Lev Chertok was spinning, tumbling over and over, high up in the Skylab's dome. Per the plan, after shocking Galkin with the live panel Mason had hurled a pyro bolt at him. The bolt flared near enough to Chertok to send him into a tailspin, but not close enough to injure him. It was only a small pyro. They weren't about to set off a major charge right here in the living space. Chertok had loosed off some bullets, but hadn't hit anyone. Yet.

Josh got going. As he flew past Galkin he dealt the cosmonaut a blow to the head with a spanner that might keep the poor guy's eyes crossed for days, but his main target was Chertok.

Chertok wasn't terrific in zero G, but he didn't suck either. He spread his arms and legs wide, the classic ballerina move to slow his rate of spin, while still clutching his AK-47. He collided with the dome wall and managed to anchor himself, blinking from the dazzle of the pyro bolt but otherwise unharmed.

Mason was coming up on Chertok from one side, Josh arrowing in from below. But Chertok didn't look even slightly fazed. He swung the assault rifle around one-handed, counter-moving with his other arm so he didn't twist in the air. *Quick learner.*

Ducking under the barrel, Josh hit him first, both his fists sinking into Chertok's gut. Chertok elbowed him in the temple. Josh saw stars.

As the AK-47 went off again Josh heard two roars of pain at almost the same moment: Mason, and Jackson. Still dizzy, Josh now howled himself as the stock of the rifle smacked into his mouth, breaking teeth.

Crap, crap .... Josh shoved himself away from the bulky Soviet and twisted in the air, spinning into a floating swath of his own blood. He saw Zabrinski wrestling in free fall with Oleg Vasiliev, both men clumsy, struggling to land blows. Below them, Galkin floated unconscious. One down at least, but goddamn it ...

Viktoriya Isayeva had one arm on a handrail to stabilize herself and the other hand in Jackson's hair, methodically slamming his face into the box the optical camera had come in. Dardenas had finally gotten loose and appeared from below and was heading her way, but surely it had to be too late. Surely Jackson was already dead.

Josh slid a screwdriver from his sleeve, grabbed Chertok and got his arm around the Russian's neck. Got the pointy end of the screwdriver to the KGB guy's throat. "*Stoy.* Stay still. Don't move, or I'll put a hole in your windpipe." Damn it, what was the other phrase Zabrinski had taught him?

Chertok relaxed in midair. "*Da.*" But his eyes still darted around, on the alert for something he could use to his advantage.

"Everyone hold still! *Ne dvigaytes!*" Here came Zabrinski, a heavy pyro bolt in each hand. He'd broken free of Vasiliev, who was careening across the compartment, hands clutching his nose and groin.

Yup, that was it. Josh shouted it too: "*Ne dvigaytes!*"

And then Yashin rocketed through the gap from the crew level, spiraling in the air as he came, a Tula semiautomatic pistol in each hand.

Panic rocked Josh. *Crap.* Wagner hadn't taken him out. *That's not good.*

Dardenas hurled a wrench at Yashin just as the KGB agent shot him. Dardenas jerked twice as bullets impacted him and wallowed in the air, floating backward. Blood flowed from his shoulder and arm, spreading into the fabric of his blue jumpsuit and ballooning gently outward.

Mason had leaped above them all, wrestling with the hatch into the Multiple Docking Adapter. If he'd gotten through, he might have jammed it shut from the outside. Then he'd have been able to suit up and go and isolate Salkov, maybe even do some serious damage to the Soviet Soyuz craft. But, no dice.

Yashin fired his other pistol. The noise was deafening as a stream of bullets sprayed through the fore compartment and across Ed Mason's torso. Ricochets clanged and clattered, and Josh cried out in alarm. Mason crashed into the control panel by the hatch. Sparks flew.

Vika released Jackson's head. She looked over at Pasha, still floating there in shock, and spat accurately at him in contempt.

Chertok turned his head carefully to stare at Josh.

Yashin lobbed one of his pistols across to Vika, who snatched it out of the air, held the barrel under Jackson's chin, and pulled the trigger with as little emotion as she might display connecting a cable. Another excruciatingly loud detonation, and the top of Jackson's head fountained blood and brain.

That was probably overkill, Josh thought, and felt the obscene, hopeless desire to laugh.

Svetlana Belyakova stuck her head through the gap from below, another pistol now in her hand. Her nose dribbled a line of blood in her wake. Her gaze arrived on Josh, but by that time Vika and Yashin were both aiming their pistols at him. Instead, Svetlana covered Zabrinski. "Everyone remain still!" she called out.

"*Damn* it." Josh released his hold on the screwdriver and set it adrift. Raised his arms in surrender, floated away from the Soviet agent.

Lev Chertok calmly swung his elbow into Josh's already-injured mouth. Pain flooded Josh's head, and when the second punch came, he could do nothing to avoid it.

Just as everything went black, Josh's final thought was: *All that, and we still couldn't warn Viv.*

Makarov

He awoke with a start to a feeling of dread. Din surrounded him. *Those American fools, what have they done … ?*

He heaved himself out of his bunk, shoved off for the doorway, and collided with a body. *Shit!* The corpse drifted away. Blood filled the air, and now Makarov had red wetness all over his hands.

It was the American, Wagner, quite dead. His throat had been ripped out.

Makarov wasn't the quickest at rousing himself from sleep, but colliding with a corpse was a pretty solid wake-up call. He thrust Wagner away in horror, exited the sleeping quarters, and almost crashed into Svetlana Belyakova. "What is happening? Are you all right?"

"Yes," Belyakova said, though blood wreathed the air around her, and Makarov only now noticed she was holding a gun. More din from above: gunfire, screams. "Stay here."

She took a cautious peek. "Your stupid Americans are getting themselves killed." Thrusting her head and shoulders through the gap, she switched to English. "Everyone, remain still!"

His Americans? Makarov didn't ask. Svetlana was gone now anyway, into the forward compartment.

Makarov glanced back at Wagner's limp, grisly corpse. It had somehow followed him out from the sleeping compartment, wafting gently in the breeze from the overactive air vents. The dead astronaut's arms flexed as if they were still questing, reaching for something. *Whatever it is, Comrade, you'll never find it now.*

Jackson and Wagner were dead. Mason was unconscious, in shock, with Yashin's bullets in his chest and burns on his hand. Oleg Vasiliev had him strapped into the comms chair and was trying to stanch the bleeding; from his quick, even movements Vasiliev had obviously been trained in field surgery. Dardenas, shot cleanly through the shoulder and arm, was floating with his face creased in agony. Zabrinski was administering to him. As for Rawlings ...

"Damn it, bring him here." Svetlana was dragging the unconscious Josh out of Chertok's grasp. "Give him to us, you want him to choke on his own blood?"

"No," Chertok said coldly. "I want to put a bullet into his stupid head. Yashin? Yes?"

"No. You can't." Svetlana shot him a look, then glowered at Yashin. "Are you both mad? Two dead not enough for you? We need the rest alive."

Yashin looked at Pasha. "Do we?"

"Yes, for God's sake, of course we do." Erdeli had hurried to the unconscious Galkin's side to check his pulse and breathing. "No more killing! No more blood in here!"

Vika propped Josh's mouth open and used a rag to scoop blood out of it with rough but efficient care. "Ugh, his teeth. But he will be all right."

"You *killed* Jackson?" Svetlana demanded, incredulous.

"Of course. Bastard tried to strangle me, and was enjoying it. Capitalist degenerate."

Makarov put his hands up to his head. "This is a disaster. Dear God, Yashin, nobody was supposed to die."

"I?" Yashin waved his hand around. "What do you think happened here? You suppose Jackson would not have choked Viktoriya Gubovna? That Mason was not ready to kill Comrade Galkin? That Wagner would have let me live, had I not slain him first? These Americans are not playing games. And neither should we."

"We defended ourselves against ruthless Imperialists." Vika's calm was uncanny. "This will not be hard to explain."

Makarov shook his head. "You *killed* them. You could have merely incapacitated them."

Yashin smiled grimly. "I saw Lev Petrovich with an American blade at his throat. I saw Comrade Galkin electrocuted and stunned, and Comrade Isayeva on the verge of being murdered by a man twice her size."

Vika glanced over at him. "But I took care of that."

"So you did." Yashin's tone was half-proud, almost avuncular, and Makarov realized they'd all been blind to the connection between the two of them.

So much blood. Sorrow overwhelmed him. These were spacefarers, just like himself and Belyakova. This was out of control.

Yashin turned back to Makarov. "We have one task, and that is to force the Americans from the Moon. You disagree, perhaps, with the First Secretary?" He meant Brezhnev.

"Of course not," Makarov said quickly. "But your methods—"

"I take full responsibility for this," Yashin said. "Just as, on the Moon, your authority will be unquestioned."

For some reason, Svetlana shot Makarov a warning look. Why? *If only there weren't so much blood in the air, I could think.* "What?"

"On the lunar surface, you are the undisputed expert. Given such expertise, I am sure you can force the Americans to withdraw without bloodshed, if that is your preference."

Holy Mother Russia. "That is my preference. But ... the surface?"

"New orders came while you slept," Svetlana said quietly. "Confirmation. Our ground strike is to proceed with all haste."

Madness, Makarov thought, and almost said it aloud.

"It is a heavy burden that you bear. But I am sure that you will acquit yourself with great glory. What are your orders, Commander?" Yashin stared at him insolently.

Makarov swallowed. "Duty is never a burden. But for now ... we must tidy up. See to the wounded. Mop all this blood out of the air. Check that nothing has been seriously damaged."

"Immediately, Commander." Yashin gestured to Vika and Pasha.

"And get Salkov in here to help." Makarov glanced at the Americans' clocks. "We are really going to the surface? When?"

"Twenty-four hours. Perhaps less."

"*Tomorrow?*" Much sooner than he had anticipated. No contingency in their pre-mission briefing had this happening so fast. Makarov turned to Yashin. "You did this?"

"I? I merely take orders. The pace of our activities is set in Moscow."

Was that true? Makarov realized it must be. Yashin could not just do as he pleased. None of them could. "So, the landers and the rest of the force are already on their way?" And must have been for days.

"The first will arrive in six hours."

Six hours? "You should have awoken me, Svetlana."

Her lip twitched. "We decided it best that you rest. Who knows when we will all sleep again?"

Insanity. Insanity.

Yashin, Chertok, and Vasiliev all stared at him expectantly. Pasha and Vika were efficiently cleaning up, but they too glanced his way. Makarov regained his composure with difficulty. "Very well. No time like the present. But we have much to prepare."

CHAPTER 14

Apollo 32: Vivian Carter
December 3, 1979

"**OKEY** dokey, then," Vivian said. "Let's get this bad boy on the road."

Two hours later, little had changed out on the surface. The Sun must have moved in the sky in the meantime (*half a degree per hour*, murmured Vivian's training), but the difference in the illumination and shadowing around Athena wasn't evident. *Long days here.*

Ellis, ever methodical, was studying the thermal blanket over the rover. His voice crackled through her headset. "Looks nominal."

Starman Jones stood back respectfully, letting them work. Although Vivian couldn't glimpse his face past the golden gleam of his visor, it was easy to tell the two men apart. Starman bounded around like a big kid, whereas Ellis was still circumspect, watching where he put his feet. Also, Jones's suit was battered and worn from months of use and multiple cleanings. Ellis's still looked fresh out of the box, aside from the black lunar soil that streaked his boots and right elbow where he'd taken a tumble earlier.

The fall wasn't a big deal. All astronauts fell ass over teakettle on the Moon at some point. With less pressure of their feet on the ground it was easy to lose track of their center of mass, and the stiff suit made it difficult to bend at the knee to recover. Vivian was surprised she hadn't measured her own length on the regolith yet.

"Visual inspection complete?" May as well do this by the book. Even though Mission Control didn't seem to be paying any attention. No instructions in her ears from Houston, no requests for information. It was disconcerting.

"Roger that. No visible damage."

"Okay, swell. Let's unwrap our Christmas gift."

Vivian's tone was laconic, but her movements were eager. She was hungry for this. Right now, their hopes for any kind of mission success depended on this rover. If they'd banged it up during their chaotic landing, or if the Reds had put a bullet through something important, today was going to suck.

The Lunar Rover had flown here folded up against the LM within a complex structural-support system. Deploying it would take a combination of braked reels and cables, telescopic tubes and chassis latches, and pins to release and lock that chassis in place. Fortunately, it was designed to unfold and come free largely by itself. Even the first time astronauts had unpacked a rover on the Moon—on Apollo 15, just a couple hundred yards from where Vivian now stood—the entire operation had taken less than thirty minutes.

They peeled away the Velcro straps and slid off the insulation blanket. "Support latches in place. Trip arm up."

Vivian's heart rate was up as well. She needed this glorified golf cart to *work*. "Deployment cable released."

She climbed the LM ladder and leaned out. "Pins look fine. Far as I can see, the package is still resting in its hinges. No obstruction, no fouling." She tugged at the D-handle of the release mechanism, and the LRV began to rotate out. "Out you come, baby."

Ellis took up the slack on the cable and leaned back. "Ready."

Vivian hurried back down to grab the other cable. "Go."

As they lowered it down, the rear wheels of the rover cantilevered out automatically and locked into position. "Smooth," Jones said.

Ellis put a proprietary hand on the rover, watching as the chassis gradually straightened out. Vivian glanced at Starman. "So. Soviet soldiers, eh? Ground forces?"

"Yeah?"

"Remember the good old days when we used to call 'em 'cosmonauts'?"

"You mean, before they started attacking us?" Jones said.

"The man has a solid point," Ellis said absently, as the rear wheels of the rover kissed the ground. "Touchdown."

Jones sobered. "The skipper can talk of war and defenses all he likes, but we're crazy vulnerable out here."

Ellis half turned, amused. "'The skipper'? Now we're on *Gilligan's Island?* Are you his Little Buddy?"

Jones laughed. "Something like that. No, not really."

"Let me be very clear," Vivian said. "I am neither Ginger, Lovey, nor Mary Ann."

"Maybe the Professor?"

"Uh. Thank you?" The front wheels locked into place, and Vivian cranked the left-hand cable reel to lower them to the soil. "Oh, you lovely, lovely thing."

They pulled out the pins to separate the rover from the descent stage, and then busied themselves installing the seats, harnesses, battery, camera. Vivian glanced at Starman. "Okay, let's get real. How many weeks of supplies do we have at Hadley? If the Soviets were able to stop any more US cargo modules getting through, how long would we last?"

Ellis grinned; she could hear it in his voice. "So now the Soviets can somehow *blockade* the Moon? With what? That would be a trick."

Well, if the world goes to war ... "I'm just spitballing. Like the, uh, skipper told us. So how long, Starman?"

"Month and a half," Jones said promptly. "Probably more, but that's the minimum margin we maintain at all times in case of a Saturn V issue on the pad. Six weeks of oxygen, water, and food, and enough power for ... well, forever."

Every LM had its own RTG—radioisotope thermoelectric generator—a small nuclear power source fired by a slug of plutonium-238—plus fuel cells, batteries, and solar arrays to operate their experiments. The two Habs would have plenty more. "No other consumables? Air filters, lithium-hydroxide scrubbers? Underwear? Aspirin? I dunno, laundry detergent?"

Starman laughed. "We've got so much redundancy that we haven't loaded out even half of the last supply drop. We don't have space in the Habs for it all. And, I'm betting the first thing NASA will do is send us yet another Container, so's we're super-duper supplied. To make it crystal clear, we're staying for the long haul."

Then, it hit her. *The long haul.*

For the first time, Vivian consciously internalized that their mission really was *open ended* now.

Already they were staying at least through the lunar night, something she'd obviously never anticipated. It wouldn't have been possible at Marius. So, another week of daylight and then two weeks of night .... But even after that, no one was suggesting that *any of them* would leave. On the contrary: at least for now, Apollo 32's orders were to stay put, conspicuously doing science and transmitting words and pictures home about it.

The White House, Congress, and NASA were sending their message loud and clear. They'd maintain the American population of the Moon as high as possible for as long as possible. Which meant that Vivian and Ellis could be here a *long* time.

Provided she could stay on the right side of Norton.

Ellis installed the footrests, and Vivian fastened the dust covers over the batteries. "Ready for prime time," she said, and stood back. "Ta-da."

Jones clapped his gloved hands together in applause. "Man, oh man. That is one lean, mean, Moon-cruisin' machine."

Despite its enhanced capabilities, it didn't look all that different from the other rovers. But it was nice of Starman to say so. "Sure is."

The rover was made by Boeing and General Motors. It was ten feet long and had a seven-and-a-half-foot wheelbase, basically a framework for four wheels and a couple of seats, over a chassis of aluminum alloy tubing. On Earth it weighed five hundred pounds, and could carry a payload of well over one thousand pounds. The seats were also aluminum, with wire webbing. Vivian would apply power and steer the thing using a T-shaped hand controller between the seats.

Its ground clearance was about fourteen inches. All around them, even on this relatively tame part of Hadley Plain, were boulders twenty or more inches high. Driving across the surface would mean a constant swerve-and-jog to avoid them. The top speed of the initial Apollo rovers was a little over ten miles per hour. This one? A cool fifteen to twenty miles per hour.

Though sometimes—often, even—that might feel a little fast for the terrain.

Vivian mimed rubbing her palms together in anticipation. "Okay, guys. Spot me."

She climbed aboard, and fastened the safety harness across her thighs. Powered up. Pressed the controller forward. And away she went.

Ellis loped alongside her. "Looks good."

"Nothing flapping in the breeze?"

"Ha ha. No."

" 'Kay. See ya." Vivian applied more power, and Ellis stopped trying to keep up.

The lunar surface was bumpy as hell, and Vivian was constantly pulling the stick left and right to avoid boulders, craters, rocks. Her PLSS backpack made her top-heavy, meaning that the lurching threatened to pull her out of the rover altogether. Her left hand strayed to the grab bar by her thigh.

She navigated a wide loop around the Lunar Module. On its far side she was briefly out of sight of both guys, and for a moment was wickedly tempted to veer off and keep going, northeast across the Hadley embayment toward the curving ridge of Swann Range.

Not forever. Just for an hour. Maybe two, tops.

Nah. Time later to be a maverick. Besides, Ellis would never forgive her.

Completing the circuit, Vivian pulled up next to her Lunar Module Pilot. She felt oddly breathless. "Looks like we're a Go."

"Looks like." Ellis clapped her on the shoulder. "Nice work."

"You want a turn?"

His visor was up, so she could see him blinking inside his helmet. Commanders traditionally reserved the driving for themselves. As Vivian certainly would have done at Marius. But now, the game had changed. "Uh, yes. As a matter of fact. I do. Thanks."

Vivian made to get down, but Ellis waved her to stay. "Check me. You're on shotgun." He clambered awkwardly into the right-hand seat and drove it from there, left-handed. While he did, Vivian studied the command and control displays. Heading, speed, power, temperature. She'd been too busy dodging rocks to give the displays much attention till now, but they all looked good.

Better than good. Perfect.

As Ellis steered them back around, Starman bobbed up and down and gave them two clumsy thumbs-up. "Very cool, guys. Got yourself the Cadillac of LRVs, right there."

The moment seemed to call for more celebration. Experimentally, Vivian lifted her arm and leaned toward him. "Hey, man. Up high."

Sure enough, Starman high-fived her.

15

Hadley Plain: Vivian Carter
December 4, 1979

"HUH," Vivian said. "This thing is a whole lot larger than it looked when I was coming in."

Norton swung to look at her, though neither could see each other's face through the golden visors. "Just between us? For a moment I was convinced you were going to augur right into this."

Vivian reached up to her chest panel to turn down his volume, and again scrutinized the fuel dump before her.

"Dump" was hardly the right word. The areas around the LMs and out back of the Habs looked unbearably messy to Vivian, but the fuel depot was meticulously clean and well tended. The four aluminum tanks gleamed in the Sun, each the size of a standard Cargo Container. The system of pipes and gauges at waist height looked like it had been installed just last week, and polished to a gleam every few hours since. Even so, Norton was checking every joint and surface with minute care, and taking a rag to any flecks of moondust.

When talking to his crew, Norton's tone was offhand, almost careless. Vivian now saw that was an act. She'd found an obsessive side to him that she could relate to.

They were out here to refuel Athena's descent stage. At least partially. To Ellis's frustration he had not been able to locate any leak or blockage in the LM's propulsion units. He'd brought in fellow Lunar Module gurus Ryan Jones and Terri Brock to help him, and then conscripted Kevin McDowell and Luis Ibarra, and not a one of them could figure the damned thing out.

Vivian glanced back across Hadley Plain. All five of those LM pilots were clustered around Athena, one clumsily kneeling and another actually lying down underneath it, and from this distance they looked like white grubs clustered around a bug.

Yesterday, they'd laid out two segmented pipelines between the fuel depot and Athena. Today, they'd flow oxidizer through the first, and maybe Aerozine through the second if they got the problem fixed. The pilots were waiting for the flow test to begin, but it looked like Norton would carry out a complete systems check before he'd attach the hoses and get going.

Then again, as both propellants were highly toxic and stored under pressure, maybe a spot of caution was in order. *Impatience is the killer out here.*

She looked again at the tanks. "So, in that scenario where the Soviets launch a ground attack on Hadley, we could weaponize this. Right?"

Norton paused. *Damn, now I slowed him down even more.* "Wow. You have a nasty mind."

"Thanks."

"But, yes. We could. Even a fine spray of this stuff onto a spacesuit would be pretty bad. Corrosive. Eventually, carcinogenic."

Combining Aerozine and oxidizer in an engine produced a spontaneous ignition. "Sure. So what would happen if you sprayed one onto a suit, and then the other?"

"I actually don't know." Norton stopped again. "They burn when they mix, obviously."

"Yeah, but only in bulk? When pressurized? Or would they sizzle just from coming into contact? Uh, keep moving, boss, or we'll run out of O_2 before we get this done."

Norton grunted and continued his inspection. "I can see where you're going with this, but I'm not sure. Let's try a test or two later."

And then he paused yet again, looked up at her. "You still want your mission, don't you?"

Vivian said nothing.

"That's why you and Ellis are so keen to fix Apollo 32's descent stage. If we were ordered to evac, you'd only need the ascent engines."

"We all agreed at dinner to keep the descent stages fueled up," Vivian reminded him. "In case we need to jump in a hurry. For some kinds of ground-level attack, we can just hop away to safety. Or use a LM for reconnaissance." She paused. "Or, hey, even spray propellant on their Commie asses and set light to it."

Vivian saw Norton wince even through his spacesuit. "Ouch." At long last he started to plumb the hose ending of the propellant pipeline into the nearer tetroxide tank. Vivian watched carefully. Who knew when she might need to do this herself?

"Yes, but, Vivian? Honestly, and I'm not trying to be a jerk, but: I see through you. It'll never happen. Marius is gone, and brooding about it won't help. Get it out of your mind and move on."

Him and Ellis. Jeez. Have they been talking? "Neat idea. Why did I not think of that?"

"I understand. I do. We've all had our own disappointments. On my second flight—"

"Uh, hey. Just don't, okay?"

Norton reached into the tool kit on the rover, and extricated a long wrench. "Fine. I could use help centering this. Eyes on the connection while I crank it?"

"Copy that." Vivian leaned in to help him get the wrench centered. "Sooo …. Like this?"

"You got it." Norton applied torque. "Okay, so you don't give a toss about anyone else's sob story. But everything's changed now. This international crisis isn't going away. There's a huge mess on Earth, and if we go to war up here, guess what? You're drafted."

"Yay."

"Want my real guess about what's going to happen? You and Ellis stay here through the lunar night. Meantime, NASA sends an unpiloted pod to rendezvous with Dave Horn and do an in-orbit refueling on his SPS engine." He leaned back to look up at her. "And then, sometime lunar-tomorrow, Apollo 32 will be ordered home, and home you'll go, back to Earth. Between now and then, you have a new mission, and this is it. This is all you've got, and maybe all you'll ever get. So, for God's sake, Vivian: make the most of it."

"Trying." She turned to look off at the bulk of Mount Hadley Delta, then around the mountain range behind them.

"We've already got geologists, and you don't have an on-base specialty."

Damn it. "You've got *two* geologists. For the *Moon?* May as well use four, now you've got us."

"Hadley is about development. Materials science. Long-term strategy. Digging dirt, not studying it. We already know this area pretty well."

Vivian sighed, and the words just came out. "Don't wanna go home."

"Really? Even if this isn't *Marius?*"

She almost kicked him. "Shit, man, don't *tease* me about that! Ever. All right?"

Norton's suit body language read "startled." "Uh, okay. Then why?"

Vivian thought about it, for longer than she'd expected.

Because I've always wanted to come here.

Because the Soviets don't get to chase us away from our dreams.

And because I haven't even seen what's over the next hill yet.

How could she say all that to Norton, without sounding hokey?

"Because it's the Moon," she said, simply. "And it's awesome."

"Now you're talking." Norton peered at the connection. "Okay, looks good. Now we open up to a fraction of a psi, and do a leak check." He pointed into the tool carrier. "That there, that's the sniffer for the leak check, grab it."

"Got it."

They did the check, then Norton toggled back to the main radio frequency. "Athena, fuel depot."

"Hey there," said Ellis. "Thought you'd forgotten all about us."

"Just getting organized. Ready to flow N_2O_4 on your mark."

"All set here. Please proceed."

"Proceeding." Norton spun a valve. Eyeballed a gauge, waved the sniffer again.

"Okay, we're seeing it come through here," said Brock.

"All good, all good," Ibarra said absently, his attention on hardware.

"I'm going to monitor you listen-only," Norton said. "And turn you down a bit. If you need us, shout. Or, you know, jump up and down."

"Jump and shout, roger that."

Norton turned back to Vivian, switched back to their private band. "Okay, let's take five. Give me eyes."

He pushed up his visor. She could see his face now, looking at her intently. She pushed up hers too.

"Okay, Vivian. You want to stay?"

"Yeah. I do. Badly."

"Then stop giving me grief, and start being a team player."

"What?"

"Listen: you're really good. No BS, I'm glad you and Ellis are here. Glad of your energy. By now, the rest of my troops are getting a little …" Norton waved his hand. A little what? Tired, cranky, depressed? Probably all three. Hadley Base had some of each. "But you're fresh. You come at this from a different angle. Some folks here listen to you, so I'm going to ask you to help me. To throw in and give this your all, rather than needling me all the damn time, trying to connive things in the forlorn hope that your old mission will magically swing back into the realm of possibility. Understand: that is not going to happen."

For a moment Vivian thought he was going to ask her to do it for NASA, or for her country. And it stuck in her craw that he'd called her "Viv," but it would be petty to bring that up right now. It wasn't his fault he wasn't Michael Collins.

Besides. Norton wasn't wrong.

Vivian blew out a long breath. "Yeah. God *damn* it."

Norton nodded. "Buchanan is top class but … cynical. He's like the father of the group, but he's losing his drive, and his attitude is beginning to spread. Starman is a good team guy, but he doesn't have the leadership gene. And Dunlap used to be core, but now all he does is bitch. I think he's losing his nerve. The others are getting mouthy and cantankerous as well. And it's gotten worse since you arrived." Norton held up his gloved hands. "All I mean is, since the Soviets took Columbia."

"You're fracturing?"

"Yep," Norton said. "All along, I've been working to make us *one* single crew, one Hadley. I've mostly succeeded. But this whole Soviet bullshit has thrown everyone for a loop. And, you and I can barely stand each other. But we're on the same side."

Vivian eyed him carefully. "Same side? And you figure that how?"

Norton looked her in the eye. "Because we both love the goddamned Moon. We both always wanted this: *to walk on the Moon.*

We're exactly where we want to be." He grinned. "Globally speaking. You don't love this valley. But you love the Moon. Tell me I'm wrong."

"You're not wrong. Obviously."

"Most of the others don't feel that way. They thrive on the challenge. They like being *astronauts*, leaving the Earth, being the future. But even the original moonwalkers, a lot of them didn't *like* the Moon. Many of them hated the place. Didn't want to stay any longer than they had to. They wanted to ace the mission, and then get home. That was it."

Vivian thought of Dave Horn, astronaut par excellence, who had zero desire to step on the lunar surface, and no sorrow whatever that his job precluded it. She thought of Jim McDivitt, commander of Apollo 9, whose mission had been to put the combined CSM and LM through their paces in Earth orbit, a challenging and dangerous engineering test flight with an overstuffed schedule. Apollo 9 had been eclipsed in the history books by Apollos 8, 11, and beyond, but it had been an engineering triumph and its crew had loved every minute. They wouldn't have had it any other way.

Norton studied her face. "I'm going to tell you the God's honest truth, Carter. And then I'm going to make you a deal."

Vivian readied herself. "Fine. Spill it."

"I want to grow this base. I want it to be *permanent*. Not to just stagnate, or, God knows, be abandoned. I want lasting structures, a permanent US human presence on the Moon beginning right here. Maybe there'll even be a city here one day."

And Norton wanted to be remembered as the first commander of the moonbase that had been the seed for that city. Well, no shame in that.

"Maybe there will be," she said.

Then she added: "I hope so. Really." Because she did.

"As for you? You want to explore. Pound rocks, make discoveries. And you can. You've got a cool new rover, you've got range, and we've got the gear to support longer excursions to territory no one's ever trodden. New mountains. Fresh regolith, all for Vivian. All for you."

"Keep talking," she said.

"You want that? Then you need my support. But you've got to give me something in return. You need to pitch in and help me keep Hadley together. Raise the mood, keep it positive. And persuade the others to pitch in, too."

Vivian nodded slowly. It all made sense. Sure, Norton still rubbed her up the wrong way, but she didn't need to like people to work with them. "Okay, then, man. Got yourself a deal."

Norton didn't try to shake on it, or anything else dumb. He just turned his attention back to the complex system of pipes, valves, and manifolds underlying the fuel dump. "Great. Thank you. Okay, so while we're here, look here down low ..."

"Woo-hoo!" came Terri Brock's voice over the other channel, and at almost the same time, Ellis said, "Gotcha, you little bastard."

Vivian keyed onto their channel. "Got what? Report."

"Found the issue."

"Defs a bullet," said Brock. "Maybe two."

Ellis chimed in a little impatiently; it was *his* ship. "Double impact right by the oxidizer shutoff valve assembly, and we're lucky it didn't sever the goddamned line rather than just kinking it. Here, Terri, hold this in place while I ..."

"Got it," said Brock. "Hey fuel dump, cease the flow, and we're gonna need to drain all these pipes."

Norton was already spinning valves. "Guys?" Vivian broke in. "Fixable? You can reach the damage?"

"Sure," said Ellis. "Just need to swap out that portion of the pipe and put a stent in. Should be a simple weld, now we know where the damned thing is."

"Well," came Ibarra's note of caution. "As simple as any weld is, out here."

"And we'll need the tanks around it drained and *really* clean first," Jones said. "Shielding for the engine. A jig because gloves just don't cut it when you're holding a several-thousand-degree flame. All that's two days to set up properly, right there."

"Nah, we can speed that up with all of us," Brock said.

"It's not something to *speed up*," Ibarra warned.

Brock tutted. "Jeez, man ..."

Vivian cut in. "Do we need to drain the ascent stage too?"

"Don't think so, but we'll confer."

Norton was grinning inside his helmet, shaking his head. "Lunar welding geeks. Got to love 'em. Let's leave them to sweat the details while I brief you on the Cargo Container area."

Vivian was still pondering. "Wait. What happens if a welding torch touches a spacesuit?"

"Oh, they'll shield everything. Write procedures, run a sim or two with Mayer before anyone puts a flame anywhere near spaceflight hardware. Between 'em, Starman, Terri, and Ibarra have done stunts like this ten times or more."

"Sure, but I was thinking of *Soviet* suits. How resilient would they be to, say, a three-thousand-degree flame?"

"Damn it, Vivian," Norton said, with admiration in his voice. "You are *evil*."

CHAPTER 16

Hadley Base: Vivian Carter
December 4, 1979

WHEN Vivian arrived in Habitat B for dinner that evening, Norton was the only one there. *Damn it, that's what I get for being punctual.*

"So, you're not married?" he said.

"Really? That's your opening gambit?" Vivian flopped—slowly—into a chair. "Is that any of your business? Sir?"

Norton looked amused. "No. It's just rare. NASA loves its astros to have airbrushed apple-pie families. I do. It's all part of the myth. But okay, never mind, sorry."

Vivian relented. After all, she was supposed to be bonding with him.

So she smiled. "I was engaged. And then came the astronaut application."

"For the record, I'm not asking."

"Understood. So, my ..." Did she have to say "boyfriend"? She shook her head and stared out the window across the bleak lunar surface to the north. Nice that they'd raised the shade on it now. She dug the view, and it gave her something to look at. "Military marriages, you know? Or proto-marriages. So, he was active military as well. And don't get me wrong, we had a lot in common, including families and flying and the ... strong desire to join the space program. We both applied to the same NASA astronaut opportunity. It was his second application, my first. And shortly after that, I realized it would never work."

He nodded sympathetically. "Still not asking."

"What does your wife do, Norton?"

"Well, that's an impertinent question."

Vivian gave him a look. "Really?"

Norton grinned. "She's bringing up three boys. What Sarah *does* might be quite the list. Maybe I should skip to what she doesn't do?"

"She doesn't compete with you, soldier, that's for damned sure."

"That's right. Not professionally, anyhow."

"And that was my deal. My … fiancé assumed that I'd back him up all the way, and become the dutiful wife once he got the call. That I'd slide into the support role. After all, his chances were *way* better than mine. Obviously. So I should support him. Makes all kinds of sense, right?"

"Having met you? Not so much."

I can't do this. Can't bare my soul to Norton, just to make nice, and have him commiserate about my relationship failures. Vivian blew out a breath. "Well, the punchline is obvious. I got into the Astronaut Corps. He didn't. That was that."

Now, Norton looked intrigued. "But how did that work? I don't mean … not you and the guy." He stopped, started again. "You split up, which I totally get, and then, what I mean is: how did you survive all the psych that NASA loves, all the screening and personality testing when they assign people to crews? After all, now you're a single woman pitching to go into space with *married guys*, and to some people—not me, obviously, but to the press and all—that might look a little sketchy. And somehow you aced all that. I just don't know how."

"Well. Me and, uh, the guy: we weren't married and divorced. We split before that point. Nothing loud and messy, no big headlines. He didn't try to sink me. He just wrote me off and went back to test piloting. What did I tell NASA? That I'd wanted to be an astronaut all my life. That everything I'd ever done was toward that goal. That I'd do whatever it took to get the job done. I was completely straight with them." Vivian looked out at the horizon again. "Guess they bought it."

"Seems legit." There was a loud clunk and a hiss of air across the room, and Norton leaned forward and peered down through the hatch. "Uh-oh. Incoming."

About time. "Well, darn. And we were having such fun."

"Want to go down and help 'em doff, clean the dust off of them?"

Vivian sat back, relaxed, met his eye. "Maybe we should both go down."

"Could we use the Lunar Modules as gun platforms?"

The ten other astros currently cooling down on the top level of Hab B after dinner looked at one another, caught out by Norton's suggestion. "What? How's that?"

Norton was pacing back and forth in the small space, scribbling with a Sharpie on a yellow legal pad. "Fly 'em with the tops popped?"

"Huh." Vivian glanced at Ellis, and could tell he was trying to imagine it too. Could she pilot Athena solo while Mayer stood precariously on the ascent engine cover with his upper body sticking out the top, swinging a weapon or tossing bombs down onto cosmonauts on the surface? It seemed dicey.

Mayer looked back at her. "You'd need to read your own numbers. While flying."

"Yes, but it's worse than that. With only the two front-facing windows I wouldn't be able to see what was going on beneath or around me. I'd be mostly flying blind while you told me where to fly, when to hover."

"And I wouldn't be able to call numbers. Couldn't see the readouts."

They tossed the idea around. It sounded crazy at first, but it really wasn't. The LMs had plenty of hover time. When fully loaded, the propellant mass in the descent stage was about eighteen thousand pounds, maybe more. The rule of thumb was that every extra pound of mass they carried down to the Moon's surface from orbit cost them a tenth of a second of hover time at landing. The detailed calculation was complex because the LM would be getting lighter as it burned fuel, but even from barnyard math it was clear that if they launched full and flew at only a couple hundred feet up, the available hover time could be twenty to thirty minutes.

"Longer than any reasonable military engagement," Buchanan said, absently, also scribbling on a notepad.

Military engagement. Shit. "Except that we already know the Soviets have at least one rocket launcher. I've looked down its barrel. RPGs are the obvious light, powerful weapon to bring down to the surface as well. We'd need to neutralize them or the LMs would be stupid vulnerable."

"Rocket-propelled grenades aren't necessarily good for surface-to-air," Buchanan said.

"Yeah, but full-up rocket launchers?"

"Look, we'll see," said Norton. "We obviously won't put anyone in harm's way foolishly. But let's be ready."

"Even if we don't use them to throw bombs, a LM would make a swell reconnaissance platform," said Flynn.

"Only for the guy hanging out the top," Vivian said. "The lack of windows again. Crap visibility."

"Yes," said Flynn. "Obviously."

"You guys are all nuts," Dunlap said. "Waging war with Lunar Modules, for real?"

"We try things," Norton said. "You want to just sit here and wait to be blown off the surface?"

"Nope. I *want* us to start evacuating the goddamn base. Show signs of a good-faith gradual withdrawal so we *don't* get attacked."

"Well, no," said Norton. "Because those still aren't our orders."

Dunlap shook his head. "And do our orders happen to include arming LMs for battle? What does Houston think of *that*?"

"Obviously, Mission Control can't authorize the weaponization of any NASA equipment," Norton said, unblinking. "This is a peaceful station."

"We're not the ones bringing the war," said Buchanan.

"So we're not going to tell 'em?" Dunlap demanded.

"As Commander, I have ample discretion to protect US lives and assets."

"Best not to discuss our defenses, even over secure radio," Buchanan added. "Right?"

"Someone should try a test run." Vivian looked at Ellis. "With a Lunar Module, I mean."

"Not you two," Norton said. "I need you for other things."

You do? Vivian's eyes swiveled. "What things?"

Epps and Flynn, Apollo 31, leaned in. "Us," said Epps. "I flew choppers in 'Nam, and this guy's seen some action too—pretty cool customer in a fight, or so he tells me after a beer. We'll set up a practice run, see what shakes out."

"Good, thank you. Now, who's figured out what we can throw at them? Anyone get any further with that? Okay, Ibarra, you're up."

171

Ibarra had been grinning with unearthly glee since the conversation started, clutching his own pad of paper and obviously itching to speak. "Molotov cocktails."

Buchanan looked doubtful. "A bottle bomb?"

"*Hypergolic* bottle bomb, thank you very much. Two bottles in one. We just need to be able to throw them."

Aerozine 50 and oxidizer spontaneously combusted when mixed. That was the whole point. Controlling that explosion within the rocket motor: that was the hard part. Norton started sketching again. "Oookay. Maybe. And unless we just drop them, we'd throw them with what?"

"We're NASA," Vivian said. "We should be able to *launch* something a couple hundred yards at an enemy?"

"Heh," Buchanan waved at Ibarra. "I'm betting this guy has already figured that out."

"A mortar," Ibarra said promptly. His shit-eating grin was back.

"Jesus leaping Christ," Dunlap said to the ceiling above him.

"Dan and I have been experimenting. We have a prototype we'd like to show you."

Ibarra passed his pad over to Norton, who looked dubious. "Wow. You've already *fired* this?"

"Not with hypergolics. But we've already faked up a smoothbore barrel out of a water pipe. The firing pin uses a small amount of our site-clearance explosive. We've made our first try at a dual-space shell in the machine shop. We're confident the membrane separating the propellants will fracture on impact, and not before."

"Fairly confident," said Dan Klein.

"Confident enough," Ibarra said.

"You were those kids who built pipe bombs in your back yards when your parents were out, weren't you?" Vivian said.

"Science fair projects," Ibarra said, at the same time as Klein said, "Model rocketry."

Norton shook his head. "Whatever. Okay, then, this afternoon let's go do some, uh, model rocketry. But we do it way far from the base and all the assets." He turned to Ellis and Vivian. "Speaking of fuel, did you guys think any further about Vivian's propellant-spray idea?"

Vivian grinned tightly. "We did some math. Pressure and spray distance and coverage and such. My original idea of combining and igniting two sprays to cause a fire or explosion won't work, but just the firehose effect of one highly pressurized and cryogenically cooled propellant at close range would be … extremely damaging."

Ellis looked wry. "Although it's fun trying to figure out how *not* to get ourselves killed or poisoned in the process. And it would contaminate the hell out of Hadley Plain."

"It would work," Vivian said. "But it would be ugly. Recommend only as a last resort."

"Well, it may come to that." Norton looked around the room in satisfaction. "Damn. Great job, everyone. Now we're cooking."

Dunlap shook his head. "Maybe literally. Good grief."

"But, guys, it doesn't all need to be so high tech," Ellis said. "What does the Moon have a lot of? Rocks. A well-aimed rock will pack quite the punch and pollute nothing. We have plenty of springs and whatever other torsion devices are around to make some catapults."

Widespread amusement. "*Catapults?*"

"No, hey, those would be easy enough and pretty damaging," said Starman.

"Going up against guns and rockets with rocks." Klein shook his head.

"I like the idea of a weapon that won't blow up in our faces," Dunlap said to no one in particular.

"Lot easier to engineer a catapult than a frigging *mortar*," Vasquez said to Ibarra.

"You think?"

Ellis snapped his fingers. "And why not an air cannon?"

"Like a potato gun?" Ibarra laughed.

"Well, *like* one. Much bigger. We'd use a length of steel pipe with a filling valve and a pressure valve and all. I mean, we already have a ton of pressurized oxygen around here."

"We used to call those drainpipe cannons," Brock said.

Ellis looked impressed. "You made those too?"

"Our mortar will fire a much larger shell, much farther," said Klein, a little defensively.

Norton clapped his hands again. "This isn't either-or, people. We're doing everything that makes sense. Big shells, small shells, and if we can build some catapults, then we should absolutely do that too. Anything else?"

"Well," Buchanan said. "If nothing's out of bounds, let's go big or go home. How about the RTGs? Anyone know how to make a dirty bomb out of a slug of plutonium?"

They all looked at him, aghast. A radioisotope thermal generator couldn't explode, but it could sure as hell emit radiation. And radiation was a killer. Sooner or later.

There's eight pounds of plutonium oxide in each," Flynn said. "And every Apollo has one, and the backhoe, too. And we have four for each Hab. That's ... actually quite a lot."

"No." Dunlap was shaking his head. "Come *on*, you guys. We're not going there."

"Pretty sure a dirty RTG would count as a nuclear weapon," said Epps. "Do we want to prove the Soviets right after all?"

"Okay, break," Norton said. "Whatever. Let's think it through, just to get a handle on what's possible. We decide later what we're *really* going to do."

"Feasibility assessment." Buchanan nodded.

"Want to help me with the, uh, drainpipe cannon?" Ellis asked Brock.

"Sure. And the catapult as well."

"There's a machine shop downstairs, right? Lathes? Tool kits, wire of various gauges, springs?"

"Of course."

"Sort the details out later." Norton looked around the room. "Okay, next?"

Buchanan was pondering, balancing a Sharpie on his fingertip. It was easier in one-sixth G. "We also need to discuss defense against whatever the Soviets are likely to throw at us. They're not going to have a whole lot of mass margin. Not much space in those LK Landers."

Norton looked at Vivian sideways. "So, that rocket launcher they pointed at you in orbit. How big was it?"

"Jesus, Rick, I didn't go measure it."

"Army bazookas were like fifteen, twenty pounds, and something like five feet long. Range was a few hundred yards. On Earth."

Ellis was shaking his head. "Effective range is really only about a hundred fifty."

"Back in Vietnam, sure," Buchanan said. "But the technology has moved on a little since then. Odds are they'll be packing something like a Strela-2. Soviet shoulder-fired surface-to-air missile."

Ellis raised his eyebrows. "Those have *fins*. Two forward steering fins and four stabilizing fins at the rear. They won't fly well here, without an atmosphere to keep them straight."

"It's not just that," Jones said. "In orbit, a Strela might lock onto the hottest thing it can find in the near infrared. But down here, every single thing the Sun hits will be radiating serious heat and glare: us, the ground, everything. No heat-seeking missile is going to get a lock. And if you don't get a lock, it's hardly even worth firing it. And, yeah, the fins. It won't fly straight, and once it starts tumbling it'll be a brick."

"A brick that still explodes."

"Does it, though? If the impact fuse at the front doesn't actually impact?"

"I agree," Norton said. "I don't think Strela-type launchers will be that big a threat on the ground. And I doubt they'll bring more than a couple. I think we're back to rocket-propelled grenades, standard issue. Relatively light. Easy to use in a suit. Ballistic trajectories. Inaccurate, though."

"We'd better hope so."

"First things first," Vivian said. "How do we even know when they're coming?"

"Radar, for anything flying in from above. We can detect them a hundred miles out if we have a clear line of sight. If they come in overland, it'll be much harder."

Vivian got up and walked to the big map on the wall. "So, here we are. We have overlooks from the south and north, but too far to reasonably bombard us from. A semicircular mountain embayment to the north and east. The rille to our west with only a few convenient crossing points. Given a ground approach, this position is really very defensible."

Norton laughed. "You don't say?"

Oh, jeez. "I'm being dumb *again*? Damn."

Norton paused. "No. I apologize. But, it never occurred to you to wonder why the US would put its first major lunar base in an embayment, surrounded by mountains?"

"I guess I assumed Hadley was chosen for its scientific interest. Apollo 15 only scratched the surface. Highlands and mares both within easy reach. Volcanic stuff, possible lava tubes. Big-ass craters not so far away. The Apollo 15 post-mission report stated clearly that a return to Hadley would be of great scientific interest. And NASA already had ground truth on it. No need for an extra flight to scope it out."

Mayer considered. "But it's sure a hard site to get out of. And therefore, into."

"It's as defensible as anywhere on the Moon," Buchanan said. "Without sticking us in a castle on a mountaintop, or some shit."

Astonishing. "NASA was thinking ahead to a possible *ground attack* when they were siting our first permanent lunar base?"

"Well, you're right: the geological interest didn't hurt. Made for a great cover story."

"The Russkies did the same," said Dunlap. "Chose their site for maximum science, of course. Copernicus is less than a billion years old, with a complex crater and central peaks, but its ejecta's going to be from deep in the crust, maybe even from soon after the Moon formed. That's a geological goldmine. It's obviously just a happy accident that a high crater rim with natural terraces, ramparts, and a long view is also majorly defensible."

"Hey, cool," Ellis said to Vivian. "You found yourself another geology nerd-brother."

"Oh, hush."

Starman chimed in. "They also chose it because it was easy to *see* Copernicus from Earth. Any Soviet citizen can look up at the Moon and immediately pick out Copernicus. They can see exactly where the glorious efforts of Communism are making their mark on the Moon."

"But if any US ground force has to clamber up there, it's a big deal."

"We considered crater rims too," Norton said. "But we balked at engineering it. Too many slopes. Complicated site surveys. Anyway. To attack us here, the Soviets either have to land close by, or forge a way in from Palus over the Bridge, unless they're going through the bloody great ditch of the rille or straight over Swann Range. So, let's put a TV camera at Bridge, another on North Complex and maybe one on Hadley Delta. A few other strategic places."

Ellis looked doubtful. "We're going to stare at a TV all day looking for movement?"

"Course not. We'll loop in Mission Control, get *them* to stare at TVs all day."

"Ah. Right." They spoke to Mission Control so rarely that Vivian had almost forgotten they existed. Which made her wonder: "We have secure radio here, right?"

"Sure, on the main radios in the Habitats, and the later M- and N-class Lunar Modules, meaning Apollo 26 and later. But not in the earlier series, or any of the suits."

Ellis raised a hand. "Wait. We surely have to assume that they'll jam our transmissions like they did in space, and that we won't be able to talk to one another. Secure radio is just encrypted. It's still the same frequency."

"Jammers are big, and take a lot of power," Buchanan pointed out. "It may not be feasible to pull theirs out of their Progress and load it into a lander to bring down."

"And if we're not jammed, they'll be listening in." Norton scribbled on his yellow pad. "Either way, we'll need to figure out a system to pass orders around when we're in action."

In action. It still seemed impossible to believe they were talking so glibly about fighting battles. In spacesuits. *On the goddamn Moon.*

Vivian shook her head. "This .... Jeez. This is turning out really freaking complicated."

"Yes." Norton tossed his pad onto the table. It bounced, kept going, and fell off the other side, and he grinned.

She sighed, and looked at her watch. "Okay, fine. Who's up for staying awake another hour to get a better handle on all this? All these preparations we hopefully won't need? And assign who's doing what?"

Everyone nodded. Sleep obviously wasn't going to come easily for any of them tonight.

"In that case, before we dig in ... do you guys have a still up here, by any chance?"

Norton looked startled. "You're planning to make bombs out of booze?"

"No, sir. Just wondering whether I'm ever going to get a drink in this joint, or if I'm doomed to stay dry until splashdown."

His eyes grew stern. "Captain Carter, we have no supplies of recreational alcohol, and no means of making it. Nor would such a thing occur to any of us."

"Safety concerns, and all," Dunlap said. "I'm sure you understand."

"We absolutely do," said Mayer. "And we'd expect nothing less."

"Also," Vivian said, "for the record: you all have terrible poker faces. Abso-fricking-lutely god-*awful.*"

Buchanan grinned.

"See what I mean?"

Without a word Starman bounced across the room, dug into a desk drawer, and pulled out a small bulb of a colorless liquid.

Norton was still worried. "Hey. Seriously. No mention of alcohol ever makes the loops or debriefs. At all. Ever. Am I clear?"

Mayer mimed zipping his lips. Vivian inclined her head. "Roger that, sir. You have our word."

"Appreciate it." He sighed and shook his head. "But frankly, I could use one too."

Starman poured a small tot for everyone, and they got to work.

CHAPTER 17

Columbia Station: Josh Rawlings
December 5, 1979

JOSH had thought Columbia Station was crowded when the initial Soviet attack force of nine joined them. It turned out that he'd had no idea.

The new Soviets began arriving at Salyut-Lunik-A two days after their abortive rebellion. The surviving captives received no warning; the first they knew was when a bunch of unfamiliar Russians crowded into the fore compartment, tugging one another out of their suits while chattering in excited Russian. It was a shock, to say the least.

Per Yashin's orders to keep the Americans secured at all times, Josh and Zabrinski were handcuffed to the metal grid floor of the crew quarters level, by the exercise machines. But they could see the Russians clearly enough through the gaps in the ceiling above them.

"Holy cow," Zabrinski said. "*Eight* of them?"

Rawlings rocked his head back and forth, peering. "Yup, think so. And Belyakova is with them."

"So, how many people *can* you cram into a phone booth?" Zabrinski said ironically. "They'll need to crank the environmental controls with this many people breathing in here."

Even if Makarov hadn't thought of that already, Rawlings knew Pasha would. "What're they sayin' up there?"

"Mostly babbling like schoolkids. Pumped to see the Moon up close. Never been this far from Earth. Impressed with Columbia. Looking forward to rolling up their sleeves and getting to work."

"On what?"

"Learning and ... studying? Serving the Rodina, anyway."

"And who are the Rodina?"

"That's the motherland, Josh. The Rodina, Mother Russia. You haven't heard them say that fifteen times a day?"

"Maybe. It's all Greek to me."

Two of the new Soviets, in white jumpsuits, had now made it down to floor of the forward compartment and were peering with interest through the grille at Josh and Danny. "Aaand suddenly we're in the zoo."

"Probably the first 'imperialist' warmongers they've ever seen."

"Well, let's not let 'em down, then." Josh forced a smile and waved the hand that wasn't restrained, converting the wave into an uplifted middle finger. None of the Russians waved back, politely or otherwise. Maybe the gesture didn't translate?

"Come." Nikolai Makarov sailed through the hexagonal gap, Oleg Vasiliev shadowing him at a safe distance with his rifle. Nikolai produced the handcuff key. "Let us move into the wardroom. It is lunchtime for us."

"Well, lead on." Josh studied Makarov's face. "What?"

"We must talk." Makarov paused. "How are you? How are your people?"

"My boyish smile will never be the same." Josh ran his tongue over his cracked teeth, aware that one of them was introducing a new, irritating sibilant into his voice. But that was fixable, and he was alive. "Doing better than Jackson and Wagner." Who'd been bagged and tagged by the KGB operatives with about as much emotion as if they were packing beef, and their corpses moved down to the aft compartment.

And Josh was functional, which put him well ahead of Ed Mason, and Marco Dardenas as well.

Ed was deteriorating, currently bandaged up and lashed to one of the bunks in the crew quarters, with a pressure-driven IV drip, and pumped full of drugs. He'd lost a lot of blood. Hadn't regained consciousness. Josh wasn't holding out much hope he'd make it through.

Marco would probably be fine. His left arm was strapped across his chest so as not to reopen his wounds. In Earth gravity he'd have been bedbound, but in zero G he could already steer himself around well enough, if painfully. Josh had ordered him to rest anyway.

"We're all great," Josh said. "How are you?"

"None the worse for your attempts to kill us," Makarov said evenly.

"Sorry we weren't willin' to be your meek little captives."

Makarov nodded. "Perhaps we should have anticipated it. And yet, all the damage you caused was to yourselves."

Yup. They hadn't put even a single Soviet out of action. Even Galkin was up and around, apparently suffering few ill effects for being conked on the noggin. "Pity. We timed it so we wouldn't have to hurt *you*, if that makes any difference."

Makarov looked dourly amused. "And also not hurt Yashin?"

"Well. Not so much, in his case."

"It does not matter. Listen now, Josh. I have good news, and I have bad news. Everything is about to change."

As it happened, Josh had difficulty disentangling the bad news from the good. But as Makarov continued it became clear that big changes were indeed imminent. Because he and Belyakova were about to head on down to the Moon, accompanied by Yashin, Chertok, and Vasiliev.

Erdeli and Isayeva would stay aboard Columbia for now, to bring the new Soviet arrivals up to speed. But, since Pasha and Vika were apparently needed on-surface as well, they'd also descend in less than a week, before the next lunar night fell at Copernicus Base. Whereupon this new team of eight who'd just shown up would join Galkin and Salkov as the full-time crew of Salyut-Lunik-A. Galkin would be in command, with someone called Okhotina as his deputy.

"This station wasn't designed for a full-time occupancy of ten. Let alone fourteen ..." Josh struggled to think. The blows to his head had made him stupid. Four surviving Americans, the original nine Soviets, and now eight more? "Or, twenty-one in all, at the moment? Is that right?"

"Oxygen is cheap," Makarov said. "Not all will live inside here at all times. And Apollo 32 brought you plenty of supplies, in addition to those my comrades bring. It will be fine."

"Matter of opinion." Zabrinski glanced up. Belyakova had begun an orientation session in the compartment above. She was speaking with authority, briefing them concisely. The new Russians were trying to stand to attention in free fall. "You're stretching this place well beyond its limits."

"And how long d'you plan to keep us captive?" Josh demanded. "Forever?"

"That is not my decision." Makarov squeezed hot water into a bulb of coffee and sucked on the tube appreciatively. He was obviously a fan of American coffee. Even space coffee, which had made Josh gag the first time he'd squeezed it into his mouth. He mostly drank tea these days. "I pray that it will be soon."

"You pray? Aren't you a godless Communist?"

Makarov looked at him thoughtfully. "I know more churchgoers than holders of the Communist Party card."

"Really?"

"And it is a figure of speech, no? It is the correct context?"

"Sure. I pray to get the hell out of here soon too."

"Well. At least you will soon not have Comrade Yashin after your blood. It is my task to take him with me. I suspect none of the incoming team has Yashin's ... volatile?"

"Volatility. Yup, a little less 'volatile' would be just the ticket." Zabrinski leaned forward. "So, my friend: who *is* Comrade Yashin, anyway?"

Makarov slurped his coffee and sat back. "That is a fine question. When Yashin was first assigned to our mission, we were told he was *zampolit*. You know *zampolit*? It means a political commissar, meant to ensure that our ideology remains correct, and that we stick to principals of Marxist-Leninist thought. On Earth there is a *zampolit* for every Red Army unit and every Navy ship, and he is always a man of rank equal to the local commander.

"But it was clear from the beginning that Yashin was different. Soviet space missions have never before had a *zampolit*, and none is assigned to Zvezda Base." Makarov grinned slightly. "We are not country bumpkins, to need such instruction, and our cosmonaut team is not a hotbed of Maoist counterrevolutionaries. We are all good, clean New Soviet Men and Women—you see this, I am sure? We are well trained in speaking the Party lines."

"And so?" Josh prompted.

"To begin with, we were believing that our Sergei Ivanovich and his compatriots were KGB." Makarov looked again at Rawlings. "You know KGB? Military security and intelligence?"

"The secret police? Yes, Nikolai, we've all heard of the KGB."

"But now it is clear that Comrade Yashin is more than that. I now think perhaps he is, or was, GRU Spetznaz. Military intelligence, special forces."

"Terrorism, infiltration, assassination," Rawlings said.

Makarov looked surprised. "*Counter*terrorism."

Rawlings waved. "All a matter of perspective."

"And you know of Spetznaz?"

"Our militaries do spend some time studying each other."

"Ah. Anyway, I merely speculate. My superiors are never free with unnecessary detail, and Yashin reveals little. But whoever pays his wages, it is clear he receives his orders from very high levels."

"Interesting." Rawlings sat back too, sipping his tea. "None of them trained with you and the other cosmonauts? Yashin, Chertok, Vasiliev? Sweet little Vika?"

"Viktoriya Isayeva did. We all knew her from the Cosmonaut Corps. Chertok and Vasiliev sometimes trained with us also. Yashin, I never met until the briefing for this mission." Makarov stopped, perhaps realizing he was growing too talkative. "Anyway. We must be careful around Comrade Yashin, and that is on my mind, as I prepare to … visit the Moon again."

"A bit different from your previous trips, eh, Comrade?" Zabrinski said.

"Yes." The Russian's eyes were troubled now. More thoughtful than Josh was used to seeing him. "Quite different."

He was worried, Josh realized. Nikolai Makarov was a very worried man indeed.

"You've been ordered to go down and attack Hadley," Josh said bluntly.

Makarov glanced at him in surprise, then at Zabrinski. "I always suspected you understood more than you claimed. But it doesn't matter now."

"So you *are* attacking Hadley. Very soon."

"Yes. Yes, we are."

"Who's in charge of the assault group? You or Yashin?"

"I am."

"Well, that's something."

"Is it?"

"But Yashin and his goons are going too."

"Yes. Obviously."

"Great. So further casualties are acceptable to you? American casualties? Soviet casualties?"

"I hope they can be kept to a minimum."

The Russian's face was guarded, but Rawlings could see the concern behind his eyes. "Nikolai. I've no way of knowing what Commander Norton's orders are. But I do know he'll obey 'em. If NASA hasn't started ferrying astronauts home yet, they're not going to."

Makarov nodded, slowly. "Perhaps they might begin, once we give them a further nudge in that direction."

Rawlings studied him. "If any are left alive."

They glanced up as Svetlana poked her head through the hatch—carefully, so as not to alarm Oleg Vasiliev in his role as armed guard—and apparently informed Makarov that she needed to bring the new team down to continue their tour. Makarov waved them in, and down they all came, poking into everything like a flock of clean-cut parrots, making comments, asking questions, and staring curiously at Rawlings and Zabrinski. Too many for Belyakova to herd effectively in the confined space, the new people bumbled into the sleeping quarters and awakened Dardenas and Chertok. Chased out with oaths in Russian and English, they nonetheless looked unabashed.

This appeared to end Belyakova's duties, because when the new students—as Josh couldn't help thinking of them—left, she tugged out a tray of food and began to heat it up. Pity, Josh thought. The pumping of Makarov for information had been going quite well.

Belyakova was off shift, relative to the rest of them. This was dinner for her, her last meal before she'd take some rest. As she sat and hooked her feet under the bar to stabilize herself, she glanced at each of their faces. "Interesting conversation?"

"Very," said Rawlings. "So, will you be going down to attack Hadley too?"

Belyakova just looked at him bleakly. Makarov gestured at Zabrinski and said something in Russian, at which she tutted and looked grim.

"What's happening on Earth?" Josh said. "At the UN, elsewhere? Do you honestly think you're going to get away with this?"

"Get away?" Belyakova shook her head. "This is peaceful occupation. Police action against unlawful American intrusion into Soviet airspace."

Rawlings laughed. "You do realize there is no *air*, Comrade?"

"I make a comparison. This is like U-2, Gary Powers? The USSR will no longer be spied upon from above, on Moon or on Earth. So our Supreme Leader has said. Warnings were given. You ignored those warnings and continued to send your illegal spacecraft into Soviet territory."

"On scientific investigations. As allowed for by the Outer Space Treaty of 1967, which *your* nation signed."

Belyakova chewed and swallowed, took another bite. Looked at him thoughtfully. "Josh. Listen. This does not have to go badly."

He almost laughed, but her gaze was becoming quite intent.

"We must work together. If you want to help yourself and your men, tell us where the weapons are. Then we can stop all this. Believe me, we want this, Nikolai and me. We, too, want only to explore. Not to fight. We want this to be over. But for that, you must help us."

"Weapons?" Rawlings shook his head.

Makarov cleared his throat. "She is right, Josh. We did not want this. But we have our orders."

"You told me you were in charge," Rawlings said. "Big man Makarov? Moonwalker, Hero of the Soviet Union, twice over? So, if you're really in charge, stop this your damned self because it's the right thing to do."

"We will be happy to stop Yashin," Belyakova continued doggedly. "We can make this end. Once you tell us what we need to know."

She leaned in, and fixed him with that man-killing glare. "Do not play the innocent. We all know the US has brought weapons into space. Powerful weapons. That is why we are here. Soviet Union cannot permit this flagrant disregard of the non-prolif ..." She looked briefly frustrated at not finding the word. "1967 treaty you speak of, between our countries."

"Weapons in space? No, ma'am. We don't have any."

Svetlana grabbed Josh's jaw with her thumb and forefinger, stared into his face. Rawlings managed not to cry out, but tears of pain sprang into his eyes from his damaged teeth. Ignoring them, he met her gaze.

Belyakova said: "We Russians were the first into Earth orbit. The first to walk in space. The first to walk on the Moon. Through this, we prove beyond any argument that Communist system is far superior to the decadence of the West. And because of this, America now runs scared. First you put your spy stations around the Earth. Now you bring your nuclear weapons here to the Moon. We well know this. And it cannot be tolerated. Could the United States tolerate it if our positions were reversed? No. You know this."

"You're crazy," Rawlings said flatly. "Jeez, lady ... NASA is a civilian organization. You'll find no weapons here—because there aren't any. Do you think we'd have thrown punches and pyros if we'd had guns? If we had nukes here, don't you imagine we'd also have brought a hand-gun or two?"

"A civilian organization filled with military men?" Svetlana's gaze drilled into him. "Perhaps that lie works in America. In Russia, we see more clearly. Wagner is dead. Jackson is dead. Mason may die soon. You, Dardenas, Zabrinski: all injured. Where does this end?"

"Well, ma'am, you tell me."

"Yes, I will tell you. It ends once we have indisputable proof of the US buildup of nuclear weapons in space. Once we have that, the world will see that our actions are justified."

Rawlings stared back at her bleakly. "No. You listen to me: you have already killed two United States citizens, maybe three, and you may be about to kill many more. I promise that this will go *very badly* for all of you. It will go badly on Earth, and here in space. I guarantee it."

Belyakova looked interested. "Yes, you say so? What will you do? What *weapons* will you use to *guarantee* that?"

At last, Makarov seemed to feel the need to support his comrade. "Do not take us for fools. For many years, we know you have small nu-clear weapons. For twenty years you have the, uh, W54 warhead."

"The what?"

"Your W54, it is fifteen inches long and ten inches in diameter, and can explode to anything from ten tons to two hundred fifty tons TNT equivalent. More than enough to turn us all here into ... vapor that glows. All very dead."

"You know a whole lot more about US nuclear weapons than I do, buddy."

Belyakova took over again. "And such devices could be ..." She gestured. "In any compartment or tank or cupboard. We could search for another month and not find them."

"Yes. For a month, or a year, or forever. Because there are *none here*."

"We will see. And so, when we *do* find them, we will prove decep-tion of United States government, and rightness of, of?" She looked at Makarov.

"Of the legality of our seizure of your spacecraft," Makarov said.

Rawlings snorted. "Legality!"

"You should tell us now," Belyakova said. "You should be happy that it is we who are asking. If it were Sergei Yashin? He has very effective methods of persuasion. Up to and including torture."

"Which Comrade Yashin would regret."

"We will see," she said again.

Makarov stirred uncomfortably. "Josh, the Union of Soviet Socialist Republics is very good at obtaining information. Your American agents are weak, so easy to turn, terrible at keeping secrets. Your whole system is *designed* to be open, and so no one can keep a secret, especially one so big. We *know* that you have nuclear weapons on the Moon."

"Then prove it," Josh said. "Which you can't, because it's simple bullshit that your bosses have fed you. It's a fairy tale, so Brezhnev can justify pushing the US off the Moon, so that you Soviets can have it to yourselves and proclaim it as a Communist triumph."

"It is not so simple, I think," Makarov said.

"It's exactly that simple." Rawlings leaned forward. "Keep them alive, Makarov. The crew of Hadley Base? I'm holding you personally responsible."

Makarov stared at him. Belyakova closed her eyes. "Please shut up, Commander Rawlings. Or I will shoot you myself."

CHAPTER 18

Hadley Rille: Vivian Carter
December 7, 1979

"UH, Vivian, you're sure that's a good idea?"

Gravel and dust sprayed up behind Vivian in a twin rooster tail. Beneath her, the Lunar Rover slid sideways. Wrapping one glove around the grab bar, Vivian eased the T-handle to the left with her other hand, steering a slightly steeper angle uphill.

Here, "uphill" meant out of Hadley Rille. It extended away beside her, sinuous and dark in the late lunar afternoon, a mile across and a quarter-mile deep, its eastern slopes in bright sunlight and its depths in utter darkness.

The slope she was driving across was fifteen degrees, tops, but even that was a challenge for the rover. And it was studded with boulders that she had to avoid, mostly by skidding around them.

Evidently, she was giving her crewman the vapors. Ellis's spacesuited figure stood upslope of her, a bright but dirty white against the black sky. She saw no stars behind him; the Sun's glare was still too intense.

She and Ellis, alternating the driving, had mastered the up-and-over of small-to-medium craters two hours ago. Next, she'd wanted a real hillside to practice on. The rille was the obvious place. Plus, it gave her the chance to take a look inside it.

Vivian knew that the sinuous curve of Hadley Rille was likely an ancient lava channel, maybe even a collapsed lava tube like those they

188

might have found in a more pristine form at Marius. One of the longest and widest rilles on the Moon. And even Ellis had casually identified the outcrops of the underlying mare basalt exposed in the upper hundred feet of the rille walls, and the blocky talus farther down the slopes. On the far side of this gouge in the lunar surface, the layering of the volcanic materials that had formed it was very evident.

Super geological. Vivian loved the place.

She cranked and skidded her way up. Eventually braked to a standstill beside Ellis, and hopped off. "Okay, man. Now you."

"Hmm," he said. "Maybe I should try something less risky. Straightforward, with some finesse."

"Sure. You be finesse guy, while I slalom the shit out of the uphills." Ellis shook his head. "Roger that."

Even through his suit, Vivian could read his body language. Ellis was unhappy with her. And she knew why: she was being impetuous Vivian, flippant Vivian, instead of taking each step slowly and carefully, evaluating it, then moving to the next.

Well, he'd have to get used to that. For Marius they'd had a detailed schedule. Now, everything was ad hoc. And Vivian was coping by throwing herself forward body and soul. Driving the rover into the rille and daring herself to get it back out. Taking care, yes, but not that excruciating caution that NASA often adopted. She needed to make quick progress.

Meanwhile, Ellis was backing up and trying to consolidate before taking each new step forward. Compensating for her.

She needed to throw him a bone. So Vivian picked up the brush to clean the caked moondust off the fenders, examined the wheels and linkages. "Okay. Let's review. What's working, what isn't? Where do we need to focus effort?"

He sighed. "Vivian. We both know this is bullshit."

She ducked her head in her suit. Stared at regolith. Took a sip of water from the straw that led to her water bladder. "Okay. Talk to me."

"Just how long are you aiming to stay here, anyway?" he said carefully.

"About as long as possible."

"You don't want to go home?"

"Master of the obvious, Pilot."

"Uh. When we got here, Hadley sucked and you hated it. You get hit on the head in the meantime?"

"We can't screw this up," she said. "If we do, we never get another chance. We have to make this count. Jump in with both feet. If we don't, we get sent back to Earth and might never get a flight assignment again. But if we accept the new damned mission, dig in and excel, fight off the Soviets, whatever the hell we have to do, maybe we get another shot one day." She paused. "That's a massive *maybe*. But I'm damned if I did all this just to get shipped home at Mission Control's earliest convenience, and dumped back in fricking Texas."

Eventually, he said: "Apollo 32 was supposed to be a ten-day mission."

"And that was the mission I wanted."

"Do you have any idea what I've put my family through in the past two years?"

Vivian had lived it too. "I have some idea."

"Do you know how many weekends and holidays I've missed? How many softball games? Dance recitals?"

Oh, right. His daughters. But, hey, Ellis had signed up for this, like the rest of them. "Well … yeah. I do get that. Sure."

"We were supposed to have been back by Christmas. My family was relying on that. On me being *there* for them, after all this. I promised."

Everything was uncertain about Apollo scheduling. Everything. Even without armed Soviet intervention. Vivian shrugged helplessly. "Well, I don't know. Maybe … you shouldn't have promised?"

He stared at her for so long that she had to drop her eyes. "What? Sorry. Again. I guess."

He exhaled long and hard. "You don't understand."

"Ellis. We're on the *Moon*. Doesn't that make up for … a missed Christmas?"

"Vivian. Please. Just stop talking."

"Okay." She considered. "While I'm busy not talking, let's loop back to the LM?"

"Sure. But I need a break, first. Give me some time?"

Yeah, I'm driving him nuts. "Will do. Come pick me up in the rover when you're ready? I'll be paying my respects to Apollo 15."

According to Vivian's original mission profile, she wasn't supposed to wander off on her own. On the exploratory Apollos, crews stuck together on-surface. Here at Hadley the vibe was different. Astronauts meandered off to do stuff by themselves all the time. Norton himself constantly came out onto the surface alone. The base was home to them, and besides, they had contingency measures: suit patches, emergency oxygen. If you needed anything more drastic than that, it was doubtful that having a buddy nearby would help you anyway.

Habitats A and B were behind her now to the south. Ahead was an odd sight: a lone Lunar Module descent stage. She was so used to the LMs at the base that seeing one without its ascent stage seemed wrong. Forlorn, naked, and abandoned.

This was all that remained of Apollo 15, the home of Scott and Irwin for a little under three days in July 1971, and with a shock, Vivian realized she'd already been on the Moon longer than those pioneers, with no end in sight to her sojourn here.

It was clear that she wasn't the first from Hadley to venture this way. There were too many boot prints in the soil. And Apollo 15's three EVAs meant she should be seeing just six sets of tire tracks, but there were well over a dozen.

At that, Vivian stopped and looked around her. Something was missing.

"Huh," she said aloud. "Weird."

"I have to be useful, Ellis. I have to have a mission. I came here to explore. I'm not about to just sit here and maintain machinery and holystone."

"Well, *that* I agree with. So what's next?"

They were back in the LM, having doffed and stowed their suits. Fortunately, by now Ellis looked amused rather than exasperated, but still, she studied him carefully. "Sure you want to know?"

"May as well get straight to it."

"Okay." She tugged out a folded map of Hadley Plain, printed from a large-format photograph taken from orbit. Mount Hadley rose brooding in the north and Mount Hadley Delta in the south, and between them was the large D of the Plain, with the meandering line of the rille forming its western straightish edge, the half ring of mountains of the Hadley-Apennines making the curve of the D.

From lunar orbit, the two Habs were mere dots. Slightly above them to the north was a black Sharpie cross marking the site of the Apollo 15 landing. Craters, large and small, covered the whole site.

"Here's us," Vivian said. "Here's the rille. Dobbs and Vasquez have taken samples down to the base of the rille by Hadley, and along it to some degree. Down here is Bridge Crater." She indicated a region close to the lowest cusp of the D. "Its bowl pushes into the rille, and its rim forms a ridge we can use to cross it. Dobbs and the others have done that already, and worked their way back up on the far side to Lonely Crater, right here, so that they were looking back toward Hadley across the rille. But they never went any farther north than that, and they certainly haven't been west into Palus. Here within the embayment, they've been to North Complex." She gestured at the region of hills and craters six miles north of Hadley Base. "They've surveyed the South Cluster fairly well on the downslopes of Hadley Delta, and sampled the ejecta from St. George. But they've never been higher up the mountain than that nearer edge of George. Now look."

Ellis made a show of checking his watch. "Aren't we missing a meal yet?"

"Hush up and look. Have they been due east to the slopes of Swann Range? Or up to the north?" The upper end of the D. "Nope. And here's the other thing."

Vivian pulled out a second photo, a lower-resolution map covering a much larger area. "The big point is that *everything* they've done—is strictly local."

Ellis whistled. "*Local*, you say?"

"Yeah. That D shape I showed you is actually a P, with a loooong stalk. See here. Hadley Rille zigs and zags down through here, between the hills, and goes past a humongous and really well-defined crater, nearly four miles across, called—and God help us trying to keep all this straight, but it's called Crater Hadley C."

"Of course it is."

"Its rim forms another bridge across the rille. And way up here in the opposite direction, beyond the top of the D? This is Crater Hadley B, which is even bigger.

"Thing is, most of the terrain around us here on the Plain is volcanic flows and ash beds. The mountains above us are more, uh, classic rock, if you follow. Highlands, probably a lot like Fra Mauro, where Apollo 14 landed. But the crater rim material from Craters C and B, that's going to be freshly exposed bedrock and freshly generated talus and ejecta from the impacts. Crushed and brecciated debris."

192

"Awesome," said Ellis.

Vivian eyed him. "Please try to look like you care."

Ellis gave way a little at her expression. "Sure, I care. I do want to do interesting stuff while we're here."

"Absolutely. And so, if the Russians leave us alone for a while, that's what we do. We pitch to do the big craters, and do them well."

Ellis was looking at the photos again. "Vivian, these are a *long* ways from here. Hadley C crater is twenty miles away, Hadley B, thirty or forty."

"We'll be smart about this. We train nearby first. The rille, the far side of St. George Crater on Hadley Delta. Then out to Hadley C, then B. Maybe even farther. We need to caucus with the geology room in Houston, get 'em on our side. We clearly aren't launching any more expeditionary Apollos for a while. So for now, for lunar geology, it's us. They need to help us get out and about and run around all *over* this area. If we do a great job, that's more ammunition we can use to persuade Houston to let us stay longer. Well beyond Christmas. Sorry."

He shook his head. "You know you're crazy, right?"

"Sure. But this is what it's all about. Let's explore."

Ellis drummed his fingertips on her photos. "You'd need to sell this to Norton first. You do realize he's the boss of you now?"

"NASA is the boss of us," Vivian said, doggedly. "And NASA wants us to pound rocks, and for the world to watch us doing it. Norton will be happy as long as we make him look good."

Ellis sighed. "Vivian has a plan."

"Can't live without one. Seriously, you don't ever want to meet Unscheduled Vivian."

"I believe you." He checked his watch. "Are you *sure* it's not time for a meal?"

"Damn, man, you're always hungry. Okay, fine."

They dug out trays, set the food to warming.

He looked at her. "Okay, what else? Come on, Viv, there's something else. I can tell."

"Yeah, but you already think I'm crackers, so I'm holding off."

"Don't hold off."

"Okay." She took a deep breath. "How about putting together a weekender?" She closed her eyes. "Maybe even across Palus?"

"Across Palus?"

"Trailer," she said. "Inflatables. Food. Oxygen. Let's go camping."

Ellis got it immediately. "Holy *shit*, Vivian."

And then—to her relief—he laughed. "Wouldn't *that* be a thing?"

Since their new rover wasn't reliant on battery power, in principle they could drive it off into Palus Putredinis with a trailer, spare oxygen, and a couple of tiny inflatable Habs, the ones all Apollos were equipped with now for emergency use. The baby Habs were cramped, claustrophobic, and sweaty, and would be no fun as accommodation, but they should be tolerable for a single sleep stop. And that approach would double, perhaps more than double, their range.

That was daunting in its own right. The idea of being eighty, a hundred miles from Hadley with only their suits, their rover, and a blow-up tent or two to keep them alive? Far away and exposed on the desolate, merciless surface of the Moon?

Daunting, but unbelievably cool. Historic, even.

"Norton will never go for it."

"I heard him specifically tell us to go do science."

"I guess he might be glad to be shot of us for a while."

"Of me, you mean?"

"Us." Ellis grinned.

"You're not taking this seriously, are you?"

"What about the Soviets?"

"They're five hundred miles away." Vivian shook her head. "No one's coming that far just to give us grief. They've already shot themselves in one foot by taking Columbia. I can't believe they'll shoot the other one too."

"Guess we'll see."

She studied him. "I'm sensing you're not all thrilled and goosebumpy about Palus Trek? Discuss."

"Might be pushing the envelope a bit, Viv. We'd be a *long* way from help. Way out past our walkback radius."

"Workarounds." She started counting on her fingers. "One: we take two rovers. Leave the old-style one at the first-night camp. Then if ours craps out, we only need to walk back to Camp One, roll home on the spare. But ours isn't going to crap out."

"Maybe."

"It's not. By then we'll have put it through its paces closer to home, and we'll know its quirks. We'll be confident. But, okay. Second workaround: we do an initial scouting trip. Find a campsite and set up a cache, with spare everything. Then we go out a second time for the overnighter itself. That gives us even more redundancy on consumables. Or. Three: absolute worst case, our pals here at Hadley can come get us. Rover sprint, or even a short-hop LM rescue trip."

"No one's going to like that last scenario."

"Yeah, whatever. But a Lunar Module bailout would be a no-other-option lifesaver. Which we won't need. Look: our rover can haul a trailer behind it under RTG power, and that packs a *lot* of redundancy. We carry lots of oxygen. We double up the baby Habs we take with us, have them with us always, even for short trips. They pack small and weigh almost nothing anyway. We could take along spare suits and PLSSs. Let's even start doing that now: travel loaded, so even our local trips are dry runs for …. Ellis, what?"

Ellis was staring at her patiently. "Vivian. I know you're itching to make a mark here. But don't let that blind you to *risk*. Don't get crazy."

"Crazy, what? Am I not talking to you about risk mitigation, right now?"

Ellis, too, started checking off points on his fingers. "Unknown terrain. In an area where we already know there might be lava tubes, a surface a fully loaded rover might break through. Micrometeoroid hits. Tumbles. Leg or arm breaks. Suit stress, two or three days without proper maintenance. Especially from regolith; we couldn't clean the suits properly in a baby Hab and they'd be in there with us. We'd get moondust into everything, maybe into our lungs, and that would be bad. Plus the added radiation exposure?" He shook his head, out of fingers.

"Jeez, man. You're no fun at *all*."

"Someone has to be the grown-up here." He grinned apologetically.

Vivian smiled back. Ellis was quoting a phrase she'd used a dozen times during training. "Fine. But let's work scenarios, okay? As … a mental exercise."

"Sure. After all, if I don't do it, you'll just put a plan together with those other geology lunkheads anyway."

"No," Vivian said immediately. "I absolutely will not. We're crew. If you're not in, if we can't arrive at a plan we're both behind, it doesn't happen. You hear me?"

"Okay." Ellis thought for a moment. "Good."

"Thank you," Vivian said, on impulse.

He looked askance. "Isn't it me who should be thanking you?"

"Nope." *Because your methodical caution might one day save my life.*

She asked Norton that night. "So, the Apollo 15 Lunar Rover. Where did it go? It should be just sitting there, a hundred meters to the east of the descent stage where Dave Scott parked it. With his red Bible still sitting on the T-handle."

"That old thing?" Norton grinned. "I requisitioned it. Replaced its batteries, gave it a scrupulous clean, end to end. That's the rover I drive around now."

Meaning Vivian had been a passenger on it when they'd driven to the fuel depot together. She'd been aboard Apollo 15's LRV, and hadn't even known it. "You took their *rover?*"

"Uh, yes? They were here three days. I've been here nearly a year. Is it a holy relic or something?"

It did seem vaguely sacrilegious. Vivian tried to make a joke of it. "Future generations of lunar historians will curse your name. The US's first Lunar Rover, stolen for joy rides?"

Norton looked baffled. "We need to know how long equipment can last here and still be operable. It's given me no problems, even after seven, eight years of baking and freezing. I was impressed."

"Okay." Vivian felt a bit bashful. "In that case—could I drive it, sometime?"

Norton grinned. "Just say the word."

CHAPTER 19

Outside Columbia Station: Nikolai Makarov
December 8, 1979

"ALONE at last," said Svetlana Belyakova as oxygen returned to the Soyuz cabin and they lifted off each other's helmets.

Makarov blew out a long breath. "Josh is right. Columbia Station is much too crowded."

"Salyut-Lunik-A," she chided him.

"Oh, of course. Of course."

"Are you all right?"

He pulled a towel from the locker behind him and wiped his brow and cheeks. "You know. Spacewalks."

Frankly, Makarov was happy to get back into his Soyuz and dog the hatch. Because of the spacewalk, but also because of the craft's familiarity: the green and gray instrument panels with their Cyrillic script; the lockers, the contents of which he knew so completely; even the blue couches, so ludicrously uncomfortable under acceleration or gravity. Even the Soyuz's tight, cozy confinement after the open volume of Columbia Station.

Makarov had never felt safe on Columbia, surrounded by Americans who—with reason—hated his guts. Better to be here. Whatever dangers awaited on the surface.

197

At the window, he took stock. Soviet ships surrounded them. More spacecraft than Makarov had ever seen in one place. It was glorious, and terrifying.

Their original attack force had consisted entirely of Soyuz, plus the Progress that had carried their frequency jammer and photographic equipment. But over the past several days a new fleet had been steadily arriving: LK and LEK Landers and Soyuz and Progress craft in a bewildering profusion, some tethered to the boom, others floating free and station-keeping with occasional bursts of their reaction control jets.

The LKs, *Lunniy Korabl*, meaning "lunar craft" in Russian, were the two-person lunar landers, a little smaller than NASA's Lunar Modules. Their cabins were more bulbous and less angular than the LMs, but the four-legged landing gear was similar. The larger LEKs, *Lunniy Exspeditionniy Korabl*, or "lunar expeditionary craft," carried three cosmonauts; half again as large as a Lunar Module, and even more pear-shaped than the LKs. All were marked with the red Soviet CCCP lettering, alongside the hammer and sickle. For some reason Nikolai had never understood, it had been deemed important that cosmonauts and their spacecraft be clearly labeled.

"I am sure you know which of those is ours." He and Svetlana were in their original Soyuz, the one they'd used to fly from Earth to lunar orbit, but they'd need an LK to get to the lunar surface. Several landers were as yet unpaired with a Soyuz. Over the past twelve hours, Nikolai had spent a great deal of time planning this assault—determining how to get multiple landers down in quick succession and have them immediately ready for EVA activity—but he'd left the logistics of exactly where each craft was currently located to Svetlana.

She grinned and pointed. "On the very boom end."

"Of course." Even from here, Nikolai could see the boom flexing with an amplitude of a couple meters, with a periodicity of maybe ten seconds. "Waving in the breeze."

"Time to stun everyone again with your docking skills."

Nikolai's first thought was that Svetlana was very relaxed for someone about to help him conduct a technically difficult descent, followed by an armed ground assault. On the verge of asking her about it, he glimpsed the stress lines around her eyes.

Belyakova wasn't calm. She was *acting* calm and casual, to try to calm *him*. Now he came to think of it, she'd done something similar right before their first descent to the lunar surface, a decade ago.

"Thank you," he said. She nodded without meeting his eyes, and they fell into the rhythm of preparing their Soyuz for flight.

Would Makarov have been able to do all he'd done, the space heroics, his two Moon landings, even the arduous planning for this lunatic expedition, without Svetlana? Without someone as unflappable and dependable as Belyakova by his side? He wasn't sure.

Belyakova was blond, compact, and strong. She glowed with strength and energy, and looked like she'd just sprung out of a Soviet propaganda video. Which was hardly an accident, since she'd been selected for the Cosmonaut Corps for exactly those qualities.

Makarov himself was square jawed enough, and looked just fine in propaganda footage. He appeared broad shouldered on film, but the angles were always chosen to make him look taller than he was. In fact, Makarov and Belyakova were the same height, though she might outweigh him based on muscle mass.

Belyakova had been selected because she was exceptional—small-town working-class heritage, a pilot of huge experience, a well-educated and savvy officer, and a woman of great personality and beauty besides. Married, but no children; utterly dedicated to her career. Makarov was equally convinced that he himself had only made the cut by having no disqualifying flaws and being above average in every required regard: physical fitness, piloting skills, quickness to learn, willingness to help others. He knew his fellow cosmonauts viewed him as bland. But wasn't it always the bland, solid men who made the grade, in the Soviet Union?

"I wish we did not have to do this," he said.

"I know. But they are the enemy."

"Are they?"

Svetlana tutted. "You let him get to you. Josh Rawlings. Didn't you?"

"He is not a bad man."

"*He* is not who we are fighting. We fight the American war hawks, those who develop the Moon as a base to attack the Rodina. We fight for our families. We fight for each other." She gave him a long look. "Do not forget this, Nikolai. When we attack Hadley Base, do not see a friend behind every American visor. They well know what they are doing here."

"And yet, still."

Her fingers moved over the instrument panels, and she completed her next sequence before speaking again. "Yes, Nikolai: *and yet still* we have our orders, and would be foolish to disregard them. The Supreme Soviet and the Politburo know more than we about what the Imperialists are doing on the Moon."

"I said that to Commander Rawlings. Wait." He flipped his comms switch. "Comrade, Soyuz TS-1 to LK-1. Preparing to approach."

"LK-1, confirm," came the prompt reply, and Makarov realized that he did not even know the name of the cosmonaut who was at this moment preparing LK-1 for them. Strange to be flying a mission with so many people he did not know personally.

Svetlana wasn't distracted. She hadn't forgotten. "And what did Rawlings say to you?"

Makarov switched to English, and attempted to mimic Josh's drawl. "'You mean you'll blindly follow orders, then blame the man who gave 'em to you? Nikolai, that's not valor. That's simple cowardice.'"

"That sounds like him. Always mind games."

"And he had it backwards in any case."

Belyakova nodded. Blaming a superior for the orders you had carried out was hardly the danger. The danger was in carrying out your orders to the letter, and then having your superior deny they'd given them in the first place. Then you became the scapegoat, the alleged rogue, the useful fool to be blamed and disavowed.

Nikolai had been about to go back onto the radio, give the order, and pulse his engines to set the Soyuz in motion toward their LK-1. Instead, he took his hands from the controls. "Svetlana. Is that what is happening to us? That we will become the useful fools?"

"No," she said immediately. "The Chairman has spoken publicly. The world knows the Americans must leave the Moon. We are merely the Chairman's hands and eyes and ears."

They had met Brezhnev twice, after their previous lunar flights, to be congratulated and awarded the title of Hero of the Soviet Union. Nikolai had brought the first medal, a gold star hanging beneath a red ribbon, on this trip for luck. The other hung over his bathroom mirror back in Moscow, partially covered by a snapshot of Olga and his children, Pyotr and Lidia. To remind him of what was truly important.

"Nikolai?"

"Yes. You are right."

He spoke his orders over the loop and fired the thrusters, and Soyuz TS-1 began its slow waltz across the empty space that separated it from its lunar lander.

As commander of this attack force, his was the first craft to move, but the others had been preparing. In the near vicinity of TS-1, cosmonauts floated on tethers or propelled themselves toward their spacecraft. As their orbit took them toward the Moon's sunlit limb, the glow from the cabins of the other Soyuz craft and landers seemed to shine ever more brightly.

A Red Fleet. A *space* fleet.

A fleet that, soon enough, would disgorge a squad of soldiers, a Red Army detachment, onto the Soviet Moon to drive away the American interlopers.

Earth shone by reflected sunlight out of his left-hand window. Nikolai did not even glance toward it. *Let us not die today,* he nonetheless whispered quietly to that grainy, fading picture of Pyotr and Lidia, a quarter million miles away.

And let us not kill too many Americans this day, either.

Makarov might think that. And in her heart of hearts, Svetlana might, too. But Yashin and his toughs were also on this trip, and half a dozen other guys Makarov didn't know. Nominally under Makarov's command, but who knew what covert orders they might have received that Nikolai knew nothing about?

His plan was good. It should go well.

But it might all be about to go very, very badly.

20

Hadley Plain: Vivian Carter
December 9, 1979

THE shriek of a klaxon flooded the confined space of her Lunar Module, punching Vivian out of a sound sleep. She lunged rightward to where her alarm clock would be on Earth, and her hammock swung left in reaction, almost spilling her out onto Ellis below. "Holy shit!"

She thrust her hands up against the new aluminum shielding across the ceiling to stabilize herself. Ellis leaped up, scanned the boards, then hit Comms. "Hadley, 32—"

A voice overrode him, Buchanan's. "Hadley crew, to stations. Hostiles incoming. Crews on EVA, move to positions. Those off shift, get up and out. This is not a drill."

Vivian jumped down and reached for the liquid-cooled garment she'd wear under her suit. Not yet capable of rational thought, she still knew what *stations* meant.

Ellis pushed the button again. "Range and direction of hostiles?"

"Landing two miles north. Approximately."

Three more questions came in at once. The only one they could disentangle was Gregory Leverton's—"Size of force?"—and it was the only one Buchanan answered. "Unknown. Come on, guys. Less talk, more action. We'll tell you more when we can."

Vivian ducked left to let Ellis swerve by to start squirming into his own LCG. "Naturally, the bastards *had* to attack while we were asleep." She glanced at the clock. "For not even two hours." No wonder she felt queasy and dog-tired.

"Our lucky star strikes again."

"What?"

Ellis shook his head, still groggy. "Um. You know."

Vivian grabbed at his garment. "Ellis, hold up. It's inside out."

"Goddamn it."

They wrestled themselves into their suits, checked comms, fastened gloves and helmets. *I don't want to think how fast we're doing this.*

Had the Soviets known that this was the off shift for the majority of Hadley's crew? Of course they had. Even though NASA was becoming more tactical with mission information and declaring less publicly, the Soviets could still *count*.

"Depressurize?"

Ellis raised a hand. "Wait. Sanity check."

"Bit late for sanity, my man."

He ignored that. Reached out to touch her helmet and glove locks, leaned in to look at her gauges. Scanned the LM, checked the control boards. Was he counting to ten as well? "Ellis. Chrissakes, I'm awake now. I haven't messed up."

"You're seriously giving me shit for double-checking?"

Vivian backed off. "Nope. Please disregard."

Yeah, one day this guy is going to save my goddamned life. Just in time for the Soviets to kill my ass.

Finally, Ellis nodded. "I am Go for depress. Concur?"

And because he'd asked, Vivian took the two seconds to triple-check her own suit and his. Power, oxygen flow, pressure integrity. "I concur. Go for depress."

"Depressurizing the hell out of this mother." He cranked the valve on the overhead hatch.

Vivian grinned. "Nice protocol, Army."

"It's the middle of the night, Navy, and I need my beauty sleep."

"You certainly do."

"Goddamned Soviets."

Fear reached for Vivian, its cold fingers caressing her neck and spine. *A military action on the lunar surface? What in hell was even about to happen?*

She pushed the fingers away. "Let's go kick some ass."

"Roger that."

Beneath them their rover bucked, its wheels hopping and bopping over the lunar bumps and rises. Every instant, two out of four of the wheels were spinning off the ground while the other two bit into the soil to fight for control. Moondust spat out right, left, and upward. Vivian and Ellis bounced off their seats and clung to the grab bars with their free hands as it surged across the surface.

Norton's voice over the loop: "Listen up. Five to ten Soviet craft have landed approximately two miles north of Hadley. Y'all know what to do. Anyone who won't be where they're supposed to be, two minutes from now, report by name only. Not location. All others, maintain radio silence. Execute the plan."

Ah, the vague joys of nonsecure communications.

Ellis glanced over to see if Vivian would respond. Two minutes? It might be four or five for them. *Whatever.* Vivian said nothing. If they were late, no one else could cover for them anyway. They had precious few people to defend such a large area, and everyone else was already moving in different directions.

The stresses on the rover reverberated through the chassis and her suit to her spine. They were still almost a mile from the fuel dump. And allegedly, two miles separated the fuel dump from the Soviets. They'd make it.

All of a sudden, Vivian pictured Josh Rawlings's face. A nice guy. And Dardenas, Mason, Wagner, Zabrinski, even the tiresome Jackson. None of them deserved to be incarcerated in their own orbiting station, courtesy of the Soviet Union.

And the Reds were coming here, now? To mess up Hadley and its crew? *No freaking way.*

If it wasn't a sizeable boulder or an especially rough crater rim, Vivian Carter was going over it or through it.

Around them, Hadley Base was a hive of activity. Two astros, presumably Leverton and McDowell, were loping at top speed toward the Apollo 29 LM, bouncing in high arcs. Three beefed-up Lunar Rovers sat outside Hab A. A driver already sat in the left seat of one, while an astronaut yanked equipment off the back to lighten it. Other astros were descending from their LMs, and two more hurried out from Hab B lugging a large piece of hardware: Klein and Ibarra and their homemade mortar. Yet another rover already bounded over the surface to defend the newest supply pod. That would be Seaton and Massey, Apollo 30.

"No sign of Soviets."

"Nope. Must be still unpacking whatever the hell they're bringing." If they'd landed any closer they'd have been easy targets while they got their attack together. For once, it helped that every EVA action on the Moon was a complex process.

Vivian plowed her rover to a halt beside the fuel dump, again flinging soil high. Ellis leaped off and kangaroo-hopped around the fuel tanks, preparing to deploy the hoses for action. Last resort. *If we get so desperate that we need to spray the bastards with propellant, we're probably already dead.*

She turned off the rover drive power and steering, jumped off to eyeball the fuel facility, and headed in toward its now heavily shielded valve-system area.

Over the last few days the crews of Apollos 25, 26, and 30 had worked around the clock to fortify those four fuel tanks against attack. Using the base's backhoe plus their rovers and trailers, they'd carried several tons of lunar regolith across to pile against the tanks, an activity that had the additional advantage of establishing a trench to the east of the base with only a couple of intact access points. In the low gravity, unencumbered astronauts might drop down into the trench and hop up the other side. Cosmonauts carrying substantial equipment or, say, riding their segmented six-wheeled Lunokhod Rovers might have greater difficulty.

Except that the Soviets were coming from the north, not the east. *Of course.*

"Ready, Ellis?"

Vivian could hear him puffing with the effort, and Ellis Mayer was a pretty fit guy. "Need a hand?"

"Nah, I'm peachy." He appeared, clutching the huge snake of a fuel hose in both gloves. "Phew. Here."

Vivian stepped up beside him and locked the metal frame around it that would keep it upright against the pressure if they did have to use it as a wacky, toxic firehose. "Gee whiz. Remind me whose stupid idea this was."

"Yours."

"Oh, right."

Norton's voice overrode their channel, terse in their ears: "Battle LRVs, go-go-go."

Vivian glanced across to Habitat A, toward the setting Sun, as the three rovers powered up and got into motion. *Slowest battle charge ever.* Though it wouldn't feel so sedate to the guys driving as they swerved around avoiding obstacles.

The rovers now looked very different. Originally skeletal and open, thick plates of aluminum shielding now protected the fronts and sides of the vehicles. Their crews might be anonymous in their spacesuits and largely obscured by the shielding, but Vivian knew them to be Norton and Jones, and Collier and Lawrence, with Feye Gisemba riding the third rover solo.

Outside Hab A she saw Dunlap and Brock setting up their defenses: shielding, a drainpipe cannon, a catapult, and a bunch of rocks and explosive packages of various kinds. Outside Hab B, Dobbs and Vasquez were doing the same thing. And way out front in a central position but well away from anything that they didn't want to accidentally blow up, were Klein, Ibarra, and their crazy mortar.

With luck, that mortar would fling their Molotov cocktails of hypergolic propellants at the enemy and not explode right there in between them. They'd only had time to make a half-dozen shells, so they'd be cautious about firing them. They'd faked up some duds with flares to shoot first, to establish range.

Also with luck, Vivian and Ellis would not be instantly incinerated due to a Soviet rocket igniting the fuel depot they were standing right in front of.

Good grief. What are we doing?

Apollo 32 should be heading home to Earth by now, basking in the glory of a ten-day scientific mission well done. But nooo.

They were still on the Moon. And, despite what naysayers like Dunlap might claim, the Moon was worth fighting for.

Vivian could see them now, the Soviets. Racing across the regolith toward her.

Racing.

"Holy crapoli," said Starman in her headset. "Dirt bikes? *Seriously?*"

No one else spoke. Nothing to say because, yes indeed: the Soviets had brought lunar dirt bikes.

The resemblance to a terrestrial bike was strong, with wheels, fenders, seat, and handlebars of similar size. The rear wheel spat up a rooster tail of soil and dust that arced high behind it. Astride each bike was a cosmonaut, his standard orange suit augmented with shiny black shielding on chest, arms, and legs.

Even as Vivian ran forward to where they'd set out their catapult two days beforehand, she was figuring the machines out. *Battery driven, must be. So, limited range? Just a few klicks?* The tires looked thick and knobby like those on Earth off-road bikes, but had to be solid rubber rather than inflated. But rubber would take a ton of damage from the day/night temperature changes. What the hell was the melting point of rubber, anyway?

Didn't matter. *Sorry, motocross cosmonauts, but you're going* down.

Each rider had a weapon slung over his shoulder, an RPG or a rifle or whatever, but they couldn't shoot them on the move. They'd need to come to a halt to pull the weapons off their shoulders and aim.

And that would be when Vivian and Ellis fired at the bastards.

Six bikes, spreading out across the landscape and angling back around so that they'd converge on Hadley in pairs: two from the northwest, two from the north, two from northeast. It wasn't clear whether the riders of the northeast pair had noticed the trench. Its edges were irregular enough, and given the normal scatter of lunar features, that long gash across the soil might go unnoticed.

The Soviets obviously had other things to keep their eyes on. Vivian guessed—hoped—that they hadn't expected such a well-organized response.

Standard Lunar Rovers did twelve miles per hour, tops. The bikes were surprisingly nimble by comparison. Twenty miles an hour? Twenty-five? Faster than Vivian had seen anything move since she'd arrived on-surface, anyway.

"There's a Lunokhod behind the bikes," Starman Jones reported on the open loop. "Just one, carrying maybe three cosmonauts. Some superstructure."

"That *superstructure* is two guns in a metal frame," came Carol Massey's voice from a few hundred yards farther forward, by the supply pods. "Guessing SPG-9s or similar. Tripod mounted."

Vivian couldn't keep the exasperation from her voice. "What the hell's an SPG-9?"

Buchanan, still in Habitat A and the only one of them currently able to hold binoculars up to his eyes, cut in. "I confirm SPG-9s. They're a seventy-three millimeter recoilless gun that fires rocket-assisted projectiles."

"Oh, for crying out loud."

"Good job we have rocks to throw at them."

"They'll need to move in a bit closer first, and keep still."

"Break, smartasses," Buchanan said. "Focus on the bikes. They're the first threat. Then converge on the fricking armored car."

Vivian didn't buy it. "Range of SPG-9?"

" 'Bout eight hundred yards," said Massey.

"Range of rocket-propelled grenade?"

"Thousand feet."

Perfect. She and Ellis would start coming within range of both at the same time. Which presumably wasn't just an unhappy coincidence.

Ellis ran around her and they busied themselves setting up his drainpipe cannon.

"Bike on far left has a rocket launcher," Buchanan reported.

"Of course it does."

With a slight lead on his comrade, the first of the northeastern dirt bikes discovered the trench. He put the bike into a sideways skid but still fell into it, dropping down to the trench floor some four feet below. Somehow, he retained his balance and began driving along it, only visible from the chest up, to bump up the slope at its end point and regain the surface. Astonishingly, his partner managed to leap the trench and keep coming. *Damn.*

But those riders would pass behind Vivian and Ellis, and those from the northwest were now angling in toward the Hadley Habs. It was the two who were coming straight at them from the north that threatened the fuel dump.

Even as Vivian realized this she glimpsed something looming over her and flinched, flinging up her arm to protect herself. But it was several hundred feet up and to her left: a Lunar Module balanced on a plume of fire, sweeping away to the north.

An ungainly flying bug. And, swaying back and forth, jutting out white above the head of the insect, were the rounded shoulders and helmet of an astronaut.

It was Apollo 31, with Epps at the controls, and Flynn literally sticking his neck out. *Off to attack the motherships. To try to cut the umbilical between the attackers and their exit strategy.*

Damn. Shit was going *down.*

"Here goes nothing." Ellis was turning an explosive charge over and over in his gloved hands, looking for its crude priming mechanism. He found it, pulled at it, dropped it gingerly into the tube of his makeshift cannon.

As it fired, Vivian saw the briefest of flashes and broadening spherical cloud of dust and gas from the cannon's base, and other than that … nothing. Nothing. "Shit, Ellis, did it go?"

"Yep." Ellis's head turned, tracking it through the air. Vivian hadn't even seen the shell leave the tube, had feared it would explode right there and then, spraying them with deadly fragments.

Ah. Steel tube. Metal fastenings on the explosive charge. Shot out using a short, intense burst of pure oxygen, which had then … ignited briefly in the tube. *Jesus, this is all much more dangerous than it sounded when we discussed it over cookies and juice in Hab B.*

The shell silently exploded in the air a couple hundred yards away. A bright flash, and shrapnel rained down on the Soviet bikes coming in from the north.

"Hmm," said Ellis.

A direct hit on the first try would have been a miracle. They'd had precious little time to practice, and these targets were moving. At least Ellis had established range.

But he had scant time to connect up the oxygen tank, pump up the gun again and launch another salvo. In planning, they'd assumed the Soviets would be running in on foot, or driving the much more cumbersome Lunokhod Rovers. They hadn't reckoned on freaking *dirt bikes.*

The cosmonauts had their legs stuck out straight on either side, keeping their bikes upright by skating their boot soles across the lunar surface. It looked dangerous and haphazard—*just like the whole Soviet space program*, Vivian thought—but it was working.

A NASA rover was speeding in toward Vivian and Ellis now, to back them up. It looked like Collier and Lawrence, but they wouldn't arrive in time.

One of the cosmonauts braked, bringing his bike to a skidding halt on the rim of a twenty-foot crater two hundred feet away from the fuel dump. Clumsily, he tugged on a strap to pull his weapon up over his shoulder.

"RPG!" Ellis called, but Vivian could see that. Rocket-propelled grenade.

As she turned, Ellis fired his cannon again. A pyro whizzbang exploded a few feet to the cosmonaut's right in a bright spray of sparks and soil, but the Soviet was already shooting.

Vivian saw a flash of fire and an almost simultaneous puff of smoke out the rear of the RPG launcher. The grenade streaked in, arrowing straight for the fuel depot. And with a target that large, there was little chance of a miss.

The grenade exploded, another shockingly bright but silent pulse of energy. Vivian relaxed and waited to be incinerated.

The fuel tank held. Shrapnel skittered across the lunar soil that covered it, some of it flying over and past it. There was no immolating explosion. Grit and gravel rattled across Vivian's helmet and arms. She blew out a breath of relief.

The cosmonaut reached into what looked for all the world like a basket, mounted in front of his bike handlebars. Vivian saw the short, curved shape of the rocket-powered grenade in his hands, and knew they could never wait for him to reload it. But the second cosmonaut had kept coming, and was nearly upon them.

A second Lunar Module flew right over her, so close that the thrum of its plume raised a cloud of dust around them. Leverton and McDowell in Apollo 29. *Uh, thanks, guys?* Vivian jumped left, so as not to be where her cosmonaut attackers had last seen her, although the dust was already dropping back to the surface anyway.

Apollo 29 dipped, right over the first dirt bike. *Holy shit.*

The cosmonaut had chosen to reload the RPG rather than drop the grenade and get moving again. It was a fatal mistake. The LM's hot plume swept him, causing two bright explosions as the Soviet's ordnance detonated in the fierce heat. Bike and cosmonaut flipped up and crashed into the ground, glowing. The cosmonaut's helmet was newly jagged; it had lost integrity.

"Oh wow, oh wow," came Ellis's horrified voice in her ear.

Boy. That had to have hurt like hell. Briefly.

First blood. As far as Vivian knew.

She dropped back and scooped up the catapult. Tossed a two-fist-sized rock into it, hauled back against the rubber, and let loose at the second bike. The rock skimmed the lunar surface like a stone over a pond, bouncing and kicking up soil, and shot past her target, but now Vivian had confidence. Her next missile was an explosive charge, and it exploded less than ten feet from the bike. The cosmonaut skidded, but stayed upright.

She'd deterred him, that much was clear. This cosmonaut had a rifle rather than a grenade launcher, and it looked like he'd given up the fuel dump as a bad job.

"He's disengaging." Ellis pumped his cannon up again.

Apparently peeling off toward the Cargo Containers. *Sure, go bother Carol Massey instead …. Wait—*

"Goddamn it, no he isn't!" Vivian broke into a run, chasing the bike. Ellis, catching on, leaped for their rover.

The cosmonaut was veering back toward the fuel dump, right at the end of the last tank. Vivian was still forty feet away but closing fast, covering the distance in long loping strides, and Elliot was just about to overtake her in the rover when, without dismounting, the Soviet soldier slapped something onto the tank valve assembly and took off again. His front wheel angled up into a wheelie as he punched the gas, or whatever the equivalent was for a battery-powered machine.

"Down-down-down!" Vivian shouted, and threw herself to the ground. Her fall forward felt agonizingly slow …

The valve blew. Plastic explosive, presumably with a fuse embedded? Whatever it was, it did the trick. The valve assembly cracked and bent, and a wave of Aerozine 50 arced high into the void, subliming and disappearing before it came back to the surface.

Vivian rolled onto her back. "Ellis? Ellis?"

He'd swerved the rover in toward the fuel tanks, which was a good call; if that end tank had exploded and thrown out serious shrapnel, he had a better chance of escaping it if he was at an oblique angle.

"Well, there goes half our rocket fuel."

Luckily, not <u>all</u> over her and Ellis. And at least the Soviet bike really was gone, now: off to the supply area.

As she watched it go, the surface of the fuel tank above her seemed to spatter in a dotted line of tiny explosions. For a moment Vivian thought it was ripping across, its metal sheering … but no, it wouldn't look like that. Those were bullet impacts. Maybe bigger than bullets. Small shells.

Buchanan's voice. "Lunokhod incoming, guys. You need to go get it, real fast."

Easy for you to say, old man.

The Lunokhod Rover. With its SPG-9s. What were they, again? And they had to stop it with a catapult and a glorified potato gun?

Dear God.

"Get up, Viv," Ellis said. "We've got to move."

Vivian gunned the rover. It leaped over rocks and the pocks of craters, heading for the Soviet Lunokhod.

They weren't alone. Collier and Lawrence were close now, coming in from the west, and Gisemba and someone else—Vasquez?—a little farther out from the east. How had Vasquez ended up in that rover? Vivian had no clue.

The Lunokhod looked like a motorized slug. Three big wheels on each side. It wasn't any faster than the American rovers, but it went straight up and over terrain that the rovers would have to dodge. That bumpy terrain was messing up the cosmonauts manning the guns, though; one guy was swinging back and forth behind his weapon, trying to bring its long barrel to bear on them while the Lunokhod bucked beneath him. The second had given up and was sitting down, firing an AK-47 at them instead.

Even as they bounced across the lunar surface, Ellis was pressurizing his drainpipe cannon for another shot. An explosive shell lay in his lap. *Really?* Wouldn't it be safer to just use his perfectly good catapult and a rock? *Boys and their toys.*

This had to be the equivalent of attacking an armored car with three golf carts. In slow motion.

Fear spiraled in around Vivian again. Her heart rate was way up, her breath coming short. *Going into battle.* One lucky shot by a cosmonaut, one screwup by an astronaut—even Ellis, or herself—and she'd be dead before she knew it.

"Wait for me to stop," she said.

She was heading straight for the Lunokhod. Bullets raked across them, pinging off their suits and the exposed metal of the rover.

"Bastards!" she shouted and swerved left and right to screw up their aim.

"Vivian, still stopping, yes?" Ellis said.

What, did he think she was going to ram the Lunokhod? *Maybe I should.* "Real soon now."

The Soviet driver tried to take evasive action. At the same time, his second gunner half stood to aim his SPG-9. From this close range they could see the break in the trigger guard and the enlarged trigger that would allow the cosmonaut to fire.

"Okay, sure," Ellis said. He rested the air cannon across his knees and picked up his slingshot. "So: when?"

For an answer, Vivian yanked the T-handle left to throw the rover into a sharp turn, and after half a second, jerked it back to jam on the brakes. And then, belatedly, called: "Hang on!"

It wasn't exactly a handbrake turn, but close enough. The rover swung broadside—on to the oncoming Lunokhod and dug into a skid. Rocks and gravel sprayed over the Lunokhod.

"Christ," Ellis said, and fired his slingshot. The rock flew the ten-foot distance separating them in an instant, and smacked the first gunner cosmonaut squarely on the helmet. In almost comical slow motion, the man threw up his arms and sailed backward off the Lunokhod.

"Wow, ouch," Vivian said instinctively. *Sympathy for the Devil?*

The Soviet driver had jammed on his own brakes now, and both vehicles ground to a halt. Even as the Lunokhod driver released his controls, he was reaching down.

A gun? No, a long pole that now telescoped rapidly outward to a length of twenty feet.

Vivian vaulted off the left side of the rover even as Ellis jumped down from the right. She was moving without conscious thought, while some calm center of her mind was still processing. *Spear. Killing stick. Like pinning a butterfly. Or at least keeping us at a distance. We should have thought of that, too.*

Then an even colder part of her thought: *Won't help him.*

Ignoring the driver, Ellis had broken into a high-stepping run around the Lunokhod, flying in long arcs. Vivian had never tried to propel herself that fast in lunar gravity, and she wasn't about to experiment now. The Soviet driver's spear was swinging around. He had the drop on her, sure enough.

Vivian leaned back, so she could skid to a halt without tumbling, and took aim at the cosmonaut just as she ran onto the end of his stick, its blunt end impacting the pipes and umbilicals over her stomach. It wouldn't have mattered much even if it had been sharp; little chance of it penetrating her life support apparatus. The aim of the pike was to keep her away while he or his colleague could shoot the shit out of her from short range.

Which his colleague was now doing, swinging the SPG-9 barrel around to aim it at her.

Ellis tossed the shell he was holding into the Lunokhod, and it exploded right behind the second cosmonaut. The blast smashed the Soviet into his SPG-9, and the explosive depressurization of his suit lifted him into the air.

A burst of rage startled her. Till now, Vivian had been appraising the Soviet threat in a cold, analytical way. She'd felt anger in orbit, when her crew had been in danger, but mostly she'd been applying her brain to the problems at hand.

Suddenly, it was different. Soviet forces were making a sustained attack on the US base and its astronauts, bringing fatal danger. All at once, it felt personal.

And this Soviet guy was poking at her with a stick while bringing up an assault weapon one-handed.

Vivian grabbed the Soviet's pike and pulled on it, tumbling backward. It jerked him forward, before he had the presence of mind to release it. His bullets sprayed past her.

She fell to the ground behind her rover. Reached up, and her questing hands found the core drill. She lifted it one-handed, almost pulling a muscle, and shoved herself up.

She didn't yet have time to find the power switch, but with a mass of thirty pounds the core drill made an excellent club.

The Soviet's faceplate didn't break, but the impact sure threw him off balance.

A NASA rover loomed to Vivian's left, startling her. She'd completely forgotten Collier and Lawrence. Now, their rover also hit the Lunokhod driver, knocking him back against his own crumpled vehicle.

Vivian tossed the long pole aside and rushed in. Swung the drill again, this time aiming for the chest where the cosmonaut's air hoses would be.

Lawrence was already jumping off the front of his rover, taking the guy down. Vivian left him to it. Leaped up onto the Lunokhod. "Ellis?"

She could hear him through her headset, grunting. And there he was, on the far side of the Soviet machine, clumsily struggling with the cosmonaut he'd initially knocked off the Lunokhod with the rock. The cosmonaut had one hand up to Ellis's helmet, the other pulling at his shoulder. Ellis was shoving, wrestling, trying to trip his assailant, while intermittently punching at the guy's oxygen hoses.

"Ahh, shit," he said, and Vivian heard a sudden loud hissing. The Soviet had yanked the oxygen purge valve on the right of Ellis's helmet, and his suit was depressurizing.

Vivian dived. Her spare arm went around the cosmonaut's neck, and they kept going, down to the ground. The Russian elbowed her, but couldn't get much force into it.

And then they were down, all three of them.

Vivian got her other hand onto the drill and pulled the actuator. The drills were rotary percussion, and the bit began to judder as well as spin. She swung it against the Soviet's helmet, and felt rather than heard the screech as the tungsten carbide bit clattered and pounded across the polycarbonate.

The Soviet immediately released Ellis and went limp. Raised his hands, palms up.

Oh, sure. Surrender now? Too late by half.

Yes, too late. In less than a second, cracks radiating outward from the drill bit, and then the cosmonaut's faceplate shattered.

The Soviet fell back, thrashing. He'd be dead in seconds. Vivian dropped the drill. "Ellis!"

Ellis reeled, his hands up to his own helmet, fumbling with the valve. "It's okay. Think I got it." Losing balance, he toppled onto his butt. "No, I don't. Wait."

His suit was clearly deflating. Was he slurring? Vivian dropped onto the ground beside him. "Hands away. Ellis, let go."

"No, it's good, I've got it closed. I think. Have I?"

Maybe. Vivian could no longer hear the hiss of his escaping air through her headset. She grabbed at the valve anyway, checked it. Shoved up his visor, but it was so fogged on the inside that she couldn't see his face. And the main pressure gauge on his chest was smeared with all kinds of dust and crap. "Wrist up, soldier."

215

Ellis raised his arm obediently. The needle on his wrist gauge was creeping back toward five psi as his life support backpack took care of business. He'd be okay.

Vivian was shaking, breathing hard, her heart racing. Damn. *Now* she was going into a shock reaction?

Well, better now than earlier. She swallowed, and tried to slow her breathing so her voice wouldn't quaver. "It's all good. You'll be fine, man."

"Course I will."

"Stay down a moment, anyway. Suck in a few deep breaths. Why not?"

"Sure thing." Ellis paused. "Uh. Did we win?"

"Good question."

Vivian glanced up at the pulverized remains of the Lunokhod, and realized Collier and Lawrence were watching them, one from each end of the Soviet vehicle, their hands down by their sides.

"Well?" she demanded. "Did we?"

They did.

Back in the Habs that evening, they pieced together the whole story.

The riders of the two Soviet dirt bikes from the northwest had attacked the Habitats. The Hadley-defending crews had stood their ground, with the mortar sending hypergolic fireballs shimmering across the lunar surface and the others launching explosive charges and boulders dangerously close to the bikes. None of the Soviet grenades had done significant damage to the Habs or its defenders. Their AK-47 fire was largely blocked by the Hadley shielding. The end result had been a standoff, and once Norton and Starman came careering in on their armored rover, the cosmonauts had thought better of it and withdrew—one of them on foot, having been knocked off his bike by a lucky shot from Starman and forced to abandon it.

With the help of covering fire from the Apollo 31 Lunar Module, Massey and Seaton had held off their aggressors for a while. Their Soviets were armed with AK-47s and explosives but little else, and had probably expected an easier time of their assignment. One of their assault rifles had overheated and jammed, and needed to be tossed aside as worthless. But the arrival of the third bike—the one that had just blown up the fuel tank—proved to be the tipping point, compounding more moving targets than Massey and Seaton could deal with. They'd lost the Cargo Container to a rocket impact. But once that was done, those Soviets had retreated as well.

Meanwhile, slightly over the horizon to the north, Apollo 29 had located the Soviet landers, but was unable to bomb them effectively. The Soviets had—sensibly—left troops behind to protect their craft, armed with at least two rocket launchers, and once the missiles started flying, Leverton and McDowell had been forced to beat a speedy retreat.

As soon as Vivian, Ellis, Collier, and Lawrence had dealt with the threat from the Lunokhod, the other Soviets must have received the order to disengage, because that's what they'd done. Retreated, loaded up, and launched, presumably heading for Zvezda Base.

Four Soviets had perished in the assault. Hadley Base had lost no one. The attackers had taken out one of Hadley's four fuel tanks, depriving them of half their Aerozine, and blown up the Cargo Container, but one of the dirt bikes had been destroyed with its passenger, and the Soviets had lost another bike and what was left of their Lunokhod Rover to the Americans.

The Soviet strike had caused significant damage, and the Hadley crew would need to ration their remaining supplies through the coming night. But the attackers had taken greater losses, and when Norton declared victory, no one was about to disagree.

Vivian had always known that one day she might have to kill, but she'd rarely given it much thought. As a Navy pilot it would most likely happen at a distance, in an aerial dogfight between her Douglas Skyhawk and a Soviet MiG somewhere over Asia. Or she'd have been ordered to shoot up hostile assets on the ground. Either way, the deaths would have been at one remove. Impersonal. And Vivian had been prepared for that.

Today had been very different.

Most of the astronauts were now asleep in their LMs, or in Hab B. Vivian was in the lowest level of Habitat A, meticulously cleaning her suit and Ellis's, double-checking everything, looking for any hint of damage or wear that might endanger them later. Ellis had offered to help, but she'd sent him off with Brock to fix up their drainpipe cannons. Just in case there was a second attack, sometime soon.

A second attack. Jeez. Hopefully unlikely, given the Soviet's losses in the first one.

If Ellis had stayed, he'd have wanted to talk about what they'd just been forced to do, and Vivian wasn't ready for that conversation. Both her coldness and her rage had been unexpected, and she didn't know how to interpret either one.

At least her hands weren't shaking any more.

"Russkie dirt bikes were pretty cool," said Starman. "Just between us chickens, I kinda dug them."

He swung himself down into the airlock area, and grinned at her. Vivian scrutinized him. "Are you drunk?"

"That would be unethical. A NASA astronaut under the influence?" He sat down beside her.

Carefully, but accurately. He wasn't *that* drunk. "I withdraw my baseless accusation."

"And I respect you for that. Am I disturbing you?"

Yes. No. "So, that bike they, uh, left behind. Can we use it?"

"Sure. Controls seem pretty straightforward. We can even recharge it. Sometime soon I'm gonna ride it around, see if I can decode the Cyrillic mumbo jumbo on the control panel. Must be all about the battery voltage, range, heading, and such, like on our rovers."

"You figure it's yours now?"

"And whose else might it be?" The "whose else" ran together a little, but otherwise Starman seemed fine.

Vivian grinned. "Okay. But: heading? I doubt it." NASA rovers had complex electronics to gauge distance traveled, averaging wheel rotations and using dead reckoning. The bike wheels jumped and spun and skidded too much for that approach to work well.

"Sure, but there are too many dials otherwise. I'll figure it out. My little side project."

"Also, you totally want to dirt-bike the freaking Moon."

"Fun, cunningly disguised as research. I knew that you, of all people, would understand, Madame Commander Geologist."

Vivian wagged her finger. "Lunar geology is critical to mission success."

"Indeed." Starman saluted. "Dirt bikes, likewise. Hey, once you're done here ... join me on the top level if you'd like a beverage of your own."

That was an appealing thought. "Maybe in a bit?"

He nodded. "In that case, carry on, ma'am."

218

"Will do, young man."

Once he'd left, Vivian wondered whether anyone else at Hadley could have raised her spirits as effortlessly. Not Ellis, much as she liked him. Ellis was calm and methodical to a fault, which made him her perfect crewman. But he wasn't necessarily the best person to bring Vivian out of a funk.

All right, Starman. That was surely enough suit maintenance for one night. She stood, carefully dusted herself down, and walked to the stairs.

Unexpectedly, she found Carol Massey in the midlevel, sitting on an exercise bike. Not pedaling, merely staring across the room. "Hey there, Apollo 30."

Massey blinked. "Hey yourself. What's up?"

"Nothing. Rough day?"

Massey shrugged. "Not so bad."

That was clearly bullshit. Vivian hesitated.

"Could have been worse, right?"

"Overall?" Vivian nodded. "We did great. Pushed the bastards away. They won't try that again."

"But we lost the Container."

Ah. Massey and Seaton had been tasked with defending it. "And some fuel."

"Nothing more you could have done about that," said Massey.

Vivian studied her. "The Container, same. You know that, right?"

Massey just looked away. Vivian thought about pushing harder. But they were both military, and she didn't know Massey that well. "So, I guess you're just goofing off, now?"

Massey's mouth made a straight line. It wasn't a grin, exactly, but it wasn't a sneer either. "Could say that."

"Got a spare moment, then?"

"As a matter of fact, I do."

"Outstanding. In that case: school me on what we need to do to batten down for nightfall?"

CHAPTER 21

Hadley Base: Vivian Carter
December 10, 1979

THE last rays of bright sunlight shone obliquely across the lunar surface, throwing every boulder and crater rim into sharp relief, and turning most of those craters into pools of absolute black. The shadows of the LMs and Habitats reached out like long fingers, knife-edged but oddly contorted by the uneven ground. Mount Hadley to the north, and Hadley Delta to the south, stood starkly illuminated on their western slopes, their eastern inclines dark against the sky. Compared to the glare of local noon when Vivian and Ellis had arrived, it was a forbidding, spooky landscape.

But they'd had little time for sightseeing. Preparing for lunar night took a lot of effort, which now needed to be done in double-quick time. The astronauts had needed to string extra power cables between the Habs and the assets. Cover and safe the solar panels and the more vulnerable experiments. Unpack and test the survival heaters, and install them into the Lunar Modules. Shield and batten everything against the brutal cold that was coming.

It was a great deal of work, in spacesuits that still seemed to fight back against them. Vivian and Ellis had done plenty of physical conditioning in the run-up to their mission, but even so, dealing with the suits day after day took its toll. Vivian's fingers, forearms, and shoulders ached constantly, and her fingertips, palms, and elbows were chafed raw. Her face was sunburned from pushing her visor up to do precision work out on-surface—like removing the plutonium fuel capsule from its graphite cask and installing it into the RTG. Where radioactivity was concerned, Vivian had wanted every last scrap of detail her eyes could give her.

Her legs, on the other hand, felt great. Somehow, they never got tired on the Moon. Vivian felt like she could run for hours, if necessary, in that strange galloping lope that all the Hadley crew eventually adopted.

But once night fell over Hadley Plain, there was no loping.

Vivian and Ellis were out on-surface for the moment of sunset: a tradition, for incoming members of Hadley Base. Vivian stood near Hab A next to Terri Brock. Ellis was over by Athena with Ibarra, having just mothballed their respective Lunar Rovers with thermal blankets.

Sunset came dramatically. One minute the Sun-sliver shone at grazing incidence across Palus Putredinis, sliced clean by the horizon. Next moment, the base and the entire plain were cast into darkness.

And at that moment, the stars leaped out. The broad swath of the Milky Way was revealed in all its glory, no longer obscured by the dazzle of the Sun's rays sparkling off regolith.

"Oh my God," Vivian said.

Brock chuckled and bumped shoulders with her. "Pretty cool?"

Vivian gulped and regained her composure. "Yes. Pretty cool." And then they all hurried for the airlocks.

And that was that, for the next two weeks.

That first sleep period after nightfall, Vivian and Ellis had to spend in Habitat B. NASA protocol, to ensure that their LM survived the transition into a cold bath of minus two hundred degrees without springing a leak. There weren't enough bunks for everyone, and as the newcomers, Apollo 32 got the floor. When they transferred back to their LM the following evening, Vivian and Ellis felt sore and on edge.

It was an eerie experience walking across a lunar surface lit only by earthlight and by the lights from the Habitats and Lunar Modules. The regolith beneath their boots seemed crunchier and more resistant. If they weren't shining their flashlights at their feet and paying attention, it was easy to trip and fall; and despite what the experts told her, Vivian was convinced that their helmets, umbilicals, and other hard surfaces must be more brittle in this deep cold.

And they couldn't be out for too long because the suit heaters would labor and eventually fail.

Most crews slept in the Habitats as often as possible. It was easy to see why. The Habs had proper beds with mattresses, which were curtained off for a modicum of privacy. It was warmer, and by God, it was definitely quieter. Athena flexed in the cold, expanding and contracting in weird ways. Their Lunar Module constantly hummed and hissed, buzzed and clinked, and sometimes, even more alarming, emitted ominous snapping and cracking sounds. There was the constant gurgle of water flowing through the heating system. The crews who'd been here for several lunar nights had stories of spontaneous vibrations starting up in the landing gear subsystem, or of the entire cabin suddenly tilting and then subsiding again for no reason they'd been able to determine.

Was it dangerous, sleeping in a LM during the cold and the dark? Probably. The Hadley crew had yet to suffer a serious mechanical failure or breach. The earliest crews had been here through twenty lunar nights by now, and all continued to sleep over in their LMs. They'd always been okay. But, as Mayer would say, *it's always "always" until it isn't.*

Naturally, special effort had gone into temperature resilience when NASA and Grumman had augmented the LMs for long stays. The engineering test models had been through a hundred cycles of lunar heat-to-cold-to-heat transitions in thermal vacuum chambers without a fail. The batteries and heaters were rugged, specced out to keep their crews alive. In the event of a breach to the Hadley Habs, or even a mundane failure of the environmental control systems, the LMs would be the crew's only lifeboats. They had to remain available and reliable even deep into lunar night.

Vivian knew the Hadley folks joked about her and Mayer. It was obvious enough. Other crews camped out at their LMs from time to time, but Vivian and Mayer were the only mixed-gender crew who religiously trooped off to their own LM four nights out of five. But their reasons were entirely aboveboard. They'd come to the Moon expecting Athena to be their home. They hadn't expected the Habs, hadn't anticipated any company on the Moon. Athena was theirs. And doggedly sticking to at least a part of the plan was comforting for both of them. *Sleeping simultaneously, not together, you jerks. It's not the same.*

The jokes were especially ironic because Ellis Mayer had never pushed the envelope with her. At all. He'd been professional throughout. Early on, as soon as he'd learned they were being considered as partners on a landing crew, Ellis had invited her over for dinner. There Vivian had met Mayer's wife, Judy, and perhaps more significantly, Judy had gotten to meet her. Vivian had liked Judy well enough, and Judy and Ellis seemed like the straightest of straight arrows. Childhood sweethearts, military spouses through the inevitable half-dozen moves cross-country. And then had come astronaut training, something Vivian didn't know how any spouse could put up with.

In training, and especially in space, in the tight confines of the CM, Mayer and Horn's banter—and Vivian's too—veered off-color, but that was a military thing. It went with the territory. Where it counted, Vivian trusted Ellis completely.

And the one tenet that Vivian and Mayer agreed on without needing to say it aloud? They had to keep Athena healthy, keep the dream alive. In principle, now they'd refueled Athena's lower stage at the Hadley fuel depot, they could fly her off to land, well, somewhere else on the lunar surface. Vivian had no clue how that could ever work out, but if they got the opportunity, Athena would be ready. Primed and pumped and lovingly cared for, capable of keeping them alive for ten days without external support.

Ellis Mayer had eaten, slept, and breathed their LM for years. If anything, his love for this ungainly cockroach was even deeper than hers. Perhaps a little less than he loved Judy and his kids, but certainly more than he loved Vivian. And Vivian was totally okay with that.

Vivian swung slowly in her hammock, staring up at the gray-silver aluminum shielding in the glow of the LM console lights. "Wonder how Dave's doing."

"You're awake too, huh?"

"Ticks me off we can't even *talk* to him."

"I'm sure he's fine," Ellis said.

"You are?"

"Well. I hope he's fine."

"He'd better be." Vivian shifted her hips, to keep her hammock swinging. "Our little submarine in space."

The silence extended. Eventually Vivian said, "If I could just reach up, grab Horn by the scruff of his goddamned unshaven neck and drag him down here, that's exactly what I'd do."

"You're sure we're not going to do that?"

Vivian had been doing the same math. "Strip out everything we don't need. Food, water. Tools, PLSSs, everything. Leave the rover on-surface, obviously. Take off. Bop straight out. Dock with Minerva. Transfer Dave, bring him straight back down here. We could do it."

"No PLSSs? We'd need someone to bring 'em to us when we landed." They'd have to suit up and depressurize the cabin, take O_2 from the LM's systems through umbilicals, while someone shoved the life support backpacks in through the hatch.

"Starman would do that for us in a heartbeat. Or Terri. Even Carol. Anyone."

"Yeah, but ..."

"I've become a fan of fuel margin," Vivian said. "One landing on fumes was enough. If we ever did it, I'd want to save all the weight we could. And Dave would have to sit his ass down on the ascent engine or lie across the cabin at our feet while we flew Athena back down here."

"We only have two umbilical ports for O_2. Ol' Dave is holding his breath for a while."

Vivian shrugged in the dark. "No worries. We land pressurized. Then pump his suit up hard before we depressurize to load the three PLSSs in. Dave can survive off a suit-full of oxygen for several minutes if he's not exerting."

"But what if we breached during the descent?"

Vivian rocked some more, and didn't respond. If they lost cabin integrity, they probably had other problems that would kill them first.

"Great plan. Shame we'll never do it."

"Yeah," she said, and they subsided into silence.

Because Dave would never just *leave* Minerva. The Command and Service Module was Horn's baby, his pride and joy, just as the LM was Ellis's. Dave would want to fly it back to Earth with Vivian and Ellis. To complete his own mission.

And if they abandoned the CSM in orbit it might tumble into a slow spin. They might not be able to dock with it again. In which case they'd have to go home in someone else's CM.

In an emergency, a standard Command Module could take five people: three in the couches, two in the storage area beneath. But for the three straight days it took to coast back to Earth, that would be hell. Five people in a CM designed for three? Sheer claustrophobic hell, and logistically challenging besides. Vivian might ask to take a drug and be comatose for the duration.

"God, I need a drink," she said.

She almost heard him grin. "I would kill for a beer."

He'd meant it lightly, but the phrase summoned the broken Soviet suits back into Vivian's mind. Four corpses still lay out there on the lunar surface. First people to die on the Moon.

Some of the guys had gone out and hauled the bodies, suits and all, into a crater out east, and no one had mentioned them since. Vivian didn't even know what Mission Control or NASA or America had had to say about it, how anyone on Earth had responded to the Soviet attack. Until now, it hadn't occurred to her to wonder. They were on secure-radio-only contact with Houston now, and Norton handled that.

We're separating from Earth, she thought. *Mentally, at least.*

"Two beers," she said.

It could be one of them, or both, lying dead and frozen in an un-named lunar crater right now. Her or Ellis, as still as the rest of the Moon. Might still be. This wasn't over yet.

"Three bottles of beer on a wall," Ellis said, unseen beneath her.

The Lunar Module creaked and popped. Vivian swayed again in her hammock as she turned over. "Goodnight, Pilot."

Vivian felt his hesitation. None of the Apollo 32 crew had ever said *Goodnight* before beginning a sleep period. This was a mission. When it was sleep time, you slept. That was that.

The LM rocked slightly as Ellis changed position too.

"Goodnight, Commander."

22

Hadley Base: Vivian Carter
December 25, 1979

"... **BUT** the missile gap between us and the Russians was always bull," Collier was saying. "Everyone with a clearance knew Kennedy just said that to get elected. The Red Scare was good for politics, but come on. Look at the Soviet space program. It's a farce. They bang shit together with a hammer and shoot it into space. What d'you think we could achieve if we didn't give a toss whether we did it rigorously and safely? Any idiot regime can shoot guys up in a tin can."

"And a Merry Christmas to you, too," said Gregory Leverton, bored.

Earlier that day the first rays of dawn had illuminated the mountaintops, then gradually angled down to graze the surface, bringing harsh light back to the Habitats and LMs of Hadley Base. On Earth, dawn and dusk were soft, gentle times of diffuse lighting. On the Moon, the return of daylight was a crashing full-frontal assault, and the Hadley structures creaked and groaned in complaint as temperatures soared.

For Vivian the dawn came as a visceral relief. Over the past two weeks she had gradually withdrawn into her shell against the endless bleak dark. Ellis, of course, was fine. Mentally unassailed, patiently waiting it out, while staying busy at the hundred and one maintenance tasks around them. Vivian might often wish she could be that calm and level, but she never would be. She'd just have to fake it.

226

Now that real light returned to the lunar surface, Vivian wanted to sing and dance. Obviously, both were untenable in their current confines. But she was anxious to *see* the Sun for herself: their two small LM windows faced west across the rille toward Palus, and all she could see were the Sun's effects downstream of them, throwing the irregular terrain into the sharpest of reliefs.

Fortunately, the Sun's return meant an immediate EVA to remove the thick thermal blanketing shrouding the LM and their rover and set out the solar panels again. And after that they'd hotfooted it to the fuel dump, and then Hab A, to help the Hadley astros bring both back up to their daylight configurations.

One of Vivian's first priorities had been to test drive their rover and ensure it had survived the night. It had: everything was fine. In a couple more days, once the Sun was higher, Vivian planned to do their second major excursion along the rille. If that went well, and everything else stayed calm, she'd pitch for Palus Trek the following week, in the second half of lunar day. So this evening she was browsing the high-resolution maps of the rille that Columbia Station had taken from orbit and correlating them with the geology reports that Dobbs and Vasquez had filed. She listened with only half an ear: the Hab conversation had been relentlessly political for so long that people were repeating themselves, and since none of them knew what the hell would happen next anyway, where was the point?

Weird that I've now been on the Moon over three weeks. More than double the length of my original mission. And despite that, it still feels like I just arrived.

Dawn had brought welcome light back to the surface, but little clarity about the future of Hadley Base. Two weeks had made almost no difference to the superpower standoff on Earth, pithily summarized by Starman as "lots of shouting and wheel spinning, and no movement."

Neither side had publicly mentioned the armed assault on Hadley Base, in the fine old détente tradition of hushing up such skirmishes. The Soviets had not admitted suffering any fatalities on the Moon. The UN General Assembly had adopted a resolution demanding the immediate, urgent, and unconditional withdrawal of Soviet cosmonauts from Columbia Station, which passed by 106 votes to 16 against the obvious opposition from the USSR and other Eastern Bloc countries. But no one was anticipating that the Soviets would be swayed by that.

Meanwhile, Soviet troops were consolidating their hold on Afghanistan, but encountering strong resistance from the mujahideen and other Afghan rebel groups, and as yet had made no moves toward Pakistan or Iran. Trade embargoes and other sanctions were being imposed, and a US-led boycott of the 1980 Summer Olympic Games in Moscow was in the cards, but Brezhnev and Reagan were still entrenched, neither one blinking. There'd been no advance and no retreat on either the high or low frontiers.

Despite that, several of the astros were incapable of shutting up about politics. Now nine of them lolled around the crew area in Hab A after dinner, drinking juice and shooting the breeze.

"The Soviets beat us to orbit," Norton said patiently. "They beat us to spacewalk. They beat us to the Moon. Aside from this base we're sitting in right now, every other significant space 'first' is notched on Soviet belts."

"Doesn't matter who does it first," Collier said doggedly. "We do it *right*. And we're still better. Guys, the Soviets aren't going to mount a ground assault on Hadley from Zvezda, especially given how we slapped 'em back the first time. It's just bluster and chest thumping. They don't have the tech. Look around. You think Zvezda is anywhere near as slick as this?"

Buchanan snorted. "As slick as *this*? Right." He glanced at Norton. "Don't get me wrong. This base is a big deal, a major achievement. But it still takes too much maintenance."

On that, they could all agree. "All the running we can do, to stay in the same place," Starman said philosophically.

"Yep. And so I bet the Soviet base takes even *more* running," Collier said, and then the teleprinter started clacking.

Buchanan stared at it, eyebrows raised. "Well, hello. Daddy's calling."

Vivian checked her watch. The teleprinter fired up several times a day to deliver schedule information, news, and messages from friends and family, but Mission Control never sent up reports during mealtimes.

Norton gestured, and Starman stepped forward to look at the emerging text. "Gee willikers. This is encoded."

Vivian looked at Terri next to her, who was gazing at the teleprinter like it was a serpent. "So?"

"That's already an encrypted and secure line. Sending a *coded* message on top of that is overdoing it some."

"Has this happened before?"

"Not while I've been here."

Everyone put their juice down, leaned forward. Some people stood up, as if expecting to leap into action at any moment. Vivian slid her photographs back into her file folder.

Starman Jones tugged a loose-leaf binder out of the bookshelf below the printer, flipped pages. "Hang tight. This may take a few minutes."

"Hurry it up," Norton said, unnecessarily. Jones's eyes were flicking between the printout and the folder and he was already scribbling on a clipboard, concentrating so hard that he may not even have heard.

No one spoke. The teleprinter kept clacking. Norton and Buchanan stepped up to look over Jones's shoulder as he worked, writing down the message in clear text. If anything, they looked perplexed rather than alarmed.

"Damn, this is *long*. Get 'em started." Jones tore off the first piece of paper, handed it to Norton, kept scribbling.

Norton turned with the flimsy paper in his hand. "This wasn't sent from Mission Control. It's from … Apollo Rescue 1." He stopped, giving time for Collier to say: "Which is?"

"Apparently, we're about to get help."

"What kind of help?"

Norton finished scanning the page. "Okay. Here's how it'll be announced in the press tomorrow on Earth, and how we're to refer to it publicly, now and in the future." He began to read aloud. "'Apollo Rescue 1 will drop critical supplies to our US astronauts endangered by the recent and reckless Soviet aggression, and provide defensive support to US assets in cislunar space.'" Norton lowered the paper again. "Whatever else we may be about to learn, this is all we say."

Jones dropped his pen and tore off the second piece of paper. "But hey, funny story: that's not what they're here to do at all. Rescue 1 is military."

Vivian looked at Starman's expression. "Military? Coming to Hadley?"

"How many of them?" Norton demanded.

Starman raised his hands helplessly. "Thirteen."

"Thir*teen*?" Brock said, her eyes wide. "Thirteen *people*?"

"Lucky for some," said Buchanan.

"How, thirteen?" Collier asked. "A bunch of LM Taxis, four or five or them?"

"No LMs at all." Starman frowned at the teleprinter paper. "Single drop. One module."

"That's not possible," Norton said. "We don't have that capability."

"Well, NASA doesn't, that's for sure," said Buchanan.

A short silence fell.

Vivian had been watching Buchanan throughout this exchange. "So the USAF has space tech we were unaware of. Tech that comes as more of a surprise to some of us than others."

Buchanan looked wry. "At my age, I'm harder to surprise."

"Bullshit," said Vivian. "You knew they could do this."

"Easy, ma'am," said Buchanan. "Eye on the ball. *Why* are they coming here?"

"Why don't you tell us?"

"If I knew, I would," Buchanan said steadily.

"Wait, break," Norton said. "*When* are these jokers coming in, exactly, Starman?"

"Oh, y'know," Jones said. "Like two hours from right now. They'll swing around the Moon once and then, bam, down they come."

"Jeez, you didn't think that was worth mentioning *first*?"

"They don't need beacons," said Starman. "They don't need tidy-up. They say they're just fine for an orderly landing. They do advise us to bring all personnel, dogs and cats indoors."

"They said that? Those words?"

Starman held out the second teleprinter page. "Sure did, Skipper. Dogs and cats."

Norton grabbed the paper, scanned it quickly. "Christ. A regular clown posse. And, no shit: *thirteen* of them."

"Gonna be a brave new world around here," said Buchanan.

"No kidding." Norton turned to Starman. "Spread the word. Wake everyone up. Evacuate the LMs, pull everyone into the Habs." Starman started flipping switches on the comms board.

"Sure hope they're bringing their own air and water," said Gisemba, logistics guy.

"And sleeping quarters," said Collier.

"Huh." Norton held the pages up to the light as if studying them for a watermark. "They'd damned well better. We can't support that kind of personnel surge in the Habs."

"They will," Collier said. "But I'm more interested in what *else* they're bringing. Because we don't need rescuing, and we sure as hell don't need another thirteen people here."

Norton was shaking his head. "Someone thinks we do."

"More manpower," Buchanan said. "Trained manpower."

Lawrence eyed him. "Trained for what, exactly?"

"Well, that seems clear," Buchanan said.

And it was, but someone had to say it aloud, so Vivian did. "Trained for war."

"Trained for war." Buchanan inclined his head. "We're obviously facing a major escalation."

Apollo Rescue 1 came in fast, and it came in hard. Vivian never even saw it until it fired retros five hundred feet up to break its speed. It didn't hover, didn't pause. Just decelerated hard in that last five hundred and walloped down onto the lunar surface.

It was still going at a hell of a clip when it hit. They felt the impact, transmitted up through the lunar crust. The Habitat shuddered. Everything rattled. Cups fell off tables. A slow oscillation followed, reminding Vivian of a midlevel earthquake she'd once experienced.

"Sweet Mary, Mother of God," said Dunlap.

"Harder impact than a supply drop?" Ellis asked.

"Oh, yeah. By far."

The impact had kicked dust, pebbles, and small rocks high into the air. They rained down now, scattering off the Hab roof.

Rescue 1 looked similar to one of their regular Cargo Containers, but chunkier and more bulbous. It had landed on the fourth side of the square made by the rille to the west, the Habs to the north, and the fuel dump to the east. Right next to the other supply pods.

As the new ship settled it subsided to the left, maybe ten degrees off true. *Their floors won't be level*, Vivian thought. *Their bunks. Bathroom.*

Then, belatedly: *If anyone could really survive a landing that hard.*

The radio crackled. "Hadley Base, this is Apollo Rescue 1. Do you copy?"

Norton stood still, apparently stunned. "Hey, boss?" Vivian said.

He shook himself and gestured to Starman, who pressed the Push-to-Talk button. "Apollo Rescue 1? Welcome to Hadley Base. This is Rick Norton, Commander."

"Roger that, and thanks," said the voice. "Which Habitat?"

"Me, now? Hab A," Norton said.

"Roger. Hang tight, I'll be right over." And the connection went dead.

Vivian rocked back. *Oh, boy. How the hell … ?*

"Well," said Terri. "That was terse. Not even an introduction or a how-are-you?"

"No names, no pack drill, even on secure radio," Buchanan said. "Interesting."

Mayer looked sideways at Vivian. "What?" he asked quietly.

"That's Peter Sandoval."

Mayer hadn't been in her astronaut group. "Who?"

"Blue Gemini guy I met in training."

"What kind of a guy?" He blinked. "Wait. *That* kind of guy?"

"Not a boyfriend."

Ellis just looked at her, and she realized her tone of voice had been odd. "Weirder than that. I gave him marital advice once." She glanced sideways. "That's not a euphemism."

Ellis did a bad job of amending his expression. "Didn't imagine it was for a moment."

Norton noticed their heads together. "What's that you're whispering about, 32? Care to share it with the class?"

"Maybe later."

"Fine. Okay, let's make ready to receive our visitor. Carol, you want to go help him clean off, welcome him aboard?"

Carol Massey looked at him in disbelief. "Say what? Me *again*? You must be kidding."

Norton eyed her, perplexed. "We rotate this duty. You know we do."

"Rotate," Massey said. "D'you want the statistics on how that's worked out?"

"Not really. Not right now."

Vivian stepped in. "I'll take it. I'm one of the newest on deck. But a quiet word, first?"

Norton looked happy to escape Massey's glare. "Uh, fine. And, sure."

They moved to the side of the room, turned their backs. "Let me do this solo," she murmured. "He might let more slip to me than to you, or the whole crowd."

That piqued his interest. "And why?"

"His name's Peter Sandoval, USAF. We were training buddies. Me, him, and Rawlings, as it happens."

"And you and Sandoval have … history?"

Geez, two for two. What is it with these guys? "Not like *you* mean. But yeah, we've had some long chats in the past. Let's just say we both know where the bodies are buried."

"Oookay. Not even going to ask you to explain *that*. Sure, you got it. But anything you find out, you'll share with me?"

"Sure thing," Vivian said, and jumped the stairs down to the airlock.

CHAPTER 23

Hadley Base: Vivian Carter
December 25, 1979

HE was taller than she remembered.

"Hi there," she said as she lifted his helmet off. "Commander Vivian Carter, Apollo 32."

"Glad to make your acquaintance, Commander. And a Merry Christmas." He was grinning like a Cheshire cat. *Hmm.*

She unseated his right glove, then shook his hand professionally. "We meet in the strangest places. The Moon's a bit out of your jurisdiction, no?"

"Little bit." He looked wry.

"How's Alice?"

This time he paused, grimaced for real. "Nope. Didn't work out. Did my damnedest."

"Sorry to hear. Don't scuff your boots on the floor. It throws dust into the air."

"Oops, sorry."

As they talked, Vivian was efficiently brushing his suit down, using a DustBuster-style device to pull as much moondust off him as she could before he doffed the suit. "So, you brought a team all this way to be our saviors?"

"To strengthen your defenses. Give you a hand defending Hadley Base."

"You're a bit late. We already handled that."

"That was only their first pass." Sandoval bagged his gloves, looked around curiously. "The Soviets seem to have gone off half-cocked, frankly. Maybe hoped to catch you on the hop, but you caught them instead. They won't make that mistake again."

"Worse coming, then?"

Sandoval nodded. "Our intel suggests that action was directed by Nikolai Makarov. Who, though a Major-General in the Red Army, has been a career cosmonaut for a decade and a half. Arguably rusty in combat. But the Soviets already have a tougher military commander on-site. More ruthless. Looks like he was sidelined for this first action, presumably in deference to Makarov's lunar experience. That was probably an error."

"And you all know this how?"

"Cannot reveal." He didn't smile. "But it's clear from monitoring launches—as best we can, without the Manned Orbiting Labs—and from general chatter that the Soviets have a dramatic buildup underway. They've got the bit between their teeth, and a point to make."

"And so do we, apparently," Vivian said.

"We absolutely do," said Sandoval. "And Night Corps is here to help you make it."

Vivian paused. "Seriously, 'Night Corps'? That's what you call yourselves?"

"I didn't name us. But by the standards of military BS, it could be worse. We're a special ops group for … military activities off-Earth. You'll hear more during the briefing that I'm about to give."

She looked askance. "And you were always part of Night Corps? Even back in the day?"

"Yep. But that information was not to be commonly known."

"Right," she said. "Sure."

"Sorry, Viv. There were things I just couldn't tell you."

"Clearly." She unhooked his PLSS and hefted the backpack over to a wall clip. Meantime, Sandoval stood and unzipped his own moon suit down the back with a confident pull. *Yep, he's trained for space, all right.* "You're better at that than I am."

"But I know almost nothing about the Moon," he said. "No bullshit this time, Viv. My team are trained for this place. I'm not."

"Really? You never expected to come here?"

235

"Could never have imagined it. Wasn't interested, frankly. Never signed up for it. I was really invested in the MOLs, the orbital stuff."

"Sooo, no offense or anything, but if you're not trained for the Moon, why are you in charge of the folks who are?"

He grinned. "Operational reasons."

"Fab," she said. "Mister Mysterious."

"Sorry … look, can I just do one big 'Sorry' and then quit saying it?"

"May as well." She stood in front of him, grabbed his sleeves, and tugged as he curled and extricated himself from the back of the suit. Yes, tall. Buzz-cut black hair. Clear eyes with laugh lines. Broad shouldered for an astronaut; the suit was tight on him. Amazing they could even stuff him into a Gemini capsule.

"For real, Vivian. I studied up on the Moon and Hadley as best I could during the past three weeks, but there's a lot I'm not going to know. Help me not screw up? The Moon is a harsh mistress, as they say."

She blinked. "Uh, literally nobody says that."

"The sci-fi novel?"

"I did get the reference," she said. "But, sure. If I see you about to mess up, I'll holler."

"Or maybe slip me the word quietly."

"Situation dependent."

"Yep." Man. They'd fallen straight back into their ready rapport of a few years back. Aside from Ellis, Vivian hadn't felt this comfortable with anyone else on the Moon. She'd forgotten how familiar and semi-flirtatious her chats with Sandoval had been. Wife notwithstanding. Dang.

Well. This familiarity might be useful in the days to come. And it was why she'd volunteered to welcome Sandoval to Hadley, right?

It was only now that Vivian realized that she considered herself a member of Hadley Base. One of Norton's team, resistant to outsiders. Circling the wagons against intruders. She'd made the transition without even realizing. And apparently all it took was a couple of Soviet attacks, plus a bunch of newcomers busting into her town with no notice.

Sandoval started unfastening his liquid-cooled garments. Vivian perched on the edge of a table. She wasn't about to get in and help him with *that*, even though he was wearing a crisp blue flight suit underneath. "Heavy, then? That landing?"

Sandoval's eyes went wide and he gripped the arms of his seat for a few moments, miming stark terror. "Think so? You should've seen it from the inside."

"No thanks. Fortunately, that controlled crashing shit is just for hotshot *USAF* astronauts."

"They never warned me how brutal that was going to be."

"For reals?"

"'Controlled decelerated landing,' they said. 'Fixed point,' they said. 'Slam into the Moon at barely survivable speed, relying on webbing and crumple zones to absorb the shock?' That, they did *not* say."

"Fascinating."

"My pilots had simmed it. But it was mostly computer controlled anyway."

He had his LCGs unfastened now. Before he could stand up and shuck out of them, Vivian put her hands onto his shoulders. Leaned forward, looked into his eyes. "Peter. Just between us. How bad is this shit going to get?"

She felt devious even as she did it, but hey. Sandoval was the super-spy around here. It was up to him to resist her wiles.

Which he apparently found easy. "Can't tell you. Sorry."

"I don't have need-to-know?"

His shoulders came up under her hands as he shrugged. "There's a lot *we* don't yet know about Soviet ordnance levels and intent. But, sure, it's likely to be bad. You should take me in to address the troops now." He paused. "Talk more later, maybe?"

"For sure, Secret Agent Man," Vivian said. "Why not?"

"Hi, everyone. I'm Colonel Peter Sandoval, USAF. Thanks for hosting us at Hadley. Looks like you have yourselves one smooth operation here, and I do apologize for barging in. It took a very serious situation to make this necessary, and no one regrets the need for it more than I."

They all watched him, mute. *He's good with a room,* Vivian thought. *Sharp. Holds everyone's attention. Runs rings around Norton.*

Though I doubt Peter would think Hadley was a smooth op if he saw how much we argue and futz around here.

"You all know the situation in orbit." Sandoval gestured toward Vivian and Ellis. "You two saw it up close and personal. A Soviet military force, hijacking a NASA scientific facility. On Earth, the news rags are calling it 'Piracy on the High Frontier.' At the UN, they're calling it a 'regrettable action.' Me, I'll call it what it was: a declaration of war."

People had interrupted Norton freely during his all-hands meeting. It was clear that no one was about to interrupt Colonel Peter Sandoval, USAF.

"It's a miracle nobody was killed. No thanks at all to the Soviets. They were hell-bent on commandeering that facility even if their actions resulted in extensive loss of life. It was only the cool heads of the Columbia crew that kept everyone safe. And then the ground assault, down here. I've seen the reports. You guys did great. Nice job.

"But we're seeing a continuing Soviet military buildup in orbit, and SIGINT is hearing a sizeable comms traffic between Zvezda Base, the Soviets on Columbia, and their keepers in the USSR. There's also an uptick of Soviet clandestine activity in Washington, DC, and around Cheyenne and the key NASA Centers. All of which indicates they plan another assault.

"Let me be honest. I doubt you'd escape another confrontation with the Soviets without a sizeable body count. No disrespect. But I severely doubt it."

Sandoval pointed briefly at himself, then waved in the direction of the glorified Cargo Container he'd crashed down onto the surface in. "Enter Night Corps. A special unit most of you are hearing about today for the first time."

Most of you? Vivian's gaze flickered across to Buchanan and Norton, but their faces were impassive. *Was that a slipup, Peter, old buddy?*

Sandoval looked around. Met some eyes. Nodded in approval, as if he was looking at the best folks he'd ever met. "Here we are. We're directed to safeguard US lives and assets. Protect ourselves and all of you. Defend the American stake on the Moon, our investment in exploration and discovery, and our national pride and world standing. Show the Soviets that we won't scurry back to Earth with our tails between our legs. You folks here, and everyone at NASA and the USAF, and throughout the US at various Centers and companies and wherever the hell else, have worked way too hard for far too long for that to happen."

Okay. By now, Vivian knew why Sandoval had drawn this assignment.

"The men of my squad, whom you'll work alongside in the weeks to come, are an elite force. Just like NASA, we're the best of the best. We have Navy SEALs, Army Rangers, Marines, and CIA operatives—every one of them extensively trained for off-Earth military operations. Our existence is above Top Secret, so you all know the drill. Don't ask us who we are, where our hometowns are, where we trained or served, what we like for dinner." Sandoval grinned. "And, God knows, don't ask what sins we committed in a past life to earn this gig. But be assured that every person you meet in Night Corps is trained for this type of action, for any ordnance that we may use, and for any activity you see us perform.

"Give us your help and support. Answer any questions we have. When the shit hits the fan, do what we say without hesitation. And once we're all home safe on Planet Earth: Night Corps was never here. You never met us. You have nothing to say. No details, ever, unless otherwise instructed.

"So. Any questions, before I brief you on what's about to happen next?"

There were none. Nobody wanted to wait longer than necessary to find out what was about to happen.

"We harden Hadley against Soviet attack. My guys deploy various defensive capabilities. You supply assistance as necessary, using the systems you're already familiar with. We work as one big team for our mutual support and protection. Clear?"

"I'm surprised I wasn't consulted about this," Norton said bluntly.

"Well, I'm surprised too. If it had been my call, you would have been. But, my bosses? Frankly, they never tell anyone anything till they absolutely have to, and that includes me."

Norton folded his arms. "Maybe we can look after ourselves just fine."

"Maybe so. Maybe sending us here was overkill. I guess we'll find out."

Norton was growing irritated. "This is a NASA base. *NASA*. Not USAF. Sure, I'm military and so are my people, but we're detailed to *NASA*. And NASA is a civilian organization."

Sandoval took his time. "And you're thinking the Reds give a damn for that fine distinction?"

"They might. They *well* might. Maybe by bringing your *elite military unit* here you've painted an even bigger target on us. Maybe doubling the occupancy of Hadley Base when the Supreme Soviet is calling for us to leave will be considered an escalation that can't be tolerated. Maybe your arrival will invite a new attack that otherwise wouldn't have come."

"I didn't see the Reds hairsplitting the career status of the Columbia crew. Or of the crew of Apollo 32, here, who got caught in the crossfire. But that aside, the whole point is that the Soviets don't know we're here. They think our module out there is a supply drop. If we're lucky, they've never even heard of Night Corps. But, hey. If they have, then maybe knowing we're on-site will give them pause."

Norton was clearly gearing up to say something else, but Sandoval raised a hand to stop him. "But, with all due respect? This isn't a discussion, and we don't get to vote on it. Because Night Corps was sent here by order of the President of the United States, and we're not leaving, because we can't." He pointed at the window. "Do you see any new launchers out there? You do not. Because Night Corps did not bring any. This is a one-way trip. We'll formulate our extraction plan downstream. For now, we're here for the duration, whether you like it or not. And we're about to dig in."

He turned to face Norton directly.

"Commander Norton, I have almost as many guys here as you. From now on we take the same risks you do, and we can't just sit tight and hope for the best. If you want my honest opinion, I think that Hadley is a soft target that's just about to get pummeled. And so we get to make it a hard target, and turn your village into a castle. My people are already deploying. Some of what they're doing, I won't share with you. Other aspects, I will brief you on fully. But here's what I need you and your people to start doing, right now …. I'm sorry, Commander, did you have another question?"

Norton had, in fact, gone very still. Now he raised his chin and spoke. "You keep calling me *Commander*. But it seems like you're saying that you're in charge now. Is that correct?"

Sandoval shook his head. "Negatory, sir. Hadley Base is still your command. Your people still report to you. Your responsibilities and accountability remain unchanged. I have written orders for us both, from our respective superiors, detailing this. You may study them at your leisure.

"You're still in charge of everything you were in charge of yesterday. But the game has switched up a little. I am responsible for implementing defensive measures for Hadley Base, and I will require some of your local expertise to implement those measures. Are we clear?"

"Yes, sir," Norton said. "Crystal."

Sandoval nodded. "Outstanding. So, let's roll up our sleeves and run through some specifics."

"As before, we expect the Soviet attack to target infrastructure. If they can render Hadley unsustainable by limiting your O_2, power, food, water, or fuel, then you have no choice but to leave. And they only need to ace one of those. Do you store supplies in the Cargo Containers till you need them? Then they're easy targets. You need to bring it all in right away."

"*In?*" Norton said in exasperation. "In case you haven't noticed, Colonel Sandoval, we don't have a lot of free space. We leave supplies outside because there's no room in here."

Sandoval scanned the room. "I see all kinds of materiel you don't absolutely need. You can't breathe furniture, spare bedding, and chemistry sets. Move 'em out. Move the O_2 and water in. And get used to having less elbow room. We need to reduce the area we protect. We can't move your fuel tanks, but we can sure as hell move the supplies. Bury them in the ravine if you have to."

"That's a rille," Vivian couldn't help saying.

"I'm sure it is, Captain."

Buchanan frowned. "Do you plan to billet your troops in here? Or equipment?"

"No, sir. From time to time a couple of my people may visit to assist. They'll breathe your air, but they won't eat your food or sleep in your beds. We have all our own supplies. Those will remain in the Bunker, which is how we'll refer to our facility from now on."

"Sounds great," said Norton. "Okay, so how about if we move some of our supplies into there?"

"No can do. Honestly, the pressurized space in the Bunker for my entire squad is less than the volume of this room."

"So, you're assuming the Habitats themselves aren't a target? They're the biggest pieces of infrastructure we have."

"Excellent question, Commander Collier. Yes, we do believe these Habitats will be targets. We're confident the Reds will leave the LMs alone. They're not about to decommission your only means of egress. So, some of your supplies can end up there, though I know how small those things are." He paused to think. "D'you usually keep the LMs fueled up and ready to fly? Or are their tanks dry?"

"Full and ready," Norton said. "In case we need an emergency evac."

"Good. That practice should continue. But we still have to assume the fuel dumps will be a prime target. We'll secure those as carefully as the Habs."

"Define 'secure' for us, Colonel," Buchanan said. "We've already reinforced their shielding with regolith. They've survived one attack already. Mostly."

"We'll add a perimeter fence and extra shielding. Plus, the Habitats and the fuel dumps will both get active protection."

"Active how?" asked Mayer.

Sandoval looked at Vivian as if expecting her to answer, so she did. "You're about to say 'ordnance,' I'm guessing."

Sandoval smiled, his mouth a thin line. "Ordnance."

Dunlap stood up. "With all due respect. This is not the duty I signed up for."

Sandoval regarded him calmly. "Meaning?"

"Perhaps some of us should rotate out, and leave you to it. More supplies for you, and you won't have us inconvenient astronauts getting in your way."

"That's your best call? Up and run? Abandon everything you've worked so hard on?"

"Abandon what?" Dunlap demanded. "Hadley Base is my duty assignment, and it's a bunch of rocks. it has no strategic value. There's no shame in tactical withdrawal."

Vivian had never seen Sandoval's eyes so cold. His folksiness and bonhomie had evaporated. "No strategic value? The frigging *Moon*?"

A long silence fell, eventually breached by Carol Massey. "You must admit this mission has changed parameters since we were assigned."

"Welcome to the military," Sandoval said. "Listen: I wasn't kidding when I said I was impressed at what you've achieved here. The first US outpost on a *new world*. You've taken a desolate valley with zero resources and turned it into a freaking *Moon colony*, the most substantial US 'first' in space."

"Sure. So?"

"*So*, if it were me, I wouldn't leave something I'd worked that hard for. They'd have to drag me out. My last assignment? MOL-7. And it was blown up by a Soviet missile just moments after I left it."

"Uh. That's hardly great support for your argument."

Sandoval held Dunlap's gaze. "*My point being* that I loved that goddamned *duty assignment*, and I deemed it important, and of the highest strategic value. And seeing it get blown apart by a Soviet missile just about broke my goddamned heart. All right?"

Oh, you're good, Vivian thought. *Was that heartfelt, or calculated? Just how skilled are you at tweaking our emotions, Peter Sandoval?*

Vivian did like him. But could she trust him?

"Okay, on that note ..." Sandoval looked at Vivian, then Terri Brock and Carol Massey, then back to Vivian. "I'm about to convey an order that I don't give a good goddamn whether you obey or not, and this will be the only time you'll hear me say that. Listen up: I've been commanded to order the female astronauts to leave Hadley Base and return to Earth. Because the US military does not condone females serving in combat roles."

Massey leaped to her feet so forcefully that she almost impacted the ceiling. Brock shook her head in irritation, and said: "I think someone missed a memo." Vivian snorted.

Sandoval raised his hands. "Understood. I've been fully briefed on the quality of the personnel here. Commander Norton gets to call this one. I, personally, do not require anybody to leave, and this is the first and last time I'll be raising the issue."

Everyone looked at Norton, who was staring squarely at Sandoval. "Well, then, I'll call it. We're a team, here, Colonel, with a wide range of skills and expertise. I'm not going to weaken that team and endanger everyone's safety by arbitrarily ordering anyone home."

"And that's good enough for me."

"Damned right."

Sandoval nodded. "Then let's move on. Radio transmissions. These will continue, even increase, and remain clear-channel. Your geologists can run around all over the surface with their hammers and collecting bags and what all, and chatter about it enthusiastically on open live radio, for transmission. TV too, as long as Night Corps and all its works are kept completely out of the picture. Your other activities—construction, materials science, solar wind measurements, counting sunspots, whatever else you usually do—those also continue, reinforcing the narrative that Hadley is a base devoted to scientific inquiry.

"But in case of enemy incursion, or anything else you wouldn't want the world to know, you switch to secure radio. Don't get cute thinking you're speaking in riddles that the Reds won't understand. Use secure radio, or say nothing at all."

"We don't have secure-radio capability in individual suits," Collier said.

"Huh." Sandoval thought for a moment. "Okay. Night Corps suits have it as standard, but we can't retrofit your suits. So, you'll just need to be *very* circumspect. Never refer to any of us by name on the clear-channel loops. Never refer to Night Corps at all. Your main Habitats have secure radio, though? Good. So, tell me this: d'you use Christian names or surnames here, when talking on the loops?"

"Either. Both. We're not consistent."

"I'm asking because I need an alias. Okay, when you're talking about Dan Klein, what do you call him?"

"Uh, 'Dan'?"

Sandoval grinned. "Sure. But does that mean you never refer to him as 'the doctor' or 'the medic'? Doc? Sawbones?"

"Right," said Klein. "They've never called me any of that. So if you want those as code names, that'll work."

"Very well. So from now on, if you need me you ask for the medic. Or the doctor, or something similar. Something generic. No need to say it's urgent. We'll just assume it is. If Night Corps hears any of those words, we respond immediately."

"Okay."

"If you have a *real* medical emergency, call it what it is: a *medical emergency*. Those words. If you need Klein, call for Klein. But if you ask for a medic, you get Night Corps, and fast. Okay?"

"Sure."

"We want to keep the element of surprise as long as possible. And once we enter a conflict situation, we give away *no* information about our locations and talk only when unavoidable, because the Soviets will track us individually by those transmissions."

Sandoval looked at his watch. "Okay. I need to head on out and shout at my people a bit. But next I'll be sending in one of my guys: Major Gerry Lin. I'd like one of your commanders to bring him up to speed in Lunar Module ops, eventually take him up for a quick spin for orientation. Gerry has flown a couple hundred hours in LM simulators on the ground, about half what y'all have done, but I don't have to tell any of you that the real thing is different."

Norton and Buchanan looked at each other. Collier said, "You already have nine trained LM commanders in front of you, and an equal number of LMPs also supremely capable of whatever you might need."

"Sure. NASA people. Some of whom haven't piloted their craft for nearly a year."

"You're really expecting any of us to let someone *else* fly their Lunar Module?"

Sandoval met Collier's eye. "You do realize I'm authorized to requisition anything and everything I want if I see an operational need? Come on. I don't want to do that. This is uncomfortable enough already. But I need my people to be prepared for any eventuality, and the LMs are the only aerial capability we have. So I'm requesting one training ride for one officer, and not requisitioning any damned thing at all."

But you'll do it in an instant if you have to, Vivian thought, and the same thought was probably in Norton's mind as well.

"My ace pilot needs to get a few flight hours under his belt, in case something comes along that I can't ask any of you to do. Or that would expose you to information that I'm not permitted to divulge. This will happen only in extreme circumstances. I trust this isn't going to be an issue."

Norton just stared.

"No issue," said Buchanan, and looked at Collier. "Sorry."

Collier looked dour. As commander of one of the two three-person LM Taxis, it clearly made sense for him to host the training run. And he knew an order when he heard one. "Fine. We'd be happy to show Major Lin the ropes, sir." He turned to Terri Brock, his LMP, who was looking right back at him, wide eyed. "Wouldn't we, Pilot?"

"I, uh, guess it would be our pleasure."

"Excellent," Sandoval said smoothly. "Thank you very much. I'll send Gerry in so's you can all get to know one another."

Ellis was calmly watching this exchange. Vivian wondered how he—or she herself—would have reacted if Sandoval had insisted that Lin take the controls of *their* LM, Athena.

That would have been a gut punch. Would she have refused?

Fortunately, it looked like she wouldn't need to find out. Or at least, not yet.

24

Hadley Base: Peter Sandoval/Vivian Carter
December 26, 1979

Sandoval

Sandoval was making a bad habit of dodgy landings. His last reentry was still giving him nightmares.

That wasn't a figure of speech. Sandoval was suffering actual, horrific nightmares that woke him up in a hot sweat, something that had never happened to him before, even after getting his F-100 Saber shot out from under him by a MiG somewhere over North Vietnam a decade ago. He was, frankly, a bit worried about them, the nightmares. Maybe he couldn't hack it anymore. But if he was losing his nerve, the timing on that was freaking *terrible*.

A few weeks back, their Blue Gemini craft had arced over the Soviet Union. Gerry Lin was a top-notch pilot, despite the way he casually deprecated his own abilities, and he'd achieved the atmosphere skip with ease. He'd done the math, checked it twice, entered the burn info into the guidance computer, and then leaned back into his Gemini couch and closed his eyes in apparent relaxation. Sandoval, by contrast, had spent the remaining minutes till the burn rechecking that math, first on the computer, then using a TI-30 scientific calculator, and a third time for luck on his aluminum Pickett N600-ES slide rule. Like most airmen, Sandoval had a healthy distrust of the new plasticky handheld calculators, which felt to him like they

246

came out of an oversized cereal box. And if anything, he trusted the fifteen-plus-year-old technology of the IBM Gemini guidance computers even less.

He'd still been muttering and scribbling numbers onto the checklist on his sleeve when the burn lit.

Down they'd gone, the atmosphere flaring into incandescence outside the tiny windows of the Gemini. Buffeted far more than he'd been on any of his previous reentries, and why? Because of the atmosphere skip? Sandoval had no idea. Minutes of terror, anyway, then a drenching relief when the drogues and main parachutes opened. A hard splash into the northern Pacific. Followed by a nauseous twelve-hour wait, bobbing in the wide ocean with their recovery lights lit, radio beacons pinging, and yellow dye staining the water around them. Until the *USS Kitty Hawk* hove into view at local noon. It was only after they'd been airlifted out by helicopter and their Gemini capsule winched aboard the aircraft carrier that Lin confessed he'd spent the minutes leading up to the deorbit burn praying rather than dozing.

The first thing they'd learned was that their fellow crew members, Pope and Rodriguez, were safe and being hauled out of the ocean by a different Navy cruiser a thousand miles away.

The second thing was that they were already manifested for launch on Apollo Rescue 1. They'd been in orbit for almost a month, would be on Earth barely long enough to recover, and then their next stop would be the Moon. It had been head-spinning. Sandoval had nearly refused, almost clammed up and declined the assignment, something he'd never done before.

But he'd trained for space military ops at huge public expense for all these years, and now it was time to pay the piper. It was go-time. And so he went.

And now he was on the Moon, and he hated it.

In Earth orbit he'd always had the capability to abort to ground in a matter of hours. Get safely back into atmosphere. The Earth was solid, pretty, and comfortingly close. But the Moon was an airless rock, pummeled regularly by other rocks, and right now he was *three freaking days* from home. That was damned daunting, and it was taking all Sandoval's wits just to look calm and confident, as if he knew what the hell he was doing.

The Moon could kill him in an instant—and it likely would.

He was exceptionally glad that Vivian was here and had apparently stepped up to be his bridge to the Hadley crew. Sandoval could be straight with her, with none of the tap dancing and posturing he had to do with Norton.

He could tell Vivian anything, if he needed to, and get an honest response.

If necessary, he might even be able to tell her how shit-scared he was of being here. Though maybe he shouldn't. Not yet.

He'd wait another day or so, see how it went.

"You're a manipulative bastard," Vivian said cheerfully, joining him once again in the suiting-up area.

"That's my job. In fact, that's how it's stated in my position description. Those exact words."

Unexpectedly, she sat down next to him. Leaned forward, elbows on knees. "So, Peter. I need to know some things, and you have to be straight with me. Is that possible?"

"Sure," he said. "Well, maybe. Depends what you ask."

"That stuff about women in combat. And not enforcing our evacuation."

"Yes?"

"Tell me that you didn't say that just to ensure I wouldn't be sent home."

Sandoval shook his head. "Why would I do that?"

"Oh, I dunno."

"Seems kind of big-headed of you to assume ..."

"Peter. Did you or did you not say that because of me?"

Sandoval met her eye. "No, ma'am. I said it because it's a stupid order, and I don't need to enforce stupid orders when I'm a quarter million miles from Cheyenne. Why create a goddamn problem where none needs to exist?"

She stared at him for a moment. "Okay."

"Okay. What else?"

She hesitated. "Well, let me ask you this. If there happened to be ... y'know, alcohol on this base, would you feel duty bound to report it? I mean, hypothetically."

Sandoval considered. "Beyond my jurisdiction. I see no reason why I'd feel required to. Hypothetically."

"Stand by." Vivian produced a plastic bottle, poured them both an ounce of hooch, and topped it up with orange juice. Handed it to him. "I cannot guarantee that it is palatable. It is, however, not actively carcinogenic."

"Understood." He sipped it. "Wow. That's truly terrible. You're sure, about it not being carcinogenic?"

"Actually, no. But this is the Moon. Radiation. Vacuum. Soviets. Ethanol is the least of your worries."

"Sounds about right." Sandoval drained the glass.

"Whoa, Tiger." She refilled him. "Job stress much?"

"With your intuition, you'd make a terrific spy." He looked at her sideways. "Who's manipulating whom here?"

"Cannot reveal."

"Can't help noticing that Norton leaves us alone together a lot."

"Yeah. He seems happy enough for me to, shall we say, liaise with the USAF."

Well, I'm happy too. "Whatever works."

She stared at him in that intense Vivian way. "Okay, next question. All that time I thought you were a rookie Air Force ascan, you were already this hotshot superhero tough guy?"

To his surprise, embarrassment flooded him. "I wasn't bitten by a radioactive spider or anything."

"You're sure? Or does your story change again next week?"

"Ouch, lady."

"And all that stuff about your wife. Was it true? Or were you just playing mind games with me?"

That hit home. "What?"

"No, really, Colonel Sandoval. How much of that was on the level, and how much was you working me for, I don't know, psych ops practice?"

Sandoval's fists clenched. Vivian glanced down, looked back up at his face. "But seriously, Peter. How does that make you feel?"

All at once Sandoval felt angry, ashamed, and vulnerable. He bowed his head. "I lied about nothing. My ex-wife …. There was no game, no playacting. I was grateful to you for your friendship, and your advice. It helped me navigate what was a pretty terrible time. And if you don't believe that? You can go to hell."

Vivian raised her eyebrows. "Wow. No more booze for you."

He didn't apologize. Just waited.

Eventually, she nodded. "Okay."

Now he could say it. "Sorry. But … that was real, Vivian."

"All right." She looked around her at the Hab, and shook her head. "This is all kind of crazy. This Moon situation."

"Yes, it is." That came out more heartfelt than Sandoval had intended, and he could tell she'd noticed.

"Not quite how I was planning to spend the holiday season, if you see what I mean."

Sandoval wanted more hooch, but that would be a bad idea. He still had to get back into his suit and return-hike across a bleak landscape in vacuum. And he hardly needed to reek of booze in the cramped confines of the Bunker, with his people close by.

He turned his glass upside down to make that clear. Got to his feet and started arranging his suit. "So, how about we talk about something normal and not messed up, while I'm getting ready for the great outdoors?"

"Sure," Vivian said.

"Good." Sandoval waved his hands, a little helplessly. "So, how've you been?"

Carter

"I don't like it, and I don't want them here."

Five of them were left in the upper area of Hab A: Norton and Buchanan, Vivian and Ellis and Starman. Buchanan glanced up. "God's sake, Rick, sit down. You're wearing a trench in the floor."

Norton frowned, but stopped pacing and leaned against the wall instead.

"He seems legit to me," Starman was at the window, staring across the lunar surface and occasionally doodling on a yellow pad. "Just doing what he has to."

"He wouldn't have been ordered to bring his squad all the way here if there wasn't a credible threat," Buchanan pointed out. "One that we can't handle alone. So maybe we should be happy they showed up. Once the threat goes away, they'll be extracted back to Earth."

"Will they?"

"I don't think he wants to be here himself," Starman said. "I'm thinking our Colonel Sandoval would rather be anywhere but on the Moon."

Norton glanced at Vivian. "Not so sure about that."

"Oh, hush," she said.

"How about we concentrate on the credible threat?" Ellis was sitting on the edge of a bunk, looking like he'd prefer to be lying in it with the blankets over his head.

"Let *them* do that. That's why they're here."

"Ellis is right." Buchanan stretched. "If the Reds are coming back in greater force, how do we help Night Corps prepare? What can we do that they can't?"

"Just about everything," said Norton.

"Hey." Starman beckoned from the window. "You have to see this."

Vivian made it to his side first, and peered out. "Huh. It's growing."

The Bunker was lengthening, telescoping outward on both ends. It was already half again as large as it had originally been, and was still expanding.

Several Night Corps astronauts were standing on-surface around it as it grew, watching carefully. One hauled a rock away before the out-moving wall could scrape into it.

Those astronauts, too, were startling. Sandoval had arrived in Hab A in a standard Apollo moon suit, but the Night Corps astros clustered around the Bunker wore much darker and bulkier suits. The NASA astronauts wore their PLSS life support backpacks out in the open. Those of Night Corps were concealed inside a black protective carapace. And, from the more purposeful, less bouncy way that Sandoval's people walked, their suits were clearly heavier than the Apollo suits. "Wild."

"Pretty cunning," said Starman.

Once the Bunker stopped swelling, it was fully twice as long as it had been previously. And now, its midsection began to bulge outward.

"That part's inflating," Buchanan said. "An inflatable Hab?"

"I guess that's how they make room in there for thirteen people."

Starman held up what he'd been sketching. A rough schematic of how the inside of the Bunker might look. Math in the left margin, figuring out masses and volumes. A neat list on the right of likely volumes for consumables, fuel, weaponry. "I'll bet they couldn't hardly move in there before. If they're carrying all the supplies and gear they need for a long occupation, there can't be much space left over. I'm betting they were stacked like cordwood for the flight here. Only room for one, maybe two of them to move around at any one time."

"Tighter than a Command Module?"

"Absolutely."

"God." Vivian winced. "Hideous."

The expandable part of the Bunker was quickly inflated. Overall, the Bunker was now the shape of a truncated T, with the metal cylinder forty feet long forming the crosspiece and the inflated portion jutting twenty feet out of its side.

"Clever." Starman smiled. "NASA should have thought of that."

"We did," Norton said, with some irritation. "We have the mini-Habs for emergency use. But they provide almost no protection against micrometeors or radiation."

"They'll mitigate that, for sure," Buchanan said. "They're likely already bracing and strengthening the inner walls."

Nothing ever seemed to surprise Buchanan. Vivian studied him again, wondering how much of what he said was guesswork, and how much he'd already been aware of.

The Soviets had obviously been planning their military action against the US for some time. It was now equally obvious that the US hadn't quite been caught on the hop, either. That Bunker hadn't been thrown together in a couple of weeks.

She looked uncertainly at Buchanan. "You know—"

Sandoval's voice overrode her, crackling out of the loudspeaker with startling volume. "Hadley Base, this is the Doc."

Norton swiveled quickly and pushed-to-talk. "Hey, Sawbones. Norton here."

"Informational: we're getting another supply drop in an hour."

"What? I have people out on-surface."

"Yeah, same. I only just found out about it myself. Be advised that the new payload will be making moonfall just twenty meters from, uh, sickbay."

That was astonishingly close. Habitats A and B were two hundred feet apart, and even that seemed uncomfortably nearby to Vivian. "Sawbones, Carter. *Twenty?*"

"Affirmative." From his tone, Vivian could tell Sandoval wasn't happy. "Accuracy should be nominal, but there's obviously a cratering and debris risk, so I need your folks under cover immediately. Make it happen."

Norton lifted his hand off the Comms button. "Cratering risk? Your boyfriend is going to be the death of us."

"Not my boyfriend. How many times?"

The radio crackled. "Hadley, you copy?"

Norton pressed the button again. "Copy, Doc. We're on it."

The "new payload" hit the ground even harder than Rescue 1. Binders toppled off shelves, and once the ground stopped juddering, Vivian found she'd been holding her breath.

Night Corps started unpacking it immediately, and to their surprise, Sandoval invited Norton and two others of his choice to come and take a look. Norton chose Starman and Vivian.

This container was larger than the standard Hadley supply drop. And it turned out that the biggest item it contained was a MOLAB, which was a vehicle the Hadley astros had all seen on paper as a design concept proposed after Apollo 11 but that none of them knew had actually been built by the military in the years since.

The MOLAB—Mobile Laboratory—was a twenty-foot-long silver barrel. Its chassis was articulated, with six-foot-high wheels on flexible axles, so the beast could negotiate obstacles with more proficiency than the rovers. The rocket launchers arrayed on its roof, plus the antenna and periscope, raised its total height to twenty-five feet above the lunar landscape.

Its cabin was pressurized. Just days before, Vivian might have scoped it out as a three-person vehicle, except that somehow Night Corps had crammed thirteen people into the Bunker. If the MOLAB had flat couches stacked one upon another with precious little clearance between them, might they get five people into it? Maybe.

Behind the MOLAB was its trailer, on which were stacked three cylinders for essential supplies they couldn't fit into the main vehicle. Neatly packed in and around these vehicles had been boxes, air cylinders, and other standard-looking supplies, that the anonymous worker bees of Night Corps were now carrying off to the Bunker.

"Can't believe you guys brought a fricking *tank*," said Jones.

Starman obviously saw strength in the MOLAB. Vivian wasn't so sure. "It's no tank."

Norton had been uncharacteristically silent. Now he said: "Looks pretty solid to me."

Was that jealousy in his voice? Maybe that wouldn't be surprising. A MOLAB would have been damned useful to the Hadley astros over the past year.

She looked at Sandoval. "It weighs, what, eight thousand pounds?"

He just grinned.

"Fine." Vivian talked to Starman instead. "Look how its wheels rest on the regolith. It's heavy, but not crazy heavy. Must still be aluminum, probably twenty-two nineteen." Aluminum 2219 was an alloy with around 6 percent copper for strength, extensively used in NASA spacecraft, and Vivian didn't know of a tougher or lighter material for such a purpose. "So, let's assume that its life support and other auxiliary stuff weighs around the same as a LM's. It doesn't have a rocket motor or tons of propellant. But there must be all kinds of weaponry inside that add to its load."

She could see Starman working the logic. "Sure, okay. So it looks a bit tanklike, but it can't really be armored or it would be prohibitively heavy, and sink in more."

"Battle tanks on Earth are, what, twenty tons? More? Help me out, I'm Navy."

"Anywhere between twenty and fifty tons. Lot of steel in a tank. Whereas this MOLAB is, well, maybe four or five tons."

"Fifty tons?" Vivian whistled. "Wow. Tanks are awesome."

Norton joined in. "And the cabling to the trailer is obviously a weak point in battle."

For a moment Sandoval looked as if he were about to say nothing—again—but they'd finally gotten to him. "Okay, fine. This wasn't designed as a *tank*. No one was anticipating a full-up lunar ground assault." He gestured upward. "Those launchers were still being jury-rigged even while we were prepping for launch. But it might still be a useful asset in a ground action."

"Better stay suited up inside it in a conflict situation," Norton said. "It might breach real easy."

"Hope it survives," Starman said. "Because it would be nice to have around."

"No kidding," said Norton.

Yup. That was resentment. Norton is pissed off.

"Who built it?" Vivian demanded. "Northrop, Bendix? General Motors? Geez, come *on*. We all have clearances, and we're looking right *at* the damned thing."

Sandoval gave in. "GM."

"Operating range?"

"Depends on crew and loading. Maybe something like four hundred kilometers total."

"God *damn*," she said.

All the hard work she and Ellis had put in planning an overnight excursion to the limits of Palus, and this frigging Air Force truck rendered their efforts obsolete at a stroke. Or it would if they'd ever get permission to use it.

Which they probably wouldn't. But it was still maddening.

Maybe Sandoval realized that. "Y'all want to see inside?"

Vivian rocked back. "For real?"

Norton looked jaundiced. "You won't show us inside the Bunker. Why is this different?"

"Because we might need your help with it. And once this is all over, we clearly won't be shipping it home. It stays here with you."

"Oh, cool," said Starman.

Vivian considered. "If you show us, do you have to kill us?"

"Yes, of course," Sandoval said.

"Then sure, let's take a look."

There were five bunks, or spaces for them. Although the "bunks" were just shelves six feet long and two feet deep. Lying on her back in one of these, the base of the bunk above would be about a foot above Vivian's nose.

There was a small head in a closet, the most confined toilet compartment Vivian had ever seen. Could someone as big as Sandoval even close the door? No shower. Lots of metal racks for food trays. And hooks around the walls, presumably for rifles.

It was cramped, especially in suits; the MOLAB wasn't pressurized right now, and both airlock doors were open. The airlock itself would only take two people at a time, and was still one of the larger spaces in the vehicle. "Wouldn't want to spend a whole lot of time in here."

"Me neither," Sandoval said.

She looked at him. "You'd need to be really macho and rugged to enjoy it."

"Vivian. Stop."

"Sorry."

But maybe a whole lot better than one of the small emergency pup tents. Maybe time to quit tweaking Sandoval and play nice. "But hey, if war never comes? I want to take this out on a field trip. Maybe even for several days. You can swing that for me, right? I mean, you'd get useful field-test engineering data out of it and all. It'd be win-win."

Sandoval gave her a half-grin. "I'll take that under advisement."

"Please do so."

They exited, and Norton and Starman headed back toward Habitat A. Sandoval turned to look at Vivian. Even without even being able to see his expression, she knew it would be quizzical. "See? It's happened again. Just the two of us. What're the odds?"

"Pure happenstance. But we may as well make the most of it. Helmets?"

He paused, then clicked off his radio and leaned in, so that their helmets touched.

"Vivian to Spider-Man," she said. "You copy?"

"Cut that out." More of a buzz than a voice, but she could clearly understand him.

"That is some base you've got there, Colonel Sandoval."

"Why, thank you."

"I'm sure you just rigged that thing up in your backyard last Thursday. Good job, man."

He pushed up his visor, and after a moment, she did the same. "You can get sunburned this way, you know that?"

"Little secret," he said. "Though I think you can probably guess this by now. Night Corps was originally intended for anti-satellite work in Earth orbit, intercepting and messing up Soviet spy satellites, and potential assaults on the crewed Almaz stations. All zero-G, short-strike operations or other missions of opportunity. It's only over the last couple years they've been training to support lunar ops. And all that time I've been on MOL duty, in orbit or at Cheyenne."

She thought about it. "And the lunar ops prep started why? Did we perceive a surface threat from Zvezda Base? Or have we had intel about this kind of Soviet assault for much longer than I knew? Come on, it's just us chickens here, I won't tell another soul."

"That's what they all say. Including me." He twisted, looked over the lunar surface thoughtfully. "Assume you're thinking about this in the right way."

"So, all along, there was a threat that NASA didn't know about?"

"Did I say NASA didn't know?"

"Including some of our NASA guys, here?"

"I honestly haven't been briefed on what any particular Hadley astronaut knows, or doesn't."

"Jeez. You're hopeless."

He grinned. "I'm paid to be secretive."

"For a moment I thought you were going to say 'Just following orders, ma'am.'"

"Yes, well. Truth be told, I'm not so great at following orders. I tend to improvise too often. But that's strictly confidential."

She yawned. "Sure, Secret Agent Man. I need to get back. I'll be seein' ya."

"Goodnight, Vivian."

She didn't say Goodnight back. He hadn't earned that yet. "Sure. Thanks."

His eyes were still on her. All of a sudden, the touching-helmet thing felt weird. A bit too intimate.

"Welcome to the Moon, Colonel Sandoval," she said, and turned to walk back to Athena.

CHAPTER 25

Mount Hadley Delta: Vivian Carter/Peter Sandoval
January 6, 1980

Carter

This was why Vivian Carter had come to the Moon.

From five thousand feet up on the shoulder of Mount Hadley Delta, Vivian and Ellis Mayer looked north over the expanse of Hadley Plain. Their rover sat on the ejecta blanket near the uphill edge of St. George Crater, with its sloping bowl, a mile and a half across, between them and the plain below.

Hadley Rille swept north in front of her and curved to the right, disappearing to the northwest into yet another tall mountain ridge. The base looked tiny. Vivian could just about pick out the Habitats, the Bunker, and the long, low tanks of the fuel dump, but the dust-covered Lunar Modules were impossible to resolve. The entirety of the US occupation spread over a site a few hundred yards square. The whole embayment of Hadley Plain was 150 square miles of craters and boulders and hummocks and small valleys. From up here the base seemed an insignificant intrusion, dwarfed by the lunar scenery that surrounded it.

Behind Vivian, Mount Hadley Delta extended up another six thousand feet, but achieving the summit would be impossible; it was simply too steep, too far, the soil underfoot too loose and treacherous.

For all that Vivian had craved her original mission, it didn't have mountains like these. The Marius Hills were a series of lava domes in the middle of a basaltic ocean, and the tallest peak was less than two thousand feet high. But Marius had more volcanic features in one place than anywhere else on the Moon. Vivian and Ellis would likely have been making significant discoveries from the first moment they set foot outside their LM.

Sigh.

"Our friends are on their way back."

Ellis had his Hasselblad camera focused in the opposite direction, up the Delta. As he couldn't use binoculars with a helmet on, the camera's zoom lens was his only means of magnifying what he saw.

"Buzzkill," Vivian said.

"What?"

Their two Night Corps minders were coming back down. Moody and Jensen. The crew of Apollo 32 might be playing geologist, but piggybacking on that, Sandoval's soldiers had hiked farther up the mountain to set up a radar scanner and a remote-controlled camera. The added altitude might give them a few more precious moments of warning in the event of a Soviet attack.

They had to give me an operative called Moody, today of all days?

In reality, Vivian had nothing against their armed guards. They were unfailingly polite and professional. And as it happened, Jensen in particular was quite good looking. "Forget it. I just hate the Soviets, for making these guys necessary."

Vivian hadn't wanted their company. The Night Corps guys had remained unobtrusive—as they needed to be, with the Apollo 32 crew sending intermittent TV and radio transmissions to Earth—but Vivian would have preferred to be out here alone, just her and Ellis.

Also, Moody and Jensen had gotten higher up the mountain than she had. That rankled.

She tried to be happy again. After all, it was still a glorious view.

"All right. Nearly time to head on down. Loop around George and take a look-see across Bridge." Their eventual route across the rille to Palus Putredinis. But not today.

Vivian cast her eye over the rover, and the equal-sized trailer it was towing. They'd agreed to take that trailer everywhere, get used to hauling it around, and to the nonintuitive way it tugged the back end of the rover back and forth. Its bulk damped the rover's tendency to hop into the air when it went over bumps but also made the steering clunky and slow to respond. With the trailer, they accelerated more slowly, braked more gradually, but didn't skid any less often.

The trailer was loaded as it would be for an extended expedition. And since Vivian had just driven it up a freaking mountain, it would be harder for Norton to tell her she couldn't drive it across Bridge and onto Palus when the time came.

Even for a day trip, the additional supplies maximized their safety. Right here, they were perilously close to their walkback radius. If their sweet LRV ride crapped out, they might not be able to make it all the way back to Hadley on the oxygen in their backpacks. The trailer was hauling way more spare oxygen cylinders than they could possibly need, as well as a couple of the emergency pop-up tents that might save their lives if the need arose.

Whether the Night Corps guys could cram themselves into one of the pop-ups was … open to conjecture. Then again, it was a bit perplexing that their smaller rover could even carry the two of them.

She looked back up the mountain, to where their escorts were motoring down toward them. The armored spacesuits of Night Corps were darker in color, designed to fade into the background. Several times over the past days Vivian had looked straight past one of Sandoval's grunts, and only noticed him once he moved. And their visors were black, which was sinister and disconcerting. To compensate for all that heat-loving blackness, those suits must be threaded with a much higher-powered cooling system than the Apollo suits. Vivian doubted those visors could be cracked by a bullet or a rock. Maybe not even a core drill.

Wow. Time to think more positively. Vivian looked out west.

The Moon wasn't just black, white, and gray. At this time of day, with the Sun at a relatively pleasant thirty-degree angle, the surface showed an array of subtle coloration. The areas to Vivian's left and right, in side illumination, were certainly a darkish gray, dropping to the precipitous black of shadow. But in the backlit zone ahead of her the regolith appeared a subtle brown, and in the distance the hills shone golden. The terrain was still too stark, too broken up and brutal to ever be inviting, but right now it was a little less intimidating.

From the base, only the nearest reaches of the Marsh of Decay were visible. From up here, she could see a lot farther. Palus was a volcanic mare, darker in tone than the region around Hadley. On its far side were the giant craters of Archimedes and Autolycus. Archimedes was the largest crater on Mare Imbrium, over fifty miles across and a couple miles deep; Autolycus, to its east, was half the size, irregular, and probably younger. Vivian could see the rim of Archimedes, orderly and regular against the skyline, and the lumpy serrated splotch of Autolycus beside it.

Although Vivian couldn't pick it out, she was also looking toward the site of an even more recent impact. Near Autolycus lay Luna 2, the Soviet probe that had been the first Earth craft to crash-land on the Moon, in 1959. On landing it had scattered a bunch of steel pennants across the surface, emblazoned with the Soviet crest. Maybe they'd vaporized on impact and maybe not, but it would be a coup for US astronauts to reach that site and clean up the Soviets' mess.

You dumped your crap here, and now the US has come to tidy it up. Because we own this region now.

But the journey itself would be the main thing. Luna 2 was eighty-two miles from Hadley Base. It would be the farthest the Hadley astros had traveled overland, and it was in a completely different geological area of the Moon.

Vivian wanted to go there. Very badly.

Sandoval

The Bunker had a raised area at its southern end: a viewpoint with steel-reinforced windows looking in all directions, with a military-grade radar antenna atop it sweeping the horizon. This was Sandoval's nerve center, and it was cramped as all get-out inside, especially when Lin was in there too.

A missile launcher now sat in front of the Bunker. To the military eye of someone used to Earth-style artillery the structure looked skeletal, every ounce of excess metal removed or shaved down to save mass, and the missile was snub-nosed with open panels, as if they'd been removed for maintenance. It wasn't aerodynamic: with no air, it didn't need to be. It only needed to be strong enough to survive its own launch, and preserve its avionics and warhead till it hit its target. And that target had to be within visual distance, IR guidance not being worth beans on the Moon. Once fired, Sandoval would have to guide it by eye and joystick.

It still burned him that they hadn't been allowed to bring tactical nukes. Although they'd had no positive intel confirmation, Sandoval was 90 percent sure that the Soviets had had them at Zvezda all along. Even if they hadn't, he was 110 percent sure that the new Soviet force would be bringing some along.

Night Corps had brought plenty of weaponry, but it was all conventional. And fighting nuclear with conventional was literally bringing a knife to a gunfight.

So Sandoval sure hoped this didn't go nuclear, because if it did, it would be game over before they even knew it had begun.

Would the Soviets go so far? Unknown. But Sandoval probably wouldn't much care if they did, because he'd be right under the first nuke.

"Hold it. Damn. We've got to send them back up." Lin frowned at his console. "Turn Moody and Jensen around."

"Why?" Sandoval didn't wait for an answer, but keyed the comms. "Hadley Delta Force, hang tight while we run some checks."

Moody's voice came instantly, calm and precise. "Delta. Roger that."

"Delta Force? Cute," Lin said, pushing buttons.

Sandoval switched out of secure radio. "Hey, Vivian. Can you hang tight and grab a few more rock samples at the crater edge? We need, uh, better coverage. Geological. You know."

Vivian paused. "Sure thing."

She was going to hate this. Sandoval knew she wanted to scope out Bridge today. She was still keen to do her harebrained camping trip out west. Even weirder, Norton was keen for her to do it too. That was probably just orneriness, because Sandoval himself was totally against anyone traveling so far from Hadley.

"Talk to me, Lin."

"I'm seeing all kinds of scatter from the radar they just installed." Lin flipped more switches. "Seemed okay when they placed it, but now … this."

Sandoval leaned over to peer at Lin's displays. The green circular screen was a mess of blobs. "Jeez, that's not right. I don't know what could—"

"Shit. Break." Lin's voice had taken on a clipped urgency. "That's good data."

"Good how?"

"No malfunction."

Ice chilled Sandoval's neck. "Aw, come on."

"No kidding. It's not us, and it's not noise or interference."

"Confidence?"

"Ninety-five percent. Plus."

Then Sandoval's screen lit up too, from the radar right above their heads. "Oh."

If Sandoval could see them, they could see him. Whatever that crap was, it now had line of sight on Hadley.

Damn it.

He flipped the all-points Night Corps frequency switch, punched to talk. "Break, break. Listen up, everyone: we have incoming, likely major Soviet incursion. All teams to action stations, Priority One. Full mobilize, right now."

He lifted his fist off the Comms button as a chorus of terse Roger Wilco's came back.

"Better not be a false alarm." Sandoval looked again at his radar display, and Lin's, trying to figure it out. "Nine? Ten?"

"I confirm nine separate craft," said Lin. "Man, our lives are never dull."

"ETA?"

"A minute or less."

"Under a *minute?*" Sandoval shook his head. "God's sakes. Maybe you and I should have just landed our asses in Russia and been done with it."

"Should've told me that a few weeks back. I could have made it happen." Lin stood, carefully. There wasn't much headroom. "But Siberia is crazy cold right now. You've got this, yeah?"

"I have the comm. Deploy, Airman."

"Roger that." Lin jumped to it, literally springing through the hatch to the lower level.

Sandoval would rather have been in the field, but his job was here, at least for now. CC&C: Central Command and Control. Direct the troops. Who were all better trained for this than he was, anyways. Supposedly.

All the while, Sandoval's fingers were moving over switches. Now he scanned the three photographs tacked above his control panel to remind himself of the terrain of this makeshift battleground. Here was the territory they were supposed to defend. There were his Claymore mines, buried against exactly this type of incursion. Sandoval was sure all his people—and Norton's—knew where they were going and what they were doing.

He still wished he was out there with them.

Even though the Moon was terrifying.

He peered out of the window. His troops were on the move, fanning out in their sky-dark armor. They stopped on cue a little short of the mines that they'd previously buried. Where the backup ordnance could, well, back them up.

Sandoval was proud of them: their training, and their abilities. They were tigers, surging forward with muscle and guile against the Soviet threat. Well trained and excellent in every way. God help the forces of Communism against soldiers like these.

Many of the Hadley astros would be out there too, in the same configuration as last time, aside from Vivian and Ellis, naturally. Those duffers with their ridiculous homemade mortar would be manning it in the same place as before, until they blew their stupid selves up. A pair of NASA astronauts would be outside each Habitat with their air cannons, which for some reason they were calling "drainpipe cannons." But Sandoval had drawn the line at having their semi-armored rovers careering around the battlefield. Norton's rovers, along with Sandoval's MOLAB, were ready but holding off, the final defense resort. Today, Night Corps would form the front line.

All of his people had guns. Guns surprisingly similar to their earthly counterparts, simply because they hadn't designed anything better. Bullets could be fired in short bursts, and even a short burst from an automatic weapon might take out a cosmonaut. A concentrated burst into a helmet or chest control panel could yield fatal results.

But the weapons needed to be carefully managed with respect to temperature. The guns his Night Corps operatives were toting had broad covers mounted on top to keep the Sun's heat off the firing mechanisms and magazine clips. This then risked the weapons getting too cold, so they also—paradoxically—had a battery-powered heating coil mounted into them. In addition, the trigger guards were extended to allow access to a glove-broadened finger.

Frankly, Sandoval thought the vacuum-modified automatic weapons were a stretch too far, but they were the type of guns military men were trained to use.

They also had mortars and rocket launchers, of course.

His troops were now arriving at their stations along the ragged line where they'd set the shields up beforehand, and were pulling them up into place, a series of small turrets set across the lunar terrain. The Moon came complete with prepackaged foxholes; the turrets were all set against crater rims. And there were more turrets than members of Night Corps, so they could advance from cover to cover, or retreat as necessary.

Naturally, the far side of all those turrets were set with explosive charges, their remote detonators at Sandoval's command, to prevent the enemy from taking advantage of them in the opposite direction.

Sandoval scanned his IR display. The Night Corps suits were designed to be thermal neutral, and it was working: they barely showed up against the rest of the sizzling hot lunar surface. His people were impossible for heat-seeking missiles to locate. The attacking cosmonauts would need to do this the old-fashioned way—by aiming. And as all Night Corps members knew, aiming and firing a weapon in a bulky spacesuit was even harder than it looked.

Comms were quiet now. That, too, that was intentional. His people knew what they were doing. Excessive encrypted radio chatter would tip off the Soviets. The whole idea was to lure the bastards in, make them think Hadley was still easy prey.

Come on in, Ivan. Come and play.

Sandoval scanned the high radar sweeps from Hadley Delta. The optical camera up there wasn't helping worth a damn, but the radar was unambiguous. The blobs had split into two strike forces. One had landed a mile north just minutes ago, while the other was still in the air, either heading straight for Hadley or intending to land beyond and subject them to a crossfire.

Either way, Night Corps was ready.

Sandoval keyed the button to initialize the launch sequence for the rocket sitting right outside his window and watched the green telltales light up on his console.

He almost felt sorry for the Reds. Because Night Corps was going to utterly kick their asses.

Meanwhile .... He pushed-to-talk. "Delta team, Hadley here. You're go to continue your nominal mission profile with all due caution, copy?"

"Copy that, Hadley," came Vivian's prompt reply.

She and Ellis didn't have time to make it back here. Best to send them—plus their Night Corps minders—off on their merry way, down the other side of the mountain. That way, Vivian would be far away from Hadley Base. Far from the coming danger.

So that was good, at least.

Then Sandoval looked again at his display.

Oh, shit.

CHAPTER 26

Mount Hadley Delta: Vivian Carter
January 6, 1980

VIVIAN putzed around at the crater's edge, doing nothing, and wondering what the hell was going on. Ellis, calm as always, was using the time to brush dust off the rover fenders and tighten straps to ensure that the rock bags were fastened securely.

Her radio crackled. "Delta team, Hadley here. You're go to continue your nominal mission profile with all due caution, copy?"

She felt a cold chill sweep up her spine. *Caution?* "Copy that, Hadley."

Vivian turned and looked up the mountain, and sure as hell, the Night Corps guys were now sprinting down the mountain.

Ellis was miming at her, drawing a gloved finger across the bottom of his helmet where his neck would be. *Okay, I get it, smart guy. No more unencrypted radio traffic.*

Jensen skidded to a halt beside her, gestured. She toggled her radio off, leaned in to touch helmets, heard his buzzing voice as he shouted: "Bad medicine! They're coming. Right now."

Obviously, Sawbones could be more candid with his own people on secure radio. Vivian looked up, down, and all around. "How long?"

"Imminent. Minutes at most."

Vivian shook her head. "From where? I see nothing."

"Some are already down, north of Hadley. Others still in flight. Two of them heading here."

267

"For *us?*"

"That's a roger."

Mayer's arm was up and pointing at a thirty-degree angle, due west. A moment later Vivian saw it too, glinting in the sunlight, and right after that the craft fired its engine to decelerate.

"Crap."

"Run for Hadley. Get going. We'll cover you." Breaking contact, Jensen pulled his projectile launcher up onto his shoulder and dropped to one knee. Thirty feet away, Moody had set up the recoilless rifle in its tripod and was dropping prone behind it.

The bulbous craft slewed in, strange and yet oddly familiar. Like a Soyuz, but with the splayed legs of landing gear, and flying almost horizontally right at Vivian. Spitting flame.

Moody fired. Silent tracer shot across the sky.

A huge upheaval, like a volcanic eruption. A flash, static in Vivian's ears, rock lifted into the air and thrown everywhere at once. And a new crater appeared where Moody had been.

"Holy shit!" Radio silence hardly mattered any more.

The Soviet craft shot past them. A line of explosions perforated the ground behind them, and their second Night Corps bodyguard perished in a spatter of fragments and upflung soil.

Both gone, just like that.

No, no, no … "Ellis, down!"

He just stood there, stunned. But no more fire came, no new explosions, no more quick deaths.

What the hell is even happening?

The Soviet LEK Lander curved around, swinging vertical and firing jets to land a half-mile north of them on the slope. Meaning, between them and Hadley Base.

"Let's go." Mayer calmly stepped up onto the passenger seat of the Lunar Rover.

Vivian was still running downslope. Ten feet shy, she jumped. Lunar gravity carried her in a gentle arc. She hit the driver's seat with both boots, absorbed the shock, fell forward. Grabbed and swung and sat. Flipped the switches on circuit breakers, drive, and steering power.

Even as she did so, the Soviet lander downslope from them sprouted an odd wing. At the same time a hatch opened in its midsection and armed cosmonauts clambered out of it.

The wing was an extension, with two dirt bikes suspended beneath it.

"Oh, man," Ellis said.

Vivian shoved the T-handle forward and the rover almost leaped into the air as it accelerated. They were on a 15 percent downhill grade, after all.

"Jesus, Vivian." Ellis reeled. His butt left the seat and he grabbed her arm to stabilize himself.

"Hang on."

"Uh, roger that?"

The rover spat soil and dust from all four wheels, slaloming down Hadley Delta. Vivian wrestled the T-handle, struggling to keep control. They bumped and slid, barely avoiding the lip of St. George Crater.

"Don't screw up," Ellis's voice dripped with tension.

"Okay. Thanks."

Two cosmonauts had already unlinked their bikes from the frame of the LEK and were glancing up the hill toward them. Their suits rendered them impersonal, their movements almost robotic.

"We're going around them, not through them, right?"

"That's the plan." But it was nowhere near that simple. The LEK had come to ground in the direct line Vivian would otherwise have taken—the damned thing had practically landed astride the tire tracks from her upward traverse. To get around the Soviets, Vivian would need to head down onto a thirty-degree slope, perilously steep, on loose ground, with gravel spattering around them. It would be a miracle if they kept traction.

But their alternatives weren't any better. To her left was a steep drop. To her right … well, Soviets.

"Ohhh." Ellis fit a wealth of emotion into a single syllable.

The third Soviet cosmonaut had reappeared, stepping away from his craft.

Carrying a rocket launcher.

Obviously.

"Aw, crap." Vivian grunted in frustration.

The Soviet fired, the muzzle flash winking. The fierce meteor of the rocket leaped the distance between him and the Apollo team, exploding silently just twenty feet below them on the slope.

Even as she glimpsed the missile's impact, Vivian was blinded by the dust spray. Rocks rattled off her helmet and pummeled her suit.

She yanked back at the T-handle to brake and felt the rover and its trailer go into a long, vertiginous skid, a slide that showed no signs of arresting itself. "Ellis?"

She'd reached forward to grab at the console, to anchor herself. Now she leaned right, and her shoulder bumped his. "Yep," Ellis said belatedly. "Still here."

Slowly, agonizingly, the rover ground to a halt. The dust cleared. Vivian took stock, then shoved the T-handle forward and to the right and took off. Almost literally.

"Vivian, shit …"

The Soviet dirt bikes were rolling steadily uphill, steering rightward to block them. Vivian slewed the rover left, taking them down an even steeper grade strewn with boulders.

"Not Hadley then," he said.

"Can't make it. Gotta run."

"Shit …"

"Ellis. Call the Soviets for me. Range and rate." She swerved around a giant rock, still heading down. *Probably can't brake at this speed, not till I level out. And I don't level out for a good three hundred yards.*

Immediately, Ellis fell into support mode. "Both bikes turning to follow. Nearest is a hundred fifty yards, on our four. Heading downhill parallel to our course. Will probably try to head us off at the pass."

He meant Bridge Crater, the shallow feature a couple thousand feet across with its substantial swath of ejecta that provided a straightforward—if bumpy—path across Hadley Rille. Vivian's goal had been clear without her needing to explain it. She'd been heading for that dodgy overpass, intending to bounce across it and onto Palus Putredinis.

It wasn't a great strategy. Once they got onto the relatively level ground of Palus, the bikes could probably catch up to the rover. But on the downhill the rover had the advantage of mass and stability, relatively speaking, and surely had a greater range. If Vivian could build up enough of a lead on this giant slope and then across the erratic terrain of Bridge, the Soviets might not have the time and energy to maintain pursuit.

"Rock," Ellis said. "Rock? … Vivian! Big rock!"

"Yeah!" Vivian had obviously seen it, the damned boulder must be fifteen feet high, but the rover had developed a mind of its own and she was struggling for control. In the nick of time she regained traction and managed to steer leftward.

She almost made it, almost skated past the boulder Ellis had been indicating, but clipped it a glancing blow with her front right wheel. "God's *sake!*"

But they kept on rolling. Bouncing around like this Vivian could barely tell what was what. It looked like the wheel was okay, but if she'd damaged the axle, or even the chassis, the whole rover might collapse to a halt at any moment.

But, hey: so far, so good.

"Pilot. Soviets?"

"We've outpaced the two. But, oh, another LEK is flying in from the west, nine o'clock high."

"Oh, come *on.*"

"Yup."

Vivian saw the new LEK now, angling in from the west. It was going to land on the far side of the rille, just where they were headed. "Hey, radio the Russians and tell 'em we're not that interesting, could you?"

"On it."

The angle of the slope eased up, and Vivian managed to slow the rover's frenetic pace. She was *really* lucky that she hadn't wrecked them yet. Bridge was coming up, but now that she was closer she could see that it was so rocky and broken up that she'd be lucky if she could thread the needle across it at even ten miles per hour.

"Dirt bikes? Call them." She couldn't see them in her peripheral vision, and didn't dare turn her head for even an instant.

"One out front. May take a couple minutes for him to converge on us."

Minutes? "Okay, terrific. Get out."

"Huh?"

Vivian braked, gestured with her free hand. "Out. Off. Scoot. Head down to the left of Bridge, where it turns to scree. Get into shade. I'll keep going. No point in the bastards getting both of us."

"No way, Vivian."

"That's an order, Pilot."

Ellis reached around behind himself for the catapult, the only weapon they were carrying. "Fine. Maybe I can work my way around and get the jump on them. Element of surprise."

"Just hide. Take cover."

"Yep, right, *that's* happening. I'm not leaving you."

"Yeah, you are." Vivian skidded to a halt. "Go! Go!"

Ellis obeyed instantly, leaping off the right side of the rover while it was still moving, and falling forward onto his knees. He hopped back up and loped away.

Vivian immediately put him out of her mind and steered onto the broad rampart of Bridge Crater.

Jesus.

The rille was seven hundred feet deep to Vivian's left, and three-quarters of a mile across. Bridge Crater was less than half a mile wide to her right, but deep, and situated more or less in the rille center. Its raised rim formed the ridge that she was now committed to driving across. A ridge more craggy and undulating than she could have guessed.

Damn it to hell.

Here came a bike, a cosmonaut straddling it with his legs stretched out diagonally on either side, like before. But this bike had a sidecar, with another cosmonaut in it, and that passenger was toting an RPG-7.

This bike must be from the second LEK. Vivian had never even seen it land. Yeah, the sidecar probably did help with stability …

Cut off at the pass. Just like Ellis said.

The other bikes were falling behind. If it had been only the first LEK, Vivian might have gotten away—

The ground in front of her erupted, flinging the rover in a long slew to the right and pelting Vivian with rocks again. God, how much of this could her suit and helmet stand?

So, her plan to go across Bridge was a nonstarter. *Screw it.*

Vivian went *into* Bridge instead. A right turn took her straight down the side into the crater, bumping and careering, the trailer fishtailing behind her. She was driving into a huge steep-sided bowl, and as its rim came up around her, she felt the overwhelming fear of being trapped. Losing her horizon was a terrible thing. *If I die here, will anyone ever find my body?*

The bike-and-sidecar combo was coming on, but more slowly, picking its way down. Vivian was opening up a lead, but the only way she had to go was down into the crater and then up the other side, and to stay in sunlight she'd have to describe a broad arc to the east.

Another grenade. Another silent explosion close by on her front right. Again, Vivian was strafed and pummeled by rocks and gravel. This one brought her to a complete halt. Her helmet was scuffed and bashed, her arms in particular had taken the brunt of the flying regolith, and she was sweating profusely, her life support system incapable of keeping up with her exertion.

Well, Vivian thought, *we know the remedy for that, don't we?*

The cosmonauts were still incoming, only a couple hundred feet behind her.

Vivian leaned on the T-handle, and drove the rover into shadow.

Suddenly she was in almost pitch darkness. She could see nothing ahead of her, but kept the handle forward, trusting to fate. The lights and gauges on her chest were spattered with dust by now and looking especially dim. Unless it was just the delay before her pupils dark-adapted. Anyway, she didn't have a switch to turn them off, so—

The rover slammed into something, probably a rock on her left quarter. Even at fifteen miles an hour the impact was enough to send her sprawling sideways across the passenger seat that Ellis had so recently vacated. She recovered herself, reached again for the rover controls, and powered it off. The console lights died.

The region of shadow she was occupying was roughly semicircular and a thousand feet across. Beyond it, in the blinding Sun, Vivian could see the Soviet bike and sidecar tracking slowly around it.

Of course, "tracking" was exactly what they were doing: following her tracks to the point where she'd passed into blackness, so they'd have the angle right for their own entry. To stalk her into the night.

The sidecar passenger turned on a flashlight, and its beam arced across the darkness like a laser. Vivian jumped off the rover, watching the light streak across the surface, illuminating rocks and rubble.

Vivian eluded it, swerving left in broad lopes. She covered maybe a hundred feet before she tripped on a rock and took flight on her own small trajectory, powerless to stop herself.

She hit. Landed on her arms and rolled. Struggled up onto her feet again.

The flashlight beam was crisscrossing the crater, and a second beam was now jutting down from her right. One of the bikes from the first Soviet lander had caught up.

Vivian's only forlorn hope had been to find a boulder large enough to hide behind and hope that the task of flushing her out of this pool of blackness would be too great for her pursuers, that they'd run out of time. That ... didn't pan out. Vivian did see light skitter across a tall, broken rock that might have sufficed, but as she ran that way the second beam pinned her.

She ducked and weaved, used its glare to guide her on, again broke into a loping sprint. But it was surely hopeless now.

Vivian didn't even see the cosmonaut who wiped her out. He'd come in on foot to apprehend her, and the first she knew of his presence was his mass slamming into her from behind. She crashed down disastrously, shouting in rage and knowing that no one could hear her. She was encratered, with no US assets in her radio line of sight.

Her assailant grabbed her and flipped her over. Vivian and the suit together were close to two hundred pounds on Earth but less than forty pounds here, and the Soviet had no difficulty turning her onto her back.

Next came a blinding dazzle as the cosmonaut shined his flashlight directly into her helmet, followed by dramatic swaths of blackness crisscrossing her vision. Vivian raised her free glove to wipe at them but the cosmonaut rocked forward and fell onto her, his knees pinning her arm and shoulder. "Get off me!" she heard herself scream with a breadth of anger and fear, and then blackness descended again, the blackness of obscurity as the cosmonaut efficiently completed the job of coating Vivian's faceplate with paint.

Blinding her. Leaving her helpless, trapped, and alone in utter darkness.

PART THREE: ZVEZDA BASE

January 6–30, 1980

CHAPTER 27

Zvezda Base: Vivian Carter
January 6, 1980

VIVIAN expected death—a kill shot through the helmet, or maybe a grenade—but the next thing she knew, her arms had been bound to her sides and her legs roped together, and she was being lifted off the surface. She could tell when they moved her into sunlight from the rise in heat in her suit, but all she saw was blackness. The constriction and helplessness were terrifying.

"Hadley Base, Vivian Carter. Captured by Soviets. Look for Ellis Mayer, still out there. Hadley, Vivian. Mayday, this is Vivian Carter in Bridge Crater. Soviets have taken me prisoner. Norton? Doc?"

She heard nothing, but she felt it when her captors broke the VHF aerial off her backpack. After that she fell silent. No point in saying anything more.

Now she was bumping painfully across the lunar surface. Her best bet was that they'd rested her suit across the dirt bike and sidecar, her feet higher than her head, and driven off. She began to slide, but someone grabbed her and kept her anchored.

It went on for a long time. Strange, to be both terrified and bored.

Vivian couldn't communicate with her captors. She could shout and scream, but only she would hear it.

The journey eventually ended, and they lifted her off the bike and laid her on the ground. "What the hell's going on?" she asked, just to hear herself speak. Her throat was dry. She sipped water from the straw inside her helmet. She'd probably lost about a gallon of sweat and electrolytes.

After another interminable pause she felt herself tilted upright, lifted and bumped, then laid down again. *I hate these bastards. I hate them so much.*

A long delay followed.

Liftoff: a shuddering, followed by a rumble that resonated through her suit. A force that tugged her down, unambiguously the acceleration of a launch. A purposeful shaking back and forth, and then a steady tilt as the craft leaned onto its side.

They'd loaded Vivian into a Soviet LEK and now she was rocketing into space, still entombed in her suit. They'd cut her out of it eventually. Wouldn't they?

She breathed deep. *They haven't killed me. They're taking me somewhere. They need me alive. I guess.*

Alive. God, Vivian wanted so very much to live.

All the time she'd been on the Moon, she'd obsessed over details. Forgetting the basics, that she was *alive*, and wanted to stay that way.

What did the Soviets want with her? Would they just eject her off-world, fly her to captivity on Earth? Or to be another hostage, back on Columbia?

Vivian didn't want to be a hostage. A bargaining chip, again. It would be mortifying.

Her heart rate rose, and her breathing quickened. Being constrained in her suit in darkness was getting to her. Sinister thoughts crowded her mind: what if they never let her out? She'd stifle and die in here. Her head told her that the Soviets would hardly go to all this trouble just to let her suffocate—but her fear centers were working overtime.

The LEK leaned back in the other direction, swinging Vivian head down. They hadn't gone into free fall—even trapped in her suit, she'd have known. The implication was clear. After arcing upward, they were angling down again. Not heading for orbit, but back to the surface.

They were taking her to Zvezda Base.

Oh, great.

Vivian shook her head, flexed her arms and legs to keep her blood flowing. Her shoulder felt raw, as if she'd only today been hit by bullets from an assault rifle. Surely an association of ideas, inflamed by the damage she'd suffered fleeing down Hadley Delta into Bridge Crater.

The vibrating thunder as an engine fired. The LEK was decelerating. They would land soon.

Vivian had never felt so alone.

The braking burn seemed long and harsh, which meant the LEK was dangerously close to the surface. *The Soviets take big risks. Wouldn't it be funny if they killed me just getting me back down?*

Yeah. Hilarious.

Landing was a slam, rather than a kiss. A gut-punching impact. Vivian might have braced if she'd known it was coming, and wasn't lying supine.

More jolts and bumps. And then silence.

Had they abandoned her in the LEK? Vivian closed her eyes, breathed long and slow. Thought about Ellis, Dave, and her Hadley base mates. Listed each in turn, wondering whether they'd lived or died.

She experimented. Her legs were still bound together, her arms by her sides. Could she loosen her bonds? Probably not, but she had nothing better to do. Though even if she got her arms free she wouldn't be able to take off her helmet, which she'd need to do in order to see anything. From how the suit felt around her body, she knew she'd been left in vacuum.

Anyway, she got nowhere. No signs of her bonds loosening.

After an interminable length of time there was another bump and sway, and then Vivian was lifted unceremoniously, turned upright and marched forward. She could feel the bouncing tread of the two men who carried her.

Okay, off we go. Following the yellow brick road to Zvezda-Town.

Whatever the hell *that* would mean for her.

They'd carried Vivian inside and lain her down. She was in a pressurized environment now, because her suit joints and outer shell were much less stiff. Someone snapped open the fasteners at her wrists and slid her gloves off. The air around her hands was cool, and Vivian flexed her fingers and rubbed them together to dry the sweat. No one stopped her.

Hands fumbled with the clamps that held her helmet on. Vivian raised her head as it was lifted clear, and there was Svetlana Belyakova.

Vivian recognized her immediately. The faces of the first cosmonauts on the Moon had been plastered across American newspapers in 1969 as part of the national, extended shock, even worse than that caused by Sputnik and Gagarin. Leonov, Makarov, and especially Belyakova—because she was a woman, and a striking one: Vivian would recognize them anywhere.

They stared at each other. Svetlana's blond hair wafted around her almost ethereally in the one-sixth gravity and the breath of the portable fan purring across the room. Vivian's hair was plastered down with sweat and her eyes watered in the sudden brightness.

Vivian broke Svetlana's gaze to glance around. The room resembled a janitorial closet in a school basement; small and square with open metal pipes and umbilicals threading the walls. Except that the walls were of metal rather than concrete, and the ceiling seemed implausibly low.

She was apparently lying on a table, alone with Belyakova.

"*Dobryy den'*, Major-General," Vivian said.

"Good afternoon, Captain."

"May I sit up?"

"Of course." Belyakova stood back.

It was hard for Vivian to push herself upright from a supine position in a spacesuit. She had to roll onto her side and lever herself up.

Belyakova half smiled. "I would have helped, had you asked."

Vivian considered smiling back, to attempt a rapport. But the last time she'd heard this woman's voice, Belyakova had been insisting that Columbia Station surrender or be destroyed. And now Vivian was her captive. "I demand you release me immediately, or at least put me in contact with Commander Norton at Hadley Base."

"I can do neither. Would you like to take off your suit?"

"So I'm staying a while?"

Belyakova nodded.

Vivian had little choice. She doubted she'd get the chance to escape. Her suit did her no good without a helmet, and her faceplate was painted over. She couldn't get out of here blind and unaided. Even if she could, she was deep in enemy territory, five hundred miles from Hadley Base.

She rolled clumsily onto her feet and wrestled with the cord that would unzip her spacesuit. Naturally, it caught. Belyakova stepped around her, freed the zip, and pulled it down her back and past her butt.

"Uh, thanks." Vivian scrunched and leaned back, sliding herself out, and Belyakova obligingly tugged it off her from the front.

Beneath, Vivian wore her liquid-cooled garment, a cotton jumpsuit, and a diaper, and that was about it. *Hey, whatever. We're all astro-girls together, right?* She stripped down to her underwear and, without comment, Belyakova handed her some wipes, a towel, and a fresh one-piece Soviet jumpsuit like the one she wore herself.

Vivian tidied herself up. "So what happens now? I'm, what, a prisoner of war?"

Svetlana was stacking Vivian's suit against the wall. "To be honest, I am not sure."

"Well, damn. If you don't know, I'm sure I don't."

"Maybe you will be treated as a prisoner of war. But perhaps Comrade Yashin will deny that we have you, and … keep this as a private matter between ourselves."

"Oh." That didn't sound good. "Pardon my ignorance, but who is Comrade Yashin?"

Belyakova looked surprised. "He is one of the leaders of our group. He concerns himself with matters of security and ideological soundness. He will be along to question you shortly, as you must know."

"I don't know anything. I don't even know why you'd assume I *would* know."

"American intelligence forces are well aware of Comrade Yashin. And you are a member of the American intelligence forces."

Vivian stared. "You have been misinformed. I'm a naval aviator and a NASA astronaut. Nothing to do with military intelligence."

Belyakova smiled politely. "As you wish. I am not the one who will interrogate you."

"And what does Comrade Yashin want to know?"

"He will need to know details about Hadley Base," Svetlana said. "The names and capabilities of the new personnel who have recently landed. And the location of the nuclear warheads the United States is stockpiling on the Moon. We need—"

"Let me stop you there. The US has no nuclear weapons on the Moon."

Svetlana did not blink. "We both know that is not true."

"I know nothing of the sort."

The Russian stared at her. "Captain Carter, listen. You are a clever woman and a fellow pilot, so let us speak plainly. In your country you have hard and soft ways of performing interrogations, no? It is the good policeman and the bad policeman?"

"Sort of. Good cop, bad cop."

"All right." Svetlana looked her up and down slowly, in a thoughtful but intense way that made Vivian want to fold her arms over her chest. "Then: I am the good cop. Yashin has sent me to befriend you, in hope that you will give me information. And then he will be the bad cop. I know this simple ploy will not fool you. But be assured it will be much more pleasant if you tell me what we need to know, rather than require Comrade Yashin to extract it from you."

Suddenly, Vivian was finding breathing difficult. *Extract it from you.* The grim truth of her situation was finally sinking in.

Vivian knew a lot about Soviet methods of interrogation. She had been briefed as part of the standard NASA/USAF astronaut training, shortly after getting her Top Secret clearance. If US astronauts were forced to land behind the Iron Curtain, it was best that they know what might await them there.

And here she was, effectively imprisoned behind the Iron Curtain. She might simply disappear without trace, her body and mind destroyed as Yashin attempted to force information from her that she didn't possess, because it didn't exist.

She felt a sudden pain in her lower lip. She'd bitten into it without realizing.

Great, now I'm torturing myself and saving them the effort.

Perhaps it was time to reevaluate her hostility toward Svetlana Belyakova. Befriending the woman would be a much better tactic. Time to good-cop the good cop.

Not that Belyakova was dumb enough to fall for that.

"Well, damn," Vivian said. "This isn't very promising, is it?"

"I wish there was a better way. But we cannot allow you Americans to use the Moon as a launchpad to hurl nuclear weapons at my country."

"The US has no—" Vivian shook her head. "This is getting old. Do we have to stay in this damp little room?"

"Damp?" Belyakova looked surprised. "There is somewhere else you would rather be?"

"Uh, yeah." Laughter bubbled up in Vivian's throat. *Careful, Viv. You may be starting to lose your shit, here. Tiny bit.* "Yes, Major-General Belyakova, I can think of many other places I'd prefer."

"You cannot escape Zvezda Base. You understand this? If we left you alone, you might perhaps put on one of our EVA suits and work out how to use the airlock. Such items are similar in your program and ours. But we shall not neglect you, and even if you departed from Zvezda, where could you go? Into Copernicus Crater? Off the highlands and across the lunar sea? You cannot fly a Soviet craft. You would walk until you ran out of oxygen and died. There is no help for you in Zvezda Base, or outside it."

"Yes," Vivian said. "I understand that very clearly."

Svetlana considered. "If I were to take you out of this room, do I have your word of honor that you will not try to escape?"

"Of course not. But that hardly matters if there's no point in me attempting it."

"We can leave this room if you will tell me the names of the members of Night Corps currently at Hadley Base."

Ah. Of course, that's exactly how they're going to play this.

Again, Vivian felt the weight of defeat and depression. She'd been in this room only a few minutes, and her nerves were already frayed. And despite Sandoval's confidence, the Soviets clearly already knew about Night Corps. "I don't know. They said they were giving us false names, nicknames and such. I doubt I've learned the real name of a single one of the new people currently at Hadley."

Technically, that was almost true. Sandoval and Lin didn't count as "new people" to Vivian, and Moody and Jensen were deceased, thus no longer currently at the base. "The KGB probably know much more about them than I do. Try another question."

"Very well. Then tell me about their MOLAB."

"Certainly. The MOLAB is the Mobile Laboratory, a big enclosed vehicle. USAF-built, from an original NASA idea that we never built ourselves. Six wheels, can probably carry a crew of between three and six. And that's honestly all I know about it because, and I can't emphasize this enough, Svetlana: Night Corps tells us almost nothing about themselves and their gear."

"But you know they have weapons. Mines, rockets, grenades."

The Soviets had probably seen all these used in battle on Hadley Plain. And even if not, it wouldn't hurt to persuade them that

Night Corps was formidably armed. "Yeah. They have a shit-ton of all those."

"And armored spacesuits." Svetlana's tone had relaxed, turned almost chatty, as if they were discussing the weather. If the Moon had any weather.

"Yep. They look damned heavy, don't they? Almost like robots, or exoskeletons. They actually call them exosuits. I think it's a joke."

Svetlana nodded. "How do they even get inside something that clunky?"

Vivian smiled cheerfully. "I'm curious about that too, Svetlana. But they don't don them in front of me, and even if I knew where the suits' weak points were, I wouldn't tell you."

Belyakova stood and stretched. "All right, then. Just tell me this one thing: is the Sandoval who commands Night Corps the same Colonel Peter Sandoval who used to command MOL-7, prior to its destruction? Meaning that Major Gerry Lin is one of the dozen or so new crew at Hadley, along with Kevin Pope and Jose Rodriguez?"

Whoa. So, the Soviets even already knew who Sandoval was.

Well, hell. Vivian couldn't think of a single reason why it would matter if she confirmed that. And in all likelihood her face had already given it away.

"If I answer, you get to show me around Zvezda Base?"

"Why not? I cannot wait to get out of here myself, to be honest."

"Then: yup," Vivian said. "Sandoval and Sandoval are absolutely the same guy. Gerry is there. Have no clue about Pope and Rodriguez. Seriously, I don't know them."

"Thank you." Svetlana Belyakova stood and pushed down the door handle. It wasn't locked. "Come on, then."

28

Zvezda Base: Vivian Carter
January 7, 1980

VIVIAN did not find the rest of the Soviet facility much more inspiring than the storage room. Zvezda Base was a series of long, narrow, inter-connected tubes forming the shape of an E, and those tubes were dingy, low-ceilinged, and claustrophobic.

NASA's presence at Hadley was distributed: a federation of two Habitats and nine Lunar Modules, plus the fuel depot and Cargo Containers. The Soviet base was—perhaps equally characteristically—centralized, and constructed out of a number of almost identical parts. According to Svetlana, the basic modular component was a cylinder four and a half meters long at launch that telescoped out to eight and a half meters when installed on the Moon, providing a floor area of over twenty-two square meters. They were three and a half meters in diameter, and weighed eighteen tons.

These modules had been soft-landed in groups, pulled into place with a "surface tug"—apparently a heavy Lunokhod tractor—and then fastened together, although whether welded or riveted was not clear. Flooring had been laid throughout, with storage space, pipes, and cabling beneath, in addition to the festoons of extra cables that hung from the ceiling so low that even Vivian bumped her head regularly.

Alongside the resulting main thoroughfares—which Svetlana called halls—were additional rooms that jutted out from the various

285

strands of the E-like carbuncles. One of these carbuncles was Storage Nine, Vivian's detention cell.

Halls One and Two formed the long axis of the E. Halls Three through Five made up the three tines, from top to bottom. Storage Nine jutted off Hall Three.

At regular intervals along the halls were bulkheads of heavy metal. All the hatches currently sat open, but could be dogged quickly in the event of a breach.

The corridors were not all level. Hall Two slanted downward at a fifteen-degree angle, with steps every few feet. Then, at the bottom left corner of the E, Svetlana and Vivian had to step down three feet to get into Hall Five, around what looked like a custom-built elbow pipeway. Presumably this was to accommodate the underlying terrain. With its tubes, bulkheads, and pipes, Zvezda Base felt more like a submarine than a lunar surface base.

Surface. Hmm.

"No windows?" Vivian asked. "Windows are against your Communist ideals?"

Wrong thing to say. Svetlana fixed her with the iciest expression that Vivian had yet seen from her. *No more jokes about Communist ideals. So noted, ma'am.*

Then, her face returned to normal. "We are underground. Mostly."

"You tunneled into regolith?" *That* would be impressive. "Or you piled regolith on top?"

"Some of both. We have dug down into the ... ejected?"

"The ejecta of Copernicus Crater?"

"Yes, yes, on the slope outside the crater. We have another station, smaller, inside the crater. But here we are outside. We dug a trench and arranged Zvezda within it, and on top of the Zvezda modules we piled more soil and dirt. To block solar radiation, and form a screen to help maintain the inside temperature through the lunar day and night."

"Amazing." Vivian pulled herself together. She wasn't a tourist. And if Belyakova was being free with information, that was surely just a tactic to make Vivian lower her guard. *She is not my friend.*

Nonetheless, it took little effort to look fascinated. "And, another outpost *inside* Copernicus Crater?"

"This, in here, is the biggest part of Zvezda Base. Kopernik crater is huge, nearly one hundred kilometers across. When I am within it and traveled well away from its high rim, I forget that I am in a crater. And yes, there is a second, smaller module on the crater floor. A base to explore that crater." Belyakova cocked an eye at her. "Scientific exploration. For all humankind."

"And who's in charge here? Who is the Rick Norton of Zvezda?" Obviously not Makarov or Yashin, because they'd arrived here with Svetlana.

Belyakova paused, perhaps wondering if this was information that should not be divulged, and then said, "Major-General Yelena Rudenko."

"A woman? Excellent."

Belyakova just raised her eyebrows, and didn't comment.

They went on. Every hall was cluttered. The Soviets had a *lot* of equipment stuffed into Zvezda Base. Each module was lined with crates and metal boxes. Even the common living spaces, with metal tables and chairs in the middle, had bags, boxes, and other units crammed beneath and around them. Generally, the health and comfort of the base's occupants seemed to have been an afterthought. Bunks were distributed haphazardly, although Svetlana assured her that there were also dormitory areas at the end of Halls Three and Four, well separated from the central mess and workshop areas.

Vivian saw no exercise equipment, and almost asked whether the cosmonauts might be suffering from loss of bone and muscle mass. She decided not to; it was clearly in US interests if they were. She noted the various instrument panels along the way, for communications, life support, and other critical functions. Each had a cosmonaut stationed next to it in a fold-up chair, some monitoring dials and switches, others reading books or magazines.

Zvezda was fairly crowded, with men and a few women, all of whom looked oddly similar. Vivian saw none she could identify as Slavs, Balts, or other ethnic populations. Despite Brezhnev's claims of Soviet equality, spacefaring was clearly an activity reserved for the Great Russian elite. Some cosmonauts studied Vivian curiously, while others ignored her. None made any attempt to speak to her. Probably they'd been ordered not to.

Svetlana seemed completely at home at Zvezda and showed it off with professional pride, emphasizing its solid construction, expansive living areas, and the quality of its equipment. Her satisfaction in the Soviets' achievements was evident. She obviously expected Vivian to be impressed, perhaps even daunted.

In a sense, it *was* daunting. Added up, these halls totaled several hundred feet of interconnected space. The mass and volume of Zvezda far exceeded those at Hadley. But to Vivian, Zvezda felt dank and oppressive, and walking through it was almost more depressing than sitting in Storage Nine.

"And this is still just a first step, the core of what will one day become a Soviet Moon city. Wait fifty years, and see what we have achieved here."

"I look forward to it," Vivian said politely, wondering if she'd survive the week. "Which one is Yashin? You'll be sure to introduce us?"

Svetlana's expression was difficult to interpret. "Comrade Yashin has not yet returned. He is still … busy."

"Busy with nefarious activities against US interests?"

"Nefarious," she said, thoughtfully. "I expect so. Would you like something to eat?"

"If I say yes, what question will you demand that I answer first?"

"I think perhaps I will leave the questioning to Comrade Yashin."

Vivian had no doubt she was still being played. Belyakova would surely slip in more attempts at tricking information out of her. *But hey, a girl's got to eat.*

"Yes, I'd very much like some food. Thank you."

A few minutes later, they were eating borscht and some kind of chicken dish, and Vivian was discovering that Zvezda meals were on a par with Apollo fare, but not as good as those at Columbia Station or Hadley Base. "This is excellent," she said, anyway.

"I am glad." Svetlana grinned.

"So, space sister. Maybe we can trade information."

The Russian eyed her. "Perhaps."

"Back in orbit, which of your good friends here fired an assault rifle at me and my ship?"

Belyakova nodded slowly. "I understand. If one of your imperialist astronauts fired bullets at a ship of mine, I, too, would be angry."

Vivian leaned forward. "Yes. Me, my crew, and a Lunar Module that I was about to land on the Moon. What was his name, Svetlana?"

The other woman nodded in understanding, but said nothing.

"Major-General Belyakova. Cosmonaut to astronaut, for the love of God, tell me who shot at my Apollo, and tell me what information you would like in return."

"Nothing," Belyakova said.

"What?"

Svetlana gazed at Vivian with her very blue, very penetrating eyes. "I will tell you freely. But be sure to remember that I did, when next we speak of trade. It was Yashin himself."

"And why would you tell me that?"

Those blue eyes again. "Because he did it against orders and should not have done so."

"All right. Thank you." Vivian leaned back. "So you are no friend to Yashin?"

Belyakova held her gaze. "If an American astronaut ever fires bullets at me, my crew, or my ship, I now trust you to tell me his name."

It seemed unlikely Vivian would witness such a thing. "Very well."

Svetlana leaned forward. "Vivian, we are human beings first, and … cops second. Yet, still we have our duty."

Vivian nodded. "And so, we begin again?"

Belyakova gave her a half grin. "And so, once again. Captain Carter, tell me where the other US base is. How long it has been there? Or the names of the Night Corps astronauts. Tell me now. Why not? Tell me, and I will allow you to take a shower, and I will also … tell you which US astronauts died at Hadley Base during Yashin's most recent attack."

Oof. "Died?"

"I'm sorry. Yes."

Vivian leaned back, and tried to breathe. Hadley astronauts she knew had died. Ellis? Terri, Starman?

Don't think about it. That's how they'll break you.

Vivian gave Svetlana a long and searching scan that began at the top of her blond head and worked its way down to her boots, missing nothing, and then exhaled long and deep. "There's no base. I know no names. Sorry."

Yashin stormed into Zvezda Base like a force of nature. The low lunar gravity made it difficult to walk with an authoritative stride, but Comrade Yashin came as close as anyone Vivian had yet seen. Close behind him came two other men, neither of whom Vivian recognized.

Vivian had never seen Yashin before but would have guessed his identity anyway. He was shorter than she might have expected, a mere inch taller than her. His hair was black and short-cropped, and his features were young, clear, and unusually bland. But when he stared at her, Vivian intuited that this blandness conveyed the absence of any normal emotion. Sergei Yashin did not think and feel as other men. Vivian had never gained a clearer appreciation of someone's cruelty merely from his lack of expression.

"Why is Carter out here?" Yashin evidently demanded of Belyakova in Russian.

In English, Svetlana replied: "Good cop, bad cop."

Yashin shook his head. Snapped his fingers. And one of the two men behind him stepped forward and picked Vivian up bodily, pinning her arms to her sides. Lifting a woman of Vivian's size was no real feat in one-sixth gravity, but for an instant Vivian was shocked that a man she did not know would lay hands on her. She cried out, "Hey!" and back-kicked him, reaching her foot as high as she could.

The man turned her and lunged forward, and Vivian saw the wall approaching. Unable to raise her arms to protect herself, she lifted her right leg and tried to brace herself. But Yashin stepped in and drove his knee into her thigh.

Whether it was an expert move or a lucky hit Vivian couldn't tell, but her leg instantly went numb. And the first man, the man still holding her almost immobile, shoved her face-first into the wall.

Vivian howled. The bang to her forehead stunned her, the pain in her nose was immediate. She writhed, lashed out backward again with her foot.

Svetlana was by her side instantly, her hand on Vivian's shoulder. "Stop it, please. Do not resist. Keep still, dear. Very still, very still."

Vivian froze. Perhaps if she obeyed, these men would not damage her any more. Was her nose broken? She didn't think so. But it was bleeding like a tap.

Then she felt a sharp sensation in her upper arm, and jerked her head. One of the men had jabbed a thick hypodermic needle through her jumpsuit and into her skin.

"What the hell is that?" she said. She tasted blood in her mouth now as well. "What did you just do?"

The man holding her in the bear hug released her, and Svetlana grabbed her so she wouldn't fall to the ground. "Here. Lean on me."

"Svetlana, what did that bastard inject me with?"

"Vivian, come."

Vivian spat blood and raised her hand to her nose. It hurt like hell, but didn't grate like broken bone.

Still, rage consumed her and she yanked free of Svetlana and whirled. The man who had shoved her into the wall took a calm step back as Vivian swung her fist, and then Svetlana got hold of her again. *Shit, this woman is strong.* "Vivian, please. Sit down."

"'Kay." Dizziness swept her, and all of a sudden, sitting down sounded like a good idea. "But what did ... he do?"

She allowed Svetlana to guide her into a chair and rest her arms on the metal armrests. Then the man appeared to her left and Yashin to her right, and before Vivian could react, they wrapped metal cables around her wrists to lash her to the chair. "Oh, shit, come *on.*"

Vivian struggled in vain. The two men picked up the chair and bundled it forward. The narrow Zvezda hall flowed past her, dizzyingly fast. Then the chair legs were back on the ground and a door slammed, and she was back in Storage Nine. Three men loomed over her, their faces shiny with sweat.

You've been drugged, dear. Stay calm and breathe.

Vivian thought that her own calm center was talking to her somehow, but then realized the words were Svetlana's. The cosmonaut was murmuring: "Vivian? Be calm. Relax, pay attention, then this will be over and they will let you rest. Relax, Vivian."

Vivian turned her head to the left, and there was Svetlana's face and blond hair, just a few inches away. "Step away from me, bitch."

Now, her vision was blurring. *Oh, God. Oh, God.* "Tell me what ... you ... stuck in me." Even her voice was failing her, coming out slurred. *Damn.*

Hating herself, Vivian said: "Sorry. Svetlana. Please. Help me."

Svetlana said nothing, but straightened and stood calmly to her left.

Betrayal. Communist bastards. Why should I have expected anything different?

Or did it even count as betrayal since she was already their captive?

"Vivian." Yashin stepped out in front of her, hands behind his back. *Every inch the little tin-pot dictator.*

"Comrade Yashin," she said. "Release me, immediately."

He looked sour at her use of the word "Comrade." It was the first human reaction Vivian had seen from her. "You will address me as Colonel Yashin. I should advise you that I am expert in extracting information from foreign agents. You cannot withstand my interrogation."

"We'll see, *Comrade.*"

"The man to your right is Lev Chertok. He has injected you with a cocktail of drugs, including a sizeable dose of hyoscine. When members of your CIA use this drug to interrogate Soviet agents, they call it scopolamine."

Pharmaceuticals were not Vivian's area of expertise. The names meant nothing, and anyway she could hardly focus.

Oddly, she found herself explaining this. "What you say? I don't know .... Scallop?" Tears sprung into her eyes and trickled slowly down her cheeks.

"Hyoscine is a truth serum," Yashin said.

"No such thing," Vivian said, indistinctly.

He shrugged. "Results are not guaranteed. But you should pray that it works, so that we do not have to move onto more drastic methods. More physical methods. More personal."

Vivian took a deep, staggered breath. Her throat was raw, and her heart pounded. "'Personal methods'? What the hell? You sound like a ... World War Two movie. Like a ... little Hitler."

She lost lock in a wave of dizziness. For a vertiginous moment she didn't know who any of them were. She talked to cover her confusion. "Always loved those movies when I was a kid. Black-and-white film. Chisel-jawed men. Daring-do."

"Which were your favorite movies?" he asked.

"*633 Squadron. The Dam Busters.* And *The Guns of Navarone. Casablanca ...*"

Vivian centered herself with an effort. Christ, whatever that muck was that they'd pumped into her, it was really good. She was already babbling and couldn't stop. "This isn't going to go well for me, is it? None of this at all."

"Tell me about the nuclear weapons."

"Show me yours first, you Soviet bastard." Vivian made a mental connection and glowered at him blearily. "You shot at me. At my Apollo. With a freaking *assault weapon.* I'm going to cut your balls off."

"Vivian, Vivian." Yashin snapped his fingers in front of her face. "Yes, I admit. We have brought tactical nuclear weapons, many of them, in response to your provocation. They are here, at this base. And this alone should assure you that the illegal American occupation of the Moon will soon end. Now, your turn. Where are yours?"

"Hadley is a NASA base. The first permanent moonbase. The *first*. We began it *weeks* before your first Zvezda component landed, and Hadley will thrive long after this shoddy piece of Soviet crap has cracked like an egg and burst into a million pieces."

Well. Yashin's drug was certainly making her talkative. Vivian swallowed, the metallic taste of blood still in her throat. Nausea swept her. She half closed her eyes, and through the haze around her, realized that Svetlana was wiping the blood from her nose and chin.

Go ahead, lady. No sense in me looking a bloody mess.

God, was Yashin talking to her again? Why couldn't he shut up? "Sorry, what you say? … What did you say? I was distracted by the good cop. She's blond as hell."

Yashin grunted, began again. "Perhaps, then, the weapons are elsewhere. Separated from Hadley, for safety?"

"No weapons. Our only nuclear materials are in our RTGs, the radioisotope thermal generators, R-T-G, so that's the acronym. NASA loves acronyms. We call them TLAs, Three Letter Acronyms. That's a joke. The RTGs power our experiments. But, no weapons, missiles, nothing. Aren't you bored yet? I'm bored."

"Tell me about Night Corps," Yashin said next, and Vivian did so in spades. She found herself telling him Moody and Jensen's names, the meager few nicknames of other Night Corps people she knew, and everything she knew about their suits, guns, and missile launchers, which fortunately wasn't much. It was a relief to get it off her chest. *It's the drugs*, said the calm Vivian that still hovered somewhere within her consciousness. *The drugs, talking. And you just can't stop talking right now, can you, Viv? You idiot, you fricking weak sister. But it's okay, but they must know all this already. Mustn't they?*

Even so.

"Oh …. Heart. Heart!"

Vivian's heart rate was dropping. Thundering even harder in her rib cage, but more slowly, its beats more erratic. *Oh, shit. Oh, shit.*

Her hands started shaking as if palsied. She stared at them in fascinated revulsion as they rattled against the arms of the chair, and missed Yashin's next question. "What? What?"

"Vivian, where do Night Corps keep their nuclear weapons?"

"God's *sake*! Night Corps have none. Their commander told me himself." She stopped, on the verge of telling Yashin she trusted Sandoval to tell her the truth about this, about everything, because they were friends, she knew him well. *Mustn't say that. And no time.* "My heart rate is dropping." Her head lolled, and she tried to focus on Svetlana. "Jesus, I'm not kidding. Check my heart. Svetlana. My heart."

Her heart still throbbed, but her blood seemed to crawl through her veins. She felt very woozy.

Svetlana pressed her fingertips into Vivian's wrist, checking the Vostok Amfibia watch on her own wrist to count seconds. Alarmed, she spoke sharply in Russian to Yashin, who merely looked frustrated.

"No nuclears," Vivian said. "'Cause that would be really dumb. I ... Antidote to this? Bet there isn't one. You utter bastards."

That's what she heard in her head, but what came out of her mouth was slurred into incomprehensibility.

And then she blacked out.

29

Zvezda Base: Nikolai Makarov
January 8, 1980

A rise of steep, craggy rock drifted by, twenty feet beneath Makarov's boots. A creak from the cable above him reverberated through his backpack and helmet. The rocky inner wall of Krater Kopernika was layered, almost terraced, and one of Makarov's idle pursuits while being winched slowly up the steepest part of the ascent was to study these terraces, evaluating how he'd climb it if he ever needed to.

He doubted it was possible. Too many sheer areas.

His headset crackled. "Nikolai, Svetlana. Where are you?"

"Ski lift, ascending." They all called it the ski lift.

"What news from the Annex?"

Makarov frowned. It would take only ten minutes for his skeletal open gondola to reach the hummocky crest of the crater wall, and maybe twenty minutes more for him to hike down the outside slope to Zvezda. What did Svetlana need that couldn't wait that long?

"Everything's nominal. Half the crews are patching up the minor damage to the landers, while the rest prepare the Annex for nightfall. What's the matter?"

"Just checking. I'm on my way out to our lander to run some diagnostics. Meet me there?"

This was alarming. Why hadn't she led with that? "What's the problem?"

"Nothing direct. It's just that with lunar night coming on I would like to go over the lander carefully. And there was that intermittent comms issue you were concerned about. We should track that down."

Makarov nodded. He hadn't raised any comms issue with Svetlana.

So, now he understood. She wanted to speak privately. And the only privacy available was within their tiny two-person lander with all comms off.

Unless their LK was bugged. He wouldn't put that past Yashin. But it should be easy to check for an intermittent transmitter if everything else was turned off.

"Agreed. Let's do that while we can."

At the crater rim, Makarov brought the gondola to a halt. While he waited for it to stop swinging so he could step off safely, he looked back over the broad expanse of Copernicus. Hell of a place. A hundred kilometers across and four kilometers deep, its floor bumpy and itself cratered. From up here, Makarov could just pick out the low, half-buried L-shape of the Annex. The LEKs lined up outside it looked lonely in the abyss. Far off in the distance rose the three rocky peaks in the crater's center, each over a kilometer tall.

Makarov badly wanted to go over there. Perhaps if someone could stop all these Cold War skirmishes, they could all get back to exploring.

He'd never really expected to return to the Moon. The Soviet leadership had mothballed Alexei Leonov soon after his historic first moonwalk, bumping him upstairs to Commander of the Cosmonaut Office and next to Deputy Director of the crew training facility. They didn't want to risk getting their history-making Hero of the Soviet Union killed in a subsequent spaceflight. There had been talk of doing likewise with Makarov and Belyakova—"pickling us in a jar," as Svetlana had privately termed it—but their skills, competence, and easy popularity among the Cosmonaut Corps had ensured them a second, ten-day trip prospecting for the site of their Copernicus Base. Then, much more recently, it was only their piloting skills that had enabled the Soviets to rendezvous with Columbia Station.

And so now Makarov was in a war zone. In space. He couldn't decide whether he'd rather have stayed on Earth, quiet and boring and with no war, or whether it was worth the risk and danger just to be back here. Were Copernicus and Zvezda worth Yashin?

That might depend on how it all worked out.

Anyway. Belyakova was waiting for him. Loping down the shallow slope he could see her standing by their LK, leaning against it with one knee raised as if propping up a bar. She nodded as he arrived. "Commander."

"Flight engineer," he said, grinning.

They climbed the ladder and crawled in through the hatch, she moving right and he left. The circular cabin was ridiculously confined, and with both suited up they had little room to maneuver. Most of the control panels were lit, telltales glowing blue or red, and above them hung a steerable light on a stalk, which Makarov twisted to aim the light at the hatch.

He closed the hatch, checked it, then checked it again. "Okay. Ready for pressure."

Belyakova reached for an oxygen bottle and spun the valve open. They brought the pressure up to two psi, held it there for a couple minutes to verify cabin integrity, then pumped it the rest of the way up.

While he watched gauges and flipped switches to bring the cabin heaters online, Svetlana disabled the cabin microphones, and then shut down communications altogether at the circuit breaker.

"Pressure holding." Glancing over, he saw she was already doing the check he'd planned to do, scanning for bugs.

Soon, Svetlana gave him the thumbs up and looked at him soberly through the polycarbonate shells of their faceplates. She didn't look happy.

They reached for each other's helmets at the same time, and with the ease of long practice, lifted them off each other's heads. He caught the glimmer of her familiar smell in his nostrils, clean and calming, and instinctively felt himself beginning to relax, even as he said: "So. What's so important it couldn't wait?"

"I didn't want you to do anything stupid when next you see Comrade Yashin."

His relaxation went on hold. "What in hell has he done now?"

"He has captured an American from Hadley. Vivian Carter."

Makarov's mind raced. "*Captured?* How did he manage that?"

"She was halfway up a nearby mountain on a geology trip during the attack. Yashin must have known that. I believe he timed our strike so that she would be vulnerable."

"Vivian Carter is *here?*"

"Yes. Locked in Storage Nine."

Makarov stared. "And Yashin is interrogating her."

"Yes."

"Hurting her?"

Belyakova glanced down at his hands, which he'd balled into fists. "I don't know, Nikolai. He began with drugs, and it did not go well. But this is why I wanted to brief you here, quietly. I did not want you to lose your temper and storm in, enraged by chivalry."

"You think I still will not?" he said, grimly. "Exactly how much damage is this idiot going to cause? When the Americans find out what he is doing …"

Svetlana shook her head. "Nikolai, Nikolai. Yashin must do this."

"But a woman, an astronaut …" He looked at her.

Belyakova shook her head. "Stop imagining me captured by Americans, Nikolai Ilyich, and how you would feel about that. It will not happen."

She knew him too well. As always. Makarov leaned back against his headrest. "You say it did not go well? Has Carter told Yashin anything of use? And, is Yashin injuring her to the point that it will be clear what he has done, once she is freed?"

"You assume a great deal," Svetlana said. "That he will ever free her. So far, she has no … permanent damage, I think."

He closed his eyes. "The Americans must know that we have her."

"They must suspect. We do not know if Carter's crewmate survived. He fled down into the rille, and Chertok shot at him. He fell, but far away. Chertok radioed Yashin to ask whether to continue pursuit and capture him as well, but once Yashin learned they had Carter he ordered them to return to Zvezda immediately."

Shaking his head, Makarov said: "What is so important about Carter?"

"Yashin believes she is American military intelligence. She trained on Earth with Peter Sandoval, Gerry Lin, and Joshua Rawlings. Her mission was diverted to Columbia Station at the last minute, to take them the large-format spy camera and other items we are still evaluating. As for myself, I cannot decide. At times she seems straightforward, even naïve. Other times, devious and manipulative."

"You've spoken to her?"

"At length. Yashin ordered me to befriend her."

"Yashin chose you for that, rather than Isayeva?"

"Carter reveres the pioneering astronauts. Even though she is an astronaut herself, she hero-worships the first Americans on the Moon. Perhaps Yashin thought that Carter might worship me, too." Svetlana grinned ruefully. "I think perhaps she even does, a little. But so far she has only confirmed facts we already knew."

Makarov studied his crewmate in the glowing light from the control panels. "Svetlana Antonovna, are we sure that the Chairman is correct about all this? Have we seen anything with our own eyes to suggest the Americans have brought weapons to the Moon? That the astronauts we have seen are even capable of this?"

She pursed her lips. "*You* believe that Chairman Brezhnev, and the entire Politburo, would lie about a matter so serious?"

He and Belyakova often disagreed about politics. "The Supreme Soviet has complicated motives. It is not always so simple to determine what is true."

Svetlana shook her head. "It does not matter. We are at war, and Yashin has assumed authority, which is within his power as political officer. And I am glad of it. I would not want the responsibility for all this on *my* head. Or yours." She paused. "If this is what our job now requires, perhaps we have been cosmonauts too long."

"Time to retire to our dachas by the Black Sea?" Makarov said sardonically. "Our spouses would thank us."

"Mine might not," she said. "How long until we slit our wrists with boredom? Three days. Perhaps a week."

Svetlana's was a combative marriage. Something Nikolai would not have wished upon her. She deserved better.

But right now, there were more important issues at hand. "Svetlana, where is our line in this matter?"

"We serve the motherland. We have no line."

"No line? If Yashin handed you his gun and told you to shoot Vivian Carter in the head, you would bless Mother Russia and pull the trigger?"

"So melodramatic, Nikolai Ilyich."

"But if he did, that would be a line. Would you cross it?"

Svetlana turned to face him, only a couple feet away. "Nikolai, stop. We do not know all that is happening. The Chairman has information, the Supreme Soviet has information, KGB Chief Andropov and his officers in the Lubyanka have information. Yashin gets his orders directly from Andropov. We know only our own small part of the picture. We cannot just *decide* that there is a line, and that our opinions outweigh everyone else's."

"So, you would shoot her. Would you shoot *me*?"

Svetlana rolled her eyes. "At this moment? I am contemplating it. Look. Carter has information, or Yashin would not have split her out from the imperialist herd. And thus, she is important. If she seems genuine to me, perhaps that is just her training. You and I both made the error of thinking Isayeva genuine. I might have spent months more with Vika without guessing she was just as brutal as Yashin. How could I already know Carter?

"And, *it does not matter*. Nikolai. These people are our enemies. You are a noble man, but you cannot leap to Carter's defense merely because she is a woman, knowing nothing of what is in her head."

Makarov nodded. "And you made sure to tell me this before I walked into Zvezda Base."

"Yes. Before you could crash in there with all your bluster, and gain even more demerits in the eyes of Sergei Ivanovich. Yashin is a dangerous man, and I need my partner."

"My *bluster*?" Makarov exhaled, forced a smile. "Very well. Always, you have more sense than me."

"Always," Belyakova said, as if that were obvious.

"Even though you would put a bullet in my head if those were your orders."

He said it lightly, trying to wash away its sting. Expecting another sharp response.

Instead, Svetlana reached over and took his hand.

Her fingers were warm, her grip strong rather than affectionate. He looked down at their hands, joined. This had happened maybe a dozen times in as many years, and always at times when he was showing weakness. When Svetlana needed him to be strong, or feared for him. Or just needed to get her own way.

He squeezed her hand back, and released it.

"And so, I think you have found my line," she said. "Do not duel with Yashin. Do not cement your opposition to him. That will not end well for any of us."

"We just nod and smile, and follow orders?"

"Do we not always?"

That made him grin. "Oh yes, of course, Comrade. Always."

She bopped him lightly on the arm and looked away, also smiling.

And yet there was so little to smile about. "Too many have died. When first we landed on the Moon, we scarcely knew that one day we would be discussing bullets to the head here."

Belyakova began setting switches on the console before her. "We never imagined we would spend a lunar night here, either. Let us see if our little craft is ready for such an ordeal."

He took a deep breath. "Thank you, Svetlana."

"You are most welcome, Nikolai. And now?" She indicated the checklist.

Makarov nodded, and reached up to restore power to the communications boxes and guidance computer.

For the next hour they lost themselves in work, and for a brief time Nikolai Makarov managed to forget about Vivian Carter, nuclear weapons, and bullets to the head.

CHAPTER 30

Zvezda Base: Vivian Carter / Nikolai Makarov
January 8–16, 1980

Carter

Once Vivian awoke again, she remained awake, for the Soviets would not let her sleep.

She regained consciousness to find a man in the room with her, and when she attempted to put her head down again, he wrapped his fingers in her hair to pull it upright. When her eyes closed involuntarily, despite the shock, the man slapped her face.

After that, she was never left alone for a moment. Three men, or maybe four, took turns monitoring her. Whenever her head drooped down onto her chest, the Soviet soldier standing guard would step forward to punch her, or yank her hair, prod her, or jab her in the arm with a knife. Never hard enough to draw blood, but painfully enough to waken her. The fear of that pain was a powerful antidote for drowsiness.

On the plus side, the fog in her brain had dissipated, and she no longer had the urge to babble. And her heart was beating well enough again. Like a normal heart, that might keep her alive through all this.

She was given water on request, but no food. She was not allowed to relieve herself, and soon soiled herself where she sat. Her guards did not stop her from speaking, unless she grew loud or irritating, but never responded. As far as Vivian could tell, none of them spoke English.

She lost track of time. She was pretty sure that the men served shifts of differing lengths to disorient her. Storage Nine had no clock, although after being wakeful for a while Vivian began to hallucinate one, its second hand grinding forward with excruciating sluggishness.

For as long as she could remember, Vivian had had a clear plan for every day. Since becoming a Navy pilot, almost every moment of her time had been scheduled and often overscheduled. Now, her days were empty. She was hungry and in pain, her deep fatigue was building, and despite her terror about what might happen next, her main emotion was a stultifying, soul-destroying boredom.

Every so often, Yashin would show up to stand before her and shout the same questions, make the same demands and the same offers, until she was at screaming point. Where were the nukes? What weaponry did Night Corps have? When had Vivian been recruited by military intelligence? She could bathe and sleep in privacy if only she would answer his questions. Eventually Vivian yelled at him to leave her alone and, unfortunately, he did exactly that for what must have been a dozen hours or more.

"Unfortunately," because her conversations with Yashin were the only times she could speak to another human being and get a response, however infuriating. Belyakova did not come back, nor did the guards react when Vivian spoke Svetlana's name. In the tedium of her eternal wakefulness she almost longed for Yashin's return, if only so she could swear at him and refuse to answer his demands.

Now, having managed to nod off and stay sound asleep for what may have been twenty seconds, Vivian lurched sharply awake to feel the sting of slaps on her cheeks and see blood leaking from a two-inch slash in her arm.

"Oh, sure," she said. "Cut me. Damage me. Then I'll have evidence of your war crimes, you bastard. Geneva Convention? Cut me again, asshole."

The soldier stared stolidly back at her.

"How the hell old are you anyway? Twenty? Twenty-two? Bastard."

Perhaps a half hour later he left the room to trade shifts with another soldier, and soon after that the door opened again and Svetlana walked in.

Oh thank God. In her relief it was all Vivian could do to not break down in tears. She swallowed, tried to glare. "What time is it? How long have I been here?"

Belyakova spoke an order to the Red Army soldier. The man snapped a salute and stepped forward.

And loosened the straps around Vivian's wrists to free her arms, before leaving the room and closing the door behind him.

Belyakova put down a fresh jumpsuit on the table in front of Vivian, and a box of germicidal wipes. "There is a toilet behind you in the corner. Please feel free to avail yourself."

Vivian pushed herself upright and staggered, the blood languishing in her veins, but Belyakova did not help her. She took her time, shaking feeling back into her legs. "Thank you."

Belyakova made no response, merely watched impassively as Vivian used the facilities and cleaned herself up, dressed again in the new clothing, and wiped down the chair where she'd been imprisoned for the last several days, drying it with the sleeve of her old soiled jumpsuit. "May I stand for a few moments? My butt is sore."

"Your … ?" Belyakova stifled a smile. "Oh. By all means."

"So now I'm supposed to feel grateful to you, and spill my guts. Right?"

"Vivian, I hate to see this happen to you. It makes me cry. Just tell Yashin what he wants to know."

"Ice queen. You've never cried in your life."

"That is far from true."

Even leaning against the metal cupboards, Vivian's head lolled. "I am so freaking tired."

"I am sorry, but you cannot sleep. If you try, I will have to prevent you, or bring one of the guards back in. It is more than my life is worth to oppose Yashin. So, just talk to me, dear. And then you can sleep. I swear it."

"I can't, dearest Svetlana, because I have nothing to say. I don't know anything. I'd invent something if I thought it would help. But Yashin would find out I'd lied, and then what? Punish me even more."

To her horror, Vivian discovered tears pouring down her cheeks and neck into her jumpsuit. "Oh, for God's sake."

So that was all it took, after being drugged and held in physical and emotional deprivation: just a few words of feigned kindness, and her floodgates opened.

Svetlana rose. Did she intend to wipe the tears off her cheeks? Even console her? Vivian held up her hand. "Don't even try to be human. I've got this."

"All right."

"I hate you," Vivian said. "All of you."

Svetlana grinned dourly. "There is no truth serum left in your body. Nothing compels you to be so candid."

"Just let me sleep, bitch." Vivian's words were harsh, but she had no strength left, and started crying again.

"I cannot. And, Vivian, I must go now. When you are ready to tell me what we want to know, say my name to your guard and he will have me fetched. They will wake me if necessary. But ask for me only if you mean it. You understand? Otherwise, you will never see me again."

Vivian took a deep breath. "Yeah. Thanks for the wipes. Good talk. Really. But now, trot off like a good Communist."

"You must sit again first." Svetlana reached for the steel cables. "I am sorry we must be enemies, Vivian."

"Not half as sorry as me." Vivian struggled to think. "Wait. Have there been any more battles? Any more deaths? What time is it, anyway? What day?"

"It is lunar night. That is all I can tell you."

"Great. Thanks so much. First woman on the Moon? Jesus. No truth drug necessary, Svetlana, I'll tell you this for nothing: I always wanted to meet you. For a decade or more. And now I have? What a goddamn disappointment."

Svetlana paused. "And I am not lying when I tell you that I hate this. Be sensible, Vivian. I beg you."

"Please," Vivian said. "I'm begging now, too, Comrade. Please just go the hell away."

Yashin said: "Today I come with a different question. And if you do not know the answer, then who does?"

Vivian struggled to comprehend. It was maybe two days since she'd seen Svetlana. Longer? By now, every word came to her through a dense fog. "What?"

Yashin leaned in. She could smell his breath. Borscht and vodka. God, what a cliché. "By now, I am in doubt whether someone as weak as you could have held out so long if you really knew anything of value. Perhaps, despite our intelligence to the contrary, you know nothing."

"Bingo. Nothing to know, smart boy."

"And yet ... despite your weakness, I believe you are very clever, Vivian. I have grown sure from your reactions that you have had suspicions about your own people, even before we captured you. So, my question to you now is, who among your colleagues at Hadley would know the truth of the secret activity going on there?"

Vivian kept her mouth tight shut. It would have been so easy.

Yashin smiled. "I see a name on your lips." He reached out, and touched her lips with his fingers. Vivian recoiled. "What is that name, Vivian?"

"Call me Captain Carter, or don't speak to me at all."

"Captain? Not Commander?"

"I am a captain in the United States Navy. I was ... commander of Apollo 32, but I'm ... that doesn't mean anything any more."

Vivian almost started crying because it was a shock to hear herself say it aloud. But it was true. Apollo 32 had ceased to exist.

Except for her Command Module Pilot. Was he still orbiting above them? All alone? God, Vivian could not bear that thought.

"So, Captain Carter: a name for me, please?"

"Dave Horn. Not because he knows anything but because I badly want you to go up and, yes, capture him. He won't tell you a damn thing either, but maybe you might feed him and lock him up in here with me for company."

Yashin looked interested. "Your lover, perhaps?"

Vivian laughed. A braying sound that worried her because insanity lurked behind it. "Much more. One of my crew."

"Where might I find him?"

She knew he was toying with her, so she tilted a finger, straight up toward the sky. A middle finger.

Yashin grinned thinly. "You do a good job of distraction, but I have not forgotten my question."

"What do I get if I tell you? A night's sleep, in a bed, lying down?"

Yashin considered. "Yes."

Really? A bed? It seemed an impossible dream. "You promise?"

Irritation swept his face. Vivian instinctively rocked her head away, sure he was about to hit her. But he merely said: "Always take me exactly at my word. No more, and no less."

Vivian knew she had reached rock bottom. She would be forever broken if she could not rest soon. Even now, the room was undulating in front of her eyes. "It would really do you so much good? One name?"

Darkness loomed behind her. Goddamn it: Yashin was right. She was weak.

Tears flowed down her cheeks. Yashin ignored them. "One name, and you may sleep."

And then Vivian's fear and cowardice truly took control. "You can't tell anyone I told you. Don't tell my people. Don't tell Norton."

He laughed. "I doubt that I shall ever speak to Commander Norton."

"Buchanan." *Oh my God, it came out, I said it.* "Norton's Lunar Module Pilot. I don't know what the hell he knows. But he knows more than the rest."

Vivian, you are scum. You should have just died. Swallowed your own tongue and choked yourself.

"Casey Buchanan." Yashin nodded.

"Yeah. Buchanan. If there's anything to be known, Buchanan knows it."

Had Vivian just signed Buchanan's death warrant? But how could that be?

Maybe he'd be the next one the Soviets made a targeted strike on, and captured. Damn.

She blinked away more tears. "And now I'm sure you'll double-cross me, and deprive me of the sleep you promised. Ask me another question, and another."

"By no means," Yashin reached forward to unlock her wrists. "I told you: take me at my word. I will take you to a bunk. I will, of course, have to handcuff you to it."

Vivian felt overwhelming gratitude. *Oh, come on. You're giving him points for keeping a promise? For* not *being a bastard, for just a few moments?*

"Lead on," she said.

Makarov

"That's her?" Makarov leaned forward. The woman shackled to the bunk was snoring slightly, her hair folded over her cheek. She was smaller than he had imagined. Almost delicate.

Then again, a lot of people looked calm and innocent when they slept.

"And she really told Comrade Yashin what he wanted to know?"

"It appears so," said Svetlana.

Now, Makarov felt weary himself. "So, the Americans *do* have nuclear weapons on the Moon? She revealed their location?"

"We can only assume so. Yashin does not confide in me."

"Damn." Makarov had been hoping, perhaps forlornly, that this was all just a made-up threat, or a misunderstanding. That war could cease, here on the Moon. "And has Sergei Ivanovich informed us what must happen next?"

"He has not. Just that this one has earned herself eight hours of undisturbed sleep."

"I should like to talk to her myself," Makarov said.

"You wish to take your turn at being the good cop?"

"What?"

"The friendly inquisitor. That is up to Comrade Yashin. I have no idea what he intends to do next. But he has the rest of the long lunar night before we can return to normal operations."

"Lunar night." He looked at Svetlana. "It is something to see, is it not?"

"I would just as soon have missed it. Trapped in here with Yashin and too many other people, and no cognac?"

Makarov looked a little smug. "You suppose that we have no cognac, Svetlana Antonovna?"

"*Armenian* cognac?"

"You know of a better kind?"

Belyakova looked around. No one was close enough to hear, aside from Vivian Carter, who was obviously out cold. On impulse, she reached forward to smooth the hair away from the American's cheek. "Sweet dreams, Vivian Carter." And then, to Makarov: "Come. It seems that my own crewmate has been keeping secrets from me."

He grinned, and they hurried away.

Carter

"Captain Carter? I am Viktoriya. Viktoriya Isayeva. Sometimes, they call me Vika."

"Go away. I'm asleep."

"You have slept nearly seven hours."

"Good. Go away." Vivian squinted up blearily, and found herself looking at a petite, very frightened young woman, standing too close to her bunk. "Uh. Hi."

"Hello." Vika stopped as if tongue-tied.

The girl looked terrified. Vivian tried to focus. "I don't know what they may have told you, but I don't eat babies unless the Moon is full. And … it's not full."

Vika glanced behind her, then brought her nervous gaze back to bear on Vivian.

"Really, let me sleep." Vivian struggled to think. "Wait, though: what day is it? What's the date?"

"The sixth day of lunar dark. It is very black, outside. And cold. But you have seen this already?"

Dark as my soul. I betrayed Buchanan. And no way to even warn him.

"Yeah. I've seen it. It's crap."

Now, Vivian became aware of the intermittent creaking from the walls around her. She sure hoped the Soviets had engineered this base as solidly as they thought.

Stranded here, in the cold and the dark, with a torturer and a bunch of dodgy women who kept trying to befriend her.

"Sixth day of dark, so … is that the fifteenth of January? No."

"The sixteenth."

Vivian rocked back. *Jesus wept. I've been here for ten days?*

Vika peered at her. "You are planning to escape?"

Uh, yeah, tiny girl. I'm just about to snap these handcuffs and smash through the wall.

"If you do, can you take me?"

"Take you?"

"Yes." Vika glanced back again. "These people, they are crazy. I want to go to America. I want more for my life than," she waved, her very gesture helpless. "This. This cold gray of Soviet. I want to be free, to live in a free country. And if you take me, I will tell the United States all I know about Soviet space. Including … nuclear space. You understand? You will take me?"

Vika began to cry silently, tears welling in her eyes and streaking her cheeks. *Oh, Jeez.* "Viktoriya … Vika. I'm not about to escape any time soon. They have me watched pretty good. Unless …" Vivian looked at her. "Unless you can help me with that?"

"What you need?" And then Viktoriya looked scared again. "No! If they discover I help you, they will kill me."

Yeah, probably. "Well, no pain, no gain. Can you fly an LK Lander?"

Vika looked surprised. "Of course."

Whoa. Jackpot.

Vivian tried to hold down her excitement. Was this too good to be true? But this girl, Viktoriya Isayeva, seemed genuinely scared.

"I have no plan, Vika. Zero. Not a clue how to get out of here. If I could, I'd do my best to take you. But you'll have to help me."

"How?"

"I can't speak or read Russian. You'll need to figure out a way to get us out. And once we get to an LK Lander, you're the boss of that. You'd need to get us into orbit, or to Hadley Base. I'll help where I can."

"All right."

Vivian thought about it. "Okay, talk to me. Where are the airlocks?"

"There are hatches at the end of each hall, so in the top and bottom corners, and at ends of Halls Three, Four, and Five."

"Okay. Which is closest to the landers?"

"The landers are farther down from Kopernik, where the ground is more flat. The hatch at the end of Hall Five is closest to them. But farthest from where we are, here."

Brilliant. "How far to the landers?"

"Two hundred yards, outside."

"We'd need a distraction, to pull everyone away from them. Maybe at the top end of the base. Can you think of one?"

Vika looked baffled.

"Jesus, Viktoriya. Come on, you want to go to America, land of the free? You want a wonderful new life? Then Step One is getting me out of here."

"Perhaps a breach?"

Vivian's blood ran cold. "A breach in Zvezda?"

"Opening a hole to space, yes. At the top. Why not?"

Why not? Vivian stared at the woman. Viktoriya Isayeva was very calm about risking the lives of her crew, and everyone else here. "You'd really do that?"

To her credit, Vika looked like she was suddenly reconsidering. "Well. Perhaps small. Just to scare, to distract?"

"And where are the spacesuits?"

"Spacesuits?"

Vivian resisted the urge to raise her voice. "Yes, Vika. Spacesuits."

"Different places. Mine is at the south end. Hatch Five."

"You only have one suit each?" Vivian said. "Then, if there's a breach, everyone will run to their own suit. Meaning that many people would run *south*."

"Oh." Isayeva pondered it.

"Come on, Vika. We need a problem that people believe they can fix, so that they will *not* run south, but north to fix it. No? And then we run south."

Vivian shook her head. This was still hopeless. Who among the Soviets was going to let her and this woman run through Zvezda in the opposite direction from everyone else, and then allow them time to suit up? "Wait, this is no plan at all. Vika, you're the one who knows Zvezda Base. How on earth can we do this?"

"On Earth?"

"Figure of speech! I just mean: how?"

"If I can get you a radio," Vika said, "you could contact your people. Maybe they can be the ones who make the distraction."

"Okay, that could work." And it would let her Hadley people know she was alive. "Good. So get me a radio." Her mind went blank. "What kind of distraction are you thinking of?"

"Perhaps a big explosion."

"Maybe so." A Lunar Module might fly over, launch a rocket close to the north end of Zvezda Base. *Wouldn't need to be a breach, as long as it got everyone's attention.*

"Perhaps a nuclear explosion. That would make panic, no?"

Oh.

Vivian looked at her. "Sure, a nuclear explosion. We could launch a bomb into Copernicus Crater. Far enough away that no one gets hurt, but still …"

"Yes, yes! That would work."

Damn it. Damn it to hell.

Of course this was too good to be true. *Of course* it was. How could she have been so gullible? "Except that NASA has no nuclear weapons on the Moon, Viktoriya Isayeva."

The girl paused, crestfallen. "Then, whatever they have, whatever they can … aim here."

Vika was good. Vivian had nearly fallen for it. Might even have done so if the US really had nukes on the Moon.

Depression washed over her. *I'm screwed. However hard I try, I'm just screwed.*

Well. Maybe not. Maybe Vivian could still trick Vika into helping her. Somehow. If only she was smart enough to figure out how.

"Okay, Vika, let's think about it. Come back again later. We must be careful, not go off half-cocked, make a good plan."

"Half what?"

"Let me sleep. Talk to me again, whenever it's safe. Bring me a radio."

Vika studied her a moment, then nodded. "I will find a way."

"I'm sure you will."

Would Vika bring her a radio? Hardly. Not unless it was part of some bigger plan.

How could Vivian do this? How to trick a Soviet agent into doing what she wanted? Vivian wasn't the intelligence officer they all took her for. She wasn't trained in subterfuge. God knew whether she'd be able to think of anything.

She'd just have to sleep on it.

But the next day, and the day after, and for many long dreary, painful days after that: Vika never came back.

Painful, because Yashin began the torture again.

CHAPTER 31

Copernicus Crater: Peter Sandoval
January 24, 1980

LAUNCHING in the first grazing-incidence rays of a Hadley dawn and flying west and low across the terminator into night was terrifying. Sandoval couldn't figure out why he'd ever agreed to it. Even though it had originally been his idea. *Well, we were just brainstorming, right? There are no stupid ideas?*

Correction. Sometimes there was *one* stupid idea, and now Sandoval had to live it.

"We need to cut this out, man," he said.

Gerry Lin looked up from the Lunar Module guidance computer, his hands still adjusting the controllers to tweak their trajectory. "What? Zooming across planets in the dark?"

"Exactly that," Sandoval said. "That, in a nutshell."

"I got this," Lin said.

"Simulators?"

Lin grinned. "Simulators. And our course is mostly preprogrammed already, by real LM pilots. Except for the hard part at the end."

The landing. Sandoval shook his head. "I must be insane. By the way, the Moon's not a planet."

"Details." Lin made a sudden correction, and the LM lurched.

"What was that?"

"Mascon. Mass concentration in the Moon's crust? Gravity anomaly?"

313

"Naw. They can't be that large."

"Yeah, okay, maybe I just read a number wrong." Lin grinned across at him.

"Where are we?"

"Still three hundred miles out."

Sandoval knew that. They were approaching the top of their ballistic arc, mostly weightless, and Lin was lining up the LM for the descent and landing. The landing that could well end with them blowing a big, bright hole in dark regolith.

Sandoval pictured the lunar surface shooting by beneath them, because imagining it was all he could do, *in the dark*.

They'd flown up and out of the embayment. Passing close-ish to Hadley Delta, hulking and smooth and nicely illuminated from the side—because what was a launch without a stinking great mountain almost in your way? Heading southwest along the line of the Apennine Range, the lower right edge of Mare Imbrium, the Sea of, what, Storms? No, wait: it was Oceanus Procellarum, the *Ocean* of Storms. Imbrium was just Showers, or Rains, or some other water word, here on the most arid ball of rock imaginable.

Sandoval still knew very little about the Moon. That was bad.

They flew on across Eratosthenes Crater and down toward Copernicus.

Going in all by myself. Special Operations Man. Earning my pay.

In the fricking dark.

Lin flicked him a glance, swaying in his straps. "Hey, man, chill out. Vivian is going to love you for this. Uh, ullage burn."

The LM kicked, and Sandoval grabbed onto his harness. "Good grief. That's just ullage?"

"Yeah. Shoving the fuel to where we need it—at the bottom of the rocket."

"Thanks, I know what ullage is. Has it occurred to you that these things are ridiculously flimsy?"

"But very cool. Beats the Bunker hands down. This, I can actually fly like a real ship."

"Yeah, but ..."

"Relax, man," Lin said. "Briefly. Because real soon we'll start the descent burn and I'll need you calling numbers. Because I can only do one thing at a time, and landing means doing three things at once, between two people. You remember how to call the numbers, yes?"

"Uh, sure."

"Sound more confident, sir?"

"Yes, Airman, I absolutely know how to do that."

"Roger that, sir. Descent burn in fifteen seconds."

"That soon?"

"Yeah," Lin said. "That freaking soon."

Without the night-vision goggles that wrapped Sandoval's face under his helmet, Zvezda Base would have been impossible to locate. He would have just tooled around out here till he ran out of batteries, or out of air, and then either froze or choked to death.

He stepped off the Soviet dirt bike and stretched, as best he could inside his armored suit. Around him the landscape glowed a dull green. Ahead, on the upslope that led to the rim of Copernicus, he could see the eerie glow of a long, low E etched into the moonscape in slightly lighter green. Zvezda Base was mostly covered in soil, and well insulated, but its outer shell was still a teensy bit warmer than the surface around it.

The night-vision goggles were military A-grade, specifically designed for off-Earth operation, and they didn't just image in the infrared. Their optoelectronics also intensified the visual light, that scant earthshine and starlight that reflected off the lunar surface. Dirt-biking it here from where Lin had dropped him off had almost been like a videogame, except that Sandoval had only one life and if he'd screwed up, it would have been game over.

Fortunately, the highlands around Copernicus weren't that terrible to steer over. High and rocky, sure, but not a whole lot harder than the uplands around Hadley.

And the Soviets had a good thing going with these bikes. Nimbler than the rovers. Sandoval had only fallen off and skidded across the surface on his butt, what, three times? Starman hadn't wanted to give the bike up, but Sandoval hadn't offered him much choice; and once Jones heard what Sandoval needed it for, he'd given way pretty quickly.

Anyway. There was Zvezda Base. And here was Peter Sandoval: one man in the pitchy dark, two days before local dawn, against the whole Soviet machine. So, it would be a great idea to not get detected.

Sandoval's exosuit was screened against IR emission. In principle he was as stealthified as an SR-71 Blackbird aircraft on Earth, and for the same reasons. And his people had done what they could in the limited time to shield the bike's battery and engine, though to Sandoval's night-vision gaze it still looked like some parts of them were warmer than the rocks around him. Until someone fired a rocket at him, he wouldn't know whether he'd been detected.

They'd studied Zvezda as best they could, analyzing images obtained from orbit as well as data from intelligence assets. If the Soviets were holding a prisoner, best guess was that she'd be in one of the storage rooms off the top tine of the E shape.

The upright of the E was the main ops area; the bottom tine, the main ingress and egress and a big functional area; and the middle hall was mostly science and workshops. But the top hall held the lab and storage space. So they'd put Vivian up there, where she'd be least in the way, rather than cluttering up a high-traffic operational area.

So Sandoval needed to make a big old disturbance as far from that area as possible. Something preferably nonfatal to everyone inside. Then he needed to loop around and see whether he had even a dog's chance of getting himself into that top hall to rescue her.

Probably not. The odds were stacked against him getting in at all, let alone out again afterward. And Vivian would hardly be decked out in a suit waiting for him. Either way, he'd still aim to inflict some damage. Serve notice that the Reds weren't safe anywhere. Even at home. Even at night.

He'd just play it by ear, and see where the chips fell.

Sandoval took a deep breath. All alone. But that was what they'd all grudgingly agreed upon, after a long and intense debate with USAF Mission Control at Cheyenne, and then another with the NASA Hadley astros, who were still grieving the deaths of four teammates plus the loss of Vivian.

Emotions had run high as the glare of day had yielded to the chill dark of lunar night. Everyone wanted a quick counterstrike on the Soviets. Everyone wanted Vivian back. But no one wanted to put valuable NASA assets in further jeopardy or weaken their defenses.

And so Sandoval had proposed his one-man sneak attack. They only had one dirt bike, after all, and a more substantial force would mean risking the LMs and the rovers to transport them. They couldn't roll the dice on that much Apollo hardware. And buddies also meant other people to watch out for and coordinate with. As it stood, anyone Sandoval was likely to come across would be a hostile.

And, having seen some of his men's bloated faces after kissing vacuum during that last Soviet attack, Sandoval would show no mercy to hostiles. None. The only reason he wouldn't blow every single last Russkie to hell was because somewhere in that Soviet complex, Vivian Carter might still be alive.

So, his goal was to make this a slow disaster, not a quick one, for whatever chance those minutes might buy her.

Sandoval fidgeted with his chest controls to adjust the contrast of his goggles as he scrutinized the area around Zvezda. He didn't want to trip over any Soviets. But if the Reds were anything like the Americans, they were unlikely to be out and about in deep night anyway.

South of the base, he saw LK and LEK Landers arrayed in ragged lines. Kinda funny that the Soviets were so haphazard about so much of their clunky space program, but tried to park their landers in a neat row. It would be a good trick once they got it right. A fine propaganda picture for *Pravda*.

He swung his leg over the bike again. *Okay, time to make my presence felt.*

Sandoval had covered maybe half the remaining distance to Zvezda when it suddenly struck him that this bike might have a transponder on it. He'd been looking to see where he might stash it if he decided to strike out on foot, and how he'd find it again after, and then realized that the Russians probably had the same difficulty. A bike lying on its side wasn't as visible as a rover. Maybe the Reds had installed a device on each, to avoid losing them.

In which case they could be watching him approach and laughing their asses off. Waiting for him to get in range so they could blow him the hell up.

Why hadn't that occurred to anyone in Night Corps? They were supposed to be a supersmart black ops group, and yet not a one of his people had thought of it.

Crap.

Sandoval braked hard, hopped off, dropped the bike to the ground, and ran right. The power servos in the legs of his suit tossed him up farther than a hop in a regular suit would, and he had to pay attention to where his boots would land. Didn't want to trip on a boulder. But after running maybe a hundred yards he stopped and took a knee to case the area again.

Any signs of activity? Nope.

Glancing back, he triangulated as best he could where he'd left the bike. In principle his suit was logging his path relative to his starting point, using data from his boots and the inertial guidance device mounted into his chest. That had worked fine in tests in the Mojave Desert, but didn't seem to be so accurate on the actual goddamn Moon.

Well, whatever.

Sandoval loped on toward the line of LEKs. This was a calculated risk. At Hadley, astronauts occupied their LMs during lunar night. Sandoval didn't know whether cosmonauts did the same. Maybe not, since the lighting on all five craft looked minimal, perhaps just enough power to keep the avionics boxes warm. Given the dubious margin on a lot of Soviet systems, maybe no sane cosmonaut would trust their lander that far. Nonetheless, there was a finite chance that Sandoval was about to bound straight into a couple of his Commie cousins.

He arrived next to the rightmost LEK, bulbous and alien. The five craft were daisy-chained with thick power cables that glowed a faint green through his goggles.

From a pocket on his left thigh, he pulled out a block of explosive and clamped it to the underside of the LEK. Its core was a Semtex composite, a plastic explosive, although currently brittle rather than pliable in the extreme cold. Sandoval didn't need to mold it, anyway. He just propped it in place, set the fuse, and moved on.

He'd been told not to disable all the landers, because that would give the Soviets no means of evacuating. This was just to make a point. Of course, when this LEK went up, pieces of it might well smash into adjacent LEKs. Sandoval didn't much care. It wasn't so long since the Soviets had fired three ICBMs right at him and his crew, and they'd only escaped by the skin of their teeth.

The Soviets vaunted their experience and superiority in space? Let 'em figure out a withdrawal plan after what Sandoval was about to do to them.

He set a charge by the hatchway at the bottom of the E, and moved on. Zvezda Base was surprisingly extensive, though most of it was below ground; Sandoval could see just the top curve of the hallway tubing, rising a few feet above the surface. Its slope was shallow enough that he could have strolled across the roof if he'd felt like advertising his presence with his footfalls. But here and there the lunar soil had been combed aside to reveal a porthole, and in other places he saw a pipe sticking up that might have been to expel waste gases but could as easily be a periscope.

So, he had to take care. Didn't want to be spotted kangaroo-hopping past a porthole, an imperialist shadow against the night. That would just be embarrassing.

He was aiming to set another package of Semtex at the wall opposite the middle tine, but en route he discovered a big square section extending above ground. From a distance he'd thought it was a boulder, but, no. And from its configuration and—helpfully—the Cyrillic lettering stenciled on its hatch, which Sandoval could read with ease, it was clear he'd happened upon the central environmental processing unit for the base.

Well, that rocked. Sandoval had been hoping to locate a slow-kill point for one of his last two explosive packs, and this would work great. Somewhere the Reds must have a propellant dump to refuel their landers, but Sandoval couldn't see it. His military intel, plus simple mass and scaling arguments, predicted that Zvezda must be powered by a small nuclear reactor, but he hadn't seen that either. The reactor would need to be separated from the main base by some considerable distance—miles, even—and they'd probably have buried the cabling to preserve it from the temperature extremes. But Sandoval wouldn't waste time searching for it, especially since he didn't want to blow it up and spread contaminants across the surface, anyway. Regardless, the US would deny that Sandoval had ever been there and blame it on the Soviets' notoriously lax nuclear regulatory processes.

But now he didn't have to look for it. He'd trash this environment control center, and *that* would give the Soviets a literal headache. They could probably fix it—they must have some redundancy, and failing that they could flee to their remaining landers, or their Crater Annex—but it might cause some useful havoc. *Turnabout is fair play, nyet, comrades?*

Sandoval fixed his explosive packet and placed the fuse. Cool beans. Now, off round to the top right corner in the however-forlorn hope of acquiring Vivian.

And then, down the slope not fifty feet away, a hatch opened to reveal a circle of dull red light. A moment later, two shadows stepped into the circle, occulting a part of that light.

A pair of cosmonauts were egressing. Hunting him? Or was this just really poor timing?

Didn't matter. Sandoval didn't wait. He hit the button on his chest that blanked out the dim lights on his chest display and the telltales inside his helmet. Then he primed his explosive packet on their environmental control center and headed on upslope.

He heard the echo and clang as half a dozen bullets smacked into his suit, so close together that they were practically simultaneous, and threw himself to the right instinctively. Sailed through the air, bounced on the regolith-coated roof of Zvezda, and clawed himself up and over.

Not much point trying to stay covert now he'd been seen. Then again, not much point in expecting to gain ingress to Zvezda either. He routed full power to his boot servos and loped high and fast. He was now flanked on either side by the top two arms of the E, and he wanted to get the hell out of *that* valley.

Mere bullets likely wouldn't damage his suit, but he wasn't going to hang around and let the Reds pump a bunch more into it. Or fire a rocket at him.

He jabbed at his chest and glanced right. Dumb mistake. The explosion that blew the LEK in half almost blinded him, when magnified by the goggles. *Ack. God's sake.* The next time his boots hit the Moon he stopped, squatted, blinked away the afterimage as best he could, and pressed the button on his chest to detonate the second explosive package.

Looked up, and there was a damned cosmonaut just thirty feet ahead and coming fast.

Sandoval jumped straight up into the air—well, into the vacuum—to throw off the guy's aim, at the same time snatching at a broad tube strapped to his side. He swung it up and fired. The grenade at the tube's tip shot off on its way and detonated on impact with the Red's chest, somersaulting him back in another potentially blinding flash of bright green that Sandoval closed his eyes for. Another cosmonaut behind the first sidestepped smartly.

Well, this was hopeless. Two cosmonauts behind him, plus one still operational ahead, and who knew how many more would spill out of this hornet's nest now?

Sandoval hit his chest a third time. He felt the rumble through the rock beneath him as the charge on the environmental processing unit went off, but didn't turn to look.

By hand, he lobbed a whizzbang at the second cosmonaut, and turned leftward away from that too, kangaroo-hopping up and over the curving top tine of the E.

For all Sandoval knew, he could right now be running across the roof of Vivian Carter's cell. She might be just ten feet below his boots. If she was, there was nothing he could do about it. So near, and yet so far.

As he leaped off the curve of the Zvezda roof a single stray bullet whanged off his helmet. He glanced back and counted the pale green blobs on his trail.

Not three cosmonauts. Five.

Damn it to shit and back. This wasn't going to work. No way.

He'd burned his bridges. Couldn't make it back to the dirt bike, couldn't flee back the way he'd come. Which was a real bummer.

Sandoval landed and kept running in the only direction left to him.

Farther uphill, toward the rim of Copernicus Crater.

CHAPTER 32

Zvezda Base: Nikolai Makarov
January 24, 1980

IN Hall Two, Chertok grunted with frustration. "Your cosmonauts are sloppy. A disgrace to the Rodina. You have really survived here through nearly a dozen lunar nights? Amazing you have not already killed yourselves."

Yelena Rudenko, commander of Zvezda, eyed him coldly. "And why do you say so?"

"I was told that night on the Moon was a serious business. That each piece of equipment could make the difference between life and death."

"As it can. Of course."

Chertok looked her up and down. Rudenko was raven haired and strong bodied, and Makarov had seen Chertok leer at her before. It was a wonder Rudenko stood for it.

Today, she did not. "Control your eyes, Comrade, and explain yourself."

Makarov stepped up to the console to support her. "Lev Petrovich, come to the point. We are the commander's guests, and you will respect her."

With his usual air of calm menace, Chertok shifted his gaze from Rudenko's body to Makarov's face. Clearly, he respected neither of them. He pointed to his screen.

Rudenko looked over Chertok's shoulder and frowned. "A motorcycle? No. All were brought inside before nightfall. All equipment was

322

accounted for, twelve hours prior to the shuttering of the base. All checklists are complete and filed."

"And yet my screen proves you wrong." The blip of the motorcycle's transponder was unmistakable, and Chertok's eyes were bright with contempt.

Rudenko muttered under her breath and went to pull a ring binder from a bookshelf on the other side of the Hall.

It was surprisingly easy to mislay one of the Voskhod-made lunar motorcycles. They could be propped up on a stand, but this was cumbersome to kick into position in a spacesuit. Cosmonauts found it more convenient to lay the bikes down, whereupon they largely disappeared from view. As the wheels and frame were generally coated with upflung soil and dust after even a short trip, a cosmonaut might walk twenty feet away, and on turning find it difficult to pick out the Voskhod amid the rocks and pocks of the surface. Also, there was the possibility of a mishap, with a bike sliding away downhill into a pitch-black crater bowl. Hence the transponder units, so that they could locate each bike using a radiofrequency signal meter.

Rudenko flipped pages. She had swallowed her irritation and her face looked as serene as always, until she came to the page she was looking for and compared it to the signal trace on the console display.

"What is it, woman?"

"Lev Petrovich," Makarov said again, in warning.

Ignoring Chertok, Rudenko turned to Makarov. "Commander, this is an emergency. That frequency corresponds to one of the motorcycles not recovered after the Hadley action."

Chertok leaped up, bouncing in a long arc across the room. Makarov followed him with his eyes. "Suit up and get out there," he said coldly, to make it clear that *he* was giving that order.

In response, Chertok shouted over his shoulder: "Inform Comrade Yashin immediately!"

Makarov looked at Rudenko. "I suppose we must."

She made a face. "You or I? Because ..."

"Where is Yashin now?"

"Interrogating the American. Comrade Yashin forbids me to enter that area."

"Me, then. In the meantime, let's station watchers at the periscopes and windows, and check for any other radio emissions on-surface."

"And the seismographs, to see whether enemy vehicles have landed?"

"You will obviously take all other measures you see fit, Commander." Makarov nodded formally, gave her a brief smile besides, and hurried off.

Makarov rapped on the door to Storage Nine and opened it without awaiting a response. He'd half-expected the door to be locked, and dreaded what he might find within.

What he found was Yashin leaning against a locker with arms folded, and Svetlana Belyakova sitting at a table resting one hand on Vivian Carter's shoulder. The American astronaut was hunched over with her hands covering her face, and when she raised her head at the interruption, Makarov was shocked to see her cheeks wet with tears, her skin blotched and eyes rheumy. She squinted up at him, barely able to focus. Then her head lolled, and she uttered a single incoherent sound.

My God, what are they doing to her? "Svetlana? Explain."

Yashin stepped forward. "No explanation is required. What is the meaning of this?"

At his tone, it was all Makarov could do not to stand to attention. Damn it, he didn't answer to Yashin. "Comrade, we have a situation. One of the Voskhod motorcycles lost during the first Hadley Base strike has ... returned."

"Returned?"

"Its signal is less than a half-kilometer south of Zvezda Base."

Yashin's eyes narrowed. "And your response?"

"I ordered Lev Petrovich to suit up for egress. I assume he will select a comrade to accompany him. Commander Rudenko is executing other precautions."

"A night attack? That would display a boldness I had not expected. Perhaps their Night Corps is aptly named."

"It cannot be a major attack," said Belyakova.

Yashin turned to her. "Because?"

"Because if it were, we would already know—"

A percussive crash, followed by a deep rumble and the clatter of metal against metal. The walls shook, and a broom slid sideways across the wall and onto the ground. A babble of voices broke out in the hall outside, and the sounds of running feet.

Makarov's eyes were still on Vivian Carter. Disconcerting to re-alize that the calm, authoritative voice he had heard over the radio during their approach to the American orbiting station belonged to this distraught, confused-looking woman.

Whatever Yashin and Belyakova had been doing to her, Makarov was sure she did not deserve it. "Has she told you what you need to know?"

"Little," said Svetlana. "She still insists—"

"Silence," Yashin cut in. "Belyakova, secure the prisoner. Ma-karov, come."

He walked out. Svetlana glanced up at Makarov. "Well? Go."

"Is she all right?"

"Go, idiot!"

Then the second explosion came, and they felt its effects immedi-ately. A breeze sprang up in the room, along with a whistling sound. Carrying clear over the hubbub of voices and other activity, they heard Rudenko shout a single, chilling word: "Breach!"

Makarov ran out of Storage Nine. The hall was chaos. Amid the running cosmonauts Rudenko stood poised and calm, a headset to her ear, speaking into its microphone. She pressed a button and a siren sounded, three fast blips, followed by her voice over the loudspeakers: "Zvezda Base: breach-breach-breach. Emergency personnel to stations. Prepare to close bulkheads. Wait for my command. Repeat: bulkheads remain *open* until my command."

Rudenko met his eye. Makarov nodded. The crew all had to reach their stations before the bulkheads could be closed, dividing Zvezda into individual areas. Everyone needed to suit up. Yashin was already gone.

But where was the breach, and who would deal with that? Makarov looked left and right. The hall had the same breeze flowing through it as Storage Nine, and the air now had unpleasant odors of oil, burned wiring, and smoke. Was there a fire?

A third explosion. "*Ty che, blyad!*" he shouted involuntarily; a strong Russian curse.

Already, he felt heavy headed. Whatever else was in the air, oxygen was no longer forming a sufficient partial pressure. "Life support sys-tems," he said, and took a few steps in the direction of the ECS station.

He bumped into a slim cosmonaut dashing in the same direction. The woman, Irina something, was an expert in the heating and cooling systems, and if …

Yes. The air was definitely getting colder, and the carbon dioxide level rising. Makarov swerved aside and let Irina go do her job.

Damnation. Even if they got the breach under control, if the heating had taken a serious hit as well they were likely all dead.

Makarov walked back to Rudenko. Strange to say, he had no role here. He had a nodding familiarity with the Zvezda systems, but had not trained in sufficient depth to be any use in an emergency. No one would thank him for charging like a bull into an area where others had more competence, and maybe messing matters up even worse.

Rudenko was speaking into her headset, giving orders and flipping switches. This was her base, and she knew every inch of it. "Can I help?" he asked.

She barely glanced his way. "Suit up. Get everyone else into suits. This is serious."

"Where's your suit?"

"Someone will bring it later." She waved him away, turned back to the board, started speaking again in a clipped, efficient tone.

What about Belyakova and Carter? Makarov turned and ran back toward Storage Nine. He burst in and almost collided with Svetlana heading out.

He looked past her. Carter was strapped into her chair with steel cables. Her head lolled on her chest. "What the hell have you two done to her?"

"She just lost consciousness, Nikolai. She's very weak. We need to suit up."

"What about her?"

"For God's sake ..." She grabbed his arm and dragged him out, and they ran down Hall Three. Makarov coughed; the air was getting even worse. They'd have to close the bulkheads soon if they wanted to preserve pressure in any of the Halls, but people were still dashing back and forth between them.

Their suits hung at the end of Hall Five. Makarov unhooked his from the wall and climbed into it. Beside him, Svetlana did the same. Fear churned in the back of his mind. This was a debacle. Zvezda was facing disaster.

They'd suited up together more times than he could count, and generally in much more confined spaces than this. By the time his head emerged out of the top of his suit, Svetlana had already tucked her blond hair into her collar and pulled her own helmet on, snapped it into place. As he reached to double-check her, he heard Rudenko crisply ordering the bulkheads closed.

That would trap both Carter and Rudenko herself. And Rudenko's suit was right here, hanging in front of him.

He turned. A hundred feet away, a cosmonaut he did not know was pulling the big door between Halls Two and Five closed. "Wait!"

"Nikolai. Helmet."

He took it, dropped his gloves into it, and grabbed up Rudenko's suit. "Get a spare for Carter and follow me."

"Nikolai, the Americans are out there. We must go and defend the base from them, and check our LK."

He doubted it. "A sneak raid. We must look after people here."

And when she didn't move, he said, "I'm going."

He ran along Hall Five and through the bulkhead. The man closed the hatch behind him, and dogged it.

Makarov was separated from Svetlana—the last thing he wanted to be, in an emergency.

Around him was controlled pandemonium. Some of the crew had suited up and were heading toward the hatch into the life support nexus. Others ran through the base checking for breaches in other places. Still more were powering down experiments and electronics boxes, closing side doors to storage halls, battening down the hatches. All now wore moon suits, giving the impression of a hive of giant insects.

Their alleged *zampolit*, Sergei Yashin, and his fellow agents Oleg Vasiliev and Viktoriya Isayeva, were nowhere to be seen. Makarov assumed they had followed Chertok on-surface to hunt for the American saboteurs.

Since he'd last seen her, Rudenko had managed to pull on a suit from somewhere. It must be one of the spares, for he saw no name on the breast.

Okay, good, then the suit Makarov was carrying would serve for Carter. He ran through Hall Two into Hall One, lugging the spacesuit behind him … and found himself blocked. Hall Three, the top tine of the E, was closed off and the way blocked by an armed guard. "Let me through, soldier. Three is not yet empty of personnel."

The Red Army man eyed him insolently. "It is now. It's depressurized. Open to vacuum."

"Helmets on. Base oxygen is now fatally low." Rudenko's voice sounded in their ears.

Depressurized. Open to vacuum.

In which case, Vivian Carter was already dead and gone.

Makarov swore, but there was nothing left he could do. And the air around him was becoming unbreathable.

He dropped the spare suit. Pulled his helmet over his head, clicked it fastened. He could not go back, and he could not go forward. He could only go out, now: through the north hatch and into the icy dark of lunar night.

CHAPTER 33

Zvezda Base: Vivian Carter
January 24, 1980

VIVIAN came awake with a gasp, clawing her way out of a confused dream of panic and suffocation. She found herself unable to move her arms and fighting to breathe, and the desperate reality of her situation crashed over her.

Zvezda Base was depressurizing, and she was alone, bound to a chair with metal cables. "Shit, shit …"

Her head pounded, and her vision was blurred. The din of a klaxon emanated from a loudspeaker in the corner of the room, then a female voice. Svetlana's? No. Someone else.

Vivian kicked upward. Her legs were still free. The chair was metal and solid and really goddamned heavy.

But here on the Moon: not as heavy as it looked.

Vivian rocked forward, set her boots flat on the floor and pushed up. The legs of the chair lifted.

Crap, no, not like that. If she overbalanced she'd tumble forward onto her face, unable to break her fall with her hands. *Stupid, stupid. Come on, Vivian, think.*

Thinking was hard. Really freaking hard. Vivian just wanted to sleep.

You'll get a long sleep real soon now if you don't get moving.

She balanced on her feet precariously, and crab walked toward the door. She could take only small steps, swinging her legs at the knee, the chair frame forcing her to bend forward painfully.

The door opened inward, so even if Vivian could reach the handle, she'd need to back up to open it. But she wasn't about to escape from Zvezda attached to a goddamned chair.

Then again, even if she made it out into the hall, someone would pick her and the chair up and toss them right back in here.

She let the chair legs drop back to the floor, and looked at her arms. The cables that wrapped them were fastened together at each end with a combination padlock. Six numbers on each. Even if they were both the same combination, Vivian could never guess it, even if she could wriggle her fingers around that far. The date of the October Revolution, perhaps? Or of Leonov's lunar landing? She doubted it would be anything so obvious.

She needed a more drastic solution.

Vivian wheezed in the thin, oil-laden air. A new wave of dizziness rocked her. She didn't have a prayer of getting free. Given a couple hours she might have propelled herself around the room and tugged open locker doors until she found a tool kit or something. But she was bound fast by steel cables to a steel chair, and even if she already had a bimetal hacksaw and lubricant in her heavily constrained hands, it would take forever to cut through those cables.

I don't want to die.

Even over that brittle ever-loving klaxon, Vivian could hear herself whoop and wheeze as she tried to suck in oxygen that wasn't there.

She would asphyxiate right here. She had maybe a minute left before she blacked out.

The door opened, and a spacesuited figure bounded over to her. Vivian squinted at the nametag on the person's chest. She couldn't focus. Peered in through the helmet instead.

"Vika," she said, and coughed uncontrollably.

Viktoriya Isayeva grabbed the chair back and spun her around. As Vivian tilted backward, she felt the legs of the chair scrape across the floor as Vika dragged her out of Storage Nine.

Hall Three was empty of people. Red lights winked out of phase on consoles on either side as Vika towed her along. Blackness was already creeping into the edges of Vivian's field of view by the time Vika

330

dropped the chair back onto all four legs, reached for a face mask on a bench, and forced it painfully over Vivian's head.

An oxygen mask, attached to an umbilical. Vivian inhaled, and nothing happened. Her eyes widened, arms straining against the cables in panic. Then the Russian leaned across her to crank a valve, and oxygen flooded Vivian's nose and mouth.

Oh my God. She wasn't going to die. Yet. "Thank you," she said into the mask, then inhaled deeply and coughed.

Vika peered at the bulkhead, reading gauges bolted to the wall. Hesitated. Then unlatched her helmet and raised it. "Integrity is holding," she said, in that little-girl voice of hers. "Steady, but very low. I think perhaps my people are recovering the station. We have little time."

Vivian just sucked down oxygen, and raised her eyebrows questioningly. The sick core of her headache was already melting, and her vision was clearing. *Pure O_2 is one hell of a drug. Miraculous. Addictive.* She felt the urge to laugh.

"If we are to escape, it must be now."

"How?" Vivian mumbled through the mask.

Vika hefted up the oxygen tank and lay it across Vivian's arms on the chair. The girl was stronger than she looked. Once again, she hauled on the chair back, dragging Vivian through the empty Hall Three dormitory to the airlock at its end.

Vivian blinked. There was her white-silver NASA spacesuit on the floor, her PLSS propped up against the wall, her gloves and helmet resting on top of the backpack.

Isayeva began to work on the combination lock by Vivian's left arm, trying one number after another, her lips moving. Perhaps there were only a limited number of possibilities? Maybe so, because the first one came free after a half-dozen tries, and Vika swiftly unraveled the cable from her arm. "Me, now?"

"What? Oh. Sure." Vika was swaying, and Vivian pulled the mask off her face and passed it over. Vika took several quick breaths, then handed it back to Vivian and went to work on the right-hand combination.

Vivian blinked at her NASA suit. She was still weak as a kitten, and it would be a hell of a job to don it. She'd need to hold her breath, dive in and up, then get the oxygen mask back over her face as soon as her head popped out the top, before getting her gloves settled and everything else ready for her helmet. After that, she could plug the oxygen umbilical into the chest sockets while she pulled the PLSS on.

It was doable. But her helmet faceplate was still covered in black paint.

"If I put that on, I'll be blind." Again.

Isayeva found the second combination, untwisted the cable around Vivian's arm, threw it aside, coughed. "I will guide you out. Can you stand?"

Vivian pulled the mask off her face and thrust it at Vika. "Yes."

"Good. Where are we going?"

At the intent look in the small woman's eyes, Vivian felt the urge to laugh hysterically. "Beats me, sister."

"We cannot go to Hadley," Vika said. "Hadley is not safe. After this, Yashin will attack Hadley, maybe bomb it. He is too angry. He scares me."

Yashin scared Vivian too. "Bomb Hadley?"

"Nuclear bombs," Vika said, simply. "After this? Yes."

Jesus, Mary, and Joseph. "*Nuke* Hadley?"

Isayeva leaned forward, peering into her eyes, maybe to see if Vivian was lucid. "Yes. Destroy Hadley. So we must go to your other base. There, I can defect and we will be safe."

"There is no other base, Vika."

"Somewhere else then. In orbit? You have another station, besides Columbia?"

"Only my Command Module." If Dave Horn was even still up there. But Vivian couldn't match orbits and rendezvous with it. She had no ephemeris, didn't even know the orbital inclination. "That won't work. No."

Vika seized her as if about to shake her, clearly on the edge of panic. "Vivian! You must tell me where we must go, or I cannot fly us there. And then we will die here. If we are *lucky*. If Yashin captures us, he is insane, he will kill us slowly, torture us to death."

What the hell was *wrong* with all these Soviets? "Damn it, Vika, there is *no other base.*"

Isayeva stopped moving. "Well. That is unfortunate."

"Vika?"

Isayeva pulled the mask from Vivian's face. "Listen very carefully. Last chance. I have already come too far. Yashin will guess that I have helped you, and then he will kill me, and you too. I risked my life for you, Vivian Carter. So please. Let us escape this hell together."

"Vika …" Isayeva was watching her intently. To Vivian, Vika's face seemed to wash in and out of focus. The tunnel vision was creeping in again. "Let me breathe …"

Vika's eyes glittered. "Tell me. Tell me now."

"All right," Vivian coughed helplessly. Opened and closed her mouth, stared right into Isayeva's face with pleading eyes. Giving her best impression of a woman who could not speak, had no breath left to speak with.

As acting went, it wasn't much of a stretch.

"Vivian! Tell me, or I will leave you here. Escape alone, take my chances. You understand?"

Vivian nodded and rocked forward: weak and shaky, with defeat in her eyes.

And as Vika leaned in, Vivian exploded upward, punching both hands into the smaller woman's face. Isayeva's head snapped back, but at the same moment her fist swung around to slam into Vivian's nose. She leaped up, her knee pounding Vivian's ribs.

So much for my helpless victim act. Vivian lashed out again. Vika raised her forearm to deflect Vivian's fist, and kicked her with full force this time, her booted foot catching Vivian's hip and propelling her into the air. *Man, she just kicked me like a football.* Vika fought like a pro. Hard, fast, and instinctive.

Vivian had almost no schooling in hand-to-hand combat. It wasn't a big feature of Navy training. Ships and submarines fought with missiles. Pilots attacked from the cockpit. The chances of a naval officer coming into close combat with an enemy was approximately zero. Her training had reflected that. Vivian had spent more time learning how to fight fires than people. Now, that lack of preparedness might kill her.

She'd gotten into a few scraps in military bases around the world as a kid, though.

Vivian got her feet under her. Vika was reaching out again, maybe expecting Vivian to flinch or dodge her. Vivian did neither, but leaped forward into the other woman's face.

She had only moments. The oxygen level in the hall was still hellishly low. Exerting like this she had time for another swing or two, after which she'd need to lunge for the oxygen mask before she collapsed.

Isayeva danced back, gearing up to kick her again. But on Earth she could have hopped up and down twice and then swung. Here, when Vika's feet left the ground it took longer to drop down again.

Vivian lunged and wrapped Vika in a bear hug. They rolled over and over in the air in a long arc. Vivian pounded the woman on the back of the head, but her skull was hard there.

They banged down onto the floor. Vika yanked her back, and tried to sink her teeth into Vivian's already-bleeding nose. Vivian whipped her head forward, attempting a head butt, except Isayeva swung to the side and Vivian's forehead met Vika's temple instead of her nose.

Her left fist caught Vika under the chin, snapping her jaw shut. Their faces were close enough now that Vivian could see the other woman's eyes swim as the blow stunned her.

But: *No air.*

Vivian shoved Isayeva away and dove back toward the oxygen mask, which still hissed and sputtered. She jumped too far and over-shot, scrabbled toward it.

Looking up, she saw Vika fifteen feet away, raising a handgun. "Crap …"

Vivian changed course. Grabbed her NASA spacesuit, and swung it up over herself. Blackness threatened to steal her away. *Need to breathe. I'll be dead anyway if I don't breathe.*

Vika fired once, twice, three times, the gunshots sounding like the pop of a toy pistol in the thin air. Vivian felt the thwack as each bullet hit the suit. *No chance of explosion,* she thought groggily. *O₂ too sparse for a spark to catch.*

The oxygen tank was eight feet away, the mask bobbing up and down as the precious air bled uselessly out. Far from Vivian's reach.

I'm done.

With an oddly attenuated beeping, the airlock at the end of Hall Three opened and someone stepped in wearing a suit, likely a man by his movements. At the same time, with a boom and a loud hiss, cold air rushed out of the vents into the sealed hall.

Vika was still aiming the gun right at her. Vivian squirmed away as the woman leaped forward for the kill.

Behind her, the man snapped off his glove, reached into the thigh pocket of his suit, and pulled out another handgun.

Okay, so that's death-squared for me then.

Vika spun. She and the new cosmonaut fired at the same moment. At each other.

Vika's bullet hit the man's chest and ricocheted off with an audible squeal. The man flinched, but fired again, the quick burst of a semiautomatic pistol.

His shots hit Vika in the thigh. Several bullets in the same place. Vika screamed, falling backward in slow motion.

The man loped toward Vivian. She watched in bemused fascination, no longer able to comprehend what was going on.

He squatted beside her. His reflective visor was down to obscure his face, but his suit patch read MAKAPOB.

Makarov held the gun out to her, grip first.

"What?"

Another trick? If so, Vivian couldn't fathom it. Behind them Vika still screamed, hands clamped around her thigh.

As she didn't take it, he placed the gun on the ground and unclipped his helmet, lifted it from his shoulders. It was Makarov all right. "Kapitan Carter."

"Yeah?"

"Kill her."

"Huh?"

"If she talks, I am dead too."

But Vivian had already grabbed the gun and kneeled up.

Isayeva had seen the danger now and was scrabbling for her own gun, which had hit the deck just a few feet away, even while she still whimpered and clutched at her leg.

Vivian fired almost before she knew it. Shot Isayeva in the head. Blood spattered, and the Soviet agent toppled sideways onto the floor.

Vivian slid the safety on and dropped the gun. "You could have done that," she said coldly.

"Take it with you. My gun." Makarov loped forward.

"What the hell is going on?"

He turned Vika over, started to unhook her life support backpack and unzip her suit. "Put this on. Get out. Maybe you will find your people—if they are still out there."

"What?"

"We are bringing Zvezda back. Others of us will be trying to get in here soon. But if we recapture you, do me the favor? Tell them you held the gun on me to let you escape. Yes?"

Vivian closed her eyes, trying to make sense of it. What the hell was really going on? Had the whole US attack on Zvezda been faked, an elaborate deception so that Vika could trick her into revealing secrets?

She raised Vika's gun. "So, Comrade Nikolai. Are you the latest good cop? How much more of this hell do I have to go through?"

Makarov looked at her, shocked. "Put the suit on, Carter. Get out of here."

"You plan to follow me? Seriously, I have no idea where 'my people' might be. If they're even here. Are they?"

He was staring as if she were demented. "Why would I follow? Put the suit on."

Fine. Whatever. Put the suit on. Figure out the rest later.

"Okay, sure." Vivian put the gun down. Helped Makarov haul Isayeva's bleeding corpse out of the suit. And dived into the back of it.

It was tighter than her NASA suit, harder to worm her feet down through the legs, and then her arms through the upper half. It had been customized for Isayeva, and on Vivian it was tight at the thigh and shoulder. Makarov helped, and while she was getting settled into it, slapped patches onto the suit where his bullets had hit it.

The suit collar was still sticky with Vika's blood. Her body looked so small and broken, lying discarded on the floor of Hall Three, her face calm in death.

Calm, aside from the red hole Vivian had put in her forehead.

Vivian pulled herself together. Her entire body was wet with sweat, her breathing still laboring despite the air that now poured into Hall Three.

Her sweat, Isayeva's blood. Who cared which was which any more?

Makarov clipped a flashlight to her waist. "Do not use this until you are far off. They will see you."

Vivian reached for Vika's gloves, wriggled her fingers into them. Makarov snapped them closed at her wrist. She prodded his arm. "Hey. Why are you doing this?"

"Because I am not a killer, and this is not right."

"Uh, what?" Vivian indicated Isayeva's corpse. Vika was certainly dead because of Makarov, even if he'd forced Vivian to fire the final bullet.

"She has already killed one of yours. And would have killed me if I had not been quick."

Vivian's spine chilled. "Who did she kill?"

"On Columbia Station. The astronaut, Jackson."

"You're kidding."

He looked frustrated. "What? It is true."

"Is everyone else all right?"

"Wagner and Mason are also dead. Others are injured."

Jeez.

Don't think about it. That's not something we can address right now.

Vivian glanced at her chest. The gauges and switches were all very different those on her NASA suit. The labels were in Cyrillic. "I've no clue what all this shit is."

Makarov pointed. "Here is heating and cooling, Both the same dial. You understand? One way for heat, the other way for cold. This, oxygen flow. Turn it up if you exert. Here is your oxygen remaining, on this gauge. This is radio. See here? On-off. Frequency. This here, internal suit lights. Turn them off until you are away. If suit breaches, patches in right calf pocket."

"Okay," she said. "But, Nikolai, I can't get to Hadley in just this suit."

She expected him to say, like Vika, "Then go to the other place, that mythical place where the United States stores its nuclear arsenal." But Makarov merely looked helpless. "I do not know what to tell you. But out there, perhaps you have a chance. Here, none."

"Copy that," she said. "And thanks."

He picked up the backpack, the life support system that would have been called a PLSS if it had been of US make. "All this is controlled by the switches and dials on your chest panel. Do not touch the settings here."

"Sure thing." Vivian could hardly reach around to adjust them anyway. Makarov hitched it onto her, pushed her toward the airlock. "Go."

"Go *where?*"

He stopped, pulled her around. "Listen. We are not all like Yashin and Isayeva. Some of us still believe in … in space, as the, as the domain for all humans, everywhere. Yes?"

That sounded too trite. What was Makarov's game? Was he for real? "I don't believe you."

"Then do not. But go."

"Where? Hadley is five hundred miles away."

"You have a day of air. Maybe your friends will find you."

They wouldn't. Vivian was sure of it. But what other choice did she have?

He looked around suddenly, maybe reacting to something in his headset radio. "You must go *now*."

"Which way? Once I'm out?"

"We are on the southeast corner of Kopernik. Keep the crater to your left. Keep going around, and then head north until Mare Imbrium. Good luck."

Just like that. "Okay. Sure. Thanks."

Moments later, Vivian was in a dark airlock. Lights glowed faintly from within her suit collar: indicators, a couple of numbers, a light on the microphone below her mouth. She located the switch on her chest unit, and flicked it. All the lights went out.

She stood in near darkness, wearing a dead woman's suit, the blood and sweat on her neck drying in the steady pulse of oxygen.

The suit smelled of Vika. Of treachery and death.

Jeez, Vivian. Don't think about that. Think about hard vacuum. Think about EVA. Which you're seconds away from.

The air hissed out of the airlock. "Turn," came Makarov's voice in her ears. "In front."

Vivian knew where the hatch controls were, from glimpsing them before she'd turned out her lights. She cranked the wheel, and the outer door began to open ... onto more darkness.

Of course. It was night out here. *Good grief.*

"Radio off until you are far away," Makarov warned. "Good luck."

Then a click, and quiet white noise.

Another click, as Vivian turned her own radio off at the switch.

She stepped out into the surface, her eyes gradually adapting. She glanced up at the partially sunlit Earth, and from reading the shadows on its face knew that dawn at Copernicus could not be far away.

Another day or so, at most. It was unlikely Vivian would live to see it.

She was not alone. Cosmonauts were all around her, three of them close by, tinkering with machinery, and half a dozen more spread out along the side of Zvezda Base.

Okay, so now it was suspicious that Vivian was walking around without lights. She turned them back on and set off, walking briskly and with purpose.

Uphill was to her left, downhill to her right. At the downhill end of Zvezda she saw a line of four Soviet LEK Landers, and the twisted remains of a fifth. So, there genuinely had been a US stealth attack. Of limited scope, but enough to give Vivian this chance at a last few hours of futile freedom. Some time to herself, at least, to come to terms with her imminent demise.

Or: the Soviets were so determined to make this look convincing that they'd torched one of their own spacecraft.

No, that was surely nuts. Wasn't it? Who even knew what was true, any more?

God, she was tired.

The wrecked lander gave her a plausible reason to head in that direction, so she did. She'd pass it, put the line of landers between her and Zvezda, then head east. She glanced up at the stars, and chose a couple of constellations to keep her on the correct heading.

The constellations would move, of course, as the Moon continued in its orbit around the Earth, and the Earth around the Sun. She tried to calculate how long it would take for the error in her heading to become significant, but blanked. Her head was too fuzzy for math right now.

One thing at a time, Vivian.

She walked to the end of the LEK line and looped around it. Damned if there wasn't now a line of the two-person LK Landers off to her right. Going any other direction might look odd if anyone caught sight of her. Perhaps one of these LKs was even Vika's. So Vivian bounced confidently on toward the LKs, then passed them and kept on going.

Vivian was easily visible, yet she was disregarded. But, in a way, she was not surprised. The Soviets relied on drills and rote learning. At a time like this, everyone would know where they had to be, and Rudenko would be directing her teams. So it wasn't the Zvezda crew she was worried about, but Yashin and his cronies. They were presumably out here somewhere too, hunting for the US team who had sabotaged their base.

Vivian might run into them at any time.

All she could do was keep moving and hope for the best.

Whatever *that* meant. She'd be lucky if she could cover even fifty miles out of the five hundred that separated her from Hadley. But, what else could she do? Other than lay down and sleep, which was what every nerve and sinew in her body was begging for.

Sure, she'd sleep. But not until she was away from here.

She walked on, glancing back every few minutes. Seemed like she'd left all the Soviets far behind. She'd turned the lights back off as she walked toward the LK line, so if there was a clock somewhere in her helmet, she couldn't see it. But it felt like about fifteen minutes before she glanced back toward Zvezda Base … and realized she was being followed.

A dim headlamp was bumping up and down on the regolith. The lights of Zvezda Base and its landers and cosmonauts were a mile behind her now, but this lone headlamp was less than a half-mile distant.

A dirt bike. *Crap.*

Could they see her? Maybe. Earthshine was actually pretty bright, now she was properly adapted. Or did she have a tracker on her? Had Makarov set her up after all?

No, damn it. Simpler than that. They were following her boot prints.

Time to pick up the pace. Vivian broke into a lope, and immediately kicked a rock with her right boot and fell. Rolled on the surface, bobbed back up onto her feet and set off again.

She headed uphill. Rockier terrain, less chance of her tracks showing, harder for the Soviet to trail her. Once she'd bumped over rock for thirty paces, she changed course again.

Despite her exertion, she was getting cold. She identified the dial that Makarov had indicated, and tweaked it a quarter turn to the right. No way of telling if that was too little or too much. She'd just have to experiment.

She loped on. For a while, she could fool herself that she was maintaining her distance from the Soviet bike. But she wasn't.

Hell.

Time to start thinking about defending herself. She had Makarov's gun, but couldn't pull its trigger effectively in a glove. She might hit the guy with a rock, for all the good that would do. Best might be to attack the bike. If she could incapacitate it and then run, it would become a straight foot race.

Yeah. Right. And who'd win that?

Up and over a hill and down the other side. Vivian had been jumping over rock for a while now—this was the lunar highlands, after all—and right now, her pursuer had no direct line of sight on her.

Looked up the next hill, took a deep breath, and began to run up it.

She covered a surprising amount of ground before she had to pause. Panting, she looked downslope, and there was her pursuer, headlight bobbing as his bike bumped over obstacles.

Screw it. Vivian clicked the radio on. "Mayday, Mayday. Vivian Carter out on-surface, seeking US assistance, come back?" No response. "Night Corps? Minerva? Anyone?"

Nothing. Maybe they could hear her, but she couldn't hear them. More likely, no one was within the limited range of the suit radio.

"US lunar forces, this is Vivian Carter, escaped from Soviet Zvezda Base and seeking help. Just to complicate, I'm wearing a Soviet suit and being pursued—"

She was suddenly blinded by a silent explosion thirty feet to her left. The Soviet on her trail had fired a rocket-powered grenade at her. Rocks and dust pummeled her suit. "Damn it!"

She glanced about her, blinking in the afterglow of the explosion. Dazzled. "Come on, eyes." Paused. Blinked. "Seriously, any time now."

When her vision returned, Vivian threw caution to the winds and ran like hell. Ducked and wove as best she could. Still heading uphill, in hopes that this would be harder going for the dirt bike and make it use up battery power more quickly. *Fat chance.*

She expected a second explosion at any moment. Expected to be blown off her feet and smashed to the ground, or pummeled with rocks from a nearby explosion. At this point a direct hit might be more merciful. She'd feel just a fraction of a second of agony.

No blast came. Her pursuer might not have many missiles. Rocket-powered grenades weighed, what? Ten pounds if it was an RPG-7. And they'd be bulky.

"Mayday, Mayday, Vivian Carter fleeing Soviet pursuit on-surface, seeking US assistance. Any freaking assistance at all."

No one could hear her. She scanned her surroundings as best she could. Hide? Or loop around to get the jump on her pursuer? Bash a rock into his faceplate until it shattered, then steal his bike? It still wouldn't get her anywhere near Hadley—

The giant bloom of a flare directly over her head, impossibly bright. "Shit!"

She leaped toward the nearest crater. Sailed through space to land on her hands and knees. "Ow, goddamn it ..."

Dust swamped her. She rolled onto her back, tried to peer into the glare. It was a plume of rocket exhaust, just a few tens of feet away. "Jeeeeesus!"

It couldn't be.

It was. An Apollo Lunar Module was coming down just fifty feet from her.

The landing wasn't pretty. Vivian couldn't watch directly—the column of fire was too goddamn bright—but even out of the edge of her peripheral vision she could see the LM lurch as it thumped into the ground, and then that insane brightness quenched, leaving only the red-hot glow of the descent engine exhaust nozzle.

A crackle in her headset. "Vivian Carter, your ride is here."

Voice seemed vaguely familiar. "Be aware: at least one hostile on my six. Has an RPG."

"I'm on it."

Gerry Lin, that's who it was. Sandoval's deputy. Okay, but what did *on it* mean?

Next moment, she found out. Lin had jumped up into the open upper hatch of his LM and was firing something. Something with muzzle flashes. Then a pause, before a much larger explosion a few hundred feet to the southwest. Rocket launcher?

Not that Vivian was doing much scrutiny. She was on her feet and running toward the LM as fast as she could. "Top hatch, then?"

"Both hatches open. Ladies' choice."

Lin had flown and landed this Lunar Module in the dark *with both fricking hatches open*? There'd been no time for him to pop them since landing. "Man, you're hardcore."

"You know it. Get up here."

Vivian was already in midair. Midspace. Whatever. "Roger that."

She'd jumped from a running start. Couldn't spend time stepping prettily up the ladder, and the steps were perilously close to that fatally hot descent engine skirt anyway. The egress porch above that ladder was ten feet off the ground, and Vivian damn near made it all the way up in one bound. Slammed her left boot down on the almost-top rung to propel herself higher, and grabbed the LM by its buggy left eye, illuminated from inside by the console lights. She got her boot onto the jutting reaction control thruster assembly, reached up with both gloves for the docking radar antenna, and hauled herself up to the LM roof.

She'd have pulled somersaults if she'd had to.

Light spilled out of the top hatch around Lin's suit. Vivian let go of the antenna assembly and scrabbled forward. "Hi there."

"Whoa, holy smokes." Lin tossed aside whatever he was holding and grabbed her.

"Hey, you told me to get up here."

"Yeah. Uh—"

"Gonna ingress head first. Out of my way."

Lin dropped clear and Vivian almost dislocated her shoulder pulling herself forward, rocking up, kicking her legs in the air, careless of the possibility of ripping her suit on the hatch. She was long past caution now. "We need to go."

"No shit."

One moment of near panic as she got wedged partway in. She hung there, then twisted and scraped by. *Maybe it helps that Vika's suit is two sizes too small. Just like her goddamned heart.*

Enjoy hell, Viktoriya Isayeva, Vivian thought as she tumbled to the floor of the LM in slow motion.

"Hold on."

"To what?"

Gerry Lin was already strapping into his harness in the left-hand position, the commander's position. Vivian already knew this LM wasn't Athena. Identical in layout and design, but the scuffs and marks, some of the paint colors … not Athena. Familiar, yet alien.

Whoever lent their baby to this crazy Lin guy to save my ass? I owe them big.

The thrust of acceleration clamped Vivian to the floor as the LM took off. She reached out to anchor herself the only way she could. Wrapped her arms around Lin's calves—*nope, that's not embarrassing at all*—and thrust her boots against the edge of the floor-level hatch.

Launching with both hatches open? *Sure. Whatever.* "Go, man, go."

"We're going."

"I'd help, but …"

"I got it."

The Lunar Module arced up into the sky.

"Where's Sandoval?" Lin said.

Once the first surge relented and the LM heeled over, Vivian struggled up, pulling herself up on the right side of the LM and buckling in. "Peter's here?"

"I brought him. He set the explosives at Zvezda."

"That was all him?"

"Guy's a regular one-man band."

"Didn't see him. I was busy getting my ass out of there."

Lin flipped switches. "Well. He'll be fine."

"We can't go look for him?"

"Where? I never got a ping from him after the explosions. Had to guess, I'd say the Reds chased him into Copernicus."

"Into the *crater*?"

"Yeah. Call numbers for me?"

"Sure." Vivian scanned the dials and switches for the propulsion system. "To Hadley?"

"Yup."

She glanced at the guidance computer. "Course preloaded?" Better be. Vivian couldn't plot a point-to-point trajectory from scratch in under an hour, and two would be better. If Lin said no, Vivian didn't know how she'd respond.

"PAD already loaded. Burn to Hadley is P85, then we do final approach on P67, just like always."

"Just like always," she said, her tone ironic. "P85, P67, that's a roger."

Lin glanced at her. "Numbers for descent right away, Vivian. It'll be fast."

Yeah, obviously. "Roger that."

Her eyes raked the panels again. She was more used to standing where Lin stood now, her own hands on the controls, but she'd simmed the other side often enough. "DPS tank pressures nominal. I'm seeing an RCS caution light?"

"Yeah, I know about that. Prep for P85." They'd transition to the program for the short arc across to Hadley in seconds.

She looked at the computer display. "Eighty-five, we're all set—"

Then came a slam up through their feet as if a giant had kicked the LM. Vivian was thrown back, her harness arresting her painfully just before she could smash into the ascent engine housing behind her.

With a sickening lurch, they went into a spin.

Vivian knew instinctively what had happened. A Soviet ground-to-air missile had just exploded at the base of their Lunar Module.

Everything was in motion in the cabin. The radar altimeter read all nines, unable to get a lock on the ground. Vivian grabbed the controls on her side of the cabin.

"Still got it," Lin said with supernatural calm, and Vivian felt pulses of thruster fire as he fought to bring them out of the spin.

She squinted at her readouts. "Thrust is all over the place."

"Yeah, DPS is hosed. Preparing to abort to orbit."

They'd lost the descent propulsion system, the rocket motor that was keeping them up. It was the right call, the one Vivian would have made if she'd been on the commander's side, but could they? "Roger on abort."

"Aborting descent stage."

Lin pressed the button. Beneath them, four pyro charges fired to sever the attachment points between the ascent and descent stages. Explosive bolts drove guillotine blades through the electrical cables connecting the two craft.

A dizzying jolt and swing as the heavier descent stage dropped away. Freed of its weight, the ascent stage powered upward. They both bent their knees to absorb the shock.

But still they lurched and yawed. "Huh." Lin fought it.

Startling, how quiet it had become. The ascent engine was a dull pulse behind them, with no alarms, no crunching or rending sounds. But they were out of control, the engine firing awry.

Vivian scanned the panel. "Ascent engine thrust only thirty percent. Not enough."

"Aw, crap." Stress veins bulged from Lin's temples and neck.

Numbers returned on Vivian's guidance computer as they momentarily stabilized. At least in one axis. "Eight hundred feet, dropping hot." Vivian's voice was steady. Just a couple of pilots auguring in, still working the problem.

Lin wrestled the controls. "Thrust is just swinging us around. I'm guessing bent pipe. Ideas?"

Vivian had been thinking the same. The engine nozzle at the base of the ascent engine motor had been compromised by the violence of the disconnect. Because of their rapidly fluctuating attitude, the descent stage hadn't sheared clean. "Concur. I got nothing."

"Then we're going in."

Landing with no landing gear, no legs. *Yeah, that's called "crashing."*

"Three hundred feet," she said. "Two fifty. Two hundred—"

"Gonna push everything, mains and RCS, even if—"

"Do it now!" The cabin surged around them, flinging them back and forth in their straps.

As they went in, Vivian realized she'd never even thanked him for coming to her aid.

"Brace for impact," were the last words she heard him say.

CHAPTER 34

Copernicus Crater: Peter Sandoval
January 25, 1980

PETER Sandoval hiked across the floor of Copernicus Crater in the dark. For a while he had turned off his goggles to minimize his power usage, but he kept kicking boulders and stumbling on crater lips, so he turned them back on and turned down his suit heating instead. It wouldn't hurt him to move faster to keep his heart rate up and keep warm.

He'd already turned off the power assists on his boots. They'd have helped him lope maybe half again as fast, but they soaked up power like crazy, and he didn't have any to spare.

He'd descended into the crater well west of Zvezda Base. The overall slope on the inside of the crater wasn't too extreme but it was oddly layered, almost terraced, on the inside. He was sure Vivian could have told him why it looked that way, but Sandoval didn't speak geology and didn't care if he never learned. He'd already seen enough lunar rocks to last him a lifetime.

He'd made it down by jumping, scrambling, sometimes digging in with a pick. Some of those jumps hadn't been the acts of a rational person. He'd had no time for *rational*. Once he made it to the gentler slope, well down inside the crater bowl, he'd looked up to see what looked like a cliff towering over him. *Whoa.* Weird to think he'd just survived that descent.

The Soviets had some kind of cable-car arrangement to winch themselves up and down into the crater. The gondola was still at the top and not moving, so Sandoval knew they weren't on his tail. But they had a sizeable contingent down here in their Crater Annex, so he wasn't scot-free yet.

The floor of Copernicus Crater was a good twelve thousand feet below the rim, and almost sixty miles in diameter. And once Sandoval hiked all the way north to the opposite rim, he'd need to haul his ass up and out. That would be no picnic.

Time enough to worry about that when he got there. If he did.

Once away from the rim the crater floor was as pocked and hummocked with subsequent smaller craters as everywhere else on the Moon. But at least Sandoval had a target to aim for: at the crater center were three mountain cones a good four thousand feet tall. He just had to get to those, and then keep going.

He gave the Soviets' Annex a wide berth. It shone bright in his night-vision goggles. Several glowing portholes, plus blue beacon indicators above every hatch and green telltales on low objects that he figured were Lunokhod Rovers. But he saw no cosmonauts, and didn't worry about them a whole lot. If necessary, he figured he could outrun them.

Sandoval trudged on. God, the Moon was boring at the best of times, and triply boring at night.

He'd killed Vivian.

He was pretty sure of it. His Semtex charges had blown more spectacularly than he'd anticipated, despite the subglacial temperature. Signs were that they'd lost environmental control and even containment in much of the base, and in that kind of panic, Sandoval was guessing no one would take the time to ensure the American chick had a suit. He certainly didn't see Vivian outside—US spacesuits were very different, their IR signatures clearly distinguishable. That meant she was still inside, and probably restrained.

If Sandoval had been a betting man, he'd have laid down folding money that Vivian Carter was toast.

He tried to console himself that maybe it was better than whatever Yashin had been putting her through. The Soviets had denied taking her captive, meaning that the KGB bastards who were really running things would have no scruples about damaging her for information.

Sandoval had met people who'd been through the KGB torture mill. It wasn't pretty.

Maybe they'd even killed her before Sandoval's acts of sabotage. That might make him feel … better? Maybe?

The hours dribbled by. Sandoval wearied long before getting to the central peaks. He stopped, sat. Checked his gauges.

Damn it. His O_2 and water use were nominal but he was still using too much power. The heavy batteries mounted in his backpack and alongside his ribs were still putting out, but clambering into Copernicus had burned a lot of energy, and heating his exosuit was draining even more. *Crap.*

As for Sandoval's own organic energy supplies, he'd eaten the energy bars mounted inside his suit collar long ago. Those were the only food he had access to, until he could take his helmet off.

Not much choice, then. He reluctantly reached to the left and stuck his tongue out toward a sticky strip. Took a big old hit of Benzedrine.

Woo. Woo! Speed freak. Yeah!

All Sandoval's nerves twitched, and he was suddenly aware of the many smells and tastes inside his suit. Above him, the stars glowed brighter. He turned his suit heaters down a notch.

God *damn!*

He resisted the urge to turn on his boot assists and tear off across the crater floor like a maniac. But he did stand immediately, bounce up and down, and then lope off.

A few paces in, he switched it up into a run.

He could go all day now. For some values of "day."

Sandoval hated amphetamines with a passion, because he loved the rush they gave him. If he'd been that kind of guy, he could easily get addicted to this shit. Without question.

But the speed—both kinds—sure made this sorry-ass gloomy Moon a bit easier to bear.

The Benzedrine was wearing out by the time Sandoval made it to the northern rim of Copernicus. It had been a tough climb, but at least dawn was on its way. Flecks of sunlight were striking the topmost edges of the crater rim far to his west, and moving slowly, so damned slowly, to illuminate them a little more. That sunlight was actually causing him grief, because when he looked that way he got dazzled and then had to wait for his scotopic vision to return before he could dedicate himself to the climb again.

He was using the headlight mounted into his helmet now, and the flashlight at his waist as well. If the Soviets had really tracked him all the way across the damned crater floor, they were welcome to take their shot. He didn't think that was too likely.

Real dawn should be here soon, and Sandoval craved the return of the light.

All of a sudden, there he was, on the crater edge. Sun to the right of him, blackness to the left.

By now he'd been on his own for what felt like forever, and on the waning dregs of the Benzedrine he'd found himself fantasizing weirdly that when he crested the ridge he'd see a glorious green valley stretched out in front of him: trees and fields, or maybe even rain forests like Panama, with parrots squawking and flapping around from tree to tree. Maybe a nice river at the valley floor, with shaded banks.

Nope. Just more goddamn Moon, its plaster-gray surface under that very partial and irritating illumination of side-angle sunbeams. Somehow, they made everything even more stark than full-on night. *This shit just never looks welcoming.*

Again, he checked O_2, H_2O, power. Yeah, the Benzedrine had obviously helped. His body was eating its own fat, rather than sucking the life out of his suit batteries. *Awesome.* But he was well beyond the rush now, his head aching, anxiety and mild depression nibbling at him. Anger, too. Anger at himself for leaving Vivian to die, even though he'd had no choice. Anger at the Reds for making him do it. Anger at the USAF for making him come to the Moon at all. God, he *hated* this place. He'd never hated anywhere quite this much.

Sandoval knew it was mostly artificial. He also knew that he'd need another hit of Benzedrine, Real Soon Now, if he was going to get back to Hadley alive. But he'd put it off as long as possible, till all his nerves were screaming. Even louder.

He pulled a radiofrequency detector from his shin pocket, and turned it on. Nothing happened, and he restrained the temptation to toss it back over his shoulder into the crater. *Come on, man. Cool the irrational urges before you do something that kills you.*

He cycled the power, and once it rebooted it immediately locked onto the transponder blip.

Sandoval stood and followed that blip up hill and down dale. As he descended off the crater rim he lost the signal as he lost line of sight, but kept moving, confident he'd get it back.

He found the transponder wedged into a crack at the top of a cinder-cone ridge. Well, it probably wasn't a cinder cone, but it looked like one. Hell, ask the ghost of Vivian what it was; Sandoval didn't really give a damn.

He peered downhill, and there on the far side of the ridge was a Lunar Rover, parked neat and tidy and waiting for him. It belonged to Apollo 30, and Seaton and Massey had made a special LM trip last week to put it there. They'd also placed the transponder so that he'd be able to find it.

Shame they couldn't have stayed there in their LM and given him a ride home. But that was impractical. You couldn't keep a crewed but otherwise unsupported LM in the middle of nowhere in night's deep freeze. Not enough power. Too much chance of a critical failure that would kill the crew.

Plus, of course, in one distantly possible scenario it would've been both of them arriving here right now, Sandoval and Vivian, and a LM couldn't carry four.

Yeah, but that didn't happen, because I killed Vivian.

Damn it all.

Sandoval gave in. Stuck out his tongue and took another Benzedrine hit. *Hey, you only live once. If that.*

All his senses erupted again, and he ran to the rover.

He felt the creak and sag as it took his weight. In this suit he weighed about twice as much as an Apollo astronaut, and all that mass was going into the webbing of one seat.

Hey hey hey, wouldn't it be funny if the seat broke?

Goddamn hilarious.

Sandoval flipped switches, checked the battery power. It all looked good. And he had four or five sets of spare batteries right behind him.

He reached back to the oxygen tank, found the umbilical, and connected it into the external feed on his chest. Now he was breathing O_2 from the rover's substantial supply, and not what remained in his suit tank. He screwed up his eyes against the Benzedrine buzz and ran the numbers again to be sure. Yeah. More than enough.

Ahead of him Sandoval had five hundred miles to travel, at fifteen to twenty miles an hour, over shit terrain. At some point he'd need to catch some sleep, because he wasn't about to literally drive himself into insanity by taking three or four Benzedrine in a row. He would drive till he couldn't see straight, slide into sleep, have godawful Benzedrine-tainted dreams, scream and shout and thrash around inside the suit, then wake up half-rested and three-quarters petrified, and drive the rest of the way home.

Without Vivian.

Shut up.

Sandoval set off. His route would take him off the highlands and onto the lava-covered expanse of Mare Imbrium, and then it should be a straight shot. Well, straightish, in the sense of having to concentrate every moment on steering around boulders and craters.

He bumped along, focusing on the terrain and his onboard direction setting. After half an hour he was already bone weary of bracing himself against the turns and the hops the rover did whenever he went over a bump. This was going to be a very long five hundred miles.

Vivian would love this. He just knew it. Out on-surface, traveling where no other human had ever left boot print or tire track? That was totally Vivian's scene. She'd be talking a mile a minute right now if she were by his side. Happy as a pig in mud.

Sadly ironic that Sandoval got to do it instead of her, alone, and hating it.

And it was for goddamned sure that he wasn't about to stop to pick up any rocks on the way.

35

Lunar Surface: Vivian Carter
January 25, 1980

VIVIAN stirred. She could see nothing.

How long had they let her sleep? When would Yashin be back, with his shouted demands and his drugs, and the pain, on top of her all-consuming fatigue?

She shuddered convulsively along her entire body, and realized that she was somehow even more tightly constrained than she'd been in Storage Nine.

Oh, dear Lord. What now?

Eyes open, but seeing nothing. Had they put her back into her NASA spacesuit, with its painted-over helmet? What sense would that make? Could you even thread an unconscious, floppy person into a suit?

No. It didn't smell right.

Her memories crept back. This wasn't her suit. She was wearing Vika's suit—Vika the Viper, that deceitful, homicidal maniac. So, if Vivian couldn't see, there was some brand-new crappy reason for that.

Vivian tried to move her head, but her helmet wouldn't budge. Wriggled her legs easily enough, but her right arm was jammed in place, and she appeared to be lying on her left arm.

Pinned by the head and shoulder? *Boy, this is fun.*

Maybe she should start panicking. Or save that for later. After all, she was still breathing.

Vivian flexed, bent her legs, and pushed upward. Wriggled her left arm out from beneath her and reached up. Yep, definitely something on top of her, but with her gloved hand she couldn't identify it. *Sack of potatoes? Probably not.*

She shoved with both arms and legs, and the encumbrance that held her down shifted slightly. *Again, again.* She pushed hard, several more times, and finally found a surge of anger strong enough to thrust it up and away.

Light spilled in through her visor.

The sack of potatoes was an astronaut. She'd regained consciousness with Gerry Lin's spacesuited torso sprawled across her upper body.

Lin was dead. His helmet was cracked like an egg, his head twisted around and jammed against the shaft of the LM ascent motor. His face was blackened and bloody. Disfigured. Dehumanized.

Damn it. He seemed like a really good guy.

Vivian was lying across the LM instrument consoles. At any other time that might have been alarming—what switches might she have inadvertently flipped? But right now it wouldn't make much difference. Most of the lights were out anyway.

It started coming back to her now. Their ascent stage had come in hard. Smashed down onto the surface base first, but much too fast. From her memories of vertiginous motion, Vivian was sure their LM had then rolled a couple of times. You didn't get to be a naval aviator without developing an innate sense of what your vehicle had just been through.

So, the LM had rolled and then face-planted, windows to regolith, its motor jutting up at a forty-five-degree angle behind her.

Vivian had been extremely lucky. Though, again, it kind of sucked that both the top and front hatches were now facing down into the lunar soil.

She took a deep breath. What next? Could she lever the front of the Module up, or apply sheer force to get it to roll over?

That's a negatory, as Sandoval might say. The dry mass of the ascent stage was maybe ten thousand pounds. She didn't know how much fuel remained in its tanks, adding to that weight. Perhaps none, since the propellant tanks had likely not survived impact; the Aerozine and oxidizer had probably spilled out and sublimated off. Either way, she wasn't about to shift the Module she was trapped inside.

Think more, Vivian.

The Lunar Module was compressible, and—as designed—had crumpled rather than shearing or tearing. Its skin was distorted, shoved inward in an odd and disturbing way. The circuit-breaker box on the left-hand side of the LM—Vivian's side, in her own LM—now jutted into the cabin. It seemed like no part of the interior was unscathed. The whole craft was distended, altered, almost eerie.

Thank God this isn't Athena. Or I might cry.

Okay, so she was trapped in an airless and damaged Lunar Module. No immediate chance of escape. Wearing a Russian suit with limited oxygen.

She'd need to cut her way out, and head off on foot again.

But not in Vika's suit.

No way. On a gut level, Vivian didn't want to keep that woman's spacesuit on a moment longer than she had to. And on a brain level it made even less sense. The Soviet suit had not a single advantage.

Given time and luck, Vivian might plumb the oxygen and water tanks into Vika's suit to recharge it. But—paradoxically for the arid, airless Moon—it wasn't lack of oxygen or water that would kill her. It was power, and her own exhalations.

To survive longer than another few hours Vivian would need to replace the batteries that would keep the suit fans turning and its environmental control system working. There should be spare EVA batteries in the rear compartment of the LM. She'd also need fresh lithium hydroxide cartridges to scrub the CO_2 out of her air. But the American batteries and LiOH cartridges wouldn't fit the Soviet suit.

Essentially, if Vivian was to survive on the stark lunar surface more than another couple of hours, she'd need the NASA PLSS backpack she was familiar with.

Even so, she would have to take that PLSS off twice a day, to replace the batteries and the LiOH canisters and top up her oxygen and water. Disconnecting and doffing the PLSS, servicing it, and then donning it again all by herself before she ran out of air was going to be a race against time, even with a system Vivian was intimately familiar with. Trying to fumble and guess with the Soviet backpack would be hopeless, even if everything else worked.

Far down the list but still significant: any Night Corps astronaut who saw Vivian approaching in a Soviet suit with "CCCP" emblazoned across her helmet would likely just shoot her.

"Ha." Vivian should be so lucky, to happen upon Night Corps. The only USAF black ops guy for several hundred miles was dead and spread across the consoles right next to her.

Come on, Vivian. Get on with it.

So: she had to seal up the crashed LM. Repressurize it. Get out of the Soviet suit and into the spare NASA suit that hung in the rear of the LM before she froze to death. Plug in her umbilicals for air and water. And then work fast to grab everything else she'd need.

Could she pressurize the Module for long enough to change suits, or were there a dozen punctures in the LM's skin? Only one way to find out.

Ellis .... Vivian experienced a surge of loneliness that bordered on panic. With Ellis's calming presence right now, she might have had a chance. By herself, the odds were stacked against her. The chances of her screwing up were ... let's face it, pretty high. Any error would take her out of the game. Even if she made every move to the best of her abilities, she'd still need to perform a bunch of actions alone that were designed to be done by two. She had no backup, no extra pair of eyes or hands, no auxiliary memory. No one to double-check her. This ... wasn't good.

Wah wah. Poor me. C'mon. Move.

She cranked and dogged the fore hatch by her feet, and the "overhead" hatch that was anything but overhead right now. Reached for the oxygen tanks and opened the valves.

This was the moment of truth. If the LM was compromised beyond all hope of holding in atmosphere, Vivian was done.

She raised the cabin pressure to three pounds per square inch and waited, watching the gauges. The numbers fell, but slowly. Enough that she could manage a quick change? She cranked the pressure higher. Four psi? The air kept on leaking out of whatever punctures the LM had, but still slowly and steadily. Five psi would have been more comfortable, but every extra pound of pressure increased the risk.

Trying to track down the leaks would take time she didn't have. She'd leave the oxygen valve open at a trickle to replace the air she was losing.

Don't think. Act.

Vivian began to rip the Soviet suit off. Gloves. Boots and helmet. Then she wrenched at the tag that would open the suit behind her. She squirmed out of the Vika-suit, even now thinking she might puke at the memory of the woman who'd once worn it, who had tried to con her and kill her back in Zvezda Base. *When I see you in hell, Vika Isayeva, you'd better hope you see me first.*

Then she was out, peeled like a grape, wearing only the Russian cotton jumpsuit Svetlana had given her back in Zvezda. She ripped that off too and was down to underwear, almost naked and freezing in a Lunar Module that might lose integrity at any moment.

Well, at least that would be quick. She'd only have a few seconds of breathless agony before she checked out completely.

She pulled on the highly absorbent underwear that would need to soak up any and all, well, emissions for however long this took. Then pulled a second pair on over the top. Yeah, that part was going to be fun. *The chafing is gonna suck.*

New overalls, then the liquid-cooled garment, lined with the tubes that would bring cold water next to her body in the scalding heat of lunar day. Couldn't live without her LCG. Hardly breathing, not checking the pressure gauge any more, because if it all went to hell she'd know right away. One rupture, and she'd have time to glance up, feel stupid, and then die.

Suit up. Go.

Vivian struggled into the shell of the Apollo moon suit and pulled the cord to drag the zipper behind her crotch and up the back. Forced herself to slow down: if the zip jammed, that was a single-point failure she'd be hard pressed to recover from. *Don't want to screw up something obvious through indecent haste.*

Okay, it was up all the way. *Cool. Girl can dress herself.* She lifted the helmet from its hook, pulled it over her head, and snapped the latches closed. Tugged on the Moon overboots while she still had fingers unencumbered by gloves.

Wait, wait. Stupid. Vivian took the helmet off again.

With the helmet on, she wouldn't be able to eat. Or talk.

Food first. She reached into the drawer of food pouches and ate everything she could get her hands on. Some of it, she rehydrated with hot water. Other stuff, she didn't waste the time, just crammed nutrients into her mouth and chugged them down. No time for dignity, barely time to chew. Vivian had little idea of what she was eating. Hardly tasted it. It was only when she feared that she might throw up that she eased back.

More water next. She sucked down as much as possible, flipping switches on the comms board in the meantime.

Lunar Modules had two high-gain antennas. One was above the front faceplate, and the other hung off the back equipment bay. Both stuck out, and the LM's crashing tumble had probably destroyed them.

Worth a shot, anyway. "Houston, this is Vivian Carter. Houston, Carter. Mayday. I am crashed. Regret to inform: Lin did not survive. Mayday, Mayday. Houston, this is Vivian Carter down in the dirt."

No response. She swallowed more water. The air pressure gauge was dropping steadily.

"Minerva, Vivian Carter. Dave Horn, come in, buddy. This is a Mayday, Vivian on-surface with no means of determining my location, come in?"

Another deep breath.

"Houston, this is ... aw, screw it."

She was wasting time. Nobody would hear her. She'd already had her one chance at rescue, and it was sheer blind luck she hadn't already perished in a fireball. No one else was about to swoop in and pluck her away to safety. The rest of this effort had to be Vivian-driven.

She put the helmet on again, and the gloves, and plugged in her umbilicals. Might as well use air and water from the LM tanks while she still could. Now, the goal was not to rip those umbilicals out by accident before she got her shit together for the great outdoors.

But she was back in a US spacesuit and away from the blood and evil aura of Viktoriya Isayeva, and just for that Vivian already felt a thousand times better.

NASA suit reacquired. Commence Phase Two. Go.

Vivian had a short but incredibly important list of items that she needed to keep herself alive. If she failed to snag any of them, she was dead meat.

"Oxygen."

There were three one-pound pressurization bottles alongside the hatch, plus a rack of high-pressure oxygen cylinders lining the rear of the cabin. She counted them, started to do math, then shook her head. *Later. Do that outside.* She unclipped them all and piled them up together.

"Water."

Portable, potable water. For this she had to be grateful to the design changes NASA had made following Apollo 13. She fished out a half-dozen heavy-duty bags, each with two-gallon capacity and a small but complex valve, and filled them from the water nozzle. Once she had each one filled, she had to massage it to get the air bubbles out, otherwise they might rupture when she went back into vacuum.

The PLSS was already charged with water and oxygen, as was the emergency purge system that sat atop the regular backpack. So that was good. But the longest possible EVA using the PLSS was ten hours. *Maybe* twelve if she wasn't exerting. But she'd be exerting, big-time. So she'd need to refresh the PLSS during the hike, with monotonous regularity. With:

"Batteries."

Also in racks in the back. But they were heavy. One battery per ten-hour EVA. How many would she need?

Well. It looked like there were only ten, so … ten it would have to be. Plenty of margin engineered into EVA batteries, right?

"Wait."

Eleven. She rolled Lin over with some difficulty, and snapped the battery out of his PLSS. *Sorry, buddy. Pay you back, someday.*

"Navigation."

The map packet, from the contingency sleeve in the back right of the LM. The book of tables, from the same place, that would help her do math. The Texas Instruments calculator would melt outside in the heat of the day, so she left that and instead took the five-inch Pickett N600-ES slide rule every Apollo mission carried. Easier to use in gloves than the calculator anyway, and not a whole lot less accurate.

Of course, what she needed most was a sextant. Not the big alignment optical telescope hard-mounted into the LM that served as one; she could hardly rip that out and tote it around with her. An honest-to-God brass sextant from the Napoleonic Wars would have served her much better. Without one, Vivian could never really be sure where she was.

"CO_2 scrub."

The canisters of lithium hydroxide, to purge out her carbon dioxide. Plenty of those, right where they should be.

Finally, she'd need something to carry all this crap.

"Cart."

The Modular Equipment Transporter, a cross between a cart and a wheelbarrow. It was about three feet tall with two wheels, and she'd pull it behind her using a draw bar. It was designed to haul cameras, trenching tools, cores, and sample bags, with lots of useful pockets, which were not at all a good fit to the stuff Vivian needed to haul. She'd need to unbolt and unclip the rods and bars that would get in her way, without weakening the cart so much that it collapsed. An ordinary wheelbarrow would have been much handier.

"Tool kit."

She opened it up, and right there on top was the core drill, that wonderful gadget that allowed geologists to probe beneath the surface and drag out long thin samples of lunar crust. Also, to kill cosmonauts. That was what she needed to get out of here: holes. Boom boom boom, a row of wide-drilled holes across the LM's skin, and then she'd punch her way out of this tin can.

"PLSS."

She wedged it in place, and reversed into it. This would normally be the point where Ellis would grab various straps and ties and thread them around her.

And that was a problem. Right now, Vivian was damned if she could locate the ties to fasten the backpack onto her shoulders. Eventually, she had to grab a mirror from the vanity kit and hold it up so that she could see behind her. Which then meant she only had one free hand.

Gah. Space is hard.

She figured it out. Looped the PLSS straps over her shoulders, anchored them and the waist belt. It didn't feel quite right. But she was, at least, wearing the PLSS and not cursing at it.

She fastened connectors, checked gauges, poked at switches. Breathed deep.

"We are Go for decompress."

She needed to let the air out of the LM before she started hacking at its outer skin. An explosive decompression would throw around all her carefully assembled survival gear.

She opened the valve. "And out goes all the air."

Her suit's pressure was holding. "Yeah, Ellis, I should have checked that first. Shut up."

She hefted the core drill from the tool kit and pulled the trigger. It started up with a reassuring vibration that she could feel all up her arms, and made ridiculously short work of the LM's skin. "Now we're talking."

Well then. Out we go.

She went, making haste slowly, aware that any damage to her suit could have serious consequences. Even a minor breach would end her. Crawling out of the Lunar Module was one of her most careful maneuvers of the year.

Finally, she stood up and looked around.

Craters surrounded her, thrown into harsh relief by the early grazing-incidence Sun. She saw no mountains nearby. Her isolation was clear. Nothing, and no one, was anywhere near her, aside from the trashed ship she'd just crawled out of. A shallow but very clear gouge marked where the LM had augured in.

She was clearly in a mare rather than an upland region. And the Sun was up, though barely, meaning she must be about as far east as Hadley, but well south. "Mare Vaporum?"

She sat down and spread her maps out. "At least I don't need to weight 'em down. Not much risk of them blowing away."

Mare Vaporum was a relatively small sea, about 150 miles across, tucked in between the southeastern rim of Mare Imbrium and the southwestern rim of Mare Serenitatis. South of that the surface was all highlands and messy terrain, so it was good that she hadn't come in there. But Vaporum was well off the direct line between Copernicus and Hadley. Could she really be so far over?

Well, sure. Hadley was due northeast of Zvezda, but on take-off Lin's program would have vectored most of the LM's thrust due east, to counter the Moon's rotation. The plan would then have had them bending their trajectory northward. But if they'd just kept going straight after they were hit, their momentum would have carried them east-northeast. Vivian couldn't clearly recall how long Lin had wrestled the controls, but if their total travel had been a couple hundred miles, that's where they'd be: Mare Vaporum.

Which meant her direct route back to Hadley was almost straight north. Over the Apennine Mountains.

If she couldn't cross them, she'd have to go around them. Head northeast over highland terrain to Mare Serenitatis, then follow its border clockwise till she reached the gap in the mountains where she could cut through into Mare Imbrium. Then all she'd need to do was follow the "coast" up and around, and down into the Hadley Plain embayment.

Nope. No way. If she was, say, right in the middle of Vaporum now, that put her at about 13 degrees north, 3.6 degrees east. Hadley Base was 26 north, and … 3.6 degrees east. That meant a distance of around two hundred and thirty miles to Hadley, as the crow flew. The level, but circuitous, route via Serenitatis would more than double that. "Out of the question. Think again."

She studied the map more closely. There were two smallish embayments on the northern side of Vaporum, either of which would bring her partway into the Hadley-Apennine chain. Then, if she could trust the contour lines on this map, she might weave her way north to Conton, a prominent crater thirteen miles across, right in the middle of the range, and continue on through a pass in the Mons Bradley Ridge …

If she could find her way.

Getting ahead of yourself, Vivian. Is this doable at all?

For the time being, just call it 250 miles, because Vivian could probably walk at about two and a half miles an hour in a spacesuit, and that made it a nice round figure.

Which was a hundred hours of walking.

"Jesus Christ." The cold sweat of fear started at the base of her spine.

A hundred hours was like ten days worth of normal EVA, although nobody slogged along on foot the whole time they were out on-surface. That's why they had rovers.

Vivian didn't have ten days. She was sealed into a spacesuit. She had until she ran out of oxygen or water, or until her power to cool the suit failed and she boiled to death inside it. Daylight temperatures averaged out at about 220°F—hotter than boiling water.

"Terrific."

How long could she last without food? People could survive for three weeks, right? "Hardly, Vivian. Maybe lying on a bed. Not while hiking all day, every day."

Seven days, maybe? Call it seven. After a week, she'd either have made it to Hadley, or died in the attempt.

Okay. Vivian had to walk 250 miles in seven days or less. Say, fifteen hours a day at two and a half miles an hour. Not deviate too much from straight, and not let the mountains slow her down.

Did she have the supplies for that?

Vivian grabbed the slide rule. Rough numbers: humans used 550 liters of oxygen a day. More, exerting. A pound of O_2 corresponded to

350 liters. Even if she used five times the nominal amount, that was only fifty pounds of oxygen. And fifty pounds of oxygen weighed eight pounds on the Moon. The tanks holding it were heavier than the gas inside. And liquid O_2 under compression took up eighty-six times less volume than gaseous. So, she had way more oxygen than she'd ever need in those tanks piled up inside the LM. She'd only take half of it.

For water, she'd need three liters a day, maybe more. Seven days at three liters was twenty-one liters, weighing forty-six pounds—on Earth. That was for drinking. Add more to top up the suit cooling. So the weight of that would be okay, too.

Add the lithium cartridges to scrub out her CO_2, the tools, and the batteries.

It sounded doable. But once Vivian had dragged everything she needed out of the Lunar Module, piled it onto the cart, and lashed it with wire so it wouldn't slide off onto the ground, it sure looked like a lot. And leaning into the cart handle with all her strength drove it home: it was freaking hard to get well over a hundred pounds of mass going in the right direction, even if it only weighed a sixth of that. Especially in a regrettably inflexible suit.

Keep up a pace of two and a half miles per hour, while towing this thing? It would be hell on her shoulders. And legs. And patience.

But, yeah. *The possibility of a successful outcome was not precluded by the data*, as one of her old instructors might have said.

She wouldn't have to drag all of it the whole way. Whenever an air or water tank ran dry she'd discard it and travel that much lighter. Day by day, it would get easier.

Except for the part where she couldn't eat anything, so she'd be getting weaker.

Doing the math for all this was almost a grim type of fun. Back to real, honest work. It beat being tortured, or fighting for her life, or getting blown up or shot down. It beat all those things by a *lot*.

"Time to get started."

Vivian had always wanted to explore new territory, blaze new trails. Be the very first to walk the new regolith, see lunar sights no one had ever seen before. No one else had ever seen this particular rock before, or that mountain, or that crater, from ground level.

Or that rock. Or that rock. Or *that* rock.

"Careful what you wish for, my dear."

The physical labor was one thing; arm-wrenching, backbreaking work, and Vivian had no way of telling whether she was really managing two and a half miles an hour.

The tedium: *that* was something else.

And, talking of waste? Not long from now, some, uh, regions of this suit were going to get very uncomfortable. "Best not to dwell on that."

And that was the last thing Vivian said out loud for a while, because talking was a waste of both breath and moisture.

It was a long slog. A very long slog. She walked all day. The terrain around her changed gradually, though more quickly than it would have on Earth. The Moon was so much smaller than Earth that the mean horizon was only a mile and a half away, and the undulating terrain often made it seem nearer. But by the end of that day, Vivian was still in Mare Vaporum. Flat. Boring. And Vaporum was one of the *small* seas.

She walked until exhaustion threatened to overwhelm her, and then … just stopped. It wasn't going to help if she fainted and collapsed.

Enough was enough. She lay down without ceremony. Double-checked her connections to air and water. Turned her face away from the Sun, and was asleep in moments.

Her first PLSS recharge was dicey. Vivian found a suitable boulder to lean against, unhooked the waist latches that held the backpack on, and shimmied out of the straps, inasmuch as anyone could shimmy in a spacesuit. It helped that the suit was big on her, presumably designed for a man. Vika's suit had been so tight that it had rubbed her shoulders, elbows, thighs. This suit flopped on her. Yet another thing that would get old in a few days.

If she made it that long. To service the PLSS, Vivian had to disconnect it completely. This left her with only the oxygen within her suit. Worse, it also removed her power source. Without power, her suit fans stopped working and the air didn't circulate. Also, the cooling water stopped flowing through her LCGs, and she got ridiculously hot, very quickly.

The first time, she hadn't completely thought all that through, and had to race against time. She'd assumed she had all her ducks in a row. Recharge the air by connecting an oxygen tank to the fill reconnector. While that was happening: change out the battery and the lithium hydroxide canister. Then came the really exciting part, which was connecting up a bag of water to the H_2O recharge connector and opening up that valve. Dodgy, because if she screwed up, gallons of precious water would vaporize into vacuum in seconds.

She needed to complete all that before she could reconnect the oxygen inlet umbilical on the front of her suit and open the shutoff valve. Then the feedwater fill connector and liquid cooling umbilical, and the power line, holy crap. And then reconnect the leads to the controller box on her chest. And then finally, while panting and waiting for her body temperature to cool to something like normal, she could drain the waste water out of her suit and fumble the damn PLSS onto her back again.

Then stand up to keep plodding across the goddamned hellscape of the lunar surface.

The first time, she nearly passed out from the heat. Even once she got it all reconnected she was so overcooked and woozy that when she set off hiking across the endless landscape, she forgot to grab the pull bar of her cart. She made it a full three hundred yards before realizing her progress was easier than it ought to be. She stopped, cursed, and trudged back to fetch it.

For the second PLSS refresh she made use of the shade of a rocky outcropping, and it went much better. Resting afterward, she stared thoughtfully across the plain in front of her.

In all the time Vivian had spent on the Moon, this was the very first time she'd been well and truly out at sea—deep in one of the mares. Hadley Base was located in the highly cratered plain of a mountainous basin, mostly ancient primordial crust: bedrock, breccias, regolith. The Copernicus area around Zvezda, not that she'd spared any time for sightseeing, was all highland volcanic ejecta. There'd been some mare basalts lining Hadley Rille, but not like these. The basaltic lava here was fine-grained, darker, very different to her eye, and the surface smoother and flatter, relatively speaking, than anywhere else she'd yet been. Similar to how it might have been around the Marius Hills, or out on Palus.

Nice to know all that lunar geology hadn't been knocked out of her brain.

She picked up a small chunk of basalt and stared at it for a moment, then slipped it into her sleeve pocket. Sample? Keepsake? Good luck charm? She had no real idea, but it felt like the right thing to do.

By her third PLSS refresh it still wasn't routine, but it wasn't a deadly semi-panic either. And she got to throw away the spent oxygen cylinder. It should have made the cart seem lighter. She couldn't detect a difference. But now she was two and a half days into the hike and suffering badly from lack of food.

She had, at least, now made it to the edge of Mare Vaporum.

Perhaps that should have cheered her. But the Hadley-Apennine range reared up ahead of her, bleak as hell and stretching to right and left as far as she could see.

Now, this hike was about to get *really* tough.

CHAPTER 36

Zvezda Base: Nikolai Makarov
and Lunar Surface: Vivian Carter
January 25–28, 1980

Makarov

On finding Storage Nine empty and Vika shot dead in Hall Three, Sergei Yashin had gone about as unhinged as Makarov had ever seen anyone go. He stormed along the halls calling curses down upon them all: Vivian Carter for being an imperialist spy; Viktoriya Isayeva for her incompetence; Commander Rudenko for her ineffectual response to the evacuation and emergency repair of the base (which, to Nikolai, appeared exemplary); and Makarov and Belyakova themselves, for running off to their LK Lander.

Because that was their story. Svetlana had agreed to cover for Nikolai, once he'd confessed to her in a few whispered sentences—even though she hated what he'd done and disagreed with his reasons for doing it. Belyakova had indeed gone to their lander after egressing Zvezda, to assure herself that it had not been sabotaged by the Americans. Nikolai, still driven by the need to confirm Carter's fate for himself, had looped around to reenter Hall Three at its far end, come across the battle scene ... and acted instinctively.

Svetlana was Nikolai's closest friend, but he'd pushed that to its absolute limit. Shooting a fellow Russian, no matter how psychopathic? Going behind Yashin's back? She'd torn bloody strips off Nikolai, verbally, and made it very clear: this would be the one and only time she would defy the KGB by lying for him.

But Yashin believed them readily enough. All the physical evidence in Hall Three supported a simple story: a violent struggle, and Carter besting Isayeva in the ensuing firefight. And for all Yashin's rage, much of the blame was his, for agreeing to Isayeva's plan. She had radioed to tell him she was taking advantage of the base's loss of integrity to run a play on Carter. And thus Yashin had ordered everyone else to withdraw from Hall Three and its vicinity … which had spurred Nikolai to move even faster in that direction.

Vika had been one of the few people Yashin trusted. His ranting made it evident that the two of them had been running covert ops on both Soviet and foreign soil for years. It was simple to glean that much of Yashin's fury was redirected grief at the loss of his partner.

Somehow, Carter had managed to overcome her obvious weakness and kill Isayeva. As a result, it was crystal clear to Yashin that he had been right all along. Defeating Vika—playing her in return, then slaying her—was the hallmark of a cold-blooded operative. Carter must be Night Corps herself, to have carried it off and then evaded pursuit by Chertok, ultimately flinging herself aboard a Lunar Module to escape.

Yashin hoped the surface-to-air missile strike had brought the LM down. Although he spent a lot of time listing the torments he would wreak on Carter if she'd somehow survived.

Makarov knew that Svetlana, too, hoped Carter had died. If she was recaptured, and betrayed Nikolai's role in her escape, he and Belyakova would spend the rest of their lives in a Siberian gulag. If they even survived Yashin's rage.

So now they kept their heads down and joined the hard work of restoring Zvezda. Waiting, in the hopes that this might soon be over, and that Yashin and the rest of his thugs might be withdrawn back to Earth.

Those hopes were swiftly dashed.

Carter

"Hadley Base? This is Salyut-Lunik-A. Hadley, Salyut-Lunik-A."

Vivian jumped, which on the Moon meant that her feet literally left the surface. "Whoa …. What?"

She was hiking through the foothills of the Apennines, skirting mountains thousands of feet tall. All she'd heard for days was the swish of fluid through her suit, the hum of the fans, and her own labored breathing and swearing.

She'd left her radio on. It used almost no battery power, and in receive-only mode no one could use her signal to track her. Now she switched to Transmit. "Columbia Station, this is Vivian Carter."

A forlorn hope. Spacesuits had relatively weak VHF radio transmitters: a couple watts of power, a range of only a few miles. They relied on converters on the LMs or rovers to boost the signal to craft in orbit, or switch it to S-band to communicate with Earth.

Vivian looked to her right and there it was, a fast-moving speck coming up over the eastern horizon, glittering in reflected sunlight. "Columbia Station, Mayday Mayday. This is Vivian Carter, alone on-surface."

Rawlings's voice came again, with no sign that he'd heard her. "Hadley Base, Salyut-Lunik-A. Hadley, do you read?"

"Columbia, this is Hadley." It was Peter Sandoval, and for a moment Vivian thought she might burst into tears. Rawlings and Sandoval. The two guys here, aside from her crew, that she most wanted to see right now. "Columbia, we read. What's your status?"

"Break, this is Vivian Carter." She gave up. No chance of her feeble VHF transmission crossing the sixty miles to Columbia's orbit. She was just embarrassing herself, in front of herself.

They weren't using secure radio, she now realized. Columbia and Hadley were transmitting in the clear. If they'd been secure, Vivian would be hearing only encrypted garble.

Which made sense. If Rawlings of all people was calling it by the Soviet name, Columbia was obviously still in Soviet hands.

A three-second pause. "Hadley, this is Rawlings. Our Soviet friends are still occupying our spacecraft, as is their legal right, considering the US's multiple acts of aggression in cislunar space."

And that, along with Josh's sardonic tone, meant that the Soviets were telling him what to say. They'd put him on a delay, too, so he couldn't veer off script.

Sandoval clearly knew it too. "Understand completely, Columbia. Proceed."

"Uh, you're requested to use correct terminology when referring to this station. Way more importantly, I'm instructed to inform you that all personnel must evacuate Hadley Base by midnight, Universal Time, on January thirtieth. After that, the local officials of the Soviet Union will conclude their decommissioning of Hadley Base, and initiate the final removal of all US materials from the surface."

January 30th? When the hell was that? Vivian had no idea what day it was.

"And what form might that final removal take?" Sandoval's voice was brittle.

"Beyond my power to say, but assume it will be definitive. As per the Soviet Union's standing generous offer, evacuating Lunar Modules may approach this station one at a time to transfer their crews into Command and Service Modules for their return to Earth. But I and my two colleagues will no longer be joining you. We choose to remain here."

The heavy irony in Josh's voice gave the lie to the word *choose*. He continued: "Hadley Base, please confirm you understand the ultimatum as presented? Complete your departure in three days, or the Soviet Union will not be responsible for the consequences."

Three days? "Crap." Vivian could *never* make it to Hadley in just three more days. Could she?

"Acknowledge receipt," Sandoval said. "Request clarification: you and two colleagues? Columbia—uh, the former Columbia Station had a crew of six."

This time, the pause that prefaced Rawlings's reply was closer to twenty seconds. The station was now already halfway across the sky—orbits of sixty-mile altitude went by fast. This conversation wouldn't last much longer before Columbia lost line of sight.

"Surviving members of the original crew are myself, Dardenas, and Zabrinski. Regret to inform that Mason, Wagner, and Jackson squandered their lives attempting the cowardly murder of Soviet cosmonauts."

Sandoval's response was immediate and emotionless. "Understood, Commander. Sorry to hear." Vivian had learned of these deaths from Makarov, back in Hall Three, but still swallowed a lump in her throat.

Sandoval again. "Returning to your ultimatum: how do we know this is not a bluff? US forces have easily resisted previous Soviet strikes on Hadley Base. Before finalizing my response, I'll need proof of your ability to … definitively remove us. Absent such proof, I'll assume it's an empty threat."

Way to go, Peter. Hold their feet to the fire.

Twenty-second delay. "Commence your preparations to depart," Rawlings said. "I'll present proof positive soon." Another pause. "Seriously, Peter; I can't say more, but I'm very confident the Soviets can follow through on this. We'll transmit an image to you in a day or two, then you'll understand. Okay?"

This sudden return to a conversational tone, replacing his former stilted delivery, chilled Vivian to the bone. Josh believed the Soviets. And so Vivian believed them too.

A 'final, definitive removal' could only be a tactical nuclear strike.

"Okay, Josh," Sandoval said. "About to lose your signal. Hang in there, buddy."

"Will do. You too," Rawlings said. "Salyut-Lunik-A out."

And that was that.

Robotically, Vivian leaned forward into the weight of her cart and began to walk again while she gnawed away at the problem. She hadn't seen the kind of launcher at Zvezda that could send a missile five hundred miles, but the Soviets could achieve a nuclear strike in several other ways. Easiest would be to stick a nuke inside an LK Lander and fly it remotely on a ballistic trajectory. The Russians were pretty good at computer-controlled operations. They'd tested a lot of their Soyuz launches that way, back in the 1960s.

Night Corps had defensive missile capability. But could they react fast enough to nail an incoming LK? She didn't know, but considering how far from Hadley she was, it wasn't relevant. Right now, her job was to keep putting one foot in front of the other.

Three days?

She had to go on. She had no other options. Keep walking. Worry later about what the hell might happen to Hadley, and her friends, come midnight of January 30th.

And about exactly how Vivian herself would die, soon after that.

Makarov

Nikolai leaned back. "You heard Sandoval's tone? They will not evacuate. They will stay and take their chances. Meaning they will have no chance at all."

"That is their choice," Svetlana said stolidly.

"So, the Americans will all die?"

"Perhaps that is inevitable."

Makarov just looked at her.

"Nikolai, they have received fair warning. As plain as we could make it, and plainer than Yashin wanted. This ultimatum is as far as Yashin is prepared to go, and we can push him no further. This must be the end of it. If Yashin were to learn what you did at Zvezda—"

"I cannot just …" Makarov shrugged, frustrated.

"You tried," she said, more gently. "Your conscience is clear."

"It is not. But perhaps there is another option."

Belyakova knew him too well. Her eyes narrowed. "Sabotage the bomb? That would be treason, Nikolai. Suicide."

"Not if nobody ever finds out."

"Oh, they would find out," Belyakova said.

"You would give me away?"

"On something so major? Yes. I love you as a friend, Nikolai. But for an error that grievous? While we are at war? That is a secret you could not possibly ask me to keep."

Makarov was silent for a long time. Then he grunted. "Again, I suppose we have found our line."

"I suppose we have. I am sorry, Nikolai."

He bowed his head. "I, too."

Carter

Vivian awoke in pain. Always, it was painful. Light lancing in through her faceplate when she moved. Her body cramped, her mouth dry. Her stomach aching with hunger.

Add to that the returning knowledge that she was totally alone and still had many more miles to hike across the sullen lunar terrain, and the stress level seemed overwhelming. It was amazing she'd managed to sleep at all.

Up without ceremony. Off again. Except that her back had stiffened up as she slept, and with every heave on the cart, it felt like whichever shoulder was taking the strain might pop out of its socket. Her thighs and ankles hurt as well.

She had just slept for six hours on the rim of Conton Crater. It had to be Conton because it was almost circular, thirteen miles across, and a mile and a half deep; the largest and most regular crater in this area of the Apennines. She was currently at an altitude of twenty thousand feet. To her west the ridge of Mount Bradley loomed another ten thousand feet above her, ominous in full-Sun glare.

And so Vivian now knew exactly where she was: halfway through the Apennines. From here she'd head along a valley oriented slightly west of north, then work her way onto a contour line at about seventeen thousand feet and thread the needle the rest of the way. Once out of the mountains, she'd eventually pick up Hadley Rille and keep it to her left for the last sixty miles home.

It sounded straightforward enough, but from the terrain Vivian had already conquered, she knew it would be hell. Following a contour line essentially meant walking across a steep slope, while weaving left and right to steer the cart around rocks and boulders.

At least today would begin with an easy downhill.

Even this was relative. The slope down Conton was a boulder field strewn with ejecta; not a scree, geologically, although it looked and felt like one. And ahead of it was the next rolling mountain she'd need to get herself across, on her way to the only sane pass through Bradley.

On, Vivian. On.

She fell three times in the first half hour. As her strength ebbed, her coordination was fading with it, and the beginnings of the days were oddly worse than the ends. Just bringing herself fully awake was a chore, so she now recharged her backpack in the middle of each hike rather than at the beginning.

She reached the valley floor, lumbered across it. "Up we go."

As she climbed laboriously uphill. her eyes smarted. She blinked impatiently and jerked her head; sweat rolled into her eyes a dozen times a day, and was difficult to clear.

But this wasn't sweat, and her eyes flooded with tears, turning the landscape before her into a watery blur. She suffered a sudden jolt of pain in her left eye, and scrunched her eyelids closed Instinctively. "Shit … damn. Ow, ow!"

She let go of the cart handle, and raised her gloved hands to her face. *Yeah, rub my eyes, why not? Shame about the helmet getting in the way.*

The stinging got dramatically worse. Both eyes now. "Ow, Jeez, oh my God ..." Vivian fell forward onto her knees.

Blind. Alone on the Moon, hundreds of miles from anywhere, and I'm blind.

Adrenaline surged through her, provoking a roar of anger and frustration. After which she sucked in a long breath, tried to steel herself against the pain and think ...

She broke into a wracking cough.

Oh no, oh no ...

Vivian knew what this was, and If she was right, she had only minutes to live. Maybe seconds? Had anyone even done tests on this?

"Gah! Shit!"

She clenched her throat against the coughing. Shoved herself around and scrabbled for the cart she couldn't see. Groped with her gloved hands. What was what? Where was anything?

Pain and shock knocked her down into a fetal position. She coughed again. *Better not vomit. Can't vomit. Not in a suit. Nope.*

This was no good. She'd never find it, not in this pain.

Vivian was out of options. She fumbled with her helmet, reaching up beside her left ear for her oxygen purge valve.

She wrenched at it. The sudden hiss of depressurization turned to a roar as air spilled from her suit. As she coughed again her ears popped. Her suit pressure was dropping rapidly.

Vivian blinked, trying to force tears into her eyes. *Clean it out, clean it out, Goddamn it ....* Still she saw only a blurry mess, and her eyes stung so much she couldn't keep them open more than a fraction of a second.

But she'd stopped coughing. Vivian rocked her head forward, found her water tube with her lips, sucked water into her parched mouth.

Purge more. DO IT.

She let more air flow out into the vacuum.

Her suit tried to compensate, pumping in more air in to maintain pressure. *No, bitch: stop that.* She reached up to her chest, twisted the dial to zero. Prevented her suit from trying to save her.

She was gasping, but it wasn't like the original caustic irritation. Now, it was just lack of oxygen.

Good.

Vivian inhaled, a long deep wheeze that felt like it did nothing at all, and held her breath. Closed the purge valve. Scrabbled again for her cart.

Okay, so the oxygen tanks are on top. Water to the left. And down here …
Must be here. Dear God. Come. On.

If only I could feel my fingers.

Somewhere along the line Vivian had stopped holding her breath, because now she was panting rapidly in a fast in-out-in-out that brought her no relief at all.

She felt woozy. Was she going into shock? Would she black out?

Need more O$_2$. But … can't.

But I have to.

Still rooting in the bag with her right hand, Vivian she reached to her chest with her left, twisted to turn the oxygen full on again.

Except, that would also turn up the air purification system.

Which was her problem in the first place. It was her air purification system that was trying to kill her.

Damned if I do. Damned if I don't.

Oxygen rushed into her suit. *Is it pure?*

Her eyes stung again, and she coughed.

Nope.

As she choked again, her searching right glove closed around a long, thin tube.

Oh, my darling. Gotcha.

Vivian reached back to the lower right of her PLSS, thrusting painfully against her suit resistance. Snapped open a plastic cover. Pulled out the old lithium hydroxide cartridge and tossed it away. As she did so, the air handling in her suit went into pause mode. Obviously.

All she had to do was seat the new cartridge in there before she died. Easy, right?

But she needed to *slow the hell down*. She still couldn't see. If she dropped this cartridge and it rolled away, she'd never find it again.

Slowly, carefully, Vivian inserted the new lithium hydroxide cartridge.

And if this one was as munged up as the last, it wouldn't make a blind bit of difference, *haha, I'll die anyway*.

There. It was in place. The air handling clicked back on. Vivian snapped the cover closed. And breathed. Swallowed hard to pop her ears, as the suit pressure changed up on her again.

Her eyes were no longer smarting, and she wasn't choking.

So. Okay, I think? Okay?

Yeah. She was okay.

The carbon dioxide was scrubbed out of her air supply using lithium hydroxide. But the cartridge must have gotten damaged in one of her falls. And as a result, raw lithium hydroxide had begun to circulate in her suit.

Lithium hydroxide was incredibly caustic. God knew what it had already done to her lungs. Vivian could tell she still had some LiOH left in her suit by the smell, but it was attenuating as the air scrubbers did their work. *Clean it out. Scrub my air. That's your job.*

Vivian was breathing again. Her vision was clearing. Her eyes ached, but she could see.

Oh, look. There's the Moon. Black and gray, and more gray, and that light plaster-of-Paris color, and boring as hell.

Just like it had always been. Eternally monochrome. Large as life and twice as dangerous.

But, hey. She was breathing.

Vivian got back up onto her feet. Repacked her cart, and leaned into the weight of it.

Once again, she began to trudge up the mountainside.

CHAPTER 37

Mount Hadley Delta: Vivian Carter
January 30, 1980

"HADLEY Base, this is Vivian Carter, do you read?"

No response. She hadn't expected one, but since there was a very slim chance that a Hadley astronaut might be in her line of sight, she had to give it a try.

She'd given up on rest periods, and had now been awake forty hours straight: walking, walking, walking, often in a daze, her stomach a single knot of pain.

It was January 30th. Hadley Base was now officially on borrowed time, and Vivian was still on the wrong side of Hadley Delta.

Initially, she hadn't been sure. Now she was. The mountain had a distinctive shape, and she also recognized the meandering ridge to its right and the slope down toward the rille to its left. She was off the rocky highlands of the Apennines and back onto hummocky mare basalts, and from here on she could no longer lose her way. A couple miles to her left snaked Hadley Rille, she had the Apennines to her right, and she was walking between them.

Which meant that, although Vivian couldn't quite believe it, she still had a slim chance of making it back to Hadley in time.

But she was cutting it awfully damned close.

Her power was fine. She still had three batteries, and if she could breathe amps, she'd be golden. But she had only five hours of oxygen left and had emptied the last water container into her suit four hours ago. Her cart now held only the batteries, tool kit, and LiOH cartridges, and it bumped high in her wake as she hurried along.

Only one mountain left to climb. Unless she could persuade someone to come fetch her.

"Vivian Carter to Hadley Base. Mayday."

If only she'd made it over the earlier hills more quickly. Cut back on sleep earlier. Not nearly killed herself breathing poison. Found shortcuts. Gone longer between PLSS refreshes, or all of the above, she might already be home.

In her heart, she knew that none of that had been possible. Just getting this far had nearly killed her.

"Vivian to—holy shit!"

From the far side of Hadley Delta, two Lunar Modules ascended noiselessly into the black on plumes of fire.

"This is Vivian Carter! Mayday!"

A third LM appeared above the ridge, its ascent stage powering up and away. All three were ascent stages, leaving their descent stages like mummified spiders on the regolith beneath.

"Damn it, don't leave me here!"

Yet another Lunar Module ascent stage launched. These were not like rocket launches on Earth, where the storm and tumult of ignition raged and a tall rocket stack hung in place and seemed to consider its options before laboring into the sky. These launches resembled fireworks, with the flare of hypergolics leading immediately to a powerful upward thrust. Lunar gravity barely impeded the craft as they abandoned Hadley to its fate, and they were already rising quickly by the time Vivian saw them. Like the others, this latest LM tilted over just seconds after clearing Hadley Delta, shoving sideways toward orbit.

So ... that was four out of the eight Modules that had been on-surface when Vivian had landed with such flair and dignity, two months ago.

Assuming they'd all survived the Soviet attack. Vivian had no way of knowing who had lived through that second assault, and who had died.

Norton and Buchanan would surely be the last to leave the base they'd established with their blood and sweat. Rick would need to know his people were safely off-surface before relinquishing his hold on Hadley Plain.

It must be gutting him. Norton had been willing to stay on the Moon indefinitely, to make Hadley the Earth's first permanent lunar outpost. To grow and mature into a living city. Deserting it must feel like a dagger driving deep into his heart.

Another Lunar Module was rising away from Hadley Base. Having seen so many launches, Vivian was sensitive to the lesser speed with which this craft rose away from its descent stage. Slower, which probably meant it was heavier. Why? Maybe they'd crammed extra people in.

Vivian's vision blurred. She was sobbing, her cheeks and neck wet.

The NASA presence on the Moon, the jewel in its crown, the very first time they'd decisively beaten the Soviets at *anything* in the Space Race, had been cut short by international politics and violent nuclear posturing. These launches were all LM ascent stages. Without the legs and powerful descent stage motors, they couldn't land again. This was the final curtain.

And there went *another* Lunar Module, pirouetting up from the surface. Maybe *that* was Norton and Buchanan, but by now Vivian had lost count.

One thing she was sure of: they were all leaving.

All but Vivian. She was still here. Left behind, after all she'd been through.

Damn it. Damn it.

It was hard to bear.

All of a sudden, all of her aches and pains rushed in on her at once.

Her hands hurt like hell. Her knuckles were raw, and she was pretty sure she'd lost three or four fingernails. Her feet were cramped, pinched, and sore. Her back and guts ached furiously. Her hair felt glued to her head in a skullcap of doom. As for the two pairs of absorbent underwear she'd put on under her liquid-cooled garments, Vivian didn't want to think about what she'd have to deal with down there if she ever got this suit off. Which would be never.

God. This truly sucks out loud.

But, even worse than that?

The Moon. Her hope and dream for so long that Vivian could hardly remember a time when it hadn't been front and center in her mind. And now, she was stuck on it. Having struggled across mountains and mares and craters for so long.

The Moon would kill her, and her body would rest here for all eternity.

Her headset crackled. "Vivian Carter, Apollo 22. Carter, 22."

She was being hailed by one of the departing LMs. It sounded like Starman's voice. "22, Vivian Carter here. 22, Carter."

No response. The LM was out of range of her transmissions.

"Vivian, if you're in the vicinity, listen carefully. A Soviet nuclear weapon will detonate imminently at Hadley. Maybe in minutes, maybe only seconds."

"Oh, Jeez. No."

"All US forces have now departed Hadley. Do not approach the base, or even the plain. I repeat: do not approach."

Vivian looked west. She saw nothing.

As if reading her mind, Starman said: "Note that the Soviet bomb is not in a missile. It's already on Hadley Plain, brought by a small Lunokhod controlled remotely by Soviets from Columbia Station. We couldn't locate it. Needle in a haystack. You won't find it either."

How big would the bomb be? *I'm finished. Am I finished?*

"Hey, Vivian?" It was Buchanan's voice, now. "If you hear me, be very smart now. Don't fly too close to the Sun. Y'hear? Best of luck, girl."

A nuclear explosion? Yeah, real funny, old man.

Starman again, impatient. They presumably had only seconds before going over the horizon. "I repeat: do not approach Hadley Base. Good luck, Vivian. Here's hoping you're alive and within earshot. God bless. 22 out."

Starman was right: such a Lunokhod would be untraceable. It wouldn't be a large rover for people but one of their smaller robotic vehicles, barely six feet long and four feet high. Plenty of capacity in one of those for a small tactical nuke. The Soviets couldn't have driven it remotely all the way from Zvezda, but could easily have dropped it off just over the horizon, or—more likely—left it behind during their second assault.

That didn't matter. What mattered was getting as far away from it as possible.

Vivian ran as best she could, hopping rather than leaping in her weariness, while paying sudden and uncanny attention to her boots. She couldn't afford to trip.

If only I'd walked slower. Or slept longer. Or not even bothered.

Thirty seconds later, the nuke exploded.

Vivian saw the flash of atomic detonation as it threw the shadow of Hadley Delta across the ground in front of her, so bright that she instinctively squeezed her eyes closed and skidded to a halt, somehow not tumbling over.

She raised her gloved hands in front of her visor. Risked twitching a single eyelid open. Okay. That quickly, the killing light had faded.

She turned to see an uncanny fountain of rock cascading skyward, sparkling in the late sunlight.

Oh my God.

No mushroom cloud, not here. No atmosphere to hold one. At the center of the detonation everything had vaporized, fused instantly. But at the outer radius of the new crater that was even now burning into Hadley Plain, up came a splashing wave of regolith, dragged from the fringes of the explosion and hurled into the air.

Fist-sized chunks of rock rained down around her.

Vivian did not throw herself to the ground. That would only increase her surface area, raising the odds of something fatally large smashing into her helmet, legs, or PLSS. Her weakest point was her helmet, and she raised her arms in a futile effort to protect it. Her mind whirled. What to do, for the best?

The storm hit her with full force. A wall of dust thundered over her, thick and brutal, and she was pummeled from every direction at once, taking blow after blow from unseen rocks, one of which plucked her up and tossed her sideways.

Vivian rolled and came to a clumsy halt, lying on her left side. Had her suit held? Were her pumps and fans still working? Yes, she could hear them again, now.

After a confused, indeterminate amount of time, the onslaught ceased. The dust settled uncannily around her.

She was still alive.

For now.

A tactical nuclear weapon had gone off, not ten miles away. *Oh, Lord.*

Hadley Base had been vaporized, but Vivian hadn't been bowled over by the blast itself. On Earth, most nuclear destruction came from blast wave overpressure, which couldn't happen on the Moon. No shock wave in a vacuum. Just the hurled debris.

But the thermal radiation? The flash burns, the temporary or even permanent blindness? Those could all have happened, but for Starman's warning. If Vivian had been facing toward Hadley, the intensity of the explosion would have burned out her retinas.

She pushed herself off the surface till she was kneeling uncomfortably upright. Around her, the Moon looked the same as always. All the dust and rock had fallen from the sky by now.

But everything had changed, and what Vivian couldn't see might still kill her.

She reached down and scooped up a handful of moondust. By now she was intimately familiar with how that felt and looked, in her glove and on the surface of her suit.

The miniscule glassy beads were new. Regolith, fused by the titanic energy of the nuclear explosion and now scattered all around her. And presumably radioactive as hell. She needed to get away from this entire area, as fast as humanly possible.

Up, Vivian. Go-go-go.

Run like the devil is chasing you.

She got up and bounded across the surface, shaking her arms and rocking back and forth in an effort to dislodge the dust that streaked her suit.

First, get out of the immediate area. Then, brush herself off properly. Then run some more.

Her power consumption, her oxygen consumption: all irrelevant, right now. Getting out of the hot zone was all that mattered.

Echoes of her long-ago Navy training flowed back into her mind. Iodine, cesium, and strontium were among the worst fission products. Right? But how long were those half-lives? How long would she need to take cover?

After even thirty minutes, that initial radiation from the short-lived isotopes should drop considerably. Fourteen days from now the dose rate from this area would have fallen by a factor of a thousand or more. But right now, distance was everything.

382

The afterimage of that nuclear light was still imprinted on her eyeballs whenever she blinked.

Live for the Moon, die for the Moon.

As Vivian came to the edge of Hadley Rille she did not even pause, just leaped down onto the steep slope and kept running, down into the V-shaped canyon.

At the base of the slope she stopped, panting, tumbling forward onto her knees again. The steep sides of the rille rose up on either side of her, fifteen hundred feet high. She wondered about all the radiation that would still be coming out from ground zero. Gamma rays, alpha particles, that whole stew of crap that emanated from a nuclear conflagration. But most of it would be line of sight.

She scooped up soil with her glove again. No glass beads on the ground here.

On Earth, they'd run drills for this all her life. Duck and cover. Then hide for two weeks till it was safe to come out again, right? Except that there'd be no delayed fallout here. No atmosphere to suck all those bad particles up into, and then shed them back downward again. But due to the direct radiation, Hadley Plain still wouldn't be safe for another week or two.

A week or two? Ha.

Vivian no longer had a base there to return to. She was starving, nearly out of water, and had only a couple more hours of oxygen. And then it would be all be over.

Unless.

Up again. No rest for the wicked.

She didn't have the strength to run any more. That would just deplete her dregs of oxygen more quickly, anyhow.

Vivian struggled upright, and began to walk along the bottom of Hadley Rille.

CHAPTER 38

Hadley Rille: Vivian Carter
January 30, 1980

VIVIAN Carter, staggering uphill in a spacesuit. She'd taken a long swig of water an hour ago, and that had been her last. Empty, now.

Even at a walk she was sucking down oxygen hand over fist, and that would run out soon too. She didn't even bother checking the gauge.

Even so, her PLSS might start running low on cooling water before she suffocated.

Her panting breath echoed in her helmet. *Dear Lord. This is insane.*

Well, sure. *Sane* was way behind her, far back over the horizon somewhere.

It was still sitting there in Bridge Crater: the Lunar Rover that Vivian had crashed into a rock while trying to evade the Soviets. That panic-stricken day seemed at the same time a hundred years ago, and just yesterday. The rover's front wheel was bent, and the whole vehicle turned askew. Most of the gear was still aboard its trailer, with other items strewn across the landscape.

Now, Vivian checked her gauge. Only half an hour of air left. But there were oxygen cylinders piled onto the rover's trailer. Lots of 'em.

O_2 was no longer a problem, but she still had plenty of others to wrestle with.

Even without kneeling again she could see that there were none of the glassy beads on the floor of Bridge. There'd likely be some radioactive dust. But she had to assume she was okay here, beyond the major fallout area and with a solid mountain and a steep incline between herself and Hadley.

She could go no farther, in any case. Her chances of fixing up the rover right now, packing everything back onto it, and driving away were, well, zero. Exhausted as she was, attempting it would be crazy.

Hopefully, its batteries and RTG would still be sound.

She brushed dust off herself as she pondered where to start.

If only I'd slept, well, any time recently, thinking would be a lot easier.

She dragged a long sausage-shaped bag off the rover trailer, and pulled at the zip that ran its entire length. A tube popped up, which she connected to one of the oxygen tanks. At the base of the tube was a small box with a gauge, a switch with a guard over it, and a dial. With two quick twists, Vivian snapped off the guard and flipped the switch, and a small red bulb lit up on the box. *Phew. Functional.*

She twisted the dial all the way clockwise.

For a heart-stopping moment, Vivian thought nothing was going to happen. Then she saw movement as it began to inflate at the end farthest from her.

Vivian had last erected one of these inflatable Habs in the Sonora Desert as part of an emergency training exercise, about a million years ago. In her memory, the thing had popped up almost immediately. This sucker was taking a much more leisurely approach. "Get a move on, for the love of God."

Inevitably, the Hab had an eighty-page NASA manual. That manual was right here now, tucked into an outer pocket. Vivian had a vision of herself paging through it with clumsy gloved fingers looking for the troubleshooting section.

But no, up it came, lengthening and thickening, and she remembered the ribald humor among the astronauts at its shape and, uh, angle of inflation. *Oh, sure, hahaha.*

Pretty soon, it would reach its full size. Such as it was.

The emergency Hab was more of a pup tent. Ten feet long, seven feet wide, five feet high, and that was on the *outside*; fully inflated, its walls would be almost a foot thick, and part of its apparent length was the ingress space at the end closest to her.

Vivian wouldn't be able to stand up inside. It was designed for two astronauts in suits lying side by side in dire emergency, with only limited life support functions. No frills. Ensuring sufficient space for a couple of weeks of supplies was far beyond its design requirements.

While it finished inflating, Vivian threw together everything she'd need: oxygen, water, food, and the small tool kit. *Especially food. Jeez.* Her hunger was killing her from the inside; she was cold, dizzy, and faint. Even the sight of the food packs was making her crazy.

At most, the Hab was intended to be occupied overnight. An Earth-style night; an eight-hour sleep period. Not three weeks, two of them in the chill of lunar night.

Right now, it was about halfway through the current lunar day. Seven Earth days left until the Sun went away, and Vivian had no hope of rescue within that time. And landing at night would be risky. Which might mean … a very long stay in this Hab. Vivian didn't know how long her current supplies could last, but she wasn't about to do the math now.

Who even knew whether the Hab would stay inflated that long? And the smallest leak might be fatal.

Whatever. For now, she opened the hatch and started piling stuff in. It wasn't easy: the Hab's entrance was too low, too narrow.

After a couple trips in and out, she halted to reconsider. She couldn't take all this stuff inside with her. Not possible. There just wasn't enough space.

Would half of it fit?

Shaking now, Vivian divided her supplies into two piles: air, water, food, CO_2 scrub cartridges. One pile she moved up outside the door. The other she transferred into the emergency Hab, packing it as best she could.

When she was done, she had a space left for herself that was barely six feet long and four feet wide, and she'd be sharing that with her suit. "Oh boy. This is going to be *such* fun."

Shaking her head, she strung cables from the rover battery and the RTG through to the external sockets on the Hab. Double-checking the storage areas on the rover to make sure she hadn't forgotten anything.

She expended more effort arranging the tanks and packages outside her front door. She'd need to suit up, decompress the tent, and grab these supplies later on, and she wouldn't want to spend a lot of time on it.

When she thought she was ready, she stopped. What would Ellis do, right now? She glanced at her oxygen level—nearly empty—and then triple-checked everything: what was inside the tent, what was outside, and what was still on the rover.

Now she noticed a small red object resting on the T-handle. As Vivian picked it up, clumsy in the gloves, a wave of unreality swept her.

It was a Bible.

You've got to be kidding me.

Somebody had come all this way, just to put Apollo 15 commander David R. Scott's Bible onto her Lunar Rover? So she could make her peace with God before expiring gracefully?

Well, whatever. She'd need some reading material. She stuffed it into her sleeve pocket. Then she crawled into the emergency habitat boots first.

Even with the hatchway still open, it was unspeakably claustrophobic. Vivian had been out in the open spaces of the mares and mountains for almost a week, and had grown accustomed to the large vistas. And for some reason, the confined interior brought back savage memories of Storage Nine. Perhaps it was the lack of freedom of movement, or maybe just the lighting: the single lamp inside the pup tent sent sinister shadows dancing around the boxes and tanks she'd be sharing the space with. "Come on, Vivian, you weenie. If you can live in a Command Module with a couple of stinky guys you can survive in here all by yourself."

And with that, it was time. "Well. Goodnight, Moon."

Vivian closed the hatch and pressurized the Hab using one of the oxygen bottles. A gauge mounted into the wall by the door allowed her to monitor the internal pressure and temperature, and also the inflation pressure within the tent's walls.

Once she reached 4.5 psi she forced herself to monitor both pressures for ten minutes before she did anything else. And then, in Ellis's honor, she waited five minutes more.

"Okay, then."

It was a scary moment. She had to entrust her life to this flimsy tent she'd just erected. Living in an inflatable Hab had seemed straightforward when she'd been considering it as an optional adventure, a camping sleepover to break up a geology trip. But Vivian couldn't even be sure that she'd set the damned thing up right.

But she was exhausted and hungry as hell, and it wasn't going to be any safer half an hour from now. "So here goes."

She snapped the latches on her gloves, pulled them off. Beneath them, her fingers and palms were red raw. "Oh, girl. Nasty. Wonder what the rest of me looks like."

Vivian wasn't in a hurry to find out. She knew she wouldn't like it. She took the helmet off.

The air in the tent had a damp, plasticky taste. She frowned at the shoebox-sized CO_2 scrubber and dehumidifier set into the wall, but didn't change its settings. She didn't want to stress her precarious ecosystem. She had no spares for anything. If something broke that she couldn't fix with the tool kit at her feet, she was shit out of luck.

Now that the moment had come, she'd stopped feeling hungry, which was probably a bad sign. She just ached everywhere, and tiredness was pounding away at her brain, which made her check the CO_2 level again. This place was going to make her paranoid.

She ate the blandest meal she could find, a risotto, but quickly felt nauseous. "Oh no, you don't. You're keeping that down."

Now, she had work to do. Again.

She dusted off her suit, and bagged the dust rags. They smelled of gunpowder, which was the characteristic moondust smell. She'd have to resign herself to getting some of it into her lungs. Hopefully not too much.

She wriggled out of the spacesuit, LCGs, and the sweaty and dirty jumpsuit beneath, which left her sitting in her diaper. A very full diaper. "Ew."

God, she was a mess, and that made her even more nauseous.

Germicidal wipes had never felt so good. Vivian cleaned up and toweled off, and bagged all the dirt. Then she cleaned the space around her, sweeping up every piece of dust she could find. Some of that dust would be radioactive, so she bagged it really well.

As she slowly ate a second meal, her head drooped. How long had she been awake? *Don't do the math.*

Tears dribbled down her cheeks. Because, frankly, the last few weeks had been kind of trying, even before she'd had to live through the past few days. And then the past few hours, and the recent minutes: God, it all sucked.

And now she'd be utterly alone for … who knew how much longer?

Vivian unrolled her sleeping bag. Tomorrow she'd clean and service the spacesuit and PLSS from helmet to boots. The shape her gear was in, that would probably take the whole day.

The day after that? She'd see how she felt. But once she was rested up and had some strength back, she'd need to go out and power up her Lunar Rover and see whether the S-band antenna and LCRU, her lunar communications relay unit, were still functional. Align the antenna toward Earth, and call ignominiously for help. Which might be a very long time coming.

And on that note, Vivian fell into a deep sleep.

Thirteen hours later, after breakfast but before she started the monotonous job of servicing her suit, Vivian picked up the Bible. She'd never read it all the way through anyway, and she was about to have a hell of a lot of downtime. How long was the Bible, three quarters of a million words? Vivian Carter: aviator, astronaut, suspected spy, and religious scholar.

As she riffled through the pages, an envelope fell out of it.

She tore it open. Inside was a single piece of paper, folded in two. The message was short and sweet.

Hi Vivian! Hope you survive your stroll back from the Zvezda Hilton in one piece, to read this.

We parked Athena fifty miles out on Palus with a full tank. Hopefully out of range of the shit that's about to hit, but watch out for residual radiation. The moondust will be even more fatal than usual.

We should really catch up sometime. Lots to talk about.

Peter

"Oh my God."

Her boys had left her a lifeboat.

A surge of relief buoyed her. She wouldn't have to call Houston for help and beg for rescue after all. At the same time tipping off the Soviets that she was still alive.

This was good.

But, fifty miles out on Palus? Vivian shook her head. She couldn't head off there anytime soon, not with the radiation levels as high as they were, and the state she was in. For now, she'd hang tight right here.

"The moondust is probably more fatal..." You don't say? Gee, thanks for that.

For an irrational moment, Vivian felt weird that someone else had flown Athena, even the short hop out to Palus. Athena was *her* ship.

Then she chided herself. *Yeah, crazy irrational.* Because Norton or Sandoval or whoever had given the order, and Ellis Mayer or whoever had piloted Athena to Palus, had probably saved her life.

Presumably Ellis. He'd have taken Athena the short hop to Palus, then gotten himself a ride back to Hadley—Vivian was betting Starman had driven a rover out to pick him up. They'd probably placed Scott's Bible with Sandoval's letter onto her rover on the same trip, since they'd have to cross Bridge on the return from Palus. The whole scheme would have taken less than a day to execute—once they'd received that final Soviet ultimatum.

They'd had a lot of confidence in Vivian, that she'd make it back this far. More confidence than she'd had in herself.

Dazzling.

"Peter, Ellis: beers forever. Y'know, assuming that I make it home alive."

The following week crawled by with excruciating slowness. After the first forty-eight hours, Vivian had mastered the mechanics of her surroundings: check the pressure, check the O_2 content, replace the LiOH cartridges as necessary. Wipe the damp off the walls, yuck. Eat. Clean herself, meticulously. Take more antibiotics for the urinary tract infection she'd unsurprisingly developed on the hike. Ensure her bodily wastes didn't escape from the sealed containers she was storing them in, sheesh. Exercise: yoga, Pilates, weight training with oxygen cylinders, with lots of reps of everything to keep up her strength and tire herself out as much as possible; after her initial very long sleep session, proper rest was hard to come by.

She was at the same time bored to tears, and jittery with the chronic fear that the Hab and its equipment would fail at any moment. She could tell almost to the second when the Sun moved far enough west to plunge the Hab into shadow, forcing her environmental system to abruptly switch from cooling to heating. Bridge Crater had been mostly in shadow when she'd been captured, toward the end of that lunar day, so this was hardly a surprise. The crater was at a much lower elevation than the western rim of Hadley Rille. Even though night wouldn't fall on the plain for several more days, the temperature outside her bolt-hole was now rapidly cooling to -200°F. Her rover, its battery, the RTG, and all the cabling and electrics were now immersed in a subzero bath.

Two days later, she had her second period of excitement: restocking. She clambered back into her spacesuit and depressurized the Hab. Opened the hatch and spent the next hour tossing out her spent air and water cylinders and other garbage, and hauling in the spares she'd left outside the door to replace them.

Once she'd gotten everything settled and repressurized the Hab again, she still couldn't doff the suit. The new stuff she'd pulled in was so cold that it would sear her and cause substantial injury if she touched it with an unprotected hand. Her suit exterior was almost as cold. Unsuiting at Hadley during lunar night, she and Ellis had followed strict protocols and used heavy gloves, and watched each other like hawks to stave off disastrous errors. Here, there was no one to watch out for her. It just wasn't worth taking the risk.

Her heating system was laboring, but she couldn't mitigate that. It was four hours before Vivian felt confident enough to crack her suit open, and once she'd gotten it off, she crawled into her sleeping bag and stayed there for ten hours. It took another full day for her lair to warm up to its previous coziness.

But that was the turning point. After restocking, Vivian felt her mood lifting.

She started scheming in earnest. She'd had a lot of time to think and figure things out, and she now knew exactly what she was going to do next. She hadn't phoned home, and had no intention of doing so.

Obviously, she would head off to Athena soon.

Less obviously: she had no intention of returning to Earth just yet.

She had a plan. And when Vivian Carter had a plan, what could possibly go wrong?

PART FOUR: OFF THE GRID

January 30 – February 29, 1980

CHAPTER 39

Lunar Orbit: Dave Horn
January 1980

FROM the Apollo 32 Command Module, Dave Horn first saw the un-piloted Agena vehicle as a moving pinprick against the stars. It grew over the next twenty minutes to become a long cylinder in an orbit slightly below his, its two red lights blinking up at him. And as he watched, its cold gas thrusters fired to nudge it into an orbit matching Horn's own.

Pretty cool. So far, the Agena was doing all the work, with help from Mission Control and Minerva's own transponder, which Horn had recently reactivated to bring him out of EMCON—emission control mode—for the first time in … more weeks than he cared to count.

Nothing in his headset from Mission Control. Using the short-range VHF transponder was a calculated risk, and almost unavoidable, but any chatter on S-band, even encrypted, would make Horn's detection certain.

In principle, Horn could control the Agena himself, piggybacking his commands onto the transponder signal. He didn't think he'd need to. He goosed his reaction-control jets, eyeballed the result, measured an angle or two out the window, and typed numbers into his guidance computer. *Sure. I can grab that thing without any further help.*

Horn didn't say the words aloud. He'd talked to himself a whole lot during his first few days alone, and it had just emphasized his isolation.

Now he scheduled a conversation with himself once per day, while tidying up after breakfast, to keep his vocal cords warm.

The Agena came closer and closer. *Come on, sweet baby. Come to Papa.*

It would've helped if the Agena had been the same shape and size as the Cargo Carrier because Horn had a ton of experience with those. But, of course, it wasn't. The Agena was a space-age classic that had been in use since the Gemini missions in 1965–66, where it had served as a practice vehicle for rendezvous. It was a cylinder thirty feet long by five feet in diameter, and probably weighed around four tons.

He was aiming to dock with it end-on, at its nearer, flatter end. Its far end was a truncated cone, the flared nozzle of a rocket motor. The vehicle was bringing Horn a couple of months more food and water in a storage compartment, but its mass was mostly fuel; it would serve as a propulsion module, the same kind they regularly bolted onto Skylabs and MOLs in Earth orbit to counter atmospheric drag and boost them back into a higher orbit. Once docked, Horn could fire the Agena's rocket engine without having to leave Minerva, via the umbilicals that passed through the docking probe, but to grab his victuals he'd have to get out there for a lone spacewalk. Was he looking forward to that or not? Horn couldn't decide. He'd be out of this tiny capsule for a while, but with quite the list of things that could go wrong.

Twenty feet and closing, and the Command Module's snout was absolutely lined up with the docking collar of his new cylindrical pal. Horn could now see the four lights on the Agena that would guide him in: two blinking, and two to illuminate the drogue. Nothing to it.

Horn grimaced. Still no end in sight to his lone vigil. *Sure hope they didn't think I was kidding when I told 'em to toss in a few dozen books and a bunch of new cassette tapes.* His health and skills might be nominal right now, but if he didn't get some new reading and listening material soon, he might go stark raving mad.

With a grating *clunk*, he docked with the Agena. Latches snapped into place. His key lights went green. He effectively had a full tank of gas again: more propulsion than he was ever likely to need.

It would be nice to go home.

But, nooo, because those weren't his orders.

Horn's orders were, in fact, the exact opposite: to use the Agena's motor to establish an orbit just a couple thousand miles away from Columbia Station. Continue his silent vigil, monitor Soviet VHF frequencies, and stage that information to Earth by squirting it at the two comms relay stations on the lunar surface.

Dear Lord, he really wanted to get away from this Command Module. It reminded him too much of his failed mission, his dead commander.

Because Vivian surely had to be dead by now. Ellis Mayer might still hold out his forlorn hope that she'd survived, but Horn was too much of a realist.

No one had heard from her for weeks. Nothing from Gerry Lin either, so the Soviets must have nailed him too.

And the Soviets believed she was dead too. They'd discussed it quite freely in their radio transmissions.

So that made it unanimous. Aside from Ellis. Poor bastard.

Damn, Horn hadn't expected to start feeling emotional about it. After all this time?

It seemed worth making an exception. Breaking his silence, because he'd never said it out loud: "Rest in peace, Vivian Carter."

And that was that.

Time to suit up, and go see what those jokers had sent him to read.

Three hours later, safely back in the cabin and repressurized, Horn fired up his brand-new engine.

Woo, baby.

And: ouch.

The rocket motor aboard the Agena was a beast, even bigger than the one in Horn's CSM. It was designed to move mountains, and Minerva was just a large boulder.

The G's were fierce. And worse, they were eyeballs out. All the major accelerations that Horn had experienced previously had been from behind, shoving him back into his seat. But for this burn he was strapped in facing the damned rocket, and so the G's were pulling him out of the couch, jamming his chest painfully into his harness straps. It messed with his breathing more than he'd expected, and felt very much like having his eyes poked with sticks. His risk of an eye hemorrhage was *much* greater with the acceleration in this direction.

"Jeez," he wheezed aloud. Fortunately, this would only be a twenty-second burn, but his next one would need to be a lot longer.

Maybe by then he could figure out a way of rejiggering one of the couches so he could face the other way.

To distract himself, Horn began to list all the ways that would be extremely freaking difficult. The main one being that he'd have his back to his control panels. *Shee-it*.

Boy, Horn would have a whole bunch of suggestions for his NASA mission debrief.

If this interminable mission ever ended, that was.

And if he was lucky enough to survive it.

CHAPTER 40

Bridge Crater: Vivian Carter
February 6, 1980

TWO days till local sunset. This was about as late as she could leave it.

Enough lying around. Time to go.

In her damp-walled and pungent Hab deep in Bridge Crater, Vivian hurried into her spacesuit, more than ready to get her ass on the road again.

She crawled out of her cocoon and gazed out over the lunar surface. Black and white and gray. It still had that savage beauty, especially in the heavily slanting sunlight of evening. But, right now, Vivian Carter was sick of it.

She'd kill to see a copse of trees or a lake. To feel the wind in her hair. Which was a shame, because she wouldn't be leaving the Moon any time soon.

Her first task was to fix the rover wheel that had smashed into the boulder. She whacked it back into shape with a rock, and jimmied at it with a screwdriver. That would have to do. The terrain was so irregular that she might not even notice the kinks that remained.

She unhooked the cables that had provided her with RTG and battery power. Deflated the Hab that had kept her alive for the past week, and tossed it into the back of the rover without bothering to pack it properly. She couldn't imagine ever wanting to get back into it. Loaded up what remained of her spare air, water, and food, and climbed aboard.

399

The rover's engine started without difficulty, and she drove slowly out of Bridge Crater. The T-handle was stiff, probably due to dust in the steering column. It wasn't exactly receptive on the turns, either. In fact, it drove like a cow.

But it sure beat walking. After the bitterness of Vivian's hike from Mare Vaporum through the Hadley-Apennines, riding the rover seemed an absurd luxury. She bumped up and out of Bridge, and back toward Hadley.

Which was the wrong direction. But Vivian couldn't leave without just one quick glance at Hadley Plain. She'd feel like an idiot if somehow the Soviet nuke had gone off in the completely wrong part of the Plain, and the Habs were still there.

She took a peek. Nope. Where the base had been, only a giant bowl remained. A stark dish carved out of the lunar surface.

It was all gone. The Habs, the fuel depot, the Cargo Containers. The bunker, all the LMs and Lunar Rovers, all the dirt and scuffle of human occupation that had surrounded them. All scoured away in an instant, annihilated in one single white-hot nuclear moment.

And in their place, an extremely neat crater a mile across, much more regular than any other and apparently lined with glass.

Eventually, meteor impacts would roughen up the area to the point where it might not be obvious that something very unnatural had happened here. After, say, a couple hundred million years.

Crazy Yashin had really done it. He'd detonated a nuclear device on the Moon, and obliterated Hadley Base and a huge volume of regolith beneath and around it into the bargain.

Vivian didn't linger. The radiation level would have dropped exponentially, but exposure was cumulative and she must have already racked up quite a total on this trip. One quick scan, and then she U-turned her rover and negotiated her way back down across the causeway and out onto the great plain of Palus Putredinis.

Her Lunar Module was easy to spot, even from many miles distant. The gold foil that wrapped its lower half sparkled in the late Sun, a startling splash of color amid the lunar grays. She saw its sharp reflected glint long before she could resolve the squatting insect shape of the LM itself. "Ah, Athena, beautiful girl. You waited for me."

And then she added: "Sure hope you're still in good working order." The Modules weren't designed to be left unpowered in the full heat of lunar day for this long.

As she crawled in through Athena's front hatch, she wanted to kiss the floor. But in her helmet, that wasn't going to happen. Yet.

It was dark inside, because the shades were drawn over its two small windows. Shining her flashlight around gave her a shock that jolted her to her core: for a mad moment she thought someone was in there with her. But it was just an empty suit. Her people had left her a spare, and while it obviously wasn't fresh out of the box, it was a hell of a lot cleaner than the one she was wearing.

That was great. She'd switch over to the newer suit for her next EVA.

The Hadley folks had also left her some weapons, which was almost funny. An RPG launcher and a bunch of grenades. Guess they'd been trying to think of everything. Fortunately, there was no one around to defend herself against.

She reached for the circuit breakers. "Okay, Athena, baby. Time to wake up."

Powering up and repressurizing the Lunar Module took several hours, and by that time Vivian was ready to eat and sleep again. The hammock was bliss after sleeping on the Hab floor for weeks, but it felt odd not to hear Ellis breathing quietly in his own hammock beneath her.

When she awoke the following day, she briefly considered phoning home. After all, she now had two working S-band antennas and a presumably functioning comms system. And people would be worrying about her.

"Nah."

Mission Control would only want to tell her what to do. And Vivian wasn't about to do what they told her in any case.

Sure hope my hunches are right. I'm going to look like a real idiot if I'm completely overinterpreting all this.

She'd certainly spent enough time in her Hab thinking about it, before committing to this plan. But it still might be worth keeping her fingers crossed.

Easy enough to justify her silence. If the Soviets were still monitoring NASA frequencies, they'd detect her right away from Columbia

Station or whatever else they had in orbit, and might take hostile action. And the most recent Soviet action Vivian had witnessed had been very, very explosive.

She was certainly curious about what had happened to all her people over the past month or more. But not yet curious enough to ask. Best to remain silent and unseen.

Instead, she donned her new suit. It was Carol Massey's spare, according to the chest tag, so it fit better than the one she'd worn to slog north over hill and dale from Mare Vaporum. *Hey, Carol. Thanks.*

Amused, it struck her that she could take her geology trip, after all. She had a rover. The Hab still seemed to be working fine. Between the rover and Athena she now had a ton of supplies. She had a spare suit, and nothing but time. She could take a leisurely road trip across Palus to Archimedes and Autolycus Craters, check out the Soviet Luna 2 probe crash site. Take samples of ejecta and everything. She'd certainly earned a vacation. Why not?

"Yeah, think I'll pass."

She had a lot do in the coming days, including some hardcore math to run on the Apollo guidance computer before lighting the LM fuse and betting her life on the answers.

Besides, she'd promised Ellis that if he didn't go on Palus Trek, she wouldn't either.

Vivian would see plenty more craters before she was done here, in any case.

Five days later, she was all set.

A day to clean up and put Athena's systems through their paces, run diagnostics, and make sure she was sound. Two long EVAs to load the LRV back into the outside bay, and even at that she'd made a half-assed job of it. The rover was designed to deploy easily, but Boeing and General Motors hadn't spent quite as long engineering the process for putting it *back*. But she couldn't leave it behind. She completed the load just before sunset.

A full day spent doing star sightings to recalibrate the reference system on her guidance computer, plus deriving a PAD for the launch, and uploading and rechecking it. Almost another full day training herself for what she was about to do, running the procedures from beginning to end and going through all the motions as best she could, to make sure she wouldn't hesitate at a crucial moment. Lunar Modules weren't *designed* to be flown solo, damn it, and Vivian was willing to bet that the dear departed Gerry Lin had trained rigorously for lone LM ops before he'd even left Earth. It was nowhere as easy as he'd made it look. If Vivian lost lock on what she was doing during launch or, worse, her descent, she'd make a spectacular crater.

Finally, she did a night EVA to finish loading everything in, filling all the free space: food, oxygen, tools, the collapsed baby Hab. Lashed the RTG back onto the outer leg of the LM. Clambered in. Closed the hatch, then spent another two hours reviewing everything one more time.

Okay. If she wasn't ready now, she never would be.

Vivian was going to shirtsleeve this one, and the hell with it. This flight would be hard enough as it was, with no help from Ellis or Mission Control, without having to do it hampered by her suit. And if she crashed again, it would all be over anyway.

If Dave Horn can hang out alone in space in a tin can for however many weeks, I can launch myself off the goddamn Moon in my underwear.

She paused to pray that the LM repair had been done right, that stent to the tubes that Ellis and the other LM pilots had spent a day and a half welding into place. Sure, Ellis had hopped Athena from Hadley to Palus, but Vivian was about to put way more stress on the engine than that. "Oh well. Nothing I can do about it either way."

She took a deep breath. "Second star to the right, and straight on till morning."

When she pressed PROCEED on the onboard computer, and the engine beneath her burst into life and shoved her off the ground, Vivian whooped aloud.

Then she frowned and focused in, reading her instruments, checking numbers. The computer was in charge for now, but she needed to keep a close eye. If Athena deviated from the course Vivian had charted, or the instruments gave wonky readings, she needed to know right away.

After a while she settled into the groove, with the fierce concentration necessary to fly a high-performance machine, scarcely self-aware at all. Before she knew it, she'd passed the high point of her trajectory and fired the jets to flip Athena around engine-first for the descent. It was one of the shortest hours she'd ever experienced.

No worries. She had this. She was a stone-cold pro. *A steely eyed missile man.* Ha.

It was a programmed descent through the modified P63 braking burn. The descent stage engine fired right back up again on command. P64 took her on final approach and pitched the LM upright so that Vivian could see where she was going and, sure enough, it was all lumps and bumps below her in the oblique light of early morning. Craters and hills she didn't know because she'd never needed to memorize this part of the Moon. Standard highland terrain, but at least there were no giant mountain ranges.

But mostly she did it on instruments. For her first Moon landing she'd been focused on what was happening outside the craft: craters, mountains, and boulders, not to mention the sizeable human assets she'd been trying to avoid. This time it didn't matter where she came down, to within a few miles, anyway. Her landing zone was close to the terminator, so if she overshot she'd be heading back into night. But she couldn't overshoot by *that* much.

She took over full manual control about as late as she could, well into the land-or-crash zone of unforgiveness. She could see the craters in sharp relief. *Wow, landing is much easier when it's nominal. Even doing it lonesies.*

She took the last four hundred feet really seriously, braking the LM to a hover while she studied the site. She leaned the Module forward and flew it on and to the right for about half a mile before she found a rocky highland surface she liked the look of. By that point she was down to a minute's worth of flying time before the bingo call.

A whole minute. Luxurious.

The landing was almost anticlimactic. Perhaps because her nerves were already shot to hell. Or maybe because it was her second time and she wasn't suffering from a holed propellant system, a severe fuel shortage, immense and scary mountain ranges, and Sun-drench.

She eyed the height and rate indicators and only occasionally risked a glance outside to check for boulders. She got the contact light from the dangling six-foot probes earlier than she'd expected, brought the Module down a notch farther, and cut power just a couple feet above the surface. Vivian had had enough hard landings.

The LM curtseyed down, rather than crashing like a pile of bricks. Barely a creak out of the landing gear as it came to rest.

"And *that* is how we do *that*. Congratulations, Vivian Carter, on your solo descent on the far side of the Moon."

Pity Mission Control hadn't gotten to monitor her telemetry. That one was about as close to textbook as it got.

On her next EVA, the Earth wouldn't even be in the sky. That should have been a lonely, alienating thought. It probably would have been, if Vivian hadn't already spent the last two weeks alone.

Her descent stage propellant tanks were nearly dry. The only way Vivian could take off now would be to use her ascent engine, abandoning the descent stage. If she launched again, she'd be leaving the Moon for good.

Which might be in a few days, or never.

Okay. Time to measure some more damned star angles and do more damned math to verify her location. Put her damned spacesuit on again and get out onto the damned lunar surface. Deploy the damned rover again. Load up with oxygen and water, her spare suit, and that triple-damned baby Hab in case she had another goddamned catastrophe.

Mount up. And go a-hunting, to see what she could find.

41

Farside: Vivian Carter
February 10, 1980

TWO hours of measuring and math convinced Vivian that she'd landed exactly where she'd intended. She was a tiny bit south of the lunar equator, and a little northeast of the enormous Heaviside Crater. "Right on the money."

If the far side of the Moon was a target, Athena was currently located a little lower and to the left of the bull's-eye. Almost exactly on the opposite side of the Moon to Copernicus Crater. And just under two hundred miles due west of Daedalus Crater.

Although, since the crater coordinates referred to its center and Daedalus was 60 miles across, that meant she was only about 170 miles from the crater rim. And hopefully what she was looking for would be on the near rim? Could Vivian get that lucky, for a change?

Only 170 miles.

When she'd originally planned Palus Trek, the distance from Hadley to Archimedes Crater had seemed enormous. And that was a mere 150 miles. Vivian's perceptions of *near* and *far* on the Moon had changed considerably.

"Of course, it'll be a lot farther if I broke the rover in transit."

She hadn't. She might have ... bent it a little, cramming it back into Bay 1. Deploying it for the second time, the chassis didn't swing out and lock quite as smoothly. Only one of the seats would straighten up properly, but that was fine: there was only one of Vivian.

She loaded up. She was tempted to leave the sad old inflatable emergency Hab behind, couldn't imagine the magnitude of emergency that could ever persuade her to use it again. But hey, she might change her mind. She tied it on the back.

The weapons? Tricky decision. She ended up loading them in the wayback, where she couldn't reach them from the driver's seat.

Finally, she powered off Athena and closed the door. Remembered not to lock it.

Only then did she look up into the sky.

"Yup, no Earth."

Yeah. That *was* unsettling.

"Ah, well." Vivian climbed aboard the rover and powered it up. "Here I go again."

She'd flown halfway around the Moon, and from the end of the lunar day to its beginning—so she'd be driving with the Sun in her face all the way. A hundred fifty miles in the rover was a mere ten hours. Vivian only had to stop once. Otherwise, she just bowled on through the highlands. No mountains, no mares. Just craters, craters, boulders, and more craters. It was comfortably dull.

As it turned out, Vivian didn't need to look for them. They found her, and before she was expecting it. She was still thirty miles from the rim of Daedalus when she saw the glint of a fast-moving object on the horizon that was probably a dirt bike.

She kept on going and soon noticed a second vehicle pacing her, a mile or so off to her right. It was a six-wheeled vehicle that looked like neither a NASA LRV nor a Soviet Lunokhod.

"Guess my rogue rover makes all the boys come running."

Vivian drove steadily, keeping her arms where they could be seen. She expected at any moment to be hailed, but her headset was silent. Nor did she attempt to contact them. Their mere presence meant that she was on the right track, and that was a great relief. She'd have hated to come all this way based on a misunderstanding.

Vivian's marked-up photograph of this area was folded and strapped to her left arm. While swerving around rocks she could only glance at it occasionally, but it looked like she was still heading in the right direction.

Daedalus Crater was dead ahead of her.

Buchanan's last words to her, that he'd thought so important he needed to interrupt Starman's warning. *"If you hear me, be very smart now. Don't fly too close to the Sun. Y'hear? Best of luck, girl."*

Not just a wisecrack. Buchanan's tone had been very serious and intent. He'd meant it as a clue. One that would mean nothing to Vivian, unless and until she'd figured out every other piece of the puzzle.

Daedalus. Thinks his way out of the labyrinth. Never flies too close to the Sun. Flies sure but steady, and survives.

Not like that crazy Icarus, who crashes and burns.

Buchanan, you wacky old dude. I guess I owe you a beer as well.

Even though I'm flying a bit close to the Sun right now, despite your sage advice.

So, thanks to Buchanan, once Vivian had realized *what* she was looking for, the *where* had been obvious.

And now she could see it. Three square Habs in a row, and sticking straight out from it, a long, low structure that extended way out into the distance, very thin and unnaturally straight against the fractured rim of Daedalus Crater.

"How the hell long is that thing?"

No one answered, and for the first time in several weeks Vivian felt a creeping fear. She'd become hardened to the risk of suit breach or some other fatal mishap, but she still wasn't immune to wariness of her fellow man. No one here would be pleased to see her.

The closer she got to the Daedalus facility, the closer in her escorts came, to her left and right. She resisted the urge to wave. Didn't want them to think maybe she was throwing something, even though it would take a major league baseball player to throw anything that far. Even in lunar gravity.

They were herding her in. By now, they must be able to tell that she was American. Or at least that she was wearing a NASA suit and driving a glorified NASA golf cart.

At last, they acted. The dirt bike swung toward her and roared in at the breakneck speed of twenty-five miles an hour. The six-wheeler accelerated, seeming to leap forward, bouncing and bumping over the terrain, often with three or four of its metal-framed wheels airborne.

Her headphones crackled with incoming VHF. A terse voice, with a distinct military/law enforcement tone. "Intruder: identify yourself."

"Captain Vivian Carter, United States Navy," she said promptly. "Also Commander Carter of NASA and Apollo 32, recently reassigned to Hadley Base."

"State your intentions."

"Rescue. To be reunited with my colleagues and countrymen, following my capture and escape from the Soviet Zvezda Base and a hellishly long journey." She might as well be honest. "Also, simple curiosity."

"Stop your vehicle immediately, and step away from it."

Vivian nodded, rocking back and forth to make the motion big in the suit. "Roger, wilco. Note that I am unarmed save for a rocket-powered grenade launcher, brought purely for defense, behind me in the rover. That's my only weapon, and I'll make no move toward it."

"Make sure you don't."

She came to a halt, and stepped down from the rover. The bike had stopped a hundred feet behind her, its rider standing up in the saddle, covering her with a weapon of some sort. The six-wheeler was keeping its distance to her right. *Lunar traffic stop. Wonder if he'll ask to see my license?*

"Step away from the rover. Arms held out. Walk twenty feet, then lie face down. Stay put. Do not move again until instructed."

"Roger that." She extended her arms out to left and right, trudged out without looking back. "Have I gone twenty feet?"

"Close enough. Down."

"Down I go." She clambered down onto her hands and knees, then straightened out carefully. "Moving rocks from beneath me to avoid damage to my radio and suit controls."

The man just grunted. Then there was silence. Vivian lay there patiently. Even if she turned her head within the helmet she couldn't see back to the rover, but she presumed that the men were checking it thoroughly. "Uh, guys? This is pretty uncomfortable."

"Stand by, ma'am. Almost done."

That was a second male voice, sounding almost apologetic. She'd become ma'am, at least, although she'd have preferred Captain.

"All clear," said the first guy.

Moon boots loped into her field of view. "All's well, Captain Carter. You'll understand our need for caution."

"Absolutely," she said. "Am I getting up now?"

"Yup. Although, you're really not supposed to be here."

"Seems fair," Vivian said. "As far as most people know, you're not supposed to be here either."

The first guy grunted again. "Smartass."

The second man reached for her arm to help pull her up. The fingers of his gloves seemed more supple than hers.

Vivian turned. Their suits were neither regulation NASA nor Night Corps; dark gray in color with a smooth texture, but when she looked into their visors all she saw was her own distorted face reflected back. Both had short, stocky rifles slung under their arms. Not exactly pointing at her, but not exactly pointing away, either.

Each axle of their rover was separately articulated. The bike was sleeker than the Soviet bikes, even though sleekness wasn't much of an asset where there was no wind resistance. "Nice wheels, boys. Lead on."

"Uh, no. Ladies first. We'll be right behind you."

"Copy that." Vivian walked back toward her rover.

For her first human interaction in a month, it was sadly wanting.

It was for all the world like driving onto a military base in Texas or South Carolina. Vivian drove up, and all of a sudden, the couple dozen astronauts standing or moving across the surface started paying *real* close attention.

The base was ringed with six of the skeletal rocket launchers, identical to the one Night Corps had installed at Hadley, and which had never been used as far as Vivian knew. A mile away were the low lines of a fuel dump also similar to Hadley's. In the opposite direction, right at the horizon, was another blocky building which probably housed a nuclear reactor, since thick cables linked it with the Daedalus facility.

An astronaut raised his hand to halt her well short of the main Hab, which was obvious by its windows and its three-level height. Alongside it were two more low buildings with no windows at all. Close by were three Lunar Modules, apparently L-class three-person LM Taxi variants, but somehow more steely looking. Well, why reinvent something that worked?

Dominating everything: jutting out from one of the low buildings was the rail, a meter wide and half a meter thick, held horizontal by a succession of solid piers two meters tall and extending far into the distance. "Impressive," she said. No one answered.

Vivian knew what she was looking at. She'd read Gerard O'Neill's 1974 article about the colonization of space along with everyone else in her astronaut candidate group. Ambitious blue-skies stuff describing huge cylindrical habitats in orbit, and as unrealistic as the *Collier's* magazine articles by Von Braun and Willy Ley in the early 1950s. But O'Neill's mass driver concept? Yeah, everyone had been in basic agreement that that could work.

The lunar mass driver catapult was designed to throw small- to medium-sized objects into space. It was an electromagnetic launch system, with the electricity producing rapidly moving magnetic fields. Drive coils would accelerate a bucket coil that, at the far end of this track, would hurl the payload into space.

By the time the payload reached the far end it would be traveling at two and a half kilometers a second, the Moon's escape velocity. The payload—*let's be honest, the missile*—would fly across Daedalus Crater, and arc on, up and out into space.

From the center of Farside, a standard trajectory would carry it toward Earth, and very efficiently. No fuel required, and no exhaust volatiles at all.

Vivian wanted to go over and touch that rail. She also felt sure that someone would shoot her if she did.

Holy shit. Her suspicions were confirmed, and in spades, but it gave her no satisfaction. Instead, she felt a simmering anger that she tried not to allow into her voice.

"Very impressive, guys. Seriously."

Was it operational yet? This weapon that the Soviets had gotten wind of, far ahead of Vivian, that could change the entire equation of the Cold War?

Soviet intelligence and suspicions about the existence of this mass driver had propelled their attacks on Columbia Station and Hadley. It had gotten Vivian captured and interrogated, and Hadley Base nuked into glowing glass. Because of her associations with Sandoval and Lin, and because she'd carried a spy camera to Columbia in her Cargo Carrier, they'd assumed that Vivian knew all about this thing, and where on the Moon it was located.

Simply put, this mass driver had already nearly gotten Vivian killed, several times over.

And its existence proved that the US had been comprehensively breaking the Outer Space Treaty for years, despite Reagan's protestations of innocence. *Damn it.*

Vivian wondered what lengths the astronauts who stood silently around her now, and their masters in the main Habitat, and *their* masters back on Earth in the USAF, Army, CIA, NRO, whatever; what lengths any or all of them would go to, to ensure her silence.

No, come on, this is still America. No one is going to kill me because I saw this.

Are they?

A hatch opened in the Hab, puffing up a spray of moondust. "Please go on in, ma'am."

When Vivian hesitated, one of the dark-gray astronaut's arms visibly twitched. The arm that held his gun.

Great. "Sure. No problem."

She walked into the confined space. Someone closed the hatch behind her and sealed it. Red lights turned amber and eased toward green, and Vivian could hear the dull hiss that meant the chamber was pressurizing.

Through her headset: "Please disconnect your PLSS and remove your suit."

The inner door had not yet opened. Vivian didn't move. Removing her suit would put her at their mercy. If they depressurized this airlock again, she'd die in agony. "Let me come in?"

"Will do. But first, please take off your suit."

They held all the cards. Nothing she could do. "Roger that."

Vivian took off her helmet and gloves, and paused. Now would be the time if they were going to do it. Or maybe that would be a waste of a perfectly good spacesuit, as her body exploded into it.

Nice.

Fine. Let's get this over.

Vivian hauled herself the rest of the way out of the suit, stripped off the liquid-cooled garments, and stood there in her jumpsuit.

The inner door opened. Three men in blue flight suits and crew cuts were waiting for her.

The first man held out a tube, which emitted a few metallic clicks. A Geiger counter. She was obviously showing residual radioactivity from the Hadley blast. She wondered how much.

As yet, no one had met her eye. This was ridiculous. "I'm Captain Vivian Carter. You?"

The first man glanced up and raised an eyebrow, but said nothing. Vivian scanned the decals on his suit. USAF. Had Sandoval known about this place all along, then? Probably.

But if so, he couldn't have told her even if he'd wanted to.

The man stepped toward the door. "Please come through, ma'am."

Vivian flashed him an insincere smile, and stepped through into the Hab.

CHAPTER 42

Daedalus Base: Vivian Carter
February 10, 1980

VIVIAN had been extensively interrogated by the Soviets. Now she faced interrogation by her own people. Though Major General Karl Johnston, Commander of Daedalus Base, hardly inspired the same terror as Comrade Sergei Ivanovich Yashin.

They sat in a small cubicle lined with lockers. An empty desk separated them, and cool, clean air purred into the room. Johnston was in his late fifties and balding and, to Vivian's astonishment, was wearing full military dress uniform. He regarded her severely. "Captain Vivian Carter. We're surprised you're still alive."

"I'm surprised too, sir. Whenever I wake up, and several times daily. Did all our people get off safely from Hadley? Did Ellis Mayer and Dave Horn make it back to Earth?" Vivian almost asked about Sandoval too. Thought better of it.

"In due course. I'll need the answers to a few questions first."

"Happy to oblige."

"Why are you here?"

Vivian gave the most direct answer she could. "Because I had to know, sir. I've been through so much already. I had to know whether my country had been lying to me all this time. Needed to see for myself."

"So you decided to just *show up* here?"

"Yes, I did. Sir."

"Captain, you do not *own* that Lunar Module you flew to Farside in, nor the Lunar Rover. They are not your personal property, to use to satisfy your curiosity."

"If I'd split for home, I'd have abandoned the rover and Athena's descent stage on-surface anyway. May as well burn up the consumables in a good cause."

"Once you regained your Lunar Module, you could have communicated with NASA Mission Control. You should have made contact and requested new orders."

"I was in a war zone, sir. I couldn't call in without revealing my location to the Soviets."

Johnston folded his arms. "Captain Carter, how did you learn of the existence of this base?"

"I figured it out for myself."

Johnston raised his eyebrows.

"Long story," she added.

"You have plenty of time."

Vivian marshalled her thoughts. "Okay, then. From the beginning, even before Night Corps arrived at Hadley Base, it seemed odd that the Soviets were so hard-over convinced that we were developing a nuclear weapons capability on the Moon. What would be the point? We argued about it a lot, us astros, particularly during my first lunar night when we were all stuck inside the Habs with too much routine maintenance to do and not enough else to think about. But it was only once Night Corps arrived that I realized what had to be going on."

"How so?"

"Night Corps was too proficient. Obviously, we all know about the USAF surveillance activity in Earth orbit. That's why we have a parallel space program, right? A defense effort, separate from NASA's civilian mission to explore.

"But then? Less than a month after the Soviets took Columbia Station, Night Corps showed up on the Moon, and they were … extremely competent. Unbelievably so."

His face was a mask. "Go on."

"Night Corps has been training for lunar military ops, in case of need. Fine. But they're too damned *good* at it. They slam down onto the surface, and within hours they've established their beachhead. They wear spacesuits that are obviously heavier and more complex than

415

NASA suits, but they're comfortable in them from Hour One. The only one from Night Corps who even stumbled on the lunar surface was Peter Sandoval. 'Well, he hadn't trained for the Moon,' you'll say. But Ellis and I *had* trained for the Moon, and we still fell down up here a *lot*. But aside from Sandoval, the Night Corps guys got everything right, all the damned time. They were supernaturally good. That's just not possible."

Johnston nodded. "Excellent men. Adaptable and proficient, and well trained."

"Yes, sir. But this wasn't their first time on-surface. They'd been well trained, *and* spent a considerable time, *on the Moon*. Obviously not at Hadley. So, somewhere else. It's obvious now that they trained *here*. I presume they'd all done tours of duty at Daedalus and rotated out, and so were available for Apollo Rescue 1 when the shit hit the fan.

"As for Sandoval, I'm guessing he was assigned to lead Rescue 1 because he'd trained so extensively with NASA astronauts. He knows how we think. He'd already met Norton and Buchanan; he knew me, Terri Brock, even Josh Rawlings. I'm thinking there's no one else who could have liaised with the Hadley crew so smoothly, and who we'd have trusted so quickly."

Vivian took a drink of water. This was the most she'd spoken aloud in many weeks. Her throat was already sore.

"At the time, I just had a nagging suspicion that something was, well, *off*. But then I got captured and taken to Zvezda, and that's when it really sank in that this wasn't some propaganda play cooked up in the Kremlin to justify a lunar land grab. My Soviet interrogators were completely convinced that the American Imperialists were installing a nuclear capability here that posed a serious threat to the Soviet Union. And these were not stupid people, sir. The cosmonauts, the Red Army soldiers, they all *knew* the US was doing something up here."

Johnston looked dour. "And you believed them?"

"Well, they were right, weren't they?"

"And from all that you somehow concluded that we had a base located here at Daedalus, and flew straight here the first chance you got?" Johnston's sarcasm was heavy.

"In a manner of speaking. You must realize that I've had a lot of time to think over the past few weeks. A *lot* of time."

"There's more?"

"If you wish."

Johnston leaned back, waved a hand.

"Okay. So, I'm in Soviet captivity, and I'm being kept awake around the clock, and going half mad, and thinking it all through. Obsessing over it, frankly. So, my train of thought: If I'm the Soviets, and I suspect that the US is establishing a covert lunar base, what do I do? Well, ideally, I'd put a surveillance platform of my own in orbit around the Moon. Scrutinize the surface from sixty miles up with some serious optics and try to locate this mysterious base. But that'll take time, and in all likelihood the US will never let me do that.

"So, instead, I—this is still the hypothetical, Soviet me—I bide my time till the Americans themselves ship a major optical instrument to Columbia Station, and then … I take Columbia. Acquiring the surveillance capability I need, without having to build it myself."

Despite himself, Johnston looked intrigued. "The large-frame camera."

"Yeah. But even before the Soviets took Columbia and got the camera up and running, they must have had a fair idea where to look. Once you know the US has established a secret base, it's clear where it must be located. Right here."

She took more water. "When we fly Apollos to the Moon, we loop around to Farside in a ballistic trajectory and fire our orbital injection burn at our farthest point from the Earth, to circularize the orbit. For trans-Earth injection, breaking orbit to go home, Apollos initiate that burn while we're over the center of Farside. That's just how orbital mechanics works, and you know that as well as anyone. If you want to launch something from the Moon to Earth using the minimum amount of energy, you launch it from mid-Farside at escape velocity, and away it goes. You might need a midcourse correction between Moon and Earth, or you might not.

"And now you've got yourself a second- or even third-strike capability."

Johnston's eyes were unreadable.

"Launching missiles from here will be a pretty inaccurate proposition. Given an Earth-based launch from Nebraska or Kansas, we can put our ICBMs on target in the Soviet Union to within a few miles. Using a ballistic trajectory from the Moon you can't achieve anywhere near that accuracy. That's what threw me off for a while: the inaccuracy and the travel time. With the best will in the world, anything launched from Farside takes days to get to Earth, and by that time the war's likely over.

"But that's not the point, is it? If the Soviets do initiate a nuclear war on Earth—get in their first strike and disable a US response by land-based ICBMs—we need *some* way of getting back at them. I realized that all this must have been initially scoped out long ago, back in the 1960s, before we had enough nukes to destroy the Earth several times over, and specifically before we were able to launch Polaris missiles from submarines. So, the logic must have been that if the Reds catch us on the hop and take out our ground-launch capability, three days later a wave of US missiles shows up from the Moon to pepper the Soviet Union. Sure, our aim will be crap. But there's no way the Soviets can stop those missiles. They'll be traveling too fast to intercept, much faster than a normal ICBM. And they'll be smaller. You can't ferry big nukes all the way out here and then launch them back because the weight would be prohibitive. You can't throw a major warhead with a mass driver. But you can throw tactical nukes. Instead of taking out major Soviet cities with big missiles, you toss dozens, maybe hundreds of the little guys. Even if each warhead is only a tenth of the size of the Hiroshima bomb, that's still pretty bad. Earlier this week I saw for myself the damage a baby nuke can inflict. And on Earth, the fallout takes out everything downwind. I'm betting that even a random distribution of small warheads across the USSR bombs them back into the stone age. You need to launch from here at a time of day when the nukes will fall onto the USSR and not the US or Africa or the Pacific, but that's trivial slide-rule math. How am I doing so far, sir?"

"Admirably." Johnston paused. "All right. In the late fifties, the Air Force proposed a moonbase called Lunex. Which, yes, would have had nukes."

"The fifties?" Vivian whistled. "Earlier than I thought."

"Von Braun's Army boys proposed something similar. Project Horizon." Johnston allowed himself to look a little self-satisfied. "But once the Soviets landed on the Moon, the Air Force was much better placed to hit the high ground running."

"Well, congratulations."

"But you still haven't told me how you knew so accurately where this base was located."

"Lucky guess," Vivian said, poker-faced.

Johnston stared at her. "That's a lot of luck. This base is six degrees south of the equator, and offset in longitude from the center of Farside."

"I know. But by less than a degree. I figured that you'd establish yourself near a crater, to make use of the natural ground elevation, defensively. And Daedalus is the largest crater, this close to the bull's-eye of Farside. You're still within a hundred twenty miles of the center. I didn't know exactly where you'd be, but remember: your people found *me*. You sent a rover and a dirt bike to shepherd me in."

This was Vivian's first direct evasion, and even as she said it, she realized how weak it sounded.

"I don't believe you," Johnston said.

"Okay," she said. "Fine. Honestly? It may have been something someone said once, something I overheard, that slid into my mind. Because when I looked at the Farside map, and saw how close to central the crater is,"—*I remembered Buchanan's odd and insistent words, moments before Hadley went up in a nuclear fireball*—"Daedalus just seemed to make sense. And I rode that hunch all the way here. And hey, if I'd been wrong, I'd just have kept looking."

Come what may, Vivian would never admit that Buchanan had leaked classified information to her. *Guess he figured that if I could live through all that, I'd earned it. And he already knew that if I did make it back, my LM would be waiting for me.*

Johnston's eyes narrowed. "And did you reveal your suspicions about Daedalus Base to your Soviet friends?"

"No, for the love of God; of *course* not. Besides, I only figured out most of this while I was wandering across the wide open spaces, and kicking my heels on Palus. In Zvezda, I was kind of busy being tortured."

Johnston sat back. "Something doesn't ring true, Carter."

"That's all I've got." Vivian stretched; she was getting stiff from sitting in one place all this time. "I mean, I'm here, aren't I?"

"Yes, Captain. You're certainly here."

"And that's all I know. So: Ellis Mayer? Dave Horn? Peter Sandoval?"

"All alive and well."

Relief washed her. "You know, sir, you could've told me that at the outset. It wouldn't have changed anything I said. Where are they now?"

"Not so fast." Johnston leaned forward again. God, why did this guy feel the need to wear a dress uniform on the Moon? That was just weird. "Next, I need you to tell me everything that happened between you,

Nikolai Makarov, Svetlana Belyakova, Sergei Yashin, and all the rest of them. Every conversation before, during, or after your detention at Zvezda Base. And I should warn you that I'm recording this debriefing."

Vivian had assumed nothing less. "My detention?" An odd way to describe incarceration and torture. "Okay."

It took nearly an hour because Johnston was intent on wringing every last possible detail out of her. By the end, Vivian was hoarse.

Johnston tapped his pencil on the desk. "So, let's review. Nikolai Makarov, a Hero of the Soviet Union twice over, risked his life to help you escape from Zvezda. Prior to that you'd seen each other only briefly, and barely spoken. And yet, one of the Soviets' most renowned cosmonauts exchanged fire with one of his own people to ensure your survival and escape?"

"That's correct, sir."

He considered. "Let me try something on you. Yashin and Belyakova interrogated you. When that failed to produce results, Viktoriya Isayeva tried to win your sympathy in an attempt to weasel information out of you. And when *that* failed, Makarov conveniently helped you escape, in a bugged suit that they could track at their leisure. Having seeded the idea in your mind that our Dark Driver capability, or something like it, existed, and realizing that you could not be persuaded by torture alone to reveal its location?"

Dark Driver? Cute. "You believe this is all just an elaborate scheme? That Yashin and Makarov sacrificed Vika's life to let me escape, so they could follow me?"

Johnston smiled grimly. "I see that you're not up to date in the latest Soviet espionage techniques. This is exactly the sort of operation that might appeal to them."

"I left the Soviet suit behind in the crashed LM. Even the jumpsuit. Everything. I brought literally *nothing* from Zvezda with me."

"They couldn't have guessed that would happen."

"I don't believe it."

Johnston nodded. "You've done a good job of distraction. But let's return to your hero worship of Makarov and Belyakova."

"Now it's hero worship? Good grief."

"It's well known that you idolize the early lunar explorers, Captain. It's something of a joke around the Astronaut Corps."

Shit, how embarrassing. "That's ridiculous."

"Is it? And if you admire our astronauts, how much more might you admire the first Soviet moonwalkers? Have you never heard of *Stockholm syndrome*, Captain?"

"This line of questioning is pointless."

He blinked at her. "I see several possibilities. One is that you are telling the truth, and are somehow at the same time extremely perceptive but very foolish, and that Makarov acted from altruism or some strange sense of gallantry. The second is that the Soviets are playing you. And the third is that they've turned you."

"You think I'm a fricking *double agent?*"

"You must admit that from where I'm sitting, it's a distinct possibility."

"No, it's not. It's stupid. It might have been worth considering if the Soviets hadn't *shot down* the Lunar Module I was attempting to escape in. If they had provided any assistance at all when I was hiking across the face of the goddamn Moon to get home, and not bombed my destination just before I arrived. No, sir, with all due respect, there is *no* angle where your second and third options aren't bullshit."

"That's insubordination, Captain."

"If I'm a Russian spy, that's the least of my worries."

Johnston paused. "True enough. However, there's also a fourth possibility, which is the only reason I allowed you to complete your approach to Dark Driver, and the only reason we're still having this conversation."

"And what's that?"

"It's the possibility that Nikolai Makarov's release of you is exactly how it appears. Meaning that his loyalty to the Soviet Union may be wavering. And that he may even be seeking to defect to the United States."

Vivian sat, stunned. That possibility had never occurred to her.

"That would be quite a coup," she said, slowly. "But I'm not sure I buy it. He has a wife in Russia. Two children. A top-niche, comfortable life. Big cars, a dacha on the coast."

"Who knows what his relationship is, with that family? Think what he could tell us. And think of the publicity. The second man on the Moon, turning his back on the motherland? That might be *bigger* than his original Moon landing."

And if Makarov did defect to the West, all Vivian's problems with going rogue would evaporate. She could write her own ticket onto any mission she wanted.

So, she nodded. "Well, sure. Anything I could do to persuade Nikolai Makarov to willingly come over to us, I'd certainly do, but I'm unlikely to ever see or hear from him again."

Johnston just stared at her.

"Sir?"

Eventually, he came to a decision. "Then you are unaware that he is attempting to contact you?"

Jeez. What? Vivian leaned forward. "Wait. *Makarov* is trying to contact *me?* On *this* side of the Moon? How could he know I'm here?"

"Excellent question, Captain. What's the answer?"

"I don't know."

But she could guess, and she had to be honest about it.

"*Damn* it. My Athena launch. They must have seen it from orbit." If the Soviets had been watching Hadley and been lucky enough to detect the flare of her launch, they could have tracked her continuously as she flew around the Moon. Her radar had necessarily been on for the entire flight, and Athena and Columbia Station were obviously going around the Moon in the same direction, at about the same speed. With Athena in their sights, it would have been straightforward to follow her path until she landed. "Oh my God, sir. I'm so, so sorry."

Well, now. Vivian was finished. She'd likely be court-martialed. Imprisoned for treason, even? What *couldn't* they do to her?

Johnston let her stew for a few moments, then said, "No. Not that it excuses your behavior and poor judgment, but the Soviets learned about Daedalus prior to your flight here to Farside. It's been evident from the chatter Dave Horn has been monitoring from Columbia Station. They discovered Daedalus Base two days before your launch from Hadley."

"Holy crap." Relief washed over her. *Luckier than I deserve.* "But ... even so, that still means the Soviets tracked me here. Right?"

"It certainly looks like it."

"When Makarov tried to make contact with me, what did he say?"

"He hailed you by name, 'Captain Carter.' Said that he had important information for your ears only, that couldn't wait."

"Did you respond?"

"And confirm our location? Of course not."

"When was this?"

"Yesterday."

422

She thought it through. "So. The Soviets have found, uh, Dark Driver for themselves, using the optical gear on Columbia Station. They probably found it at lunar dawn, from the contrast as the terminator went across it. And so Makarov knows, or guesses, that I've made my way here. If he hailed you, he must be in orbit, at Columbia Station, or free-flying. Either way, Belyakova is probably with him. He doesn't fly without her."

"And?"

"I don't have an 'and.' I'm just trying to put it together." She thought about it. "If he calls again, you want me to speak to him?"

"Yes."

Vivian ran her fingers through her hair. *Could really use some sleep soon.* "Okay. So, remind me: when did you say Sandoval and Night Corps would be arriving?"

She enjoyed the startled look on his face. "What?"

"Sandoval. When does he arrive? Is Ellis Mayer with them, or was he ordered home?"

"I don't follow."

"You think I can't do *math*? If the Hadley folks had ripped every single thing out of the Lunar Modules on-site, they *might* have been able to launch everyone to orbit. But I doubt it. And they left a LM for me, on the remote chance I'd make it back, compounding their problem.

"And, let's be real. Sandoval would never cut and run and leave the Moon to the Soviets." *And he wouldn't want to leave me, not if there was the smallest chance in hell ...*

Best not to say that. "And Dark Driver *is* here. I didn't know it, but I bet Sandoval did. His secondary objective must have been to defend this facility. Night Corps wouldn't just withdraw with a military engagement ongoing and US assets at risk. They'd come to reinforce Daedalus Base."

Johnston said nothing.

"So, rather than evacuate to orbit, a contingent from Night Corps has been making its way here overland in the MOLAB. They're following the terminator around. Outrunning the Sun and driving into lunar night would add a complication they don't need. So they'll have kept pace with the Sun's illumination as it swung gradually around the Moon. And since morning broke here just a day or so ago, they'll show up any time now. Right?"

Still no reaction from Johnston.

"You're really going to make me do this? Fine. The Moon is six thousand, seven hundred eighty-six miles around. So the dawn line travels around the equator at two hundred thirty miles per day. A little under ten miles an hour. The MOLAB can easily keep pace with that, especially if they cheat and swerve up to a higher latitude. Follow the light. Use solar power to supplement the RTGs. They're coming with the Sun."

Johnston almost smiled.

"If it was me, I'd travel behind the terminator with the Sun at my back at an angle of fifteen degrees, like the Apollo exploratory missions use for lunar ops. If they're doing that, they'll show up in about twelve hours.

"Sandoval will definitely be with them. Ellis wouldn't have wanted to leave the Moon without me. Maybe they forced him, but just now you wouldn't tell me where Ellis was. If he was back on Earth, there'd be no reason not to tell me. I really hope he's with them. And maybe Buchanan is, too, because"—and why the hell not just say it, because by now even the Soviets knew—"If any NASA guy has known all along what you're up to, it's Casey. I heard his voice as the Hadley folks launched to orbit, but it could easily have patched through Starman's LM."

Vivian had a burst of wicked inspiration. "As a matter of fact, that's why I came to Daedalus. I deduced that many of my team would be en route, along with my current CO, Colonel Sandoval. And so I headed here too, to rendezvous with him."

Johnston leaned back in his chair. "Captain Carter, you're a prize bullshitter."

Without blinking, Vivian replied: "Thank you, sir. So, when did you say they would be arriving?"

"About seventeen hours from now," Johnston said. "And Ellis Mayer is with them."

Vivian blew out a long breath. *Thank God.*

Johnston looked at his watch. "I'll need to keep you under lock and key, Captain Carter, at least for now. We can't spare anyone here at Dark Driver to supervise you, and I obviously can't have you wandering around by yourself. We'll need to wait and see how this Makarov matter plays out. After that I'll be seeking further guidance from my superiors, but I'd expect you to ship home very soon. After that, you're someone else's problem."

"Yes, sir. How long until Dark Driver is operational, if I may ask?"

"I'm not authorized to tell you that, Carter."

"Fine." She yawned. "This place where you're about to lock me up: there's a bunk in it, right? Wake me when Sandoval gets here."

"Or when Makarov calls," said Johnston.

"Yes, sir. Either way."

CHAPTER 43

Columbia Station: Josh Rawlings
February 10, 1980

IT was very obvious when everything changed.

Rawlings had been on duty when the excitement level among the Soviets on Columbia suddenly spiked. Soon after, when the station swung around to acquire line of sight with the Earth, Galkin, and Okhotina had escorted him away from the comms board while they conducted a long conversation with their masters on Earth and with Yashin at Zvezda. They'd discovered something, and if Rawlings had possessed Zabrinski's proficiency in Russian, along with supernaturally acute hearing, he might have known what it was.

Truth be told, Rawlings did not dislike the current batch of Soviets. They were very different from Yashin and his goons: solid cosmonauts, with evident scientific and technical proficiencies. They were keen, organized, and proficient, and worked their tails off. Armed guards still remained vigilant, but faded into the background to the point where Rawlings sometimes forgot they were there.

But Galkin, Okhotina, and the rest were obviously under orders to tell the Americans nothing about what was going on. They received no news from Hadley, Zvezda, or anywhere else. Rawlings, Dardenas, and Zabrinski had their duties—to help keep the station operational, while the Russians performed their obscure mission of surveillance and research—and that was exactly what they did.

So Rawlings was doubly surprised when, at dinner two days later, cosmonaut Katya Okhotina said: "We have located your secret base. Your military base on the dark side of the Moon. You knew of it already, I think?"

Dardenas sighed. "For the hundredth time, there is no military base."

"Also, the Moon has no dark side," Rawlings muttered.

"Ah, so this is a natural formation, you think? A, perhaps, quirk of lunar geology?"

Okhotina floated a black-and-white photograph across the table. Rawlings grabbed it.

At first, all he saw was standard lunar terrain: a heavily cratered highland area, its features stark in the local dawn. And then, close to the leftmost of two major craters he spotted a long, thin line, and four rectangular formations along it: three at the eastern end, and one well off to the west.

"What's the scale of this photo?" Rawlings demanded.

Okhotina told him.

"That can't be right." The thin line was over half a mile long, and the buildings were *not* small: each was at least twice the size of the Habs at Hadley. "Holy cow. And this isn't yours?"

"Our only base is our scientific center at Kopernik. This illegal installation is all yours."

Dardenas shook his head in disbelief. "Not NASA's doing. I promise you that."

"We believe that it is United States Air Force." She gestured at the photograph. "You know what this is, yes?"

"I have no idea," Rawlings said.

"Of course not," she said sarcastically. "I am sure you have never heard of a rail gun, or perhaps it is a mass driver. I am sure you could not imagine that such machinery could throw a missile into space. That you are ignorant that Farside would be the perfect place for such a weapon, or that a warhead launched from there could easily be targeted at the Soviet Union."

"I've honestly never thought about it. I mean, I know what a mass driver is, but ..."

"You found this using *our* camera," Dardenas said suddenly. "The large-frame camera that Apollo 32 brought to Columbia Station."

427

Rawlings looked at the photo again. *Jeez.* "If this is publicized, it'll cause the US substantial embarrassment. Substantial *international* embarrassment."

"Additional embarrassment, yes," Okhotina said.

"Additional?"

Okhotina leaned forward. "I am now permitted to tell you that NASA has evacuated its base at Hadley Plain. Immediately afterward, to prevent its secrets falling into Soviet hands, your people destroyed the base in a nuclear conflagration to cover your tracks."

"That's crazy," Rawlings said. "Hadley was a NASA facility. It had no secrets, and there is *no way in hell* that it had nukes either."

"They were perhaps brought by the USAF military forces that arrived later. An elite black operations group called Night Corps. You know Night Corps?"

"Nope. This is … Katya, where on Earth did you get all this nonsense?"

She smiled in satisfaction. "From your television evening news programs. The US has already publicly admitted the existence of Night Corps and its operations on the Moon, once my country published photographs of its activities at Hadley. They are no longer there. The nuclear explosion destroyed Hadley Base almost a week ago. The world now sees the evidence of what your country has been up to for all these years. It cannot be argued away anymore, and our own defensive operations are seen to be justified. Your President denies that the US destroyed its own base, of course, but once we also reveal the existence of the mass driver, he will lose what remains of his credibility."

"Wow." Rawlings sat back.

Dardenas frowned. "Is that mass driver operational?"

"We do not think so, but we cannot afford to take any chances. This is a very dangerous act, of your country. Very dangerous to the world."

"Your country is the danger to the world, lady."

"Hold up, Marco. That doesn't help." Rawlings turned to Katya. "So Hadley was evacuated? Everyone from Hadley Base made it out safely?"

"Of course. It was always our goal that you should evacuate peacefully. Your crews were allowed to approach Columbia Station, one by one, to collect Command Modules for their return to Earth. This was our promise, and we honored it."

"They came and went, and we never knew?"

"If it were up to me, I would have told you. Still …" She shrugged.

"And Vivian Carter returned to Earth with the others?"

Okhotina paused. "The Apollo 32 astronaut? I regret to tell you that Carter is missing, presumed dead, following a military action on the surface long before the evacuation."

"A military action?" Rawlings said. "Jesus Christ … what happened?"

"That, I am not informed of."

Rawlings sat back, thunderstruck. Dardenas grimaced. "Hey, Josh. 'Presumed dead' is not the same as 'dead.' There's still hope."

Katya pursed her lips. "Hope? She disappeared over a month ago. And … it is the Moon."

"Yeah." Rawlings gave a deep sigh. "I'll need a moment, here."

"Why are you telling us all this now?" Dardenas demanded. "You're being very free with information, all of a sudden."

"Comrade Galkin directed me to speak with you, and for two reasons. First, it is important to him—and to me as well—that you understand that your detention here was not in vain. That your own government has deceived you, and your situation here is their fault and not ours. That the Soviet Union has behaved truthfully and correctly throughout."

"Huh," said Dardenas.

"There is no reason for us to be enemies," Okhotina said, simply. "The more you help us, the sooner this can be over. We have got what we came for. As soon as we can operate this facility without your help, we will argue that you should be freed, to return to Earth."

"Home?" They looked at each other. This was their sixty-ninth day in captivity.

"So far, you are barely cooperative," she said. "You provide little information that we do not directly ask for. If this changes, if you complete your instruction to us, why would we need to keep you here longer? Of course, you could choose to stay voluntarily."

"Voluntarily." Rawlings looked around him. "You know, even before you Soviets barged in here, I was already itchin' to get the hell out and go home. Now, even more so. Lady, I'll be hauling ass just as soon as y'all say the word."

Okhotina smiled. "Then give us your wholehearted cooperation, Josh and Marco, and perhaps we will be able to say the word sooner rather than later."

CHAPTER 44

Daedalus Base: Vivian Carter
February 11, 1980

VIVIAN did not find her house arrest onerous. They restricted her to a tiny compartment, barely wider than the bed and only four inches taller than her, but it was all hers. Everything was scrupulously clean. Air and water were freely available, and nobody was interrogating or torturing her. She wasn't risking agonizing death over the smallest error. She could use the waste management unit whenever she needed, clean up afterward, and sleep without interruption. She'd stayed in worse hotels.

And she could catch up on a month's worth of news, leafing through the stack of teleprinter flimsies Johnston had left her. Not that *that* was particularly relaxing.

South central Asia had become a military quagmire. Backcountry Afghanistan was a mess of regional warlords, none of whom took kindly to the imposition of Soviet-style socialism. The Red Army had faced extensive uprisings and was finding it tricky to maintain their hold on territory. They also suffered constant sabotage from mujahideen cells, who were knocking out power lines, air terminals, and radio stations.

The mujahideen were not going it alone. The US had been sending them military aid, in the form of CIA advisors and weaponry, since the 1978 April Revolution when the Afghan Communist Party had taken over the country. Such US support had increased manyfold once the Soviet army breached the Afghan border.

430

But that was just the beginning of the story. Despite their challenges in Afghanistan, the Soviets had now invaded Pakistan.

It made sense. They were suffering shelling and rocket attacks from Pakistani forces on the border. Afghan insurgents were trained in Pakistan, and many of their attacks were being coordinated from Pakistani soil. And so, the Soviet 103rd Guards Airborne Division had spearheaded a blitzkrieg attack through Peshawar all the way to Islamabad, annexing the northern part of the country.

Now the gloves were off, and US troops were pouring into southern Pakistan at Karachi and spreading into the Sindh and Balochistan regions. The hope was that the superpowers would limit themselves to this proxy war on Pakistani soil, and that calm heads would ultimately prevail. But there were no guarantees and plenty of disaster scenarios. The rhetoric between Brezhnev and Reagan was escalating as quickly as their military buildup.

With all that going on, relatively little attention was being paid to matters off-world. The US had protested the Soviet military attacks and the nuclear destruction of its lunar base. The Supreme Soviet had contemptuously dismissed the allegations and countered with evidence of Night Corps' activities at Hadley, which the US had been forced to admit. The Soviets' counterclaim that the US had nuked its own base after withdrawing from it was believed in some quarters. On both the earthly and space conflicts, the United Nations was hopelessly split.

It was all a giant mess.

The other somber note was that Vivian now had the leisure to mourn the astronauts who had died at Hadley in the second assault, meeting their ends even as Vivian was being chased down and captured.

Rick Norton was dead, his helmet blown open while defending his base. He'd been the first to step out onto Hadley Plain to stay, and now his atoms would remain there for eternity. Jim Dunlap, Apollo 22, who hadn't wanted to fight and just wanted to go home to Duluth, Minnesota, had been killed in an explosion. And Dan Klein and Luis Ibarra of Apollo 27, with their enthusiasm and can-do attitude and their ridiculous homemade mortar, died together when a Soviet rocket blasted that mortar position to smithereens.

It was a mercy no more of them had died, considering the ferocity of the second Soviet attack on Hadley. Night Corps had led the charge and borne the brunt, and had presumably suffered their own casualties, but Vivian wasn't cleared for those details. Either way, she figured their blood was on Soviet hands: Yashin, Chertok, Isayeva, and all the other nameless Soviet soldiers in the attack.

But then there were the more perplexing Russians. Svetlana Belyakova, who'd appeared to harbor genuine sympathy for Vivian's predicament but hadn't raised a finger to protest her ill treatment at Yashin's hands. And Nikolai Makarov, who had surely pulled punches in the first Soviet assault on Hadley and had come to Vivian's aid at Zvezda Base, shooting one of his own people in order to set her free.

Makarov, who'd insisted that the Hadley crewmembers receive warning of a nuclear conflagration they couldn't possibly evade.

Makarov, who had apparently tried to contact Vivian *here*, here at Daedalus Base, although the attempt had not been repeated, or Johnston would have summoned her. Wouldn't he?

The MOLAB containing Sandoval, Ellis Mayer, Terri Brock, Casey Buchanan, and four members of Night Corps, rolled into Daedalus-Base seventeen hours later. One of the first people to greet them once they'd unsuited and entered the Central Habitat was Vivian Carter. "Hey, guys. What kept you? Was traffic bad?"

As one, their jaws dropped.

Vivian was not a hugger. On this occasion, she made an exception.

Ellis, she noted, was shaking as he hugged her back.

She'd been permitted to watch their approach from the main window of Central Hab. The MOLAB looked like hell. Its metal tires were so bent and pocked that it wobbled as it rolled. It had bashes and bumps all over it, and its paint job was scorched from all its time in the Sun.

The men and women who climbed wearily down from the MOLAB looked almost as hard used. Their suits were blackened with ground-in moondust that no amount of brushing could remove. The suits all had visible scuffs, frays, rips, and tears, and Terri Brock's helmet had a big ding on its side as if someone had chucked a rock at her.

And once they unsuited, they all seemed to have aged a couple of years since Vivian had last seen them. She'd never noticed lines around Terri's eyes before, or those wrinkles on Ellis's forehead. Buchanan had acquired a hacking cough, perhaps from the dust, and took a seat whenever he could. Sandoval kept stretching and twisting his right shoulder, like he had a muscle cramp he was trying to work out. Every single one of them looked as if they hadn't slept properly for a month, which may have been true.

But the difference in their behaviors on arrival was crystal clear. Buchanan and the four Night Corps grunts barely spared a glance for the Daedalus Habs or the immense rail of Dark Driver that led off to the horizon. Peter Sandoval, Ellis Mayer, and Terri Brock gawked around with intense interest, taking in the height of the buildings at the rail's closer end, the different-style rovers, the bikes parked in a neat row, even the scuff marks on the walls.

So noted, guys. Buchanan, and Sandoval's people, had been here before. Ellis, Terri, and Peter himself had not. Vivian felt vindicated.

"So, how was the journey?"

"Dear God," Ellis said. "It was a nightmare."

Seven men and one woman had traveled slightly over halfway around the Moon in a MOLAB built for short-range excursions with a crew of four or five. They'd been crammed in, hot-bunking the available sleep spaces. Generally, two or three of them had suited up and hung onto the outside of the vehicle just to escape from the overcrowded cabin.

"I fell off the damned thing half a dozen times," Terri said. Which explained the helmet ding.

"Maybe a whole dozen," Ellis said, and Terri poked him in the ribs with her toe in retaliation.

Peter, Ellis, and Terri had come to hang out in Vivian's cubicle. If space was tight, no one mentioned it; they'd all suffered worse. The room smelled pleasantly of soap, shampoo, and brandy, as the new arrivals were fresh from well-earned showers, and it turned out that the Daedalus crew even got a liquor ration. A *small* liquor ration. But they were all out of practice.

"How did you decide who stayed to crew the MOLAB? You guys picked the short straws?"

Ellis just gave her a look, and didn't bother to respond.

"I asked for volunteers." Sandoval sipped at his drink. After their first toast, he'd managed to make his second shot glass of brandy last almost an hour. "I wasn't going to condemn anyone to a tiny vehicle for weeks on end unless they *wanted* to be there. There wasn't much competition for the slots. By then, most of the Hadley crew were ready to get the hell home. And most of my folks didn't want to stick around any longer, either."

She eyed him. "Because, after all, your Night Corps people had spent plenty of time on the Moon on previous trips. Right here."

"Cannot confirm."

"Bullshit, man."

Sandoval raised his glass and touched it to his mouth, like he was doing it for the communal experience of pretending to drink, rather than actually drinking. "Ellis refused to ship out if there was a chance you were alive. Said he wouldn't leave without his commander."

She winked at her Lunar Module Pilot. "Dang, Army. Can't shake you, can I?"

Ellis looked embarrassed. "You'd have done the same."

"I absolutely would." Vivian didn't remind him that a few days after landing he'd been itching to get back to his family. Perhaps that urgency had diminished once Christmas had come and gone. Whatever. She was thrilled he'd stuck around.

She turned back to Sandoval. "Buchanan?"

Sandoval's expression was guarded. "There's nothing for Buchanan on Earth any more."

"He's dying," Vivian said flatly.

"Yes."

"Of what?"

The guys looked at Terri, who grunted. "Bunch of things, but mainly radiation. Early on, they had an unexpected solar storm. Normally, we can predict space weather pretty good. The particle detectors onsite ... I mean, the ones we used to have. Anyway. Four months in, Buchanan was out on-surface when the main flux hit. He couldn't get to cover quick enough.

"Normally that would have gotten him flown straight home. But Buchanan didn't want to go, and he persuaded Norton, Dunlap, and Jones to cover for him. Since then he's had all kinds of joint issues, and the moondust bites his throat even worse than it does ours."

"He chose to die here, on the Moon," Sandoval said. "Norton wasn't gonna take that away from him, and neither am I. His wife's dead. No family to speak of. Why waste the gas to take him home, only to drop him off in a VA hospital? Maybe in a full G he even dies sooner. And

Buchanan has irreplaceable experience. So, screw it. He wants to stay? He stays."

Vivian nodded. "And what's your angle, Terri?"

Brock shrugged. "It's the Moon."

"Well, yeah?"

"Always wanted to come. Never thought I would. A hundred times, it looked like I'd get kicked out of the program or passed over. Now I'm here, but I doubt I'll ever get the chance to come again. So I'm not leaving till they force me off-surface."

"Fair." Vivian fist-bumped her. "Moon sisters."

Sandoval shuddered. "I don't know what the hell you see in the place. It's ugly as shit and it still frigging terrifies me. But Terri is lunar hardcore, and has mean engineering skills."

Brock grinned. "Thanks for bringing."

"Sure thing."

Vivian stretched, knocking into Ellis. "Okay. So much for—"

A bang on the door of the small compartment made them all jump. Sandoval spilled brandy in his lap. Vivian leaped up to yank the door open.

It was Johnston, in a plain blue flight suit this time. "Carter, come now."

"Makarov?"

"Horn. He'll speak only to you." Johnston turned on his heel. "*Now*, Carter."

"Hey, Viv. You made it."

"Christ, you're *still* up in orbit?"

"Yep, sad to say."

"Jeez, people." Johnston spun his finger in the hurry-up gesture, and pointed at the clock. With only a brief window before Minerva went over the horizon there was no time for small talk.

"Yeah, yeah." Vivian turned away from him. "So, Dave, what's up?"

"Funny thing. Nikolai Makarov pinged me on my last pass, with a message. He needs to talk to you. Him and Belyakova. They're close by."

Close by. "On the ground? Near my current location?" Even over secure radio, Vivian wasn't about to name Dark Driver, nor the crater it was located by.

"Roger that. He'll meet you on-surface, since he obviously can't approach the base. You can bring a buddy for safety, but only one. He doesn't want to see any weapons. He'll speak only to you. A matter of the utmost importance. Wants to save lives on both sides."

Vivian glanced at the countdown clock. Three minutes till loss of signal. "What are his coordinates? Did he seem sincere? What else do I need to know?"

"They're at latitude minus zero point five, longitude one seventy-nine point two east. Sincere? Sure, I guess. Makarov also emphasizes this is an unofficial visit. His superiors and colleagues are unaware. He needs to keep it that way. Oh, and if anyone approaches who isn't you? They blast off and don't come back."

Mayer shook his head vigorously. Vivian ignored him. "I'll be there."

"The hell you will," Mayer said.

"Oh hey, you've got Ellis? Tell him hi." Then Horn's signal disappeared over the horizon.

Vivian scribbled numbers onto a pad with a Sharpie, did quick geometry. "They're parked eighty miles away due north, almost on the equator line."

"It's a trap," Terri said.

"I don't think so," said Vivian. "But I could be wrong."

Brock looked at Johnston. "Do we attempt to capture? Or just kill them quietly?"

"What?" Ellis looked at her in shock.

Brock's expression was bleak. "You didn't see Norton's face after those bastards blew out his helmet. You didn't have to carry Klein and Ibarra's bodies to storage."

"No, I just got shot and fell into the rille and had to stagger home on emergency O_2."

Sandoval overrode them. "Terri, I doubt Makarov and Belyakova were in the strike squad that penetrated Hadley's perimeter."

"So they just gave the orders."

"Nah. Likely Yashin."

Terri gestured at Vivian. "And Yashin and Belyakova *tortured* Carter. What hell is wrong with you?"

"Stand down," Johnston said. "All of you. We need to find out what they want."

"No way," Ellis said. "Terri's right. Vivian is not going back anywhere near the Reds."

Johnston looked irritated, clearly not used to his orders getting this much blowback. "Stand *down*. These are prominent cosmonauts. World famous. Maybe they want to defect, or give us intelligence we can't get any other way. We need to consider this."

Goddamn it, Vivian hated siding with Johnston against Ellis and Terri. "Correct. I have no choice."

"And she's not going alone," said Sandoval.

"She's not going at all," Ellis said. "But if she is, I'm going with her."

"No. That would be me. That isn't up for debate."

"I'm her damned crew."

"And I'm Night Corps. End of story."

Terri's face was red with anger. Now she took a step toward Vivian. "Why the hell … ?"

"Terri. They'll talk only to me."

"Oh, sure. Because they trust you? No. The Soviets *want* you. Either to retake you, or kill you."

"Not these Soviets."

"I don't buy that," Ellis said.

Brock took a deep breath. "Vivian, your judgment is compromised."

"No, it's not." Vivian held up her hands. "Guys, guys. Makarov and Belyakova didn't fly around the Moon just to terminate me. Ellis, Terri: I appreciate it. But if they want to tell us something this badly, we need to hear it."

"And if I don't like what we hear, I end the contact," Sandoval said.

Vivian turned. "Wait, what? End?"

"Sure. One way or another."

"Peter, 'unarmed.' That's the deal."

"That's not what I heard."

"Come again?"

"Horn said that Makarov doesn't want to see any weapons. I can arrange that."

"Christ, Peter, you know what he meant."

"It's nonnegotiable." Sandoval looked at Johnston, who was clearly exasperated. "You wanted to say something, sir?"

"Yes. I said we would *consider* this. It's a highly sensitive situation, and this planning is premature. We'll need to run it by Cheyenne."

"No, we won't."

Johnston's irritation reached a whole new level. "I beg your pardon, Colonel?"

Sandoval stepped up and met his gaze. "Your charge is to develop and defend Dark Driver. If you detect an aggressive Soviet approach, you get to take whatever action you deem necessary. But mine is to engage and neutralize the Soviet threat to the United States' presence in cislunar space. A negotiation with highly ranked Soviets falls within my purview."

"You're joking."

"No, sir. Right now, there's no direct threat to Daedalus Base. The cosmonauts revealed their presence and requested contact. So it's a white-flag scenario. It's my responsibility to assess their intel and take appropriate action. And the longer we make them wait out there, the greater the chance their absence will be noted, putting them at risk. It'll take hours to relay the request to Cheyenne, up through the Chiefs of Staff and to the White House and back down. We don't have those hours. This is an operational decision, and I'm making it."

Johnston drew himself up. "I outrank you here, Colonel."

"No, sir. I'm outside your chain of command." Sandoval reached inside his jumpsuit to an inner pocket and drew out a slim envelope. "My authorization is signed by the President of the United States."

"Hot *damn*," Vivian said.

Johnston did not take the envelope. "A word in private, Colonel."

"By all means." Sandoval's expression was bleak, and as he left the room with Johnston, his eyes flicked over to Vivian. "I've got this. Go suit up."

CHAPTER 45

Farside: Vivian Carter
February 12, 1980

AS she skidded across the lunar surface in Peter Sandoval's wake, Vivian had to admit that Starman was right: the Moon bikes were pretty cool. If only that guy in the lead would stop spraying her with dust and gravel, she might almost be enjoying herself.

She steered off to the left and, getting the idea, Sandoval slowed to let her parallel him. Now she was out of his rooster tail, it was much more tolerable.

But it still required concentration. They were bumping along at close to twenty-five miles an hour. Vivian constantly tugged her handlebars left or right, sticking out one boot or the other to scuff across the Moon's rocky surface and keep herself upright. She couldn't go any faster, and would have liked to slow down. She was sweating more, and breathing harder, than when she'd hiked across the Hadley-Apennine chain.

But they had to move fast, and even so, it was four hours until they saw the Soviet LK Lander perched on the edge of the crater known as Lipsky V.

Their suits orange against the bleak Moon-gray, Makarov and Belyakova were easy to spot. As Vivian braked to a halt and sat up to regard them standing just twelve feet away, she thought: *At least no one has pulled a gun yet.*

Dismounting, she laid the dirt bike on its side with care. She didn't fancy the walk back if she broke it. She'd done enough lunar hikes for one lifetime.

Easy enough to tell the cosmonauts apart by their posture. On instinct, Vivian walked to Belyakova and stuck out her hand. "Hey. No hard feelings. I guess."

Vivian's radio wasn't on and it was doubtful that Belyakova could lip-read English. Either way, Belyakova studied her up and down in her usual way—perhaps, this time, looking for weapons—and then raised her gloved hand.

They shook, clumsily.

Vivian stepped over to Makarov. He clasped her hand with both of his, which felt threatening, as if he might be about to fling her across the regolith, but she figured he didn't realize how it might be perceived.

Sandoval stayed put. He wasn't about to shake hands with anyone.

Vivian leaned in to touch Makarov's helmet with her own. "Thanks again for breaking me out of Zvezda, Comrade."

"You are welcome, Kapitan." The refracted buzz offered little indication of his feelings.

"Does Svetlana know?

"Yes."

Sandoval dug into his thigh pocket and pulled out a mess of cables, all connected to a small box. Once he and Vivian had straightened them out their function was clear: four comms cables leading to a central hub. Vivian plugged one jack into her chest panel, and offered two more to the Soviets.

The connectors on those were Soviet standard. Even through spacesuits, Vivian registered Makarov's surprise.

He plugged in, and after a brief hesitation, Belyakova did likewise. Sandoval's voice came through loud and clear. "Better than the helmet-touching nonsense, I think. And impossible to eavesdrop on us."

Still looking at the connector, Belyakova said: "Your intelligence sources are good."

"Always, Comrade."

Even with the cables, they had to stand close. It was oddly intimate, peering into three other helmets from a few feet away. Two Russians, two Americans. Two orange suits, and two white. "Makarov, you hear us?"

"Of course."

Vivian nodded. "So. Hi. What's up?"

"We bring information," Makarov said. "Simple information, but at great risk. Colonel Yashin will destroy your military base here, as he destroyed Hadley. He intends to deorbit a Progress Module, to impact directly upon it. Within this Progress will be a nuclear warhead. The mass driver your country is constructing will be destroyed, and everyone at your Daedalus base will die. You must evacuate it immediately."

Another nuke? Jeez. "How—"

"That cannot happen," Sandoval said crisply. "First: we have insufficient craft at Daedalus to evacuate all its personnel. It's not a USAF mission requirement to allow a complete withdrawal at short notice. Second, abandoning the base would allow your country to appropriate its capabilities. We have no guarantee that this is not a ruse to achieve just that. So, no dice, Major-General."

Vivian studied Makarov's face. "Yashin will really do this, you think? How soon?"

"Of course. He has already returned to Columbia Station to supervise the operation. The ensuing nuclear explosion will complete his mission. Then he will render Columbia Station inoperable and return to Earth. When? As soon as he can."

"What happens to our Americans on Columbia then?"

"They will be taken back to the Soviet Union, to be questioned further as spies."

"Spies? You've got to be kidding me."

"And why would you choose to inform us of all this?" Sandoval demanded.

"I warned you once before," Makarov pointed out. "It was I who insisted that Hadley receive a fair warning, at much cost to myself. This time, Yashin has overruled any such warning. And so now I come to you … more quietly. I do not crave the loss of American life."

"You defy orders, and risk yourselves to do so?"

Vivian touched his shoulder. "Peter. Let me."

She looked at Belyakova. "I might believe Nikolai. You, I have no reason to trust. Why the hell are *you* doing this? You have one minute to convince me."

"She—"

Vivian tapped her gloved knuckles against Makarov's helmet. "Not you, Nikolai. I want Svetlana to tell me why one day she helps Yashin break me, and another day she helps you warn me. The truth, fellow spacewoman, or we're done here. Sixty seconds."

Svetlana spent the first ten seconds staring at her. Then she said, briskly: "You are right. If this were only up to me, we would not be here. But Yashin might have killed Nikolai already if not for me. I must make my choice. Our present course is a calculated risk, the lesser of two evils. And also, I do not desire unnecessary death."

"And also? That's your postscript?"

Belyakova's gaze bored into her. "Your soldiers at Daedalus are aiming a gun at the head of my country. I should care if they live or die? Would you, if the Soviet Union was threatening the United States with nuclear devastation in this way?"

"You're right. I might not. So, again, why are you here? If you prevent the base's destruction, that threat still exists."

Belyakova exhaled, obviously irritated. "Because we are no longer welcome persons to Comrade Yashin, and I think that he may kill *us*."

"Ah," Vivian said. "Self-interest: *that* rings true."

"I believe there must be a better way to assure the base's removal," said Makarov.

Sandoval spoke up. "Major-General Makarov, Major-General Belyakova, do you hope to defect to the United States?"

Belyakova snorted. "Of course not."

"Because of your families?"

"Because of our whole lives."

Makarov nodded. "I fear for my family, of course I do. My wife, Olga. My two children, Pyotr and Lidia. But I have no wish for them to grow up in your country, away from everything they know."

"You wouldn't prefer to raise your children in freedom?" Sandoval asked.

Belyakova glared at him. "You think yourself free?"

Makarov raised a calming hand. "Please ..." He looked at Vivian. "I have some hope that there are those, back home in the Soviet Union, who will not look kindly at what Yashin does here. The first use of nuclear weapons, in war between our countries."

Sandoval was losing patience. "And yet, Yashin is presumably acting under orders from *the Soviet Union*."

"Orders may come from several masters," Makarov said.

"What the hell does that even mean?"

"Peter, hush. Svetlana—you, too." Vivian reached out, clasped Makarov's hand. "Let the grown-ups talk. Go on, Nikolai."

Sandoval recoiled in irritation, nearly dislodging his communications jack. Belyakova made a growling sound. Makarov said, "Comrade Yashin receives his orders directly from the Lubyanka. From the KGB, perhaps even from the mouth of Yuri Andropov himself. Svetlana and I do not talk with such people, and do not hear such conversations. Our orders from Baikonur and Moscow are vague by comparison. Support the mission. Take all measures necessary. I think that, back on Earth, many are ... waiting to see what happens before they decide how to jump. Hedging their bets? That is the phrase?"

"Sure."

"It is the Soviet way. The left hand and the right hand, operating separately."

"This is also the American way," Svetlana said to Vivian. "For you clearly knew about Daedalus Base all along, despite your lies at Zvezda."

"God's sake," Vivian said. "Give it a rest. *You're* here to negotiate with *us*, remember?"

"Vivian didn't know," said Sandoval. "And she still wouldn't, if .... That doesn't matter. Yes, NASA and the USAF keep to themselves. There still aren't many at NASA who know the full story. So, left hand, right hand, whatever. Can we move on?"

Makarov nodded. "I agree, this is not simple. But your secret base and its weaponry must go. They cannot remain on the Moon, threatening our country, threatening détente."

"Détente?" Sandoval laughed.

"But not like this, by bomb. Not in a way that invites US nuclear retaliation against Zvezda Base."

To Makarov, Vivian said: "As it happens, I agree with you and Svetlana. Daedalus Base can't remain."

"I don't think you get to decide that," Sandoval said, his voice brittle.

Vivian looked carefully at each of them in turn. "You know what, Peter? I think that, between the four of us right here, perhaps we do."

Sandoval breathed deep. "I wish there wasn't a need for Daedalus Base. But the Soviet Union has ICBMs targeting our cities. We need to keep one step ahead, to protect ourselves. That isn't hard to understand?"

"It is not at all hard to know that we must prevent you from completing this step," Svetlana said.

"If it ever does come to war, Major-General, the United States *will* win. You can be very sure of that."

"Peter …"

"It must not come to war," Makarov said.

At the same moment Svetlana said, "We already are at war."

"Not Afghanistan, not Pakistan," Makarov said. "Forget those places. We can do nothing about the Earth. We can only do the best we can, here and now."

"Right," said Vivian. "This situation, *our* situation, can't be allowed to escalate any further. Can we at least all agree on *that*?"

Sandoval began to speak, then stopped. A long silence fell, the silence of an airless waste. Even the hum of the fans in Vivian's suit appeared to still.

Makarov said: "There is a time to stay quiet and obey orders, and a time to be dissident, no matter what the consequence."

"Dissident?" Sandoval said, quietly.

"Nikolai, please." Svetlana's voice was almost a whisper.

Makarov said nothing more.

"All right," Vivian said. "Nikolai, Svetlana, can Yashin even pull this off without you two? Crash a Progress right on top of Daedalus with such accuracy? You're his rendezvous experts."

"We Soviets are expert at deorbiting material to a precise location," Belyakova said. "How else could we have built Zvezda Base? Precise *landing* is not such a trick. Orbital rendezvous is more difficult, and we have been performing even those by automated methods for years."

"But perhaps if you stay in the loop, you can deliberately misprogram the deorbit burn."

"After which Yashin will shoot us both in the head," said Svetlana.

Vivian looked from one to the other. "And so …. What would you suggest we do next, Comrades?"

"You should evacuate your base. Go to orbit. Save yourselves."

"No," said Sandoval. "Next option?"

The Soviets were silent. Sandoval's eyes flicked to hers. Vivian knew what he was thinking, and now he said it. "Well, we could just capture you."

"You could try," Belyakova said calmly.

Still Vivian still saw no weapons. But it was too much to expect that Belyakova didn't have a trick or two up her sleeve. Metaphorically

444

speaking. "Wait. Let's talk that through. Maybe it's not such a bad idea. If we were to capture you, you could claim it was against your will. Would your families be safer if you were captured than if you defected?"

Makarov looked puzzled. "So, we flew here ... why? How could that be explained?"

"You came to see for yourself? Verify from first-hand reconnaissance?"

"Just like Vivian did," Sandoval said dryly.

"There may be other ways we can fake it," Vivian said.

"We will hardly agree to come *into Daedalus Base* with you," Belyakova said incredulously. "Sit under a bomb? No. And we do not wish to be captured. We have warned you, done our human duty. It is more than you deserve. Did you warn *us*, before your cowardly attack on Zvezda? Did you ensure that no deaths would result? No."

Vivian did not look at Sandoval. How might Belyakova react if she discovered that the solo saboteur, the specific *you*, was standing right in front of her?

"Let us not forget in all this that *you* are the ones building an illegal military base here." Svetlana was almost spitting the words out. "A base designed to scatter hundreds of nuclear warheads indiscriminately across the Soviet Union."

Sandoval shook his head. "Hey, Vivian? This is hopeless. They've delivered their message. Let's let them go their own way. Head back to Daedalus and figure out a plan."

"Hold up. Maybe there is a way for us all to get what we want. Soviets and Americans. You and us. But it involves considerable risk. More, perhaps, than you may want to consider."

They all looked at her.

Vivian took a deep breath. "You might not like this, but hear me out. Help me brainstorm it, even.

"We need to go up there. Into orbit. And take care of the threat ourselves." She looked from face to face. "If Yashin must be prevented from doing this, *we* have to prevent him."

Belyakova just stared.

"We need to pool resources," Vivian argued. "We can't do it without you. You can't do it without us. And maybe in the end we all get what we want."

"Perhaps we cannot do it at all," Makarov said.

"Hear me out," Vivian insisted, and began to explain what she had in mind.

"No," Sandoval said immediately.

She ignored him. "Nikolai. Columbia Station, and the Soviet ships. What's their on-orbit configuration, right now? How will Yashin do this?"

Without looking at Belyakova or Sandoval, Makarov kneeled clumsily. Picked up a rock, and drew a series of arcs. "Partly, I will be guessing. Look here. Listen."

Once they started, Makarov and Belyakova were surprisingly free with details. Vivian could see Sandoval wishing that he had a notepad or a cassette recorder to capture it all. After a while he loosened up, and they began to discuss it, all four of them. *There are no stupid suggestions.* Everything was on the table. Or, at least, in the dirt.

Eventually Nikolai went back to the lander for two oxygen bottles. One for Belyakova and himself, which they took turns to attach to the feed on their chests with a short umbilical. The other for Vivian. Sandoval refused to accept O_2 from the Soviets.

Whether astronaut or cosmonaut, they were all natural problem solvers. The problem took precedence over everything else. And when, forty-five minutes later, Sandoval beckoned to Vivian, she passed him the O_2 umbilical and he plugged it in to get a replenishing blast of oxygen so that they could talk for even longer.

"Okay, then," said Vivian eventually. "Everyone happy?"

Predictably, Sandoval replied, "Not at all."

"But we're doing this anyway?"

"Yes."

She looked at Nikolai and Svetlana. Both nodded, the latter with less enthusiasm.

"Hey," Vivian said. "What's the worst that can happen? That I end up captured again?" She yawned ostentatiously. "Big deal."

"It'd be a big deal for me," Sandoval said. "I already had to fly across the Moon and kick a hornet's nest for you once."

The cosmonauts turned to look at him.

"Yes, that was me. Sorry about Zvezda."

"I told you so," Nikolai said to Svetlana, in English. She replied with a curt phrase in Russian, probably an expletive, then said: "I knew it was you. It fits your profile."

Sandoval looked intrigued. "You've read a file on me?"

"Of course."

"Sandoval has a file?" Vivian demanded.

"Simple as a felt boot," muttered Svetlana.

"You both have files. And we have read them." Nikolai stood. "And now we could report that some of the assessments in your files are incorrect, and for the better. Except that this conversation never took place, yes? Let us go."

"You have not read files on us?" Svetlana asked, apparently genuinely curious.

"Nope," said Vivian.

The Russian shook her head, perplexed.

Sandoval stood. Even now, Vivian could see second thoughts moving behind his eyes. "Okay, then. Take good notes, Captain Carter. Stay in touch."

"Always, Colonel."

"And good luck."

"And to you," Makarov said.

"Yeah. Thanks for the oxygen."

With that, Sandoval disconnected from the O_2 cylinder and the comms link. He gave Vivian a long look, reached out to touch the arm of her suit. Then turned to walk over to his Moon bike, and rode away without looking back.

Vivian watched him go, swallowed, then turned to Makarov and Belyakova. "Well, hey. Lead on, Comrades."

The three of them walked across the surface toward the bulbous, awkward-looking Soviet LK Lander.

CHAPTER 46

IF the Soviet lander looked odd from the outside—like an onion on splayed stilts, and disconcertingly smaller than an Apollo LM—that was nothing compared to the cramped, cluttered mess of its inside. Peering in from the ladder, Vivian had a moment of panic. "Jeez, guys, this is never going to work."

"Wait." Svetlana, already inside, was disconnecting pieces of electrical equipment, jerking wires loose with scant ceremony. She picked up a wrench and passed it to Vivian. "See this box? Lean in, unbolt it here and here. It goes out too."

"We'll have to toss out a hell of a lot more than that." How could the Soviets function in this disarray? Vivian supposed their training told them where everything went, but to her eye, the inside of the lander looked like a junkyard.

A junkyard she'd shortly be taking off in.

Well. Their Soyuz craft had a pretty great safety record. The LK and LEK Landers were close cousins, and the Soviets still had yet to suffer a fatal failure in either—that Vivian knew of.

Half inside and half out, Vivian helped Svetlana to strip the LK's interior of all the parts it apparently didn't need, tossing them out onto the surface. Makarov was still outside. Through the frame of the lander she could feel him unbolting stuff from its externals, a banging and

448

vibration separate from the efforts of the women within, that echoed through her suit.

After about an hour she and Makarov wriggled in, and the Soviets sealed and repressurized the LK. It took another half hour for them all to squirm out of their suits in the confined space. Only one of them could move at a time, and Vivian found herself half-lying across the Russians in a way that would have been embarrassing if her sensibilities hadn't been so blunted by the events of the past couple months.

It was weird how that worked. Being in intimate confines with Makarov was somehow okay. By now, Vivian was used to sharing cramped spaces with guys. But Belyakova? Who'd held her hand while Yashin had pumped her full of scopolamine, and stood by, blank faced, during her torture? That was much harder, and Vivian subtly tried not to let her skin come into contact with Belyakova's, lest it shrivel and die.

But eventually the three of them slumped back with the weariness common to all astronauts after a long EVA. By now they were stripped down to their jumpsuits, stained dark at the underarms and pelvis and across the chest, and hiding little. Vivian's skivvies extended down to her wrists and ankles, while the cosmonauts' stopped at the shoulder and thigh. Vivian couldn't help noticing that Svetlana was seriously cut, her skin muscular and tanned even after all this time on the Moon. Yet another reason to hate her.

The smell of their sweat mingled in the air. Makarov checked his watch. "Well. Mathematics to do, no?" He opened up a book of tables and took out a slide rule and pencil. Belyakova boosted herself up using Vivian's shoulder, to position herself at the eyepiece of a sextant mounted centrally above the instrument panels. Just where it was in Vivian's LM. Interesting.

"Sure, comrades," Vivian said. "Do your thing. Take me to space."

She added: "Willing to check your math. Or do anything else you need."

Neither responded. Makarov said a couple of words in Russian, and Belyakova nodded and reached over to set switches.

The Soviets had fallen back into their mission rhythm. Vivian sat back, breathed, and waited—and tried to stay out of their way.

Launch was much more dramatic than in a Lunar Module takeoff. The lunar gravity meant a thrust of only one-half gravity, just as it had when Lin had rescued her from near Zvezda. But half a G was still three times more than Vivian had experienced in the weeks since. And added to that was an unnerving lateral vibration as the LK Lander wobbled on its tail of fire and reached up into the sky.

Nikolai sat to her left, Svetlana to her right. Vivian lay curled into a ball, uncomfortably crammed between them. The vibrations directly behind her from the LK's main engine went from a throbbing rumble to a teeth-rattling buzz and back again every twenty seconds. Neither Russian remarked on it, so maybe this was normal? It sure freaked the hell out of Vivian.

The LK rocked forward, orienting itself for orbit. Although Vivian braced herself as best she could, her butt still left the floor and she bounced into Svetlana's thigh. Embarrassed, she tugged herself back into position. Svetlana glanced down, her eyes unreadable.

Soon the main engine thrust eased up and the Russians freed themselves from their harnesses. Nikolai began a series of star sightings to confirm their course, while Svetlana ran numbers on the guidance computer. Vivian did her best to keep out of the way.

She was mildly nauseous, as she always was when entering weightlessness. For her two launches off Earth she'd popped an antinausea med. Today she hadn't been offered one, and was damned if she'd ask. She also felt the beginnings of the mild congestion that came with zero G, and was relieved to see that Svetlana's and Nikolai's cheeks were already showing the puffiness that almost everyone experienced in orbit.

Out of the small window, Vivian saw the Moon's dark curving limb and the stars beyond. They'd already passed into orbit night; the terminator hadn't made much progress since Vivian had arrived at Dark Driver.

For now, Vivian was a supernumerary. But soon she'd have work to do.

Soon, she'd be taking her second spacewalk, without even a gas gun to guide her trajectory. And then she might find herself up against Yashin again.

Nope. *That* prospect wasn't nerve-wracking. Not at all.

Svetlana pointed. "There. TS-1."

Nikolai grunted, didn't even look. He obviously knew what he'd see.

The uncrewed Soyuz grew quickly in the side window. Vivian's eyes widened. "Nikolai?" He still wasn't looking, trusting to his radar.

Belyakova poked her arm with a finger of steel. "Please, do not talk right now." Then she turned to Makarov and said, in English for Vivian's benefit: "I read seventy-eight degrees off."

Sure enough, the Soyuz was orbiting almost sideways on, its docking hatch facing left, its solar panels like stubby wings. Nikolai nodded.

They were close enough to the Soyuz to see when its reaction control jets fired in yaw and pitch to turn its nose toward them, then again to stop the rotation.

It still wasn't perfectly aligned. "Fix that?" Nikolai said absently, and Svetlana leaned across him to pulse the Soyuz's thrusters until they were approaching it head on.

Vivian watched with professional interest. They were controlling the Soyuz remotely from the LK, lining it up for docking as they approached. The Soyuz had a transponder to provide range and rate information, but neither Russian called numbers. Nikolai glanced at the computer, checked the radar, and applied corrections with the LK's thrusters. Svetlana sent occasional adjustments to the Soyuz. Both made it look effortless.

Svetlana, at least, seemed alert. Makarov appeared half asleep, but this was obviously an illusion. He never overcorrected, made no obvious errors, and Vivian had to admit—just to herself—that the two craft were sliding together more quickly and smoothly than her own crew might have done it. *First guy I've met who might give Dave Horn a run for his money.*

The drogue of the LK kissed the probe on the Soyuz, and Makarov blipped his engine, propelling the LK decisively up against the larger craft. With a crunch, the docking latches sprang.

Svetlana scanned readouts that Vivian couldn't decode. "Capture. Hard dock."

Nikolai leaned back and grinned, suddenly looking twenty years younger. He plucked a towel from under his seat and rubbed the back of his neck. "One down, no?"

They opened up the hatch. Nikolai soared in ahead, and Vivian followed on Svetlana's heels into the Soyuz. *Chalk up another experience I never imagined I'd have.*

After the ruthless confinement of the LK, Soyuz TS-1 seemed spacious. The ball-and-bell appearance of the craft now made sense. The globular area Vivian had just entered was the Orbital Module, eight feet across, with a single removable couch and an array of equipment crammed in around its walls: control panels, comms equipment, cupboards, life support gear, cameras, plus a small window. Beyond the OM, another hatch led into the bell of the Descent Module, the only part of the Soyuz that returned to Earth at mission end. It contained three uncomfortable-looking blue couches facing an array of control panels, and not much else.

It was cold in the Soyuz. The air tasted metallic, and the fans and water pumps made so much racket that Vivian again worried that something was wrong. But the Soviets looked around in calm satisfaction.

Nikolai threaded himself into the Descent Module and strapped into the center seat, his knees folded up higher than they'd be in a NASA craft. "And now," he said with a quiet glee: "More mathematics."

"Do you need the toilet?" Svetlana asked her.

Well, that's direct. Vivian looked around. "Wouldn't say no. Uh, where?"

The Soviet opened a drawer in the lower left of the control panel, and pulled out a hose and funnel apparatus connected to a storage can with a rubber cover. "Valve, here. Hold it like this." She demonstrated. "Wipes, here. Need me to stay?"

"Um, no. I'll manage."

"All right." Svetlana looked around thoughtfully. "Do not touch anything else."

"No, ma'am. Wouldn't dare."

Svetlana left, looking sour. Well, she bugged the heck out of Vivian, too. She liked Makarov well enough, but perhaps it wasn't surprising that she was having difficulty bonding with Belyakova. It was all Vivian could do not to needle the Russian spacewoman even more. *Screw her. I've never been a girl's girl anyway.*

Twenty minutes later, once everything was stowed and they were all scrunched into their seats, Nikolai jettisoned the LK Lander and initiated the burn that would take the Soyuz to rendezvous with Columbia Station.

"All right," he said, as soon as the burn was over. "Now, Vivian, look. Here are the circuit breakers, up at the right. Here are the status lights. These are all green, so everything is okay."

"And if one turns red?"

"Then everything is not okay. But this screen, here: this is where you look. This shows your attitude, X, Y, and Z axes."

It was a crappy monochrome display, yellow words and numbers against black. The orientation diagram and the numbers, Vivian instinctively understood. But not the words.

"Left hand, left joystick," Nikolai continued. "This translates you forward, back, left, right, up, down. Like this," he mimed the actions. "But we are on a course, so I cannot push anything now without changing our trajectory."

"Copy that."

"Right joystick is for orientation: roll, pitch, and yaw. Just how you think it would be. Up-down, or left-right, or twist it." He touched this joystick lightly, causing the Soyuz to sway around each axis in turn. "See: when you let go of the joystick, the movement stops. You do not have to compensate the other way to stop a roll. Automatic."

"Sure. Though the joystick looks a bit different from the controls I'm used to."

Actually, a lot different. Vivian was pretending a confidence she didn't feel. Having all those indicators in a language she couldn't read was … disconcerting.

"Now here, let me show you how to work the periscope."

It was between the seats; an optical device with adjustable mirrors that extended beyond the outer skin of the Soyuz, to aid in docking. "Cool," Vivian said eventually.

Svetlana looked at her watch. "Many hours yet. So now: guns."

"I still can't believe you guys carry *guns* in a spacecraft."

Belyakova eyed her, unblinking. "Because American astronauts never land in Siberia."

"Wolves," said Makarov. "Bears. Cosmonauts can sometimes come down far from cities and have to survive twenty-four hours, or thirty-six, before they are found."

Svetlana's lips pursed. "Nikolai."

"Ah yes, sorry. What I meant to say: our Soyuz craft always land on target, due to our superior Socialist navigation skills and equipment."

Vivian grinned. "So. Guns?"

There were two: a nine millimeter machine pistol, and a three-barrel shotgun of a type Vivian had never seen before. Also, a machete and a flare pistol. Vivian studied them all. "Okay, fine. And now, the ultimate deterrent?"

Svetlana looked at Nikolai. "I still am not happy about this."

"I hope she does not need to use it."

Belyakova muttered something in Russian. It sounded like a curse, but then again, so did most things she said.

Nikolai leaned over to indicate a set of switches under protective covers. "Here is the manual self-destruct for this Soyuz craft. Fifty-one pounds of TNT."

Vivian looked at Svetlana. "We have range safety and self-destruct mechanisms on the Saturn V as well, sister."

"It can be primed from the cabin?"

Vivian paused. "Nope. Not from the cabin. Shaped charges in the third stage, irreversibly safed once we reach orbit. Uh, so where are your explosives, exactly?"

"Under the floor." Nikolai reached down in between them. "Well. I cannot pull up the panel, but down there, beneath and between our couches."

Fifty pounds of TNT, right under my butt. Excellent.

"Okay," Vivian said. "I'm ready to suit up again now."

Svetlana was taller than Vika, so her spare suit was a better fit than the last Soviet suit Vivian had worn. The Russian spent a while coaching Vivian on the suit controls, lending her confidence. In hindsight, it was a miracle Vivian had survived even a short EVA in Vika's suit.

Meanwhile, Nikolai stretched out across the Descent Module cabin and, to all appearances, went to sleep floating in weightlessness, his arms folded. Vivian wasn't fooled. She was sure Makarov was wide awake and running scenarios. That was certainly what Dave Horn might do in the moments prior to a highly stressful encounter.

Sure enough, Makarov opened his eyes just before Belyakova glanced right and said: "Columbia on the radar."

"Salyut-Lunik-A," Vivian corrected her. "Your terminology is faulty, Comrade."

Svetlana grimaced but said nothing, merely propelled herself back to her couch and began to set switches for the coming rendezvous.

Columbia Station looked a lot different in mid-February than it had in early December. Back then it had seemed shiny and radiant, a platinum jewel sparkling in the dark skies above the Moon, its boom decorated with a neat row of equally bright Command and Service Modules. Trim, orderly, and all-American.

Now, Columbia's external surface was banged and pitted. No Apollo CSMs remained, replaced on the boom by a motley selection of Soviet space hardware. Four Soyuz craft, two silver and black, and two that dingy dark green, rubbed shoulders with the blisters of two LK Landers and the bubble of a LEK in a haphazard display. A battered Progress cargo vessel, of similar shape to the Soyuz but with no windows, hung on the boom's end. Another much newer blue Progress was clamped directly to Columbia's outer skin like an ungainly barnacle.

When Vivian had last seen Columbia, the station, its boom, and the CSMs had seemed rigid and immovable. Now, every part of it appeared to flex and writhe as the vibrations from various craft torqued the boom. The oscillations were slow to damp out, and each movement of one Soviet craft forced the rest to stir uneasily. Nikolai's docking at their assigned station halfway along the boom, followed by Svetlana sticking her spacesuited upper torso out of the hatch to tether them manually, provoked the Soyuz craft on either side to quiver and shift. And once they were docked, Vivian noticed that Columbia Station was precessing as it orbited.

The X shape of the solar arrays was damaged. One of the four 40-foot-long array wings had sheared off at the beam fairing, leaving a jagged edge close to the mount. The other three wings were dirty and dinged up. One was even slightly bent, but probably still functional.

In Columbia's wake, behind it in orbit and a half-mile distant, the hulking Apollo 32 third stage had acquired a steady end-over-end rotation lasting two or three minutes. As the Moon passed by beneath, it appeared to bob up and down as if wallowing in a gentle tide. Everything Vivian could see appeared to be twisting and squirming in slow motion.

"As if I wasn't feeling sick enough already."

No one could hear her. Her radio was set to receive-only. She and the Soviets were suited up, and the Soyuz was depressurized. She heard Nikolai and Svetlana talking in relaxed Russian, but understood none of it.

Svetlana flipped circuit breakers, which turned lights off in groups on the instrument panels. Nikolai secured his pencils, clipboard, and other floating objects.

It was go-time, and with shocking suddenness they were gone, Belyakova clipping her tether to the boom rail and propelling herself out into space, and Makarov right behind her, swinging the hatch closed. Neither had spoken to Vivian for the past half hour, and neither even acknowledged her as they egressed.

Vivian was alone in Soyuz TS-1. One of Nikolai's last actions had been to secure the shades over the windows; for temperature control, but also so that no one would glimpse the orange flash of Vivian's Soviet spacesuit inside a supposedly empty Soyuz. She peered carefully around the sides of the shades and watched the two cosmonauts haul themselves hand over hand along the boom, heading for the Multiple Docking Adapter fifty feet away at the fore end of Columbia Station.

Half a dozen other Soviet spacewalkers were working out in the void, ferrying boxes and crates from Columbia to their other Soyuz craft. Evidently stripping the station of anything that might prove useful.

Somewhere around here, either inside Columbia or out here, would be Yashin, Chertok, and maybe others responsible for Vivian's torments and humiliations at Zvezda.

She swallowed. Deep in enemy territory again. The plan that had seemed almost straightforward when they'd formulated it near the rim of Lipsky V just hours earlier now seemed crazy. Two and a half months had surely transmuted Vivian into a lunatic.

Then she remembered Josh Rawlings, and Zabrinski and Dardenas, who'd been incarcerated here for that whole seventy-five days, and her own crewman who'd orbited the Moon alone for just as long, and strengthened her resolve.

It was time to act. Well past time. She could do this …

Vivian froze. *What the hell is that?*

A bright sparkle, above and ahead of Columbia Station, in a higher orbit. Columbia was gradually overhauling it. As she watched, it fired a thruster. "Aw, crap."

Something large and new was approaching, and it was way too early to be Night Corps.

Vivian was still trying to control her nausea as all these space fronds undulated in a gentle current around her. Now the sickness arrived in her stomach. *Reinforcements? A new Soviet station?*

Well. *That* certainly wasn't factored into their plan.

A plan that might be about to go seriously south.

CHAPTER 47

Columbia Station: Josh Rawlings/Nikolai Makarov/Vivian Carter
February 12, 1980

Rawlings/Makarov

"An Almaz station?" Makarov frowned. "Why was I not informed? And why are these men bound like this?"

"Bound" was an understatement, to Rawlings's mind. He, Dardenas, and Zabrinski had been trussed up like turkeys by Chertok and Vasiliev, then lashed together with cables. They were back-to-back-to-back, each man facing outward, and none capable of using their hands or feet. They'd then been set adrift, free to turn in the air, bounce off the floor and walls, and generally bang into things. Whenever they drifted to a standstill or got pushed against the air outflow vent by the fans, a KGB guy would float by and give them another shove.

The Americans were a three-man rubber ball, and this remorseless set of random collisions throughout the cabin had already lasted six hours. Rawlings's knees, shoulders, and face were thoroughly bruised, and he knew the other guys were doing no better.

He could tell that Makarov and Belyakova were shocked at Columbia Station's appearance. The place had gone downhill since they'd left. As its commander, Josh felt every new breakdown, degradation, and failure as an almost physical wound, and that didn't count the layers of grime that encrusted many of the surfaces. But from Makarov's face it seemed that the overall effect was quite strong. *Yeah. My command here is kind of trashed.*

Yashin floated through the hexagonal hatch from the crew quarters. With a shiver, Rawlings remembered how this bastard had rocketed up through that hatch, firing as he came, during their abortive attempt to regain control of the station. Even without pistols Yashin was dangerous, his eyes restless and manic. "And why should you believe yourself entitled to such information, Nikolai Ilyich?"

Makarov frowned. "As commander of this—"

"That ship sailed long since, Comrade. You and Rudenko may bicker for seniority at Zvezda if you wish. Here on Salyut-Lunik-A, I now command. Perhaps I should arrest you for obstructing my authority, and tie you to," he gestured, "those fools."

Makarov held Yashin's gaze for a long moment, then turned to Okhotina. "Report."

Promptly, Okhotina said: "We have received new orders. The plan has changed. We will shortly decommission Salyut-Lunik-A. The Almaz will replace it, to maintain permanent control of the lunar equatorial orbit for the Rodina."

Makarov nodded. "I see."

The Soviet Union kept several crewed Almaz-Salyut stations in Earth orbit. They were the Soviet equivalent of the USAF's Manned Orbiting Laboratories, with the same functions. Surveillance. Defense. Potential anti-satellite activity.

And each of those Almaz stations was armed with an external cannon, to defend itself against US attack. This new Almaz, the first to be propelled into orbit around the Moon, would surely be just as well armed.

Its arrival complicated matters immensely.

Nikolai glanced at Svetlana. She wore a distant frown, as if focusing on a crossword puzzle. She didn't look back at him.

"Free these men," he said to Okhotina. "Are we savages? By all means handcuff them to a rail, but having them bang around and suffer injury is unconscionable."

Okhotina propelled herself toward the three men.

"Disregard that order." Yashin drew his pistol.

The breath snagged in Makarov's throat. *It comes to this, so soon?*

Okhotina halted herself against the communications chair with her forearm, her other hand on Zabrinski's chest to hold them steady. She waited, looking back and forth between Makarov and Yashin.

"It little matters what happens to the Americans now," Yashin said. "They have reached the end of their usefulness, and they will go down with their ship."

Makarov stared at him in shock. "You intend to deorbit *Salyut-Lunik-A*? And with these three *inside*? Are you mad?"

"Careful, Nikolai." Svetlana's voice was barely more than a whisper.

"I told you I would use a Progress: yes, I know. I thought it prudent to misinform you." Yashin eyed him speculatively. "In case you became tempted to commit any treasonous activity."

"Treasonous?" Belyakova almost barked the word. "Guard your accusations, Comrade Yashin. They may come back to bite you."

Yashin grinned, which made him all the more menacing. "Perhaps it is Nikolai who should take care, lest he join the Americans on their journey. You have always loved your landings on the Moon, have you not, Comrade? What more fitting way to end your career than with one final, glorious descent?"

Yes, Yashin was quite mad.

Makarov glanced at the Tula semiautomatic in Yashin's hand. He believed its safety catch was still on, but that would slow Yashin by only an instant.

Makarov held his stern expression with difficulty. Everyone was looking at him: Yashin, Vasiliev, the three Americans, Belyakova, Okhotina.

Then Yashin laughed and lowered his gun. "Ah, Nikolai Ilyich, your face. We need no further unpleasantness, I think? If we stand together in this, all will be well. Do you not agree?"

A cosmonaut entered the fore compartment through the upper hatch, tugging his helmet off. It was Pasha, Pavel Erdeli from the original team. Behind him was Yuri Galkin, also removing his helmet and gloves and eyeing the gathering with concern.

"Always I strive to avoid unpleasantness," Makarov said, his throat still tight. "These are our confirmed orders, then? To eradicate the American mass driver base with an atomic weapon fastened to Salyut-Lunik-A? Are we also ordered to …" he gestured at the Americans, astonished he even had to speak the words, "end these men's lives in the process? I understood that we would take them home for further interrogation?"

Zabrinski was glowering. Ah, yes, he spoke some Russian. Makarov had almost forgotten.

"I recommended this course, and my superiors concurred. Cleaner to wipe the slate. After all, these men now know a great deal about our personnel and operations. Having them aboard a Soyuz for the return to Earth poses an unacceptable risk."

Makarov gave a curt, if reluctant, nod. "Very well. You may be right. Meanwhile, how long until the Almaz rendezvous? What remains to be achieved by then?"

Yashin nodded approvingly. "Now you are speaking sense, Comrade. As our orbital specialist, you must oversee the final approach of the Almaz."

"Not the programming of the Columbia deorbit burn?"

"That has already been handled in your absence." Yashin gestured at Erdeli and Galkin. "Straightforward. Beneath your notice."

"As you wish."

Okhotina glanced at the clock over the comms unit. "Shortly, we will pass into orbital dark. Once fully loaded, the two Soyuz of Salkov and Royzman will undock and leave lunar orbit for home. In another hour, around the start of the next orbit day, the Almaz will take up station twenty meters from this Salyut-Lunik. Comrades Yashin and Erdeli will arm the bomb, and then Erdeli and I will transfer to the Almaz, to bring it up to its full complement of six. The rest of you will return to Earth aboard your Soyuz craft, by original crew." Meaning Makarov, Belyakova, and Vasiliev would be in one Soyuz and Galkin, Chertok, and Yashin in the other.

While the American Farside base glows as radioactive as Hadley, with dozens of men dead, Makarov thought. *So methodical, our Soviet machine. So matter of fact.*

"And not a moment too soon," said Belyakova. "For my part, I cannot wait to put this messy business behind us."

Yashin's eyes glittered. "Nor can I, Svetlana Antonovna. Nor can I."

Makarov lowered his eyes in apparent acquiescence, but his thoughts were whirling.

The plan had been for him and Belyakova to enter Columbia Station, determine the location of the Soviet nuclear device, and inform

460

Vivian either by radio or by signal light from the wardroom window of Columbia Station. Most likely, the device would be already installed aboard its Progress. A simple "Yes" flashed in Morse code would confirm this, whereupon the follow-up signal "Now" would let Vivian know the coast was clear and that she could safely proceed to it. A "No" or "Inside" signal would mean that the device was elsewhere, perhaps being prepared within Columbia.

Given the opportunity, of course, he would send a longer message. He might even radio Vivian if they gained control of the comms board, with sufficient confidence that no other Soviets would be listening in. Their secondary objective was to disable the Soviet radar, either at the board inside or by sabotaging the dish on Columbia's outer skin, to allow Night Corps to approach undetected.

The location of the nuke, and the Soviet strength at the station, would define Vivian's next move. Before leaving Lipsky V Crater, they'd scoped out a variety of scenarios. In most of them, Vivian would either proceed covertly to where she could do the most damage, or if that proved impossible, hold tight until Makarov and Belyakova regained control of Columbia, or Night Corps stormed in.

Unfortunately, they'd based these scenarios on what they'd heard at Zvezda. They had anticipated a drawdown of personnel on Columbia—and thus a limited Soviet crew to distract. And Okhotina, at least, was a friend: Svetlana had trained extensively with her before being assigned as Makarov's crewmate.

Now, all bets were off. Yashin had kept his cards close to his chest, and Makarov and Belyakova had been outplayed. They could not have anticipated the arrival of the Almaz, nor guessed so many cosmonauts would still be on EVA, constraining Vivian's mobility. Nor that their own actions would be monitored so thoroughly that they'd have no freedom to signal her. If Vivian's presence were discovered, he and Svetlana might face summary execution by Yashin.

But if Vivian received no signal, she would surely just hide in the Soyuz until Sandoval and Night Corps arrived.

And whatever happened after that would be out of Makarov's hands.

Carter

Nothing from Nikolai or Svetlana, and an incoming Soviet craft nearly as large as Columbia Station? Vivian could wait no longer. She had to act.

In her borrowed Soviet suit, Vivian inchwormed her way along the boom. Rather than rely on gas guns, the cosmonauts performed EVAs using a system of dual tethers. Fasten yourself by the first tether, head off where you needed to go. Fasten the second tether. Go back and unclip the first, bring it with you. Go forward until you reach the limit of your second tether. Clip in. Repeat. Clunky but straightforward and, with care, fail-safe.

Surely the nuke would be in the new Progress attached to Columbia; the older Progress on the boom was likely the original craft containing the jammer. So Vivian headed for Columbia.

The Almaz was getting nearer, smoothly dropping down into Columbia's orbit. Vivian had never seen one before, but it looked just as she might have expected: a cylinder fifty feet long and fifteen feet in diameter, not dissimilar to the USAF MOLs.

It would be within docking range soon. About to go into orbit night, they'd do the final approach once the station swung back into sunlight.

How long before Sandoval could get his Night Corps group operational and off-Moon? Two hours from now? Four? Vivian had no way of guessing.

She continued on, latching her tether clips alternately onto handholds and rails while the lunar surface beneath her passed into darkness. She'd hoped to take advantage of orbit night, but in the reflected light from the mostly sunlit Earth, she felt like her orange Soviet suit glowed like a beacon.

Vivian couldn't gain access to the Progress. Its hatch was closed up tight, and when she prodded at the keypad it lit up with an unhelpful array of nine green zeros. She'd need the keycode to attain access—and she didn't know it.

Instead she inspected the Progress's engine, and attempted to determine how the craft was clamped. If she could release the Progress and shove it off, it would take a while for the Soviets to retrieve it. Extra points if she could screw up its propulsion system.

She came up empty on both ideas. The Progress was bolted secure-ly. She might fetch a wrench from Makarov's Soyuz and set to work, but it would take time, and be evident as sabotage even from a casual glance. Ideal might have been to haul over some of the self-destruct explosive and find some way to detonate it, but that would be quite the technical challenge. Firing one of her guns into the rocket noz-zle would probably be futile. And any of these activities would attract more Soviet attention than Vivian could handle.

"Fabulous."

She couldn't dally. If this Progress contained the nuke, only select-ed Soviets would be allowed near it. If someone checked up on her, or showed up to access the Progress themselves, her goose was cooked.

Vivian headed back along the handrails, trying to adopt a body language of confident purpose. She glanced around, establishing where the other Soviets were. They seemed busy. Vivian might look more convincing if she could find some big chunk of payload to heft around.

No point now in attempting to sabotage the Soviet radar. They'd be actively using it to monitor the Almaz's approach. Taking it offline would immediately betray her presence. And the Almaz's radar would detect Night Corps anyway.

She briefly considered entering Columbia. If no one was inside the Multiple Docking Adapter she might be able to doff her suit and hide somewhere.

And then do what? Vivian wasn't James Bond. The likelihood of *that* plan having any success was approximately zero.

The Almaz was still on its inexorable approach. It could not dock with Columbia directly, but cosmonauts had already exited it and were setting one of their inflatable airlocks in place.

"Okay, babe," she said to the inside of her suit. "Back to base camp." Time to figure out her Plan B.

Hand over hand, tether connection by tether connection, Vivian inched her way back toward Soyuz TS-1.

Uh-oh.

Her way back was blocked. Three cosmonauts were now clustered around the Soyuz just inboard from Makarov's on the boom. She couldn't get by without drawing their attention.

All the while, Vivian had been hearing intermittent Soviet com-munications over the radio, businesslike but orderly, as the Soviets coordinated the stripping and evacuation of Columbia. But now came a sudden din that made her jump. It was Yashin, and he was shouting.

She glanced out and down. She couldn't see the incoming Night Corps craft yet. But based on Yashin's tone, the Soviets had picked them up on radar.

Suddenly, it was all systems go.

The cosmonauts who'd been methodically setting up the inflatable docking tunnel between Columbia and the Almaz sprang into more vigorous action, pulling the tunnel aside and out of the way.

Even while they were doing that, the Almaz fired thrusters and began to rotate, swinging through 180 degrees in space.

The docking tunnels on Almaz-Salyuts were on the aft section, Vivian knew. The armaments were on the fore section.

Serious armaments, too. From both ground-based intelligence and space-based observations using the DORIAN telescopes on the MOLs, they knew each Almaz was armed with a large rapid-fire cannon. Likely the same Rikhter cannon used on their Tupelov-22 bombers, it weighed forty pounds and could fire between a thousand and five thousand shells a minute at fifteen hundred miles per hour. Each shell weighed half a pound, twenty-five times as heavy as the AK-47 bullets that had struck Vivian's suit back in December. If one of those shells hit a suit it would smash a limb, blow a hole, or just kill its astronaut outright. Even the Night Corps exosuits might be compromised if they took shells from the Rikhter.

Its disadvantage was the limited maneuverability of its aim, and the noise and vibration its firing would inflict on the Almaz crew. But Vivian had no doubt that, if Night Corps was coming in, the Soviet cannon would deal them a devastating blow.

And as if that weren't enough, a cosmonaut was egressing from the Almaz upper hatchway carrying the long tube of a shoulder-mounted rocket launcher.

And Vivian still couldn't even see Night Corps yet.

She definitely had to move. *Don't wanna be caught outside when this storm hits.*

With all this activity, hopefully no one would question a cosmonaut rushing purposefully toward a Soyuz. And glancing along the boom again, she saw that one of the Soviets who'd been blocking her path had now entered his Soyuz, with a second man following. With luck, they'd all be aboard by the time she made it there.

The Almaz was still rotating, but there was no doubt that its turn would be complete by the time Night Corps arrived. And then those cannon shells would carve their way through their Lunar Modules' aluminum walls like a hot knife through butter.

Damn it, this inchworming was too slow. Vivian needed to hustle.

She unclipped her tether, and did not reclip it. Hauled herself hand over hand along the boom. Another thirty feet to go. As long as one hand always had tight hold and she was vectoring parallel to the boom, she'd be fine, right?

She glanced up. Ahead of her, the third cosmonaut had disappeared into the Soyuz. The hatch was shut. And the hook holding it to the boom was now unfastened.

Wait a goddamn minute—

She was only twenty feet from the Soyuz when its commander fired the thrusters. Fast blips of plasma from four jets, two on each side. The blast was aimed directly back toward the boom, but it was bright and close and scared the living crap out of her.

But Vivian's reactions were good: rather than shoving herself away and losing her grip, she clamped tight with both gloves to pull herself in, and closed her eyes.

She didn't feel the heat, felt nothing but the throbbing vibration of the boom through her gloves. When she opened her eyes, the Soyuz was thirty feet out and still backing up.

"God *damn* it, Soviets have *no* health and safety protocols."

Now the question was, had those jets heated the area of the boom separating her from TS-1? Applying her glove to white-hot metal would end her. The silicone coating her palm would bind and burn through, breaching her suit.

It didn't look white hot, or even red. But caution was in order.

The Soyuz was rotating, fifty or sixty feet distant. Which, since the craft was twenty-four feet long and about thirty-five feet from wingtip to wingtip of its solar panels, still seemed too close. But she was out of time.

Vivian launched herself forward. Floated across the boom section the Soyuz had just departed from, without touching it. Reached Makarov's Soyuz, and grabbed at the hinge clip holding it to the boom. *Whoo.*

Pulled herself into Soyuz TS-1 and did the next best thing to slamming the door behind her. "Goddamn this war."

Okay, the hell with keeping a low profile. Vivian opened the shades and peered out. The departing Soyuz had wasted no time in dropping into a lower orbit to pass the Almaz and haul ass away from Columbia. It looked like a second Soyuz would disengage imminently.

How could Vivian help Night Corps?

Also, what could she do to avoid being seen as an enemy combatant once they arrived? She was wearing a Soviet suit and inside a Soviet craft. Night Corps couldn't know it was Vivian aboard. They'd just see a big old curvy bug with "CCCP" painted on it, and shoot the crap out of it like all the rest.

Well. Wait and see, I guess.

CHAPTER 48

Columbia Station: Josh Rawlings
February 12, 1980

"**THEY** cannot get here in time." With some satisfaction, Yashin leaned back to pluck the three-man rubber ball of Rawlings, Dardenas, and Zabrinski out of the air, and turned it to grin into Rawlings's face. "You hear? Help is on the way for you, likely Night Corps craft from your Daedalus Base. But still two hundred miles distant. An hour, perhaps? Maybe more? By the time they arrive, Salyut-Lunik-A will be on its way down. Just like this."

Using the wall for leverage, Yashin raised his legs and shoved, hard. The three men shot across the fore compartment and slammed into the floor, Zabrinski howling as he bore the brunt of it. They ricocheted upward, heading straight for Belyakova.

Swearing, she grabbed Dardenas's leg and threw her weight backward to arrest their motion. She glowered at Yashin. "You are quite sure of that? There is still much to do, and it is a dangerous distraction to have these three idiots bouncing around. We must fasten them in place for the descent now." She started to untape the Americans. "We will handcuff them to the grating. Where are the keys to the handcuffs? Give them to me."

Makarov looked at Yashin. "I still do not approve of this, leaving the Americans aboard while the station is deorbited."

"Your hand-wringing is noted," Yashin said, and then to Belyakova: "Very well. But one at a time, and keep them apart. Then prepare to evacuate. Nikolai Ilyich, if you could turn your attention back to the Almaz approach?"

In his relief at being released, Rawlings almost missed Okhotina smoothly passing Belyakova a gun.

Svetlana was still berating Okhotina, and snatched the handcuff keys from her. Okhotina raised her hand at the same moment, as if preparing to defend herself against a blow, and that was the moment when the pistol passed between them. Easily visible from Rawlings's perspective, but from Yashin's angle, Belyakova's body would have blocked the handover.

Josh's heart began to beat faster. *Well. This is interesting.*

He looked around. Oleg Vasiliev floated in the corner of the cabin with his AK-47. With the Americans restrained he had no need to cover them constantly, but he could still swing it around and fire in an instant.

Rawlings meekly allowed himself to be repositioned by Belyakova. She glared down into his face. "Do *nothing* unless I tell you to. Don't even blink. You understand me?"

"Yes, ma'am, I do."

"Very good," she said, put her hand over his, and winked solemnly. *Holy shit.*

Josh glanced at the handcuffs. Sure enough. Despite the savage show Belyakova had made of relocking them after passing the chain through the grate, the cuffs were loose, locked at their widest setting. Josh could slide his wrists out whenever he needed to.

He watched as she moved Danny and Marco in turn to the grate at ten-foot intervals. Belyakova looked into Zabrinski's eyes as she fastened his handcuffs in the same way. He, too, would be able to shuck them at a moment's notice. Dardenas, however, was positioned too close to Vasiliev; with a rueful look, Svetlana was forced to attach him securely.

Zabrinski caught Rawlings's eye and looked away. Dardenas looked frustrated.

Well, hey. In the words of the immortal Meat Loaf: two out of three ain't bad.

Something was about to go down. Civil war among the Soviets? The cosmonauts double-crossing Yashin? How dangerous a game was that?

For now, the why doesn't matter. Figure out your move.

Josh judged distances and angles. Makarov and Erdeli were huddled around a Soviet computer the size of a door. Erdeli held a clipboard covered in figures. Makarov was studying it and asking questions, prompting Erdeli to punch numbers into the computer and read out the answers. Yashin was at the comms board briefing the Almaz crew, watching Makarov out of the corner of his eye. Galkin and Chertok were up in the dome, prepping suits. Vasiliev floated comfortably on the far side of the compartment, holding the rifle across his lap.

Hunky Nik and Blond Svet were a team, with Okhotina apparently in their camp. Opposed would be the KGB trifecta of Yashin, Lev Chertok, and Oleg Vasiliev, with almost all the firepower. What would Galkin and Erdeli do?

Svetlana was obviously relying on Rawlings to come hurtling in to back up her and Makarov, once the chips were down. Which he would. Any enemy of Yashin's was a friend of Josh's, and the alternative was a sharp nosedive into the Moon at well over a mile per second—

And that was all the time Josh had to think about it, because the very next moment Svetlana drew her pistol and fired two shots into Vasiliev's chest at almost point-blank range.

There was no shocked pause, no cries of alarm or disbelief. Most of the Soviets moved immediately, as if they'd been waiting for this. Yashin's gun was back in his hand as he ducked behind Erdeli, and Galkin surged down from the hatch at the top of the dome, also drawing a pistol. Robbed of a clear shot at Yashin, Belyakova streaked across the compartment, racing Chertok for Vasiliev's rifle. Makarov had shoved Erdeli away and was swinging at Yashin. Okhotina pulled out a gun of her own and fired once at Yashin, missing, then turned to cover Galkin, who was just ten feet above her. She snapped out a couple of words in Russian and Galkin looked startled and turned his pistol aside.

Jeez. Way too many guns. Rawlings slid his hands free and shoved himself upward. Zabrinski was also on the move, barreling into the hapless Erdeli and knocking him into the brawling pair of Makarov and Yashin as they fought for control of Yashin's Tula pistol.

The fore compartment of Columbia was only twenty feet across, and the crowding and confusion immense.

Vasiliev's body rolled gently, fountaining blood. Chertok and Belyakova slammed into it at the same moment, wrestling for the rifle. Josh came up on them from beneath and swung his elbow into Chertok's mouth, once, twice. He felt a tooth break. *Payback, pal.*

As Chertok reeled back, still clutching the barrel of the AK-47, Belyakova turned to aim her pistol at Yashin again, shouting in Russian and then English: "Stop! Everybody, stop still!"

Nobody stopped. Yashin was pummeling Makarov's face with the butt of his pistol, swinging the cosmonaut's body between himself and Belyakova as a shield. Erdeli was shouting at Yashin, arms outstretched, apparently begging him to stop. Above them Zabrinski had threaded the needle between the battles and was arrowing toward Yashin feet-first when Galkin shot at him. Okhotina loosed off two shots almost simultaneously, and a bloody hole appeared in Galkin's face, snapping his head back and sending him tumbling. Zabrinski crashed into the wall, apparently unconscious, drifting up into the dome.

Somehow, Chertok had retained one hand on the barrel of the AK-47 while pounding his other fist into Rawlings's stomach. Josh, winded and coughing, braced against the wall to get some leverage. Belyakova turned back and banged the barrel of her pistol into Chertok's eye.

Josh grabbed the stock of the AK-47 and pulled, pivoting it in Chertok's grasp, and grabbed at the trigger. The din was huge as bullets raked Chertok from thigh to shoulder. Blood sprayed.

Across the way, Makarov's head lolled. Yashin had one arm looped around his neck. He swung the Tula and fired two quick shots across the compartment, and Belyakova screamed and thrashed, her limbs jerking.

"Release the rifle." Yashin was turning in the air, still holding firm to Makarov, but his pistol was aimed unerringly at Josh's face. It was like looking down the barrel of a cannon. Reluctantly, Rawlings released his hold on the AK-47, and pushed himself away from it. "Restrain her."

Belyakova was tumbling over and over, her face screwed up in a rictus of agony, alternately shrieking and whimpering. Okhotina seized her arm and dragged her down toward the floor, and Josh reached out to help guide her. It looked like she'd taken a bullet to her side and another to the thigh.

Yashin said something in Russian. In response Okhotina retrieved Belyakova's pistol and tossed it up to him, and then her own.

The AK-47 was turning lazily end-over-end in the center of the compartment, and drifting down toward him. Josh watched its approach with a kind of fascination.

Rather than attempt to cover everybody, Yashin now held the barrel of his pistol to Makarov's head. His lips were slightly parted in a feral expression that was almost a smile. "Please: Commander Rawlings, Comrade Okhotina, I invite you. Take the rifle. Just reach for it. See what happens."

"Love to, you bastard," Rawlings said, not reaching for it. Okhotina had one arm clamped around Belyakova to hold her still while pulling at her bloody jumpsuit with the other hand, trying to assess how badly she was wounded, and ignored Yashin completely.

Belyakova went quiet and limp. Alarmed, Rawlings pried open her mouth to check her airway. In zero G, injured people could easily suffocate on their own blood. But Belyakova was still breathing, though ragged and shallow. "She's going into shock." Blood soaked her jumpsuit from pelvis to right knee: plenty of blood, but not a huge welling balloon of it. Not a femoral artery hit, then, but still bad enough. Should they tourniquet her? "Talk to her, Katya. Keep talking. Comrade Yashin, can I fetch the medical kit and manual?"

"No. Stay where you are."

Strange: just a couple months ago Rawlings had head-butted this woman in an attempt to regain the station from her, and now he was trying to save her life. He wished he could get to Zabrinski, still spinning slowly in the upper area.

Yashin gave Erdeli an order in Russian. Erdeli gaped. Yashin repeated it, and shoved the barrel a little harder against the unconscious Makarov's head.

Erdeli turned to the Soviet computer and flipped switches. A telltale lit up in red. Erdeli pressed a button to turn it green. That seemed almost anticlimactic, but Pasha backed away as if he'd seen a snake. Two seconds later, the NASA comms board went dark. He stared at Yashin.

"What the hell did you just do?" Rawlings demanded. No one answered him. Instead, Yashin gave Erdeli quick orders in a brisk monotone.

"Katya? What's happening?"

Okhotina was tearing strips off her own jumpsuit to wind around Belyakova's leg. "I do not know."

"Be silent," Yashin said.

Erdeli retrieved the AK-47 and shoved it to Yashin, who looped it over his shoulder. He pushed off, propelling himself into the dome.

Josh took stock. Makarov, unconscious and still in Yashin's grasp. Belyakova, badly wounded but now whimpering again. Zabrinski: shot, silent, and adrift. Almost no blood in the space around him, which was ... encouraging? Rawlings wasn't sure. Chertok, Vasiliev, and Galkin: all dead and bleeding copiously in all directions. Erdeli: unscathed, following on Yashin's heels. Dardenas: still handcuffed to the rail below and staring around in horror.

At Yashin's command, Erdeli preceded him through the hatch into the Multiple Docking Adapter. Yashin had pocketed the Tula, and held the AK-47 in one hand, preparing to pass Makarov's unconscious body through into the docking adapter.

"Not Nikolai."

It was Svetlana Belyakova. Her left hand clutched at her side, but her right was held out to Yashin in supplication. Sweat dripped off her face, and blood still spilled into the air around her. Her teeth were gritted against what must be immense pain, but her eyes were clear.

She spoke alternately in Russian and English. "Do not take him. Do not kill him. I beg you, Comrade. This one thing. Give him back to me."

Yashin's smile dripped with venom.

"You hardly need a hostage at this point," Rawlings added. "Be magnanimous in victory."

"Perhaps it is fitting." Yashin released his hold on Makarov, made a handwashing movement, and used his booted foot to send the cosmonaut gently down toward them.

"Thank you," Svetlana gasped.

"Oh, do not thank me yet, Comrade. The best is yet to come." Yashin pulled himself out of the forward compartment, and slammed the hatch closed.

As Svetlana reached for Nikolai's body, sobbing in pain, all the lights went out inside Columbia Station.

For the first few minutes, it was literal bloody chaos. As Rawlings fumbled his way around in the pitch black, still panting with pain and exertion, he breathed other people's blood into his mouth and twice bumped into corpses. Or perhaps the same corpse twice.

By Josh's count, there were nine bodies trapped here in the dark. Of those, only Okhotina, Dardenas, and Rawlings himself were essentially unharmed, and Dardenas was still chained up. Belyakova had presumably lost consciousness again, because he couldn't hear her whimpering and Okhotina was talking to her urgently in Russian. Makarov would still be out cold, and presumably Zabrinski was too. And then there were the three corpses.

"Jesus, what a goddamn mess," Rawlings said. "Katya, where's the key to Marco's handcuffs? In Svetlana's pocket?"

"I am busy, damn you."

Looking after Belyakova. "Yeah, that's nice, but the air handling went out with the lights, and we don't have long. I need Marco's help. Find me the damned key. Now."

Astronauts on EVA carried penlights. Rawlings didn't have one and, right now, was blanking on where he could find one. By propelling himself to the wall and fumbling his way around it, he arrived at the comms board. By feel he located the circuit breaker, but of course that didn't work: Yashin had turned off the power from outside. Christ.

There would be lights in the suits. Or near them. Most of those suits were up past the hatch in the Multiple Docking Adapter.

A corpse banged into him, soaked in blood all down its side. Chertok, then. Rawlings thrust it away, resisting the urge to put all his force into it. It wouldn't help if he hurled a dead body into Okhotina. Speaking of … "Katya, the damned key!"

"*Mudak!*" she spat, evidently a Russian curse.

"She's got it," said Marco at the same time. "She's here with me. Best she takes this slow but sure, yes?"

"Yup." Inspiration struck at last. "Ah!"

Rawlings twisted himself around, aligned himself by muscle memory, and pushed off. That memory was pretty reliable. His outstretched right hand fetched up against the edge of the hatchway into the crew quarters and he pulled himself through. "So damned dark."

Above him, someone retched. *Perfect. Just what we need.*

Makarov coughed and cried out as he regained consciousness, and Rawlings heard him bang into something hard. Okhotina called to him in Russian at the same time as Dardenas said "Oh, ack, space puke."

"Sorry," Makarov said, indistinctly.

Rawlings kept going, through the door into the sleeping quarters, and found his bunk. He had a battery-powered reading light mounted above it, and when he pressed the switch its faint bulb dazzled him. "Let there be light."

Unclipping it, he thrust himself out of the sleeping quarters and into the personal hygiene cubicle, grabbing tissues and wipes. Spun, applied his feet to the wall, and headed back up. Around him, shadows loomed and lurched. A space station in near-dark was pretty forbidding.

Back in the fore compartment, in the faint glimmer, he saw Marco en route up to Zabrinski. Katya was going toward the spare suits. Was the air already getting stale, or was it just all the … human fluids staining it up?

"Here, let me." Makarov took the wipes from Rawlings, and started chasing down his own vomit, which made Rawlings start to feel nauseous himself. "I am sorry."

"Don't sweat it," Josh said. "Glamor of space travel, am I right?"

He pinned the reading light up over the dead comms board, and tried to think. Corpses floated ominously around him, casting their macabre shadows across the walls. *Horror show. Jeez Louise.*

"Zabrinski's alive," said Dardenas. "Grazing bullet wound to the head, far as I can tell. Not much blood. Do we have a doctor in the house?"

Rawlings didn't honor that with a reply. "Let me guess. Hatch jammed shut?"

Marco wrenched at it. "Yeah, but good."

"Okay, drag out whatever suits we have." He peered up at Okhotina. "Which you're already doing. Marco, give her a hand. Oxygen tanks, everything. Batteries, can we splice one up to a fan and try to blow some of this goddamn blood away? At least attempt to scrub some CO_2 out of the air with the suit systems?" He shook his head. "Will that help? Anyone have any idea how long we can keep on breathing in here?"

No one responded. The grim despair in the air was almost as tangible as the blood. Still so much blood.

Shit. Was this hopeless? Rawlings looked over at Makarov. "Hey. Nikolai, buddy. Talk to me. What's happening? Is anyone left out there except goddamn Yashin and Erdeli?" Damn, he was saying "goddamn" a lot. Well, perhaps he could be forgiven for that.

Makarov had actually done a pretty good job of swabbing up the air after himself. Now he looked soberly back at Rawlings. "The propulsion module is already connected to Columbia Station. Yashin and Erdeli will be arming the bomb now, I think, and then will go to their Soyuz and set off for Earth. Then the module will fire. Long before Night Corps gets here."

"So, what you're saying is that we're freaking doomed."

Makarov rubbed his head gingerly, looked up and around without much hope in his eyes. "Well. There is still Vivian Carter."

CHAPTER 49

Columbia Station: Vivian Carter
February 12, 1980

THERE it was. Morse code, from Columbia Station's only window.

Truth be told, Vivian hadn't been paying close attention. She'd assumed that they'd screened the wardroom window, because twenty minutes ago it had gone dark. But no: now she noticed the blink of a light from its exact center and focused in hard.

—PPED IN HERE. NO POWER.

No power? Whoa.

After a pause, the message restarted. YASHIN ARMING NUKE. COLUMBIA TO DEORBIT ONTO DAED BASE. TRAPPED IN HE—

Vivian didn't wait, but shoved off to look out the other window.

Damn it.

In the last moments of lunar night, two shadowy figures moved across the pale skin of Columbia Station, inchworming in slow-but-steady Soviet style toward the Progress.

So. The nuke was in the Progress. Yashin and another cosmonaut were on their way to arm it. After which Columbia—the whole station, not just the Progress!—would be deorbited by a propulsion module, to land on Dark Driver. Killing the dozens of Americans there, including Ellis Mayer. Plus Rawlings and his astronauts, plus Makarov and Belyakova …

476

Night Corps wasn't going to get here in time. And even when they did, the Almaz would be waiting for them.

"Well, shit."

Vivian thrust herself in the pilot's seat of the Soyuz.

"Time to make some noise."

The two cosmonauts were now at the door of the Progress, one with his body half-inside. Arming the bomb.

How long did Vivian have? Columbia Station was now back in sunlight, crossing the western face of the Moon. In fact, they'd passed over Copernicus Crater just a few minutes ago. The most fuel-efficient way would have the deorbit burn begin at the exact opposite side of the Moon to Dark Driver. But the Soviets didn't need to be fuel efficient. This would be a fast one-way journey, with little additional braking or maneuvering necessary. They weren't soft-landing the damned thing, after all.

With Night Corps on the way, Yashin would press the button as soon as he could. Then leap aboard a Soyuz and be gone.

It was all down to Vivian.

She strapped in, cranked circuit breakers, and picked up the stick that would help her prod switches she couldn't reach. Ran her eyes over the cryptic displays. Glanced out the window.

"Soloing a Soyuz, based on several whole minutes of instruction? Shouldn't I have staff for this kind of crap?"

Before she could change her mind, Vivian pressed the switch to release the hinge clip that held the Soyuz on the boom. Unlikely she could ever reattach it, because that took two people: on arrival, Svetlana had hooked them up manually while Nikolai drove. In that one moment, Vivian had already burned her bridges. She had no idea what would happen after the next few minutes, no broader plan to save herself.

"One-way trip, Captain Carter." She looked up and around. "Well. Here goes."

TS-1 was on the move, tracking crabwise in fits and starts. *This tub needs* way *more windows*. Ideally, she'd take the time to properly orient the thing and then edge in, but this wasn't a leisurely NASA maneuver. The clock was ticking.

At least she picked up the maneuvering pretty quick. Accustoming herself to TS-1's controls was no harder than shifting from one type of jet fighter to another. More challenging was that Vivian had no transponder information, no range and rate cues. She'd be doing this on visuals alone.

It might have been more terrifying if she hadn't done something very similar two and a half months ago, wearing just a spacesuit and propelling herself with a gas gun. Having the shell of the Soyuz around her provided at least the illusion of protection.

Besides, Vivian wasn't planning to rendezvous. She was planning to crash.

Crashing was surely easier.

The Soviets hadn't seen her yet. She blipped the jets again with her left hand, and the Progress slid down out of her window. Then applied roll and yaw with her right controller to turn the Soyuz face-on.

You're going to go crush 'em while their backs are turned? Lovely, Vivian.

Yeah. I'd feel worse about it if they weren't arming a frigging atom bomb to blast several dozen Americans off the face of the Moon.

Her radio crackled. Someone bellowed in Russian.

Ha. No comprendo. Ich spreche kein Deutsch.

The cosmonauts at the Progress reacted simultaneously. One swiveled, looking for the threat. The other, more quick-witted, thrust himself sideways into the void, relying on his tether to save him.

Vivian shoved her left joystick all the way in, and the Soyuz surged forward to slam into the Progress.

The roar and shriek of tormented metal filled the cabin. The collision threw Vivian into her straps. The side of the Progress buckled inward right outside her window. But Vivian hadn't hit it head on but slightly low of center, meaning that the impact flipped her Soyuz dizzyingly forward and up into a roll. "Damn it!"

That roll lasted a less than a quarter turn because something caught. She felt a terrible grinding in the frame of her Soyuz as it swung back in the opposite direction. "Gah …!"

Her pilot's intuition kicked in. The lower flared skirt of TS-1 had gotten itself jammed up into the Progress's skin and torqued as far as it could go, and then been yanked back in the other direction. She was caught. "Shit."

Still, from what she could see of the Progress, she'd mashed its side in pretty good, and crushed at least one of the cosmonauts in the process. She'd had no concern that the nuke would detonate; you could drop most nuclear weapons onto the ground, even from an airplane, and they wouldn't explode unless they were somehow forced into supercriticality. Pounding on one with a Soyuz-sized hammer wouldn't do that. Sane engineers designed nukes not to explode when dropped, knocked over, or accidentally included in train derailments. But the Progress's engine and guidance system couldn't have survived unscathed.

But Vivian was now a sitting target. Could she break her Soyuz free of the Progress? She narrowed her eyes, gripped the left controller, and applied full thrust.

Nope. Evidently not.

Red lights flashed all across her console. On some intuition, she looked up. Hatch open?

Oh, for God's sake.

Yeah. The Soyuz was open to space on the far side of the Orbital Module, where Vivian had originally entered.

The black of space turned orange. A cosmonaut was hauling himself into Vivian's Soyuz. Probably a really pissed-off cosmonaut.

Let me guess.

Yashin was *fast*. Even as Vivian unbuckled, he was swarming into the OM headfirst like a bullet, clutching a familiar weapon in his right hand. *AK-47? Shit.*

They'd come full circle. Except that Yashin was much nearer, and probably *really* mad.

He was only ten feet away from her now and powering forward, blocking Vivian's only way out of this Soviet deathtrap. *Ohmigod, Vivian. Do something.*

She shoved the right controller all the way over, hit her straps to free herself, and jumped left. Yashin twisted, kicking out as the rocking of the Soyuz threw him off his game.

His AK-47 came up. One bullet might not fatally breach Vivian's suit, even at this close range. Several at once surely would.

He was right there, head and shoulders through the hatch into the Descent Module, rifle held parallel to his body and pointing straight at Vivian. His patch said "Яшин." Sure enough. Yashin.

Vivian was screaming with rage and fear as she tried to pull herself out of the line of fire of that damned AK-47. The Soyuz stopped moving, at the limit of its freedom to swing in place.

Yashin fired. Bullets clattered in the confined space, the impact vibrations echoing through her suit, which was pressed against the Soyuz wall. She felt the separate thuds in her legs, shoulders, and back as his bullets struck her. Some of their power was mercifully blunted by their first or second ricochet, but it was still like being kicked by several mules at once.

Aching, roaring, Vivian grabbed up the closest weapon she had to hand. Barely aimed it. Pulled the trigger and closed her eyes.

The flare exploded, bright and brilliant even through her eyelids, with a thunderous shock that bounced off all the hard surfaces and echoed through her suit.

As Vivian dropped the flare pistol and reached up to grab for the barrel of Yashin's rifle she *felt* the flare's radiance along the left side of her suit. Opened her eyes for a fraction of a second, and in the uncannily bright, tight hellscape of the Soyuz interior saw Yashin's gloves reaching for her. An instant later he rammed her back, banging her helmet against the instrument panel.

Vivian was pinned. She kicked out, but with little force. She thrust her hand downward, scrabbled at the thigh pocket of her suit.

The flare was burning out, but there was a giant globe right in front of her face: Yashin's helmet. His hands reached for her umbilicals to twist the valve on her air supply. "No you don't, you bastard ..." But she couldn't stop him, and a moment later the whine of the fans in her helmet ceased.

She wrestled her thigh pocket open, dug her hand in, and yanked out Belyakova's gun. The nine millimeter pistol looked small in her gloved hand, especially against the looming threat of the KGB cosmonaut. Worse, she couldn't pull the trigger, could never get her gloved finger into the trigger guard. It would be like trying to thread a needle with a sausage. "Damn it! Shit!"

"I will enjoy watching you die," said Yashin, and his words echoed in the eerie silence of her helmet. "And listening, too." He reached for her chest-plate, turned her radio back on.

Now, he could hear her scream, and feast on her pain and desperation.

"Screw you," she said.

The next moment, he swung a hammer at her faceplate. He was still holding her helmet against the instrument panels with one hand, both wedged into the small space of the Soyuz Descent Module, and the hammerhead crashed against it right between the eyes. The polycarbonate held. It might take several blows to break through. How many? Of course, she might suffocate first.

He swung again, in exactly the same place, and the hammer bounced off. "Are you afraid, Vivian? I am enjoying your fear."

Yeah. Thought so. "You're repeating yourself, dipshit."

She wasn't sure he'd even seen the gun in her hand. Vivian poked the safety down with her thumb. Grabbed one of Makarov's pencils and slid it through the trigger guard. Clamped the muzzle of the pistol to his helmet with her right hand, anchored it in place with her left against the recoil, and yanked back with the pencil.

It shook her hands, the vibration. The noise clattered into her helmet too, because by now she was shoving up against him and they were pressed together, her helmet and his. She pulled on the pistol to fire again, and a third time and a fourth in exactly the same spot, and then the pencil broke, the two pieces flying off in opposite directions.

Yashin swung the hammer, and it crashed into her visor again. She heard a splintering crackle, and got ready to die.

No sudden pressure drop. No blood boil. That sound wasn't her helmet. It was his.

Yashin's faceplate cracked all the way across, and breached a fraction of a second later. She heard the sharp snap of shearing plastic, followed by the whoosh of expelling air.

Vivian opened her eyes, and watched dispassionately as Yashin died in bubbling, asphyxiating agony, their faces just inches apart.

Her rage revived. She shoved, driving his body away, back into the OM. But that wasn't far enough, so Vivian kept on going, pushing him back, tugging his drifting arms down by his sides so that they couldn't catch on the hatch.

"Get out, you sick bastard. Out. Out!"

Vivian threw him out into space with his jagged helmet gaping. Narrow ribbons of blood still spilled out into the void before they eerily boiled and then froze in an instant, to become a scatter of macabre crystals.

"Goodbye, asshole."

God. I hurt everywhere.

Sanity returned. Vivian fell back into the OM and twisted to look down at herself. Her suit was scuffed and greasy, with large, ragged gashes on both shoulders and her right thigh where the inner layers of her suit showed through. She jabbed her chest controls and the fans in her helmet started up again, but her suit pressure was still dropping.

It was compromised. She had leaks from the bullet impacts, probably several. "Oh, shit."

Patches? Where the hell would the Soviets keep suit patches? Cupboards surrounded her in the OM. Patches could be literally anywhere.

Then she heard Makarov's voice in her memory, from that superfast suit briefing in Zvezda before he'd shoved her into the airlock: "If suit breaches, patches in right calf pocket."

Vivian reached down to that same pocket on this suit. Lo and behold, there they were. She pulled out four of the large quick-adhering patches and applied them to her shoulders and thigh.

"Come on. Come on." She squinted. The pressure gauge stopped its slump and slowly, grudgingly, began to crawl back up. "Yeah!"

Okay. Breathe. What next?

Christ, what a mess.

Debris surrounded her, chunks of metal and plastic of various sizes, smashed up by Yashin's hail of bullets.

Yashin's AK-47 was still in the OM, bouncing off the walls. She ignored it, instead pulling herself back into the descent stage with its couches and instrument panels.

Those panels were devastated. Every screen was smashed. Whole rows of lights glowed red, while other areas of the boards no longer had power at all. The central couch where Vivian had sat was broken, split, and fractured. Bullets had even ricocheted into the food supply, because tubes of what looked like borscht and a chicken dish were leaking red liquid and brown paste into the cabin.

This Soyuz was never going anywhere again, at least not under its own power. And since she was apparently now welded to Columbia Station, that was bad.

Vivian got her legs beneath her and shoved herself back through the OM. Cautiously, she leaned out the hatch into space. What had been happening in the rest of the universe, while she'd been fighting for her life?

A mere few hundred feet away was the dark, hostile tube of the Soviet Almaz station, half again as long as Columbia, but not as wide. Bursts of shells erupted from its closer end, the path of those shells clearly delineated by tracer.

So, Night Corps was incoming, and facing a hell of a barrage.

A barrage Vivian could do exactly nothing to prevent.

CHAPTER 50

Lunar Orbit: Peter Sandoval/Vivian Carter/Josh Rawlings
February 12, 1980

Sandoval

Three USAF Lunar Modules screamed in toward Columbia Station.

Well, Sandoval thought, *not a literal scream*. No sound in space. But he was hearing a lot of high frequency noise through his headset, and they were going at one hell of a clip.

"Radar shows the Almaz is moving in," said Pope from the second LM. "Damn it."

"Sonovabitch," Rodriguez agreed, from somewhere behind them both.

Sandoval glanced at radar. Columbia ahead, the Almaz beyond it and getting closer. Pope and Jaffe in LM-2, maybe ten miles back. Rodriguez and Doyle in LM-3 beyond them.

At worst, they'd figured on facing off against the usual Soviet collection of small missiles and grenades. At best, Vivian and the Soviets would be creating a giant ruckus as a distraction, or might even have retaken the station. But an Almaz? Against Sandoval's three puny Lunar Modules, their skins barely thicker than a soda can?

To put it mildly, the odds were not in their favor. Unless they could neutralize the Almaz, they had no hope of applying pressure at Columbia Station.

"Range and rate, yeah?" Brock said, impatient.

"Yes, sorry," Sandoval said, and started chanting numbers in that low drone that NASA astronauts seemed to find so comforting.

He'd rather have had Gerry Lin at the helm. But Gerry was gone, killed in action by the same Soviets that this Lunar Module was now plunging toward.

If he couldn't have Lin, Terri Brock was a damned good alternate. She had more LM experience than Pope or Rodriguez, or even Dark Driver's lead pilot, Doyle. Ellis had volunteered, but an edge had developed between them that Sandoval found unhelpful, plus Ellis was too close to Vivian for an action where she might be in the line of fire. Terri Brock's chops were current and she was super alert; congenial but not afraid to argue with him when necessary. When the pace got hot, Sandoval wanted a pilot who'd just do the right thing without worrying what his reaction might be.

And so there they were, Sandoval and Brock, plunging into battle together. It was military policy to keep women out of combat situations, but screw that. Sandoval had authorized Vivian to head off to Columbia Station with actual Soviets, and he was more than happy to be piloted right now by Brock. This was Sandoval's battlefield, and he'd direct it as he saw fit. His superior officers could give him shit about it later. If he survived.

The fear that had plagued Sandoval on the lunar surface had disappeared. The Moon was terrifying. This? Sandoval had *trained* for this. Long and hard, in Earth orbit. He'd been designing and simming zero-G conflict for years. He barely knew shit about the Moon, but he'd written the book on weightless combat. Literally.

He was worried about Vivian, though. She was likely in a heap of trouble at Columbia. The plans had been strong, but Vivian and her cosmonauts obviously hadn't pulled them off. Soviet comms were alive and well. Even now, Sandoval could hear chatter on their frequencies. Worse, he'd heard that chatter surge when his strike force flew into range. So much for the element of surprise. This strike would be a lot hairier than they'd anticipated.

But Night Corps still had some tricks up their sleeves.

He looked again at the radar. They were zeroing in on Columbia and the Almaz pretty good. As with most rendezvous, they were coming up at it from underneath in an elliptical orbit that would intersect that of the captured station.

485

It was time to finish this. What Sandoval and the others in this combat zone did in the next hour—maybe the next few minutes— might define the US future in space.

"We'll need to avoid their space cannon thing as long as possible," he said.

"Yeah, because ducking and weaving while attempting to match orbits is totally doable," Brock retorted.

"Do what you can."

"Will do." She glanced at the guidance computer. "Okay, time to slam on the brakes."

So saying, she swung the LM around feetfirst and lit the rocket motor. Strong G's pushed them toward the floor. This was the risky moment: exposing their rocket plume, setting themselves up as a target for a missile with an infrared seeker. But they had no choice. To come in fast, they needed to brake fast. A quick, hot burn to decelerate, then they'd flip the ship around again.

Sandoval read out the range and rate. They were just a few miles from Columbia now. Approaching fast, but not too fast. "By the way, you're pretty good."

"Damn right."

"I'm going up top now. Okay?"

"Sure. Don't fall out."

"Roger that."

Sandoval flipped open the hatch above them and shoved himself up, taking care not to bang the complex system of pipes on his back into the hatch edge. Good job the upper hatches on the USAF LMs were wider.

He got gloves onto the rocket launcher they'd mounted up there, and swung it to point at the Almaz.

"LM-1, this is LM-2: no missile launches detected," came Pope's voice. "We're going into braking burn soonest. You have eyes on us, Three?"

"Two, Three: we confirm eyes. You're go for braking."

"Copy, Three," Pope said.

"Break, break," said Sandoval. "Tracer fire incoming from the Almaz."

Here it came, a fast dotted line in space. Bright bursts arced in a ballistic trajectory. Right now the shells were streaking past Sandoval's LM-1 at a considerable distance, but the stream was stepping closer all the time.

"Brock, evasive maneuvers on my mark."

"Roger."

Sandoval grinned savagely. "But let me pop one on the bastards first."

He aimed, as best he could. And fired.

"My missile away."

He heard a crackle, pressed a button to mute it. The Soviets had brought their jammer online, rendering the NASA frequencies unusable.

But Night Corps didn't use the NASA frequencies. So Sandoval just stopped listening to those.

He glanced back to see LM-2 go into its braking burn, then swung eyes-forward again. He didn't see an explosion from the Almaz.

"You missed," Terri said.

"Yeah, Pilot, I copy." He glanced left. "Uh—mark."

"Look on the bright side, you didn't hit Columbia either. Going into avoidance mode."

Sandoval could tell. The LM was already whipping viciously in response to her jet firings. "Oy." Belatedly, he clipped his tether.

Despite Brock's maneuvers, the Rikhter tracer stream veered sharply toward them.

"Hostile missile launched," said Brock. "Get inside."

"Not at us." Sandoval could already tell. That rocket was for LM-2's hot burn. "LM-2, missile incoming. Maximum evasive action. LM-3, be aware: hold off from braking burn."

"Sawbones, get your ass *in here now.*"

He pulled himself back in, acid in his throat. The Almaz had changed the game. He felt cheated.

"Shells incoming!" she shouted, and the cabin jolted. Half a dozen splashes of fire erupted in a line from above their left window to down past the forward hatch. Electronics sparked. "Ah, shit!"

Sandoval had shouted out too as the shells impacted. He leaned back to glance behind him. Sure enough, the Rikhter shells had torn almost instantaneous paths through the front and back of the LM. He must have been bracketed by two of them. A direct hit would have ended him. "Terri?"

"Nicked," she said calmly.

Alarmed, he glanced down at the deep furrow across her armor at upper gut level. That shell had ricocheted off her and blown a foot-wide hole in the cabin behind and to her left; Sandoval could see space through it. "Hell of a nick. Suit integrity?"

"Holding."

He'd already guessed that. In space combat, troops wearing exosuits generally had only two possible statuses: Uninjured, and Dead.

He scanned the instrument panels, some blown out and dark. "Are we okay?"

At the same moment, Pope in LM-2 said: "Had to abort the braking burn. We'll overshoot. Sorry, boss."

"Brock! Are we okay?"

She waggled her right control. The LM responded sluggishly. "Not dead yet. Somehow."

Redundancy. "Good." He took a deep breath. "But we won't last much longer. We'll have to go in light and blow that thing up. Could be a suicide mission."

"Hell with that." The lines around Brock's eyes were tight. "Think of something not-suicide."

Yet again, they saw the flare of the rocket launcher from above the Almaz. "Damn. LM-3, LM-2: disengage, fly on by. We'll go in alone."

"Oh, great," she said.

"Disengaging," said Rodriguez and Pope at the same instant.

Sandoval estimated angles. "Time for our party trick. Ready for pyros?"

"This is going to be freaking uncanny."

"Ready or not, Pilot?"

"Sure. Uh, fire away. This is completely safe, right?"

Sandoval flipped the cover off a red button, then set two dials next to it using a code only he knew. "To be honest, it's never been done with actual people aboard."

Brock swiveled to stare at him in alarm. "You've got to be—"

Sandoval hit the red button with his fist.

Pyros fired under the floor, above them by the hatch, and under the battle LM's skin to left and right. Guillotines sliced through cables. Compressed air shot through metal pipes at impressive pressures.

And the Lunar Module broke apart around them.

"Holy craaap!"

Sandoval reached over to hit three switches on Brock's chest panel. He felt weird doing that, but she was battle-armored from helmet to boots anyway. He glanced down: their exosuits were now connected at the waist by a broad rigid spar of the same armor. He and Terri were literally joined at the hip.

Which was good, because the LM's floor, lander legs, and rocket motor had already spun off fifty feet below them, the engine nozzle still glowing red. Large aluminum chunks of the Module were drifting away more slowly to their right and left. The instrument panels that had been in front of them moments ago, with the windows beside and hatch beneath, had been thrust up and away as a single piece, and that whole unit was turning lazily over and over, the two bug-eyes of the windows swinging around to blink at them in reproach every few seconds.

Just like that, they were out in space. "Wow," said Brock with deep reverence.

"Heads up," Sandoval said tersely. "War zone."

He fired up the jetpack on the back of his suit, which cofired the identical one on Terri's back through the cabling in the spar that connected them, adjusted course using a lever on the spar, and away they went. Soaring upward, black against the stars, toward the Almaz.

Sure enough, moments later the Soviet missile hit the hot descent stage engine that was less than a half-mile below them, silently blowing it to smithereens.

As they swooped in beneath the Almaz, Sandoval could see the wide aperture of its surveillance camera, the Soviet equivalent of the DORIAN system on his MOLs, and was darkly amused that right now he and Brock must fill its field of view.

The Almaz crew were likely too busy for routine surveillance. At least one was operating the Rikhter cannon. Streams of shells studded with tracers still arced across the sky, maybe at LM-3 as it flew by. And as he and Brock approached, Sandoval had glimpsed two cosmonauts in orange suits floating above the Almaz, one holding the rocket launcher, the other supporting him with further ammo and presumably acting as spotter.

"Helm's yours," he said. Their comms ran through the rigid spar that held them together, so the Reds couldn't detect their signal, and they'd been sailing merrily along with only occasional thruster corrections. But even without Brock saying anything, he could tell she was impressed that he'd set a course for the Almaz by eye that had largely gotten them right up to it. Sure, Sandoval was a rookie on-surface. But up here? Close-range orbital mechanics? Lunar three-body problems? This was right in his wheelhouse.

Though, in return, Sandoval was impressed at how calm and matter-of-fact Brock was. She glanced up appraisingly as the Almaz loomed over them. "Target area? Arrival speed?"

Sandoval pointed. "Two-thirds up. None of your fancy NASA braking. Just a fast, hot burst at the end so we don't bounce back to the Moon. Doesn't matter if we hit hard."

The Rikhter cannon was at the fore end of the Almaz, while its camera system, propulsion, and life support system would take up the aft half.

So, two-thirds of the way up would put them against the crew compartment. Quick kill. With the men he'd lost on the Moon, two of his best friends in LM-2 and LM-3, and Vivian stuck on Columbia Station, Sandoval wasn't about to cut the Soviets any slack.

And Brock realized it. "Head shot, then."

"Problem, Pilot?"

"Hells no."

Sandoval had guns strapped to his legs, but left them where they were. Instead he reached down to a bag at his left waist and pulled out a big, chunky tube.

Worry in her tone. "That a nuke, sir?"

"No. Damn near as good, though."

The knobs and dials on the tube were garishly colored and over-sized, for easy use under low-light conditions with astronaut gloves on. Sandoval pushed buttons.

"Impact in thirty-ish seconds. Orders? Last requests?"

Sandoval glanced up. More like twenty-five. They were coming up on the Almaz at such a clip that he'd be terrified if this was his first rodeo. "You have steel balls, Brock."

"Yeah. After we hit?"

"Run like hell. Next stop Columbia. You're driving. I'll fix anything you screw up."

"Ha."

Just when Sandoval thought Brock had left it too late and was about to hit the retros himself, she fired their jets at full power. On the verge of slamming into the Almaz's hull at twenty feet per second, they were thrown forward against the front of their suits. Sandoval distinctly felt a blood vessel burst in his left eye.

He fired up the limpet mine and it leapt out of his hand and adhered soundly to the Almaz.

With the remains of their considerable momentum they banged into the hull just above it and spun away. "Okay?" said Brock.

"Perfect. That mine fires in ten seconds, by the way."

"God *damn*." She'd already canceled out most of the spin, but they were heading upward. "Soviets?"

"On it." As the two orange spacesuits came into view, Sandoval fired three quick blasts from the grenade gun he'd just pulled up from his thigh. One of his grenades caught the nearer cosmonaut in the chest and flared, its explosion throwing the man backward.

"Wrong guy," she said.

"Oh well." Ideally, he'd have killed the one holding the damned rocket launcher. He'd instinctively drawn a bead on the closest target. "Hit the gas, damn it."

Brock lit the candle, and this time the G's were from the rear, pushing them up, up, and away.

The surviving cosmonaut was still swinging the long barrel of the rocket launcher around when the mine exploded. It bloomed like an improbably bright flower, its detonation giving a simultaneous mule kick to the Almaz. The Soviet station yawed, impacting the cosmonaut's boots and knocking him flying, till he reached the end of his tether and swung in a swift arc to thump into the skin of the Almaz. The rocket launcher sailed from his gloved hands.

Beneath the Almaz, all kinds of gear spewed out of the jagged hole from Sandoval's mine blast. Boxes, tools, trays, a disembodied helmet. The explosive decompression had put the Soviet station into a slow spin, and the Rikhter had stopped firing. If any cosmonauts had survived, they'd be plenty busy for a while. "Threat neutralized. Next?" Sandoval looked forward. Brock's trajectory wasn't bad, but they'd miss the station by a good margin. Still better than his own first attempt at something like this, training in Earth orbit—but he might not mention that. "Taking the helm."

He'd expected snark, but Terri just said, "Roger." She rocked back, breathing deep.

Sandoval blipped the jets to make the necessary corrections. "You okay in there?"

"Holy crap," she said. "We killed an Almaz? Just like that?"

And two, maybe four cosmonauts. Sandoval didn't care. "Just like that. Eyes on Columbia, now …. Huh. What the hell's going on down there?"

Carter

"Oh my God." Had the Almaz depressurized? Big gash in its side. In a slow roll. "Hallelujah." But she still saw no sign of Night Corps. What the hell was going on?

Then, between Columbia and the stricken Almaz, Vivian glimpsed the unmistakable flare of jets. Something was approaching Columbia at speed, something that was neither a Lunar Module nor a solo astronaut.

She'd seen one LM explode, and another two flash by. Had one of them managed to score a number on the Almaz, in passing?

If so, this might be the evacuating crew of the Almaz, bearing down on her. What did she have left to defend herself with?

Well, she had an AK-47. And a flare pistol. A shotgun. Even a goddamned machete.

Coldly and calmly, Vivian ducked back into the Soyuz to fetch them.

Sandoval

"Cosmonaut," Brock said tersely. "With an AK-47. Second cosmonaut floating nearby, probably a goner. We can hope."

"I see him." Sandoval swung his gun up. "Slow us down. LM-2, LM-3: we have eyes on Columbia. Two Soyuz and a Progress on the boom. A second Progress attached to Columbia. Soviet propulsion module on Columbia's base. One hostile in view." Only one? No comms at all on Soviet frequencies, and the jammer had stopped jamming. What was up?

"He's not firing," Terri said.

"Yet." Probably waiting for them to get closer. As soon as Sandoval saw the AK-47 muzzle flash, he'd blow the guy away. Maintaining his aim with his left hand, Sandoval reached down to his right thigh and pulled out a second limpet mine.

"Wait, you're going to bomb *Columbia*?"

"Maybe. There's a nuke in that Progress, Pilot. Right now, I'm ready for anything."

"And three of our people aboard the station. And Vivian, somewhere."

"*Columbia* is dark. Our guys could be dead or gone already." Sandoval swallowed. "Terri, Vivian's likely the dead one we see. Tried to take the nuke out, but couldn't." Meaning the guy in his sights had probably killed her. His finger itched.

But he didn't know for sure. Couldn't pull the trigger till he did. Even though that meant breaking radio silence, and putting himself and Terri at risk.

"Damn it."

He flipped switches on his chest, and pushed-to-talk on all three relevant frequencies, in the clear. "Columbia, this is Night Corps."

They saw the AK-47 waver. "Peter?"

Holy shit. "Vivian? If that's you, drop the goddamned gun."

"No problem." She scooped up what looked like a fistful of weapons and shoved them back through the hatch beneath her, into the Soyuz. "*You* blew up the Almaz?"

"Break, report. Status aboard Columbia?"

"Back in US hands, with our friends' help. But the power's out and the hatch is jammed. They're trapped in there. Yashin's last gasp." She pointed at the drifting corpse. "Meet Yashin."

"Way to go, girl," Brock said.

Astonishment in Vivian's voice. "Terri? *You're* here?"

"Where else would I be?"

Jeez, ladies. "Cut the chatter. Any other hostiles around?"

"None nearer than the Almaz. That I know of."

"Yeah, we decommissioned the Almaz," said Terri.

"I saw."

Sandoval shoved the limpet mine back into its pocket and holstered the gun. The seething restlessness of combat still swarmed in his veins, and he was almost sorry there was no one else left to kill. "Okay, we'll head for the docking adapter—Whoa!"

At the same time, Brock said: "Ohh, crap," and Vivian gave a short yelp.

Beneath them, Columbia Station lurched as a rocket plume shot from its base.

The propulsion module was igniting.

Rawlings

Inside Columbia, Rawlings felt a jolt as the entire station pitched up around him and yawed left. The Soviet propulsion unit had activated.

Its burn would take them out of orbit, setting them on a course that would intersect the Moon's surface right at Daedalus Base, blowing them and everyone else to hell.

In minutes, their fate would be sealed.

Rawlings was going down with his ship, along with Dardenas, Zabrinski, and the three good Russians who'd put their lives on the line to defy Yashin and help them.

And there was exactly nothing Rawlings could do about it. Columbia Station had small thrusters to change its attitude, but they were currently powered off and Rawlings knew Yashin would have disabled them anyway. Was there any other way to drive Columbia Station off course as it plummeted toward the lunar surface? Even a small lateral thrust might save Daedalus, though the end result would be the same for Rawlings and his crew.

The only thing he could think of was a deliberate explosive decompression. And he didn't even have anything aboard that could cause such an explosion.

But maybe someone else did.

"We need radio," he said. "And we need it now."

Carter

As the Soviet propulsion module fired, Vivian immediately felt the surge of its acceleration and grabbed the hatch rim, teetering on the brink of being tossed out into space. She swung dangerously, her boots thumping into cupboards inside the Orbital Module.

The lunar surface tilted up toward her. The station was already turning. The throbbing vibration of the module's thrust purred through her gloves.

Vivian's Soyuz flexed and wallowed, but stayed attached firmly to the Progress. They were already opening up separation from the crippled Almaz. *Damn it.*

Yashin had programmed the burn, and set it with a deadman's switch so it would go ahead unless he canceled it himself. Of *course* he'd do that. And now Columbia, the Progress, Vivian's Soyuz, and Vivian herself—they were all going down together. They'd smash onto the surface in what? Ten minutes or so?

She'd probably prevented Yashin and Erdeli from arming the nuke. But the kinetic impact of Columbia Station would still annihilate Dark Driver and slaughter Johnston and the other USAF astros, plus Ellis and Buchanan. Death would be mercifully instantaneous, but Vivian still had several minutes left to ponder its approach.

She glanced into the Soyuz cabin. She might be able to blow Columbia off course by detonating her Soyuz's self-destruct. A final, desperate act.

Vivian wouldn't die watching the Moon surging up to pulverize her. She'd have to die sooner, knowing she'd done everything she could to ensure Ellis's survival. Assuming the self-destruct circuits even still worked, after all the bullets that Yashin had sprayed around.

Vivian's last resort. And she'd know within seconds whether she'd need to use it.

She flipped the switch on her radio. "Minerva, Vivian. Hey, Dave? I need a miracle here, buddy."

Horn's voice rang in her ear. "Roger that, Commander. I'm on it."

CHAPTER 51

Columbia Station: Vivian Carter
February 12, 1980

SHE looked up and there he was, a silver speck rising from his hiding place behind the abandoned Apollo 32 third stage, half a mile back in orbit, and by now noticeably *above* her, as the triple-goddamned Soviet propulsion module continued its inexorable braking burn.

Minerva was moving *fast*. Much faster than the usual Dave Horn deliberative maneuver. Way faster even than his return with Athena to pick up Vivian on that long-ago day of the original Soviet attack on Columbia.

"What're you gonna do?"

"Don't ask. Buckle up."

Buckle up? Vivian was still hanging half out of her hatch, her upper torso in space, watching shit fly all around her. "Roger that."

She slid inside, threw herself across the Orbital Module and back into the shot-up, beat-up Descent Module. The commander's seat was unusable. She spun backward into Belyakova's right-hand seat, lashed herself in as best she could, peered out of the window.

Here came Minerva, roaring in *damned* fast. It was somehow flying toward her butt-first, because she could see the SPS engine cone. "Jeez, Dave. You found yourself an Agena?"

"Hush. Concentrating."

Minerva wasn't pointing right at her. She'd have worried if it was, because—orbital mechanics being what they were—that would mean Horn was about to shoot right on by. What he was actually doing was plunging into a slightly lower orbit to overhaul her, at which point he'd surge back up to rendezvous.

Of course, since Columbia's own current "orbit" would soon become a ballistic trajectory homing in on Farside like a brick, Horn didn't have a lot of time.

Horn was figuring this out, literally on the fly. He could easily screw this up. Very easily. Super easily.

The Soviet propulsion module was a minute into its braking burn. The Moon loomed queasily in Vivian's window.

Oh my God.

Fear gripped her. She didn't want to die like this.

Live for the Moon, die for the Moon.

"Mayday, Mayday, this is Josh Rawlings in Columbia Station. Vivian? Night Corps? Anyone?"

The signal was faint. She gulped, answered confidently. "Hey Josh, Vivian here."

"Vivian! Thank God. Where are you? We're trapped in here without power. I'm communicating through a suit radio. And the propulsion module is firing—"

"Break-break, Josh. I know. No time. Hold on. Have everyone strap in, anchor themselves, right now. Your ride's about to get *real* rough .... Whoa, holy *shit!*"

"What? Viv, what the hell is happening?"

She'd asked for a miracle, and Command Module Pilot Dave Horn was bringing it. Or maybe he'd just annihilate them all even sooner. He'd already been surging in like a bat out of hell. And now he was flipping his craft end over end to come in Agena-forward. As he did so he fired up Minerva's SPS, the rocket motor at the base of the Command and Service Module, meaning he was *still* accelerating, Jesus H. Christ ...

Horn was going to ram Columbia Station.

Great for saving Dark Driver. Crap for saving Vivian and the Columbia crew.

"Columbia, Vivian. Brace for impact."

The Agena's rocket lit moments after the CSM rocket flickered out. Horn had just gone from a brutal eyes-in acceleration to an equally painful eyes-out deceleration. So he wouldn't ram at full speed. But still …

Horn's voice, calm in her headset: "Impact in five seconds. Hi guys. Miss me?"

"Hi yourself," Vivian said, and then Horn plowed into Columbia Station, Agena-first.

A crash, a titanic shaking, and everything went hazy as Vivian's head banged against the back of her helmet, whiplashing her neck painfully. She heard two screams at the same time, one her own, the other the transmitted shock of grinding metal. The Soyuz thrashed around her as if buffeted by a heavy sea. Would this collision shake her loose, throw the Soyuz clear? If so, whatever happened to Columbia Station, Vivian would still crash onto the Moon.

But, no, the buffeting continued. She was still attached.

"Ow, God's sakes," she said. "Dave? Dave? Josh?"

"Stand by," Horn said laconically. "Trying to figure out which way is up."

All Vivian could see out her window was stars. "Can I help?"

"Yeah, be quiet for a moment."

She felt a vertiginous swaying and another lurch, and then everything stabilized. They were still accelerating, but sideways now. The G's were pushing her painfully to her right, into the Soyuz wall.

She tried to figure that out. Accelerating … where?

More so than before, that much was clear. Perhaps two G's? But in which direction?

Safety be damned. Vivian unbuckled and crawled painfully along the side of the Descent Module into the globe of the OM. Used to seeing it in weightlessness, the section of cupboards where she'd used the facilities a few hours ago had become the floor.

"Columbia Station, report."

Nothing. That wasn't good.

"Peter, Terri?" Also nothing. Also not good.

The hatch at the far side of the OM was still open to space. It seemed a hell of a lot farther away than it used to be.

A smart astronaut would tether herself, about now. Vivian had no tether handy. She'd earlier disconnected the one on her suit. It was out on the boom somewhere.

Without actually pulling herself out the hatch, which would be a step too far, all she could see was … stars. *So unhelpful.*

She opened the drawer and pulled out the hose from the waste management system. It was pretty long. She looped it around her ankle, tied it off as best she could. "Bathroom tether."

The G's eased, which made her feel even more queasy. Dizzy, she wondered whether she'd given herself a concussion against her own helmet. "No throwing up, babe. Hang in there. Damn, I hurt."

"Vivian, Josh. You all right? You're not making any sense."

Vivian's microphone was live. She'd have to get out of the habit of talking to herself. "Pretty much. How about in there?"

"Don't know. It's dark. Are we still crashing?"

She laughed, a spikey sound more painful than humorous. "I dunno, man, what are the odds?"

"We're going up," said Horn. "But, even so."

Vivian heaved herself half out of the hatch, took a look. "Yeah, no kidding."

The Agena had speared through the weaker unpressurized waste tank area between the crew compartment and the propulsion module. Minerva was still attached to it. The Soviet module was still firing. Minerva's SPS rocket engine was firing. The combined crashed mess of Columbia, the Progress, the Soyuz, and the CSM-Agena was heading off upward at what looked like a forty-degree angle to the lunar surface.

As she watched, the SPS engine cut out. "Dave?"

"What?"

"Report."

"Working it. Taking star sightings."

"Minerva, you dry on fuel?"

"Nope. Saving the rest for contingency."

"Contingency?" That was almost funny. Almost.

"Vivian?" That was Josh's voice. "Please tell us what the hell is going on?"

"Columbia, Vivian. Dave Horn drove Apollo 32 into Columbia Station, shoving it off course and turning it. Forcing the Soviet propulsion unit to blast us into a higher orbit. So now we're going up, not down."

Vivian took another look and grimaced. "However, it's visually apparent that our trajectory is seriously elliptical. Horn is taking sightings to determine whether our new orbit will still intersect the lunar surface."

"Oh," Rawlings said. "Uh, roger that. What happened to Yashin?"

"He died."

"Died?"

"I blew his helmet open my own self."

"Break, break," came Horn's terse voice. "I'm overloaded here. Anyone have a guidance computer handy?"

Crap. "My Soyuz is dead," Vivian said.

A new voice came on the line from Columbia Station. "Major Horn, *dobryy den'*. This is Nikolai Makarov. May I be of assistance?"

"*You* have a guidance computer?"

Rawlings cut in. "Regrettably unpowered."

Columbia Station's main power rack was in the airlock module. The jammed hatch prevented the Columbia crew from reaching it. But Vivian was outside Columbia, just forty feet away from the outside of that airlock. She could *see* the damned thing.

"I'm starting to really hate spacewalks," she said.

"Say again, Vivian?"

The Moon crawled by beneath her. The terminator back into dark was fast approaching. By now, Columbia Station must be at least a hundred miles above the surface. The Soviet propulsion module burn looked like it was fading, but everything was still shaking around like crazy.

Both Vivian's shoulders, her neck, and her right leg all hurt like hell from the bullet impacts. Many of her muscles felt wrenched out of their sockets. But …

No rest for the wicked. "I said: hang in there. I'm on my way."

"Belay that," said Brock. "We got this."

"Got what?"

"Sandoval and I are inside the Multiple Docking Adapter."

"You *are*?"

"We said we were heading here."

"Yeah, but—"

"Restoring main power breaker," said Sandoval, and at the same moment the headset crackled really *loud* and Josh Rawlings gave a most unprofessional whoop.

"You're welcome," said Terri Brock.

Working against time in far from ideal circumstances and in separate locations, the best orbital mechanics experts of the US and the USSR determined their ephemeris and calculated a correction burn. The resulting orbit was still elongated, but survivably so. Its lowest point took the smashed-together conglomerate craft down to a gut-churning nine miles above the lunar surface. Now outside again, Vivian watched the craters, rilles, and mountains of the Moon pass beneath her without blinking.

By the time they reached their crazy orbit's highest point an hour later, Makarov and Horn had agreed on the parameters of a second burn that would—once again—exhaust the SPS rocket motor but would put Columbia, plus its Soviet and NASA appendages, into a much saner 140-mile by 90-mile ellipse.

And there they'd remain, astronauts and cosmonauts looping the loop around the Moon together, until someone came to rescue them.

CHAPTER 52

Eagle Station: Vivian Carter/Nikolai Makarov
February 17, 1980

IT took the surviving Americans and Soviets the rest of that day to stabilize Columbia Station. Makarov and Okhotina tidied up blood and bodies and made their wounded comfortable, while Rawlings and Dardenas restored the station's systems. Still outside, Peter Sandoval, Terri Brock, Dave Horn, and Vivian Carter cut away the wreckage of Soyuz TS-1 and the grisly remains of Pavel Erdeli, and wormed and hammered a path into the crumpled Progress module to confirm that the nuke was safe, not armed, its containment not breached.

After that, they'd transferred into Columbia Station, helped to take inventory and plan how to ration their little remaining food, called home to report ... and then, exhausted, had tethered themselves to whatever anchor points were available, and fallen asleep.

Four days later Apollo Rescue 2 arrived from Earth, this time a genuine mission of mercy. It consisted of a Skylab, pristine and shiny, similar to Columbia Station, with a crew of four, two of them trauma surgeons, and an orbiting fuel depot almost the same size as the Skylab. The NASA astronauts knew nothing of such a depot, but Sandoval admitted it was a familiar component of the USAF's presence in space.

Horn and Vivian, along with Makarov and Okhotina, refueled the Minerva CSM and their two remaining Soyuz craft and—after much deliberation and back-and-forth with both Houston and Baikonur—devised a schedule of burns everyone could agree on to transition the small flotilla of US and Soviet craft down to a more nominal circular orbit.

As Dave Horn said, somewhat tongue in cheek: it was much easier when they'd been left to themselves to figure it out on the fly.

Makarov

"Comrade Nikolai, a word."

Makarov turned as Vivian Carter floated through the hatch into the fore compartment of the new Skylab, with Peter Sandoval close behind. "Ah, Vivian." He gestured about him. "I like this one much better."

"I bet. Don't get any bright ideas about stealing it, though."

"That's really not funny," Rawlings said, from the comms board.

"Oh, hey." Vivian looked around. "Anyone else in earshot?"

"Don't think so. Two of the Eagles are out taking pictures of the Soyuz craft. One's tending to Svetlana. One's asleep."

"Good. Nikolai, we need to talk about, well, a whole bunch of things before you blow out of here."

Makarov, Belyakova, and Okhotina had been ordered to break lunar orbit and return to Earth within twenty-four hours. Makarov was glad. They had Svetlana strapped up and connected to a pressurized IV; Yashin's bullets had just missed her lung but broken two ribs. She was stable, and should pull through, but Nikolai wanted to get her to a real hospital as soon as possible, and get on with ... whatever the hell was going to happen next. Face whatever music awaited him, and get back to his real life.

Hopefully.

He looked from Vivian to Peter and back again. Their expressions were serious. "Should Svetlana hear this too?" It would give him an excuse to get back to her. He felt lost without her at his side.

Vivian grimaced. "Let her rest. Girlfriend needs her beauty sleep. Brief her later, as you see fit."

"Very well."

Rawlings floated up out of his chair. "Want me to split if y'all are talking secrets?"

"No, stick around," said Sandoval, and to Makarov: "How much do you know about what's going on in the Soviet Union right now?"

"Very little."

"So you're not aware that Andropov has ousted Brezhnev?"

Makarov frowned. "'Ousted'?"

"A coup, Nikolai. Leonid Brezhnev has been removed from office. After fifteen-plus years, he is no longer the big boss of your country."

"Nonsense," Makarov said automatically, and then frowned. "Really?"

"You guys don't get much news," Vivian said ironically.

Makarov's contacts with his own Mission Control had been limited to logistical matters. "No. *Yuri Andropov* removed Brezhnev?"

"Sure did," Sandoval said. "It came as a surprise to us as well. We had our eyes on several guys jockeying for position. Suslov. Kulakov. Chernenko. But I guess we never paid enough attention to Andropov."

"To be fair, no one has ever vaulted up to become Chairman of the Presidium directly from being head of the KGB," Vivian said. "That's quite a feat."

"Allegedly, the orders to invade Afghanistan and then Pakistan came from Brezhnev," Sandoval said. "Andropov publicly opposed both military interventions. He was one of the few. Now that everything is falling apart in south central Asia, that's making him look pretty smart."

"It is falling apart?"

"Yep," Vivian said. "The Red Army is getting its butt kicked. Regret to inform."

"But ... Yashin was getting his orders directly from Comrade Andropov."

"Right. Our people are telling us that Andropov was behind *all* this lunar escalation. It was Andropov, through the Soviet espionage machine, who first suspected the existence of Dark Driver. But now Yashin's out of the picture," Sandoval grinned at Vivian, "and everything's gone south for the USSR up here as well, Andropov is blaming Brezhnev for all this, in addition to the Asian debacle."

Sandoval glided to the wall, anchored himself easily by his foot. Makarov reminded himself that the American had a great deal more zero-G experience than he did. "Brezhnev's health has been failing for years. He smokes too much, drinks too much vodka. Recently he's been suffering from emphysema and chronic bronchitis, and his heart isn't going great guns either. Indications are that he's been fitted with a pacemaker. We've seen him suffer from speaking problems and coordination issues at public events, so he may have had a stroke or two."

Astonishing. "You know all this?"

"We do."

The last time Brezhnev had pinned a medal on him, Makarov had recognized that the man smelled strongly of cigarettes and was getting old and a little feeble, but if all this were true, the US was amazingly well informed.

Apparently, Vivian noted his bafflement. "Nikolai, much of that is obvious just from seeing him on TV." There, again, the Americans had the advantage over him. In Russia, only the great speeches were televised. Makarov was well aware that the Soviet publicity machine was carefully curated. He found it tedious, though sometimes amusing when watching the hagiography and hero worship of himself and his fellow cosmonauts. But, how else to keep a country the size of the USSR stable?

"And so, it was pretty easy for Andropov to argue that all this was Brezhnev's fault. That his decisions were dangerous and not to be trusted, and move him out of the way."

Makarov nodded slowly. It was a lot to absorb. "And so it was Brezhnev who became the useful fool."

"Brezhnev the scapegoat," Sandoval agreed. "He's been invited to spend the rest of his days at his dacha. Yuri Andropov is in the driver's seat now."

"Then this is not over yet." Nikolai wondered whether they understood that. "Chairman Brezhnev might have been open to reason, to compromise, but Andropov? Yashin is gone, but Andropov has many more Yashins. And Dark Driver cannot remain to threaten my country." Had all their efforts, and Svetlana's pain, been for nothing?

"I agree," Vivian said. "That Dark Driver has to go, I mean."

"Many other people agree," Sandoval said.

"They do *now*," she said, pinning him with a glance.

"I mean back on Earth."

"I don't get it." Rawlings was shaking his head. "By the way, Nikolai, I'm just as in the dark about all this as you. At least it explains why this precious pair were spending all that time on comms, while the rest of us were cleaning up. We figured they were just goofin' off."

"Dark Driver was a gamble," Vivian said. "The USAF, the Senate Armed Services Committee, Nixon, and now Reagan. They'd all counted on completing it before the Soviets even learned it was under development."

"Stealing a march on the Commies," Sandoval said. "Uh. No offense."

"As it is, well. The Soviet Union now has cast-iron evidence that we—the US—have initiated a massive step forward in the militarization of space. If that goes public, it creates a huge public relations issue for the Reagan White House. If they'd managed to make it operational before it was discovered, it would be a different matter. The President could take the glory as a master strategist, keeping the country safe. Revealed while it's still under construction, he just looks like a bumbler."

Rawlings clearly wasn't convinced. "So what? If Reagan carries on denying it, folks will believe him. Lots of people love him, and hate the Soviet Union. Uh, again, no offense, Nikolai."

"You're forgetting what year it is," Sandoval said.

"1980?"

"Election year. Reagan barely beat Carter in 1976, and now he's up against the same guy for reelection in November. We've had the oil crisis, the Iranian hostage crisis, and Three Mile Island, all over the past year and all on Reagan's watch. A lot of people feel that he's too combative. That his foreign policy is too aggressive. He's on shaky ground, and he can't afford to let the information about Dark Driver come out now. Have the country find out he lied? Have the *Soviets* be the ones who reveal it? The Democrats would make hay with that. Reagan's got to know he'd lose the presidency in the fall." Sandoval shook his head. "If we could have kept Driver under wraps for another year, it would all have been fine."

"Fine for you," Makarov said.

"Yes, Comrade. Fine for me, and my country."

Vivian shoved him, dislodging him and sending him floating off across the fore compartment. "Thanks, Viv. That was real mature."

Vivian grinned and turned to Nikolai. "Long story short: they've struck a deal."

"Who have?"

"Reagan and Andropov."

"You're kidding," Rawlings said. "Already?"

"Four days is a long time in politics."

"Vivian may have had something to do with that." Sandoval reached the far wall, pushed off, and floated slowly back.

Makarov looked at her. "You?"

"Or, or: it may be just coincidence," Vivian said.

"Coincidence that two superpowers are doing just what you pitched to Young, Kraft, and the NASA Administrator?" John Young was the Chief Astronaut, a veteran of Gemini and early Apollo. Chris Kraft was the Director of the Johnson Space Center. "What are the odds?"

"Whatever," Vivian said. "Besides, it was *you* who then pitched it to the Air Force Chiefs of Staff."

"What have Reagan and Andropov agreed to?" Rawlings said impatiently.

Vivian gave them the rundown. Through the Soviet state-owned media, Andropov had publicly denounced the actions of political officer Sergei Yashin, whose mental health issues were clearly exacerbated by the stresses of spaceflight. The Presidium of the Supreme Soviet dissociated themselves entirely from Yashin's unauthorized acts of nuclear vandalism and murder on the Moon. They'd announced that Yashin's actions had far exceeded his mandate.

Counterbalancing the criminal behavior of Yashin were the prompt and selfless actions of Heroes of the Soviet Union Makarov and Belyakova in supporting Communist ideals by safeguarding Soviet assets and extending the hand of friendship to NASA astronauts in peril.

Through its occupation of Columbia Station, Andropov claimed that the Soviet Union had merely sought to defend its right of precedence. In the spirit of international brotherhood and peace, Andropov announced that they now generously relinquished that right.

Soviet troops began to withdraw from Pakistan the same day.

In the same magnanimous spirit, Reagan welcomed Andropov to power and praised his initiative, expressing a desire for cooperation in space. He proposed mutual investment in two areas: a Soviet-US collaboration at Copernicus Crater, building on the initial steps the Soviets had made there, and a second US-Soviet base, to be constructed on the Moon's far side. He revealed that the US had already been searching Farside for prospective sites for a science station and sensitive radio telescope array for astronomy, free from interference from Earth broadcasts, and invited the Soviets to participate.

Daedalus Base was never publicly mentioned. As part of the back-room deal, Dark Driver would be dismantled. While the Cold War would undoubtedly continue on Earth, the exploration of space would henceforth be a peaceful activity with joint support by both superpowers.

It was quietly accepted by everyone that US Manned Orbiting Laboratories and Soviet Almaz stations would be established in lunar orbit—eyes in the sky—each capable of monitoring the other's actions on the surface. "Trust, but verify," in Reagan's memorable phrasing. In addition, both nations expressed a willingness to restart the long-stalled SALT II: strategic arms limitations talks.

Rawlings nodded. "So, everyone gets to cover their asses."

"Maybe." Vivian sobered. "Nikolai? What will this mean for you? Will you be safe when you get home, with Andropov at the helm?"

"I have no idea," Makarov said.

"But he's a hero," Rawlings objected. "Again. Didn't you just say that?"

"Yes, and he got to be a hero by fighting Andropov's guy every step of the way," said Sandoval.

"End result: Dark Driver will be decommissioned. And the Reds will never answer for what they did to Hadley, or to my Columbia Station. Am I right? Seems like a pretty sweet deal."

"Or for blowing up my MOL-7," Sandoval reminded him.

"And we'll never be called to task for sabotaging Zvezda and blowing up an Almaz," Vivian said dryly. She took Makarov by the arm and turned him to face her. "Nikolai? Time to choose. If you want to come to the US, we can help you. There's still time. We'll make it work."

Now, even Sandoval looked dubious. "How, exactly?"

"We'll figure out how. And negotiate to get your wife and kids out too."

"My wife would never leave." Makarov dropped his gaze. "And ... Svetlana will never leave, either. I will be all right."

Vivian looked at him for a long moment. "Whatever you say. Though, maybe you could visit? International cooperation and all. See the bad old imperialist nation for yourself?"

"Nikolai?" From the hatch, Belyakova floated up toward them, hair tousled, her left arm strapped across her body. Pale, but moving. Makarov's heart leaped at the sight of her.

Life was much too complicated.

"Should you be up?" Vivian demanded.

Belyakova eyed her. "Should I not?"

Vivian shook her head. "That is *such* a Svetlana response. You're going to be just fine, aren't you?"

"Sorry to disappoint you." Svetlana looked from face to face. "What is happening? What have you all been talking about?"

Carter

"After all this?" Sandoval said, "I'm done with vacuum."

Vivian looked at him sideways. "Can't hardly blame you."

After some further discussion, Makarov had ushered Belyakova away, and Rawlings had beaten a strategic retreat back to Columbia Station. Leaving the two of them alone in the wide open space of the Eagle Station forward compartment.

It was almost disconcerting. This much clean, free, space, with only two people in it? And no one attacking them? Vivian had the urge to race back and forth between the walls, set herself spinning in midair, just for the joy of it. Be Rocket Girl for real.

She hadn't died. Neither had Josh Rawlings, or Peter Sandoval, or Ellis and Horn.

Some had. Rick Norton. Dunlap, Ibarra, and Klein. Gerry Lin. Moody and Jensen.

But most of them would live to tell the tale. It could all have been so much worse.

She tried to focus on what Sandoval was saying.

"I mean it. Once I get my feet back on Earth soil, I'm staying there. I'll put in for a ground assignment training future MOL crews at Vandenberg, and Night Corps crews at, well, doesn't matter where. And once my time in the Air Force is done, I'm guessing I've racked up enough military miles that one of the commercial airlines would give me a shot."

Vivian smiled. "Really? The great secret agent and military hero Peter Sandoval is going to ferry pudgy businessmen around on Pan Am?"

"Uh, yeah? Sure."

"Let me know how that works out."

He gave her a patient look. "Vivian. My point is: once we get ourselves back to Earth, back to normality?"

"Normality." She pretended to look confused. "We had a briefing on that once. I didn't take notes. It sounded boring. What about it?"

509

"I'm thinking that we might have a future together."

Damn. And just like that, Colonel Sandoval goes in for the kill.

Was not watching out for that. Might not be as smart as I think I am.

"Huh." Her mind whirled.

Well. Maybe, just maybe, it wasn't a crazy idea.

Flying, and then spaceflight, had been Vivian's life, her all-consuming passions for a long time. Years. And even after this, she wasn't done. Unlike Peter, she wasn't ready to commit to staying in atmosphere for the rest of her life.

Space was addictive. Even now, the Moon was addictive. But once Vivian got back to Earth, it might be a while before she'd get assigned to another crew.

She'd have time to kick back. To not have every day planned out and filled with peril. Time to focus on something other than hardware. And Peter was a good guy. Brave, smart. Solid. Perhaps even easy on the eye. And one of the few guys Vivian knew who wouldn't be blind-sided by her stubbornness and dedication, her love of spaceflight.

Peter was waiting, watching her think it through. Not pushing her. So at least he knew her *that* well.

She grinned. "Maybe. Once we're back in real gravity, and we have real forks and knives again … maybe we could go for dinner. And then take it from there. See whether there's any chance of, well, anything. Once we're away from all *this*."

Sandoval smiled back in relief. "A chance is all I'm asking."

"But …. In the meantime, you know I'm going with Ellis, right?"

His expression switched around with almost comical speed. "Wait. *With* Ellis?"

Vivian peered at him. "Yeah. With Ellis."

Sandoval just looked at her.

"Uh, because he's my *crew*? Sawbones, this is Apollo 32, do you read?"

"Really?" Again, he broke into a grin. "Oh! Sure, 32. I read you five by five." He thought about it a little more. "Wow. You're a real operator, you know that?"

"Takes one to know one." Vivian leaned forward. "And it's just dinner, when we get back to Earth. We're clear on that? Until we figure out an up and a down?"

"Dinner would be great. And, hey. Have a blast with … your crew."

"Thanks, man." Vivian nodded. "Certainly plan to."

CHAPTER 53

Moonfall: Vivian Carter
February 29, 1980
Mission Elapsed Time (Hours, Reset): 109:45:00

THE Marius Hills stood alone and silent, as they had for a billion years: four large cinder cones, and beneath them a web of lava tubes, dark and undisturbed.

A craft appeared in the sky above. It approached in a long arc, spewing fire to decelerate, at times almost coming to a standstill over the rocky surface, before nuzzling down to a near-perfect landing in between two of the main cinder cones, and—as it eventually turned out—less than a half mile from the most easily accessible of the lava tubes.

Inside the Lunar Module, Ellis Mayer wiped sweat from his neck and turned to Vivian Carter. "That was a bit casual. I wasn't even sure you were paying attention."

Vivian grinned. "Sorry. It was my fourth landing, and only one of those was technically a crash."

"Huh. Well, okay, then."

"To remind you, I wasn't at the controls for the crash."

"Sure. It's all good."

"Yes. Yes, it is. Houston, be advised that Apollo 32 has landed at Marius Hills on its mission of exploration and scientific understanding."

CAPCOM responded as promptly as the Earth-Moon distance allowed: "We copy you down, Athena. All indications are that you are Stay at T-minus-one."

"Houston, 32, that's a roger on Stay."

Vivian glanced at Ellis. "Well, then. Let's get to work."

Ellis released his harness. "Roger that."

Out of the window, Vivian could see the broad swelling shapes of the cinder cones. No forbidding mountain ranges, no mighty peaks. No other lunar craft, no base, no tangles of cables or piles of garbage. Pristine territory.

From close orbit above came the voice of Dave Horn: "I copy you down, and see you on my scope. Godspeed at Marius Hills, Athena."

"Thank you, Minerva." Vivian paused, still drinking in the harsh terrain, then smiled. "Hey, Dave? Thanks a *whole lot*. Stay in touch. We'll see you again real soon."

"Looking forward to it, Commander. Enjoy."

Ellis looked at her sideways. "So, pop the top? Standing EVA to check it all out?"

A glow of quiet joy filled her. "You know it."

Vivian Carter would get her Moon, after all.

ACKNOWLEDGEMENTS

Moon-sized thanks are due to my agent, Caitlin Blasdell of Liza Dawson Associates, and to the whole crew at CAEZIK SF & Fantasy who helped bring this book to life: Shahid Mahmud, Lezli Robyn, Christina P. Myrvold, Leylya Udimamedova, Marne Evans, and Debra Nichols, plus Mickey Mikkelson of Creative Edge. I'm also extremely grateful to my valiant beta readers who read all or part of *Hot Moon*, and/or provided specialist help on some aspects of the story, among them Karen Smale, Kelly Dwyer, Stephen Blount, Ken Carpenter, Rick Wilber, Chris Cevasco, Jeff Petersen, and Tetyana Royzman. Any blunders that remain should be assigned to me alone.

Hot Moon has been a long time in the making. I started writing it in mid-2017, and the first complete version went out to my agent and beta readers in October 2019. Of course, soon after that the world was plunged into the coronavirus pandemic and everything ... slowed down, quite a bit. While COVID-19 was far too gloomy a topic to refer to in a Dedication at the front of the book, I'd certainly like to salute the heroic efforts of medical professionals of all types, supermarket workers, and the many, many other essential personnel who kept (and, at the time of writing, are still keeping) the country going under working conditions ranging from unenviable to horrendous. Hats off to all of them.

DRAMATIS PERSONAE

Americans

Apollo 32:

    Vivian Carter—Commander (CDR)
    Ellis Mayer—Lunar Module Pilot (LMP)
    Dave Horn—Command Module Pilot (CMP)

Columbia Station:

    Josh Rawlings—Station Commander; Apollo 21 CMP
    Gary Wagner—Flight Engineer; Apollo 22 CMP
    Danny Zabrinski—Flight Engineer; Apollo 26 CMP
    Marco Dardenas—Flight Engineer; Apollo 27 CMP
    Curtis Jackson—Flight Engineer; Apollo 30 CMP
    Ed Mason—Flight Engineer; Apollo 31 CMP

USAF Manned Orbiting Laboratory-7:

    Peter Sandoval—Commander
    Gerry Lin—Flight Engineer
    Kevin Pope—Flight Engineer
    Jose Rodriguez—Flight Engineer

Hadley Base:

    Rick Norton—Base Commander; Apollo 21 CDR
    Casey Buchanan—Deputy Base Commander; Apollo 21 LMP

    Jim Dunlap—Apollo 22 CDR
    Ryan "Starman" Jones—Apollo 22 LMP

Allen Collier—Apollo 25 CDR
Terri Brock—Apollo 25 LMP
Ron Lawrence—Apollo 25 CMP

Bill Dobbs—Apollo 26 CDR
Christian Vasquez—Apollo 26 LMP

Dan Klein—Apollo 27 CDR
Luis Ibarra—Apollo 27 LMP

Gregory Leverton—Apollo 29 CDR
Kevin McDowell—Apollo 29 LMP
Feye Gisemba—Apollo 29 CMP

Joe Seaton—Apollo 30 CDR
Carol Massey—Apollo 30 LMP

Ben Epps—Apollo 31 CDR
Jack Flynn—Apollo 31 LMP

Soviets

First Assault Team:

Nikolai Makarov—Soyuz TS-1 Commander
Svetlana Belyakova—Soyuz TS-1 Flight Engineer
Oleg Vasiliev—Soyuz TS-1 Technician

Yuri Galkin—Soyuz TS-2 Commander
Sergei Yashin—Soyuz TS-2 Flight Engineer
Lev Chertok—Soyuz TS-2 Technician

Pavel Erdeli—Soyuz TS-3 Commander
Viktoriya Isayeva—Soyuz TS-3 Flight Engineer
Boris Salkov—Soyuz TS-3 Technician

Other Named Cosmonauts:

Katya Okhotina—Soyuz TS-5 Flight Engineer
Yelena Rudenko—Commander, Zvezda Base

APOLLO LUNAR LANDING MISSION SEQUENCE

Mission Series specifications

G-series: First US landing. 2-man landing crew, 1-day stay, 1 EVA

H-series: Precision landings. 2-man landing crew. ,-day stays, 2 EVAs

J-series: Scientific investigations. 2-man landing crew, 3-day stays, 3 EVAs

K-series: Hadley Pioneer LMs. 2-man landing crews, indefinite stay

L-series: "Lunar taxis." 3-person landing crews, indefinite stay, descent engine refire capability

M-series: Enhanced expeditionary LMs. 2-person landing crews, descent engine refire capability

Apollo Missions—Destination / Designation

Apollo 11—Sea of Tranquility / G-1

Apollo 12—Ocean of Storms / H-1

Apollo 13—(No landing) / H-2

Apollo 14—Fra Mauro / H-3

Apollo 15—Hadley Rille / J-1

Apollo 16—Descartes Highlands / J-2

Apollo 17—Taurus-Littrow / J-3

Apollo 18—Schroter's Valley / J-4

Apollo 19—Tycho Crater / J-5

Apollo 20—Gassendi Crater / J-6

Apollo Applications Program—
Destination / Designation, Personnel

Named Apollo crew members are stationed at Hadley Base, aside from those who remain in lunar orbit.

Apollo 21—Hadley 1 / K-1   Rick Norton, Casey Buchanan
(Josh Rawlings/Columbia)

Apollo 22—Hadley 2 / K-2   Jim Dunlap, Ryan Jones
(Gary Wagner/Columbia)

Apollo 23—Hyginus Rille / L-1

Apollo 24—Censorinus Crater / L-2

Apollo 25—Hadley 3 / L-3   Allen Collier, Terri Brock,
Ron Lawrence

Apollo 26—Hadley 4 / M-1   Bill Dobbs, Christian Vasquez
(Danny Zabrinski/Columbia)

Apollo 27—Hadley 5 / M-2   Dan Klein, Luis Ibarra
(Marco Dardenas/Columbia)

Apollo 28—Rimae Bode / M-3

Apollo 29—Hadley 6 / L-4   Gregory Leverton, Kevin McDowell,
Feye Gisemba

Apollo 30—Hadley 7 / M-4   Joe Seaton, Carol Massey
(Curtis Jackson/Columbia)

Apollo 31—Hadley 8 / M-5   Ben Epps, Jack Flynn
(Ed Mason/Columbia)

Apollo 32—Marius Hills, Hadley 9 / M-6   Vivian Carter, Ellis Mayer
(Dave Horn)

TECHNICAL AND POLITICAL BACKGROUND

A Red Moon by 1969?

In *Hot Moon*, the Soviet Union beats the US to the Moon, landing a single cosmonaut on the lunar surface two months ahead of Armstrong and Aldrin's Apollo 11 landing in July 1969.

There's a strong vein of plausibility to this alternate timeline. The Soviets were indeed trying very hard to beat the Americans to the Moon, and we've only recently come to appreciate just how close they came. As mentioned in the media during its fiftieth anniversary commemoration, the Apollo 8 mission in December 1968 was completely reformulated at the eleventh hour to orbit the Moon once the US got wind that the Soviets were on the verge of sending a cosmonaut on a looping lunar trajectory. We now have comprehensive information about the technical capabilities and schedule of the Soviet space program, including full details of their N1-L3 lunar program (N1 super-heavy launch vehicle, enhanced Soyuz spacecraft, and LK lunar landers; for a compendious description, see *Challenge to Apollo: The Soviet Union and the Space Race* by NASA historian Asif A. Sidiqqi). And in *Two Sides of the Moon*, co-written by Apollo 15 astronaut David Scott and pioneering cosmonaut Alexei Leonov, Leonov states his conviction that if Chief Designer Sergei Korolev had not died, the Soviets would have maintained their former development pace and beaten the United States to the Moon. As in *Hot Moon*, Leonov himself would have been a prime candidate to make that trip.

The survival of Sergei Korolev is the point of departure for the *Hot Moon* timeline. In our history, Korolev died on January 14, 1966. Falling

519

foul of the Communist regime in his earlier life, he had been sentenced to hard labor in 1938 and spent two years in the Kolyma gold mines in Siberia, which led to long-lasting health issues. His death was probably due either to internal bleeding or heart failure during an operation to repair a cancerous tumor in his intestine, though sources differ on the exact cause(s).

What is well documented is that there were no Soviet launches for a year after Korolev's death, and that basically everything fell apart. In *Epic Rivalry: The Inside Story of the Soviet and American Space Race*, authors Von Hardesty and Gene Eisman note that Korolev's demise was "a serious blow with immense consequences," his passing "left the Cosmonaut Corps in despair," and his successor Vasili Mishin "lacked Korolev's charismatic style and wide experience." In the coming years the N1-L3 program suffered several critical disasters, and cosmonaut Vladimir Komarov lost his life in Soyuz 1 in April 1967—an event which caused another eighteen-month hiatus in the Soviets' spacefaring plans. Once the Soviets lost the race to the Moon, N1-L3 was canceled in 1974.

But it needn't have happened that way. If Korolev had not been so ill in the first place, or had pulled through—even, perhaps, if he'd had different doctors—the Soviets' destiny in space might have been very different.

If Sergei Korolev survives, it changes everything. A faster pace, fewer disasters, higher morale among the Cosmonaut Corps, and the Soviets are in it to win it.

Politics of the 1970s

In our timeline, having won the Space Race, the US bowed out of further lunar exploration after Apollo 17. However, given a greatly changed political will, the technology already existed to exploit an *increased* investment in orbital and lunar spaceflight, further lunar exploration, and the establishing of a permanent NASA base on the surface.

Could we have afforded it? Yes. The amount that the US spent on the Vietnam War would have been more than enough to continue and dramatically extend an Apollo-style program, with billions to spare. By the end of Apollo in 1972 the US had spent around $25 billion on the program. The total direct cost of the Vietnam War was $168 billion, and the estimated indirect costs to the US add up to a great deal more. Naturally, dollars spent on the space program don't just disappear into the vacuum: they flow into American industry and technology and American salaries, and parts of those dollars then return to the US Treasury through taxes. *Hot Moon* doesn't dig deep into Earthly politics, but it's clear that a Soviet triumph in the Space Race, a swift withdrawal from Vietnam, and aggressive investment in aerospace R&D funding leads to a greatly different US economy and mindset in the 1970s.

In my timeline I assume a complete US withdrawal from Indochina, and that the whole of Southeast Asia falls into the Soviet sphere. Nixon never resigns in disgrace, and Reagan defeats Carter to become President in 1976, four years earlier than in our world. The Cold War continues even more belligerently, and the situation in Afghanistan in 1979 flares up a little more promptly and unfolds differently than in our history.

Secret Space: The USAF Space Program

The USAF's Blue Gemini program and their Manned Orbiting Laboratories (MOL) for Earth surveillance were under development in our timeline, with extensive details only fully declassified in 2015. Some of these preparations were quite advanced: eight astronauts were selected for USAF MOL Group 1 in November 1965, five for MOL Group 2 in June 1966, and a further four in June 1967, for a total of 17. Seven of these men transferred over to NASA in August 1969 as NASA Group 7, and all later went on to fly on the Space Shuttle.

In our world, the MOL project was canceled in June 1969. One can easily imagine that it would have been extended if the Soviets had landed on the Moon the month before. The original MOLs were designed to have a crew of two USAF astronauts and operate for a month at a time. I've postulated that, given a further ten years of development, the MOL Project will evolve to a four-man crew and surveillance stations permanently in orbit; given the technical complexity and sophistication of the MOLs, this would be far more cost-effective.

Project Blue Gemini, as a separate Gemini development track, was formally canceled in 1963 by Secretary of Defense Robert McNamara, since its military and technical requirements would be met by the maneuvering and spacewalk activities baselined for NASA's Gemini flights. USAF experiments were incorporated into NASA missions: for an example, the Astronaut Maneuvering Unit—jet backpack—carried aboard Gemini 9 was originally developed by the USAF to enable its astronauts to investigate Soviet satellites (as described in *NASA Gemini 1965-1966* by David Woods and David M. Harland). The official name for the Gemini spacecraft that would support the MOLs was "Gemini B," a variant that would have a hatch in the heat shield to enable crew access to the MOL. (A refurbished Gemini capsule with this added feature was launched into orbit uncrewed and then successfully deorbited, to prove that such a hatch would not compromise spacecraft integrity and risk killing the crew during the fiery heat of reentry.) However, had the MOLs come to fruition, with USAF crews launching regularly to orbiting facilities, it's hard to imagine that the Air Force would refer to their core two-man spacecraft as anything other than "Blue Gemini."

In addition, the Air Force proposed a lunar base named LUNEX in 1961 that incorporated an Earth bombardment system. This wasn't originally based around a mass driver, but by 1979 it might well have been. Mass drivers were first proposed (for more benign purposes) by US physicist Gerard O'Neill in 1974, and the technical details were well understood. [The Wikipedia "Mass Driver" article is quite good, and the mass driver in *Hot Moon* would look very much like the first image currently on that page.] With military-industrial level funding, the development of prototypes and then a working model should not have hit any major snags. Such a mass driver could not have launched warheads in the megaton range, but the consequences of peppering the USSR with thousands of battlefield tactical nuclear weapons would be dire for the Soviet population and infrastructure. If implemented, the threat might have formed a significant deterrent, in addition to the Earth-based ICBM capability.

For their part, the Soviets launched three Almaz ("Diamond") military surveillance stations into Earth orbit in the early 1970s, "disguised" as Salyuts 2, 3, and 5. The Almaz stations were indeed armed with gas operated rapid-fire revolver cannons, essentially machine guns. These were modified from Earthly Tu-22 bomber tail-guns, and were capable of firing at a rate of up to 2,600 rounds per minute. They were tested on orbit on at least one occasion.

And so, by 1979...

In its Apollo Applications Program, NASA made plans for more extended stays on the Moon. These were based around variants of their existing Lunar Module: a LM Taxi enhanced for longer occupation, and a Shelter that was LM-shaped but with its ascent stage and fuel tanks replaced with supplies and equipment. This would have been followed by the LESA lander (Lunar Exploration System for Apollo), to support six astronauts plus a six-wheeled MOLAB (Mobile Laboratory). Plans for all these were shelved once Apollo funding was curtailed, but had NASA been funded to pursue these plans at full throttle, they could well have established a lunar presence based around Habitats plus associated Lunar Modules by the end of the 1970s.

The Soviets also had plans for a permanent lunar base in a very different style, to be called Zvezda, and the Zvezda Base described in *Hot Moon* is modeled on those plans.

In my description of the Apollo and Gemini spacecraft, Skylab stations, Lunar Rovers, spacesuits, and various other pieces of relevant technology I've made extensive use of publicly available NASA documents, blueprints, and manuals. Substantial information about the USAF Manned Orbiting Laboratory program was declassified by the Department of the Air Force in 2015 and is also publicly available online. Details of orbital mechanics, rendezvous, and communications are accurate; despite what you see on TV science fiction, it really *is* that difficult to maneuver in space and even to talk between spacecraft. Some technologies and processes have been simplified or improved, of course, given the decade of further development by the time *Hot Moon* begins, but my postulated improvements seem modest compared with (say) the increase in functionality of Apollo in 1969 over Gemini in 1965-1966, or the increase in the capabilities of Apollo 17 in 1972 over those of Apollo 11 in 1969. And if we had gone that route, humans might be on Mars today, and perhaps even beyond.

BIBLIOGRAPHY

In researching and writing *Hot Moon* I made use of a wide variety of books and online resources. First, the books:

The US Space Program

Aldrin, Buzz, and, Malcolm McConnell. *Men from Earth*. Bantam Books, 1989.

Baker, David. *Apollo 13, Owners' Workshop Manual*. Haynes Publishing, 2013.

Baker, David. *International Space Station, Owners' Workshop Manual*. Haynes Publishing, 2012.

———— *NASA Moon Missions, 1969-1972 (Apollo 12, 14, 15, 16 and 17), Operations Manual*. Haynes Publishing, 2019.

———— *NASA Skylab, Owners' Workshop Manual*. Haynes Publishing, 2018.

———— *Rocket, Owners' Workshop Manual*. Haynes Publishing, 2015.

———— *US Spy Satellites, Owners' Workshop Manual*. Haynes Publishing, 2016.

Cernan, Gene, and Don Davis. *The Last Man on the Moon*. St. Martin's Griffin, 1999.

Chaikin, Andrew. *A Man on the Moon*. Penguin, 1994.

Collins, Michael. *Carrying the Fire: An Astronaut's Journey*. Bantam Books, 1974.

David, Leonard. *Moon Rush: The New Space Race*. National Geographic, 2019.

Donovan, Jim. *Shoot for the Moon*. Little Brown, 2019.

Hadfield, Chris. *An Astronaut's Guide to Life on Earth*. Little, Brown, 2013.

Hansen, James. *First Man: The Life of Neil A. Armstrong.* Simon & Schuster, 2005.

Irwin, James B., with William A. Emerson Jr. *To Rule the Night.* Hodder & Stoughton, 1973.

Jones, Tom. *Sky Walking: An Astronaut's Memoir.* Smithsonian Books, 2006.

Kelly, Scott. *Endurance: A Year in Space, a Lifetime of Discovery.* Vintage, 2018.

Kranz, Gene. *Failure Is Not an Option.* Berkley, 2000.

Ley, Willy, and Chesley Bonestell. *The Conquest of Space.* Viking Press, 1950.

Light, Michael. *Full Moon.* Knopf, 1999.

Mendell, W. W. (ed). *Lunar Bases and Space Activities of the 21st Century.* Lunar and Planetary Institute, 1985.

Nelson, Bill, *Mission.* Harcourt Brace Jovanovich, 1988.

O'Neill, Gerard K. (ed). *Space Resources and Space Settlements. Technical papers derived from the 1977 Summer Study at NASA Ames,* NASA, 1979.

Pyle, Rod. *Amazing Stories of the Space Age.* Prometheus, 2017.

Reynolds, David West. *Apollo: The Epic Journey to the Moon, 1963-1972.* Zenith Press, 2013.

Riley, Christopher, and Phil Dolling, *Apollo 11, Owners' Workshop Manual.* Haynes Publishing, 2009.

Riley, Christopher, David Woods, and Philip Dolling. *Lunar Rover 1971-1972, Owners' Workshop Manual.* Haynes Publishing, 2012.

Ryan, Peter. *The Invasion of the Moon 1957-1970.* Pelican, 1971.

Schirra, Walter M, Jr. with Richard N Billings. *Schirra's Space.* Quinlan Press, 1988.

Shetterly, Margot Lee. *Hidden Figures.* William Morrow, 2016.

Woods, W. David. *How Apollo Flew to the Moon.* Springer Praxis, 2008.

Woods, David, and David M. Harland *Gemini, Owner's Workshop Manual.* Haynes Publishing, 2015.

The Soviet Space Program

Baker, David. *Soyuz, 1967 onwards (all models), Owners' Workshop Manual.* Haynes Publishing, 2014.

Brzezinski, Matthew. *Red Moon Rising.* Holt, 2008.

Burgess, Colin, and Rex Hall. *The First Soviet Cosmonaut Team: Their Lives, Legacy, and Historical Impact.* Springer Praxis, 2009.

Hardesty, Von, and Gene Eisman. *Epic Rivalry: The Inside Story of the Soviet and American Space Race.* National Geographic, 2007.

Johnson, Nicholas L. *The Soviet Reach for the Moon.* Cosmos Books, 1995.

Scott, David, and Alexei Leonov. *Two Sides of the Moon: Our Story of the Cold War Space Race.* St. Martin's Griffin, 2006.

Siddiqi, Asif A. *Challenge to Apollo: The Soviet Union and the Space Race, 1945-1974.* NASA History Series, 2000.

Lunar Science

Bedescu, Viorel (ed). *Moon: Prospective Energy and Material Resources.* Springer, 2012.

Bussey, Ben, and Paul Spudis. *The Clementine Atlas of the Moon.* Cambridge University Press, 2004.

Spudis, Paul D. *The Value of the Moon.* Smithsonian Books, 2016.

Wilhelms, Don E. *The Geologic History of the Moon.* US Geological Survey, 1987.

The Cold War

Gaddes, John Lewis. *The Cold War: A New History.* Penguin Press, 2005.

Ware, Pat. *Cold War, 1946 to 1991, Operations Manual.* Haynes Publishing, 2016.

Westad, Odd Arne. *The Cold War: A World History.* Basic Books, 2019.

Soviet Culture

Kaiser, Robert G. *Russia: The People and the Power*. Pocket Books, 1976.

Remnick, David. *Lenin's Tomb: The Last Days of the Soviet Empire*. Vintage Books, 1994.

Solovyov, Vladimir, and Elena Klepikova. *Inside the Kremlin*. Star Books, 1986.

Willis, David K. *Klass: How Russians Really Live*. Avon Books, 1985.

As for the online resources, NASA has released a huge amount of information about the Apollo program, all of which is freely available online, and none of which I had to pull any dayjob strings to get my hands on (my work specialty is X-ray astrophysics, which is almost as far away from the human spaceflight program as you can get and still work for the same agency).

Two critical resources were the mission transcripts from the original Apollo missions: the *Apollo Flight Journal*, David Woods (editor), at *https://history.nasa.gov/afj/* , and the *Apollo Lunar Surface Journal*, Eric M. Jones (founder and editor emeritus), Ken Glover (editor), at *https://www.hq.nasa.gov/alsj/* . The first contains the complete transcripts from the flight portions of the Apollo missions, annotated with a wealth of commentary, photos and videos, and the second contains similar transcripts and information from every moment of the lunar surface activities. I also made extensive use of NASA's *Project Apollo Archive* at *http://apolloarchive.com/*, and the *NASA Image and Video Library* at *https://images.nasa.gov/* .

Easily Google-able on the NASA History Division site at *https://history.nasa.gov/* you can find the original press kits and Mission Reports for all the Apollo missions, along with operations handbooks and other deep and extensive technical information on the Apollo Command and Service Modules, Lunar Module, Skylab, Lunar Rover, Saturn V, spacesuits, tools, unified S-band communications, propellants, and escape systems. The same site contains the declassified military plans for the US Army's Project Horizon and USAF Lunex Project, and documents discussing the possible use of nukes in space, along with historical US assessments of Soviet manned spaceflight and lunar programs, the plans for the Apollo Applications Program, and more additional photo and video information than you can shake a stick at. It's a research rabbit hole you could get lost in forever. I'm lucky I made it out alive.

I also found valuable resources at *http://astronautix.com/* , *https://space. stackexchange.com/* and *https://gizmodo.com/* , and made heavy use of the USAF Lunar Charts (particularly the LAC series) at the Lunar and Planetary Institute, *https://www.lpi.usra.edu/resources/mapcatalog/* , and the 1:1 Million-scale maps of the Moon at *https://planetarynames. wr.usgs.gov/Page/Moon1to1MAtlas*.

CPSIA information can be obtained
at www.ICGtesting.com
Printed in the USA
LVHW010829100622
720904LV00002B/2/J